RO

"Rodrigo Fresán is the new star of Latin American literature. . . .
There is darkness in him, but it harbors light within it because
his prose—aimed at bygone readers—is brilliant."
—Enrique Vila-Matas

"I've read few novels this exciting in recent years. *Mantra* is the
novel I've laughed with the most, the one that has seemed the
most virtuosic and at the same time the most disruptive."
—Roberto Bolaño

"A kaleidoscopic, open-hearted, shamelessly polymathic storyteller,
the kind who brings a blast of oxygen into the room."
—Jonathan Lethem

"Rodrigo Fresán is a marvelous writer, a direct descendent of
Adolfo Bioy Casares and Jorge Luis Borges, but with his own
voice and of his own time, with a fertile imagination, daring
and gifted with a vision as entertaining as it is profound."
—John Banville

"With pop culture cornered by the forces of screen culture,
says Fresán (knowing the risk to his profile of 'pop writer,'
even coming out himself to discuss it), there's nothing left but
to be classic. That's the only way to keep on writing."
—Alan Pauls

TRANSLATED FROM THE SPANISH
BY WILL VANDERHYDEN

THE INVENTED PART

RODRIGO FRESÁN

OPEN LETTER
LITERARY TRANSLATIONS FROM THE UNIVERSITY OF ROCHESTER

Library of Congress Cataloging-in-Publication Data: Available.
ISBN-13: 978-1-940953-56-4 | ISBN-10: 1-940953-56-1

*This project is supported in part by an award from
the National Endowment for the Arts*

ART WORKS.
arts.gov

Printed on acid-free paper in the United States of America.

Text set in Caslon, a family of serif typefaces based on the designs
of William Caslon (1692–1766).

Design by N. J. Furl

Open Letter is the University of Rochester's nonprofit, literary translation press:
Lattimore Hall 411, Box 270082, Rochester, NY 14627

www.openletterbooks.org

For Ana and Daniel:
the real part

THE INVENTED PART

Writing is not crypto-autobiography, and it's not current events. I'm not writing my autobiography, and I'm not writing things as they happen to me, with the exception of the use of details—thunderstorms and that sort of thing. No, it's nothing that happened to me. It's a possibility. It's an idea.
—JOHN CHEEVER

I had as yet no notion that life every now and then becomes literature—not for long, of course, but long enough to be what we best remember, and often enough so that what we eventually come to mean by life are those moments when life, instead of going sideways, backwards, forward, or nowhere at all, lines out straight, tense and inevitable, with a complication, climax, and, given some luck, a purgation, as if life had been made and not happened.
—NORMAN MACLEAN

People say it's not what happens in your life that matters, it's what you *think* happened. But this qualification, obviously, did not go far enough. It was quite possible that the central event in your life could be something that didn't happen, or something you *thought* didn't happen. Otherwise there'd be no need for fiction, there'd only be memoirs and histories, case histories; what happened—what actually happened to you and what you thought happened—would be enough.
—GEOFF DYER

There's a story, always ahead of you. Barely existing. Only gradually do you attach yourself to it and feed it. You discover the carapace that will contain and test your character. You will find in this way the path of your life. [. . .] You learn to alter your life. [. . .] Everything in plain sight.
—MICHAEL ONDAATJE

We see parts of things, we intuit whole things.
—IRIS MURDOCH

No serious attempt will be made to enter into competition with reality.
—ROBERT MUSIL

Author here. Meaning the real author, the living human holding
the pencil, not some abstract narrative persona [. . .].
All of this is true. This book is really true.
—DAVID FOSTER WALLACE

Is that the noblest objective of a work of fiction? To convince the reader
that what you're writing about is really happening? I don't think so.
—JOSEPH HELLER

It all really happened.
—BRET EASTON ELLIS

Indeed, it had now become hard for me to remember
just how things really had happened.
—CHRISTOPHER ISHERWOOD

I'm not sure that what happened to me yesterday was true.
—BOB DYLAN

All this happened, more or less.
—KURT VONNEGUT

Nothing actually happened.
—JAMES SALTER

Always lie.
—JUAN CARLOS ONETTI

Can I call this a novel?
—MARCEL PROUST

This is not a pipe.
—RENÉ MAGRITTE

THE REAL
CHARACTER

Thursday, June 4th, 1959

How to begin.

Or better: How to begin?

(Adding the question mark that—nothing happens by chance—has the shape of a fish or meat hook. A sharp and pointy curve that skewers both the reader and the read. Pulling them, dragging them up from the clear and calm bottom to the cloudy and restless surface. Or sending them flying through the air to land just inside the beach of these parentheses. Parentheses that more than one person will judge or criticize as orthographically and aesthetically unnecessary but that, in the uncertainty of the beginning, are oh so similar to hands coming together in an act of prayer, asking for a fair voyage just now underway. We read: *"Lasciate ogni speranza voi ch'entrate;"* we hear: "Once more unto the breach, dear friends, once more." And good luck to all, wishes you this voice—halfway down the road of life, lost in a dark woods, because it wandered off the right path—that the gag of the parentheses renders unknown. And yet—like with certain unforgettable songs, whose melodies impose themselves over the title and even over the signature lines of the chorus, what's it called? how'd it go?—this voice *also* recalls that of someone whose name isn't easy to identify or recognize. And, yes, if possible, avoid this kind of paragraph from here onward because, they say, it scares away many of today's readers. Today's electrocuted readers, accustomed to reading quickly and briefly on small screens. And, yes, goodbye to all of them, at least for as long as this book lasts and might last. Unplug from external inputs to nourish yourselves exclusively on internal electricity. And—warning! warning!—at least in the beginning and to begin with, that's the idea here, the idea from here onward. Consider yourselves warned.)

Or better still: To begin *like this?*

And, just below, the following.

Light made for making. The sudden yet not unanticipated appearance of a landscape.

Moving from the general to the specific, to the individual, to the "hero" of the thing.

The kind of beginning—the solid foundation and articulation of an entire world on the page and between its lines, before its inhabitants make their entrance, moving left to right—considered obligatory for novels of the nineteenth century. Novels by authors who, in many cases, have been completely forgotten, but only after writing beginnings that remain unforgettable—anybody out there remember an author named Edward Bulwer-Lytton, a novel called *Paul Clifford?*—like "It was a dark and stormy night . . ." Novels that, in the twenty-first century, many readers—not too many, fewer all the time—explore with the joyful, retro-vintage wonder of someone who has to learn to breathe anew. To breathe *like this*: the way they breathed back then, opening and stepping inside one of *those* books that have the scent of book and not, as noted, the scent of machine and electric engine, of speed and lightness and short sentences, not for the wise power of synthesis but on the crass basis of abbreviation. To breathe differently, slowly and deep down inside. To breathe in books that readers, with any luck and if they're lucky, will come to enjoy like the pure oxygen of a green forest after a long time lost in the black depths of a carbon mine. That forest, that place you should never have left and to which, welcome back, you return, running like only children can run. Like running children who are pure knee: their own knees the most important part of their body (always moving, always scraped) in an adult world, known fundamentally from the height of those fierce and loving giants' knees. Like enlightened children who run, not yet thinking that someone is watching them run. Children who run, unaware that, unfortunately, for a total lack of fortune, there will soon be a uniform and a proper and respectable and harmonious way of running, for they'll know themselves watched and judged and compared to other runners. But not yet. And to run is to read. And may you be of great velocity, you readers who run like you once ran, when you weren't yet able to read but wanted to learn so badly, like a celebration of muscles and femurs and kneecaps and tibias and exhilarated laughter. Without shame or shyness or fear of what you'll say and what you'll see. Without the discomfort you'll feel, a few years down the road, at early parties, at first dances. Dances that are like running in place: because all you really want is *to stay still*; but please, without our stillness being too obvious. And, so, adorning it with slight twitches of arm and leg and a disheveling spasm of head. All those tremors, those intimate little earthquakes on the edges of improvised monosonic dance floors in order to—it's a little bit simian, really—digitize, with seeing eyes, intense as invisible fingers, what really matters: to tirelessly watch the way he or she moves. As if you were reading them. As if you wanted to memorize them, to recite later, alone, in the dark, lying down but as if running. That boy or that girl who moves *so good*, while we try to move the best we can. And to not think about how we're moving, how ridiculous we look when we see ourselves dance, and maybe that explains the humiliating proliferation of mirrors in dance clubs, mirrors that quickly make you stop dancing and send you to the bar to spend a small fortune on successive colorful cocktails with too much water and ice. Something—watching ourselves dance, finding ourselves outside ourselves, to one side of ourselves, like those strange yet familiar objects you have to look at up close—as unsettling as hearing our own recorded voice, or discovering our profile in a photo. Or, it's been said before, in one of those multiple-angle mirrors, when we force ourselves and are forced to try on and buy new clothes that never fit how we hope. Clothes that don't change us, that aren't a disguise, that only make us more ourselves, and so we groan. We sound *like that*? We look *like that*? Horrifying revelation: no, we do not look and sound how we think we sound and look. An effect similar to one you sometimes feel when you read something you wrote a long time ago. Something you understand as written, but can't understand why and in what circumstances you wrote it. Or more horrifying and illuminating and even less comprehensible: you can't understand how it was you were able to write something of that style. How is it possible to spend so much time learning how to write to end up writing something *like that*? No, please, say it isn't so, that it didn't come from us, that we never thought—and went so far as to write—something *like that*. And, presently, *that* is *here* again, like a ghost of Christmas past, to torment and ensnare us.

But there's still plenty of time to worry about these issues and, you'll ask, what was the purpose or reason for opening the door to let such a digression come out and play. Easy but not simple: because *that* is how grownups think (jumping from one point to another, like drawing/connecting dots) when they feel particularly childish and allow themselves be carried off by gusts of ideas, like loose pages swept away by a storm. Better: *that* is how (and there are people who take drugs for years to try, without achieving it, to think *like that* for a while) more or less grown up writers think twenty-four hours a day, seven days a week, twelve months a year, to infinity and beyond. So, wanting to think *like that* for a little while; because if the effect is too prolonged, the whole thing loses its charm—and gets worn out and takes too much work— and then it doesn't make any sense to say things like "You can't imagine the trip I had."

But—here and now, so close, as close as everything that's already happened—enough of this.

Better: listen to the wind blow, though really the wind doesn't blow.

The wind does something else, something for which a precise, exact, correct verb hasn't yet been created.

The wind—more than blows—runs.

The wind is running over itself.

The wind is not circular; it is a circle.

So—there we go, here we come, running—there's a beach at the border of a place called Sad Songs. And there's a boy running on this beach. A beach that opens onto a forest or a forest that opens onto a beach, depending on how you look at it, looking at the one, looking at the other. A deep and lush forest and a long and narrow beach that is, really, a thin line between water and salt and wood and chlorophyll. A line that's about to be crossed by a boy.

And, note: here it says "boy" when maybe it should say *little boy*—that oh so practical pairing of words that conflates size and age. But knowing already who and how digressive this *little boy* will be when grown up—and for reasons that have to do with transcendence and for the way it tends to prefer the most *universal* version of everything it touches and topples and breaks—it'd be better, just in case, "boy" . . . "The boy" . . . "The Boy" . . .

And The Boy is at an age that's hard to specify.

The first of those ages/borderlands: between three and four years old or between four and five years old. That year—a perfect imperfection in the texture of time—which actually lasts two years, or something like that, a period when, all at once, so many things happen. The Boy's features haven't yet ceased to be the ones they've always been; but they've already begun to be the ones they'll be until that second two-step—around eleven or twelve— from one territory to the next. So, staring at him produces the nauseating sensation of looking at a blurry photo, and, besides, The Boy never stops moving. Not even when he sleeps. The Boy is what's known as "a restless child," though the existence of a "restful child" has yet to be discovered; because it's common knowledge that children only settle down, as if in a micro-trance, for the few seconds it takes them to decide where to take their restlessness and create unrest next.

So here he comes. Running. Breathing through his mouth from the effort. As if he weren't on his feet and moving, but actually sitting still. And yet, all the same, on his feet and moving. The same way he'd feel later on, holding any one of his many favorite novels. Eyes open wide, one of those books that, with time's rapid passing, time's running, charges you the entrance fee of learning everything all over again: a brand new game with rules and—you've been warned—a breathing all its own, a rhythm you have to absorb and follow if your goal is to climb up on the shore of the last page.

And that beach, immortal, has been there for millennia; but it's only been recognized for a few years (as many years as The Boy's age) as a beach for mortals, appearing in guidebooks for beachgoers and people who enjoy lying down to change color and mood under a sun that was once a precise clock or fiery deity for those who beheld and worshipped it. The beach is, then, one of those beaches between prehistoric and futuristic. A beach with no time, no nothing, no name. No billboard saying "This is a beach." Not a single sign christening it with names as unoriginal as "New Atlantis" or "Sirens' Point" or "Dulce Mar." Its name simply that of the nearest town, which itself corresponds to some third-rate hero of the independence. And yet, The Boy's parents, feeling themselves colonists and founders, insist on calling it La Garoupe, referencing that other beach for connoisseurs and that other exclusive couple, a great inspiration for the two of them. One and the other—famous beach and celebrity couple, fantasizing that their distant yet powerful radiations reach them, The Boy's parents—far away in time and space and consciousness from The Boy, who will come to them soon, in a possible novel; but let's not get ahead of ourselves, let's not run too fast and so far. Now, this beach, like one of those beaches where you might never have been, but that you probably drew at some point when you were a kid. A zone, white and horizontal, but never straight and true. A yellow sun over-head. Splashes of aquamarine for the sky and of sky blue for the aquamarine water. But no. This is not the blue known and *pantheonized* and trapped by the wood of pencils or the metal tubes of oil paints. It's an ancient blue, a blue that has nothing to do with the blue children use to paint sky or water, or with the perfect blue of the greatest Indian gods. It's a blue that's always been there, and yet, for The Boy, there's the sensation that all of this—like a tablecloth—is spread out every morning and folded up every night, like a stage that sets itself anew with each sunrise. One of those beaches that—able to raise and lower its temperature at will—could just as easily be an African desert as a Siberian steppe. Here the sea is not even the sea—it's the mouth of a river opening into the sea. The water is not fresh, not salty, not—now you see it, up close—blue, not brown. The beach is white and wild and it's mid-day, the precise hour when everything loses its shadow and gains body. And that's the moment when, glowing, The Boy, to whom many adults ascribe a rather shadowy character, runs out of the dunes, which are sparse and small.

Everything, as far as the eye can see, seems frozen in the exact instant of a flash. A postcard of red pupils slowly developed. There's a rock outcropping and above it, yes, a deep forest. But the beach is narrow and seems to come to an abrupt end. More than a beach it's the sketch of a beach, or of something that someone, after thinking about it a little or not much at all, decided to leave unfinished, moving on to look for another view to paint.

So The Boy is running across the hot sand (just two or three meters of thick sand, stones and shells crushed by the tides of centuries and, yes, more parentheses, forgive me, and there's nothing to forgive) and the curiously pleasurable pain in the soles of his feet makes him run faster and stranger. Running like—it's already been said—children run, almost coming undone. The Boy doesn't scream, but his whole body quivers like a scream, like a silent scream, until he reaches the shore's damp sand and calms his feet, and the pleasure of its relief gives meaning to the pain. "I can well understand why children love sand," a philosopher wrote some time ago, a philosopher whom The Boy will read some time later; but The Boy already agrees completely.

This boy—now that we see him up close, now that we've been watching him for a few minutes—is, really, the opposite of what we thought in the beginning: he's a restlessly restful boy. He likes being immobile, to move for the pleasure of stopping. He likes to spend long minutes staring at fire or water (later, The Boy will never be able to pin down, despite not being a boy anymore, whether water and fire are entities or vegetal, animal, or mineral organisms; nor will all the explanations and definitions that he's been offered over the years satisfy him entirely) and he likes, all of a sudden, as if pierced by an arrow of desire, charged with quivering energy, to stand up and run off in any direction, to feel the exuberant joy of wearing himself out until there's nothing left to do but stop, to stand still.

That's why he's running now. Running like that Roadrunner the Coyote can't stop chasing; because that uncatchable Roadrunner is, first and foremost and when all is said and done, the only thing in motion in that panorama of minimal desert lines. And it's the Roadrunner who makes the Coyote move. And The Boy likes thinking of himself as a roadrunner and that behind him are coming, oh so much slower, two young adult coyotes, a man and a woman, his father and mother, no doubt about it.

And his father and mother have no strength, or they have the kind of strength—weak, slight, miniscule, in decline—parents have at the equator of long vacations. So they're not The Parents and, ever since they became parents, they've felt themselves reduced, diminished, as if some parasitic and alien entity were absorbing their vitality. The father and mother don't chase The Boy. No, the father and mother are dragged along by The Boy. The father and mother drag their feet, and a wicker basket, and an umbrella, and towels, and their own bodies. And the father and the mother are dragged by The Boy. As if he were steering them, lassoed, pulling them along, strangling them with an invisible and inseverable rope around their necks. And it's not like the mother and father have tried to sever it, but it's also not like they haven't thought many times about *what* it would be like to cut it. And—presto!—magically return to the past, to those other beaches, where The Boy only existed as a pleasant and egotistical fantasy. The father and the mother return, further away all the time, to The Boy as a mere idea that occurred to them every so often. An idea to enjoy for a while and then hide away under lock and key (one of those keys that you can't ever find when you look for it and that, with the aid of a pair of parentheses, seems to become invisible) in the drawers of a more or less possible future, always yet to come or, at least, a lateral future, in the possible variation of a possible future. This is what every father and mother in the universe dreams when they close their eyes, though none of them ever confess it. Right there. In that instant. Before falling asleep and dreaming of any other thing, of free falling or being naked in public—the greatest hits of the common nightmare. But first, like the trailer for a movie that will never premiere. About what it'd be like to not be parents. To wake up on a planet where there wasn't someone resting—yet restlessly moving and making noise—in the next room. About times when they went to bed late or not at all. Times when the next morning was a sort of luminous sequel to the previous night, when, before collapsing into bed, they bought a freshly printed newspaper and sat down to eat breakfast in a bar and read aloud in loving voices things like how a group of scientists with a lot of time on their hands (as much time as they had) had come to the conclusion that, in past millennia, children always bore a close physical resemblance to their parents. They argued that this was the genetic and narcissistic mode by which the species had insured its survival: primitive beings protect and love better and don't discard something that reminds them of themselves. Now, it's different, now it doesn't seem so necessary: the resemblance between parents and children has diminished significantly, statistically speaking, because human beings love each other more or pretend to, or feel themselves culturally and sociologically compelled to do so. And so The Boy looks nothing like his parents. And, true, it's a cliché, a tired perspective: you don't get to choose your parents. But it's *also* true that parents don't get to choose their children. And it's worth wondering whether they, if granted access to other models, would have chosen this one. Or if he would've chosen them. And how did his parents choose each other in the first place: did they feel identical or complementary or did they see in the other what they wanted the other to see in them? The way things have been, they understand now—though they don't dare admit it openly—was all a misunderstanding. A mirage disguised as an oasis. Now the effect has faded and what's left isn't its memory, but the certainty that what passed between them is already in the past. Now they feel that what ties them together is, maybe, what they like least in themselves reflected in and through the other, not in the glass of a flattering mirror, but through the unforgiving lens of a magnifying glass, where everything appears elementary, my dear. And that The Boy is nothing but the result of that sudden, precise distortion. Some really irreal thing. Something that, at times, seems like the undertow of a dream, slipping away just as you try to catch it. Something that happened but couldn't have happened. And sometimes The Boy's dreams overlap with his parents' dreams, producing a strange phenomenon: The Boy dreams he's running on a beach without them and his father and mother dream they're running on a beach without him. And they're all *so* happy. And yet the next morning they understand that they can't live without each other; that, though less and less, they still need each other; that now, nothing and nobody can or will ever be able to separate them or untie the knot of their lives.

And yet, the invulnerability of that instant of pure love doesn't last long; and now The Boy is trying get away from them, running. And his father and mother follow him, stumbling like sleepwalkers, repeating his immense little name, angrier all the time, adding his last name in order to achieve, they think, an air of greater authority, of scholastic strictness. His father and mother say his first name followed by his last name and then—realizing it's not working, sounding more schoolish still—his last name followed by his first name. The Boy hasn't started primary school yet. But he's already learned that, coming from his parents' mouths, first name followed by last name and last name followed by first name mean that the grownups' patience is wearing thin, that his childhood is wearing them out.

(And his first and last name won't be revealed here; because writing them and reading them would be the same as making that boy disappear and having him—catastrophically and violently, not by art of magic but by art of witchcraft—supplanted by that adult he became, a man everyone recognizes and about whom so much has been said and written recently; the disappeared man who appears everywhere, the man so many wanted to meet and so few know and whom, because of that, they read now without comprehension or enjoyment, but just to be hip, up-to-date, deformedly informed.)

His first and last name leap across the sand like more or less domesticated pets or, why not, better, like stuffed animals that don't bite or shit or die. As if they were chasing their own heels; and that's why The Boy runs even faster, under flashing rays of sunlight. They're not going to catch me, The Boy thinks, they won't catch him. But they catch him. And they catch him in a way that doesn't figure in The Boy's plans—they get tired. They look for and find a place on the sand. They spread out their towels. They toss two books down on top of them, two books that have the same title and author on the cover and the same characters inside, but are different editions. They plant and open their umbrella and uncap their thermoses of iced tea mixed with some liquor. His mother's book has various lines and paragraphs underlined throughout its pages. His father's book suffers abundant corrections and numbers and notations in the margins and, on the last page, a list of words including "flapper," "bob," and "crack-up." And both the readers and the books sit down to read, facing the sea, and off to one side, The Boy, feeling not chased but ignored, caught, stops and retraces his footsteps. Slowly, not in a straight line, but with elegant swooping curves, spinning around himself, delaying as long as possible the Kodak Moment of the three of them together once again: father-mother-son; an organism with three heads and three bodies and yet, even still, indivisible as long as decisions of a radical and final nature can be avoided. And, as already mentioned, decisions are about to be made. All of them. All at once.

The father and the mother and The Boy are—The Boy understands and repeats it as one indivisible word—*onvacation*. And, whatever it means to be *onvacation*, it is, fundamentally, to be elsewhere. Together all the time. And let's see what happens, let's see if something happens, let's see if the internal climate, encouraged by the fine external weather, improves. The mother and the father are there, incommunicado (far away from everything and everyone, inaccessible; the closest extant thing to mobile phones that, at the time, only appeared in movies with a-go-go spies dancing among miniskirts), and doing all they can to communicate. But soon, shortly after arriving, the father and mother find themselves found out and exposed and wanting only to go back to the big city, where it's a lot easier for them to lose each other in order to find themselves.

It's the first days of being *onvacation* and The Boy hasn't adjusted to the new rhythm—some gentle moments, others accelerated—of the new routine yet. Everything is new and everything is strange and The Boy misses his toys that the buckets and shovels cannot replace. The Boy never liked plastic and he misses the metal. The metal of that little tin man with a suitcase most of all. A toy that turned out defective—it doesn't go forward when wound, it goes backward—and that The Boy insisted on keeping anyway and not exchanging for another one that functioned properly because, intuitively, he likes its defective defense mechanism. Being dressed and ready for the future and, nevertheless, only being able to project itself into the past. And there are days when The Boy almost convinces himself that his toy is the only model that *actually* functions properly, while the rest, the ones that move forward, are imperfect, manufacturing errors, failed trials for something that only his little man has achieved. And The Boy has been chosen by fortune, by fate, because the toy came to him and him alone. A tiny tourist who travels backward to the table edge and, there, executes a half-turn and returns to the opposite edge. Never falling off, courtesy of a simple yet effective invention. A catch on its feet that keeps it from toppling into a void full of chair legs, but that doesn't stop it, time and again, from peering down into the abyss, so the legs of those chairs can tell it a story.

His father and mother—on the edge of a different abyss, their story almost told—no longer miss anything and play by themselves and inhabit a pure present. They don't move backward (because the past deceives, distorts) or forward (because tomorrow you never know). So, the reign of the minute-to-minute. A slow slide, like skating across very thin ice or along the treacherous edge of a cliff. Knowing they lack the primitive technology to keep themselves from falling and crashing down on the crags of their mutual disappointment: because love is a sickness—they self-diagnose with a strange mix of sadness and relief—and they've already been cured.

The Boy doesn't know it yet; but he suspects it without being able to explain it. Or explain it to himself. Having that rare capacity that some children have to perceive everything, to soak it all in: yeah, yeah, yeah, the father and the mother have already made one of *those* decisions. It's the dawning of an age when The Boy will go back and forth between them, one side to the other. And, every so often, they'll get back together just so they can split up again. Respecting the spasmodic but strict rhythm of a new calendar where the seasons become secondary, almost banal. Something useful only for that rare breed of children, the disappearing models of that démodé species: children who still live with *both* parents in the *same* home.

On the other hand, for the more numerous members of that new race of children—these recent mutations—weekends and vacations will be the new ways to divide and explain time's passing. Long days. Far longer than their twenty-four numbered hours. And each one of them itself seemingly divided into three days: the day of the morning, the day of the afternoon, and the day of the night. Three acts, precisely and perfectly delimited. Like tragedies and comedies. Or like both at the same time; because as a child, in one day, you can cry your eyes out before lunch and fall asleep laughing after dinner. For a child, each day is a lifetime. What time is it? Who cares? His parents don't care, they—even imposing this custom on some of their friends, as if the gesture implied a secret code granting access to a sect of the chosen—wear their watches facedown. The lens and hands facing their wrists. Inside out. With the supposedly original affectation of people who say they don't care about time and its passing when, really, fugitives, there's nothing they care about more than time and its passing and passing through and being passed through by time. And The Boy doesn't care; his life hasn't yet been reduced to hours and strict external schedules and is still ruled only by the rituals of eating and sleeping and waking.

(Many years later, The Boy who would no longer be a boy—but who would always feel like one when discovering new and surprising things—would read, dumbstruck, that there had been a time when a general and universal time didn't exist. That the abstraction of a uniform time for everyone was successfully imposed and assimilated as recently as the end of the nineteenth century; when clocks were coordinated according to the arrivals and departures of transcontinental trains, so people would arrive at the station on time and not miss the train and, in the end, before long and all of a sudden, everyone agreed that it was twelve noon when the bronze tolling of the bells and the steel whistle of the locomotive could be heard.)

The father and the mother and The Boy came to this beach on a moribund train, on one of the last trains of a derailed country. And—The Boy doesn't know it yet, but in a way, as already mentioned, he feels it, senses it—another train is approaching at top speed. Filthy smoke and adulterous fire spewing from its chimney—The Divorce Express. A vehicle representing a time of great change. A train not connecting distant places, but separating them with a series of barriers, wandering rails onto which, every so often, a poet shrouded in his own verses will throw himself or a damsel in distress will drop a flower. Stations where there's nothing to wait for because nothing showed up a while back, and it's here to stay. And that explains the lack of imagination of this summertime vacation, where nothing ever seems to happen. Where everything seems fine, but in the worst way possible. Where the smiles of his father and mother are always thin and tense, like the moist cut left behind by a very sharp knife or like the cold blade itself. Either way, it's all the same. The cut, the blade: one ends at the exact point where the other begins—the smiles of his father and mother wound and are wounds. As he decodes those smiles, though he doesn't understand their language, The Boy smiles—his is still just a smile—and doesn't know why he's smiling. But he smiles just in case, cautiously, and that's why he feels the irresistible urge to get away. To run and not stop. To consider himself from a slight distance, to gain a little perspective, to take a few steps back. The whole ". . . they understand that they can't live without each other; that, though less and less, they still need each other; that, now nothing and nobody can or will be able to separate them or untie the knot of their lives." (Many years later, The Boy would read, in a novel whose protagonist goes mad in a more or less civilized way, sending letters to the living and the dead, to celebrities and strangers—the sentence "Seashores are good for madmen, provided they're not too mad" and, looking up from the book, he'll say to himself: "Exactly. That's right. My parents were mad, but back then, they weren't *too* mad yet. Two or three summers later, well, now that's a different story . . .") But that would be a complex novel, a novel with complicated breathing. Here and now, on the beach, The Boy's "preoccupations" are more childish, but just as hard to resolve. Many of them—The Boy lacks and is lacking words, ways of putting them together—more intuited than verbalized and thought; others only came to him later on; but he'll evoke them, always, as part and parts of a childhood without clear limits or border. Things that, at times, seem to drive him just mad enough, because here, on the beach, he's not "too mad" yet. Random samples that, if translated into an adult format, would sound more or less like this:

* Why does Superman appear to exert himself equally—the same muscle tension, the same knit brow—when he picks up a car or alters the orbit of an entire planet? Which leads to: Is it really something positive for humanity that Superman and his friends—read: Batman & Company—watch over us to such an extent and so efficiently? Isn't it a little disturbing that every time the Man of Steel and the Batman are momentarily neutralized by one of their many archenemies—read: Lex Luthor or The Joker—neither the police nor the army nor the citizenry can do anything about it? And the way they limit themselves, resigned to the contemplation of the application of their superpower or mega-ability, and do nothing but pray for the, fortunately, inevitable and never too late recovery and shining victory of the guardian, until the next adventure, when everything starts over again and again and again? (Much later, The Boy would regard the increasingly absurd evolutions of multifunctional mobile phones and their "social" applications as "pocket superheroes we can't live without and depend on, never imagining that they might be super villains.")

* Whose fault is it that there are so many red Sugus and so few green Sugus in packs of assorted candies?

* Why do his parents seem to want to kill him with an overdose of Patty Hamburgers with Maggi brand mashed potatoes?

* Why don't the members of the expedition to Skull Island in King Kong choose to bring a dinosaur back to civilization, something with a smaller brain and simpler appetites—a bit more attractive and impressive as a spectacle—rather than a giant, unstable, blonde-obsessed monkey? And why in these Japanese monster movies does someone always stop in mid-flight and turn around and raise their arms and scream, immobile, just to be squashed by a giant reptilian foot?

* How is it possible that the yoga his mother practices—terrifying visions of her with a foot behind her head or her head between her legs, the plasticine elasticity of her whole body—is good for her and not the opposite?

* Why, at every single one of the childhood shows his parents take him to, is there a terrible moment when the actors or speakers come down from the stage with little hops and, shrill-voiced and giggling, head straight for him to make him participate—coerced and in front of everyone—in something that he never wanted, wants, or will ever want to participate in, with *everyone* watching him?

* Where do the holes in cheese come from?

* And wouldn't it be much more comfortable and logical to put socks on inside out, with the stitches on the outside?

*Why do the people who sing "Happy Birthday" always seem to be thinking about something else, and some don't even sing, but just move their lips without making any sound; just like, he'll soon learn, when they sing the national anthem for school activities? And why do some of them sing with undisguised hatred, as if wishing the worst on you, as if mocking the fact that you're celebrating the passing of time, of your own time?

* Who are the people who decide the colors of countries on maps and globes? And is it possible to get a job doing that?

* Why do the digits on the hand have specific names and those on the foot do not? (A question made more intriguing when in high school he discovers that, in English, the digits on the hands are called "fingers" and those on the foot are called "toes.")

* Is the halo around Jesus Christ's head the graphic representation of a powerful migraine caused by the crown of thorns?

* Why does everyone go to such pains to figure out who their babies

look like, when it is perfectly obvious that babies don't look like anyone, like anything, except babies?

* Is Jell-O animal, vegetal, mineral, or interplanetary?

* OK, he gets why Barbazul murdered successive inquisitive spouses, but why did he kill the first one?

* Why are jokes so difficult to retain—both impossible to remember and impossible to forget—and dissolve so quickly in our memories? (An enigma that will grow with him and, as an adult, will be translated into a "Is it possible that jokes are made of the same material as dreams?")

* And why is it that in genie tales—so much more interesting than fairy tales—the third and final wish is never "I want three more wishes" and on and on to infinity, a strategy that would make it possible for him to include absurd wishes like that the best student stop understanding lessons, that the water in the pool turn to Coca-Cola, or that the weekend last an entire year, or—too many wishes—that there be peace and love throughout the world, even between his parents?

* And why do we call them fairy tales when they're really witch tales?

* How is it that Cinderella's glass slipper doesn't break when it comes off her foot and falls down the stairs?

* What does Coca-Cola taste like—did the taste of Coca-Cola actually exist?—and how is it possible that so many different people agree and coincide on their love for that soda pop?

* And that great mystery, the one his parents have never been able to clear up: of all foods, why is asparagus the only one that transfers its flavor to the smell of pee, negating even the pee smell of pee?

And the last one, the one he's just added to his list:

* Why are there red and blue flags waving on beaches—not on this one, which, as mentioned, is a wild, undomesticated beach with no sign of being exploited or exploitable—reporting the liquid and elusive humors of the water, but not the moods of the sand, always quick, where his parents often behave more unpredictably than the climate or the currents and where so many things take place that are, to The Boy, inexplicable?

There are dozens, hundreds of questions like these dancing in The Boy's head. And, of course, not all his "preoccupations" are so *sophisticated*. There's also his fear of fat women; who, for him, are not just evil, but, in lingua-Disney, *malignant* or *malevolent* or *maleficent*. But the evil has already been done or the evil function already activated. And The Boy is already not all that rational and already thinks like one of those antique windup tin toys. Like his favorite toy. A toy—though The Boy can't even imagine something like this yet, that things cease to be—that will soon pass out of production. About to be discontinued, like those clever tops or cymbal-clanging monkeys. A model retired for preservation by collectors: a runaway sleigh surrounded by the eternal manpower of politically correct toys and the sound and fury of electronic and computerized monstrosities preparing to land and invade.

And, though The Boy doesn't know it, there are many children like him. There, outside. Developing in secret and ready for the assembly line. Like aliens who have infiltrated terrestrial homes, waiting for the signal to activate and start doing their thing, to the joy of specialized psychologists. Children whose childhoods will be modified by the serial separations of not-so-serious parents. Children who, suddenly, to keep from thinking about how *strange* all of that is, will start to think about things stranger still, to think a great deal, all the time, in order to think as little as possible. "Hey, here come the new Kids of Divorced Parents. Invite Mommy and Daddy to the party!"

And soon the intensity of the virus will increase forever. And more questions, questions that grow as he grows, without that meaning they get more profound or less playful:

* What's a comma doing putting itself between two numbers? Was mathematics created just to drive him crazy, a universal conspiracy in which everyone pretends to understand something that's clearly incomprehensible and has no sense or logic? And what makes a psychotic so sure that 2 + 2 makes 5, while a neurotic knows that 2 + 2 makes 4 but just can't handle it? And what about the person who always thinks that 2 + 2 equals 1 + 1 + 1 + 1, or the exact number of times you have to let the phone ring before answering or hanging up?

* Why, in TV shows and movies, can the fastest speeds only be expressed in the slowest motion?

* What happened—and, yes, he's really going to like horror movies, those sympathetic to the monsters—to Dracula's clothes and cape when he turned into a bat? Did his cape and the clothes also vampirize and then reappear when the Count regained human form? Wrinkled, stained?

* Why is the Miss Universe contest always won by a woman from planet Earth?

* Why do people put photos of loved ones on refrigerator doors? Do they think of them as cold matter or food to be warmed up?

* Why do singers in heavy metal bands sing with such high-pitched voices when, by definition and intention, their voices should be deep, metallic, heavy?

* Why do zombies' victims always get caught, when the undead or unliving move so very slowly and without any apparent urgency? Why do zombies need to feed on brrrrrrrrains so badly if consuming them doesn't increase their negligible intelligence one iota?

* Why is it that extraterrestrials—instead of abducting global heads of state, eminent scientists, or great artists—always opt to take country bumpkins or sad neighborhood hairdressers, or pretty much whoever is passing by, staring up at the sky?

* And why do the people who used to stop and help accident victims—undead? Martians?—now just film the accident with their phones and upload it to YouTube as fast as they can? Which leads him to:

* Why do famous sex addicts who check into clinics to overcome their illness—after rampaging through various harems of long-legged, perky-breasted goddesses—never get caught by their wives with "normal," unattractive, or even old women?

* Why are girls so afraid of being spied on in their underwear, but not of being seen in a bikini, and why do they always say "I don't know what's going on with me" when really they know perfectly well?

* And why are women's feet—under sheets and blankets, even in summer—always cold?

* In the instant of death, the soul departs through the soles of the feet; is that why anyone who gets hit by a car, in the air of a final, truly fatal leap, loses their shoes, which always land several meters from their body?

* Why is it that there are so few clocks in the most modern airports and that everything sold in airports is more expensive than it is outside?

* Why is it that now, later on, when people sing "Happy Birthday" they seem to always be thinking about their own birthday, about how many

they've had, how many they've got left, about whether or not they are *happy* birthdays?

* Why is it when people tell you "It's not your fault," what they really mean is the exact opposite? (Even though the word "fault" had never entered your head; and now it's there, forever, yours from here onward, always?)

* Or why are there more people every day who stop in doorways or at the foot of escalators or at exits to mass transit to consult electronic devices?

* Is it really true that dreamers in Nordic countries—and those in charge of their frigid hotels—consider themselves more evolved for having renounced sheets and sleeping under pure eiderdown?

And even though the thing about * King Kong and the thing about the * asparagus and the thing about the * feet and the soul and the shoes continue to perturb him a great deal, like tentacles from the depths of childhood (and, in the former case, will always, over the years, produce in him a strange and scientifically unjustified calm, confirming, or at least convincing him, that his intestines are still functioning as they always have because the thing about * the asparagus keeps happening like clockwork), the most intriguing question of all is *that* question. A question planted in childhood but that, with time's passing, keeps inexorably reaching out its roots into the earth, where one day we'll all be buried to feed the trees so they can grow, a question that Google will never have an answer to:

* Do they like me or not like me or still like me or no longer like me or did they ever like me? Does she? Does he? Do any of them? Do I?

But he has a while before he'll have to ask himself about all of that. (Here it comes, from so far away, so far away that it's as if it were coming from an alternate dimension, from a possible maybe and, ah, another parentheses like an expansive wave. And The Boy doesn't yet possess the knowledge necessary to resist the flood that, within a few years and *to be continued . . .*)

And meanwhile The Boy would keep on wondering—there again, in that present, *onvacation*— * how does the sun start to set, to drop from the top of the highest wall? And how, as it lets itself go and falls, shadows begin to reappear. * What color are shadows? The Boy wonders. Because clearly they're not black, not exactly. Not gray either. Shadows are the color of whatever they cover and change: because, in the shadows, everything acquires a shadowy tone and a shadowy air. And yet, so far, that's not a problem. Shadows—new shadows, shadows that last until just past midday—are brief, a sketch of shadow. It's hot, the sky is blue, the sea is darker blue—a blue made turbulent and brown by the river mouth—and the sand is yellow. Everything so fragile, so easily broken. And the oxygen is like pointy flakes of snow that sting a little when breathed in.

And The Boy drops down next to his parents. It's colder there, next to them. Lower temperatures. As if his parents were refrigerating the air around them. And The Boy feels the exquisite sensation of clean sweat drying on his skin and, suddenly, his body receives a jolt of electricity. And he's moving again, back on his feet, jumping and waving his arms and squawking like a crazy, crazy bird. "A bird crazier than a crazy bird," The Boy thinks and laughs and almost asks himself, with a strange fear, if he just made up a joke, or something like that, and he promises himself not to forget it. And he keeps on honking, making noise. Whatever it takes, anything to break the bellicose truce that his parents had settled into: the calm that precedes the storm that precedes the hurricane that precedes the tsunami that precedes the crack that'll split the world that precedes the black hole that'll devour all light that precedes the darkness that precedes nothing—because after the darkness there will be nothing left. *The End.*

Later, with the running or rolling of the years, The Boy will learn how to neutralize and ignore the call of that abyss: opening a book, plunging inside, the freest of falls, closing the cover on reality, behind him now not in front, and opening his eyes. And he'll always marvel at the fact that whenever he picks up a book for the first time—he's been told that the same thing happens to other people with firearms—he'll always be surprised by the fact that, no matter the number of pages and type of binding, he thought it'd be lighter or heavier, but never *like this*. And then it'll seem logical and narratively appropriate that each book *feels* unique and different and special. But there's still time before that. Before reading and writing. There's still about half as much life as he's already lived. So, as a protest against the slowness of his learning (with each passing day he incorporates ten to twenty new words whose meaning he doesn't know or just senses; which doesn't keep him from savoring their sound, from the pleasure they create inside his mouth when he repeats them; today, this today that he's remembering now, he's heard and tried out for the first time the word "parentheses"), The Boy keeps moving. The Boy—before the time of sitting down to read and write, of moving in a different way arrives—runs and spins and leaps and dances and falls down just for the pleasure of standing up and running and spinning and leaping and dancing and falling down again.

And his parents watch him with a mix of surprise, resignation, and fatigue: The restless Boy is also, according to his pediatrician, a boy with "a proclivity for accidents."

In his short but accident-ridden existence, The Boy has already passed through the following predicaments: a) a difficult birth in which he almost died or, actually, did die for a few minutes, first, strangled by his own umbilical cord and, again, when a nurse dropped him on the floor (he doesn't know this yet, he doesn't remember it, they'll tell him a while later, and "a while" is the chronological unit that tends to mean a quarter of a century, or something like that, right?); b) an undesired encounter with a giant cactus; c) a never entirely elucidated episode on a tricycle also involving a truck, two motorcycles, and a wheelchair; d) a fire; e) a flood with a short circuit to boot; f) another fire; g) hand-to-hand combat with one of those mutant dogs that are trained to kill and that, nobody knows how, escaped its muzzle just as The Boy was passing by (see bite scar on left heel; see dog missing an eye); h) a poisoning with cleaning products that, to the emergency room doctor's bewilderment, should've killed any living organism . . . and on and on until z) the time when, a few days ago, a clam shell clamped itself to the middle of his forehead where, now, there's a mark in the shape of a smile and, soon, any minute now a) it'll all start over again, alphabetically, like that rotating series of names given to Caribbean hurricanes.

That's life, that's *his* life.

A constant and generalized rehearsal for a death that debuted in the first second of his existence and whose silent applause can and will continue to be heard until the final instant of the final bow, which, in his case, if everything goes well for him and badly for the rest of humanity, will be an incessant *enter/exit ghost*. Meanwhile and in the meantime, a defenseless and all-powerful and enslaving tyranny of successive disasters (and the cold planning and execution of that one Oh So Particular Great Disaster that will put him in the eyes and mouths of everyone) along with the disaster of his parents as intermittent background music. (Several chapters down the road, inside the horizontal parentheses of a divan, a psychoanalyst will interpret this succession of childhood cataclysms as a system that he used, unconsciously, to keep his parents together through the adversity of their marriage, making them stay together so they thought they were protecting him from catastrophic mishaps when really he was protecting them and keeping them together as a couple.) Parents who, in turn, found themselves surrounded by mercenary armies, at the mercy of their own increasingly defeated and worn-out emotions. Another chapter in the saga. The same chapter as always with more incorrect corrections, with multiplying errata, with a lack of orthography and courtesy.

On the beach, under the sun, the father and mother read the same book. It's not the first time they've done this. That's how they met: the two of them reading the same book. On a train, the most romantic of all modes of transit. That same book they never stop reading. And, of course, there's no better argument than that for putting a conversation in drive and taking a ride down the tunnel of love. But as tends to happen with everything that seems charming in a romance's initial hours, this ritual of reading separately together—of reading the same book but different books, at the same time—now just produces a kind of irritation. The kind of annoyance we experience when, after a long time, we still feel obliged to do something that we obliged ourselves to do in the first place. And, then, you can't help but wonder, why am I doing this, damn it, damn it, how did I get here, could I be more of an idiot?

Besides, the father's and mother's chosen book isn't the most appropriate for the times that are passing, for the times that they're dragging themselves through. A book that begins on a beach and narrates—in exquisite detail, with painful elegance—the simultaneously vertiginous and gradual apocalypse of a marriage, envied and deemed perfect by many. The book is, also, an indisputable classic. Which means neither of them can stop reading it; but both fantasize that the other tires, surrenders, or retreats in terror from the cruel and revealing mirror of those pages. Give up. And leave me in peace to read it on my own and by myself, right? None of that for the moment. And his father identifies with the novel's male protagonist and his mother also identifies with the novel's male protagonist. Because the novel's *female* protagonist, the male protagonist's wife, is mad or, if you prefer, "disturbed": that subtle and elegant and polite and somewhat vintage way of saying that someone is completely and absolutely batshit insane. And both protagonists suffer equally. And, in the opening pages, they are on a beach. And she's too mad for a beach to make her "feel good." Or maybe it's just the opposite. Maybe The Boy's father and mother identify with her and not with him; because it's distinctly possible that he has something to do with her madness. Or maybe the lack of clarity and precise identification is related to the different editions and translations that they're reading. The father's copy has the photo of an old-fashioned swimmer on the cover; the mother's has the touristic poster of a beach on the Côte d'Azur. And the father and mother don't know it yet, but they're reading different versions of the same novel in the same way that they're writing different versions of their marriage and the imminent allegations of their defense and/or prosecution. Because the book's author decided, almost desperate, just before dying, to alter the temporal flow of the plot—which wasn't initially linear, but sinuous, present and past and present—and to reorganize it chronologically. To see—he'd just put so much work into those pages and nobody seemed that interested in them, considering them a successful failure or something like that—if, that way, the novel improved, if it was appreciated more, if it sold better. His instructions were followed post-mortem by his literary executor. The new version was considered inferior and he reverted to the original, to the one that—just like real time—moves forward and backward and forward again. But for a few years, in English and in translation, both versions existed at the same time. And The Boy—when he was no longer a boy, when he was able to read and compare them, multiple times—was never sure which his mother had read and which his father had read. Who moved straight and true from past to future and who was left spinning in place. It doesn't really matter, he'll think. What matters now is, yes, the absence of his backward-walking tin toy, and that his father calls his mother "Zelda" and his mother calls his father "Zeldo." With toxic affection. And, when The Boy asks why they call each other that, they tell him that it has to do with the book, with the characters in the book, with the book's author and his wife, who are like the characters in the book, though not exactly. The revelation that nonfiction and fiction can be one and the same gives The Boy a massive headache, more or less the same kind of pain that, as mentioned, movies with space-time storylines will also give him. A beatific and Jesuitical aura, another question to archive alongside * Superman and * King Kong and * fat women and * the powerful odor of asparagus in urine. And maybe, he'll think, it's all because his parents miss their toys *too*. Because his parents have more toys than he does, he thinks: silver pillows, plastic masks, glass contraptions full of colored liquids that rise when enveloped by the warmth of a hand, pendulums of multiple balls that strike each other one by one or two by two or three by three, a blue wave held captive inside an acrylic rectangle that rocks back and forth, exotic musical instruments that they don't know how to play, but that are so pleasing to look at, psychedelic kaleidoscopes, lamps of cold lava; and who knows what other toys they have hidden away, under lock and key.

Here and now, in the absence of all of that, his father and mother start once again to argue. To "debate," they prefer to say. And The Boy covers his ears to keep from hearing what he can't stop hearing. Ears covered with hands, he knows, is not necessarily a wish granted.

So The Boy decides to get away and go out into the water. Before going in he touches his bathing suit, as if checking over his superhero uniform. It's blue with a small white anchor and it fits him the way bathing suits fit all children—very well. He is still far from adolescence and further still from the prime of youth (when bathing suits can fit really badly, and it's oh so *vital* that they fit really well), or from old age (when they always fit really badly, but nobody cares anymore). The Boy enters the water like someone entering an unfamiliar place. With caution, cold and hot. And, the water up to his waist, he brings a hand to his mouth and tastes a—might such a word exist, might it belong to the same language as *onvacation*?—*saltysweet* taste. Behind him, his parents are still "debating." Random sentences reach him. Like pieces of torn letters, difficult to read. Like letters ripped apart by someone who barely reads them and later attempts to put them—torn and in tatters—back together to read again, fantasizing about the impossibility that maybe now they'll say something different. And it's the distinctive sound more than the diffuse yet easily graspable meaning of those stray words that disturbs The Boy. Things are not going well. Things are getting worse. And among all those stray words there's one that appears more and more frequently. A shy word. A name more uncommon than rare: Penelope. His mother sings it, mockingly: because the name came from a song. His mother says it over and over and, each time she pronounces it, she instinctively raises her hand to her belly and caresses it or gives it a few light taps or points at it. The name "Penelope" produces a different effect in his father: he hears it and stares at the mother's belly—as if he were penetrating it with Krypton rays—and then looks up at the sky and closes his eyes. Penelope—it's clear, much clearer than the water there before him—is already, though invisible and miniscule, a powerful presence that makes everything around her, his mother and father, unsettled and nervous. His mother: nausea, dizziness, insomnia, rapid fluctuations in body temperature, and sudden changes in blood pressure. And his father: nausea, dizziness, insomnia, rapid fluctuations in body temperature, and sudden changes in blood pressure. Penelope is a volatile reactant. Problematic Penelope is a problem even before being born. Penelope—*enfant du hasard*, Sarah and Gerald Murphy, the vague inspiration for the very novel that his mother and father are reading, would have said, on another beach, in imported yet admirable French—wasn't planned. Penelope wasn't planned and yet . . . The Boy—an exhausted and exhausting experience—was more than enough to make them parents; to level-up in the video-game of life, to perpetuate the race, and keep their family name alive; to be hip among hip young parents. Being a young parent, at that time, at least for a while and out of the blue—really out of the blue—has the same charm as dying young and leaving a good-looking corpse. But without having to die. Being a parent makes you legendary for a very brief period of time. But it's better than nothing, and how many times does life give you the opportunity to feel seriously legendary and a true creator? The problem—the problem of Penelope, the problem that is Penelope—is that it's no easy thing to settle who has the blame and who is to blame: the spermatozoid or the ovum? So, then, their words—including the name "Penelope"; because even though the exact technology doesn't exist yet and not enough months have passed to fire waves into the mother's belly and bounce them off the guest and send back the echo of an image and a sex, they already know it's a girl and that she'll be called Penelope in honor of that popular song—increase in volume and intensity. And they escalate into tuneless yelling. Here we go again, father and mother yelling, yelling at each other.

Which propels The Boy away from the shore, out into the water.

And he tries not to think about what happened last night.

About the thing with the knives.

Something The Boy would like to believe was a dream, but knows was not. And that now, in his memory, has the unforgettable clarity of one of those laminated illustrations from fairy tales and witch tales, right-hand pages facing left-hand pages, overpowering the as-yet meaningless letters.

There, yesterday, in his bed, in the darkness broken by the light from the hallway. And, first his father and then his mother, staring at him, thinking that he's asleep. (In the future, he'd read in a novel that parents start as gods and end up myths, and that, between one extreme and the other, the human forms they adopt tend to be catastrophic for their children.) So, now, divine and devouring and already catastrophic, his mother and father, silhouettes in the room's doorway, holding knives in their hands. Big dangerous knives. Mother and father clutching those knives and maybe thinking, The Boy thinks, about whether or not they're going to do it, about whether they'll dare do it, while he pretends to be submerged in boyhood dreams, so he can remember everything, forget nothing. Because, for a while longer, his memory is still the implacable and miraculous and reliable memory of a boy with little to remember. A memory still safe from the forgetfulness that will come with high school; when and where his previously infinite recall capacity will constantly be tested with names of heroes whose uniforms are far more boring than those of superheroes, with mathematic tables, dates of battles, and useless equations that'll never be of any use to him, but that might serve the secret function of burying primordial matters and more essential lessons under an avalanche of public and external information. Unforgettable and instantly memorizable lessons like the one from the night before. The lesson of the two knives. The lesson that for a few seconds fills his eyes with tears, but, luckily, there's nothing "used up" more quickly than tears—hot under his eyelids and then, a few centimeters below, already cold on his cheeks. Those parents, his parents, are like the parents in those stories who take their children into a forest and abandon them—once upon another time, there can always be once upon another time—so they can go back to living happily ever after.

The Boy doesn't know how to swim yet—he'll learn to read and write before he learns to swim—and won't know how for many years. His sporting specialty is drifting along on solid ground, crossing and lying down in dry riverbeds, intuitively understanding floor plans and blueprints of houses and apartments. He is, yes, a city boy. Not only does he not know how to swim; The Boy doesn't know how to ride a bicycle, kick balls with any precision, or climb trees. So, ah, the intoxicating sensation of doing something new, something he doesn't know how to do yet, but might along the way. Step by step, feeling how the swelling strangeness of the river spilling into the sea wraps around his ankles. Then the water is up to his chest, his neck, his chin.

And then something happens.

The Boy feels it, but doesn't understand it. The perpetual motion motor of the—and again, could this word, a close relative of *onvacation* and *saltysweet* exist?—*riversea* changes gears, accelerates. And, suddenly, his feet no longer touch bottom. The Boy remembers a TV commercial. Black and white— barely four channels back then—and maybe that's why black and white is the color of his nightmares: black and white is much more frightening. In the commercial—an advisory notice, filmed in first person POV—a person enters the sea, on a crowded beach. You hear the sound of people on the sand and the heavy breathing of someone swimming in water that is too deep. Now you also hear the sound of a whistle, warning the swimmer he's gone too far from shore. And, all of a sudden, the swimmer starts to shriek, to flail, to thrash the water—a few drops land on the camera lens, his eyes— around him in terror, and, yes, to drown. The swimmer goes under several times, comes back up for air, screams for help, gasps, and, in the end, is reclaimed by the abyss that subsequently fades to black, to darkness. Then a startling voice says something about being careful when going in the water, something like that.

Something similar happens to The Boy now, but in color, colors so brilliant they hurt his pupils, and nobody—no whistle or shouts, only the distant monotone buzz of his parents' "debate"—even notices. Extra! Extra! The Boy is drowning. He swallows water. He spits water. He sinks to the bottom and, from there, kicks off hard and returns to the surface. There's an airplane in the sky, he can see it, could they see him from up there? Looking out of one of those circular windows, thinking: "Look, down there, it looks like that boy is drowning . . . Do we tell the flight attendant so she can tell the captain so the captain can do *something*?" There's a sky and an airplane and

The Boy fills his mouth with oxygen, oxygen that won't last long. Just long enough for the automatic reflex and defense mechanism of imagining himself there above, far away, flying, grownup and looking out the little window and wondering if that little stain of color in the turgid water that is him might be a someone in trouble. An airplane like something to hold on to, to keep from sinking. And airplanes carry life preservers under their seats. But they won't be any help: he'll be too tired soon; he won't last much longer.

And The Boy is not (again, The Boy's references are still limited and fundamentally childish, though exceedingly multipurpose, already foreshadowing the possibility of a consummate referential maniac) like the beaten but unbreakable ACME-brand-sponsored Coyote. *Like this*, the coyote feels just *like this*—thinks The Boy, and he paddles and pedals the invisible bicycle of wet submarine air—when he discovers that the ground is no longer there; that he has gone out too far in pursuit of the Roadrunner; that there's nothing out there but the total nothingness of the precipice and the long vertical fall, a fall he'll survive just so he can fall again, condemned to being unbreakable just to keep on being beaten.

And no, that isn't The Boy's case, beyond the innumerable "accidents" he's already lived through: right now he's a fragile boy and his time is running out. And children's time tends to be brief; even though, sometimes, they make it seem so elastic, almost eternal. And his life has been so short that there's not enough archival material to carry out that obligatory projection; the one where "in the moment of death your entire life passes before your eyes in a matter of seconds." Because, instead, what occurs is a capricious change of film. Fear is impossible to command; fear doesn't follow orders.

And what The Boy watches now—as if he were sitting in a movie theater, just after that traumatic moment between the previews and the beginning of the movie when some pale old women walk through the rows of seats, collection boxes in hand, collecting coins for a foundation that looks after orphans and the homeless—is the blockbuster of everything that might happen if he makes it out of this predicament alive.

The Boy remembers, imagines himself in a movie theater. The Boy is happy, ready to receive his dose of illustrated and animated joy. And suddenly, more cartoons, everything becomes a little less Mickey Mouse (not the atypical and disobedient Mickey Mouse of *The Sorcerer's Apprentice*, but the same, though he wouldn't dare say it, goody-goody and kind of obnoxious Mickey Mouse as always, so much duller than the hysterical Donald Duck) and everything becomes a little more . . . a little more Bambi. Here the Coyote's explosives and perpetual resurrections don't matter. Here everything is somber, and Dickensian; The Boy doesn't know what *Dickensian* is yet, but he's suffered through it already with *Oliver!* The Boy is alone in his seat. And before the movie starts, that other commercial, more frightening than the drowning one. A commercial that's not an advisory notice, but a solicitation. A commercial designed to raise funds for a children's foundation. There, on the screen, a lost boy, holding onto the railing of a bridge that spans a highway. A national Oliver. Face streaked with tears and dotted with snot, a popular singer's plaintive voice crooning lines like "In this exact moment . . . / There's a boy in the street / There's a boy in the streeeeet." And what frightens The Boy more than anything isn't the lost and abandoned little boy to whom he'd give all his toys in a heartbeat, except for his little traveling tin man. And, no: what worries him isn't that he'll end up like that boy in the street, what worries him is "In this exact moment . . ." That terrifying precision. And the fact that—especially since it's the first show of the afternoon, the matinees or early shows tending to be the ones The Boy frequents—there's always some-where, according to that song, no matter what time it is, where everything is, *exactly*, that dark. And that that darkness—a darkness The Boy sometimes, always a surprise, discovers upon leaving the movie theater, in the winter, when the sun goes down so early on Sundays, as if accelerating the arrival of Monday and the return to classrooms—can find you. It's a contagious and sticky darkness, a darkness that you step on like a piece of chewing gum, so hard to dislodge from the sole of your shoe later on. A darkness with no timetable. Like right now, though scarcely past midday, a flash of shadow dazzles and illuminates him in the Cinemascope of that beach. Suddenly, The Boy sees everything. He understands everything all at once. Like when leaving a movie you stop in front of the movie theater doors. Back then, movie theaters (by the time The Boy leaves behind his long adolescence, this custom won't exist anymore; just like scratched copies of movies, out of focus movies, movies with asynchronous sound and image, or movies that burst into flames like vampires under the light of projectors won't exist), in addi-tion to the movie's poster, also exhibited stills from the movie. Moments that someone considered ideal for attracting the indecisive, tempting them to enter. Photos like illustrations from books that don't help you understand what they're about or what story they tell. Photos that The Boy looks at again when he leaves, after the movie is over. (Photos that before long won't be of animated animals, but of actors and actresses. A young woman with a dress made of little metal pieces. Another young woman—even younger than the last, closer and nearer—in a cemetery under the rain. A man riding a camel. And monkeys and monoliths and spaceships frozen in the amber of a frame that someone specially selected to tempt passersby.) Photos from which The Boy had already deduced a plot the moment he entered and that now, before going home, he repositions in the order of a story that often ends up being more disappointing than the one he'd imagined before the lights came down and the screen lit up. He understands now—looked at from a distance, as if they too were photos from a movie he just watched—that his parents . . . are just a couple of scared kids, because they're only now realizing that they aren't kids anymore, they're grownups! And that they don't want, don't know how, to be grownups! And that they never really will! And that, no matter how many toys they buy so they can keep on playing, nothing will save them from that reality! They'll be, at best, wrinkled children with porous and brittle and breakable bones! Right now! In the street! On the beach! In the water! There's a boy! In trouble! The force of that revelation takes his breath away, makes him long to go *onvacation* forever, to drink the water, to swallow the water, to fill himself up with the water and overflow, as if his body were a vessel. To successfully premiere, to great critical acclaim, something that previously—watching a movie or trembling from a clap of thunder or reacting to the slap of a scream or the scream of a slap—The Boy has only had small previews of, brief trials of: the taste of fear, the taste of his heart beating everywhere, the runaway taste of his heart in his mouth. An aftertaste between metallic and carnal. Someone might point out that *that* is the taste of the adrenaline distilled by the body. But no, it's something else. It's as if the adrenaline were radiating throughout his entire body, as if it were shaping it.

Is this the most important thing that's happened to him yet?, The Boy wonders. (Who knows, he responds; and, at the other end of his story, decades later, he'll say yes, when he realizes that the most transcendent events *take place* in the past but only *happen* in the future, when we're truly cognizant of their importance, of the influence and weight they've had on everything that has and will come to pass. And it's that which happens *after* that makes the *before* sad or happy. We need to know where we're coming to in order to fully understand the texture of where we came from. We have to traverse great distances without precise compasses, dragging ourselves far and wide across an immense and simultaneously forever-fleeting present. But it's during childhood that there's the least separation between what is and what's felt. There, the present is nothing but a narrow door separating the future from the past, and there's no distance to reflect on it, because there's so little experience to compare it to, there's almost no space at all between what's done and what's perceived. Maps aren't yet necessary and the possibility of monsters on their borders roars louder there, everywhere. And that—the sensation of an eternal moment—is something he'll only experience a few times in his life, like variations on the same taste, the aforementioned taste of fear that loosens the baby teeth he's not yet lost. The taste of waiting in a hospital emergency room, the taste of realizing you can't live without someone, the taste of the real possibility of leaving it all behind, the taste of closing a book never to open it again, the taste of particle acceleration disassembling the puzzle of life in another century, another millennium. And The Boy can almost anticipate, predict all those fears to be trembled at, with the precision of a visionary, far away from any switch that could turn off such brilliance. A brilliance that's strange and out of place, like a diurnal lightning bolt, like the ghost of a ghost. Again: maybe, when you die so young, what passes before your eyes isn't everything you've lived but all the fears you never got to experience, all those fears that make you feel more alive than ever. Like how now, surprise, in the liquid center of terror, comes the inexplicable urge to laugh. (That slapstick reflex that forces us to think that there might be something funny about horror, like—on the plasma screen of a future TV—the vision of all those spectators and family members looking up at the sky and wondering for a few seconds, openmouthed and wide-eyed, if the *Challenger* is supposed to give off so much smoke and separate into so many parts, so suddenly, there above in the blue.) That's how The Boy watches himself, like an *in situ, in tempo* catastrophe. (The Boy doesn't know it yet, but he suffers from a slight but decisive cerebral anomaly, a result of *r*) a fall down the stairs in the home of his paternal grandparents. More an effect than a defect. Something that alters the rhythm of what's called "persistence of vision": his is slower, making him see everything in slow motion, image by image, frame by frame, word by word. Persistence of vision that, added to his eidetic or "photographic" memory, will end up—with time and according to critics and scholars—"having a decisive influence on his style and vision.") So, all action like a freeze-frame that slowly unfreezes. Like those drawings on the borders or in the corners of the pages of some books that, flipped through rapidly, with the stroke of a thumb, seem to melt into a spasmodic flow, like an old silent movie where everyone appears to be walking across an electrified floor.

And then—more of an attack mechanism than a defense mechanism; after all, he's still a boy—The Boy forgets all of it.

He erases all memory of things he's not yet experienced (all those barely adult versions of those eternally childish questions); because now a shift in the water's gears pulls him, as if on a raft, back toward the shore, to the continuation of his story, to his present life that lacks such complications and such long sentences and such inopportune parentheses. With the relief comes the forced amnesia, the obligation to forget everything he saw and understood. He senses he has to leave all of that in the water, throw it all overboard, to make up for the lack of wind in his sails and to be lighter.

The Boy becomes who he was, who he must continue to be, so that, with the years, he can turn into who he was during the brief eternity of those two or three terrible and definitive minutes. The Boy has saved himself and has never experienced anything more gratifying than the feeling of the almost liquid mud lapping at the soles of his feet. The water is up to his neck, his chest, his waist, his knees, and he's out, taking one or two or three steps and falling down next to his parents. On his back, breathing deeply, arms crossed, rays of sunlight like ecstatic pinpricks on his skin. It's not that he's happy. It's something else. It's beyond happiness—you have to pass through happiness and come out the other side to know what it is The Boy feels now—something that has no name. It's the raw material that happiness, among other things, is made of. It's that raw and primal happiness that, over the years, proves irretrievable, and its memory—like a happy bison on a Cro-Magnon cave wall—is all that's left of it. A souvenir over which we superimpose, in vain, the whole succession of happinesses—diluted and convoluted with preservatives more artificial than natural—that will or won't come, or that we'll pass by or won't know how to see, or that won't ever even make it out of their caves. Happinesses that are false, in every case, like copies and imitations, like the postcards we resignedly pick up upon leaving the museum. Reproductions, falsifications. Believing that if you try hard enough, if you stare at them without blinking, the act of thinking about being happy can, for a while, convince us that we are happy.

The Boy laughs, but he laughs not by laughing but by making a strange, loud sound. A unique and new laugh—the one he started to laugh when, eternal moments before, he thought it his best and last laugh—of someone who departed and has just returned from somewhere far away. The laugh of an extraterrestrial back on solid ground. The laugh of someone who has come back from the dead and lived to tell the tale, to write it down, and, then, alter it, improve it, add the invented part. The invented part that is not, not ever, the deceitful part, but the part that *actually* makes something that merely happened into something as it should have happened. Something (everything to come, the rest of his life, will spring from that there and then, from *that exact moment*) more authentic and valuable and pure than the simple and banal and often unsubtle and sloppy truth.

The Boy's laugh makes a lot of noise and, for once, his parents, annoyed and distracted—The Boy won't let them read or debate—yell at him simultaneously.

In complete agreement.

In perfect synchrony.

Magic. Abracadabra. The same word, a verb (that could be the name of a faraway place), and also a command and, in addition, an absurdity impossible for him to put in practice at the moment.

But it doesn't matter, he doesn't care.

The Boy, with the laugh of a broken motor, happy to be running again, stands up and, still laughing, walks toward the trees, toward the house, and obeys.

This is how it begins.

Over the years (here and there and everywhere, in airports and hospitals and particle accelerators; in the ever-longer and more diffuse spaces that stretch out between one book and the next; before vanishing in order to be able to be in all places) the man who was once that boy, The Boy, will be asked the same question over and over again: "As a writer, where do you get your ideas?" An almost obligatory question, which he answers (which he'll always answer) with eternal vagaries or certainties forgotten the next day.

Then, unavoidably, unable to avoid it, when answering those questions, he'll put on a parentheses face, he'll invent something, anything, when answering how he invents the invented part. The invented part—an oh so insubstantial cloud that, nonetheless, manages to make the sun shut its mouth and stay quiet for a while—is nothing but a true shadow projecting itself across the real part.

And between parentheses, once again, he'll bring two more parentheses together.

Like this:

()

And the result has the shape of an aerodynamic vulva (he doesn't like the word "vulva," he'll think as he thinks it; find another, he'll write on the page).

Or of the mysterious seed of what will one day germinate.

Or of a future device yet to be turned on, inside his head, never to be turned off and to keep on working until his last day, ceaselessly broadcasting that signal, even though, more than once, he'll try, in vain, to turn it off.

Turn it on then.

And what we see now is something that looks pretty much like this:

(((((((((((())))))))))))

The device and the vibrations it gives off.

The concentric eccentric waves indicating the exact point in the pond where the rock we threw from here, from the eccentric present, just sank. And another childish but timeless question, also unanswerable: why, whenever we're standing on the shore, do we feel that irrepressible and reflexive urge to throw a rock into the water? A mystery. A sneaking suspicion, yes.

The rock is the cause and its waves the effect: what gets told based on what happened, the story before and behind History.

The rock is the invented part that, subsequently, comes to form part of the truth.

And, wearing that parentheses face, that writer who'll always be that boy will wonder—in silence, within the absolute silence of those parentheses where no outside sound can get in and be heard, forever—why it is that they never ask him something far more important, or, at least, more interesting, than: "As a writer, where do you get your ideas?"

Why do they never ask: "What made you want to be a writer?"

The parentheses are the future.

THE PLACE WHERE THE SEA ENDS
SO THE FOREST CAN BEGIN

I

The first thing they film, of course, is the library. Close-ups and wide shots and zoom-ins and zoom-outs where they can read titles but not names. Or vice versa. Though, of course, some legible titles automatically trigger the smaller-lettered name. Or the other way around. Action and reaction. Alpha and Omega. A serpent eating its own tail or strangling itself with it. Bookshelves upon bookshelves. And it's worth wondering whether it's the shelves that hold up the books or the books that hold up the shelves. Or both. Books standing up, books on the floor, books lying down, books lying down behind books standing up, books kneeling, books reclined and inclined, as if praying to other books above them, but below other still-higher books; despite the fact that their position means nothing and reveals less in terms of their quality and prestige and impact and how much they're admired by those who read them. There are no clear hierarchies or obvious favorites; there is no alphabetical or chronological or geographical or generic order. All together now, all mixed together, and the books reach the ceiling and even climb the stairs like some kind of polychrome kudzu vine; turning the wooden stairway into a stairway of books that at one point came from wood. Books that came from wood and to wood they'll return. Books shifting like ladders in an ascent without summit or terminus. Books climbing for nothing but the pleasure of continuing to climb and continuing to be read until the final step, not of a library but of a *liferary*—a life made of books, a life made of lives. Yes: the library like an organism, alive and in constant expansion, surviving owners and users alike.

A library without precise limits, where you never find the book you are looking for, but always find the book you *should* be looking for.

A library that, sometimes, lets itself fall (there are documented cases) and, while adding or removing a book, the owners are crushed to death, which is by no means a happy occurrence, though there are definitely worse deaths, more banal and less enlightened ways to die entombed.

A library that, every so often, drops to the floor the ripe fruit of a book, as if it'd been pushed by the hand of a ghost or its owner, who isn't a ghost exactly, but . . . And the book falls open and there you read, for instance, like right now, underlined years ago with one of those synthetic inks that highlight everything with an almost lunar glow, something like "Do not be cross because our characters do not always have the same faces; they are being true to life and death." Or something like "There is folklore, myths, facts, and all the questions that remain unanswered." And, next to that sentence, trapped in a comic strip speech-bubble not connected to any mouth, the irregular print, handwritten and small, but so readable and so read. The handwriting of someone who kept writing by hand despite the existence of increasingly light and smooth and plasmatic keyboards. The handwriting more of a mad scientist than a sane doctor (Slow Writer Sans Serif Bold?), adding, in red ink on the margin of the black on white quotation, a "And those unanswerable questions are nothing but the folklore and myths and facts of a private life, a very private life: PLEASE, DO NOT DISTURB."

A library of books covered in dust. And they say that domestic dust—90 percent of which is nothing but dead matter shed from human beings—is an important factor in the effective conservation of books. So, best to not dust them fully or frequently and, ah, poetic and literary justice—we shed ourselves so that our books may remain inviolate, and from the dust of our stories we come and to the dust covering our books we return. We return to a library—like all libraries—where we pause as if contemplating the noble ruins of a lost world or the raw materials of a world waiting to be discovered.

A library where, every so often, by accident and as if in the aftermath of an accident, disoriented by the shock of impact, someone arrives for whom books and, above all, the accumulation of books is an unfathomable mystery. Because for many people, books get used up and worn out and it makes no sense to keep them. They take up so much space, you have to store them, and they're heavy, and oh so dirty, and though no one would say it out loud, they're too cheap to really be something good and good for you. And, so, a library that might well provoke its accidental visitors—with an odd mixture of respect, unease, and contempt, as if referring to invulnerable and abundant cockroaches, a plague, or a virus—to ask you "But seriously, you've read *all* these books?" Visitors ask this because they don't dare ask themselves the questions they really *don't* want the answer to: "How is it that I've read so few books? How is it that there are barely any books in my house and that most of them are books of photos, some with photos of houses that also have libraries where there are barely any books except books of photos, and why instead of books, books of writing, do I have so many photos of people whom I should presumably love unconditionally but who, to tell the truth, when I think about it a little, after a few drinks, seem to be real, authentic . . . ?" They're the same uncouth tourists—never surprised by the quantity of crosses in churches or bills in banks or food in markets—who seem so amiable and pleased and presumably interested, but maintaining a safe distance from the troubling local fauna, when, in the next breath, they ask you "What are your books about?" And, yes, it's for these people that the electronic book has been invented, which—hallelujah and eureka!—has succeeded in putting television and print in communion: to download and not load down, to acquire and accumulate and never open, never turn a single page. And so that—so pleased that two thousand titles can be held in one hand—the books aren't there all the time, in view, their deafening silence a reminder of all you haven't and won't ever read. All those horizontal and vertical lines, full color and black and white. And the answer to the previous question (the envious incredulity that someone has been able to consume and process all that paper and ink) is "*Yes*, I have read *all* of them . . . Got a problem with that?" And, at the same time, the answer is *no*. Because there are books you buy to save for the future, as if you were stashing away food for a great drought or a new ice age. Or to cling to or to cover yourself with, in the pods of a spaceship, searching for a new home, while outside everything explodes and fades away and goes out. Books that, though they haven't been read and, maybe, won't ever be read, perform a critical, indispensable function: they are the past and the future and also the present of imagining (another form of reading, after all) what they tell, what they're about. Not of judging them, but intuiting or divining them from their covers, the photos and brief biographies of their authors, and the synopses written on their broad or not-so-broad backs and inside their slim or not so slim flaps. Books that, after a while, though they haven't been read or might never be read, exude a telepathic fragrance that has an odd effect on their owners: giving them the feeling that, at night, when they're asleep, these books tell each other their stories in the softest, yet most deafening of voices and that, yes, it's like you've toured and traveled through them and admired them without ever wanting or needing to open them. Sometimes, you think, it's enough to look at a book—to stare at it—to feel that you've already read it. Without reading it. The Japanese even have a word to capture this symptom and state of mind: *tsundoku*, to buy a book and not to read it, watching books collect and pile up, until the *tsundoku* grows into a tsunami, and even then . . . But for this to happen or to be felt, first you have to buy the book. Such black and white magic isn't achieved in public bookstores but in private libraries, alone, *now* you see it *now* you don't.

A library that's been organized to survive on the margin, but not in the margins of those photographs of pages, those repositories of written words. Devices that you can't smell or lend or steal or throw against the wall; that don't even allow for a surprise re-encounter with something (note or photo or snippit) inside; that won't even help us understand someone's nature when, having just arrived to someone's house, we go into their library to scan the titles, as if decoding the unconscious stains of one of those psychological tests, and even in movies, every time a library makes an appearance, we crane our necks trying to decipher the vertical names on the horizontal shelves.

A library with too many incarnations of *Tender Is the Night* and *Tierna es la noche* or—according to the translation—*Suave es la noche*, and even one *Tendre est la nuit* and *Ночь нежна* and *Yö on hellä* and *Zärtlich ist die Nacht* and *Գիշերը և անուշէ* and *Tenera è la notte*, all of them by Francis Scott Fitzgerald and by Фрэнсис Скотт Фицджеральд and by Ֆրենսիս Սքոթ Ֆիցջերալդ.

A library where, as a kind of decoration, as if punctuating the discursive flow of the books, there are also: a first edition LP (sealed, wrapped in a black case, never opened) of Pink Floyd's *Wish You Were Here*; a relatively new yet instantly vintage digital camera (with one of those stickers—the kind stuck on old travel trunks on its metal side that says "Abracadabra"); and a small and primitive and timeless tin toy. A little windup man, carrying a suitcase, with no need for batteries or switches. One of those objects seemingly designed to provoke in everyone who sees it the irrepressible urge to pick it up. And to turn the key protruding from the suitcase. And to make it walk. And, surprise: falling under its spell, the bewitched will soon discover that this toy (a defect, or maybe not), instead of moving forward, moves backward, that it only runs in reverse, as if retracing its own trajectory. And, next to the toy, a postcard reproduction of a painting that shows a clock with its insides spilling out. Springs and gears, cubist curves and, better, it's high time to start the engines of the story that'll be told here and press *play* and *record* and look into the viewfinder like someone spying through the keyhole of a door that opens right here.

And, moving across the library, camera in hand (along one wall there's an enormous corkboard with an infinity of small papers pinned up like butterflies, where quotes by writers are written. Two come into focus: "Writing fascinates me because I love the adventure inherent in starting any text, because I love the abyss, the mystery of that line of shadow beyond which lies the territory of the unknown, a space where everything is suddenly very strange, especially when we realize, like children with language, that we have to learn everything all over again, the difference being that, when we were children, it seemed to us that we could learn and understand everything, whereas when we are at the age of the line of shadow, we see that the forest of our doubts and questions will never be illuminated and, in addition, that all we'll encounter from here onward are shadows and darkness. So the best we can do is keep moving forward, though we understand nothing . . . The books that interest me are the ones the author started without knowing what they were about and finished the same way, in the half-light.—E. V-M." and "All literature carries exile within it, whether the writer has had to pick up and go at the age of twenty or has never left home. Probably the first exiles on record were Adam and Eve. This is indisputable and it raises a few questions: can it be that we're all exiles? Is it possible that all of us are wandering strange lands?—R. B." And a poster with a sloppy but effective cut-up/collage: Edward Hopper's painting *Room by the Sea* with the foamy and salty crest of 神奈川沖浪裏 by Katsushika Hokusai hanging out its door). The first thing the young woman says is something like "Ugh, I hope we don't open by showing the books and the desk and all of that." And the young man, watching the young woman watch, film (or record?, thinks the young man, who has the constant propensity to correct and edit himself), says something like "Don't worry: it's the first thing we're filming and recording; but it won't be the first thing that'll be seen in the film." And then the young man shuts his mouth; why does referring to what they're making as "the film" sound a little pretentious even to him?

So, what will be first then? What will be shown first so it's the first thing seen? What will they open with? With that toy, as a wink to the writer's oft-cited phrase about how "The past is a broken toy that each of us has to fix in our own way?" Or with the study's circular window that gives the impression of being inside a kind of space pod with views of a curtain of pine trees, their backs to a shelf of water and sand, to Jupiter and on to infinity? Or better, with the pure and unadulterated landscape. A landscape is always a good opening. The exact place: the sea, the forest, that line that is the precise point—the period and new sentence—where the sea ends so the forest can begin. And over the piles and beams and stairways of wood and concrete and steel, the house that, when the tide rises, is transformed for a few hours into an island the way Cinderella mutates into a dancing protoprincess at midnight. As if by the magic of art.

The young man (The Young Man, from here onward; read and perceive his capital letters, even if you do so in a hushed voice, as if the letters were experiencing a slight shift of atmospheric pressure, of existential intensity, like when an elevator takes off all of a sudden and we're in the middle of a sentence and then whoops!) thinks that it'd be a good idea to set the camera up on a tripod and record and open with exactly that—the sea rising around the small dock. A dock like an unfinished bridge, like a path that someone just traced in their mind, thinks The Young Man; but he doesn't dare say this, not to her. He says yes, he finds the energy to say yes, that they could use that place, that scene, later on, sped up, as a credits sequence. The tide rising and isolating the house that suddenly seems to be floating on top of the water. "It's not bad . . . But it should be at sunrise or sunset, right?" the young woman suggests (The Young Woman, from here onward; read and perceive her curving capital letters, even if . . .), acting like she's doing him a favor, like she's granting him his last wish. And, to make the idea a little bit hers, so he doesn't get all the credit, The Young Woman adds: "Plus, it fits well with what he was saying about the way he changed his approach to writing and his style. About how in the beginning, when he started writing, he just waited for ideas to come to him fully formed, like passengers at the end of the dock; and then, later on, the difficulty and challenge and doubt of having to go searching for them under the sea, to rent a boat and row out and put on a scuba suit and go down and pull them up from the depths and put them together like the debris of a shipwreck, right?"

"He" is the writer (The Writer; read and perceive and blahblahblah and whoops!), the subject of their documentary (the film). And The Young Man, with an enthusiasm he doesn't feel, but has learned to fake to the point of almost believing it himself whenever he's with her, says: "True. Perfect. Great idea." The Young Man is always trying to guess what The Young Woman is thinking; to anticipate her ideas and desires. But it's no simple task, it's hard work: it's like trying to guess a song that's playing somewhere nearby from nothing but its bass line, reverberating off walls and floors, from a long time ago, in another age.

The Young Man is six months younger than The Young Woman. It's not a decisive difference and definitely not insurmountable, clearly, The Young Man and The Young Woman now being halfway down the road and in that nebulous area without reliable maps, somewhere between twenty and thirty years old. But to The Young Man those six months seem a terrible and definitive six months. Like those months so long ago: like when he was still ten years old and she'd turned eleven and he was watching her from the opposite shore, something growing at the height of her breast, under her dress. A breast that's changing and pluralizing—breasts. As if that part of her body had been submitted to a bizarre experiment with gamma rays or something like that. And all he can do is watch it, watch them, watch her, she, who's someone else now, while he's still the same as always, or even worse—he, at that time, is even smaller because she's already grown bigger. That's how he feels as he watches her now, The Young Woman, breasts and all. More than watch her, he *contemplates* (a much more poetic verb, they say) her, as if he were appraising, with a mix of fear and admiration, a natural phenomenon that's drawing ever nearer. And that, it's easy to anticipate, will lay waste to everything. And, especially, to that poor boy who waits with eyes wide and mouth open, smiling who knows why, almost flying through the air, pulled away by the spiraling winds. The Young Woman leaves The Young Man speechless or bestows on him a kind of eloquence where everything he says is nonsense. The Young Woman takes The Young Man's breath away or suffocates him. Either way, though it's not exactly the same thing.

Aha! The Young Man is in love with The Young Woman. An unrequited love that, he thinks, is something like what people who have lost an arm or leg must feel. Not the ghost of something there then gone, but the ghost of something never possessed yet oh so longed for. That violent and sad love, downfall of the greatest monsters. Of Dracula and Frankenstein's monster and The Mummy and The Phantom of the Opera and The Werewolf and The Creature from the Black Lagoon and The Fly and King Kong and so many other mutants who succumb to the most passionate radiation of all those Beauties. A love that's not blind, but does hallucinate. A love that's not wrong, but that is, from the beginning, an error. A love that's badly aimed and only hits its target when it misfires, when it ceases to be love in order to have been love and can be looked at from a certain distance and, accordingly, discovered to have always been an unrequited love.

And The Young Woman is not in love with The Young Man; because The Young Woman saves her love for nothing more and nothing less than the Great Themes. For ART. For LITERATURE, for all the capital things she thinks about in ALL CAPS. Caps not limited to initials. Caps that reach the middle and final letters too, and even get surprised by the lack of capitalized punctuation symbols. Look at them: The Young Man and The Young Woman are literary animals. They live to read literature and dream of making a living off of a literature based in reading. And they know that modernism (when anything was possible), postmodernism (when everything had been worn out), and post-postmodernism (when, since everything had been worn out, anything was possible) have already passed. And so, now, they're waiting for the new thing, for what's next, for their own moment and the corresponding era that corresponds to them. Like those surfers at sunrise, on top of their boards waiting for the perfect wave, The Young Man and The Young Woman know their golden moment is approaching: the possibility of attaining the beach, triumphant and chosen, releasing rodeo-cowboy whoops while here comes the sun to illuminate everything, to make everything beautiful just because it's illuminated.

The Young Woman possesses a beauty that, when The Young Man is feeling between lyric and epic, he likes to think of and describe to himself as the kind of beauty that could lay waste to empires. The kind of beauty that—in order to transcend a bas-relief on the wall of a ruined temple—needs the madness or inspiration of one or more men to make it legendary, to leave its name in History. But that's not true; it's just what The Young Man wants. A vain and pointless attempt to convince himself that he's the man who'll raise her to the heavens and turn her into a constellation and a legend. Really, lacking a better adjective (and because of the added automatic reflex of the Clark Kentian glasses she wears and—secretly—doesn't need), The Young Woman's beauty might be best described as indie. The Young Man also has an indie look. Which is pretty much like saying that The Young Woman is beautiful and The Young Man is not. The Young Woman is the personification of feminine grace. The Young Man is funny. The Young Woman has been blessed by the gifts of the universe. Everything and everyone who meets her, when they meet her, think, generationally: "Uh, she's like a mix of Natalie Portman and Anne Hathaway." But really she's something else, something better, more classical and more modern. The French have the perfect word—both in its letters and sound—to define her nature. What was it? Ah, yes: "*gamine*." The Young Woman is very gamine. The Young Woman is like Audrey Hepburn in a role—a young girl gets a job at *The New Yorker* and runs into Salinger and Capote and Cheever in the elevators?—Audrey Hepburn was never offered: that of an exquisitely un-fair lady whose hobby is breaking hearts into tiny pieces without doing anything. Hearts that, when stepped on by her high- and sharp-heeled shoes, sound exactly like eggshells underfoot. Or, more precisely, like the little bones of very soft and fragile animals, delicate organisms that would never even survive the instantly-disposable sketch of a possible animated drawing. And as The Young Woman walks by, hearts tremble and split apart, all on their own, as if self-destructing. Next to her, lackluster, The Young Man is nothing but an entertaining, sympathetic caricature. Like one of those characters in millennial comics where the superhero has been replaced by the antihero; where there's no place for physical or mental powers anymore; and all that's left is a guy with his hands in his pockets and a two-day beard, walking down the street of a fishing town, and—the hook buried deep—being dragged into the depths of a dive bar, the only bar that stays open in the offseason.

But odder couples have ended up loving each other in some of the great minor successes of indie cinema; so The Young Man thinks all is not lost, and wants and needs to believe it. The Young Woman doesn't think about such things, she doesn't believe in those movies and, even less, in the barely alternative songs on their soundtracks. More than that—The Young Woman doesn't even consider herself indie. The Young Woman prefers to think of herself more as vintage, like the wayward daughter of a functionally dysfunctional Zen Jewish family, with a monosyllabic surname that sounds like a brand, and various child prodigies. Despite the fact that, yes, The Young Woman's parents flaunt two lengthy patronymics of Calabrian origin, like a shrill and shrieking operetta. Surnames that, put together, one after the other, make everyone who hears them laugh. And then they ask her to repeat them, over and over again—The Young Man, too (but just the once, because he saw what it did to The Young Woman and . . .). So, for reasons more than obvious, The Young Man avoids the subject of names and surnames in her presence. For The Young Woman, on the other hand, The Young Man's surname is *perfect*. And she'll never forgive him for it; because there are times when The Young Woman feels it might be possible to fall in love with something as volatile as a surname. A surname that, alone and when nobody can see her think it, she's dared to try out with her own name and found that it fit just right. A surname that, combined with her name, would be a great name for a writer.

The Young Man and The Young Woman discuss some technical details; technical details that just a few generations back would've required several years of university training to understand and that now seem as natural as chewing and swallowing. Something instinctive and intuitive, a rapid dance of fingers across a keyboard or a screen that, if you let it, will even speak to you and give you instructions, like an oracle, with a metallic and chrome voice.

The Young Man and The Young Woman speak in low voices, voices that bow their heads and hunch their shoulders to seem and sound lower still.

The Young Man and The Young Woman speak in low voices because they don't want—they're afraid—Penelope to hear them. The writer's sister. The Writer's Sister from here onward. Or better: The Madwoman. Or even more apt: The Mad Sister. The Writer's Mad Sister. The Writer who's missing and yet present everywhere, because of something he did (or, better, un/did), which has made Penelope, for reasons that have to do with blood and the law, the guardian of his memory. Penelope is the protector and executor of his life and work in the event of his death or—versions and theories abound, going from the magical to the scientific, from Einstein to Nostradamus—in the event of whatever his current diffuse and unknown and unprecedented situation is. And so, like the parenthetical directions in a play: (Enter Penelope.) What's Penelope like? Penelope—The Young Woman assures him with the voice of an expert—was once beautiful. Very. "Striking," she says. But, now, Penelope is like one of those houses that, due to neglect, has had its doors and windows left open for too many days and nights. A wide-open body, exposed to the elements and the scourge of animals that came and stayed a while and left, leaving behind an ecstatic trail of destruction because they were permitted everything. "It kind of reminds me of what happened to Jessica Lange," The Young Woman says. And when she says this, she seems, to The Young Man, more like Audrey Hepburn than ever. And he has to lower his gaze: it hurts his eyes to look at her. But the pain passes instantly because, from outside, comes the voice of The Writer's Mad Sister, who doesn't talk so much as shriek to herself. And sometimes she grabs The Young Woman by the shoulders and asks her, "Are you an Hiriz or a Lina?" And roams from the house to the shore, wrapped in a kind of waterproof fisherman/ scientist's jacket, her head covered with a rubber hat and her face muzzled by one of those masks surgeons wear when entering or touching or removing a human body's discordant organs. The Writer's Mad Sister seems to be singing in shrieks "Here comes the bride . . . Here comes the bride . . ." The effect—presumably involuntary—she achieves is that of a kind of nurse from a gore/slasher vacation movie who's out looking for seashells and starfish that she'll later use to stick into the eyes of kids who are always in the wrong place at the wrong time. And The Young Man and The Young Woman discover that if there's anything worse than delving into a writer's life, it's the writer's sister standing guard over it. Because it's not like The Writer chose his Mad Sister as the sole executor and guardian of his work and memory. The Writer never thought about posterity, about what came after the novel of his life. Nothing mattered to him less than the red tape of his ghost and memory. And it wasn't like, he thought, many media outlets would be all that interested in invoking him and remembering him or exploring him like a freshly unearthed archeological site. The Writer wasn't a hallowed or universal writer. The Writer was just a writer, more recognized than recognizable, and that was enough for him. And so The Writer never married or had any children because—he began to plan it when he was barely more than a child himself; it's partly why The Young Man and The Young Woman idolize him—he chose to devote his life to literature. Almost right away—without parents and with a sister whose profile and face were fairly out of focus—The Writer discovered that being alone made everything easier. All the time in the world to read and write. Both activities designed for a lonely man—as he said in one of his many appearances on a "literary" TV program, when he was young and the producers called him because his first book sold well and "plus you say really funny things"—"who doesn't want to leave behind a slew of widows or progeny signing memoirs full of resentment about how much they suffered in the shadow of the despot who used them in his fictions without asking their permission and blahblahblah."

And that's one of the many video clips—that a programmed and automated search engine locates in the wrinkles of the web and downloads on their screens—that The Young Man and The Young Woman have selected from abundant archival material taken from late-night TV shows. Shows always recorded at seven or eight in the morning, in cold studios with minimal, abstract scenography, seemingly assembled from random junk. Programs with names like *Ex-Libris*, *Loose Pages*, or *The Library of Alexandria*. Programs always hosted by pale men (and every so often by an ex-model with intellectual pretensions who considers herself the muse of a generation, of a generation as brief as it was small) who look like they've been granted one last chance in front of the cameras; men and women cognizant of the fact that, if they don't attract too much attention and read and repeat the books' jacket copy with a modicum of care, that opportunity might last for decades.

From all those hours and hours recorded in a variety of formats—from celluloid, to video, and even to digitalization for mobile phones and tablets—The

Young Man and The Young Woman have selected a handful of what The Writer tended to refer to as "my minimal maxims," which he repeated again and again throughout his books. So, a curious effect. An audio-visual effect. A kind of slippery passageway between fiction and nonfiction. Like someone who sounds—simultaneously, a twofer, a special offer—like the ventriloquist dummy of a ventriloquist. And The Young Man and The Young Woman are going to toy with it, splicing together similar sentences from different periods (like that timeless and constant and strange addiction to quoting Faulkner, a writer he almost never read), establishing an idea with The Writer looking young and more or less successful and finishing it off with The Writer looking older and more remote and, then, showing that same sentence, almost verbatim, appearing in the mouth and the role of one of his characters. There, The Writer, enthusiastic and upbeat and assisted, perhaps, by a chemical stimulus. There again, The Writer already revealing an aspect that seems to anticipate what the newspapers would call, with catastrophe-sized typography (The Writer's Mad Sister cut out those headlines and framed them, and they're already starting to assume that faded, yellowish hue), his "particular acceleration and molecular volatilization." The one and the other—the same yet different—saying exactly the same thing. The Writer as a, yes, particular writer, made and unmade of particles.

At first, this kind of credible video credo that they're putting together produces a kind of dizziness in The Young Man and The Young Woman. And then—when they find another instance of The Writer repeating the same thing as always—an idiotic laugh. As if they'd inhaled some kind of strange gas, while—always careful that The Writer's Mad Sister isn't nearby—they finish his sentences in loud voices, almost word for word. Many of them completely absurd and childish in their immodesty and, to tell the truth, difficult to frame and fairly damaging, far removed from the context in which they were uttered. Listening to and watching a good portion of those statements, The Young Man wears an ugh-face and The Young Woman wears an agh-face. Faces that people tend to wear when dealing with the discomfort produced by someone else's enthusiasm in those who have never experienced such enthusiasm. It's clear that The Young Man and The Young Woman have never felt anything like that. The feeling that—at least at various different moments—The Writer felt about the craft of reading first and writing later and then reading again. And The Young Man and The Young Woman are dying to feel it and live hoping to experience it just once, at least once. And for The Young Man, that total mutual lack is a moment of rare communion and synchronicity with The Young Woman. A moment that, paradoxically, he wishes would stretch on for hours, forever. To be the same in their ignorance and lack of feeling. But it's a wish that doesn't last long. Nobody wants to be less than and no lasting love can be built on the foundation of a lack. And The Young Man also feels like a bit of a traitor. Laughing at The Writer behind his back while looking at his rewound and fast-forwarded and freeze-framed image. It's like laughing at a God while standing before his image. But, hey, The Young Man and The Young Woman, sinful worshipers, don't want to deny or sweep under the rug all those things that The Writer said in the past and that they keep hearing in the present. The idea—projecting into the future—is not to protect and polish the memory and image of The now-invisible Writer. The idea is to present them without sleight of hand. Without editing them. So, The Young Man and The Young Woman have tried to find the most recurrent "minimal maxims." And, only in secret, do they celebrate that, over the years, more time elapsed between one and the next of The Writer's books and, as a result, there have been fewer interviews about and with The Writer and fewer statements that, near the end, after having written something he called "a more than six-hundred-page manual of funerary etiquette disguised as fiction," were almost monosyllabic or eloquently cryptic, things like "The dead have certain obligations. Could one of them be to remember us?" or "When they die, the dead forget us so we remember them better," or "It's not true, the thing about death and solitude, about death as the final and definitive act: we all die together, and death drags along the living and kills them little by little and so the living go on dying, almost without realizing it until it's too late." And The Young Man and The Young Woman have even developed a system for ranking themes and quotes that, piously, might be considered obsessions or, if you like, convenient calling cards.

To wit:

* The aforementioned thing about the dock, about the boat that used to arrive full of passengers/stories that he just had to describe and, now, the thing about the boat that no longer comes, the one about the boat lost in

the fog or sunk among the sharks, and—renting a small boat that rocked too much in the treacherous currents and putting on the uncomfortable and complicated scuba suit—about the laborious and asphyxiating deep-sea scuba dive, searching for broken storylines and loose ideas and bringing them up to the surface to see what might be made or unmade of them.

  * The thing about his logical irrealism being the flipside of everyone else's magical realism: "If magical realism is realism with irreal details, then logical irrealism is its twin opposite: irreality with realistic details . . . And yet, is there anything as irreal as so-called realism? Those stories and novels with dramatic pacing and a perfectly calculated and managed sequence of events. Like *Madame Bovary*. Or the neat structure and the precise pacing of most detective novels. But reality isn't like that. Reality is undisciplined and unpredictable. Real reality is authentically irreal . . . There is more realism and verisimilitude in a single day of the free and fluid and conscious drifting of Clarissa Dalloway than in the entire prolix and well-measured life and death of Anna Karenina. So, with so many writers who say they are committed to reality, I opt to present myself as a writer fundamentally committed to irreality. Ah, the committed writers . . . Those who say they write to contribute to the understanding of reality, those who insist that they write to help people, to guide them as if they were a lighthouse . . . The signers of the Mephistophelian pact who have sold their artistic soul for the immediate advantages and benefits of describing things as they are never realizing that this forces them to limit themselves to a handful of supposedly universal things suitable for every audience and reader . . . The enlightened to enlighten . . . Never realizing that literature is the most shadowy and solipsistic and egoistic and bourgeoisie activity that exists. It requires calm and comfort and solitude and, of course, every man for himself. Let the readers NOT come near me. The practice of literature isn't an NGO, my little friends. And, if it is, it's a self-help NGO. Of helping yourself. And if that works for someone, great. If not, then sorry not sorry: better to dedicate yourself to doctoring without borders, ethical legal practice, volunteer dentistry . . . Literature doesn't serve reality. That's why it's fiction . . . But let's get back to the idea of realism. To that whole fallacy of literature as reality's faithful mirror . . . A lie, impossible. Reality doesn't function like it does in supposedly realist books, it doesn't respect such dramatic pacing, neat sequences of events, one after

another in perfect and functional formation . . . In fact, every time I decide to submerge myself in those great nineteenth-century trilogies or quartets or quintets or sextets or septets, what I do is subvert that false realism—like that of those paintings whose only objective is, vainly, to resemble a photograph as closely as possible—by reading the various volumes out of order. That way, paradoxically, they're revealed to be far truer: as if, like in life, you met someone when you were forty years old and shortly thereafter, trustingly, they told you about their childhood; or a while after someone's death we, as if at random, ran into that dead person's first love. So, pleased to meet you and pleased to meet you again."

* A statement by Kurt Vonnegut about how writers are "specialized cells in the social organism" and "like canaries in coal mines, they anticipate the lack of oxygen." Another by John Cheever about how "literature is the only consciousness we possess." Another by Francis Scott Fitzgerald about how "The test of a first-rate intelligence is the ability to hold two opposed ideas in the mind at the same time, and still retain the ability to function." To which, smiling, The Writer adds: "I have a hundred opposing ideas here inside, at the same time. Does this make me a genius or just ingenious? Am I exceptionally gifted or exceptionally dull? Or do I have both conditions, opposites, at work inside me simultaneously? That could explain *everything*."

* A scene from a theater performance in a story from his first book, in which a young actor and a young actress recite lines like "The drug, which was all the rage and was called Cat, produced the strange effect of accelerating your body and mind while making you feel that everything around you was growing thicker, denser. You were like a pogo-punk infiltrating *Swan Lake* and, arms and legs outstretched, moving around on pointed toes, nights became long as days."

* The one about the theory of the glacier as the counterpart to Hemmingway's theory of the iceberg ("That there is a great deal below the water but, *also*, a great deal above the water, right?")

* The innumerable references to The Beatles' "A Day in the Life" (and the cover of *Sgt. Pepper's Lonely Hearts Club Band* as "the radiation of my childhood and responsible for my referential mania"), to Stanley Kubrick's *2001: A Space Odyssey* (in particular the scene in which HAL 9000 "erases his

memory while singing, terrified, 'Daisy Bell'"), to that electric and ghostly and bony line from Bob Dylan's "Visions of Johanna."

* The thing about "my surprise at how, all the time, less of what's written outside the country is read inside it and that it's only read when that foreign writer is published by a small local publisher and thus 'discovered' by some local critic or academic, no matter that the book has already been circulating there for years. As if foreign writing is only worthy of consideration after being appropriated and nationalized. And, sometimes, there are even discussions that establish absurd connections and comparisons—convinced to the point of fanaticism, insisting on impossible chronological influences of something written there on something written here—with some national writer, more a sect writer than a cult writer. Someone, generally, already conveniently and comfortably dead, and hence possible to manipulate. Someone who, no doubt, neither read nor knew of that generally far-superior foreign writer."

* A remark about young editors "who carry on lives very similar to those of writers in the 20s, from party to party; while today's mature writers are more like editors in the 20s, like Maxwell Perkins—home to work and work to home, making as little noise as possible."

* A response in a *Paris Review* interview (that venue where writers convince themselves *a posteriori* of everything about which, a priori and during, they have no clue, working in the dark, the madness of art, etcetera) of Harold Brodkey, where they ask him what his "literary ideal" is and he says: "Ideals are for greeting cards. I am trying to change consciousness, change language in such a way that the modes of behavior I am opposed to become unpopular, absurd, unlikely." And then The Writer adds: "Brodkey is an interesting case, a case to be studied, an example to admire but not to follow in what he does with "the madness of art" and with what happens when you're devoured by your own style beyond all possible digestion."

* And William Gaddis's answer, in the same magazine, when asked about the supposed "difficulty" of his work: "Well, as I've tried to make clear, if the work weren't difficult I'd die of boredom."

* A memory of "the first book where I felt I was reading someone who was *also* writing—and whose characters were narrating and narrating themselves,

literally and literarily vampirized—was *Dracula* by Bram Stoker: a novel that is, also, a writing machine. [. . .] I wrote a story about that novel, about *reading* that novel, and that story is the most autobiographical I've written. Another book that made an early and similar impression on me was Jack London's *Martin Eden*. Or, above all and more than any other, *David Copperfield* by Charles Dickens. Books with protagonists who are writers and, also, heroes. Other people's autobiographical novels that for me, subsequently, became autobiographical, because suddenly they were a fundamental part of my life and of the books I'd one day write. Yes, the discovery that someone else's existence can contain and narrate our own."

* "The most frightening and exciting moment of my life as a reader? Many. But maybe the one I remember best is reaching the final pages of the last volume of *In Search of Lost Time* and, after an unexpected, infrequent paragraph break, reading as the narrator/author Marcel confesses, almost uncomfortable yet proud: 'I had something to write. But my task was longer than his, my words had to reach more than a single person. My task was long.' And, of course, what Proust is referring to is precisely *that*, what we're reading when he tells us he was aspiring to something else. All of history—not of writing but of writers—in one line, in one brief line."

* More: "Or that other moment, in *The Ambassadors* by Henry James. That 'Live all you can . . . Live, live!' (book five, chapter II) with which, in France, the traveler and messenger on a supposed rescue mission, the mature yet not so experienced Lambert Strether, suddenly feels that he understands *everything*. And that now he'll never be able to go back to who he was, and yet he doesn't have much life left to try to become someone else. As advice, we must agree, it's not much deeper or wiser than what we tend to find inside a fortune cookie. But in the middle of a Henry James novel, one of his last novels, that almost desperate order and demand, acquires another kind of weight and resonance. To put it another way: it's one of those moments in which literature, the act itself of making literature, reveals things that life does not and will never be able to make sense of on its own. Hence the importance and existence of literature. Good fiction—if we know how to take advantage of it—is an instruction manual for our own nonfiction . . . and while we are on the subject, in *The Ambassadors*: I agree with those who insist that the 'little nameless object' manufactured in Woollett, Massachusetts, and

to which Strether refers without ever identifying it with precision, is *not* a chamber pot, or shoe polish, or clothespins, or a small alarm clock. No. The small nameless object is a toothpick manufactured by a one Charles Forester, who soon, as the novel indicates, had a monopoly in America on the product in question. But let's change the subject: because nothing causes me more pain than talking about teeth, about my tumultuous odontological history."

* More still: "Or how in *Moby-Dick*, in chapter 85, 'The Fountain,' where, suddenly, the shadow of Melville, at his desk, is like an unexpected cloud cast across Ishmael's sea. Melville, who, so near and so far, tells the reader that, as he writes those words, the precise instant, the exact and 'blessed minute' hanging between parentheses is '(fifteen and a quarter minutes past one o'clock P.M. of this sixteenth day of December, A.D. 1850).' *Call me Herman*, indeed. A humble deus ex machina that contents itself to offering the time and the date, as if taking a breath and gathering strength for the final duel and ultimate shipwreck that only one man will survive so he can tell the story of the novel."

* From another interview. Question: "Do you think you've created a school?" Answer: "Yes. But my school accepts only the best 'special' students, who have learning difficulties because they're too busy understanding things not included on the syllabus or as part of the coursework, which never includes materials like Brain Exercises or Inexact Sciences. Students who during recess dedicate themselves to running in slow motion and staring at their snacks until their eyes start watering, until the snacks turn transparent; and who come to the teacher with their hand raised but always refer to him as 'Your excellent and decapitatible majesty' and then, subsequently, ask a question that seems punctuated by an exclamation more than a question mark."

* And he goes on: "It's about continuing in that role, to have some absolute and almost divine power over others, one of my speeches, from the highest balcony of my palace (but without any need to shout or gesticulate, unlike all those politicians who seem not to have realized that it's no longer necessary, that we have excellent amplification systems and giant screens so that you're seen and heard in other kingdoms), would include what I'm going to say next: 'The work is memory and the memory can only be that which the religious call soul. But it's not something that ascends into the heavens, but

rather rots on Earth; even though it can be rerecorded over the memories of those to come. In an ideal order of things, in a world so much better than our own, everyone would be obligated to write a diary or a memoir or an autobiography or, at least, a journal of random impressions. Thus, in that far better world and in that ideal order, everyone would not only know how to write. In addition, we'd all be good writers, lucid in the face of our own story and—revising it day after day, polishing the good and the bad—we'd learn how to improve it and correct it before reaching the end, before it's too late. We'd be better people and, as such, better characters.'"

* And next: "But, clearly, writing isn't easy. Writing is a discipline that becomes more difficult every day. It's like what happens with a camera lens. Or with the human eye. At first, everything appears upside down, head down, feet up. And it's the machine and the brain that take charge of straightening it, righting it, and giving it some logical meaning. But it's a deceptive meaning. An illusion. And so, at any moment, everything can come crashing down and expose the deception in all its clumsy obviousness. So you have to be carefuller and subtler all the time. Perfect the lie and the way you take a piece of reality and turn it into fiction. And, warning: the majority of the people whom we consider liars—the best and most professional and believable liars—never lie to us. Ever. What they do is lie to themselves over and over again until they believe their own lies. And then they relay those lies to us as unquestionable and categorical and absolute truths. Writers, of course, are the extreme and artistic versions of these specimens. Writers who serve no one but themselves. Writers who only serve themselves. And, moving along, since we're on the subject: the thing about how, according to the aborigines, every photo taken of you steals a piece of your soul is a lie. No. It takes you a while to realize, you've been in a trap for a long time, a trap you only become aware of when it's already too late. The truth is that every photo you *take* steals a piece of your soul. If you look carefully, without blinking, without your eyes going click, everything turns out to be the opposite of how it seems. So the writer's task is . . . It seems like I don't really know what I'm trying to say . . . Next question."

* A recommendation of Pink Floyd's *Wish You Were Here* and Bach's *Goldberg Variations* by Glen Gould (his second version, almost a farewell) as "an ideal soundtrack for sitting down and remaining seated and writing.

[. . .] Perfect music for trying to attain that thing Fitzgerald said, that thing about how 'all good writing is like swimming under water and holding your breath.'" And "Big Sky" by The Kinks as "the best way to kick-start every workday. [. . .] A kind of supplication. An Our Father who is, indeed, in heaven because he is the heavens. And also a way to remember that, while a good part of the writers of my generation wanted to be U2, it's not bad at all, better in fact, to want to be The Kinks. True, the tours would be more uncomfortable and less spectacular. And the loneliness of the backstage hall-way before the instant glory of those hundred meters. But better to be like Harry Nilsson than like Bono. Do any of you have even the slightest idea who Harry Nilsson was or is? Or Warren Zevon? And, just to be clear, I'm not talking about their dissonant and clever self-destructive epics but about their constructive intimacy in the moment of composing subtle and perfect songs. The exquisite way they assemble and disassemble verses and choruses and bridges so their poetry can cross over to the other side where you're wait-ing for it. So, that's how I think about the writing of stories and novels. A particular balance of feelings and sound and phrasings and word games. And the Greek Choir holding hands and singing 'He goes around saying he'd rather be a rocker than writer, doo do doo, doo do doo, doo do, do doo do doo, doo do, doo do . . .' In the end . . . Where was I? Ah, yes, I'll find an easy example: better to be like Ray Davies than like Bono, I think. And I'm repeating myself. I insist. The Kinks. The ones of 'You Really Got Me,' Right? But I think more about a song like 'Big Sky.' In 'Big Sky'—like Harry Nilsson in 'Good Old Desk' singing to his divine desk; or Warren Zevon in 'Desperados Under the Eaves,' feeling down and listening to the sound of the air conditioner, which suddenly inspires a final and majestic crescendo—Ray Davies invokes, without getting too anxious, a sort of unknown deity who doesn't care much about us. Bono, on the other hand, time and again desper-ately kneels down in intense prayer to someone he knows well—to himself [. . .]. Staying on topic—and band—I can't think of a better song than 'Days,' also by The Kinks, as background music for lowering the blinds at the end of a workday. But it might be better to listen to Elvis Costello's crepuscular version and not The Kinks' original . . . Ray Davies. Thank you . . . All of a sudden I remember that once, a long time ago, Ray Davies rescued me from a University lost among the Iowa cornfields and made it possible for me to go to New York, to hear him sing 'Days.' I was there, as a sort of guest writer in an academic B-movie. And I couldn't leave that place. I was held captive by the bureaucratic spell of a special visa that didn't allow you to travel around the United States unless someone took responsibility for you. So I found out that Ray Davies was going to play in Manhattan. And I'd never heard or seen him live and in person. And I needed to see him and to hear him. So I tracked down the number of the hotel where he was staying, I was able to get them to put me through to his room and he answered and I explained the situation. He had to talk to the Dean so they would let me leave, so I could go to his concert. Of course at first Ray Davies thought it was a prank being played by some malicious friend, and then, to verify that I was an authentic fan, he made me sing several of his songs over the telephone. Not the easiest ones. No hits. Songs like 'Polly' or 'Too Much on My Mind' (one of my all-time favorites) or 'People Take Pictures of Each Other' or 'Art Lover' or 'Scattered.' And I knew all of them. But pretty soon he got tired and hung up. A few days later, thanks to a message he sent to the Dean, I left heading east. Ray Davies invited me to have tea with him; he gave me a ticket, and said, 'This is as far as we go and we're never going to see each other again, right?' A true gentleman, yes. An artist who merely raised an eyebrow above the Darjeeling-perfumed steam that rose from his cup and smiled somewhere between amused and sad when I mentioned, indignant, the gall with which, at that time, Blur and Oasis and Pulp stole and falsified his style and songs, reveling in money and fame and barely acknowledging his genius and tute-lage and mastery. There are no writers, no writers of books like that. And if there are, I'm not aware of them. There are no fans of writers like that either. Fans of musicians are happy to know their songs and to howl them at concerts or inside rooms with doors shut tight. Fans of writers, on the other hand, are more dangerous: fans of writers want to write, to write something of their own and, with their own writing, to rewrite the other and what the other has written."

* Something that John Banville said to him once, as they walked around the outside of Martello Tower in Sandycove, about how "style goes on ahead giving triumphal leaps while the plot follows along behind dragging its feet." Later he wondered whether it might not be possible for the style to go back a few steps and lovingly lift the plot up in its arms, as if it were a brilliant and

complicated child, and turn it into something new, different: into a stylized plot, into the most well-plotted of styles. It was Nabokov, and he almost always agreed with Nabokov, who postulated that the best part of a writer's biography didn't pass through the record of his adventures, but through the history of his style. Style as an adventure and adventure as style, yes.

* Something he once told someone, while they walked around the outside of who knows where: "The gods of one religion frequently become the devils of the religion that follows it. Something similar happens with writers, with the writers of a prior generation when they are evaluated by the writers of the generation that follows them."

* Answer: "What would I like as an epitaph on my gravestone? Easy: my name, the word 'Reader,' and the years 1963-1,000,000,000 and increasing. And it's not that I want to live that long; but, warning, the code for the impossible second number passes through the word 'Reader.' Which is to say: more time, all time, to be able not to continue writing but to continue reading . . . When I was very young and still concerned with things like my photo on the jacket flap of my books, I once posed wearing a black T-shirt where, written in white letters, it read 'So many books . . . so little time!' . . . I bought it in a New York bookstore that no longer exists. The T-shirt no longer exists in my closet either. It disappeared along with those other T-shirts: one with the legend 'Likes Like/Like Likes' and another with a reproduction of the cover of *Sgt. Pepper's Lonely Hearts Club Band*, where a friend who designed album covers had inserted my face next to that of William S. Burroughs. But the thing from the first T-shirt—I still think that. It's extremely unfair that, clearly, neither I, nor anyone else, has the time, *all-the-time-in-the-world*, to read everything you need to read first in order to write later. To write the best that anyone can write . . . Faulkner, without going any further. I have him here, all the Library of America tomes, waiting. I read him a little and poorly in my adolescence, in deficient translations (which, also, might bring me to all the time I lack to *reread*, which is like a glorified version of reading) and there he remains, waiting for me. To read? Or not to read? Now? In summer or winter? Is it better that the climate and temperature of the external landscape correspond to Faulkner's South? Or just the opposite? Next year? Is my writer DNA ready to receive such an explosion and, maybe, find itself changed forever? Who knows? Faulkner is there and there Faulkner stays,

howling, like one of those dangerous wolves with one foot tied to a chain whose exact length is unknown. So how close can you safely get without him jumping on you and eating your face? Or, unbeknownst to you, chewing through his own foot and lying there, waiting for you? A lone wolf. Never forget how Faulkner responded to Hemingway suggesting that writers unite and make themselves strong, like doctors and lawyers and wolves. Faulkner mistrusted writers who came together and formed groups and generations, saying they were doomed to disappear, like wolves who are only wolves in packs, but are nothing but docile and harmless dogs on their own, dogs that are all bark and no bite."

* His propensity for citing books' original titles, provided that those books are in English (because he doesn't speak any other language and because French "makes me panic"), and the idea that "*The Great Gatsby* has nothing to teach you. The only thing *The Great Gatsby* has to teach you is that neither in your lifetime nor in all your remaining reincarnations are you going to write a novel as perfect as *The Great Gatsby*. But you can learn a great deal from the imperfection, the victorious fall, from the crack-ups and roughness of *Tender Is the Night*, Francis Scott Fitzgerald's *Wuthering Heights*" (on the tape where The Writer says this, you can clearly hear the screams of The Writer's Mad Sister howling "*Wuthering Heights* is mine! And that novel you wrote about that foreign family was mine too and about me!").

* Something about how he's somewhat tired of "being considered a pop-writer; but better that than a poop-writer, right?" and that "I'm as pop as Jane Austin was in her day, irrefutable proof of the power of fiction. Don't forget that she, considered today the high oracular priestess of the matrimonial, died at forty-two, a virgin and still living with daddy."

* A clarification about how "more and more, as a reader, I enjoy the books that interest me least as a writer. It's a true pleasure to read something you'd never write and that others write so much better than you. I guess, I hope, it has something to do with maturity. Something like, remember, being young and dreaming of having a girlfriend identical to you, a mirror that understands and comprehends everything. The primal effects of beaches in movies of and about writers like *Julia* or *Betty Blue* and reading epistolary exchanges, the kind of letters no one writes anymore. Letters like those elaborate set designs, now obsolete, replaced by a blue—infinite and celestial

and divine and digital blue—screen, where you can project everything that happens inside your head into the air. Letters to be read and reread, folded and unfolded, letters of so many writing couples. But, as time passes, you discover that this mirror does nothing but reflect, with clinical and merciless fidelity, your own defects, your insurmountable flaws, your tics and cracks. So, it's no surprise that, later in our lives and work, we fall in love with our opposites, with virgin territories where everything is yet to be discovered and where the most foreign of languages is spoken. So, as writers, we start off learning from what we'd like to be and end up learning from what we'll never be, because there's neither time nor space to start over and strike out in a new direction. We begin by telling the stories we were told and end up telling the stories that are worth telling. But maybe this is all nonsense, maybe I'm lying to myself in order to fool all of you."

* One of those quotes longing for bronze or marble, but without sacrificing a certain humor or something like that: "Literature is a long-distance race and, at the same time, a race without an end."

* Another tape, another TV program, a table, a few chairs, three guests and the woman hosting the thing, a sad backdrop composed of cubes with writer's faces on their faces, all the faces of writers who, whether you like it or not, have to be there, no surprises. The Writer says: "A writer is a kind of Frankenstein's monster. A model to assemble. A life made of multiple lives. A minimum of four: the life comprised of what is written, the life comprised of what is read, the private life, the public life . . ." Then one of the other guest writers interrupts with "Once again the same crap as always" and the hostess smiles nervously and the tape stops there, cuts off, and . . .

* A theory of the reader/writer: "As far as the formation and/or deformation of a writer, I believe the process is a lot like the formation of the reader. When we start writing, as children, the most important thing is the hero, identification with the hero. We fall in love with the boy or girl in the story, and then take it upon ourselves to find out if they've starred in other adventures. So, stacks and stacks of comics and Sandokan, the Musketeers, Nemo, Jo, etcetera. And there/here is as far as most readers go (and they can stop here, no problem). To continue the adventure, into the jungle, a new reader appears. A slightly more sophisticated reader, with a particular interest in the structure of the adventures and, later, a particular fascination with who

created them and under what circumstances—with that living ghost called author and with the distinct possibility of other similar authors. The final and most evolved stage of reader—and writer—is one who, in addition to all the foregoing, is also concerned with and enjoys a particular style. That's the only way you can fight back and make peace in our digital and pluralized times, electrified by writers who narrate but don't write, by writers who simply recount but on whom you can never count when you need them the most. And there are few writers—the truly great ones—who make their style come through in their prose and, also, in what their prose tells. And thus, the miracle of a plot and a style all their own—unique, nontransferable. If there is a goal, it is certainly that—to have plot and style make space and time for a new and personal language. That the invented part of what's told *also* be the way that fiction speaks and expresses itself. But—warning—never forget that the style you achieve is always—though *a posteriori* you try to convince yourself of the opposite, that everything was coldly calculated—just a detour along the way. Style ends up being nothing more than the hangover that follows a bender. What's left behind and provokes a headache and so let's see what we can do with this. Style is the successful distillation of a failure, the glorious, unforgettable accident. A laboratory problem, like in *The Fly*, like in *The Hulk*. That's the only way to understand the expansive yet Prussian digression of Saul Bellow or the novelistic mutation of Shakespeare in Iris Murdoch. A thing you find when you're looking for something else entirely." And yes—The Young Man and The Young Woman realized this while reviewing the tapes—The Writer sometimes confuses the order and skips a few steps in his evolutionary cycle.

* More: "People read less and less and, thus, read worse and worse. Readers are more . . . unrefined all the time. And so there are more and more readers who think that everything written in the first person singular inevitably happened to the author. Or that it's what the author thinks. That's why someone like Donald Barthelme spent a good part of his career not entirely discrediting the Donald Barthelme character who said, 'Fragments are the only form I trust,' and yet incessantly clarifying that Donald Barthelme was not that Donald Barthelme character."

* The Vonnegut relapse and the ambition to, one day, be able to write a Tralfamadorian book because "Their books were small things. The

Tralfamadorian books were laid out in brief clumps of symbols separated by stars. Each clump of symbols is a brief, urgent message describing a situation, a scene. We Tralfamadorians read them all at once, not one after the other. There isn't any particular relationship between all the messages, except that the author has chosen them carefully, so that, when seen all at once, they produce an image of life that is beautiful and surprising and deep. There is no beginning, no middle, no end, no suspense, no moral, no causes, no effects. What we love in our books are the depths of many marvelous moments seen all at one time."

* Another response to another question in another interview: "What do I like most out of everything I've written? Probably that first line of that story that begins like this: 'Then it happened, the thing that, inevitably, had to happen and that, of course, should never have happened and yet . . .' No! I take it back. Can I change my answer? Yes? What I like best is the beginning of that other story: "Dun dun dun da-DAdun da-DAdun.'"

* "Will I ever be able to write something in which a character who is NOT a writer appears? Difficult. Doubt it. Don't think so. I have a completely romantic notion of the figure of the writer. The kind of notion that, I suppose, others have—when they're children—of the figure of astronauts or sports stars or firefighters, or, poor things, presidents. It was really strange: I always knew I wanted to be a writer. Even before I knew how to write. I read a survey recently regarding the age when the literary calling manifests. It concluded that 30% of writers surveyed had felt it between zero and ten, 38% between ten and twenty, 24% between twenty and thirty, 6% between thirty and forty, and 2% from forty onward. I never had a plan B, never a doubt, I was born formed and deformed. So, in my case, the thing about "be careful what you wish for because you might just get it" turns out to be true. The gift and the privilege and the condemnation of never having to renounce an initial vocation, a childhood fantasy. And, subsequently, the strange guilt of feeling that you have to, always, live up to such an exceedingly lofty wish you were granted. And to grow up—in school, in the park, with family—surrounded by people who don't have the slightest idea what they'll end up being while I was absolutely certain what I'd end up being, because I was already it. A kind of terrestrial-extraterrestrial. To me a writer is someone who flies off to the far reaches of the universe, fights for something, wins, and brings

it back to shine a little light in the darkness, but without ever having to leave home. I always wanted to be a writer, which is why—everything seems to point to it, and I can't say it bothers me—I'll always want to *create* writers."

* A proposal: "How has nobody yet thought of doing a sitcom like *Seinfeld* or *Louie* but with writers? Writers are so much funnier and more pathetic than standup comedians. The fauna surrounding them: agents, editors, journalists, critics, academics, booksellers, aspiring writers . . . And the settings: festivals, award ceremonies, presentations, domestic life . . . I am sure it'd be a great success. Or, at least, it'd be very entertaining in the most terrible sense of the word, right? I propose a title: *Typos* . . . Ah, the things I think of, my God . . ."

* "Do I believe in God? No. At least not in any of the models proposed by any of the great religious texts. But *yes* I do believe in a kind of Great Narrative Power. In a Generative Entity of Awesome Plotlines. I can't not believe in that. I can't not believe in the notion that there's someone out there, working, scheming, ceaselessly thinking: *let's see what happens.* I felt it again not long ago while reading a book about the turbulent origins of World War One, and the perverse way in which all the small pieces of the thing fit together. World War One, which at that time was nothing more and nothing less than The Great War; nobody could imagine there would be a sequel, just a few years later, with far-superior special effects. And yet it's clear that *yes,* someone could imagine it. Someone with a lot of imagination."

* And, for now, the farewell: a final throwback interview with The Writer where he looks at the camera and says in a low voice: "I'm getting more tired all the time of going places where they ask me, always, where I get the ideas that I write, and never ask me how I came to the idea of being a writer. [. . .] I'm more exhausted all the time by everything that a writer supposedly has to do in order to be considered a writer. To be a judge. To be judged. To observe and be observed at one of those roundtables. [. . .] Offer opinions about a reality that, in truth, is what interests you least, or what should interest you—a creator of fictions—least. [. . .] Was it William Faulkner who said that a writer who doesn't write tends to do morally reprehensible things? . . . I don't know. [. . .] I like writing more all the time, I like being a writer less all the time . . ."

All of that and much more.

And the search engine The Young Man and The Young Woman have programmed never stops sending them new takes and sequences of The Writer. Several per day. Splinters and seeds and bricks. Files they open every morning—between expectant and hopeful, please, no more, right?—like misplaced Christmas presents. And everything arrives there. To a small portable computer with nearly infinite capacities. The Young Man and The Young Woman put all those words in the mouth of a single face, a changing face. And they're already tired of so much watching and listening and tinkering, betting on how long it'll be before the writer says the word "epiphany" again.

The Young Man and The Young Woman are hungry and yet, at the same time, already a little scared that, not the witching hour, but the hour of making sandwiches is approaching. The Young Man and The Young Woman have been camping out next to the house that once belonged to The Writer and now belongs to The Writer's Mad Sister. And it's not a simple thing: day after day they find themselves forced to pitch and unpitch the tent according to the schedules of the powerful and not entirely predictable tides. It would've been easier to pitch it in the forest, but The Writer's Mad Sister warned them that the forest is off limits, that nobody is allowed to enter the forest. The sea in front of the house—which is a sea that mixes with the mouth of a river—is decidedly bipolar. Sweet and salty, calm and temperamental. Now you see it now you don't, and, yes, it's easy to understand why The Writer's favorite painting was or is Edward Hopper's *Room by the Sea*. And there inside, The Young Man and The Young Woman remove slices of ham and cheese from a small portable refrigerator. And they start to construct sandwiches that are increasingly complex and baroque with ingredients bought at a convenience store. In gas station about two or three miles inland (where, to The Young Man's despair, they can't obtain carbonated cans of Qwerty or Plot or Nov/bel or Typë or DrINK). There and back along the road, riding a foldable designer bicycle that The Young Woman brought. Sandwiches like Giovanni Battista Piranesi's prisons, which housed the chained and perpetual prisoners of Guiseppe Arcimboldo. They're so sick of those sandwiches—The Young Man and The Young Woman wonder if the enormous crabs that drag themselves up on the shore are edible, but can't even work up the energy to find out—and the "moment of the sandwiches" melts into the "moment of falling asleep." An act that's always fascinated The Young Man because it implies, simultaneously, action and rest. Moving—falling, asleep—in order to stay immobile. And it's a moment that, now, never fails to cause a kind of growing and excited restlessness in The Young Man. Even more because The Young Man and The Young Woman sleep separately, each in their own sleeping bag, next to all their electronic equipment, which, fortunately, occupies less space all the time, because the future is no longer the exploration of infinite outer space, but the reduction of the space taken up on Earth. All of it designer. Even the aerodynamic tent, something of a lunar module, that wraps the two of them in a larval embrace. And that gives the whole situation an air of white wedding, outside, under the heavy breathing of the sky, as The Young Man seeks to synchronize his own respiration with that of the universe, to achieve the effect of a lullaby. The Young Woman achieves it immediately. Sleep. For The Young Man, it's not so easy. So, The Young Man—who'd always been such a light sleeper it was like he was levitating—already knows that The Young Woman talks in her sleep and says strange things, that she repeats the verb "fall" and the place "swimming pool" over and over again. And says them with a softness that makes everything rise and lift and his dreams, his waking dreams, fly even higher as his body temperature spikes and . . .

Let's say it quickly so we can get it out of the way: that's when The Young Man toys with the idea of masturbating. But he's never been very good at masturbating. He's not easily turned on. He needs elaborate stories. Context. Even in the early stages of puberty, half-opening copies of *Playboy* and *Penthouse*, The Young Man always preferred the black and white correspondence section to the satiny centerfolds, whose nudity always seemed too dressed up. The Young Man was much more excited by those long letters from supposed readers (but, The Young Man imagined, probably composed by editors shut inside a poorly lit windowless room) that told, with hairs and gestures and sweat and fluids, stories of pizza delivery boys seduced by horny housewives and high school teachers pursued by crazed students and cousins who haven't seen each other for years and the omnipresent girlfriends of best friends and male bosses to be dominated and female bosses who are dominatrixes. And, yes, The Young Man could write a fan letter about The Young Woman.

When this happens—and this kind of painful and censurable and, in the end, censored ecstasy happens every night—The Young Man starts counting sheep and makes them jump over a fence, in reverse, like a movie being played in rewind. So he tries, more or less in vain, to calm himself in the present by remembering what his world was like before meeting The Young Woman and before the figure of The Writer brought them together and stuck them inside this tent.

Know this: The Young Man and The Young Woman come from a country where a dead or disappeared writer is quoted more often and more accurately than a living and apparent writer. It happens sometimes; it happens more all the time. A dead writer can always be exhumed and rediscovered, he's not going to protest, and his relatives always seem ready to exchange what he was for what he might be. And The Writer—whose activities had diminished in recent times—isn't just a dead/disappeared writer now. Really, now, The Writer is something far stranger—a lost writer. Someone whose disappearance/loss/trance has been, first, a news story of global impact and then something stranger still: a cross between a scientific aberration and atmospheric phenomenon to which many periodicals and newspapers now devote daily space and attention on par with what they devote to meteorological forecasts and horoscopes. Because The Writer has mutated into a strange kind of climatological-astrological omen. And there are more and more people who look to the sky to be guided by his sporadic appearances, much the way sailors marked their course by locating the North Star or the Southern Cross.

The Writer has become, yes, a good story.

So something has to be done and soon. And so the editor (whose brief participation here and his still lower moral standing make him undeserving of the capitalized The Editor) received The Young Man in his office one morning and immediately accepted his proposal because it was the kind of proposal that's impossible to turn down: The Young Man offered to pay (The Young Man just received a small but sufficient inheritance from his grandmother) for the trip and to finance a film to be included in an anthology of some of The Writer's unpublished work and other random pieces published in magazines and cultural supplements. The only thing The Young Man asked of the editor was a letter of introduction to The Writer's Mad Sister (who for him was not yet The Writer's Mad Sister). The only condition of the editor (who was the son of The Editor, of the first, only, and original editor of The Writer; The capitalized Editor who was struck down by the lightning bolt of a heart attack when he found out what had happened to The Writer in Switzerland, underground, top secret and classified) was that The Young Woman be part of the crew. And at first The Young Man resisted, but in the end he agreed: his firm opposition dissolved into blushing acceptance when The Young Woman walked into the office. The Young Woman was the editor's niece, she worked in the office as a proofreader (and as an object of desire for more than one author who would sign off on any clause when she was the one who handed him the contract and touched his manuscript), but, above all, The Young Woman was an unconditional fan of The Writer. First, without even having read him; because The Writer was the only one who didn't try to seduce her (and that's why The Young Woman allowed herself, at her uncle's request, to be photographed with him; and she even experienced the theretofore unknown anxiety of wondering and worrying whether, with the years, in the photo's caption it would simply read ". . . with an unidentified young woman"). Second, because one day The Writer brought her a copy of Fitzgerald's *Tender Is the Night* as a gift, telling her to "read it as if it were a negative polarity self-help book—here's everything you should *not* do for things to go well in your life. It's also a kind of more or less secret formula for forgiving your parents for everything. Besides, it's very well written." And third, because then she read The Writer. And it's not that she fell in love with him. But she did fall in love with the character of a woman who went in and out of his books, in different times and circumstances, in different swimming pools and cities and even planets—and that produced in her the irrepressible need to know more, to get a little closer. So she asked her editor uncle—having saved enough to cross the ocean—for a kind of safe passage to go visit The Writer's house. Her editor uncle was happy to oblige provided that The Young Woman look through The Writer's drawers to see what she could find. And an initial instruction: rumors of an entire novel about the story of the lost arms of Venus de Milo; of another novel with the Nazi architect Albert Speer as protagonist; of a novel titled *The Beatles* (like that, with the *s* crossed out), telling the story of a young foreigner who goes to the Abbey Road recording studios to witness firsthand the end of the greatest rock band of all time.

The editor didn't say anything—not to The Young Man or The Young Woman—about the more than a little flammable character of The Writer's

Mad Sister. The editor suspected that The Writer's Mad Sister might be a lesbian. Or a nymphomaniac. Hence, The Young Man and The Young Woman as carnal decoys. The editor limited himself to introducing them and bringing them together, dictating a letter to his secretary, sending it via email, and informing them—the next day—that The Writer's Mad Sister had agreed to their visit provided that the documentary (The Film) set aside enough time and space for her to tell "my version of the story." The Young Man and The Young Woman accepted without giving it much thought. Besides, the editor—who at one time wanted to be a writer, but paused too long at the station of copyeditor when he married the daughter of the branch president of a popular soda company—always enjoyed manipulating people until he felt like they were his characters. And The Young Man and The Young Woman are ideal material for him, because they make him feel kind of legendary, something like Maxwell Perkins (though he has no clue who Maxwell Perkins was) protecting, more in terms of publicity than in terms of literature, the memory of an author who is his because he inherited him, while at the same time getting a kick out of watching from outside what will come of this whole experiment, this combination of interesting variables. More than once, thinks the editor, the history of great literature has been sketched out in smudged manuscripts that nobody would've hedged their bets on. And that is, for him, the precise point where publicity and publishing converge in what, for him, is and would be a miracle: to get one of those housewives who is also a single mother and a war orphan who has written a universal bestseller while waiting for her kid, who has some exotic illness, to come home from a school she can no longer afford, etcetera. The Young Man and The Young Woman—like periods and colons and ellipses—are not that exactly, but they are something. A promising or, at least, intriguing beginning.

The Young Man has wanted to be a writer for as long as he can remember and The Young Woman wants to be something greater still: she wants to be immortalized, she wants to be the reactant that detonates the cosmic explosion of a great artist, she wants to be a muse. And there's no better way to combine and fuse both vocations than a digital camera and a foreign assignment. That's why others exist: so that we convince ourselves that, for a while, we can stop thinking about ourselves when really, in that moment, we're just thinking about what others think of us.

Now, on the other side of the tent's fine membrane, The Young Man hears a sound that's difficult to classify: the sound that jumps from the waves on the beach to the trees in the forest?, a poorly latched window that always dreamed of being a door? Or, maybe, The Writer's Mad Sister roaming her domain like a joyful lost soul who has never taken pity on anyone and is already preparing the takes and testimonies that The Young Man and The Young Woman will find themselves forced to shoot and record the next morning? In fact, since their arrival a couple weeks before, The Young Man and The Young Woman have barely been able to investigate the memory of The Writer, because The Writer's Mad Sister demands that the camera and microphone be pointed at her all the time; she, of course, feels that she's "the true heroine of the story" and ceaselessly "reveals" her "inevitable and decisive influence" on each and every one of The Writer's books (especially "the one where all he did was exploit my temporary in-laws, using my confidential reports and clandestine videos"), and gets lost in meandering autobiographical monologues like "My parents named me Penelope when they could've easily given me a female version of Ulysses. Does that exist? Because if there is something that's characterized me throughout my life it's perpetual motion and never sitting down to wait for anyone. Or, they could've named me after one of the many goddesses of war, at least they're mythological . . . But no. It had to be Penelope—and all because of that then-popular song by a fucking Catalan singer who, I'm sure you don't know, didn't even write the whole fucking song, but went around, for decades, singing it as if it were his. But the music is by someone else. And every time someone asks my name and I say 'Penelope' they start humming that shit about the brown leather handbag and the little high-heeled shoes and the Sunday dress. And I never had any of that: not the purse, not the shoes, not even a dress for a given day of the week . . . But, well, another of the many things for which I have to thank Mommy and Daddy who, knowing them, for obvious reasons, wanted to name me Zelda. But, setting aside the demented aspect of the thing, Zelda would've better defined and synthesized my condition as secret-female-artist-exploited-by-famous-writer and . . . Here I am, another woman in the shadow of a man who incessantly steals the spotlight. Here, lost, in a sort of museum to my brother and that my brother built himself, yes it's true, with my money, with my blood diamonds . . . Really, if we're being honest, it's not a museum or a pyramid. Nothing of the Pharaohs or the spirit of immortalizing the subject. My brother wasn't that obvious or that banal. His was something much humbler and yet, at the same time, much more arrogant. What my brother erected here (with my financial support, let's be honest) is a sort of personal theme park of his own past. "The palace of my memory," he called it. This house is exactly the same, in his recollections, as the one on a beach where, when he was a boy, he spent several vacations with our parents. I wasn't there. Or yes: I was about to be born. 'The origin, the opening line,' the great fool said. The exact place where everything began and where he wanted to return, and to stay, so that everything would remain . . . And all that remains here, now, is I."

Thinking about what The Writer's Mad Sister says helps The Young Man close his eyes at last. Wanting to fall asleep, again, trying to achieve (that verb "achieve," applied to reaching the peak of an activity where the less you think the better you do, always seemed out of place to The Young Man) sleep. But it's not easy. The Young Man heard once that human beings, having come from water, think better near water. He can't confirm it, but one thing is clear to him: he thinks *more* near the water, as if the water were an excellent conductor of cerebral electricity. Now, electrocuted, trying to convince insomnia to give him one night's rest, The Young Man can't help but think that the whole thing with the documentary (The Film) won't be more than another dead-end alleyway, worse, a circular corridor. The documentary—The Film to which he'd attributed the psychochemical properties of a detonator, the magic words to make or break the spell—as yet another reason to suspect that, maybe, his gunpowder has always been and will always be wet. The Young Man, it's been said before, wants to be a writer more than anything. Even more than he *wants* The Young Woman; something he could, no doubt, succeed at more quickly and easily than he could with a novel or a book. A masterpiece that would erase the barriers The Young Woman has built up and transform her into one of those blushing damsels in a salon lit by complicated candelabras. But no. Not yet. And it'll be a while, a long while, it seems. Because, of course, The Young Man does write. But The Young Man isn't a writer, because (as much as he tried to convince himself to the contrary with a multitude of arguments, despite what happened during that brief aerial episode with The Writer, which he doesn't dare confess and remembers more and more as an unconfessable and unforgivable sin whose punishment has been written like an eleventh commandment: "Thou shalt not write") he knows that he's not a *true* writer until he's been published and passes through bookstores to see how his book has been displayed and, when the employees aren't looking, moves it to the most well-positioned tables. Things like that. Having something behind him and everything in front of him, knowing that he'll never get anywhere. But, at least, he'll be on the way, moving. Now, The Young Man inhabits that terrible moment in the life of any writer, any prewriter. A zone without limits where *everything* seems worthy of being told, *everything* could end up making a good story, *every* horse looks at you with those bet-on-me eyes. But it's all a dreamer's dream. A desert of deceptive fertility where nothing germinates. Just titles, first sentences, endings, dedications, epigraphs (of which, like in The Writer's books, there will be, for many people, too many), acknowledgements (which, like in The Writer's books will be, for most people, too many; but The Young Man has been reconsidering their inclusion ever since The Young Woman told him that, "I don't believe them, they're false, they're acknow*lie*dgements"), and speeches, and even cover designs for editions with various publishers and in various languages. On particularly feverish days, The Young Man goes so far as to imagine the reviews of his books and a blurb for the back cover from a writer he admires. All of it meticulously compiled in small print in the increasingly numerous notebooks (Moleskine, of course) that he carries with him everywhere. Notebooks that—when he opens and rereads them—produce in him the frustrating unease of someone trying to recall dreams and make some sense of them. All meaning seems to escape him like sand, like water, like air, but then, to keep from having a breakdown, he tells himself it doesn't matter: everything those notebooks contain—he consoles himself, he justifies himself—will look really nice on the far side of the years, in the first displays of the great exposition of his life. And The Young Man likes to believe that this stage—this centrifugal rite of passage of empty suits that never fit right when he tries them on—is an inevitable transition, a kind of hormonal disorder that drives the body and face and voice and mood and personality mad. An electric dance—a flash of lightning like in animated drawings—that'll drift into a more or less challenging and harmonious choreography. Something temporary—a fever that attacks all writers when they're young—never suspecting that this is an affliction that'll never quit, that'll always be there, poking its head out every so often throughout the years, disguised as writer's block, as why sit in here when you could go walk around outside. But The Young Man doesn't think about the future because the future hurts—each day that passes is another day that he hasn't finished a book he hasn't even started yet. And The Young Man has tried everything to finish starting something. From particularly lyrical and inefficient therapies like copying out a beloved writer's text letter for letter to feel those words spill from his fingers, to running out into an open field on a stormy day wearing a metal helmet on his head, praying to be struck by a bolt of lightning. A celestial finger of light, an energy whose effect will translate into him getting back to his feet transformed into a Balzac Machine (who would even fabricate and select the type of paper and typography of his books) or a Dickens Machine (who would self-publish and chase pirates between book tours where he'd give performances "acting" out parts of his novels) or, if nothing else, into a more intermittent Stendhal Machine who, it's true, left many things unfinished or just begun, but who *also* wrote *The Charterhouse of Parma* (supposedly unfinished as well, sure) in just a few weeks. And this last one is *such* a childish fantasy: imagining and hoping that, once activated, he'd no longer experience the boundless *horror vacui* of paralysis when—though the books and years pass by—he'll always go back there. To The Ground Zero. To the pistol shot inaugurating a never-ending race. To charging out of the trenches firing in every direction, hoping to hit the target of the blank white page or the black computer screen. In his lowest and darkest hours, The Young Man wonders—adoptive child of an adaptable time—if he wants to be a writer more than he wants to write.

Of course, The Young Man attended various writing workshops—like someone crawling on their knees to Lourdes—of different flavors and styles. He can count them, in the impenetrable darkness of the tent, on the fingers of one hand.

Thumb: the one with the guy who, in the living room of his apartment, had a punching bag with a photograph of Hemingway on it that he punched and punched, while sweating and talking constantly, but between pants about courage and grace under pressure and recalling that one time he'd charged at the bulls in Pamplona, because the bulls never charged him.

Index: the one with the guy who had a small bust of Shakespeare on his desk that he turned to with the wink of an eye and a "Will," and who explained to them "the methodology for constructing plotlines out of chess moves."

Middle: the one with the guy who made them stroke quartz crystals "until the idea comes."

Ring: the one with the guy who considered it essential that first they read (buying them directly from him, "to avoid falling in the trap of publishers and the market") all his books in order to "comprehend the mystery of literature."

Pinky: the one with the guy who insisted "that everything begins and ends with Chekov." Which caused The Young Man a lot of anxiety: because The Young Man read Chekov, enjoyed Chekov, but never understood what his genius was. And he understood even less all the people who wanted to write like that. Those endings that were *so open*, where nothing was resolved and where all you seem to hear was the voice of the wind slipping in and running around. Endings where, for example, a man and a woman meet beside a museum stairway, with the whole sky above their heads, just to say goodbye to each other. And that's about it. A prologue and a selection of Chekov stories put together by Richard Ford gave him a secret hope. There, the American started by saying pretty much the same thing The Young Man thought: Chekov wasn't interesting. But, then, Ford admitted his error and joined the Russian's fanatical and fiery followers. Even worse, Ford turned into the worst kind of fan—the converted fan. The Young Man had read a Spanish translation someone had recommended, two English translations, one into the French (with the help of a dictionary), and even a Russian original which he'd limited himself to staring at, as if those Cyrillic letters were, yes, quartz crystals. But The Young Man only managed to see, as if through one of those windows with emerald-green glass, simple people having simple (ah, *the* word) epiphanies that are, generally, tepid and tenuous and almost ungraspable, like the smoke of the flame bidding farewell to the candle. One night, in the middle of a workshop, after one too many drinks, The Young Man dared to say (repeating something The Writer once said) that any one of Chekov's disciples seemed to him superior to the master. Everyone laughed at him. He walked out and never went back. And Ishmael Tantor walked out with him. His literary best friend—or something like that. They met in that workshop. Ishmael Tantor was massive, weighing more than three hundred fifty pounds ("You see: in my name, the whale communes with the pachyderm; very appropriate"); he was the son of a renowned lawyer, in his final year of law school, already considered a kind of prodigy in the subject; he insisted that he'd signed up for the workshop "to meet girls," and admitted without shame that he'd read very little. "You don't have to read so much," he said. "All that reading just confuses you and steals time from writing. And you don't have to write so much either." Ishmael Tantor—"for obvious reasons"—claimed that he'd only read, albeit multiple times, *Moby-Dick*. "You don't need anything else. That's where everything came from and where it'll all return." Ishmael Tantor had never offered to read anything during the workshop sessions. Until one night when he was the only one left who hadn't "presented," and he pulled out a stack of wrinkled pages from the inside pocket of a Canadian lumberjack jacket that he never took off, even in the summer, and announced, "I'm going to read a little thing I wrote in the bar on the corner, before coming . . ." He cleared his throat like a trumpet and then . . .

There was a sixth master workshopper—like one of those sixth fingers that some people are born with that's removed as soon as possible—whom The Young Man considered the best of all. A sad man who'd published a single novel—considered at the time precocious proof of genius yet to come—at a very young age, and who only seemed happy when talking about the other peoples' books. Someone who just had them read and made them think about what they were reading and who, at the end of one session, told them that he was very sick and that he wouldn't be able to host the workshops anymore, sending them off with a "I wish you all the best in the world." A short time later, in the pages of a cultural supplement, where suddenly everyone seemed to be commemorating him simultaneously, The Young Man discovered that the writer had died. Before long, The Young Man thought, he'd be claimed by the writers The Young Man liked to refer to as "The Resurrectionists": always young and ready thieves of literary bodies, dividing up the dead in order to resurrect them in their own image and dimension, deforming them into something they'd never been and something they were unable to deny or resist. Like that, until the absent writer ended up functioning as a kind of antecedent to those present individuals who adore him for precisely that reason—because he gave them a reason to be. Living writers who only seem to like dead writers whose work, they feel, resembles their own. So, they read them just long enough to convince themselves of that resemblance. And The Resurrectionists went around, facing off under standards of ghosts (my dead writer is more alive than yours), writing in the mode of this or that dead writer, acting as official mediums and channelers of an increasingly capricious memory, and elaborating curious cosmogonies where there seemed to be no place for different or international writers. Because everyone and everything seemed to emerge only and exclusively through the window of that bottom-less black hole that devoured all light, ceaselessly digging with the fanatic dedication of Snow White's dwarves. Pick and shovel. Heigh-ho sounding a lot like *Sieg Heil*. But not even then. To The Young Man's surprise—maybe because he wasn't sufficiently experimental, though not exactly traditional either—nobody robbed the sad writer's tomb. And, yes, The Young Man—desperate—fantasized about exhuming him and bringing him to his house and sitting him down in the basement rocking chair and killing in his name. Or proposing articles on his work to journals and magazines. Or dedicating a blog to him. But The Young Man was a noble fellow or, at least, possessed high indexes of guilt and shame in his literary DNA.

And it follows that, to overcome such a temptation, The Young Man had opted for a secret storyline. Inventing, inside his head, an entire literary system to which—every night, like tonight, when he was unable to fall asleep, to let sleep take him, a couple more verbal variations, along with "achieving" sleep, of what the act of sleep does—he added details and stories, with the same devotion and love others gave to assembling gigantic electric train sets. An entire unconfessable universe—an entire literature, with its lives and works and deaths and breakdowns—where he, like the final piece of a puzzle, would travel alone and only arrive at the end. On the seventh day of his creation. Not to rest, but, then, to be ready to write and to begin and to finish and to publish. A universe that—set to the rhythm of ancient cabalistic dances—grew out of inertia and ended up containing him so that, initiated and included, the inverse movement could take place—absolute contraction after so much expansion. And that, in the end, leaves him alone and divine and all-powerful and ready to give birth to a Great Work. And there are times The Young Man thinks he's on the right track. And other times he feels he's going off the rails into an abyss with only himself at the bottom. He's read of madness like this; and has even admired novels that tell the story of a man who ends up going to live inside his own head, in an imagined city that will end up swept away by the whisper of fire and the voice of the wind. But The Young Man tells himself—he wants to convince himself—that it's worth the risks, the necessary hazards of any great enterprise.

So now, in the tent, The Young Man opens his notebook again and with the help of a small flashlight reviews and revisits his kingdom, the only place he feels himself a creator and creative. Outside, again, that sound that, now, could only be that of a lost boy. The cry of a child prodigy. A staccato of tears and moans, intermittent, but precisely and rhythmically intermittent—like a wail that's communicated in Morse code. The message of someone who is sinking into the waters of his sadness. The sound frightens The Young Man a little. So, better to distract himself, to think of other things. The Young Man reads and takes notes and watches The Young Woman sleep. And there is a certain comfort in watching her with his eyes wide open while her eyes are tightly shut. Like that—there but elsewhere, so near in her remoteness, between dreams—The Young Woman seems less aware of her beauty. Because he's no fool, he knows, knows in the same way he knows that there's no life after death and that sooner or later bad people get what's coming to them: The Young Woman spends her life constantly thinking—at least in a tiny but important part of her brain—about how beautiful she is. Some women are like that: they know they're beautiful, though in an unconscious way, all the time, that's how they're programmed. When she's asleep, it's like that part of her is deactivated and The Young Woman transforms into, merely, a beautiful girl who doesn't know that she's beautiful, because, maybe, she's dreaming that she's inside a burning building, or flying, or naked in public, without that making her think that her nakedness is beautiful. When she's asleep—her lips half-open and letting escape a whistle that sounds like the wind in a black and white horror movie—The Young Man can concentrate on the only thing about The Young Woman that might be considered, by dull and inferior beings, an imperfection. The Young Woman has a birth-mark at the base of her neck that, in the beginning, The Young Man said to himself, had the shape of a country. He drew it from memory, searched for it on an atlas, and he found no nation with borders to match it. The Young

Man went further. He considered provinces, states, communities, districts. Not there either. So, he decided, the shape of that mark must correspond to the shape of a city. An even more difficult mission; but The Young Man had already spent several months marking maps, and something told him that the city might be in Central Europe. Buildings with stone giants holding up balconies and imperial eagles alighting, motionless amid rooftop winds and walls with bullet holes and sad trees and windows with dirty glass that seem always recently rained on and "Sooner or later I'll find it. And when I do, like someone breaking a curse and casting a spell, that'll be the city where we'll live together," The Young Man says to himself. Meanwhile and in the meantime, that city, more imagined than imaginary, is where all his literature transpires. His cosmogony. At times, of course, the whole thing rebels and is revealed to have a "texture" quite similar to that of *Playboy* and *Penthouse* letters. Dispatches to himself that are seriously masturbatory, yes, for sure; but then The Young Man wants to believe—and subsequently believes—that his is an epic form of masturbation. The mother of all masturbations. Masturbations like those of ancient gods, spilling their semen and breast milk across the dome of the skies and giving birth to galaxies and nebulas with names of their own and myths for everyone. A brilliance that The Young Man manipulates and scribbles down and crosses out as if he were dealing with delicate physics and chemistry formulas, orchestrating and disordering highly volatile elements. Blocked in his writing, The Young Man writes writers. A cast of proper nouns that he makes strange and sets in motion, marching them from here to there—like the lead soldiers of his childhood—pitting them against each other in eternal battles. Duels without the first blood of sharp knife-fighters. Intrigues in ruined palaces. Men and women. Young and old.

A few examples:

The DJ Tomás Pincho (who found success in the U.S., recording *Iron Martin*, a rap-dub-clank version of the national and telluric poem about a fleeing gaucho).

The young and acerbic blogger, alias Florida Boedo (writing posts where she reveals embarrassing details about intellectual life and reproduces the phrases of others that she makes her own, like what Saul Bellow said in Stockholm, in 1976, receiving the Nobel, that thing about, "We must not make bosses of our intellectuals. And we do them no good by letting them run the arts. Should they, when they read novels, find nothing in them but the endorsement of their own opinions? Are we here on earth to play such games?" and over and out and I hate all of you, all of you).

The successful and popular barrio writer Rigoberto Paponia (who starts out writing about his neighborhood, then about his street, then about his house, next about his room, later about his desk, and who, these days, is working on a macronovel about his hand and the pen that his hand holds, without that preventing him from pretending not to know any of the residents on the street where he still lives).

His nemesis, the academic Edith "Ditta" Stern-Zanuzzi, who, clutching her lectern at the university like the rudder of a ghost ship, combats Paponia's costumbrist-existential zeal. Ditta, with her throwback bohemian look that makes her not passé but vintage. Ah, Ditta: to whom The Young Man devotes special attention, not at the time of creating her but of re-creating her. Because Ditta (unlike a good part of his mythology) is inspired by someone real. Someone who laughed at him when—wandering from one literary workshop to another—he attended one of her canonical lectures. And, raising his hand to ask about The Writer (absent from the complex diagram that Ditta just finished presenting and imposing on the audience like an unmovable Table of the Law), she burst out laughing and made fun of him, in front of everyone, for daring to mention such an absurd name, so out-of-place on her Parnassus. Ah, Ditta: her colleagues accuse her of "copying" foreign ideas for her publications. Ah, Ditta: glimmers of Susan Sontag and Joan Didion and a pinch of Nora Ephron or Fran Lebowitz (that's where she ends up and that's where she takes a stand and that's where she stays; because Ditta will never read Deborah Eisenberg, Renata Adler, and so many others because "I have no time for what gets written outside my country") when, every so often, she has to create/insert "something ingenious" somewhere. So, to her young and beautiful followers, the so called *dittettes*, Ditta—feared and admired—is "a genius" and "gorgeous," and she seduces them sapphically yet platonically, with small but intense home seminars, on her floor where, between one theoretical jab and the next, she serves "homemade croissants." After a while, one veteran *dittette*, tired of making the pilgrimage to that three-room Mecca, feels she has the necessary support and attempts a coup d'état, which, inevitably, fails: Ditta is seemingly always two steps ahead, not due to intelligence on her part but to ineptitude on everyone else's. So, in addition, fearing reprisals that always come from the most unexpected angles and always via some intermediary, the majority of her detractors only dare to whisper, off the record and after one too many drinks, that "in her essays, Ditta is always rehearsing and never performing and it's possible she'll never even make her debut." At most, at very most, she gets parodied in some end of semester performance where students in the upper level courses put on a little vaudeville. And, of course, only a man can *play* Ditta.

The fashionista Facundo Anastasia (who one afternoon, armed to the teeth, goes into a Global Congress of Literary Workshops and shoots up some two hundred proto-storytellers "because they wear striped and faded T-shirts over their guts; and their sweaters are horrible; those light blue V-neck sweaters, like big and fat and old schoolboys, those sweaters writers in my country wear until the day they die.")

The gay performer Maximiliano Persky (another blogger, who thinks that everyone is gay even though they don't know it and, there, on the screen, demands they come out of the closet "right now, or if not . . .").

The author of "absolutely realistic" detective novels Bang-Bang Comisario, in whose books the killer is never one of the characters and only appears on the last page, passing by, stopped for a minor crime, turning himself in, tired of waiting in vain to be caught and locked up.

The Octogenarian Esfinge Tevas (whom, in the beginning, he considers the typical awkward woman who, at book presentations, asks to speak in order to torment the audience with eternal and amorphous sermons, not letting go of the microphone for long minutes before being silenced and reduced by whistles and forcibly removed from the place. Until one of Ditta's enthusiastic and ambitious students in the Department of Entropy and Numbers decides to follow her from bookstore to bookstore, to record each and every one of her interventions over the course of a couple years, to transcribe them, to put them in writing, and she discovers that Esfinge isn't ranting, she's reciting an ingenious and avant-garde "post-finneganian" novel. A novel that's published under the title *Questions for the Author* and becomes one of those inexplicable bestsellers that everyone buys and talks about without ever reading).

The Sumerian cyberpunk GygaMesh.

The *bon vivant* and *happy few* Apollo Dionisio, whose storylines pause for pages and pages every time that one of his creatures eats and drinks.

The omnipresent and inevitable supporting actor, everywhere and in every group photo, Constancio Tiempos (who specializes in writing obituaries that always begin with an "I met X . . ." and who, it's rumored, also wrote up his own obituary, with a first line that reads, "I knew Constancio Tiempos . . .").

The cultural supplement soldier with literary aspirations, Epifanio "Snoopy" Williams-Taboada (whose articles and reports about other cultures began, invariably, with long and heartfelt descriptions of the climatic state of everything around him, even concluded with the next day's meteorological prognosis. The thing about "Snoopy" came to him from "It was a dark and stormy night," supposedly).

The mysterious and anonymous and multimedia MacTypo (whose books, with their artisanal designs, were nothing but a chaos of different typographies and random photos that "the reader has to reorganize according to her own life experience and later upload to a secret site that she came to by following clues I leave in the hollows of trees in different parks in different countries.")

Cash Krugerrand, the literary agent whom everyone derides in public but dreams of having (and being possessed by) in private.

The illustrious Lucián Vieytes (who suffers from a narcissistic form of arteriolosclerosis that causes him to remember only himself and his own work and, with time, even to believe that he's the author of books like *The Brothers Karamazov* and *The Magic Mountain*, from which he recites entire pages from memory).

The Intellectualoid (a surprising masked fighter who emerges from a troupe on a successful TV show and becomes a reporter-printmaker celebrated by Edith "Ditta" Stern-Zanuzzi and by Rigoberto Paponia; who, in forums and magazines, devolve into a kind of "I saw him first" and "He's mine" argument).

The compulsive anthologist Bienvenido "Come Together" Tequiero (who is putting together an "anthological anthology of anthologies").

Baby Valencia (avant-gardist/terrorist who threatens other writers so they'll write his books for him and who even kidnapped the daughter of one writer, and put a bomb in the car of another) . . .

The list is enormous—the names and faces get mixed up and confused more than once—and it keeps on growing. And, of course, it includes a symbolic clone of The Writer: one Arturo Merlín who inhabits the catacombs of an abandoned metro station where, presumably, he continues coming up with stories that nobody can read. And tonight, his eyes growing heavy, The Young Man arranges and composes something terrifying in the air under his eyelids: for once Paponia gets up the nerve to leave his house and go beyond the borders of his neighborhood, and climbs to the top of a tower and throws himself off (though it isn't entirely clear that it's a suicide; there are those who venture that Paponia might have had a dizzy spell caused by the vertigo of going up, for the first time, in a building over one story tall) only to, fatal coincidence, crush Stern-Zanuzzi. Ditta, who—with her disarrayed blonde mane of *de luxe* homeless, always whipped not by the wind of history but by the fan of her hysteria—was passing by on her way to a conference organized by and about her. Ditta who—her obituaries will emphasize that she was working on compiling her kitchen recipes, Chicken a la King with interpolated apples and all of that—insists on claiming that she's been in all the right places and present at every transcendent moment, to bear witness and provide testimony. Ditta who, having been, if you believe her, just passing through, was in the radiation and on the battle fronts and at the ground zeros, wrote books about herself and Chernobyl, about herself and the toxic Tokyo metro, about herself and the fall of the World Trade Centers, about herself and shopping malls erected with narco money so the narcos can blow them up later—falls victim to the most barrio and absurd of deaths, almost a joke, a bad joke. This puts The Young Man in a tricky dilemma: are Paponia and Stern-Zanuzzi now united and reconciled by the connection of that fatal coincidence? Massive double funeral or a reigniting of hostilities between young factions, the followers of one and the other, at odds more than ever? Has practice buried theory or has theory precipitated the fall of practice? High culture crushed by low culture? Someone jokes that it's too bad that Ditta isn't alive so she can write a book about herself and Paponia's death.

And one thing begins to become murkily clear to The Young Man: almost without realizing it—he realizes now—he has begun to depopulate his landscape. The Young Man strolls through his literary world as if he were trimming new buds and withered growth, wrapped in a yellow wind.

The Period of Contraction has begun. Soon, he understands, the only one left will be the poet (never poetess, because The Young Man suffered greatly seeing The Young Woman's face when he called her a "poetess") and underground beauty Miranda Urano, in whose name many colleagues have taken their lives or given up writing verse. The Young Man's idea is that, in the moment of the reverse Big Bang, in the return to the absolute moment of the beginning now translated into the end, into a Genesis of apocalyptic modalities, Miranda Urano, in light of the revelation that he was the secret god operating that machine, falls to her knees and gives herself to him like an offering. And they live happily ever after. But we're not there yet, dreams The Young Man who's already dreaming, almost asleep. In that borderland moment when the eyelids seem transparent and what's lived fades into what an insomniac brain freed from the bonds of logic can imagine. In that silvery instant, all of us are experimental, avant-garde. And, just before descending toward those heights, The Young Man relives faithfully and in detail his encounter, months before, aboard an airplane in trouble, with The Writer. Remembering the internal turbulence and the storm outside, The Young Man grinds his teeth in embarrassment (few things are worse than the inerasable and increasingly detailed memory of something that made you feel really uncomfortable, trapped in the air) and, luckily, immediately, the airplane is a different airplane. An airplane piloted by Miranda Urano, wrapped in a tight, black latex outfit, her body oh so aerodynamic. An airplane full of atomic bombs that she'll drop on all the writers The Young Man created. And the Earth will burn, enveloped in the radiation of black and white explosions. And, then, a handful of survivors. Not his creations, but castaways from his increasingly distant childhood: protagonists of movies he saw some Saturday afternoon, on TV, in the days of only four channels, days when you had to stand up and turn a dial to watch something else. He sees it for the first time and he sees it several times on a cycle, a Saturday afternoon broadcast, where various random titles from different genres play in succession. The program starts just after midday and shows a western, a war movie, a comedy, a historic movie, and in the evening, a horror movie. And the horror movies are his favorites and, among them (classical and aristocratic monsters of the Old World of Universal Studios and, from the New World, tentacular monsters of American International Pictures, where everything grows or shrinks), there is one that stands out, set on one of the small Marshall Islands called Bikini Atoll where, in the aftermath of some nuclear tests, a group of men and women—the men with lab coats and military uniforms; the women, who at first seem serious and disciplined, but always have bathing suits close at hand that they won't hesitate to model for the enjoyment and distraction of the scientists and colonels—are besieged by giant telepathic crabs that devour not only their bodies, but also their minds. One by one, without any hurry. The Young Man dreams about this and, in the dream, he remembers what frightened him most when he was little, in his nightmares, in an immense little bed with room enough for every terror: the creaking conversations between the crabs and the way in which their voices (in The Young Man's dream, one of the crabs already has the unmistakable voice of The Writer's Mad Sister) infiltrate the brains of humans and drive them mad. Convincing them that nothing could be better than a walk on the beach. Tempting them, tempting him, with a "Don't you want to know what gift the tide has brought you? Is it a good story that you want, that you're looking for, that you need? *We* are the greatest story of all! Something worth dying to be able tell and to write." Deep and salty voices inviting you to a party of open pincers poised to snap shut. Voices near the reefs, under the moonlight. Mutant voices on a beach, on another beach that, beyond the years and the distances, borders this beach, where these crabs sing now for him alone and they sing come, come, come, here I am, I've been waiting for you for so long, where have you been, it doesn't matter, you've come back at last, welcome home.

II

Sing, O goddess, the wrath of Penelope. A ruinous wrath that caused her family countless sorrows; but that was, it seems, of great inspiration to her brother, who's now more particular than ever. A brother transformed into particles, courtesy of the God particle and now, all of him, stardust, *blowin' in the wind*, floating here and there and everywhere, high above in the Big Sky looking down at this little Earth. * And like the dysfunctions in satellites provoked by hysterical solar storms, he appears, without warning, like those parentheticals directing a histrionic and operatic ghost to enter and exit the most innocent of crime scenes. Lo, here he is, incorporeal yet omnipresent, interfering and interceding and—sheltered by the alibi of *le mot juste* and all that—obsessively repeating ideas and judgments. Projecting himself like the loop of a video that no search engine can locate to download and edit; a video from a security camera where he enters the frame and, after overpowering a fragile scientist, shuts the door and, alone and inside a laboratory, as everyone first orders and then begs him not to, presses a button so that everything, including him, is set in motion and spins and spins and spins until it provokes a nauseating vertigo behind the eyes. Being a nuisance, yes. Polishing a single piece to excess—tactical interventions?, voodoo pins?, inserts of more or less precious stones?, invented parts?, asterisks like jagged little black holes, like little gears looking for something to turn and set in motion?, warpath footnotes that don't resign themselves to the bottom of the page, climbing through lines to insert themselves wherever they like, wherever is most convenient?, parentheses that here are the pure present, the right now, the unexpurgated material that later will be organized and, consequently, distorted for the best possible understanding and structure?—like, appearing again, in those other stage directions, not for the actors but for the audience, soliciting or demanding *laughter and tears and applause*. Here then, mixing his indeterminate present with the precise place and exact time that already passed, that already was. History is nothing but an agreed-upon hallucination. The colorful wallpaper that distracts from and conceals a gray wall covered with damp stains that reveal very different things, depending on who is looking at them. A passing order, an attempt to evade the idea that, in reality, everything happens uninterrupted and with endless sequencing problems and—because really there is no time—with all times at the same time, with everything happening at the same time. So, History—miniscule subgenre of capital-T Time—like a collective and recollective madness that millions of people agree to believe in to keep from going mad. Dates of birth and death, names of battles, surnames of prophets and dignitaries, celebrated and bronze-etched phrases, taglines as props to lean on and stand up and repeat to achieve the automatic Nirvana of a good student, repeating day after day what gets repeated to you, so you don't have to repeat the year. But it's one thing—a sure thing—to memorize, and another entirely different and more dangerous thing to make memory. So that's why remembering what happened is more like rewriting than rereading. Memory is a receptacle of opaque crystal. Impossible to discern against the light how full or how empty it is; how much is missing and how much is left of the past it contains. And the past is so much easier to recount if it is taken out from inside—from that past that itself contains the same past in an insatiable exercise of self-cannibalism—with the forceps of a complex and always meager and slight and fleeting present. Pulled out from inside screaming. Wrapped in the moist placenta of a first cry or one of those laughs that sprays saliva onto whoever's not laughing and who won't be laughing now: because—warning, warning—this is the most inside, the most secret of jokes. Nothing more and nothing less than that instant, suspended between nothing and everything when a writer spends an eternity of seconds thinking of what he'll subsequently put down in writing. A map of unfathomable distance separating the measures of the cerebral score from the arrival of the fingers to the goal of the keyboard. Coming out of the same body but from a different source, in a different font. And, to state the obvious, that font is American Typewriter, right?; because that was the script on his first typewriter. And because Penelope's brother was (is?) a writer, always, with a particular and often criticized interest in American literature, and over and out for a while and . . . Receive in your eyes a postcard from the always irascible and redheaded Penelope, years ago but as if it were right now, coming across the ocean, descending from the Olympic heights of an ancient continent to the, by comparison, juvenile underworld of a city called Abracadabra. A city built on the ruins of a civilization that one fine day—without an explanation or goodbye note chiseled in black stone or engraved in green jade—up and left, abandoning temples and pyramids and altars where offerings of warm hearts were made to gods with long names made up almost entirely of consonants. * And, ah, poetic and intuitive justice of the names and places, their irony so urbane right from the start: because—Penelope is about to discover—nothing happens, nothing really moves, the hand that reaches into the magic top hat comes out empty of rabbit or any trick at all, there, in Abracadabra. And, suddenly, Penelope remembers a song from her adolescence. One of those catchy songs, so catchy in fact that you never remember the singer, but always the chorus. How'd it go? Ah, yes: "Abra-Abracadabra . . . I wanna reach out and grab ya . . . Abra-Abracadabra . . . Abracadabra." Who wrote it and who sang it? A mystery. * "Abracadabra," written by Steve Miller and performed by the Steve Miller Band (from the eponymous 1982 album, number one in several countries). Fasten your seatbelts. Turbulence. Deploy the landing gear. Flaps down. * Here we go. Flashes and sparks and turn off all electronic devices except, of course, the unpluggable brain that, they say, keeps on functioning for an eternal instant after the heart has broken forever. * Unceasing. Flat line. Straight lines, one after another and all in a row. No paragraph breaks, like a rolling stone with no direction home, like something—another reference to another song—"really vomitific," like something asking time and again how does it feel, how it feels, if it feels something and then, there, the nausea of Penelope—her heart wrecked for as long as her brain can remember—tied to her seat like Ulysses to a mast. Penelope tied to the seat of a latest-generation air ambulance, specially hired by her new family-in-law. * And Penelope, who never excelled at the oily and slippery art of diplomacy, never saw two words less suited to go traipsing around holding hands than "family" and "in-law." Or maybe she has, but probably not, the family should be the site and sanctuary where the law doesn't enter, where it's left outside, asking to be let in and, of course, the problem is that someone always opens the door and invites it inside and welcomes it "like another member of the family." **Not long now, just a little while, all landing is inevitable, and Penelope's ears are covered, and, in back of the aircraft, watched over by a doctor and nurse, her husband breathes mechanically, deep in a coma for two weeks now.** * The story, of course, doesn't begin here. But this is a good starting point, as good as opening—like in those black and white films of Hollywood's golden age—with a map filling the whole screen and, across it, a line that draws itself from one point to another. And, like in those same movies, lines of text rising from the bottom of the screen and climbing, like a sunrise, to the highest point, explaining everything that happened before, a long time ago in a galaxy far far away. But all at the same time, as if all times were the same time. Backward and forward and up and down and, also, to the right and the left and at oblique and sharp and steeply ascending and descending angles. A lot like the tumbling, head-over-heels deluge of speech that spews forth after drinking multiple liters of truth serum, but, also, like the panoramic and encompassing way the gods think, leisurely reflecting on a landscape where past and present and future occur simultaneously. "All good writing is swimming under water and holding your breath." Who said that? Francis Scott Fitzgerald? In a letter to his daughter, Scottie? If that's true, then reading this is like drowning, like not breathing, like discovering that when you stop breathing (or breathe in that cosmic and abysmal way that astronaut David "Dave" Bowman breathes in *2001: A Space Odyssey*) there's another way of life, a strange way of life, narrated from that even stranger way of life, the one he's living now. Penelope's brother. The way that Penelope's brother—deified thanks to science—watches her, from everywhere and nowhere. In person but absent, in the third-person. As if in telling her story he were reading his own mind. As if his most intimate thoughts had the external texture of a voiceover. Thus, Penelope in a summary of lived experience that can't get too far going in reverse. Because, to do that, would be to run the risk of falling into that delirium of summarizing sci-fi sagas where we understand absolutely nothing of what we claim to process and comprehend: billions of light years, everything taking place on a planet whose name is something that sounds like an onomatopoeia followed by a number, from the boom of its Big Bang to the terminal moan of its Little Crash. Information overload. For that reason, he—the also exceedingly cosmic—will have to resign himself to explaining how our heroine ended up aboard this airplane with a man whom, presumably, she still loves, though he's floating between the two ellipses of a deep coma. And love, definitely. But not love like love in Jane Austen's novels (where marriage is that ocean of happiness into which the complex river of falling in love spills out), but love like love in George Eliot's novels (where love is nothing but that tidal wave awaiting the go-ahead to break over the supposedly solid ground and transform it into the quickest of sands). It all depends on where you land on the wheel of fortune of feelings. A matter of luck or justice or chemical forces whose elements haven't yet been synthesized. There's no instruction manual, no list of ingredients, no precise formula—love is the most inexact of sciences. And love can be the well just as easily as what fills the well, without ever filling it entirely. In Penelope's case, love isn't one thing or the other. Penelope's love is a heavy and ominous spade. Pure exercise to exercise the musculature of the heart, aware how difficult it is in this life to be granted the gift of being able to say, like Catherine Earnshaw, that "I *am* Heathcliff!" The nonreturnable gift of loving someone so much, to the point where you end up feeling that you're them and they're you. An inseparable whole. A warm and symmetrical two-headed monster. A miracle for the two lovers that is an aberration of nature for everyone else. But no. * It's not that these kinds of things don't happen outside of books: it's that these kinds of things don't happen in any book that isn't Emily

Brontë's 1847 *Wuthering Heights*. Penelope's bible. And, also, her declaration of ultimate principals and her rebellious battle-hymn against *Tender Is the Night*, which her parents never stopped reading and stealing and tossing over their heads and that, now, her brother never stops studying and shaking and putting together and taking apart in search of some secret meaning and order that'll help him understand everything. There inside, running through fog and moor, like in Fitzgerald's novel first and then in her parents' telenovela, another pair of oh so fou lovers. But compared to Dick and Nicole, Heathcliff and Cathy are much more active and seem always seconds away from exploding or blowing up. The tempestuous always imposing itself over the tender and, for her, *Wuthering Heights* is more than a book to always return to—it's a book to never leave. Penelope has read everything that the Brontë sisters wrote and even what the Brontë brother wrote, and a good part of what's been written about them and him; but she always goes back to Emily and her single novel, her singular novel. The only novel that poor Emily wrote; though there are rumors, corroborated by the latest investigations of biographers, that she wrote a second one and that Charlotte threw it into the flames. Pages too wild, wilder even than those of *Wuthering Heights*, they theorize. And so the older sister decided to protect the posterity and reputation of the younger sister; but there are some who think she did it out of pure envy. And Penelope agrees: there's nothing more dangerous than older siblings who claim to be protecting you and who, to keep you from falling down, chain your foot to a wall and, yes, can even end up burning inside your head the first novel that you never managed to write. And nothing bothers Penelope more than those interpretations claiming that Cathy and Heathcliff are actually stepbrother and stepsister. And that their passion is nourished by something as coarse as second-degree incest when, actually, it's a love beyond love. A love for which love is nothing more than the gate to a labyrinth of straight lines, or a launch tower to the stars, or the highest diving board from which to leap to the bottom of all things. "You have killed me," says Cathy, more alive than ever and just before dying, to an agonized Heathcliff. Here outside, for

Penelope, as far as feelings go, everything is more crass and insubstantial and fleeting and as if anesthetized. Ordinary love is, in the words of Cathy, "like the foliage in the woods: time will change it, I'm well aware, as winter changes the trees" and it bears no resemblance to the "the eternal rocks" beneath the roots. Here, in the real world, Penelope likes to say that "if the heart could think like the brain thinks, the heart would stop immediately." Voluntary victim of a sudden heart attack. Tearing open the shirt, sending all the buttons flying, to flip the secret switch that marks the end of all heartbeats and of the immediate echo of the next heartbeat. Heartbeats like footsteps on a stairway that climbs and climbs and climbs to, in the end, open on a wall with no exit. A wall that, when you fail in your effort to tear it down, ends up breaking your heart in a thousand pieces. And this last thing is what Penelope says in a bar called Psycholabis—after the presentation of a book by her older brother—to the man who will be her imperfect and immediate future husband. He has the air not of a Hollywood leading man, but the look of one of those variety show actors who used to entertain spectators between one movie and the next around the beginning of the past century. "Live Number," they called it. Real people like a special effect contrasting with the false two-dimensional realism of locomotives pulling into French train stations or cowboys robbing American trains. The man is named Maximiliano Karma and not Heathcliff (and oh how it fascinates Penelope that Heathcliff is at once both name and surname, and even breed of a single being, and unique sex). And the man—Penelope will soon realize—is closer to an unstable and pendular Edgar Linton, who'd have felt much more fulfilled and happy and at home, not far from there, dancing and strolling from one house to another in a Jane Austen novel. Nothing then of an "I *am* Maximiliano!" And Maximiliano asks Penelope for her phone number and Penelope (somewhat out of boredom, mostly to annoy her older brother, a little bit also because she lives in a state of perpetual sexual arousal, one of those smoldering fires, small but impossible to entirely extinguish) gives him a long kiss, with tongue, in and out, transmitting her mobile phone number in Morse Code. Penelope learned the little taps and dots and lines of the S.O.S. at a very young age, so she could communicate with her brother through a wall, in the adjoining room, in the engine room of their childhood, the shipwreck of their parents' marriage, she and her brother clinging to a lifeboat, children first, the woman going down with the man, and *save our souls*. And, surprise, Maximiliano decodes it and, at the end of the kiss, enters Penelope's number into his phone (one of those crazy-expensive satellite phones) without taking his eyes away from hers. And Penelope's mobile phone rings and vibrates at the height of her left breast, just above her unexpectedly and unconsciously pierced and electrified heart. * And, yes, such small yet simultaneously immense acts are sometimes more than enough (because his anecdotal valor is almost inexhaustible) for that eternal spark to become a forest fire of variable duration and beds burn day and night. A little water after a while, not to extinguish anything, but to learn about the flames. Who are you? Where'd you come from? How'd you get here? Those things. Penelope is, of course, the sister of The Writer. And Maximiliano Karma idolizes him, not so much because he likes his books, but because he wants to be like him, without really knowing, of course, what he's like. Maximiliano Karma belongs to that generation of kids who're dying to be writers and to be read but who don't really bother to read or write. And Maximiliano wants to earn *that* diploma that justifies him and at the same time definitively transforms him into the black sheep—but a well-combed and sweet-smelling black sheep who wins awards and appears on TV—of his affluent family. Maximiliano Karma is the piece that doesn't quite fit in the puzzle of their tropical dynasty. An anomaly in the system, an error in the programming of his family who believe that to stay is to succeed and the failure is to leave, to create distance and to distance yourself. Or something like that. The Karmas don't know how to deal with the subject and they prefer to think that: "Maxi is on vacation." But Maximiliano has come to this city to a) to establish himself as a novelist, b) to leave behind unsavory and narcotic company in his home city, and c) to meet girls who are less repressed—of their own volition or from their parents and uncles and aunts having implemented an efficient brain- and body-wash—than his cousins and cousins' friends. So far, a lot of c) and little or nothing of a) and b), because, let's be honest, what Maximiliano writes is not very good and what he puts up his nose is superlative, courtesy of a friend who, long distance, from his big little homeland, sends regular shipments of chemical powders to season his physical exploits. Back home

Maximiliano was and continues to be here what is commonly referred to as "a social user." And, of course, the problem is that his social life is a size XL and his successive stints in rehab don't shrink it. One day, at an exclusively family baptism (where the godfathers and godmothers are, always, other Karmas, giving birth to bicephalous relationships like godfather-uncle and godmother-cousin; anything to avoid bringing in an outsider or someone external to the family and thereby degrading the purity of the increasingly tangled ties, or provoking the discomfort of "having to meet strangers and learn new names"), Maximiliano Karma is revolving and evolving in one of those synchronized country dances. What do they call those dances that are kind of a competition, or sport, or it-seems-like-we're-doing-something-all-together-and-having-fun-but-really-we're-fighting-to-the-death-for-something-but-we-don't-and-never-will-know-what-it-is? * Square Dance: popular dance with four couples (eight dancers) arranged in a square, with two on each side, starting with Couple 1, who faces each other and moves to the left until they get to Couple 4. Couples 1 and 3 are referred to as the "head," while Couples 2 and 4 are the "side." Each dance begins and ends with a sequence of "called-moves" in the square formation. Almost a Karma family tradition. Penelope (who's of the school that we-dance-separately-everyone-on-their-own-but-together-in-a-way-almost-spiritually-and-in-perfect-harmony) won't believe her eyes or her muscles when, at the weddings in Abracadabra, she'll see all of them move out as if onto a battlefield, smiling, showing their teeth, ready to win just so someone else loses, while in the background, but everywhere, a song plays in which an imbecilic cowboy without a rodeo asks you not to break his heart, his "achy breaky heart." And Maxi, his nostrils white, yells to his cousin, asking "how many grams" her little premature baby boy weighed, born just seven months after the wedding, but with the unmistakable and healthy appearance of a full-term, ninth-month old baby. That's when the family intervened and sent him to "study abroad" in The Old World. As far away as possible. Far enough to allow his immediate family to tell other relatives and acquaintances that Maxi (as his family refers to him; Penelope prefers to call him Max) is making it big in the salons of ancient and cultured cities. And, ah, Maximiliano Karma's life is so frenetic that his work isn't enough for him. And so he starts several blogs under different names, and leaves himself infinite comments—insults, praise, offers to meet up and get to know himself at bars and beaches—with so many different personalities and sexes and ages. Automatic and alkaloidic writing. Fast and almost stamped with a style that—reading between black lines and, above all, between lines of white—reveals itself to be inseparable from the rhythm of lines and inhalations. Thus, the experimental subterfuge of a series of "(In)complete Stories" (to wit: stories that begin but never end). And a series of short "Elementary Novels" that, due to their pathological obsession with detail, courtesy not of deep readings but of surfing the oil-slick waves of Google, Maximiliano Karma likes to define—though he's never opened one of the Frenchman's books—as "Proustian." What are they about? They're about things like the incremental growth of the iceberg that the *Titanic* ends up running into. Or about the slow yet constant growth of the tree in Bois de Boulogne (check whether it was a walnut or a chestnut) where, leaving Jimmy's, the mega-endowed playboy Porfirio "Rubi" Rubirosa crashes his Ferrari 250 GT, and dies. * For a second, Penelope wonders why Max chose that tree and not, for example, the much more literary tree (a banana tree, spinning through the air, and another tree) struck by the Facel Vega Sport driven by Albert Camus, who thought there was nothing more idiotic than dying in a car accident. A good question indeed. A more than pertinent question. And yet like most questions of the kind that contain their own illuminating answer, the question soon dissolves and allows whoever formulated it to go on as if nothing happened, blowing in the wind where there are no answers, just wind. Or about the tongues of fire slowly and feverishly licking the body of Joan of Arc. Or about the blank fifth bullet that's loaded in every firing squad (so that each shooter can convince himself that his is the dead round and that it's not his turn to kill) and that flies to bury itself in the chest of Gary Gilmore's smile. Or about the eternal and placid time of the horse when, one day in 1568, the dull Michel Eyquem de Montaigne mounts his steed only to be thrown off and get to his feet transformed into simply Montaigne—into something brilliant. Maximiliano Karma, of course, has never read that thing William S. Burroughs said (Penelope will hear the phrase for the first time, several months later, from Lina's lips, in another bar, on another night, on the other side of the ocean, in Abracadabra) about how "they call something *experimental* when the experiment has gone wrong." But the members of the latest and juvenile generational avant-garde, who don't hesitate to adopt Maximiliano Karma as one of their own, haven't read William S. Burroughs *either*. Why? Because talentless people tend to come together to create and seal off small and sectarian worlds, in an attempt to convince themselves of their own genius by having it reflected in the narrow and inexact mirror of others just as mediocre as they are. A mirror that's nothing but a thin layer of mercury, not magic, but a deception, always telling you you're the brightest and even the prettiest and that you look so much like it. You look just like people who don't seem to find it sufficiently experimental and avant-garde—could there be something more avant-garde and experimental?, what more do they want and need?—that entire worlds have been built, worlds more perfect and daring than the one in which they themselves were created, with slightly less than thirty letters and slightly more than ten symbols. Because, for them, Maximiliano Karma functions as a kind of rare specimen and—last but not least—as a generous payer of ethylic and ancient bar tabs and almost compulsive purveyor of maximum-purity controlled substances in the bathrooms of those same bars. Maximiliano Karma and Penelope go into just such a bathroom in just such a bar. Then, while snorting straight white lines, cut out across the lowered top of the toilet, Maxi tells Penelope that he's "working on" a novella titled *The Russian and the Butterflies* and that it's about the bizarre relationship of an FBI agent, whom J. E. Hoover has given the mission of spying on Vladimir Nabokov during his Lepidopterist wanderings through the hills and forests of the United States. Maxi never read *Lolita* or *Speak, Memory*—though, like with all his previous works, he's gathered all the information he needs from Wikipedia entries—he explains to Penelope with that strange and savage pride of those who haven't done something, who haven't done anything. * And maybe—why not write it instead of describe it—Maximiliano Karma is much more inspired when it comes to the act of inspiring through his nose. "The first time I got high it was like being kissed by an angel," Maximiliano Karma tells Penelope. "There are some people who take drugs to be somebody else and there are some people who take drugs to be more themselves. That seems to me like a good way to divide and classify the human race, right? . . . Me, on the other hand, I take drugs to be the person I used to be. That person who I was the first time I got high. When I knew everything and understood everything, really. And the best part is that you keep taking drugs, more all the time, seeking to recover that first feeling of the first time. But soon you realize that it's something irretrievable. From then on, you continue taking drugs to keep from believing that it's irretrievable. Taking drugs turns into the search for something that you know you'll never find . . . '*Pura vida, hermano*,'" continues Maximiliano Karma, with the voice of someone who is quoting but convinced that few will recognize the quote, an uncredited quote tossed into the air by the voice of the man whom Penelope already thinks of as Max. And from there, coked up and vertical (now it's his tongue that plays at line-dot-line between her legs), to the horizontality of the flat that the parents of the obligatory child prodigy bought for him in a counterculture but designer neighborhood, with an immense bed in the middle of the living room. Is Maximiliano Karma a great lover or did Penelope previously have bad luck when it comes to sex and its positions? Neither the one nor the other. But, for her, hooking up with Max is an anatomically and geographically and economically functional relationship: moving in with Maximiliano Karma allows Penelope to escape the (for her) oppressive vigilance of her older brother, to leave behind the forest and the sea and install herself in the big city, to rely on limitless funds for her vices and pleasures. And, along the way, to learn—while correcting her boyfriend's disorganized and barely original originals on the screen of a gigantic latest-generation computer—that she, though she doesn't write, is a much better writer than he is. And that consequently Maximiliano Karma, Max, could end up becoming a good part of the novel of her life that, maybe, one day, when she has nothing left to live for, she'll decide to relive in writing. Meanwhile and in the meantime, at some point (it's impossible for Penelope to pinpoint a date and day and month; surfing the crest of a designer psychotropic wave) they decide to get married so that, thereby, Maximiliano can consummate, while consuming and consuming himself, what, for his family, is the ultimate transgression—a civil and nonreligious wedding, without relatives, without even notifying the family. It's worth pointing out an additional provocation: Penelope (though she looks eighteen) is almost thirty years old, and no matter how counterculture or transgressive you are, the third decade is a complicated age for women when it comes to what they've not yet done, when it comes to what they have yet to do and what they might never get to do; get married, for example. Whereas Maximiliano Karma is twenty-five. The festivities (dubbed by Maximiliano as the Release the Kraken! Party, to which a literary fanzine devotes a special issue and which ends up being possible to follow live on the blog of the rather retrograde avant-garde, already mentioned) last many nights. On the fifth or sixth, Penelope and Maximiliano collapse—like vampires running from dawn but *also* from night—in a room with the blinds drawn. Twenty hours later, Penelope wakes up and Maximiliano does not. A week later, the air ambulance, carrying the new bride and the husband-in-suspension, lands at the airport in Abracadabra. And there is the whole family-in-law. All of it. The Karmas. All of them. Indivisible. United. Half a degree of separation between one and the next and, with the passing days, Penelope will never comprehend if they're together because they love each other, because they need each other, because they need the other's gaze to be themselves, or because—following that dictate of mafiosos and courtiers—it's best to keep your enemies close at hand. Nor will she ever understand what fluctuations determine the rotations of the enemy-of-the-moment or the fool-to-belittle among the Karmas. Week after week, the role of the guilty or the klutz will be passed from one to the other, like a relay race, and one or the other will carry it for a few days until they can pass on their "title" to the next to be condemned and slandered. No matter what, everything stays and will stay, always, within the family. The family that now is, presumably, hers or the one she belongs to. Either way, the Karmas, like one of those hallucinatory hallucinations coated in that humid and vertical heat (in the airport the hot air envelops Penelope like a gift, like an offering to be sacrificed) that always seems to grow in the distance where planes land and take off. The Karmas, like one of those mythological creatures with too many heads saying and thinking the same thing. Better to speak a lot and say little. And not to ask questions so they don't ask questions. The answers are always flammable material. So the Karmas function like an echo chamber. The Karmas, like an acoustic social network, but in person, always plugged in and preferring to say "We must go" rather than "I must go." The Karmas—pluralistic, gestaltic, more like subsidiaries of a constantly expanding franchise than members of a family—always move in groups. In small but overwhelming migrations. Filling entire theaters when they decide to go see a movie. One night Penelope almost believes she's going to be able to escape and go see the closest thing to an "art" film ever shown in Abracadabra (nothing too extreme; not Andréi Tarkovsky or Terrence Malick, but, at best, Woody Allen or Wes Anderson). But, somehow, in a way that she doesn't entirely understand, as if abducted, she ends up being dragged along in a Karmatic tide, from the door of the shopping mall multiplex to a theater showing a movie where cars race and explode or an animated movie, both in 3-D (hard to tell them apart, maybe the point of separation being those girls wrapped in racing latex or those fierce princesses ready to do whatever it takes not for a prince but for a kingdom). While, in the seats, everyone speaks loudly and chews with Dolby dentures and gets up over and over again. It's clear—Penelope already learned this, sitting down to watch TV with a handful of Karmas—that their ability to concentrate for more than a minute or two is nonexistent, that they don't care how the movie begins and how it transpires and how it ends, a story can begin or end at any moment. And, a mystery to Penelope, none of the kids take the opportunity to make out or cop a feel in the darkness; instead they ceaselessly consult their small and glowing screens, sending one-hundred-forty character messages from one theater row to the next. But she doesn't complain either—she's been lucky. After all, the Karmatic tide has pulled her into a theater. Because, more than once, as if blown off course by a secret, idiot wind, they all end up in some random place. An amusement park or a popular bar, whose attraction lasts a month or two at most. And when they get home and their parents ask them what the movie was about, the young Karmas respond: "Sex on the beach" or "A rollercoaster." No, it doesn't matter where they go. The important thing is to go somewhere other Karmas have been before and to be the first to arrive somewhere other Karmas will come later. Like sliding across the echo of an echo. Many. All of them. Together. The final destination is just a temporal and geographical accident. But there they go, taking over an entire restaurant (generally in a golden and grandiose hotel) when, once in a great while, they go out to eat. Or, on occasion, howling as they board the first or business class of a Jumbo 747, or the first class deck on a Caribbean or Mediterranean cruise: the latter being the Karmas' preferred mode of transport (they come aboard with suitcases full of autochthonous foods and regional ingredients "so they won't miss them") because there, all together, they feel that they've commandeered the ship, that the voyage belongs to them and is under their command. And that corners and stairways abound where they can bad-mouth—on the sly, but with soft and affectionate voices and wide eyes, an awkward simulacrum of astonishment and incredulity—that one Karma who took forever to come down to dinner. Or to come lie out by the pool. Or who swears someone pushed him down the stairs. Or that someone slipped a powerful laxative into his multicolored cocktail with its little paper umbrella. They rarely disembark on solid ground, and when they do, it's only to occupy an expensive and bad restaurant, a tourist trap where the maltreatment they receive from the wait staff is understood by the Karmas as a demonstration of prestige and quality and sophistication, which they remunerate with exaggerated and absurd tips. And, yes, when they return to the port of embarkation, they discover that one of the Karmas who boarded with them is missing; but nobody seems that interested in or worried by the disappearance. Or when, once a year, all the Karmas gather on Mount Karma to stage a kind of family Olympics with sports and party games where more than one person—something to do with catharsis and the fact that, for once, anything goes; preferring to compete among themselves because, they intuit, outside of their own circle they'd always be losers and so better to be taken down within the family and inside that controlled environment where the winners alternate so that nobody feels too bad—ends up crying with rage or with broken arms or panic attacks or minor concussions. The places, in reality, are what matter least and before long they acuire, for the Karmas, the poor resolution of those illustrated backdrops in front of which photos used to be taken. What matters is that familial multitude that—within a few centuries, in order to perpetuate its existence—will teletransport en masse to Jupiter and beyond. But that's still a long way off. Now, in the airport, in Abracadabra, Penelope remembers having seen fewer people at Hitler's rallies in Berlin or Beatles concerts in New York. Maximiliano's family (her family now) receives Penelope at the foot of the runway, in a pyramidal and pre-Colombian formation, lined up in generational order. And at the apex, the point of the pyramid, far above all the rest (and nobody can be so tall, thinks Penelope as they carry Maximiliano's stretcher down a ramp at the backside of the aircraft) smiles a woman, a cigar in her mouth, her body small yet absurdly tall, wrapped in a blazing red and yellow poncho. A woman with silver hair, cut short, almost shaved, a few glints of gold in a smile more teeth than smile, fixed in the center of a senescence, but of a senescence like that of Clint Eastwood. A vigorous senescence. A vintage senescence. That woman hasn't aged so much as fossilized into someone who will endure for millennia. It's not that she's shrunk, rather that she's been distilled to her most pure and powerful essence. And she's a woman who, Penelope discovers and learns, is *that* tall because she's mounted on a horse. And she doesn't even consider getting down. "I am Mamagrandma Karma, I am ninety-five years old, I think; my birth certificate was lost and never found. In an earthquake or a revolution or a fire. Knowing when I was born is unimportant, because that only serves to specify your age when you die. And I'm not planning on dying. Life is very short, but also very wide," the woman says to Penelope. "And this is Horse. Yes, the name of my horse is Horse. And period. Because I like to call things by their names," thunders Mamagrandma while patting her steed. And it's difficult for Penelope to tell where Mamagrandma ends and where Horse begins, and from then on and until her last day in Abracadabra, rare will be the time she'll see the immortal old woman not moving around on four feet. Then— another Hollywood reference, because maybe everything is starting to acquire a particularly irreal air, irreal for Penelope—it occurs to her that Mamagrandma is like a bastardized cross of Bette Davis and Emiliano Zapata, Marlon Brando's Zapata. And it'll become more than obvious to Penelope that this chronobiological aberration has had a devastating effect on the wide and winding family circle. Mamagrandma should be dead and buried already. But Mamagrandma has the vigor that many have at fifty. So, the second row of her children, almost in their seventies already, appear to have the mental maturity of capricious adolescents. Maximiliano's parents suddenly seem to Penelope like blurry and imprecise sketches: a mother who appears to be floating behind a stupefied and stupefying smile, and a father who looks like he's always more than ready to take off running to anywhere that isn't here. While Mamagrandma's grandchildren, in their forties, have the envious and competitive mannerisms of insatiable children who never make it past the age of ten and spend their lives looking at the other, at what the other has, at what should, always, be theirs and only theirs. On the other hand, all the great grandchildren (nearly all of them premature until, as already mentioned, Penelope realizes that this is nothing but a euphemism thinly veiling a "shotgun wedding") seem to be the age they actually are. But it's impossible to be totally sure, because they live inside that atemporality of people plugged into social networks and comparing models of mobile phones with more applications all the time, dreaming of the day when they'll be able to do everything between one screen and the next, without the interference of flesh and blood. Meanwhile and in the meantime, they use their tablets to enter virtual boutiques and buy things almost blindly, stumbling around, "because it's the best when boxes of clothes and devices show up at home and you don't even remember what you bought and then it's like they are presents from somebody else and . . ." Their almost lyrical eloquence when it comes to spending money and their command of technology is as astonishing as their lack of knowledge about almost everything else. Some of them—the girls—think they can get pregnant if there are sperm floating in the pool water, or, of course, when they make love for the first time, punctually and implacably fertile, or if they're not married, like all the innocent yet equally culpable girls in all the novels they don't read and all those telenovelas they do see. The boys think that the *Star Wars* saga takes place just after the fall of the Roman Empire "or after King Arthur." Their parents love them automatically and remind them unceasingly that they've never "bad-mouthed" each other in front of them. Which doesn't imply that they haven't bad-mouthed all the other parents. That's why these great-grandchildren—every Sunday, leaving mass, Penelope will watch them the way one looks at an alien species, a deep-sea phosphorescent fish—never stop sending each other highly classified electronic messages, exchanging information that might end up being useful for blackmailing their progenitors. So happy that technological progress has advanced, but at the same time descended to the almost subterranean levels of their language, with moronic abbreviations, short words (and even so it's still hard for them to find and give voice to these words, and, when searching for them, they always look up at the sky, their pupils suddenly beatific, as if expecting divine intervention), and the legitimization of orthographical errors. Communicating phone to phone even though they're right next to each other. * The faithful and written transcription of a phone conversation between two Karmas—read and take the plunge at your own risk—is like Beckett floating through the smoke of an opium den. Nothing is straight, everything is sinuous and, on occasion, the true reason for the call (generally to hatch a plot or report a scandal or confirm a lie or deafening rumor) finally shows up forty minutes after the first ring, after absolutely everything else has been discussed. From the state of the weather to courteous and cloying exchanges before the bile and the hemlock and the thunder and the lightning are released, always striking those who are absent, those not participating in this conversation because they're having another one, talking about those who are talking about them. The modus operandi is always the same: 1) One Karma bad-mouths an absent Karma to another Karma; 2) if that Karma doesn't seem in agreement or complicit with the comment about the Karma who isn't there but shines in absentia, the first Karma will slip in a tentative jab aimed at the other for being a "coward" or for "not being up to date on the situation" to, subsequently, 3) call that Karma who had been bad-mouthed at the beginning of the cycle to say that the other Karma, the one who wanted no part of the scheme, had been the one to say what he himself had initially and originally said. It seems complicated, but this infectious and toxic cycle is of a monstrous simplicity and efficiency. Soon, a frenetic vaudeville ensues, everyone has taken shots at everyone else, but nobody wants to admit they've been hit or wounded, much less take responsibility for the twisted shots they fired from the shadows. And so the monthly phone bill of one Karma would easily be enough to feed a small African village for an entire year. Exchanging—like trading cards or comics—classified and top-secret material that they'll be able to use to blackmail and threaten their progenitors if their demands are not met. They're like scale models—more modern—of ancestral perfidy and malice. They're ready to bloom like those heavy-scented flowers that blossom in the middle of the trash. Uncontainable growth that their parents—knowing what their kids are like because that's how they were; knowing how their kids will turn out because that's how they are—attempt without ever really succeeding to control, pruning back excess shoots and removing thorns, like undisciplined bonsais with delusions of grandeur. Opening and closing—without interruption, arbitrarily—the sluicegates of gifts and privileges, turning them into nervous creatures, worried that their many siblings and numerous cousins might have more than they do. As a result, each and every one of them, through the years and experiences, is sunk to varying depths in a domestic terror of complex protocol. * Nobody says what they think, though "to think" might be one of the most-thought verbs and one that will, inevitably, be brought back over and over, never really being set aside, as we'll see here, thinking about the Karmas. One says only what one is supposed to think in line with what's supposedly thought of one, or better, in line with what one thinks others think of one. Thinking of others—something that can be understood as a form of generosity, but also as an avaricious deformity—is not the same thing as thinking about what you'd like others to think, especially about you. But that's what they think about. Nothing else. But all the time. Before long, Penelope will realize that she's never thought so much in her life as she has in Abracadabra. And that she never thought about so many people who are, at the same time, so insignificant: the Karmas. All the time. Them and about them. The Karmas like a leitmotiv and like a mental block that rejects all thought that's not its own or about it. Thinking about what their personas are thinking about. Constantly. In a transparent yet palpable silence that can be studied—against the light, with squinted eyes and almost flat-line pupils—like one of those X-rays that reveal something unexpected. The Karmas thinking that saying what you think is the same as chewing with your mouth open. So, for them and from them, the bare minimum: random and figurative phrases. Nothing abstract. Everything figurative. The cloying sweetness of postcard illustrations. Hearts, kisses, flowers, never permitting the uncomfortable quirk of a double meaning. Norms so white they appear transparent. Simple things like "It's cold" or "It's warm" or "Too bad" or "Good" or "What time is it?" or "Is it warm or cold?" and, the automatic and public invocation of good wishes for all and, in a whisper, the hope that theirs are the only wishes granted, even the ones that wish the worst for everyone else. And, of course, absolution every Sunday, at mass, kneeling but with heads held high, which shouldn't be taken to mean that they look up and tremble and beg forgiveness from the heavens. So, the added sensation of hearing the distant sounds of an old machine being operated by someone who forgot long ago what the machine was meant to do. It doesn't matter: they keep checking it over and oiling it because there's nothing more frightening—more panic inducing—than thinking that at some point it'll be replaced by a new machine and a new instruction manual. And the sound of the machine, because it's familiar, is so relaxing. No one says anything to the person who wants to tell them something. Everything arrives via bizarre swerves, the unanticipated ricochet, laterally and sinuously, never in sincere, straight lines. If you concentrate, Penelope swears, you can even see trajectories of the slivers of dotted lines, where a name does or doesn't go. Or the poisoned arrows that, as if suspended in midair, connect or separate the initials of some to or from the initials of others. An always-alarming tom-tom, taser and laser, weaving a red spider web, like the ones that surround and enclose cursed relics in museums. Leave no trace and don't touch, yes. But nothing is safe from being torn apart by the always-soiled hands of evil thoughts. Penelope can never decide whether their mode of communication is very primitive or very sophisticated: A tells C what he or she really wants but doesn't dare tell B, hoping that, almost right away, C will communicate it to B as something that A said and, when B confronts A and asks if A really thinks it, A will respond that it was something he or she overheard D say when Z . . . Like that, everyone repeating what's been said, nobody saying anything. But they never stop talking, making sounds. And, as the weeks pass, Penelope mistakes the fact that—one at a time and always alone—various Karmas approach her and entrust her with things they'd never even tell the priest on Sunday, for a kind of privilege. But in the end, she'll learn that they tell her these things because they think of her as something like the tower in a castle where nobody ever ascends, or worse, the sewer where nobody ever descends. There, in her ears, they discharge the sewage of their forbidden thoughts and desires, convinced that, even if Penelope says something, nobody will believe her anyway, because she's not a true Karma, whatever the papers say. So, Penelope emerges from these confessions like someone submerged in a fever, and they force her to take long and heavy naps. The kind of nap that she wakes from with a saliva-soaked pillow and the aftertaste of nightmares where she's always like Vincent Price in those demented and libertine Poe adaptations, running down the stairs of a castle in flames—what could the curtains in Roger Corman's films be made of that burns so long and so well?—and reciting flammable lines and embracing corpses buried alive, while everything sinks into the cursed swamps in the depths of a B-movie studio. And during her first weeks in Mount Karma—as a hobby, or therapy, or whatever—Penelope, as if driven by a fever, writes and traces initials and lines on the walls of her room. A diagram where the Karmas are connected by the power of their hate and envy. An arrow connecting one of the boys who said this or that about one of the girls. Different colors to calibrate the varying intensity of their statements. Green, yellow, orange; but never achieving red; because self-destruction is poorly regarded and sullies everything, and who will tend the gardens then and, finally, because it'd spell the end, and for the Karmas the idea of anything ending results in vertigo, ending is for the unwashed masses—why end when you can go on. But before long, for the recently arrived Penelope, it's impossible to retain true clarity, the arrows crisscross and skewer each other, the diagram grows and expands like metastasis of the most terminal variety, like those allegedly simple instructions for assembling impossible furniture. And Penelope can't help imagining travelers of the future arriving to Earth and discovering this carnivorous family tree and wondering what it means, but suspecting that it must be a manual of military strategy developed during the great battle that brought about the end of everything in the world, or something like that. Mamagrandma and Horse approach Penelope and, from above, hard riding crop in strong hand, the woman says to her: "I don't know who you were before, but I know who you are now—one of us . . . I imagine you'll be tired from the trip. What would you prefer: to go to a hotel or to come home with us? Perhaps you'd prefer to be alone for a while, to take it slow. We're a bit much, aren't we?" Penelope smiles, exhausted, and answers: "Maybe it'd be best to go to a hotel, because . . ." "Say no more," Mamagrandma interrupts, "we're headed home right now." And she adds:

"Welcome to the Karmas." * And Mamagrandma says that word, "Karma" not like it's a surname but like it's a whole planet or, maybe, a black hole of dark matter capable of devouring entire galaxies in seconds. And, in that brief initial dialogue, Penelope glimpses the molecule of everything to come, the Karmas' essential protocol—force you to do what they want while attempting to convince you it's what you want; always say "thank you" with the inflection of "you're welcome"; tell you again and again that you've arrived not to the end of the world, but to the purpose of the universe. For Mamagrandma—and everyone who lives under her regime for that matter—Karma is the Alpha and the Omega. And everything that exists between one point and the other—and everything else, everything outside—has no meaning and no reason to be. What's outside (those outside) doesn't make any sense (don't make any sense) because it isn't (because they aren't) like what's inside. Its only utility is that of being, when the moment arrives, opportunistically blamed for some untoward thing that one of the irreproachable and untouchable Karmas has done. The Karmas never admit fault and, finding themselves forced to do so—and only in front of other Karmas—they offer explanations the way someone asks for the court's understanding because they're an orphan, never mind the fact that they're on trial for murdering their parents. And soon they're absolved, there inside, by those on the inside, where it matters and by the people who matter. The outside world and the people in it are nothing, forgettable and dispensable. A lower world. A vulgar antechamber to the paradise they inhabit and have created in their image and semblance. And the Karmas—Penelope discovers—are like the characters in *The Exterminating Angel* but without any anxiety about not being able to leave the room, not caring if they ever get out. Why? What for? We're just fine in here, where there's no chaos, where everything has an order, where everyone knows everyone else and the variables of disaster—the sins, the shame, the betrayals, the S and M and L and XL miseries—are covered up and kept under wraps and contained. Yes, the Karmas are content to be who they are. But Penelope never trusted that oft-cited opening of Tolstoy's that talks about the uniformity of family happiness. Family happiness doesn't speak in Esperanto, but in very different and, sometimes, incomprehensible and irreconcilable dialects. Tongues sharper and even harder to listen to and understand than those of the supposed and also Tolstoyan singular plurality regarding what unhappiness does to bloodlines. For it's well understood that the most miserable and egotistical acts are often committed and forgiven in the name of the family itself, no intermission or drop of the curtain, always soliloquizing with a choir in the background and for the supposed good of all. "I did it/I do it/I will do it for your own good" is the malevolent phrase that some fire at others, never face-to-face and point-blank, but stabbing each other in the back while exchanging those little Christian love pats as mass draws to an end. Again and again. Smiling and with the best intentions, and best intentions are never wrong, never in error. For that reason, at least in public, nobody can reproach anybody for anything. And so the apparently invulnerable happiness of the Karmas is a turbulent happiness, full of cracks. The happiness of the Karmas is like the happiness of a volcano that knows it's always on the verge of erupting, when least expected, at any second or whenever it feels like it. A happiness that, just in case, it's better to avoid getting too close to. And Penelope is too close for too long, and she feels dizzier all the time from the subterranean fumes of that toxic and asphyxiating happiness. A happiness that's more an inertial, automatic, and mechanical reflexivity than a learned manual and muscular reflex. For Penelope—who always thought that happiness was something you achieved after a long race, after crossing the finish line—that kind of happiness, ready-made at the starting line, like a trophy to be claimed without any effort or prior training, strikes her as something suspicious and almost indigestible, capable of provoking visions, of making you hear voices or see things that aren't there. And, yes, more than once, Penelope is almost certain she's seeing things she doesn't hear and hearing things she doesn't see. But there they are and there they ring out on Mount Karma. Absurd ideas, unbelievable beliefs. Listening to give them interest-free and limitless credit. Seeing to believe them, to follow them with blind and uncertain footsteps. Penelope writes down everything in notebooks, on pieces of paper. Putting all of it in writing, she thinks, is a way, for a few seconds, to cast the spell of convincing herself that she's there for a reason—to bear witness and warn humanity about what's going on there. Some days she feels like a chronicler of antiquity, wandering past broken temples and twisted columns, when the whole world—it was enough to travel a few kilometers—was another world entirely, a new world. Strange customs and foreign commandments. For Mamagrandma and her progeny, Karma traditions are law and Karma laws are tradition. So, as a word, "Karma" is black and magic. Like a possessive and possessing symbol. Like a standard waving in the wind and, yes, there are flags flying on high in Mount Karma—a K crowned by a pyramid. And all "foreign" (which is to say: of a different surname) men who marry a Karma girl have to sign a document authorizing the inversion of surnames. So that, immediately upon the document being stamped by the notarial seal, the bride's surname will precede the groom's—their children will always be, first and foremost and when all is said and done, Karmas. **And now Penelope (by law, not religion; "We'll work that problem out and the problem of getting you impregnated by Maxi too, of course," smiles Mamagrandma, revealing perfect, sharp little teeth, like the mouth of a dangerous rodent was living inside her mouth) is a Karma. Also, it's true, the recently landed Penelope is experiencing the effects of being suddenly exposed to such sensationalistic organisms and substances. Penelope—dizziness and cold sweats—feels like one of those bewitched fairy tale, or witch tale, heroines. Princesses or village girls who can point to the exact instant they were ensnared by the words of a spell, but who find it impossible to figure out when and how the knot of the curse that keeps them there, captive, will be untied. And it's clear that she's not awaiting the arrival of some Prince Charming. Because, here, in her case, Prince Charming is *also* Sleeping Beauty. Penelope, suddenly, it's not that she's Cinderella; but she has more than enough stepsisters. And—among and above all of them, like one of those hysterical and perfidious blondes at the head of a pack of blondes in those teen movies—Hiriz. "Hiriz with an H and a Z," Hiriz clarifies; the first thing she says to Penelope, as if indicating a decisive difference between her and all other Irises, properly written, that might exist around the world. It won't take Penelope long to realize that** the Karmas' orthographical liberties, when it comes to their names, are a kind of barely subliminal revindication to justify their awful orthography. The Karmas always felt that writing was a reactionary form of the telephone and now, again, they are delighted by the arrival of all the small cellular screens where writing badly is looked on favorably, using fewer letters, spelling words as if they sounded like sounds from comic books and dog-call whistles and snapping fingers and grinding teeth and names and surnames and nicknames (Penelope has witnessed conversations where all that was said was one noun after another, pure predicating of the subject, no verbal predicate). And one of the few orders of the outside world that the Karmas obey without resistance or complaint, as mentioned, is that of never exceeding one hundred forty characters, when speaking or writing. For the Karmas, writing more than one hundred forty characters is almost like writing a novel. Conversations between Karmas correspond to a nearly immobile script, perfectly practiced and with minimal alterations. Names and private events annulling planetary milestones and thus September 11th, 2001 was "the day of Carmelita Karma's debutante ball, which her father was unable to attend because he was in New York, and because of the thing with the planes and the towers they suspended all the flights; and when he called to tell her, his wife didn't believe him and still doesn't believe him." A succession of eternal and circular and perpetual-motion conversations, subjects that you get on and off of like the cars of a train going nowhere, going around and around unceasingly, by rote, along rails where it already passed and will pass many times more. So, an isolated question like what time is it—depending on internal moods and external climates—can result in a brief and decisive answer of "No" or, sometimes, in long and sinuous monologues where what ends up being discussed has nothing at all to do with the hours and the minutes. Example: "The time when—you remember?—Aunt Inmaculada came out to feed the chickens and Concepción shouted to be careful because there'd been a fox loose and then Uncle Evangelio . . ." There are afternoons when Penelope feels that what she hears is an epic and absolute form of déjà vu: not the sensation that she heard all of this before, but the absolute certainty that she heard it just yesterday, and that she'll hear it again tomorrow, in the same place, at the same time, in voices that are the same or different, it doesn't matter. The people can die or change, but the roles inside the Karma family drama, the characters, will always be the same. The ones who start singing all of a sudden for no reason. Or the ones who declare that, "We must go to Israel to see some Jews" and then ask "Why did the Jews settle for being the chosen race? We're better because we're the chosen family. And we chose ourselves, without the help of any God." The same thing happens with the storylines—the names change, but the surname and what is said and done stay the same. And, no, the Karmas don't read novels; novels are why television was invented, telenovelas, which they all watch every night, at home, and it's like taking a break from the exceedingly closed-circuit telenovela of their own lives. For the Karmas there's nothing more real than their own reality and nothing more irreal than external reality, except when that reality is invoked, of necessity, in order to—again, never forget it, keep it clear, you can't take too many precautions against it—accuse somebody who isn't a Karma of having done something to a Karma. So their own bad and shameful thoughts are assigned to some more or less distant person. Projection of projectiles as a kind of variation of a Voodoo ritual where there's always a doll at hand to be stuck with needles and tattooed with responsibilities. Is Penelope a doll? Seeing and analyzing her for the first time, in the airport, her nose quivering like the nostrils of bloodhounds picking up a fresh scent, the Karmas never really figure it out. Penelope is a new mixed breed. A coin suspended in the air and nobody knows—heads Karma, tails not Karma?—on which side it'll fall. One thing is definitely clear—Penelope is strange. And the news that (when they ask about her family to see what and how much this newcomer is worth and whether she'll be able to contribute any valuable relatives to the lush and endogamic and forever burning Karma family tree) Penelope's parents died years ago because of "political issues" makes her stranger still. And that Penelope's brother, her only living relative, is a somewhat well-known writer, prompts the Karmas, unsettled, disconcerted, to change the subject, as if changing the channel with the remote control of their highly controlled existence. Some of them, secretly, keep *watching* for a while, a few minutes more: the idea of having a writer in the family makes them feel a little perverse. And, in the end, special: none of their acquaintances know a writer, much less have a writer close to their family. But then they change the channel, in search of a better show, something less complicated, more entertaining, with a laugh track. Because to say "writer" to a Karma is to provoke an immediate eruption of the word "bohemian." In the beginning, Penelope finds the marker charming in its innocence. And she's almost tempted to tell them, to further enhance the "bohemian," that her brother rides a horse and doesn't even know how to drive. But Penelope finds out quickly that the Karmatic definition of the term "bohemian" doesn't correspond to *fin de siècle* European salons, but to a cocktail made of a mix of "alcoholic," "atheist," "sissy" (never gay or homosexual; and there are no homosexuals or gays among the Karmas, not because they don't exist, but because they don't acknowledge them as such, preferring to categorize them as "bachelors with many girlfriends we never see"), "intellectual," and, worst of all, people with limited economic means and nonexistent social standing. Provided that it isn't the person responsible for that popular book—never the writer, because the author doesn't matter at all—that everyone's reading, turning its pages, as if by social dictate. Moving their lips. As if having a conversation. Because, if reading can't be made into a topic of conversation or status symbol, what's the point? And besides, reading is an activity the Karmas immediately associate with boredom, melancholy, and, even, the preliminary symptoms of a suicide. Books—which "are all in black and white"—are, to the Karmas, even worse than black and white movies. * (One night, Penelope gets excited because a TV channel is showing *Citizen Kane* and she tells Hiriz that she has to watch it, and, after a few minutes, Hiriz stands up and says goodnight with a: "I'm really tired of watching tennis. Besides, Rosebud is definitely his mother, his mommy, right?") And seeing Penelope reread, over and over, as if it were the Old Testament, her worn copy of *Wuthering Heights*, produces in the Karmas a feeling of anxiety and wariness they've never felt before. They have rarely seen someone they know well up close in the act of reading. An act that, the Karmas know intuitively, is nothing like paging through society magazines full of big photos and brief captions. They can only understand Penelope's apparent attachment to that book by thinking of it as a thing she must have inherited from her dearest grandmother (the Karmas formulate this hypothesis aloud, in affected voices) or been given her by a secret lover (the Karmas venture this possibility in authentically conspiratorial whispers). And then they wonder (in medium-volume voices and with average prejudice) if Penelope might be bored or depressed (which she is, in fact, but not because of reading) and even go to the trouble of striking up conversations that they deem literary. Ah, the poor Karmas who, so devout, never read the Bible, which is the best thing that the religion they've chosen has going for it. The best part of what they believe in is a book, but they resist believing in it, because the Karmas don't believe in books. The Karmas listen to the Bible at mass, like a radio transmitting from who knows where, what do they know. Some of them even prefer to close their eyes, because watching the priest read disturbs them. They prefer not to see him, and to think of him as a very skilled and inspired ventriloquist's dummy. One Karma girl approaches Penelope and confides in her that "I read a book, but it wasn't a good experience. So I didn't do it again. It was *traumatic*." Right away Penelope picks up the Karma girl's emphasis when she says "traumatic," and the embarrassment accompanying just saying the word "book"; as if it were wrong, transgressive, unfit for a young lady. For the Karma girl, "traumatic" is clearly a complex word that she doesn't often say (and that's why she says it with the sort of pride of a good student more graced with a good memory than blessed with authentic interest or curiosity) and "book" is something she thinks only every so often, and it makes her wonder why such strange things—like thinking about a book—occur to her. Penelope, interested, can't help wonder what the title of the volume was that expelled her from the world of reading forever. Some cryptic or experimental title? Something long and winding and full of nooks and crannies? "I don't remember," responds the Karma girl with a trembling sigh, her eyes the deepest blue of the most superficial contact lenses, long hair dyed blonde, vainly invoking the ghost of Farrah Fawcett. And that says it all, no point going beyond that microstory. But then Penelope, more dazzled than dumbfounded, thinks: Ah, this is just the type of being for whom the concept "air head" was invented; the idea of a cranium inside of which spins, tirelessly, a wind that moves nothing but vibrates everything, a Transylvanian and thereminic wind, like an old Universal film . . . *The Incredible Empty Woman*, who one night, in a laboratory in black and white . . ." * And yet, with a shiver, like every time she confronts the absolute, doubt and fear rise inside her: "But maybe it's me who is the primitive specimen," Penelope says to herself. "Maybe this girl—who's like a character out of Jane Austen, who'll never know who Jane Austen was—is much wiser than I am; much happier and more carefree, able to remove and discard, without doubts or second thoughts, entire pieces of history and art and music and in this way contemplate, with equal interest, a sublime painting by Leonardo or that infamous Korean ballet dancer on YouTube. And decide that the Korean is much more pleasing and less complicated. Because there's no need for context or prior knowledge to enjoy the Korean. The Korean begins and ends in himself and isn't part of any Renaissance or belonging to this or that school of painting. And, yes, maybe there's nothing better than not feeling the obligation to read all of Shakespeare. Or Dickens. Or Dostoevsky. Or Stendhal. Or Borges. Or James, where those prekarmatic ladies exclaim things like 'Oh, I must confess; I don't want to know any more . . . The more you know, the less happy you are.' And avoiding the temptation (James again) to go around asking questions, to classify and divide people, thinking of Isabel Archer in *The Portrait of a Lady* as an innocent, ingenuous victim of the vampires who surround and corner her, or, to the contrary, as a proud fool who's beyond saving and deserves everything that happens to her and much more. Or thinking of Kate Croy in *The Wings of the Dove* as someone who may not be a bad person, but just a person who behaves badly. And, ah, the sudden complication of understanding (of reading and understanding) that being bad and behaving badly frequently have the same effect on everyone else. And that if you behave badly more than two or three times in a row then you're already a bad person, period. Being able to walk through Vienna thinking only about apple cakes and not about *The Third Man* or about Hitler or about Freud or, even, about that Klimt poster kissing dorm-room walls. Turning down, already at the port, without even coming aboard to inspect the cabin, a voyage to so many places, but a voyage that's understood and acknowledged to lack a final destination. Saying no to the frustrating experience of knowing that there will never be enough time to know everything." Penelope wonders if some Karmas might not benefit from an encounter with a Buddenbrook or a Forsyte or a Salina. If Hiriz would, for example, recognize herself in the voracious and insatiable Undine Spragg, in the noble and well-written reflection of some of her unsavory defects; and if this might not help her correct them or, at least, recognize them, seeing them written better in the elegant third-person of a character than in her own vulgar first-person. Probably not. And, of course, there was always the possibility that the confrontation with the far better written portrait of a different surname would have a, yes, traumatic effect on the Karmas. "So, who knows, maybe it's better to stay home and become a total expert on where you came from and ignore everything else, unless it's something that, once in a great while, crosses paths with that minimal yet graspable experience. Not trying to find yourself in the universal, but sitting down and waiting for the universe to come find you. And if it doesn't, no problem: could be that the universe isn't all that interesting, and not that you don't interest it. 'Once upon a time . . .' Again and again. Focusing a telescope on the microscopic. Being a wild dwarf star, and maybe being someone who is better and more fully capable of facing his own life, without so many complications and instruction manuals drawn up by minds vastly more powerful than our own," Penelope trembles, she trembles all the time. And she recalls one long night of cocaine and the Discovery Channel when she saw, between one line and the next, a documentary claiming that a study of African tribes had determined that the life expectancy of the tribes' members had diminished notably after they learned to read and write. Also—an incorporeal voice informed over a landscape of huts and desert—they slept less and worse. All because, suddenly, they were able to live other lives, to think more. **And Penelope thinks too much, trembling more all the time—the Karmas like a new and impossible-to-synthesize drug on which it turns out to be difficult to be succinct and of which Hiriz is its most pure and powerful strain—almost terrified by how much she thinks *like this*, more all the time: in concentric and ascending and descending circles, as if a slow spiral staircase had been injected into the high-velocity elevator of her brain. And besides, Penelope** says, giddy, a notable difference: that Karma girl, traumatized by a single book, is not like Hiriz. That girl doesn't know what she wants, but she's perfectly acquainted with what she needs (a husband, money, children, more money); while Hiriz believes she knows what she wants and couldn't care less about what she needs. And what Hiriz wants is absolutely everything. And she wants it to be more and better than what the other Karmas have. There are even moments when Hiriz wishes not that she'd read all the books Penelope has read, but, *yes*, that she knew enough about them to be able to make a certain impression on the eventual "bohemian" from the capital or foreigner who might fall across her path. But it's not like that diminishes her dream either. For Hiriz, that's just a battle to be fought once a great war is won.

* Meanwhile and in the meantime, for the rest of the Karmas, Penelope's case (having a writer as a brother) is even more disconcerting (mildly disconcerting, like everything external and alien and that, for that reason, fortunately, can be forgotten right away) but ultimately insignificant. A two-person family? That's not a family. Parents disappeared over "political issues"? Boring and, of course, they must have done something and it wouldn't be a surprise if they had it coming, and period, and moving right along. Limited possible storylines. Just a few drops of false piety and a sound like *oooh* . . . And that's it. No space in the mega-micro world of the Karmas for external matters. Everyone is occupied—in a baroque flowchart fit for one of those unbearable sagas with gnomes and wizards and kings and dragons—with betrayals, rumors, competitions, barely hidden enmities, and shameful secrets. Secrets everyone knows and discusses as if they were discussing the always changeable state of the climate's constant fluctuations where a summer storm or a hurricane, with a woman's name or the label of something that's desirable and de luxe just because one or another of them possesses it, is always on the verge of breaking out.

"Hiriz is the name of an Egyptian goddess," Hiriz continues and Penelope, who knows a great deal about a great many things, thinks "Horus, falcon head, considered the founder of civilization, version of Phoebus and Apollo in the Valley of the Nile." And she wonders why such a Catholic family (as Maximiliano had once warned her) gave its offspring the poorly spelled appellations of pagan divinities. But better, just in case, not to say anything.

And that "better, just in case, not to say anything" will become, immediately, one of the various commandments for Penelope to live by during her stay in Abracadabra. On Mount Karma, more than speaking or talking, one recites or one proclaims. Not high poetry, but innocuous statements, seemingly bottled in absolute emptiness. Clichés. The Karmas communicate among themselves with phrases prepared and practiced and repeated many times. Tribal slogans that flail about like someone walking through quicksand or across a bridge made of glass. Nothing that vibrates, nothing that causes cracks or helps you sink. Talking about what they see, but not about what they think. But, for Penelope, saying nothing, often, is the same as thinking everything. And soon Penelope—who doesn't talk much; because when she talks she gets the uncomfortable feeling that she's talking to herself, which doesn't bother her, she'll realize, with two or three drinks more inside than on top of her—will discover that she can't stop thinking about Hiriz. Is it because—as will become obvious—Hiriz can't stop thinking about Penelope? Sure, that's part of it. * But, also, there's something else: writers tend, as an occupational hazard and occupational habit, to categorize everyone they meet the moment they meet them, to synthesize them into a possible character. Those who aren't writers but who so badly want to write (Penelope's case) are even worse in that sense—they don't categorize, they judge. They spend their time taking notes for possible novels and hypothetical stories. Loose phrases, more or less detailed descriptions. But such an activity and reflex isn't an easy thing to exercise in Abracadabra, among the Karmas. The Karmas are all the same, they say and think and do the same things. They're of an absolutely unique and original uniformity in their instinctive discipline. Resembling each other makes the Karmas invincible among themselves, because nobody wants to slander their double, their triple, their quintuple. In this way, if all of them are unpunctual (because the Karmas' perception of time is really more elastic, making their favorite verbal conjugation the gerund: to say that something is being done without implying that it has to be finished, and in that way to float in an eternal during) then none of them are unpunctual and the whole idea of punctuality annuls itself. The myth of the eternal beginning. To be beginning all the time; because it allows them to avoid the frustration or disenchantment of an ending that failed to live up to their expectations, that will never correspond to the infantile fantasies of "Once upon a time . . ." Delaying for a year what is done in a week, or a day. Taking years to quit or get fired. And feeling forever young—you age little when a minute stretches out for months—suffering the paradox that their adult problems always retain a childish though increasingly wizened air. The Karmas know nothing about the crises of the thirties. Or the forties. Except when it serves as justification for the occasional outburst or passing madness. The fifties—in terms of age or marriage—are nothing but the perfect excuse to board another cruise ship. The Karmas are residents of their own private Shangri-La. To leave it—establishing a kind of comparison with the deadlines and obligations and defeats of the other mortals— is to dissolve, to lose everything gained, to not be special. All the better . . . Penelope will meet Karmas (Hiriz will be one of the most bizarre mutations of this syndrome) who studied—or so they claim— law, nuclear medicine, odontology, political science, oceanography, astronomy, and even gave themselves to the priesthood with the ambition of becoming Pope, without earning a single diploma to certify it or accredit them. Karmas who tell you, automatically and courteously, "at your service," knowing perfectly well they'll never do what you ask. Karmas who tell you "in a *little* bit" meaning they're not prepared to do something anytime soon but at some point, who knows when, maybe in a future incarnation. And, always, in a diffuse plural. Saying "We should do . . ." but not doing it and, automatically, implicating everyone in their nothing. And Penelope—who had previously mistrusted people who used too many augmentatives in their speech, exaggerating everything and overstating importance and size—soon discovers that there's nothing more dangerous than diminutives. Diminutives that endow everything with a false humility and childish flair; but that are nothing more than the jaws of a shark with multiple rows of teeth out of which emerges a little voice that says things like "But what a goody-goody you are." The exception being Mamagrandma, who seems to spin around on top of herself, tirelessly, like a force of nature, like a whirling dervish (Penelope will ask herself more than once if Mamagrandma might not be some indefatigable species of vampire, feeding on the fluids and energies of her descendants), the rest of the Karmas move as if in slow motion, like the happy prisoners of the golden amber of their comfort and privilege. "But a group portrait makes no sense," Penelope thinks. So Penelope chooses a single Karma to encompass all of them. Penelope chooses Hiriz. "Good material," thinks Penelope, like everyone who wants to write but isn't a writer thinks. But Hiriz is *really* good material. Hiriz is a Karma, yes; but she's also a Karma on the edge of something. Hiriz is unstable; as if her obligatory satisfaction with who she is and where she comes from is balanced atop a fault line in a tectonic plate that trembles in the night, when it thinks that nobody can perceive and calibrate it. Hiriz lives in that eternal moment that precedes an earthquake that only the birds and dogs perceive. So Penelope will sketch her the way maps were sketched in antiquity: not like now, from above and with satellites, but from the edges and along the shores, from outside moving inward, step by step and stone by stone. In her own environment. Up close. Penelope—like a faithful cartographer who's *also* a daring adventurer—will follow her and film her and record her and portray her. And describe her in detailed and exhaustive dispatches that (at the request of her brother, who, insatiable even at a distance, was always demanding fresh "doses of H," will soon declare himself Hiriz's "number one fan") she'll send in digitalized files through the air and across the waves. * And, yes, sometimes he—here above, everywhere and nowhere, center of an electromagnetic storm of quasars—imagines that he was still down below, writing, tempted and attracted by the power emanating from Hiriz, whom he might turn into his provincial Emma Bovary, into his starry-eyed Anna Karenina or, better yet, into the less-remembered but equally powerful and oh so frivolous Gwendolen Harleth Grandcourt. Hence the repetitions, the persistence, the more or less subtle variations—time and again, without apologies for those who deserve them—of the way that Hiriz acts or doesn't act or the way the Karmas think or don't think. Hence too the single perception of one Karma, transmitted first by Penelope and then received by her brother, who made and continues to make adjustments, now that he has eternities at his disposal to find *le mot juste*, to trap the precise instant, in the blink of an eye, that might stretch on for years. Maybe this way, thinks Penelope, time passes faster, time passes and life goes on. Hiriz is Maximiliano's older sister. "So now you're my little sister," she tells Penelope, who doesn't entirely understand the logic of this new relationship, but, once again, better, just in case, say nothing. Penelope, to begin with and even though she speaks her language, doesn't really understand anything Hiriz tells her. Hiriz talks the same way doctors write—her letters and words are incomprehensible. It's as if Hiriz's voice * (exceedingly sharp and with an accent that's odd, almost but not entirely foreign, like a remote-controlled telephone operator that you ask for the time and date and that responds with clipped diction, as if each word and number were complete sentences or ideas) were a few seconds delayed in making it from Penelope's ears to her brain and, once there, it took a few more seconds to get translated into the same language. * (Hiriz has even managed to transfer and translate the sonic quality of her voice into writing: her emails and tweets—of which you might end up receiving thirty or forty a day—are plagued, as often happens with illiterates who remain illiterate though they've learned to read and write, by emphatic caps, by ????, and by !!!!, and by exceedingly personal orthographical errors and implausible consonant abbreviations that adhere to the invisible and microscopic language of gnawing coleopterans.) Hiriz—Penelope understands right away that nothing could be more fitting than her name being derived from Horus and can't look at her without superimposing over her face the feathers and beak and aquiline look of a bird of prey that's impossible to satisfy—must be forty-some years old, though various plastic surgeries have already given her a much older and more worn out look. Hiriz evokes one of those houses with an uneven floor that someone has tried to domesticate/decorate with modern DIY furniture. Massages and peelings and oh so many nautical miles accumulated on countless health cruises, and so many meters of altitude in alpine spas, and so many hours of folding and stretching herself according to the latest variety of yogaerobics, have given Hiriz's body and soul the texture and the color and the mannerisms and the stupid but limitless evil of a perpetual cheerleader, determined to execute the best and most spectacular pirouettes only to, always, sooner or later, fall down in front of everyone at the worst possible moment, in the decisive instance. Hiriz isn't happy, because to be happy first you have to relax. And all her "spiritual journeys" to India or to the East or to Africa haven't done her any good either, journeys that Hiriz always returns from loaded down with photos where she appears embracing—with certain tension—exotic and hungry children (if there's such a thing as "loving racism," Hiriz has discovered and patented it, Penelope thinks when she sees them) and with suitcases full of tunics and dresses to sell to her cousins and sisters-in-law. In a situation where many women in her position would choose to take a lover (ideally a tennis instructor or singing coach; someone to have on the payroll), Hiriz, due to fear of what'll be said if she's found out, or due to demented bravery, not caring what anyone thinks, has decided to madly love herself. Which, of course, isn't easy. So, Hiriz lives in a state of constant tension and it's more than likely that, on the day of her death, she'll be struck by an unbreakable rigor mortis in the second of exhaling her last breath. At some point, Hiriz will confide in Penelope and, in a fragile voice, she'll confess that there was a horrible childhood incident she never recovered from. As Penelope prepares to receive a terrible flashback of rape at the age of seven or something like that, Hiriz bursts into tears and tells her "one time Mamagrandma told me my haircut didn't flatter me. It was my nineteenth birthday. And I swear I've never been the same since." Penelope decides not to tell Hiriz that she thinks childhood and its tragedies would be hard pressed to reach the age of nineteen. That that wouldn't be a childhood so much as—the noun suddenly turning into an adjective from fatigue—childish. But Penelope decides to stay quiet, to refill her glass, and to keep listening, hearing as little as possible. The truth is, Hiriz's childhood was as perfect as it was unsatisfactory, she could almost swear that one time "I had an orgasm," and she's certain that she's recently suffered multiple "emotional traumas." Like when, kinetic and obsessed with losing weight, she chained herself to a stationary bicycle at the country club gym when they tried to make her to go home. Or when an excess of weight loss pills convinced her for a few hours that Jesus Christ had appeared to her and asked her to plan the menu and choose the guest list for the last supper. Hiriz is also someone who couldn't be described as dull (a condition) because she'd lacked the means for cultivation and development and had grown up under fixed environmental conditions; but yes, she could be written off as ignorant (a choice). And Hiriz has embraced her total lack of culture as if it were a summa cum laude distinction. So Hiriz's brief and elementary educational trajectory * (and that of the rest of the Karmas, who have always traded in the idea of general culture for that of particular culture: for obsessive and increasingly complicated specializations in themselves that leave no free time for anything else) has been garnished with honorary degrees, awarded in exchange for donations to the schools. Hiriz always circles all the options on multiple choice tests ("I was always taught that you have to get along well with everyone," she explained) and it's impossible for her to concentrate on Renaissance Florence, on Waterloo or Hiroshima, or on the Big Bang, because "not a single Karma appears in any of those stories." Now, Hiriz doesn't know what to do with her life; but Hiriz thinks she can do everything. Penelope has known attenuated versions of the same species on the other side of the ocean: those unconditional Madonna fans who devoutly love and adore and envy her as a role-model for her firm body, for the fantasy of her young lovers, for her choreographies that are strenuous but easy to imitate in some future wedding, and, in a subliminal and shameful way, for giving them the hope that someone that artistically mediocre, if they learn to claw and scheme, can become a world-famous artist. But Hiriz's case is much worse. It's not that Hiriz is pursuing eternal youth, she's pursuing something that's even more impossible: Hiriz wishes she'd been born male; because, if she had, her life would've been so much fairer, so different, other.

* (The Karma women don't work. Or, better, they work at trying, in vain, to convince everyone that they do work. Or, best case scenario, that they're engaged in exceedingly protracted and theoretical and not at all practical university degrees, where they knock off only a class or two each year, just so they don't end up without a major or with someone insisting on giving them a degree that, of course, isn't good for anything but work.) Hiriz is convinced that she knows more about everything than everyone. Her areas of expertise go from baking to building cyborgs, passing through trade law and the import of heavy machinery. But she has never—Hiriz thinks and a few times even says in a very quiet voice—been given the space she deserves and requires (a space, in her mind and on her map, more or less the size of a thousand soccer stadiums lined up one after another), all because of her sex, nothing more and nothing less, because of her condition as a woman in a world supposedly governed by men.

An exception is made for Mamagrandma, who rules over everyone, regardless of gender or species or whether they're vegetal or mineral or animal. So, only her, Hiriz alone, convinced of her own polymorphous genius, similar to that of Leonardo Da Vinci. But, actually, Hiriz is more like the desperate Connie Corleone in *The Godfather III*, but with very little common sense. Hiriz is a secondary character with a longing for a movie of her own, which has almost turned the power of her frustration into a kind of achievement. Her successive defeats function like the antimatter of a victory that only she believes in. Hiriz is an exceedingly successful professional failure and—desperately seeking the favor and approval of Mamagrandma, dreaming of being her successor without daring to admit it even to herself—has done nothing but triumphantly fail, in a big way, better all the time. Hiriz has founded, alternatingly, a daycare for the children of friends and relatives and another one for poor and orphaned children (but these are suspiciously happy and nice poor children, always with a melodious song on their lips, as if they'd escaped from a local production of *Annie*, to whom Hiriz suggests games like "Now let's imagine what it'd be like to play with that toy that we're never-ever-ever going to be given, okay?" Hiriz's own children, for their part, dress up for Halloween not as zombies but as "little beggars, because they're scarier"); a store for interior décor (to furnish the houses of friends and relatives); a delicatessen warehouse (to supply the parties and lunches and dinners of friends and relatives); a boutique where she tried to sell her own designs (and to dress her friends and relatives); a travel agency in order to make friends and make peace between family members. And her brief stint in local politics—thanks to the one decisive boon of a famous last name—ended with the suicide of the mayor she was working for as "personal assistant." Before hanging himself from a rafter in his office, the poor man left a brief note—where it read one single word: "Unbearable"—that led many to believe that he could no longer bear the guilt or dishonor or extortion related to some embezzlement or corrupt dealing or secret life. But those who were close to him and knew him well were perfectly aware what and whom he was referring to. None of the preceding has prevented Hiriz from designating herself as absolute consigliore of her family, as someone who tirelessly gives unsolicited advice, hurling it at you aggressively and with terrible aim, like a knife or grenade, never hitting the target. And the advice Hiriz gives is always related to one of Hiriz's own flaws. Example: if she has problems with her children, she'll immediately start giving you advice about how to avoid problems that you must, surely, also have with your children; even if you don't, it doesn't matter. If you avoid Hiriz, it isn't, for her, something personal—because she can't even conceive of the possibility that someone doesn't want to be around her—but a perverse generalized misanthropy, or, in her words "one of those people who likes to be alone so they can do who knows what when no one is watching." So, Hiriz—who after every trip, on the pretext of dizziness and vomiting and even visions that she tries to decode, goes to see a friend who she's designated as an expert "but very Catholic" Tarot card reader—doesn't hesitate to recommend to the recently landed Penelope that there's nothing better for cramped joints after a long flight than "filling the hot water bottle with water . . . but, careful, the trick is to use mineral water." So, Hiriz knows how to do everything you don't know how to do; but following her imprecise and complex instructions always results in destructions that are oh so simple in their precision. Her inexhaustible talent for ruining everything she embarks on and, subsequently, sinks, has made it so the Karmas—who defend each other just so they can attack each other; the Karmas are enough and more than enough on their own, like the Montagues and Capulets, but with the same last name and without the deaths, because there's no external or extra-familial enemy worthy of their attention and blood—consider Hiriz a kind of beneficent spirit, restless and enterprising, though all her good, in theory, enterprises don't take long, in practice, in her lack of practice, to end, and to end badly. Hiriz—to define her militarily—is collateral damage and enemy fire. And her most recent "achievement" (because Hiriz's disasters, somehow, end up being flexible conversations at tense dinner tables) has had something to do with her thinking that she can develop a special food for cattle. A diet that, she swears, would make them bigger and more productive. It makes no difference that Hiriz knows nothing about cows, or bulls, or about what they eat, or even what they are for and what they do. Hiriz invested "a little funds, a little savings" in a hundred head of cattle (Penelope hears about this on the way from the airport to Mount Karma, Mamagrandma's matriarchal man-sion) and created, all on her own, a race of colossal mutant bovines the color of emerald fluoride. A fierce and anabolic breed that reproduce at a vertigi-nous rate and have developed an insatiable carnivorous appetite, prompting them to slaughter each other with raw bites and eat each other in a revelry of bovine cannibalism. Not embarrassed, but still, trying to make sure nobody finds out, Hiriz released the cows into the fields of an abandoned ranch. And they've since turned into a regional menace and multiple horses have been found decapitated and raped; "In that order," specified a local veterinarian. At first it was all blamed on the Chupacabras or some other rural superstition; but before long a few children from poor families (who are now threatened with a "If you don't clean your plate, the Giant Green Cow will come get you") went missing. Before long, a rival rancher (who almost ends up getting lynched by his humble ranch hands) is held responsible, and the Karmas organize hunting parties every weekend to go out and kill "mad cows," they laugh. There's only one left, apparently. One gigantic and totemic and mythic green cow. A mythic green cow like a symbolic white whale. They tell Penelope, floating in jet-lag, all of this (Penelope thinks it must be a joke, or some kind of legend, more rural than urban) and a lot more besides, as if she were being incorporated, on the spot, in the role of guest actress with opportunities to earn the spotlight and improve her standing, into a melodramatic novel that's been being written for centuries, into a telenovela with no end in sight. But it's kind of strange, something far away but suddenly so close: Penelope has the sensation of having traveled not to another country but to another world. A place where they speak her language, but she doesn't understand anything they say. Or maybe it's that her planet has been invaded. Someone hands her a stack of something like five hundred photos, so she can "Get up to date and learn everyone's nicknames and relationships." * (And Penelope is amazed by the quantity of grandfathers/grandmothers and sons/daughters and grandsons/granddaughters who have the exact same names and, when asked why that is, they say that they're already accustomed to those names so they might as well go on using them and "that way you don't have to embroider the nuptial trousseau and the towels again, and it saves you time because when you go out to the lawn between the houses and call the family together for a general meeting—you only have to call two or three or four names.") Someone else gives her a gift (Penelope will find out soon that the Karmas are constantly giving each other gifts to publicly demonstrate how much they appreciate one another despite the fact that they secretly detest each other). It's a dress. Something she'd never wear, two sizes too big; and Penelope starts to get worried: what class of organism is capable of giving clothing to a person they've never seen or met? The atmosphere in this new world is breathable, yes; but Penelope is short of breath even though her head weighs as much as one of those specially designed suits for descending to the bottom of the sky or the bottom of the ocean. Bright fluorescent fish brushing against her as she sinks or shimmering dead star dust getting in her eyes as she floats weightlessly: too many people around her, too many people simultaneously talking and breathing inside this powerful dual-traction pickup truck and inside the other seven pickups—all seemingly ready for a safari, with multiple accessories hanging from the roofs and sides—and inside the futuristic ambulance carrying Maximiliano, all following her, at medium velocity; because at the head of the caravan rides Mamagrandma on Horse, releasing little yips, across the asphalt and dirt, heading "home," they tell her. Mount Karma * (a gigantic construction where colonial Spanish architecture seems to meld, hysterically and syncretistically, into the baroque lines of Italian courts and the posterior faux Bauhaus inlays; Penelope is startled by an ominous wrought-iron K above the entrance gate before a long zoom to a window) is surrounded by an intimidating number of small replicas of the main mansion, where the rest of the family reside. Like small satellites orbiting a sun, more dictator than king. The houses are always full of people, the doors always open, and it won't take Penelope long to ask herself if they might not all be connected by a secret network of tunnels and passageways. Mount Karma is the belly button of the world and any departure—if it's not to one of Mount Karma's outposts, at sea or on the mountain—becomes a complicated affair, even attaining heights of absurdity and physical comedy and slapstick. For the Karmas, just the act of getting into vehicles to be taken outside their sphere of influence turns out to be somewhat disorienting. So they spend hours and days and weeks deciding where to go, moving around like blind, headless chickens. And once outside, somewhere foreign, they only feel comfortable going in and out of stores with names of big and expensive brands, held up by more than holding enormous shopping bags that keep them, with their weight in gold, fixed to the floor. The possibility of visiting and touring cathedrals and palaces, of contemplating museum pieces and landscapes that don't belong to them, just provokes dizziness and fear and the sneaking suspicion that there's an entire foreign—possibly better and more interesting—world outside their own. * So, better, Paris is Chanel. London is Burberry. New York is Donna Karan. Only Rome is, yes, the Vatican, where flocks of Karmas confess at prepaid papal audiences in order to emerge, clean and pure, as if levitating, heading off toward Valentino. Which isn't to say that the Karmas are a migratory species. The Karmas opt to move as little as possible, never alone or in pairs, and always as close together as they can. Never getting too far away. Never losing sight of each other. Never feeling unknown in the multitude or the desert of the metropolis. Mount Karma as Acropolis and Great Pyramid and Great Wall of China. In Mount Karma's central hall, above a table so long and with so many seats that it seems like an optical illusion (a table that fits the most intimate and closed and pure nucleus of the Karmas, the brothers who married sisters, the cousins who married cousins), there is, as if levitating, a painting. A painting, three meters tall and two meters wide, the portrait of a man with the air of an enlightened biblical prophet, dressed half killer-cowboy and half bullfighter, his eyes flaming, a smile burning on his lips. "It's Papagrandpa," they tell her in a sacred and reverential whisper, as if they were scared the painted figure could hear them. "Ah, where is he? Is he here?" Penelope asks just to ask something, because she remembers Max having made some mention of the mysterious Papagrandpa. And different Karmas offer her different answers: Papagrandpa died helping put out a fire in the convent, or in a train catastrophe, or a hunting accident, or from a heart attack on the sixth hole. The most audacious, in low voices and with cactus-juice breath, risk insinuating something about a young second-rate movie star (the most extreme versions, in whispers even more whispered than usual, speak not of an actress but of an actor), about an escape to Monaco, or about a problem with a local gangster and a new face and something about the FBI's Witness Protection Program. One of them, almost speaking in tongues, claims to have seen Papagrandpa ascend into the heavens spurred on by a herd of zebus. It doesn't matter, it's all the same, true legends are only legendary if nobody agrees on them, on what might have happened, on what what happened might come to mean. * Penelope looks and looks at the painting and it reminds her of something, it recalls something, and then it dawns on her: in his portrait,

Papagrandpa is dressed just like Napoleon Bonaparte in that portrait where he appears, imperial, crowning himself. Which reveals, in an indirect way, the inferiority the Karmas feel confronting the fragility of their roots in the Old World. Almost nonexistent. Better not to talk about that. A pack of outlaws who came to that foreign shore to seek their fortune. And so the Karmas—especially the females, suddenly Penelope's stepsisters and stepmothers—instinctively faint in the presence of any two-bit European aristocrat, and dream of marriages, titles, castles, and coats of arms. But no luck yet. All attempts to plant a Karma girl—including Hiriz, hence her time in a Swiss boarding school—in the bosom of some diminished yet respectable family have so far been fruitless. But they haven't lost hope. And, if the Karmas had an insignia and family crest, it'd bear the motto that sustains them: "None against None, All against All." A foolproof survival technique: the impossibility of sudden and fatal face-to-face and out-in-the-open duels in exchange for an eternity of slander, like fetid subterranean currents concealed by liters of perfume and flowers and incessant cordiality and, consequently, there's very little that gets said that Penelope and anyone who isn't a Karma can trust. It's never entirely clear where this feeling comes from and why it is felt.

What is clear is that Hiriz "adopts" Penelope, installing her in her pool house and taking her everywhere. Like a new accessory. Like something she bought or was given and can't stop showing off to everyone. And everyone treats Penelope with *—was it, again, William Faulkner inside a wrinkled white linen suit, with bourbon on his breath, who said it?—the suspect kindness of people who are only kind because they dare not be otherwise. The mornings pass, slow and identical, in the local country club where Penelope (who starts taking lessons in little sips, because "it's what you do") finds herself obliged to wear little white dresses and indolently carry a racquet or (Penelope never rode a horse) to stroll through the stables swathed in those attractive and tight-fitting breeches the color of marble, to the smiling and unspeakable despair of Hiriz and her friends/cousins. Because it's clear that Penelope has the best ass and best legs and best tits for hundreds of miles in any direction. And—the horror, the horror—Penelope doesn't even go to the gym. She doesn't need a trainer or trainers to stay in excellent shape. Hiriz's husband (who originally responded to the name Ricky, but who since their nuptials on Mount Karma is just "Hiriz's husband") and male cousins and male friends admire Penelope and admire it and admire them (Penelope's parts) with the awkward slyness of schoolboys. In other words: they look at nothing else, because they enjoy it and because they think they have to enjoy it. One of them secretly photographs Penelope's ass with his iPhone and sends it to all his friends, who hold a high proof alcoholic drink in one hand and sensually stroke their stoplight-yellow or metallic-rose neckties or pinch the small green crocodile at the level of their left nipple with the other; and is there anything more unsettling then wearing a reptile at the height of your heart, Penelope wonders. One of them, who they say, euphemistically, in low voices, had "some complications" at birth, watches Penelope and squeezes and strokes, up and down, a golf club he'll never use to hit a golf ball. Of course, you see, it's not considered proper for Penelope to go up and talk to him or talk to any of them. To any man. Operating orders, manual of instructions, rules of engagement: women with women talking about women and the occasional man, and men with men talking exclusively about women. So that when, in the afternoon, following a lunch as long as a nightmare, Hiriz drags Penelope to the private clinic where—connected to machines, perforated by cables and catheters—the comatose Maximiliano lies, the erotic intensity that Penelope exudes almost without realizing it threatens to turn all those young men, married in a hurry or hurrying to get married, into drooling beasts or masturbation machines. Max never dedicated himself to anything so fully and with such discipline as he did to floating in that limbo and pondering who knows what, Penelope thinks. Maybe, Penelope says to herself, Max is concocting another of his rudimentary fictions where almost nothing happens, one of his comma-ridden comatose novels. On top of that, the clinic in Abracadabra is more like a five-star Las Vegas theme hotel than a hospital. The nurses move about with the indolent and untouchable air of choir girls, the doctors (like derivatives of synthetic Dean Martin from the unscripted late nights of The Rat Pack) have the diction and smiles of masters of ceremonies and the oily charm of sharks, supposedly domesticated, but . . . And most disconcerting of all for Penelope: here nobody commands or demands hospital silence, yielding instead to a hospitable din. Everybody yells in the hallways and hugs and bursts out laughing. Many visitors are dressed in tennis uniforms or riding outfits (Penelope realizes that the clinic is something like an annex of the country club) and priests abound, almost one per patient, going in and out of rooms, exchanging ideas, in elegant robes of a dignified Armani cut. All of them, with that Catholic and apostolic and Roman enunciation that always reminds Penelope of the diction of the snakes and hypnotists and hypnotized snakes in the most vintage animated drawings. All of them moving here to there with that characteristic glide, as if there were little wheels hidden under their habits. The Karmas have a suite rented in perpetuity: two expansive rooms on the bottom floor with views of a garden where—without anybody daring call attention to it, because she's one of the clinic's principal donors and founding shareholders—Mamagrandma is riding Horse, releasing yips into the afternoon air. In one room, the smaller of the two, the body of Maximiliano pulses regularly and mechanically. In the other room, wide as a tennis court, there are various armchairs, tables, a bar, and two fifty-inch plasma TVs, always on and broadcasting indistinctly a telenovela that's been around for several decades and god-awful soccer matches featuring local teams who appear to be playing a different game, a sport whose rules imply touching the ball as little as possible and running as slow as you can and making passes that are precise only in their imprecision and never kicking the ball into your opponent's goal. The women, all together (and, of course, nothing to do with a militant feminist compact or the exchange of intimacies that can always come back to haunt you, like instant gossip attached to a boomerang), play poker and drink from tiny glasses that they subsequently, surreptitiously, refill (the brevity of the drinks is commended and the staggering quantity never condemned) over and over until they imagine themselves right there, in a near future or remote past, accompanying, so alive, the death throes of their husbands. And, ah, the unutterable but obvious disappointment when one of them experiences a miraculous recovery and gets better and then they have to delay the debut of their mourning dresses, or worse, use them at the masses for dead outsiders (various, a complex tangle of prayers specially designed, by religious chapters, to help the soul of the departed advance a little bit further, deeper into the overabundant mansions of Paradise) where they don't get to be the weeping starlet, but, merely, the supporting crybaby. The men, all together, drink from glasses the size of pitchers—sucking on them like baby bottles, their round childish faces, almost like baby faces, but babies that Francis Bacon never painted—and assess and discuss Penelope's ass again and again. And the truth is that, in Abracadabra, for once, Penelope is happy to be a woman. And that the men limit themselves to looking at her ass; because being a man would mean receiving constant vigorous handshakes or little pats on the back and full-toothed smiles and full-eyed stares and let's see *quien es más macho* when it comes to a staring contest, and that's the way they pass the minutes, the hours, the Karma men. The Karma women * (who, truth be told, are the ones who most inspect and discuss the asses and breasts and operations of other women with a forensic gusto learned from series like *C.S.I.*, and how is it that there's no *C.S.I. Abracadabra*, they wonder) are, by choice and prized surname, trophy wives, more covetous than covetable, who soon start to rust and the men are oxidized hunters who incessantly penetrate with telescopic pupils younger prey that are forbidden, although you never know. * The composition of the Karma females? A simple way of distilling them would be to say that they're crazy or stupid or evil in varying proportions. Some are crazier or stupider or eviler. But those three personality traits repeat, one imposing itself over the others. But Hiriz is special: she's 100% crazy and 100% stupid and 100% evil. Which, of course, goes unmentioned. And Hiriz, just as much as the others, likes to describe herself as "very pretty." In Abracadabra, on Mount Karma, if someone says that someone is "very pretty," it's advisable to take off running and not look back. And it's during a wedding, under a moon the color of hepatitis, that Penelope hears one Karma say to another Karma: "Penelope is very pretty." Fortunately, in the next instant, the anesthesia of deafening music. From a sound system of *discoteca* capacity surge, non-stop and as if on an infernal loop, Julio Iglesias and Luis Miguel whispering and wailing rancheras and tangos and boleros and (is Penelope delirious?) euphoric Red Cavalry battle hymns; some of those indistinguishable Italian pop-crooners with voices putrefied by the breezes of San Remo; and that infernal Nordic trilogy made up of the Spanish versions of ABBA's "Chiquitita," "I Had a Dream," and "Thank You for the Music." This is what Guantanamo must be like, Penelope says to herself. And Penelope drinks. * Penelope feels like a bee that's been stung by a wasp and, to get herself to feel this way, she realizes, first she has to drink a lot. In Abracadabra, Penelope understands alcohol's true value as a legal drug. Like a blanket of soft wind that envelopes you and rocks you gently (its fingertips of air lightly grazing your back) and makes the so-slow time of Abracadabra pass, not faster, but yes, as if it were moving at least, and advancing into the future. Nobody ever knows what date or day of the week it is. And Penelope wonders if this might be the result of having been born with money or if the Karmas might always be like this, no matter the size of their bank accounts. Lina will explain to her: "they don't need to learn or remember that kind of thing because that's what servants are for; to be asked and to remember for you." In any case, on any date, Mount Karma always seems to be in the nineteenth century. And it doesn't take Penelope long to realize that her status, within the Karma ecosystem, is complex: she's not a wife (which is just fine and right quick now, if you please) or a widow (even better, and like the crowning award after a long career, something like the Nobel for best spouse). Penelope isn't one thing or the other. But whatever she is, Penelope *should* and *must* be a virgin 2.0. Reconstituted. Untouchable. Immaculate. Her sex like a new Maginot Line and all of her being given to worshipping the memory of Maximiliano; though there's no scientific evidence that, right now, in the room next door, Maximiliano even remembers Penelope. In other words: Penelope shouldn't even speak a man's name because, Hiriz explains, "it could be misinterpreted." And Penelope confirms this when she casually says, to say something when she has nothing to say, something simple and without innuendo, something everyone understands: "yesterday in bed I watched a George Clooney movie." And even that . . . George Clooney. In bed. What's that supposed to mean? They look at her strangely, they look at her fixedly, they look at her with eyelids drooping like blinds that are always drawn so curious people can't see—but only imagine, and discuss—what happens behind them, on the other side, like the beginning of another movie that she also watched in bed, Martin Scorsese's acclaimed adaptation of Edith Wharton's *The Age of Innocence*. A movie that's set in 1870, but it's as if everything were happening last week or next week on Mount Karma, where, like the characters in the movie and in the opening scene of the novel, everyone appears to be going to a performance of *Faust* at the New York Academy of Music, not to see what happens on stage—that's just background music and drama—but to watch each other, hanging in balcony seats, like intriguing and intrigued gargoyles, through small binoculars, behind flickering fans. "Don't say such things, Penita. Problems have arisen between spouses over less," Hiriz tells her. * And on Mount Karma, if the undesired anomaly of a divorce is occasioned, it's immediately dressed up as widowhood, an uncertain widowhood but widowhood nonetheless: exes disappear, they don't frequent the places they used to, they're not invited anywhere, you cross to the opposite sidewalk when you see them coming, they aren't spoken to or looked at and, sooner rather than later, they die or they leave Abracadabra. And the Karmas believe in life after death (paradise is like Abracadabra but with worse serving staff, they fear) but they don't believe that there's life after or beyond Abracadabra. And for the Karmas, leaving Abracadabra is the same as dying. And so, pretty soon, the divorced Karmas (always innocent and victims) have convinced themselves that they're grieving widows and melancholy widowers. The memory of the dead husbands melting into the amnesia of the ex-husbands or, even, the living husbands whom they sometimes treat like amusing automatons or Pekinese lapdogs. Those little dogs that, few realize this, were adopted as ideal companions and perfect alibis by women who move infrequently or not at all. Little dogs that bark are preferable to little children who bite and yet they barely pay any attention to them though they obsess over demonstrating the exact opposite. Little dogs for courtesans and aristocrats way back when and for these Karma ladies and/or widows of today, almost always immobile, almost swallowed up by sofas and divans, accumulating gases and—this is the true and unspoken raison d'etre for those little dogs— needing someone to blame when some flatus slips out. Some of them speak to their Pekinese or Chihuahuas or whatever they are with high and infantile diction. Some even answer themselves in a different accent, as if it were the dog answering them: "Are you a little hungry, my little one?" "Yes of course, Mommy mine . . . And after eating we can watch a little TV. Something with doggies, please." There they all are, sharing with their pets the open secret, the barked secret: women play at being submissive females—but pull the reins and invisible strings—so that their husbands, alive or dead, having failed or lost the game, holding the disconsolation macho-man trophy, allowing them to present themselves, in theory, as alpha males, but in practice, as submissive and broken by the guilt and excuses of people who've been caught in something better left unmentioned. Husbands to whom they say, with servile sweetness, "My king," barely concealing the blade of a well-oiled guillotine, always ready to let it drop and dethrone. "Family is the greatest asset," Mamagrandma frequently thunders, stabbing her spurs into Horse's flanks. And Penelope—who was married under a separation of assets agreement; because Maximiliano's disobedience had its limits—discovers that, though there's nothing more she wants, she cannot separate herself from that one enormous asset, dark and gelatinous and tentacular like the Great Cthulu. When it comes to feelings, Penelope only ever believed in the passion of Heathcliff and Cathy in *Wuthering Heights* * (Penelope's favorite authors are Emily Brontë and Cipriano de Motoliú, the first to translate the novel into Spanish and who in 1921—capturing yet not domesticating the theoretically untranslatable, according to its author, "provincial adjective"—came up with the brilliant idiomatic transposition of *Cumbres Borrascosas*, first for the house and then for the novel's title). But, suddenly, Penelope finds that now she's like a sacrificial priestess in a familial religion overflowing with prayers and commandments and festivities. Penelope, now, is floating in a *spyish* or *widowy* twilight zone or something like that. Whatever Penelope is, the Karmas don't reproach her for it—they're very happy to have a reason to go to the clinic to drink and laugh. * A sick person in the family is like a sort of medal, an inexhaustible subject before and after death, an excuse to consult patient doctors and perverted, but always polite priests. A sick person is something that happens, that takes place. A sick person is an event and something to do. To tell the truth, though it shouldn't be told: for the Karmas, Maximiliano is a much more pleasant and well-mannered and sympathetic and socially acceptable person now that he's in a coma. And the days and weeks and months go by. And multiple baptisms and first communions and weddings and birthdays and funerals take place. Events you attend to see and be seen, to criticize and be criticized, to see the straw in the other's eye, to cast the first stone though you're not without sin.

And there's always some Karma of second or third or fourth or ninth degree of separation and parentage being born or dying or reproducing somewhere. And when the festivities die out—that brief limbo when nobody is born and nobody dies and everyone has gotten married—it's possible to catch sight of the Karmas, like stray dogs, infiltrating or taking over the celebrations of others, shouting, drunk and drinking, looking at younger boys and girls with eyes like long-nailed fingers, demanding the orchestra play old hits that are totally misses and almost no one remembers now. There, all of them dance as if possessed, because you have to dance. Penelope too; but never with strangers or more or less close or distant acquaintances (especially if they're married or single or divorcees) and always with harmless and inoffensive little Karmas: little or pubescent boys who are still sadistically and "traditionally" subjected to the debut of their first pair of long pants as a rite of passage when their classmates have been wearing them for years. * And subjected time and again by their elders, well into puberty, to the same interrogation, with the same insistence with which you wash a brain to later dry out a future assassin: how old are you? What school do you go to and what grade are you in? Do you have a girlfriend? What's your favorite sport? Who do you love the most: Mama, Papa, or Mama-grandma? Little big kids who—while the aunts spend their time watching little Karmas of the feminine sex with an almost infrared gaze, whom they always imagine levitating in a fit of nymphomania—at the same time, that same night, will mentally undress their aunt/cousin/etcetera incessantly, just to confess it at mass on Sunday. And, of course, be forgiven. On the spot.

* Perhaps that's why the Karmas are such believers in Catholic modality: the Catholic God offers many advantages, allowing you to sin first and be, promptly, pardoned after. The Karmas' god is like one of those products that cleans and disinfects and covers up all bad odors, often the smell of sulfur; because Penelope has seen and heard Karmas do and say things that would provoke boiling panic in the most devout Satanist. And that god is the glue that helps and forces them to stay united despite rifts and internal conflicts. And it's not an irascible and capricious god—like all those gods ascending and descending from Olympus—in mythological and Dynamation movies, interacting with mortals, manipulating them like chess pieces. The Karmas' god—for

the Karmas—is almost an employee. He's for everyone, yes. But he also belongs to them. *Our* father, yes. God belongs to them and—they're convinced, they believe in this—dedicates his free time, exclusively, to worrying about them, to solving their problems, to washing and drying and ironing out their sins. Because the Karmas have invested a lot in him—majority shareholders of God, Inc. **And that, without a doubt, is why the Karmas give so much to charity (an act which is nothing but a charity project for themselves, so they can say they do charity, so the whole world knows, to make it seem like they do something) and have several on-call priests ready twenty-four hours a day and even take them on trips to be used for quick confessions and masses in hotels and airports.** * Fact: once, the Karmas managed to postpone the departure of an airplane, because, having already checked their luggage, they decided that they had to go pray in the airport chapel, not hearing the repeated and exceedingly urgent calls over the loudspeaker, beseeching them to please, right?, come to their gate for departure. **For generations, the Karmas have tried to produce a religious figure of their own, a Father Karma, to no avail—the few candidates who took the plunge were quick to abandon the seminary when they discovered that the "vow of poverty" and the obligatory formative work in remote and primitive missions weren't for them.** * At a birthday party, surrounded by young Karmas, Penelope hears one of the family's salaried priests preach: "Boys, every time you masturbate, you expel an average of fifty million spermatozoids. This is like aborting fifty million babies. Imagine how many Our Fathers you'd have to pray to be forgiven." **Which is not to imply that—in the absolute certainty of their faith, in the absolute conviction that God believes in them and only them—the Karmas don't feel occasional doubts about the application of their faith and creed. Some sporadic temptation toward extreme and sectarian millennial alternatives. The whole thing about, for example, suddenly and without warning ascending to the heavens. End Times, The Reckoning, The Rapture, Up, etcetera. There are Karmas who are betting that they, as the chosen few, are the only ones who, one radiant morning, will be raised up into the stars. Some Karmas, on the other hand, prefer to think that the truly blessed will remain here below to enjoy an entire world all for themselves, while the second and third class souls will** be lifted up and crushed together between the clouds for all eternity. Hiriz, of course, believes she's found the perfect solution: "First I'll stay here all by my little self with all of it for me and, when I die, I'll go to heaven." Hiriz tends to apply that same kind of practical/blasphemous reasoning to all faith "in which Jesus doesn't play a role." Islam: "Ugly clothes and the women always covered head to toe. Impossible to believe in that. Why take care of yourself and exercise if you're forced to go around covered up all the time?" Buddhism: "I'm really good at meditating because it's easy for me to think about nothing . . . But the truth is it's hard to believe that a god would be fat like that. A god who can't slim down? After all . . ." Hinduism: "What's the fun in being reincarnated if you can't remember anything from before? Plus, if things go wrong and you come back as a pig . . ." Judaism: a slightly more complicated subject for Hiriz because of the origins of the Messiah who "luckily, saw the light and came over to our team." In the meantime, while they await Judgment Day, when without a doubt they'll be absolved and rewarded, Hiriz and the Karmas cross themselves, and their rapid and precise movements recall more an earthly masonic countersign than a sincere gesture of love for the divine. * It doesn't take Penelope long to see this and see them and record footage of them on her little camera. Because her brother asks her for more and more "Karmatic material." Penelope's brother follows her life in Abracadabra as if it were his favorite TV series and—he doesn't and won't tell her this—even plays with the idea of moving all of it to a neighboring country, make a few changes, and putting it all in his next book, assembling a whole *Light Inhuman Comedy* around the Karmas. And, now, later, with the book already written, he—because now everything happens simultaneously, like "marvelous moments" in the books of a certain race of extraterrestrials—thinks about it again . . . No: what he really thinks about is the moment when he came up with the figure of a little freak nestled in the voluptuous bosom of a family. A boy with a helmet onto which he's mounted a camera so he can track and capture and take advantage of a non-stop motion picture of his family, in the creation of a kind of "total and *vérité* telenovela." And the memory of inventing that boy leads him directly to the memory of another boy, a real boy, a nonfiction boy also holding a camera in his small hand and focusing it on him, on the beach, asking him serious and adult questions in a high-pitched and childish voice. And this memory hurts him so much—even though he's no longer made of nerves or muscles or heart or brain—that it's as if a lightning bolt were nailing him to the sky and wrenching a scream out of him that, instantly, turns into a hurricane in the Caribbean or a tsunami in the Pacific or into one of those earthquakes that, to prove the nonexistence of one true God, brings down the celestial cupola of some renaissance cathedral and, suddenly, fades away. And he dies a little with it. He's brought low, amid tears and angels and spilled blood. So Penelope films them in churches and chapels and even in private mass in their homes, with the anthropological and zoological and Martian eyes of a combination of Margaret Mead and Dian Fossey and John Carter. Penelope records the pious air of their arrogance. The almost moving way, as mentioned, that the Karmas believe in God because—they're certain, there's ample and irrefutable evidence—that God believes in them. Otherwise, the fact that they are so fortunate, that their fortune continues to grow, is inexplicable. * (Note: the Karmas believe in God but *also* fear black cats, walking under ladders, broken mirrors. For the Karmas, all the superstitions—as much the "brand name" as the "artisanal"—have equal value and power, though they don't dare admit it.) Hence the almost pagan debauchery at weddings and baptisms once the religious part of the program has concluded. Then, they chew on animals and empty bottles and dance almost in ecstasy, as if the end of everything in the world were on its way. There, Penelope drinks a lot and her alcohol tolerance provokes comments between condemning and admiring. Penelope never seems drunk, even if she is—she doesn't stagger, she doesn't vomit, she doesn't fall—and the only symptom of obvious alcoholic intoxication is that she becomes talkative and sharp and clever and biting and venomous. So, after the holy chalice and between glasses, Penelope tries to torpedo their armored and unsinkable mystical certainty with the blunt iceberg of comments like "How is it possible that, after killing his brother, Cain was banished to the Land of Nod, to the east of Eden, and that there he interacted with its inhabitants and even got himself a wife if, supposedly, Cain and Abel and Adam and Eve were hitherto the only members of their species?" or "If everyone was asleep, how did Matthew hear Jesus pray in the Garden of Gethsemane, at the foot of the Mount of Olives, and write down everything he said with such precision?" or "Is Jehovah the bad cop and Jesus the good cop in the great precinct of the heavens?" or "How can you believe in all of . . . *that*? Don't you realize that the times of Jesus, when Jesus existed, were times that preceded rationalism and scientific thought and that, basically, everyone was crazy and going around proclaiming strange and impossible things? And that everything you continue to believe and read was written by lunatics who, were they alive today, would be under lock and key? Don't you realize that all religion is like the echo of a madman's scream?" But nobody gets the hint when they hear her say these things. The Karmas have probably never heard anything about the Land of Nod. The Garden of Gethsemane, yes; but as something of the past and on one of those tours of the Holy Land where they went all together, inseparable, more like invading fanatics than devout tourists. The Karmas leave Mount Karma so they can return to Mount Karma and there, canine and Pavlovian, all you have to do is mention the names of New York, Paris, Moscow, London, or Rome for each and every one of them to bark a "Mount Karma" or, as a great concession to the immensity of the planet, an "Abracadabra." So the Karmas listen attentively to the nomad Penelope, yes, but they don't pay her the slightest attention. They smile at her with glazed-over eyes, as if they were using the sound and not the meaning of Penelope's words to think of other things or, better, of nothing at all or—the men and women both, for very different reasons, but coinciding on the common ground of their covetousness—about Penelope's ass. * So they let her "express herself." Because Penelope doesn't speak, rather, since they understand little to nothing of what she says, "she expresses herself"; as if hers were some kind of "modern" discipline. And the Karmas always say, *mawhdern*, dragging out the *o* into an *aw*, and inserting the silent yet always oh so expressive contamination of an *h*, with a blend of humor and derision, as if *modern*, in itself, were already a *mawhdern* word. In the beginning, Penelope enjoys the affectation and even celebrates it as a rare form of not so sophisticated Karmatic humor; but pretty soon Lina will shatter her illusion, telling her that it's just a random catch phrase from a lame TV show. But note: this mistrust of the modern does not compel the Karmas to counterattack with an ardent defense of the classic. No, the classic (which they tend to associate with an outmoded model) doesn't interest them. What prevails with them is the traditional, taken to mean family traditions and, specifically, Karma family traditions. A whole complex web of laws and clauses in permanent collision and contradiction. Example: it's very bad to look at Penelope's ass, but that's Penelope's fault, because it's her ass, and they think it shamelessly calls attention to itself, and that's why they look at it. And, after a few minutes, they ask Penelope if she wants to dance. So there, at baptisms and first communions and weddings, Penelope *also* "dances very differently." Penelope, *additionally*, dresses very differently. Penelope is, yes, unequivocally and definitively and terminally *mawhdern*. While the men wear anything with logos or suits somewhere between metallic and reptilian, and the women wrap themselves in identical dresses so that nobody can criticize or make fun of anybody else, Penelope's style might be described as banshee alien-goth. Something closer to the evolutions and tours of Patti Smith & Kate Bush * (who, yes, had a very young artistic debut and found global success with a single called "Wuthering Heights;" Penelope doesn't really know how she feels about that) than to the plastic synchronism of Madonna and her plagiarisms. And Penelope whirls around and around, over everyone and everything, like a kind of rolling protest, during that inexplicable medley of children's songs by some teenybopper band (Bulimia and the Little Skinnies?), who all the adults celebrate, clapping their hands and giving little kicks in the air, as if it were a sonic version of a rejuvenating tonic. To top it all off, Penelope doesn't put her hair up in one of those turban/beehive hairdos, petrified with a highly rain- and wind-resistant spray, that all the women her age seem to wear for these occasions. * (The aesthetic/ethical equation is, always, vertical hairdo + horizontal eyelashes + oblique words; and once Penelope saw one of the Karma women without makeup and got the disturbing sensation of a face drowning before the merciless iceberg of its own reflection, a face whose features abandon it at full velocity to secure a place in one of the few remaining lifeboats. But it almost never happens. The Karma women almost never allow themselves to be seen like this. In general, careful constructions, the face like a false backdrop and a curtain to fall and conceal everything. Makeup of a style that says, "All right, Mr. DeMille I'm ready for my close-up" and fake eyelashes onto which they scatter, impaling them, entire swarms of yellow, kamikaze butterflies. And on the dance floor, Penelope's long red hair like a red whip, lashing anyone who comes too close (and there are more then a few husbands who risk a casual brush) to the hits of a local rock band, Manjar, internationally famous because they insist, time and again, song after song, always the same, on the lyrical audacity and poetic transgression of rhyming "*amor*" with "*amor.*" See them dance. Men with gunfighter sombreros and peplum belts sporting their initials and, sometimes, American friends/associates whom they introduce as tycoons, but who never seem ready to remove their hats sporting logos of baseball teams or tractor manufacturers. Women wearing dresses that sparkle with sequins and gemstones and metallic appliques and the shoulder pads of comic book heroines. Hiriz's husband—Ricky, who almost never speaks, but when he does open his mouth and says things that Hiriz will sooner or later say, as if he were a ventriloquist dummy always in the vicinity—approaches Penelope and says that it would be better if she didn't move her arms so much when she danced because it "shows your age." "Bat arms," he diagnoses. And releases little flying rodent shrieks. The "problem" is that Penelope's arm muscles are much firmer than Hiriz's and her husband's arms and Penelope never sets foot in the gym. And Hiriz's husband, Ricky, studies Penelope with a mix of lust and contempt, trying to balance, on a low and almost secret channel, the discrete but disturbing homosexual impulses that he feels on full-moon nights and the impossibility of ever forgetting that hot morning when, upon leaving an Abracadabra shopping center with Hiriz and some friends, weighed down with heavy bags, a blast of heat dropped him to his knees on the asphalt of the parking lot in front of Hiriz. * The heat in the parking lots of Abracadabra shopping centers is like the heat in *Lawrence of Arabia*: a Cinemascopic heat that strikes you on the head like the gavel of a supreme and not so courteous judge. Ricky falls down and Hiriz drives the temperature even higher. Hiriz, who kept right on talking about some formula she'd discovered to turn something or other into who knows what. And, his embarrassment equaling his fear of mockery (which would translate into a reliable and eternal retelling of the incident across dinner tables and decades), Ricky decided that the only way he could hide his "debility" and change the sign of the anecdote was, right there, kneeling and in pain and exaggeratedly emotional, to ask Hiriz to marry him. After all, it solved a problem: once they were married, people would stop talking about certain of Ricky's somewhat "delicate" mannerisms. Ricky's eyes fill with tears, too often, after a few too many drinks, and he even lets slip things like "I'm so well-endowed that every time I have an erection I get dizzy from the quantity of blood flowing to my privates; that's why I carefully manage each one of my sexual relations" or "I don't understand why you have to wash your hands after going to the bathroom. You should wash them before; because there's no part of my body more impeccable and free of germs and bacteria than my dear Rickyto-Rickyton." Hiriz, seeing him like that, on his knees, said yes; because she always liked people on their knees, because there was no other candidate in sight, because Ricky's last name was "right." And it was clear that Ricky was a weak and easy person to manipulate—because she has suspected for a while now that she's incapable of loving anyone but herself (the sight of certain Hollywood stars on late night DVDs are merely the initial excuse to touch herself)—and because it would automatically make her the leading lady in the cast of her family during the months of preparations for a wedding that would require the deployment and strategy of the landing at Normandy. Ricky, in that moment, thought to himself that nothing happens by chance and that, after all, Hiriz would be the perfect screen, prestigious and the envy of many, in the event that his propensity to follow men at the gym with his eyes moved on to the next stage of following them—and catching them—with something more than his eyes. * (In certain circles in Abracadabra, they tell Penelope, one doesn't marry men or women; one marries surnames and families; and they're not surnames like Rothschild or Vanderbilt or Rockefeller or Kennedy, but infinite variations of Gómez and Gutiérrez and López; Ricky's last name, for example, is Fernández-Guzmán. And there's something moving in the fact that, an unspeakable secret, many Karmas are made uncomfortable by their original and strange last name and, secretly, long for something "normaler and easier to remember, something like Pérez or Navarro or Cardona.") And so everyone celebrated another wedding being added to the calendar (it wasn't easy to find an open Saturday) and it was a magnificent wedding though inevitably marked by the aesthetic of the eighties. * (Hiriz, many years later, paid a small fortune to have all the photos from the event Photoshopped—when the time came she'd do the same with the photos of her children's first communions, asking the photographer to slip in, between the branches of the trees in the garden, the face of Jesus Christ blessing the occasion—to alter her hairdo from the time that made her look, her hair in a spike, like a sort of lightning-rod fan of Duran Duran and A Flock of Seagulls and Culture Club. While she was at it, she took the opportunity to make her eyes blue and whiten her teeth and boost her breasts and iron out wrinkles that she had then but doesn't have now. Photo operation and a miracle: the young Hiriz from the photos looks more like the Hiriz of today, not that she looks younger, but like a different Hiriz, this Hiriz: an Hiriz like the avatar of Hiriz, *reloaded & second life*, etcetera, irrefutable proof that she was always like that and, as such, never had plastic surgery.) And everyone—apart from the bride and the groom, who seem somewhat disconcerted because suddenly everything is coming to an end and, at the same time, it seems that everything continues and will continue across the decades: what was sold to them as a climax turned out to be a brief preview of a long act—celebrates now as if the Apocalypse were upon them and they have to make the most of it, because the days will stretch out eternally until next Saturday, until the next wedding. A wedding is a wedding is a wedding and, as night falls and shifts into morning, the drunken men embrace each other and sing old-time ballads in which all women are unfaithful and evil and fatal and abandon them, but "luckily I still got my friends." My Karmas. * (Are the Karma men unfaithful? Of course. Though not exactly. Theirs is an infidelity that doesn't come from desire, self-destruction, boredom, or the need to escape without being forced to leave. No, the Karma men succumb to any more or less interested woman without a second thought, because they fear that, if they resist, their actions will be construed as "faggotry," as a recognizable trait of closeted homosexuality. The Karma women, for their part, have nothing to do with the songs dedicated and sung to them. Just the opposite: they do nothing, limiting themselves to the most hysterical and unconsummated flirtations, and dream a great deal and wide awake, waiting for the inevitable hour of their revenge, of forgiving and reducing the repentant man to a castrated puppet ready to make all their whims a reality. Unconfirmed Abracadabran rumors abound, Lina tells her, of "very well-to-do families" where the señoras are "attended" by professionals. And whispers of swinging parties— styles and transgressions take about a half-century after arriving to the rest of the world, like everything besides the latest cars and electronic devices, to penetrate the moral barriers of Abracadabra in general and Mount Karma in particular—where the Karmas put their car keys in a bowl and pick them out blindly to see who will leave with whom. Which is clearly still total nonsense, because the Karmas are all for one and one for all. It's also unfair to consider the Karmas passé for arriving late to this type of little game: that particular ceremony doesn't correspond to a decade but to an age, an age when the owners of those car keys, forever young and the latest models, start to comprehend, hearing odd noises in their engines, that they've already passed the midpoint on the highway of their lives, and get desperate for some kind of rebirth. But those screamed whispers are never entirely confirmed for and by Penelope. She's not really that interested either. The true lies that the Karmas throw at each other like loving daggers are more than enough for her, and best not get too close, because their aim isn't exactly precise when, as warned, they choose to sacrifice some passerby.) **And those who are not direct or indirect Karmas are "sympathy" Karmas, or people who'd give anything to be a Karma and turn into useful and, yes, sympathetic underlings and Karmatic accessories to be exploited for a while and later discarded and replaced by new voluntary volunteers. *** And Penelope (who, if she were to write seriously some day, to write something beyond the increasingly numerous ship-wrecked and in-a-bottle messages that she emails to her brother from Abracadabra) always said she'd like to write like Joan Didion, who, after all, is for her a legitimate Californian descendent of her beloved Emily Brontë. Author of poems like "The Prisoner" that Penelope recites in a low voice, because they seem oh so appropriate in her present circumstances: "Oh dreadful is the check—intense the agony / When the ear begins to hear and the eye begins to see, / When the pulse begins to throb, the brain to think again, / The soul to feel the flesh and the flesh to feel the chain!" Yes: the terrible and agonizing confirmation in her ears and eyes and heart and brain and soul and flesh of knowing herself to be chained. She feels like her, knowing she isn't her, but certain she'd really enjoy being like her, being her, consuming herself, letting herself go for the love of art. But Penelope (who doesn't dare think that she'd like to write like Emily Brontë for fear of being struck by a punishing bolt of lightning for such pride and audacity) discovers that wishes, when they're granted outside of stories, are always granted in a twisted and malicious way. Yes: so Penelope doesn't write like Joan Didion, but feels like someone written by Joan Didion. Like those women in Joan Didion's novels, lost in the tropics, prisoners of a landscape that's nothing but an equally febrile but hotter version of the British moors and wastelands of the Heights, making and unmaking time, as if suspended in a thick syrup pierced by light the same way and with the same tonality that rum bottles project across walls of airport bars when they catch the sun while airplanes that are never yours take off. And one afternoon something happens. One afternoon Penelope meets Lina. On the as yet imprecise date that she meets Lina * (Penelope finds herself obliged to check the date on her mobile phone almost every hour to remember what time of year it is, to keep from getting lost in a calendar full of tunnels that always open on anniversaries, birthdays, saints' days), Penelope is going crazy. "*Volviéndose loca*" as they would say in Abracadabra. And Penelope never understood that Spanish expression: "volverse loca," which literally means to "return crazy." Because, if you think about it a little, one "goes crazy," moves away, loses oneself, never to return to the more or less sane person one once was. So, Penelope moves through the hallways of the clinic like a too-lucid zombie. A zombie conscious that it's more unalive than it is undead. And there's no point or use in going out and eating brains. Because the Karmas' brains aren't nutritious or fortifying brains. Her own brain, she struggles to think, seems now like a big muscle that gets less use than all the small muscles she uses to conjure a perpetual and vacuous smile. Her brain, she's almost positive, experiences less activity and inventiveness than Maximiliano's. If Maximiliano's comatose brain is at a comma, hers, Penelope thinks, is at a period. And very few satisfactions worth remembering, waking up in a more and more uniform memory; because today is the same as yesterday and tomorrow will be the same as today and all the days are Groundhog Day in Marienbad, Loopländ. And what was the most transcendent and exciting thing that happened to Penelope in Abracadabra before meeting Lina? Easy to locate yet so difficult to accept: the night before—or maybe some night last week three months ago—Penelope killed a mosquito, big and plump with blood. And, ah, the triumphant and intimate satisfaction of discovering that little red stain on the wall, the next morning, after having tolerated its sharp buzzing in the darkness for so many hours. So similar to the deafening buzz of Karmatic lunches and dinners. There, they yell a lot to say very little. All of it lies so that, without realizing it, the truth shines between the lines, codified, as if written in invisible ink, like transparent stigmas tattooed on diners' foreheads, visible if they squint their eyes and concentrate a little. You don't need to be a telepath or diviner to know what a Karma thinks of another person: because what a Karma thinks and doesn't say is, generally, the opposite of what they say they think. During those eternal lunches or dinners, Penelope speaks little or can't stop speaking. The monosyllables of agreement are nothing but a product of the renewed surprise of hearing again, as if recorded and reproduced, the same conversation as yesterday, as last week, as the month before and the decade to come. The same names and nicknames (that they bear, ineradicable, from the elementary school playground, and whose inventiveness rarely surpasses something like "Skinny" or "Fatty" or "Hairy" or "The Dwarf" or the almost onomatopoetic "Chungui" or "Pupu" or "Teti") starring in the same stories as always that, in general, evoke almost childish episodes: falls, stumbles, silent-film humor. In general, Penelope manages to let her mind go blank, to take off on an astral voyage, to silently recite parts of her favorite books to herself. Sometimes she prays, just in case, just in case there's something up there that might help her. But there are times when she decides she's going to talk and launches into long and irrepressible rants. * Penelope's fiery mouth, words spinning around inside, sparking, like Pop Rocks, the urgent need to spit it all out like a flammable and pyromaniac dragon. Incinerate everything and everyone in honor of Ladon and Fafnir and Godzilla and all the Disney reptiles that were, always, the best, the most well-illustrated. Penelope, like a plumed serpent baring its fangs and gnashing, poisoning, furious, the apparent and false tranquility—that detente like an eternal siesta—that surrounds and smothers her. Pure delirium and absurdity to, for a while, suffocate the story of what happened when Froggy bumped into Freckle-Face at aerobics class. Those moments, of course, make her the favorite "aunt" among the kids and, especially, among Hiriz's kids, on the edge of adolescence and with a slight artistic restlessness. * At a baptism, after a few too many drinks, Hiriz, with a mix of unspeakable pain and barely concealed scorn, says to Penelope that, "As hard as I try I can't understand why my children love you so much." And, as mentioned, Penelope provokes certain confusion among the adults who, already, consider her an extension of Maximiliano: a/another bad influence, but who, unlike Maxi, isn't even a Karma in the first place. And the truth is that the Karma kids don't love Penelope. Love is too much to ask from creatures whose affective systems are already affected, functionally, by things that have nothing to do with the chemistry of pure emotions but with the speculations of materialism and convenience. But they do consider her "novel," a bizarre trend, a comfortable form of external catharsis created by someone else. Someone to "make trouble" for them, because they don't dare. So, they admire—in addition to her body—her unexpected rebelliousness and unpredictable and transgressive diatribes. Especially at religious and "traditional" events. Cutting remarks that they'd never dare utter (because nothing could be less in their interest, because "Look how Maximiliano ended up"), but that they collect in secret and exchange via telephonic and mobile text messages, like children's trading cards or quasi-pornographic postcards. * A few brief examples: "Seven days? If He's God why didn't he do everything in one day and boom?"; or "How do you explain that Adam and Eve are always portrayed with belly buttons if they weren't ever inside a belly?"; or "Is God a woman?"; or "Don't you know that the waltz was a rural dance that Viennese aristocrats used to consider obscene?"; or, in the middle of a First Communion, "How is it possible for someone who hasn't yet reached the legal age to vote, or drive a car, or drink a gin and tonic, or have sexual relations to confirm their belief in someone who resurrects the dead and multiplies fish and bread without first being allowed to peruse the other pages in the catalogue containing Buddha and Mohammad and Vishnu?" And other medium-sized examples: "If you think about it a little bit, Jesus Christ is like an imaginary friend and protector of childhood for people who refuse to grow up and leave him behind, right? And the thing about the Baby Jesus taking the place of Santa Clause on Christmas . . . Isn't that a bit *too much*? Who in their right mind can think and believe in a newborn, recently expelled from between the legs of the Virgin Mary, head still wrapped in the most visionary of placentas, like a headscarf through which he already sees his painful and obligatory unhappy ending, could take up distributing gifts throughout the entire world to well-behaved little ones who, above all, never doubt his improbable existence. I prefer Batman. Batman has the same historical substance as Jesus Christ. One is as true as the other. In fact, Batman is realer than Jesus because, at least, we know the last names of his creators. And the most important, notable difference of all: Jesus Christ's father forces him to die in his name and without it being entirely clear why and to what end, and announces a second coming that, everything seems to indicate, will be postponed indefinitely; while the masked man of Gotham City kills in the name of his murdered parents, and you can always count on him. Besides, Batman's disguise is much better than Jesus Christ's, right? Jesus Christ's is like the cheapest Halloween costume. Jesus Christ is a zombie! In fact, Jesus Christ would make a magnificent super villain, an ultramonster: part zombie (because he comes back from the dead and "devours" the brains of his followers), part vampire (because he "converts" them into his own kind), and part Frankensteinian monster (because he is "assembled" from parts of the ancient legends that preceded him), and part alien (because . . .)." And other examples long as stories: "The whole thing about not putting your elbows on the table . . . Poor children . . . By chance do any of you know where the whole thing about it being bad to put your elbows on the table comes from? No? Do you want to know? Yes? To begin with you have to realize that it's got nothing to do with good or bad table manners. Absolutely not. It's something that comes from the Middle Ages and that, though it might seem incomprehensible to you, like so many other things from the past, no longer has any reason to exist. The past passes, little ones. Wait and see. In the Middle Ages, the poor didn't even have tables. And much less a dining room. Just a long board that they rested on their knees or on a pile of rocks or on a couple of tree stumps. Really, their elbows couldn't even reach that board, it was too far below them. The nobles and aristocrats, on the other hand, did have rooms to dine in and solid and well-appointed tables, and so they enjoyed the rare privilege of that obvious and evident structural function of the elbow—point of support, resting them on the table . . . It's not that it's bad to put your elbows on the table. Just the opposite. But the poor, the poor can't do it, they're not allowed to, they're not worthy—it's not an issue of manners but of standing, of social standing. Elbows are only for the rich and powerful. And it's not that the poor who dare put them on the table are bad mannered; rather, they're out of place. And, of course, if a poor man were caught resting his elbows on some rich guy's table, that, yes, would be considered bad manners. And they'd probably punish him by cutting off his arms. But History and the passing of time put things in place and, paradoxically, today there are all these rich people of supposedly exquisite manners suffering and not allowing themselves to rest on their elbows and never really understanding why. In short: The blue bloods . . . And do you know where blue blood comes from? No? All right. It just so happens that rich people were almost never outdoors and so they were quite pale and their blood looked very blue in their veins; their subordinates, on the other hand, spent their time working in the sun and that's where they got their perfect tans and their blood that was so ordinary and red, when it spilled, when they cut a finger with a hatchet or fell in front of a plow, or a horse gave them a loving kick in the head . . . But getting back to the thing from before: the rich could afford themselves the luxury of resting on their elbows; on the other hand, as I've said, it's a more than obvious anatomical function; because if it were improper, then kneeling down in mass and making use of your inferior elbows, resting your knees on the ground, would be akin to blasphemy, right? In short: resting your elbows on the table is a privilege of the upper classes; not resting them is a stigma of the lower classes. Know this: you have spent many, many, many years behaving like poor people . . . And that's it. And, with elbows resting on the table, they lived happily ever after. And since we're already on the subject: why do you guys consider it rude to read books at the table, but not to read little screens?" And Penelope calls attention to herself, and doesn't add that forbidding elbows from touching the table would remove a good number of author photos from the face of the earth; including that one of E. M. Forster, her brother's favorite: Forster with his head between his hands, held up by both forearms resting on respective elbows, with the pen in the air, far from the manuscript, and with an almost despairing look. "*This* is exactly what it is to be a writer, Penelope," her brother said. And then he told her one of his favorite anecdotes, also about Forster, that was a perfect match for his favorite photo of Forster, and in which, when a friend accused him of "not facing facts," the writer responded: "Don't tell me to face facts. Facts are like the walls of a room: to face one you must have your back to the other three." Yes, deciding what part of reality to face was, also, one of the many more or less secret ways of being a writer. To choose is to invent. And, on Mount Karma, Penelope didn't have much to choose from. Reality, on Mount Karma, was a circular wall, a wall, slow as a turtle eating its own tail and stinging itself with its own venomous stinger because that was in its nature. But most serious of all—and something Penelope has less control over all the time—are the comments of a personal and intimate nature. For example, in light of the fact that all the young Karma women push out an average of five children, and tired of hearing time and again that this fecundity can only be due to—always amid smiles and blushing and never in words—the frequency of their sexual activity and how "well attended" their husbands keep them, Penelope can't help but theorize, aloud and with a drink in hand, like a detective in a Victorian library surrounded by suspects, that "perhaps it's all just the diametrical opposite: maybe all of you, due to your own lack of desire or their lack of interest, make love so infrequently that, when a sporadic and unpredicted spark comes along, you don't have any kind of contraceptive on hand and . . ." Penelope says things like this and hears herself say them. And says to herself that she can't believe what she's hearing herself say. What's going on with her? Whose voice is that? Who's the sinister puppet master hidden in the shadows tugging at her tense vocal cords? How did she turn into a diabolical and acerbic doll? What can be done to stop her, to shut her mouth? So, trying to fix things a little and talk about something near and dear, Penelope ends up causing more problems, being problematic. Because the only thing that she happens to think of (really the only thing that interests her) is, please, can they all agree and tell her once and for all how it was that Papagrandpa died or disappeared or ran away. And so, again: those unequivocally Karmatic looks. Fury contained in the name of a supposedly good upbringing that's nothing but a repressive muzzle. Or that other look, typical of the habitat and its inhabitants, that reminds Penelope of the look of a deer in the headlights. And the other even rarer Karmatic look. Almost exclusively Hiriz's. A look that's like that of a deer driving a car. A look that accelerates toward another look that, likewise, can only be described by ascribing it to another non-human species. A strange and seemingly absent look accompanied by a smile. A thin smile but, at the same time, the smile of a shark with double rows of teeth. A sleepy shark that never really falls asleep (Penelope suspects that the consumption of relaxant and antidepressant pills by the tense Karma women is sufficient to keep multiple pharmaceutical companies in business) but that doesn't even exhibit the frontal lobe activity of a shark. No, hers is closer to the parasitic geniality of the fish that feed off what clings to the backs of great and majestic whales or the leftovers discarded from the magnificent ships passing by overhead. And the unmistakable sensation that, behind that mask of amiable understanding, everything Penelope says is being stored away to later be repeated and dispersed and discussed and criticized and condemned. For this reason, she listens to Penelope not attentively, but with the fidelity of a recording device. And, later, rewind and play. And saying everything about her that they never say to her (because she's Maximiliano's wife after all and Maximiliano is the direct grandson of Mamagrandma and a man), but that's exactly what Penelope hears, in the eloquence of her silences, as if she were reading a movie's secret and alternate subtitles. And that's where Penelope is and that's where she stays: in her interminable film-loop, *Interlude / Day / Clinic / Maximiliano's Suite*. Surrounded by Karmas, with a doctor entering and exiting and saying "Trust in the Lord" and a priest explaining "Right now Maxi is enjoying the company of the angels for a little while longer, but soon, thanks to our prayers, we'll have him here again, happy as ever." Penelope, then, feels the irrepressible desire to insert one of her comments classified as "the strange things Penelope says." Something about, for example, how it's been proven that it's bad to pray for the recovery of the sick; because it won't take the sick people long, even if they're true believers, to feel bad when the prayers don't make them better, and they'll realize that they're not worthy of God's attention and care; and then they'll get worse and worse until they die in an abyss of uncertainty, blaming and, why not, reproaching the Father who has abandoned them. Also, she could point out that there's nothing more contradictory than asking the creator of all things to change the course of something—a business failure or a failed marriage, for example—while at the same time repeating, over and over, the thing about thy will be done on Earth as it is in Heaven. Is there anything more blasphemous and sacrilegious than praying to a god to change their mind? Over and over again? All the time? But Penelope doesn't say anything. The TV is turned to a news program that they watch—before the fourth telenovela of the day comes on—like microstories and brief flash fictions. All the bad news about things that always happen somewhere far away and that generate comments like "Thank God things like that don't happen to us" or—like when the terrible visions of a tsunami in the Pacific are shown—a conciliatory "tsunamis are really good for the crops." But reference and attention to extrakarmatic reality is fleeting and before long they become the subject once again. * Again, though it's unnecessary: the first thing that most interests the Karmas is the Karmas; the second thing that most interests the Karmas is what everyone else (mostly Karmas) thinks of the Karmas; the third thing that most interests the Karmas is, again, the first thing that most interests the Karmas—the Karmas. And it's then that it occurs to someone, in that hospital suite, while dealing cards for another hand of the interminable game of canasta, that it wouldn't be bad for "Maxi and Penita" * (Not long ago Penelope discovered that *that* is the nickname that's been humorously pinned on her. And that it has as much to do with her name as with a "That girl causes us such *penita*." And that the *penita*—Spanish diminutive of pena, meaning sorrow—or "small sorrow" that she causes them really has nothing to do, as they want to make her believe, with her condition as quasi-widow or half-wife, but with Penelope herself, with who and how she is) to get married by the Church.

And in three Saturdays is the miracle of a weekend with no wedding sched-uled. And that available day must be a divine omen, an order from the heav-ens. "Hallelujah," exclaims the priest on duty and the doctor, solicitous and well remunerated, adds: "I don't see any problem. We can transport all the equipment to the gardens at Mount Karma and . . ." On top of Horse, lean-ing in through one of the suite's windows, Mamagrandma calls for silence and says that nobody has asked Penelope what she thinks about getting mar-ried by the Church. "Would you like that, Penelope?" She asks, staring at her. Penelope, graciously, responds in a low voice that "Better not, at least for now; because we don't know very well how things will go with Maximi . . ." "Perfect. Say no more. Next month we'll have a wedding," thunders Mama-grandma. And, there outside, she empties her pistols at the sun. Then, all of them—like suddenly activated machines, like a perfectly oiled assembly line and, for once, fast and expeditious—begin to make lists, to plan almost mili-tary maneuvers, to calculate timelines. For the Karmas, punctuality is some-thing they only put in practice for first communions and weddings and baptisms and funerals. Hiriz, of course, will put herself in charge and per-sonally design—based on a purchased model, because Hiriz never starts any-thing from the beginning or carries out anything to the end—the bride's dress. "Luckily, with Maxi the way he is, you won't have problems with him seeing the dress before the ceremony," Hiriz says to Penelope. And Penelope believes she's witnessing a miracle: Hiriz doesn't normally allow herself to make jokes, but, not only that, the joke is quite good. And Penelope laughs with enthusiasm and for a while her bursts of laughter—almost a desperate snort—frighten her a little. But no: it turns out that—Penelope realizes when her sister-in-law looks at her taken aback and slightly offended—Hiriz is being serious. And Penelope feels that she's going to be sick. And that, if she stays there, she'll end up killing one of the assembled Karmas (Hiriz if she had to choose) or that they'll kill her. Probably, the former first and the latter later. And suddenly, in the room, an abrupt change in atmospheric pressure, like a change in voltage intensity. Everything seems to shut down so it can start up again. As if a new program were beginning that coincided with the beginning, on the TV, of the telenovela that all the women and all the men (because, curiously, it's not frowned upon for the men to follow the evolution of those absurd storylines; maybe because, probably, it's one of the only things they can talk about with their wives) have been following for years, night after night, while swallowing the pills that correspond to that particular time of day. It's called *Storms of Ecstasy.* * And though Penelope would never admit it, he—who floats above all the truths of a mendacious world, reviewing all of it like someone revising more or less rough drafts— remembers that his sister first came to *Wuthering Heights* not aboard the original novel, but riding a telenovela-esque, Venezuelan adaptation from the seventies, bad but well-meaning and respectful and— with false exteriors recreated in the studio, with cardboard rocks and a fog machine—arranged to evoke and powerfully transmit the cold and gothic air of moors oh so far from the tropics. And Penelope watches the telenovela on the hospital TV and thinks she perceives, beneath successive layers of a storyline that, after so long entangling itself, has already spun out of control, diffuse but identifiable glimmers of Heathcliff and Cathy, and she wonders if someone might not be mocking her or, perhaps, sending her a compassionate and complicit wink, words of encouragement barely hidden amid everything those leading men and heroines and villains said. Not because she feels particularly moved by this telenovela (or by that other telenovela from her childhood that showed her the way to the book of her head and heart), but because there, in the almost secret pocket of her leather jacket, she always carries, inseparable, her passport. She never leaves it behind for fear that it'll disappear. Or that they'll make it disappear. Or— almost out of her mind—for fear of not having it on hand when her employers (the CIA, MI6, KGB, an oriental triad referred to as Dragon?) decide, in the end, to swap her for some Karma spy and liberate her and, ha, ha, ha, the things that occur to someone in the first stages of what, if she's not careful, could end up being the infinite voyage of madness. And it's not that Penelope thinks she can't leave. It'd be a matter of simply going down the stairs, hailing a taxi at the door to the clinic, and saying "Airport." But at the same time, the truth is that it's increasingly difficult for Penelope to do anything outside the program, different, that isn't the same thing she did yesterday and the week before and for the past two or three months. Penelope almost panics when she breaks her routine, alters her ritual, modifies the most natural yet bizarre of cycles. Penelope feels as if she's spent years without sleeping or years without waking up, either way. In a kind of dawning twilight that, she read once, is something like what the newly blind experience. The half-light of people who, ignoring warnings for some incomprehensible reason, have lost their sight from, defiant to the point of stupidity, staring at an eclipse and—with their biological and photosynthetic clock suddenly and completely confused, out of time at all times—now don't know when it's time to get in bed to sleep or to sit down in a chair to work. At times, Penelope almost convinces herself that she no longer sees anything and, other times, that she sees too much, but always the same thing, the same people. Yes, Penelope is karmatizing. And this is like a one-way ticket. So she leaves, swaying, as if along the hallways of a ship in the storm and—slight transgression—on her way to the clinic bar, she passes in front of a room with the door open. There inside, a young woman with an unusual look for Abracadabra (as if ten mixed races were rotating around in her face) holds the hand of an old man. Accustomed to serial similitude, to the near cloning of features and styles of the Karmas, the sight of the young woman who looked so different almost makes Penelope cry. Penelope thinks—without being able to understand how it is that she's thinking it, maybe already irremediably contaminated by her overexposure to the religious pulsations of the Karmas—that "That, that is exactly how I always imagined the Virgin Mary" or, to feel a little closer to herself, to keep from losing the little that's left of her trangressive fuel, adds, "or Mary Magdalene." The young woman—whose name, she'll soon learn, is Lina—looks at her and smiles and, pointing to the old man in the bed, says: "My father . . . My adopted father . . . He always had such a bad memory, so it was already too late by the time we realized he had Alzheimer's." Penelope doesn't know if it's a joke, but—like someone suddenly looking at something they haven't seen in such a long time, like a castaway glimpsing his rescue approaching on the horizon—it is funny. Like things she used to laugh at before coming to live among the Karmas, who laugh at everything in general, but at nothing in particular, and whose sense of humor, like everything, is something serialized, collective, without any kind of singularity. So, suddenly, they both laugh, belly laughs, as if possessed, while a nurse in a painting on one wall of the clinic insists, in vain, index finger over her lips, asking for a silence that they'll never grant her. Suddenly, unexpectedly, Penelope meets Lina and, again, once more, she feels as if all of her neurons are reaching out and communicating and talking all at the same time after having stayed far too quiet. For Penelope, Lina—after so much time coexisting with people who talk a lot about what they're going to do and do so little in relation to everything they talk about doing—is a person who does things without announcing them, much less postponing them. The Karmas—for whom saying that they're going to do something is the same as doing it—would definitely consider her deranged and, probably, a "drug addict." Someone definitively *mawhdern*. Lina likes to say that she never uses drugs, but that, when she was a girl, due to carelessness on her parents' part, she ate a basket full of peyote buttons that her grandmother had gathered to prepare who knows what kind of ancestral medicine: "So now I'm like Obélix, who fell in a pot of magic potion as a boy. I don't need to take drugs. I don't need to take trips all over the place. I live, hallucinating all the time. Yippie." Penelope, on the other hand, finds a twin—yet different—sister in Lina. Unlike Penelope, who always acts on intuition, Lina, with her constant psychotropic-Giaconda and Cheshire-Cat-always-traipsing-through-the-branches smile, seems to have all her actions planned out down to the millimeter. Always. And she acts them out tirelessly and with a kind of urgency: as if she were crossing items off a list and tallying notches in her belt. * "Less blah-blah and more do-do" is one of her most recurrent phrases; "the inscription on my coat of arms," she points out. And Penelope enjoys her so much that she doesn't even dare ask herself what Lina is doing there, in Abracadabra, why she hasn't gotten far away from there. And when it occurs to her she immediately puts it out of her mind, as if she were hanging a painting to cover this imperfection of Lina's, as if she were hanging a painting of Lina. And—another difference in their appearance—if Penelope is very pretty, then Lina is beautiful. The difference, though subtle, isn't just noteworthy but also decisive. And it's not that Lina isn't—she is—very physically attractive. But, unlike Penelope, Lina doesn't get stared at. Eyes don't fix—in the beginning and whenever possible, to the point of becoming a kind of satire—themselves to certain, impossible to ignore, parts of her anatomy. Lina is appreciated in her entirety; like how for someone who goes into one of those Renaissance churches with a deceptively simple façade and, looking up from down below, without warning but already an inkling, is a miracle, and in the heights of the cupola . . . * Looking down at her, seeing a * tattoo on her left heel, "my footnote," she jokes. Lina—Lina's face—is like too many influences melded together into a single style. A modest Catholic saint with eyes lifted to the heavens whose *pentimento* is unable to conceal the pupils of a pagan goddess, always staring defiantly at anyone who dares look at her. Another miracle, yes. Lina dresses in traditional fabrics and colors in unthinkable combinations, like—according to the latest research—the plumage of the most dangerous dinosaurs. But her features have the sharp edges, Penelope thought and still thinks, of a fallen woman from Biblical times, or something like that, crossed with a feminine Frida Kahlo. A Frida Kahlo without the back problems and the mustache. An authentically fake Frida Kahlo and, really, like a Frida Kahlo played by a beautiful actress, born in the babelish Hollywood hills, just so she could one day play Frida Kahlo and, months after her debut, thank the Academy. Lina is an exotic beauty but of an exoticism that's immediately assimilable (and envied, and desired) by women and men accustomed to the parameters of normality and the ordinary. Even Hiriz, when she discovers Penelope and Lina chitchatting (*definitely* an Hiriz verb) at a table in the clinic bar, can't keep—distinctive and frequent and telltale indication that she perceives something she doesn't like but would like to be or have—her nose from quivering, as if sniffing, and the scars of her latest plastic surgery become more pronounced in a Botox furrowing of her brow, resulting from a pain similar to those brief yet intense migraines caused by an oversized bite of ice cream. Penelope had seen similar symptoms in a few sharp-nosed habitués of Psycholabis, sniffing out, when they've got nothing left in their pockets, who has drugs, who can slip them something to insert in some orifice. A kind of ecstatic agony, much like athletic discipline and Zen exercise and divinatory art. In Hiriz, all of that too; but not in the service of a controlled substance, rather due to an out-of-control addiction to herself. And the need to believe—with the ravenous desperation of someone committed to an odious diet—that everyone loves her and wants her, because before and after her there isn't, nor could there have been nor will there ever be, anything better. Hiriz needs to believe that there's no purer or better heroine than her, and that meeting her has to be the closest thing to loving her, and not being able to live without her. Hiriz was raised like this and grew up convinced that it was so. During recesses at school where she reigned like a little, monstrous queen. At the tennis club and on the equestrian field where she pretended to play (with her tanned instructor, Pinto) and rode poorly (a horse she christened Wimbledon); but it doesn't matter when you're gripping the racquet handle and holding the reins tight. In a marriage, as inevitable as it was convenient, as suitable as it was predictable, to Ricky, whom everyone calls Fido, but whom, after a few drinks, and beginning to shimmy around in a strange way, everyone starts to call Lassie. But recently * (the face is the soul's mirror; the face is the mask that the soul puts on every time it has to face itself in the mirror) Hiriz's magic mirror turns away. And doesn't answer to her. And the world has filled up with younger women who, she could swear it, are laughing behind her back because they know *something* she doesn't. Because they grew up more- and better-informed and unlike her, who never talked about sex with her mother, who received all her education in that regard from nuns, and who arrived to her wedding night only equipped with what she'd learned in romantic and not pornographic movies and who, the next morning, sat down with her family feeling a mix of unease and disappointment, wondering how the story would proceed and if it was in fact essential that it continue. Now, every time a Karma girl is born instead of a Karma boy, Hiriz suffers. Hiriz can barely tolerate the sight of the earthly and carnal nymphets that several of her nieces have become. They're laughing at her, she's sure of it, every time she says or does something. Or, even worse, when she gives them some political/strategic advice concerning what clothes to wear and what makeup to put on in order to attract "good candidates" for "matrimonial selection." So, finding Penelope and Lina, together, is a new blow/disgrace for the already staggering Hiriz, more unsteady all the time in the midst of her own earthquake. Renewed evidence that she's lost control. Because, Hiriz assumed, Penelope was hers. Penelope was the living or semi-living inheritance of Maxi. That was the only way she could put up with her and, though not love her exactly, appreciate her as an offering who was obliged to obey her and listen to her and always back her up and admire her and only her. This was not part of the plan. This is not fair. There they are, Penelope and Lina, laughing. And, no doubt, they're laughing at her; because paranoia— like patriotism or that bastardized form of patriotism, politics—is the final refuge of losers and the mediocre. So, that thin karmatic ice that Hiriz always walks on—tiptoeing and trembling, all those hours as a powder puff in childhood ballet for naught—opens under her feet to swallow her, to cover her in darkness and fury and rancor. And—another "childhood episode" of hers—spit her back out like something bitter and embittered; as if Hiriz were one of those tumorific hairballs that cats expel every so often with indolence and satisfaction. And, back in this world, transfigured by her fury and desperation and maliciousness, it's not that Hiriz isn't who she was, rather, now, Hiriz is Hiriz raised to the millionth power. An XXL Hiriz. An Hiriz, half feathered-bad-omen albatross and half tarantula, equally poisonous and poisoned. If Hiriz was a bit scattered and confused by her own delusions before, all of a sudden, she's a complete madwoman, thirsty for vengeance and focused on a single objective. Though to call her "madwoman" is excessive and unfair, not to her but to madness—all madness demands a certain discipline and nobility and creativity. Hers is, merely, dissatisfaction raised to cosmic and chronic heights. A thirst she's been suffering and putting up with for decades—obliged by clan rules and traditions—and that now finds a target and perfect victim in Penelope. The problem is that Hiriz doesn't have the Shakespearean loftiness or inventiveness when it comes to revenge. Her form of evil is banal. An evil more indulged than inherited. The miserable and miserly evil of someone who, walking along a beach, pretends not to notice that they're tromping on sand castles. And it's that Hiriz's courtesan and conspiratorial education has, basically, passed through the degraded and predictable versions of the Isabellian dramas of tabloid magazines and telenovelas. * And, since she was little, Hiriz has brainwashed herself with the subliminal dictum and the barely unconscious intuition that the true protagonist and brightest star—far above any mass-produced and dull romantic couple—is none other than the telenovela's "bad girl." Best of all to be the bad girl. So Hiriz's idea of vendetta barely has any effect on Penelope at all. Because what Hiriz chooses as a form of vindication and punishment (it tends to happen: the righteous choose punishments for others that they themselves would find terrible, and more often than not the others are, simply, too busy worrying about something else) is to choose and modify for Penelope the most hideous wedding dress ever seen. And there goes Penelope, as if wrapped in morphine cotton swabs, stuck inside a wedding dress that looks more like a wedding cake. And as she walks down the aisle, in her wake, in the corners, the standard rabid flirtation of those who know themselves restrained Monday through Friday and on Sunday, too. And who, during Saturday celebrations, loosen up just a little, just enough, to what would certainly be considered trangressive in weighty Victorian novels. And there they are: childish pageboys too closely resembling court dwarves; honorable women playing at being dishonorable women for a few hours, expressions clouded by the alcohol and too-tight dresses impeding the flow of oxygen to their brains; hysteria among the wisterias; fragments and anecdotes that are never complete but that, nonetheless, will be discussed in whispers for years to come and completed in accordance with the degree of imagination and malice and sickness of whoever is telling them. But, there, Penelope could care less. In fact—in terms of her reflexive and automatic narrative sense—it seems right and appropriate to her. Before, Penelope was locked in the bathroom for an hour. Nausea and dizziness and a whiskey double. And there she goes, moving down an interminable aisle of Karmas. And there, at the end, Max waits for her, comatose, strapped to a vertical stretcher. And, on the other side of the altar, a plethora of priests. Five or six, one for each congregation. Penelope has heard them debate the unsurpassable virtues of each of their "teams" more than once, as if they were soccer clubs. And in recent days, Penelope has been a sideline witness to tiresome discussions regarding who would be the one to officiate the act in question. Finally, Solomon-like, Mamagrandma decided to cut the event into several pieces and divide them up. So, for Penelope, the ritual acquired an air of that "We Are the World" video clip in which each person sings their own part trying to surpass in delivery and emotion the people who went before and come after. And Penelope bites her lip to keep from laughing when she discovers Lina, climbing in the highest branches of a hundred year old tree, like a bright-colored paparazzo, taking pictures and filming her for her brother, damn him. And Penelope tries to concentrate on what each priest is saying in sibylline and apparently pious voices. But no, nothing will be revealed. The way nothing, religiously, is explained now by a band of priests who are preparing to bless this holy union never to be broken, in sickness and in health, until death does them part. And, yes, these are the same people whom, after a few too many drinks, Penelope has heard laugh uncontrollably, competing over which of them "did better" and "had better ideas" in their brief stints as missionaries in aboriginal jungles. "I memorized the routes and schedules of the planes that flew over the village and predicted when God would pass over their heads again," one said. "And I gave them small portable radios and told them that God would speak and sing to them from there inside and, of course, when the batteries ran out, they had to come to the church to get them and ask for them on their knees and pray for them," another said. And now they were there, all together: Bob and Bruce and Michael and Ray and Stevie. They are the world. Or, at least, they are the spiritual leaders of Abracadabra and of the Karmas, who watch it all with a mix of beatitude and calculation. They're priests, but they don't seem to be true believers, thinks Penelope. There are five of them and they seem, always, to move around as if connected by an invisible cord. Might they be secret brothers? Might they have once been bank robbers à la the Dalton Gang? Penelope, then, thinks so much that she doesn't know what to think and remembers having seen them enter and exit a small cabin with stained glass devotionals in the windows—almost one of those giant dollhouses for rich girls—on the edge of Mount Karma. Five priests executing strange and complex and agile choreographies under the moon or sucking in helium from balloons and then rehearsing, between giggles, castrati Bee Gees harmonies. Penelope—who'd be much less frightened to discover them carrying inverted crucifixes covered in the blood of virgins and wearing masks of billy goats—suspects that they are laughing at everything and everyone. And that terrible day is drawing nigh when they'll break the Shakespearean spell that keeps them soft and invertebrate creatures, fragile gelatinous deep-sea fish, feeding off the crumbs of confessions, and recover their authentic nature as conspiratorial Richelieus. And then, with the fury of hunchbacks storming down from bell towers, they'll run through entire audiences with axes and knives. Maybe, Penelope almost wishes, right now, why not, right?, as she advances toward the altar and toward a Maxi plugged into machines whose little noises turn the triumphal nuptial march into something softly ambient. But no: nothing ends and everything continues and the "upper class" weddings in Abracadabra conceal, barely, the backdrop of an Olympic discipline that's lived Saturday to Saturday, where everyone battles for the gold and the silver and the bronze. So there they all are, the perpetual guests, same as always, waiting for the conclusion of this liturgical and excessively long part where they're merely extras or supporting actors and for the start of the long period where they get to be stars, dancing or drinking or rolling down the stairs to then bounce up like a spring and begin to sing or vomit alcoholic speeches, wrapping their arms around the first person to come in reach. Now—organized by Hiriz, who presents them from the microphone with that directorial and solemn attitude of people unaccustomed to microphones but who, subsequently, discover the renewed pleasure of giving orders and asking for attention at full volume, beginning with a "Yes . . . yes . . . yes . . . one . . . two . . . three . . ."—a choir of little Karmas butchers the "Ave Maria." Hiriz tends to approach these artistic productions of hers with enviable and frightening euphoria, but their results—just like with her business ventures—leave much to be desired. It's not like the Karmas are visionary entrepreneurs. To the contrary, generation after generation languish comfortably on a soft cushion—geese on top of goose down—of family businesses that pretty much function by inertia and monopoly. So, what the Karmas do is to work, more or less, what Monopoly is to doing business—a game, a hobby, a passing activity with no timetable, a sport of minimal physical and mental requirement whose principal preoccupation is redesigning business cards and stationary for positions that they don't and won't ever occupy. (Penelope could swear that a Karma man once gave her a card where, under the name in gold relief, was written "Gotham City Commissioner," but maybe she was drunk.) And the greatest aspiration and achievement for these professional non-executives, on a financial level, would be a currency of their own with an internal circulation that, of course, would be called The Karma. * And, yes, they talk a lot among themselves about money, and about the global economy, and about futures markets; but Penelope—despite encountering advertisements on almost every corner with the imperial K of the Karmas and the slogan "We Are Everywhere"—never manages to fully understand what it is they do, what they produce and sell. And when she asked Hiriz about it, all she got were vagaries; but expressed with a rare and almost theatrical eloquence, as if Hiriz were addressing, with a mix of sarcasm and protocol, a fledgling ambassador setting off on his first foreign assignment. For once, Penelope thought then, Hiriz seemed well-spoken, well-written: "The thing we manufacture is a very small thing . . . But we do it much better than anyone else. We nearly have a monopoly on its production and . . . It's not that it's something inappropriate or embarrassing. In fact, we refer to it constantly, with familiarity and cheekiness, almost. And yet it's still a small and trivial thing, almost ridiculous in terms of domestic applications . . . It's something . . . how to put it . . . Kind of banal." Shoe polish? Clothes-pins? Some bathroom equipment to sit down on to think and purge the thoughts you never have anywhere else? Toothbrushes? And then Hiriz changes the subject, the way a radio in a moving car changes stations on its own, and starts talking again about her "projects" which are "far more interesting." But it's been said before and will be said again: what happens when Hiriz tries to actually do anything is something else entirely. Everything is possible, anything can happen such that, in the end, nothing happens except a substantial quantity of money is always wast-ed—millions of Karmas—and written off on taxes as charitable donations. And so the apocalypse always comes too close and too soon on the heels of the genesis of any of her projects. From there, even in light of the Karmas' particular apathy, there's always a certain expectation when it comes to one of Hiriz's undertakings; knowing that, sooner or later, it will end up a topic of conversation, an anecdote with background laughter; because if there's some-thing the Karmas like, it's laughing, especially laughing at others when they're not present; so, at the massive family gatherings, all of them try to put off going home as long as they can so that as few people as possible will be left laughing behind their backs. In this sense, they appreciate Hiriz for her "creativity," such a perfect fertilizer for mockery. And yet, to tell the truth, they all laugh at Hiriz because they all fear Hiriz and what Hiriz might end up becoming when two or three Karmas of the previous generation die off and they end up decoding a series of last wills that make her, mysteriously, all-powerful, when Mamagrandma dismounts Horse for good. But these things go unsaid, barely thought (who would even dare to imagine that Mamagrandma could have an expiration date?) and, meanwhile and in the meantime, while they can, they laugh at Hiriz, slightly nervous, the future is overrated, a third act that never comes. And they still recall Hiriz's show—written, produced, directed, and starring her—that she called "a Catholic version of *The Diary of Anne Frank.*" One afternoon Penelope watched, unable to believe her eyes and ears, an old video of the thing. In that particular approximation of the classic, the character of Hiriz is—she tells Penelope before giving her the VHS as if it were a relic—a little Catholic friend from Anne's school, Yvonne, who has "the bad luck of going to visit her just when the Nazis come . . . The poor girl is captured and as they're taking her she whimpers, 'Ye art mistaken . . . I am like you. This is a mistake. The one you seek is upstairs, listen to the sounds they're making.' The Nazis go up and find Anne and her family. But they don't pay attention to the poor and unfortunate Yvonne . . . And they take her, too . . . And I still get upset remembering it." To Penelope that unexpected "ye art"—understood by Hiriz as a mark of quality and prestige—makes her shudder. And, now, with the "Ave Maria," Hiriz has made and unmade Schubert just like she did then to the great little Jewish martyr. Devout shrieks trying, in vain, to ascend to the heights. All the Karmas, of course, smile, thinking of any other thing and once again Penelope admires and envies this tribe's capacity for abstraction; an ability to be but not to be that surpasses even that of the comatose Maximiliano. Penelope, on the other hand, cannot. None of it passes her by. Penelope sees and hears *everything*. Penelope feels that she's floating, that she's taking off, that it's all like in a movie, and then—at the climax—comes the fleeting moment of the flashback, like one of the few cards in a board game that grants you brief sanctuary. * Maybe not to rearrange, but to explain everything that came before in one long memory invoked while Penelope advances toward her "I do"? To point out that, in the moment of your wedding, not your whole life, but everything that led you to that wedding, to that other *petit mort*, passes before your closed eyes? Or is it too late for such sophistry and explication of this chaos? Penelope soars and, so as not to fall from the clouds of this undefined present, Penelope clings to the solid ground of her immediate past. Soon, in front of everyone, Hiriz and Ricky will dance an approximation of the mambo that they took classes for at some point. Ricky, supposedly—there's an absolute Karmatic consensus on this, but, as tends to happen to her, Penelope can't tell if the Karmas are mocking or celebrating, because often it's both things at the same time—is "a master of tropical dances." And there, on the dance floor, is the only place where Hiriz allows him to play at being the macho man who carries the rhythm and leads the steps, circling around him with the sort of post-coital peevishness of someone who has made too much noise faking her orgasm. But Penelope has already seen Ricky do his thing at multiple weddings, and the truth is that his art is very disconcerting. Ricky—without sacrificing a certain languid Nereidic air—*mambas* like someone blighted by the evil of San Vito suffering a heart attack during the "*de pelicula*" version of the great San Francisco earthquake. * In other words: an earthquake that lasts not seconds, but many minutes, to show off its next-generation special effects, so the victims can do a lot of running. And it's not the historical San Francisco earthquake, but the coming and ultimate and final earthquake; an earthquake that he, Penelope's brother, now of the atmosphere, is capable of provoking with a snap of invisible fingers, if he so desired, mobilizing tectonic plates as if to make them dance a far superior but equally catastrophic dance as Ricky's. Finishing her studied choreography *à deux*, Hiriz always comes over to Penelope, exaggeratedly out of breath, to explain: "I had to take classes to be at Ricky's level and so I could dance with him. Because it was risky to let him loose and at the mercy of women who also dance. As you know, Ricky would be a prized catch for any woman." And Penelope trembles. Penelope—she realizes it all of a sudden—has been victim of a different earthquake, for months now. Penelope is its epicenter. Penelope can't stop trembling. And she always wonders, studying her, if Hiriz is completely crazy or, maybe, completely happy. If she might have managed to put aside all collective reality, leaving it far behind in order to throw herself into the arms of a private irreality, a much more gratifying and powerful experience than any drug or religion can offer or provide. So now Penelope travels back in time, trying not to lose her footing. It's easy to stumble when remembering, yes; but looking back produces less vertigo than looking at the present moment, which seems to stretch out like a carpet of virtually identical days that'll only be survived, as if in an attempt to differentiate them, by playing the game of the oh so elusive seven differences. Because the differences are slight: grapefruit instead of orange for breakfast, sometimes it rains a little, things like that. The rest—and weddings are understood here as a kind of gift, a wedding gift, yes, but also a welcome/farewell gift, that special day for each and every bride, even though all the weddings are virtually identical—will be an accumulation of hours and decades that all seem to last the exact same amount of time. For the Karmas, as mentioned, time is not only relative; time is, also, irrelevant. The Karmas have no sense of time because they consider time to be a complete non sequitur (something that, in addition, has the bad manners of showing up without calling ahead or imposing conditions without asking first) except when it comes to celebrating birthdays, anniversaries, and saints. So, for them, time is something that's turned on and off at will. Like electric lights or sexual desire. And turned on and electrified, remembering it almost immediately but as if already protected by a varnish of the mythic, Penelope, a few steps from the altar, evokes her first days with Lina. Penelope remembers laughing, laughing and that with Lina she can't stop laughing, and that Lina tells her "It's my fault. I can't help but say funny things, even though I'm a stand-up tragedian and not a stand-up comedian." Lina tells Penelope that she doesn't know when she was born, that she was deposited in a doorway, that she's adopted, and that, because of this, "I read the entire horoscope section every day and pick the sign and prognosis for the next twenty-four hours that best suits me." Lina is, also, a sensitive soul, but sensitive in her own unmistakable and singular way, between poet and freak. Example: in a science-fiction movie, when many spectators see that the actor playing an extraterrestrial has forgotten to remove the watch from his wrist and criticize it as an unredeemable defect, Lina prefers to believe that the extraterrestrial "took the watch from our planet on a previous visit, because he really liked it, and that he enjoys using it and knowing what time it is while he's here, right?" Lina explains to Penelope that her adoptive family is Jewish. The Libermans. And that the Jews of Abracadabra are even more conservative than the Catholics of Abracadabra: "It's forbidden to tweet on the Sabbath, and they're not allowed to drive Volkswagens, drink Fanta, or wear Puma or Adidas sneakers, because they're all considered Nazi inventions." And Lina listens with a smile to Penelope's familial blues and explains to her that, "in Abracadabra, the seven capital sins multiply into seven million provincial sins." Lina swears to an increasingly paranoid Penelope that her family has no relation to the Karmas, at least in the last five generations, but that "I, being adopted, can't make any promises: who knows, I might be a secret and compromising Karma, discarded as far away as possible; in other words: a Jewified Karma, something like that. Best disguise ever. They'll never find me." Lina, also, knew Max in high school. They studied together and Max asked her out more than once, but—preexisting condition, Maxi was not yet Max—he had to introduce her to his parents and Mamagrandma.

Lina chose to pass up the opportunity. She had enough in her life with the Orthodox Libermans to not want to add the fervent Karmas. "But I can understand why Maximiliano was attracted to you. Obviously you remind him of me. And that he couldn't conquer me," Lina tells Penelope, very seriously. Penelope regards her in a disconcerting silence. Then Lina bursts out laughing. It's a horrible laugh that sounds like "Huahuahua" and seems to burst out of someone else entirely, someone who is, maybe, perfectly unaware of her beauty. And, as such, she—maybe as a self-defense mechanism, or to protect those she encounters from a brilliance that makes them lose orientation and crash into a wall with a smile—permits herself the humble gesture of letting herself be imperfect. A laugh—Penelope realizes—that's fake and exaggerated and is Lina's way of being human. Lina's laugh is the mole that makes her unforgettable and, yes, Penelope will end up sleeping with her, once, out of love, out of sympathy, because it'd been eons since she'd had any sexual activity (since that one night that lasted several days when several of Max's transistors melted together beyond all repair), because Lina is not a Karma. And because the first time Penelope saw her naked—she who'd never felt anything resembling a sapphic longing, not even riding the alkaloid crest of the whitest night—she remembered the words of a writer she read once and whose name now escaped her: "I want to rip her arm off. I want to sleep in her uterus with my foot hanging out." And no, just in case, better to be clear: the quote does not belong to William Faulkner; but it does belong to one of his bastard yet legitimate progeny. One of the best and most pure-blood and purebred of all. One of those writers of the American south, flinging sentences like Molotov cocktails concocted with one third gasoline, one third swamp water, and one third all the sweat that Penelope and Lina left on those sheets that afterward they twisted and rang out without their laughter ever ceasing. And Lina has two personalities, two lives. In the morning she manages a jewelry store that belonged to her mother. The place was, provincially and familiarly, referred to as "La Señora de los Anillos," and it specializes in wedding rings. Lina decided to take a spin running it and renamed the place "The Lady of the Rings," and now it offers rings of elven and druidic and gothic persuasion. Rings ideal for weddings that sooner or later end in swords and sorcery because, as Lina says, "married life is nothing but a very complicated game of role-playing, right?" When the workday is over, Lina mutates, transforming into the princess of local counterculture. Every night, she puts on her show in an unequivocally and decidedly *bohemian* café in the center of the city. There, Lina dramatizes and soliloquizes the life and death of Joan Vollmer, the unfortunate wife of William S. Burroughs who took a bullet fired by the *Naked Lunch* author to her temple while playing a game of William Tell. That night, after finishing her hospital-recreational duties, on the pretext of a headache, Penelope escapes from Mount Karma and arrives at the bar Carpe Noctum. Lina has put her name on the list and Penelope is greeted by the bar owners. Two foreigners—one skinny and sad and the other massive and expansively happy—whose nationalities appear to have faded away like those passports with worn out covers and pages that won't fit even one more stamp. Professional foreigners. "They look like first rate B-roll actors at the premiere of *Casablanca*," Penelope thinks as the short one leads her to a table and the giant serves her a tall glass filled to the brim with rum while all the while the jukebox plays some kind of pop supplication, something that talks about intermittencies of the heart, something like that. On the stage, with a red hole in the side of her head, Lina is sitting in front of a TV that broadcasts nothing. Lina is Joan Vollmer, sitting in front of a TV, broadcasting her death and life from the depths of the pre-Columbian netherworld. In the body and voice of Lina, Joan Vollmer is hating on the beatniks and refusing to resign herself to be a minor member in the body of the beat. * And right away he gets it: Lina—who, unlike Hiriz, is a masterful performer of herself, someone you never really get tired of watching; because it turns out to be impossible to totally believe her, because you can never really trust your eyes and ears—is not a great actress. All her charm—of which, granted, there is a great deal—passes exclusively through her, through her persona. But—after only a few seconds of starting to watch the digital performance that comes to him via Penelope, he gets it—Lina isn't doing justice to the person that Joan Vollmer was and the character that she could be. Joan Vollmer as a sort of Megamix, where parts of Penelope and parts of Hiriz and parts of Lina mix together: the fury of the centuries, the eternal dissatisfaction, the artistic temperament that's nothing but a single, unrelenting bad mood, functioning as a kind of tormented manifesto of aesthetics and ethics. Joan Vollmer as the universal woman (this really *does* seem to him to be Lina's great idea, an idea that he'll guiltlessly rob) and goddess of the afterlife watching over everything, her face illuminated by the cold phosphorescence of a screen that tunes in a single channel, broadcast from a celestial and ancient and circular hell. Joan Vollmer—eighteen years old, subtle but nice curves, heart-shaped face, upturned nose, the first among her friends to use a diaphragm, married to a certain Paul Adams, and yet free and impossible to pin down—jumping from hotel to hotel and from bed to bed. New York in the early forties. Sharing an apartment with Edie Parker, girlfriend and first wife of Jack Kerouac. "You have to cook eggs over a low flame," Joan Vollmer repeats time and again, that being the extent of her domestic wisdom. "And you have to be very careful to make sure the flame stays lit," she adds. But Joan Vollmer is like one of those uncontrollable forest fires visiting a big city. Insatiable. Joan Vollmer is the fire and the wind. And she drives her professors mad with unanswerable questions in the Barnard classrooms and writes things in the margins of her copy of *Das Capital* like "Maybe Marxism is dynamic and optimistic and Freudianism is not. Is one more useful than the other? Why do you always have to choose this or that?" Every week, Joan Vollmer buys *The New Yorker* and reads it from cover to cover. She clips out her favorite cartoon from its pages and carries it with her, inside her purse alongside a few folded bills: it's the drawing of a disconsolate man who says, "My mother loved me, but she died." And Joan Vollmer's laugh makes almost everyone laugh. But almost everything that makes her laugh isn't funny to anyone else, she complains with a mixture of bewilderment and pride. More pride than bewilderment as she repeats to herself, in the most vertiginous and lofty of low voices: "Nothing is foreign to me. Everything is mine and for me. I am Alpha and Omega." Joan Vollmer who doesn't hear so much as see classical music while discussing Plato or Kant or while reading Proust, for hours, in an increasingly arctic bath. Joan Vollmer, who discovers she's pregnant and drives herself mad (they find her walking through the dirty rain of Times Square, talking to herself, playing with her hair), and they take her to Bellevue Psychiatric Hospital and she gives birth to a little girl who is quickly sent off to live with her grandparents, a girl who might later say, "My mother loved me, but she died . . . ha . . . ha . . . ha . . ." Although it'll be a while (but not that long, really) until then and right now Joan Vollmer is more alive all the time and takes an underage lover whom she instructs and trains and educates and makes get good grades. But Joan Vollmer—undisciplined and untrustworthy when it comes to putting birth control methods into practice, several abortions—decides that what she needs now is a unique man, a real man. Is William S. Burroughs "a real man" or is he "a unique man"? Is he a capitalist or a Freudian? William S. Burroughs is William S. Burroughs. William S. Burroughs begins and ends in himself, like her, and he moves around the rooms of the flat on 119th Street with the slowness of a fragile pharaoh or the speed of an indestructible extraterrestrial. William S. Burroughs is older than all the others and he knows how to use chopsticks in a Chinese restaurant and gets good tables in the Russian Tea Room when they get those irrepressible and amphetaminic urges to eat borscht. William S. Burroughs is able to invent stories on the spot that are impossible yet plausible in their details—like when he says "I flew for Franco during the Spanish Civil War"—and it's Joan Vollmer who pays his bail when, April 1946, he's incarcerated for the consumption of drugs and the falsification of prescriptions. It's also Joan Vollmer who scores him a little heroin when William S. Burroughs—fallen pharaoh, lost extraterrestrial—comes out of the cell shivering, in the grips of an abstinence syndrome that's not at all an enjoyable experience, because "to abstain" is a verb that never has and never will interest him. And, almost immediately thereafter, it's William S. Burroughs who rescues Joan Vollmer from a new stay in Bellevue and from then on they're inseparable. William S. Burroughs likes to say—with the voice of a gangster—"My old lady this . . ." and "My old lady that . . ." And, like him, Joan Vollmer is also interested in drugs and the Mayan codices in the Museum of Natural History where, walking room to room, they receive the blessing of gods with names made up of more consonants than vowels, and then take off for Texas. The idea, the plan, is to find a cheap and isolated farm and to plant and harvest and sell marijuana. There, Joan Vollmer discovers that she is pregnant and asks William S. Burroughs if he wants her to have an abortion. "No way: abortion is murder," responds William S. Burroughs. Neither of them, it's fair to surmise, is built for outdoor labor. The only one who seems happy there—amid the cyclones and oil drilling towers and the big, long automobiles with horns mounted on their hoods—is little William S. Burroughs Jr., also known as "The Little Beast," who runs among the plants, fleeing his own shadow while his parents look at him the way you look at a cloud: asking yourself what shape it has, what it reminds you of, if it brings rain, or if it will be broken up by the sun, and perhaps already suspecting his tragic and cursed fate; because there's no way he could have exited William S. Burroughs, entered into Joan Vollmer, exited Joan Vollmer, and turned out fine and with good handwriting. "Bill should be writing instead of going around here with a shovel on his shoulder," Joan Vollmer wrote to Allen Ginsberg. And nothing turns out fine; soon they are considered *personas non grata* by the farmers, and in 1948 they take off for New Orleans and buy a house with what they got for the farm. Joan Vollmer finds pharmacists willing to sell her Benzedrine inhalers, William S. Burroughs fantasizes about cultivating out-of-season vegetables or cotton, or something like that. But, again, planting isn't his thing. And his friends start to sell their manuscripts to publishers hungry for the new flavor, manuscripts that he edited and helped them write. And what's this nonsense about the Beat Generation that he starts to read (or maybe he dreams and is delirious, maybe they are anticipatory and paranoid visions, leaning on the bar in a Colonia Roma cantina, like a roaring gladiator surrounded by armored lions) in newspaper clippings that they send him from the U.S.A. If anything is certain it's that he belongs nowhere. He was born alone and he'll die alone; but solitude is not a simple thing. Where is your work? How to catch it? Where did they—the policemen who enter his house and find marijuana and heroin and various guns and take him to the second city precinct and behind bars again and on to a hospital, in custody, detox—come from? William S. Burroughs, shackled and howling, sees spheres in the air that remind him of pre-Columbian calendars and he decides that the answer to all his questions is, *must be*, in Mexico. From now on—ignoring the future summons of multiple judges—he'll be a professional fugitive separated from the U.S.A, a loose piece and expat, a perpetual motion machine, an invisible man who—with his family—crosses the border in September of 1949. The Mexico City sky is immense and of a blue ideal for eagles to dance with serpents in their beaks. Under their wings, millions of inhabitants move incessantly from here to there, like random scenes of a movie waiting, in vain, to be edited, for someone to give it some coherence, some storyline. Here comes the Satanist and volcanic Aleister Crowley to scale Popocatépetl and Iztaccíhuatl and in so doing attain the 36th Masonic order. There, somewhere nearby, returning from its new home, a golden angel alights atop a column and William S. Burroughs watches it without closing his eyes, so as to miss nothing, from the balcony of an apartment at 37 Cerrada or Medellín. Or was it 210 Paseo de la Reforma? It doesn't matter. My house, your house, William S. Burroughs is in his house. The whole city like a sprawling mansion overflowing with bedrooms, limitless, a mixture of past and future where, at sunset, pistols sing with the sweet voice of lead and silver. For William S. Burroughs, Mexico is like the Old West. The maximum sentence for riddling someone with bullets is eight years; but cantina gunfights abound where, in the end, the dead are the only ones condemned. "This city has the highest rate of violent deaths in the whole world. And when a Mexican kills someone it's usually his best friend—friends are more frightening than strangers. And the good thing about killing a friend is that afterward you can cry for him and get drunk in his memory," someone explains to them with the diction of a tour guide. Concluding: "No Mexican really knows another Mexican." And this last bit seems perfect to William S. Burroughs because nobody will complain about not knowing him, about not knowing what's going on inside his head without first understanding that William S. Burroughs is quiet so as not to frighten: his visions are of a dangerous caliber and he always aims and fires at the blackest of targets. In Mexico, William S. Burroughs feels for the first time that he has finally found the place where nobody is interested in or worried about banning William S. Burroughs. Everything goes, going is everything, and I couldn't care less, my children. And no one cares that you go around stoned up to your eyebrows or full of firewater. Nor do they care if you frequent gay bars like El Chimu and come out with an adolescent on each arm, heading for the first alley in a neighborhood that is like an aristocratic landscape fallen into disgrace. Two dollars a day is more than enough to sate appetites and thirst and vices. And, granted, it's not so easy for Joan Vollmer to acquire Benzedrine inhalers; but she gets her fix from thyroid pills and getting drunk starting at eight in the morning thanks "to the evil spirits that sell you a quarter liter of tequila for barely forty cents." The dealers in the place—names like Dave Tercerero (or was it actually David Tesorero, and William S. Burroughs and Joan Vollmer listen poorly and transcribe worse?), or the colossal Lola La Chata—round out their earnings selling fake silver crucifixes, and pharmacists sell you morphine with gold-toothed smiles. William S. Burroughs and Joan Vollmer are blasted all the time and there's not a lot of time or desire left over for sex. Which doesn't worry William S. Burroughs but bothers Joan Vollmer, who can't handle her partner's Taoist chemical reclusion and yells at him that, please, they should at least go out and walk their ruined selves through the ruins near Plaza Mayor. Joan Vollmer escapes to Cuernavaca and William S. Burroughs accompanies Dave Tercerero on his annual pilgrimage to the church of Nuestra Señora de Calma, patron saint of thieves and traffickers, in the eternal and unfathomable outskirts of the city. They walk almost eighty kilometers in two days and enter the basilica surrounded by beggars and cripples, crutches in the air and one-wheeled wheelchairs and, there, Dave Tercerero takes the opportunity to conduct some business while William S. Burroughs feels more depressed with each offering he hears made and each prayer he witnesses. What do all these people believe in? How can they believe in a virgin who made water flow from the earth? How can there be so many virgins, all of them the same, yet different, sprouting up between the rocks, like mushrooms more hallucinated than hallucinogenic, cradling the bloody bodies of their sons, crowns of cactus thorns on their heads, eyes rolling to the heavens as if struck by the always demanding and yet impossible to define will of our Father, as if already anticipating his imminent flight with no return trip or landing? When he gets home, his prayers have been heard: Joan Vollmer has come back as if nothing had happened. She has come to understand that they are parts of a single gestational organism and, as proof, she demonstrates it to everyone who visits them—North American students from Mexico City College, Jack Kerouac and Neal Cassady—by performing an exercise: Joan Vollmer and William S. Burroughs split apart, each with a pencil and two sheets of paper divided into nine squares; they take position on opposite sides of the room, they draw inside the squares, and more than half of the images turn out the same. One day, they think, they'll attain the communion of absolute similitude and will be one, the transformation will be complete and they'll be called Joan William Vollmer Burroughs, Jr. But everything passes: William S. Burroughs, according to descriptions of those who see him, looks more like a scorpion all the time, a desiccated scorpion. And he has paranoid dreams where he gets in gunfights with policemen dressed as mariachis, and wakes up and goes out wandering aimlessly only to wake up the next morning in a hotel. And then he goes out again to keep drinking and before long you know when William S. Burroughs is nearby because of the odor of urine from the uremia dancing in his intestines. He can smell himself as he writes about how he smells, about what comes out of his body, about what he puts in his body. As if it were a circuit, a short circuit. And money gets scarce and everything tastes like tortillas because they're only making enough to buy tortillas, which they cover and fill and wrap around whatever they can, with whatever there is and whatever's leftover, and now William S. Burroughs dreams that, possessed by a "troglodyte gluttony," he eats William S. Burroughs Tortillas that are sold in kiosks, "one after another, on the sidewalk, gorging himself, overflowing with enchiladas and sopes, carnitas, horrendous pastries, soft candies, fly-covered breads, a Chinese coffee, fried fish, chorizos . . . is there really someone who ingests all that junk?" William S. Burroughs chews words and spits out letters to his distant fellow travelers where they read things like, "Mexico is not simple or bucolic. Mexico is basically an Oriental culture that reflects two thousand years of disease and poverty and degradation and stupidity and slavery and brutality and psychic and physical terrorism. It's sinister and gloomy and chaotic, with the special chaos of a dream. It's my home and I love it." And William S. Burroughs loves the apartment they move to. 210 Orizaba. And it's there that he starts to write in earnest, for real. *Junky.* Memories of a dope fiend that he invokes while sticking himself with full syringes. Language is a virus that he injects into his vein and William S. Burroughs eats virtually raw meat and kicks cats and spends his time at a table at Bounty (could it be a young Mamagrandma there, leaning on the bar, who invites William S. Burroughs to hold her revolver, a skull stamped in the silver of the stock?), a bar where they serve food starting at sunrise in order to be able to respect the law of only serving alcohol with food. The food is bad and the alcohol alcoholic. Vodka or tequila or gin is what William S. Burroughs drinks. He likes transparent liquids and Burroughs quits the drugs but moves on to full bottles. And empty tortillas. And on Thursday, September 6th of 1951, William S. Burroughs—after fantasizing out loud about a new escape to the South, where he'd live off his marksmanship and by hunting wild animals—pulls out a Star .380 and announces to the assembly that "it's time to perform our act of William Tell, we're going to prove to the boys what a good shot I am." Joan Vollmer smiles a twisted smile and puts an empty glass on top of her head. Later William S. Burroughs will say that he doesn't know what happened or why he did it. He'll remember having been possessed by an "Ugly Spirit." And he'll say that it was Joan Vollmer's death that ended up making him into a writer because it "brought me into contact with the invader, the Ugly Spirit, and maneuvered me into a lifelong struggle, in which I had no choice except to write my way out." Years later, without giving credence to the various eyewitnesses, William S. Burroughs will attempt a banal and innocent explanation—the words of a reverse convert, the need to stop believing the unbelievable but verifiable—to cover himself, as if in a disguise, with the most pedestrian version of what could've happened: a simple and terrible domestic accident, while cleaning the pistol he was considering selling to a friend, a slip, a bang. And William "Billy" S. Burroughs Jr.—who was there too, part of the fatal tableau vivant, who died so young, after having recalled everything in a pair of desperate books, and who would've been so much happier with parents who were less "cool" and if he'd never had anything "interesting" to recall, closer to Mount Karma than to Interzone—will write much later that what his mother put on her head was "an apple or an apricot or a grape or me." But there it is and there it remains—suspended in a wrinkle in space-time—the empty glass, spinning on the floor, beside Joan Vollmer, finally fallen and for once motionless, ready to be interred in grave 1018 A-New in Panteón Americano, on Avenida México-Tacuba and, from there, in 1993, due to lack of payment and maintenance, moved to niche number 82 class R. Blood spilling from her head. From the temple and not the forehead, the way Lina portrays it for artistic and aesthetic affects, because a third blind eye between two eyes that no longer see is better. And one thing is certain, undeniable: you must be very careful of the spirits you invoke for the love of art, the ugly spirits, the malignant spirits always given to poetic justice and tragedy. It's not good to mess with the reality of the dead. Rewriting their reality is like playing with a loaded gun. **And so Penelope doesn't see how a Karma in charge of the event's security (following the instructions of "Señora-Señorita Hiriz") gets ready and takes aim and fires at Lina. Rifle and silencer and—plop— Lina falls from above, camera in hand and camera that falls from that hand to film her final images, like with all war correspondents: Penelope in white beside the vertical stretcher that holds Max, and, then, sky, a few clouds, green leaves and flaming petals, and, finally, dirt marched across by a funereal retinue of ants honoring the recently fallen. And Lina makes almost no noise as she disappears into a huge rosebush. Lina sinks into the flowers and the thorns. And the whole scene is like an old silent movie with a simple and efficient effect. Cut a few meters of celluloid. And stick it back together. And what was there is gone. And Lina is gone. Her body will be quickly and discretely removed by the servants—who take care of the things nobody wants to take care of—and abandoned by the side of some road somewhere.**

And, when it's discovered a few days later, swollen by sun and heat, it'll be written off as just another of the many victims of violence between rival narco gangs in Abracadabra. And, yes, the autopsy will reveal traces of illicit substances floating in Lina's blood; so (the girl was a drug addict and a degenerate and a delinquent, yes) a follow up investigation won't be necessary. And outside all the preceding—what just happened, what and who (the life of Lina, life, Lina) has ended forever so that eternity (the immortal death of Lina), can begin—Penelope arrives to the altar repeating over and over, as if she were praying, in the quietest yet most deafening voice of her thoughts, something she read in a book once. Not her favorite book, *Wuthering Heights*, but in a book very close to it, a direct relative of her favorite book. * "Reader, I married him . . . Reader, I married him . . . Reader, I married him . . . Reader, I . . ." (the first line of chapter thirty-eight / conclusion, Jane Eyre, by Charlotte Brontë, 1847). And standing, facing Max, listening to the things that the priests say, like a relay race, passing one sentence to the next runner to be completed and carried on, Penelope could swear that her past and future husband opens his eyes and looks right at her and shakes his head. Twice. And then smiles the saddest smile she's ever seen. And it's one of those moments. * One of those moments like ice. Like crystal. Frozen skates with glass blades sliding across thin ice, and after months of heavy and solid nothing, everything is suddenly so fragile and breakable and ephemeral. And then something snaps inside Penelope and outside Penelope and, if this were all a movie, it'd be the instant when the ambient sound drops to zero so the volume of the protagonist's thoughts can be turned up. And all Penelope thinks about is running away. And she runs. And, at first, the Karmas watch her run with borderline delight, smiling; because she reminds them (though they *never* remember the name of the actress) of one of those stupid comedies—with fireballs and flaming meteorites and other various and sundry special effects—they go see in the cinema when there's nothing playing that's worth seeing. Movies that, every so often, provide spectators and guests (scandalized yet not too scandalized, because it's a comedy, and besides it's understood that everything will turn out fine and that the lack of resolution will end up consuming itself) with the vision of a runaway bride, fleeing her own wedding, taking off at full speed with her white dress lifted and held up over her knees by hands wrapped in delicate lace and silk, the complex hairdo falling harmoniously, the veil detaching from the headband that holds it and, suspended for a few seconds in the midday air, the bouquet being launched in any direction and caught by an old lady or a little girl. By some non-Karma from whom they immediately snatch the bouquet and stomp it to nothing. There Penelope goes. A bride, unbridling herself in front of everyone. Dismantling herself like a Cinderella at 12:01, but during the day, not the night, and not inside a carriage about to become a pumpkin, but in front of all the guests at the great ball and with a prince who can no longer pursue or desire her. How funny, how fun, how instantly anecdotal and, yes, another ideal reason and perfect excuse to once again talk (badly) about the good Penelope. And knowing that everyone is laughing because they think it's a joke. "That crazy Penelope." And so, with their phones, they capture Penelope running away, as if in the fastest slow motion. And nobody dares do anything, because doing something would mean having to stop recording. **And, almost to the edge of the garden, Penelope makes the closest thing to a gesture of affection, of immediate nostalgia. Penelope stops and turns and fishes out her mobile phone (which is slipped up under her white nuptial garter) and frames the shot (it isn't easy, they are so many) and takes the picture. And they remain there, fixed, like fossils of glass and metal, on the small display—all the Karmas. Together, buzzing like a hive of forever-vacationing bees, pretending they're posing for one of those court painters who won't pass up the opportunity to slip a hidden and coded message of contempt for his employers into a corner of the canvas, or conceal it among coins and medals.** * Penelope, with the years—and like in that troubling dream where a woman without a name of her own, sheltered only by her married name, returns to Manderley—will turn on that permanent snapshot, far away, in the house on the beach by the forest (here he sees her, reads her); and she'll ask herself what might've become of them and then answer herself: "Nothing. Same as always. Just the novelties of births and deaths, some replacing others, and that's it, and maybe one of them, one of those horny adolescent nephews from back then, once in a great while, will wonder, as if looking at a mirage, if I was real and where I might be now." But at the time nobody goes after her. They're unready to act confronted by the unexpected and, when something like this happens (Penelope in flight, smaller all the time on the horizon, taking on the liquid texture of a mirage, veil and dress swirling in the wind, making her look like a plume of smoke ascending vertically to the heavens), the Karmas prefer not to act, expecting that everything will get back on track, like so many other times. To intervene would be to involve yourself and, the horror, even be considered complicit. So, better to live and let live and look the other way, while Penelope can only look ahead. Soon she crosses the border of Mount Karma and only a few times has she experienced geographically such a stark sensation of an end—the green gives way to desert in a matter of centimeters and the power of the sun increases overhead and everything spins. * And, maybe, this is where a description of that new and empty landscape that opens and closes over Penelope (who finds herself playing with the idea of going back, but who, she realizes, has lost all sense of direction) would fit well. But he—among the clouds, in a place where there are no more editors or suggestions—prefers to make use of the comfortable device, which he so admired in other writers, in other places—of the ellipsis: in the beginning, that prehistoric bone spinning in a second of millennia into a spaceship and near the end of *Sentimental Education*, when we are told that Frédéric Moreau "traveled" coming to know "the melancholy of the steamboats, the cold of the dawn under the tents, the tedium of landscapes and ruins, the bitterness of interrupted friendships." How much time elapsed? What time is it? Answers: enough and no time. Penelope, now, then, is outside of everything and beyond time's reach. In the desert. Where everything is simultaneously near and far. The desert where nothing enters yet everything fits. The desert that T. E. Lawrence liked "because it is clean," but that really is something else. Something different, though the confusion is understandable and even excusable—the desert is something that can't get dirty. The desert is like an immense room that cleans itself unhurriedly and unceasingly. There's no water in the desert, because nobody needs it, except for the fools who dare enter and who will soon be rung out, cleaned, swept under the heavy carpet of sand. And Penelope, playing the fool, is thirsty.

And remembers that she heard somewhere—Discovery Channel? History Channel? National Geographic Channel?—that when there's no water the best thing to do is put a stone in your mouth and suck on it like a candy, to stimulate the production of saliva, to take advantage of your own water before it turns to sweat and evaporates. Penelope looks at the ground and it's such a deserted desert that it doesn't even offer up any pebbles. The ground is a single horizontal plane interrupted, every so often, by a tooth of rock the size only a dinosaur could accommodate. So what Penelope does is bring words to her mouth. Actually, the words are already there, descending in a cascade from brain to tongue, bouncing off the cupola of her palate like the footsteps of the faithful in a friendly cathedral. Words that she always liked, in various languages and from varying times, enough words to end up configuring a language of their own, final, and hers alone (* Psyche, Viento, Book, Huna, Nit, Manitou, Bimbo, Oslo, Jazz, Niet, Manga, Menorah, Pomeriggio, Tedio, Bourbon, Genji, Topo, Fog, Milonga, Sexo, Genesis, Tos, Biji, Dandelion, Coral, Dicen, Madrigal, Amour, Laúd, Opus, Vispera, Dandy, Tul, Mississippi, Satori, Underground, Mann, Scuola, Frappeé, God, Tulpa, Revival, Moorland, Clown, Clone, Stop, Go, Etcetra . . .), the curves of their letters like the curves of their DNA and what're those things called, Penelope wonders. Penelope pointing at one of those balls of straw that roll along, pushed by the wind. Penelope talking to herself: "You know . . . Like the ones that always appear on Main Street in westerns, just before and always on time for the final duel between one gunslinger with a star on his chest and another dressed all in black . . . Here comes another one . . ." * Note: Salsola Pestifer or Salsola Kali or Salsola tragus. In Spanish they bear the none-too attractive name of estepicursor or running or rolling plants, originally from the Eurasian steppes, their restless seeds traveling on boats that leave Russia heading for South Dakota. Plants that overrun and erode the terrain where they wander, absorbing water and taking it with them. A better name, he—who feels somewhat like this himself—thinks, is the name of the family to which all the plant's varieties belong: "diaspora." And, better still, the much more graphic and physical common name: tumbleweed. And Penelope tumbles and rolls and falls and it's already night, dark and perfect. And Penelope is delirious; but it's not the delirium of talking out loud and saying some random thing, it's the delirium of maintaining the most absolute silence. And soon, where before it read "sun" now it reads "moon" and everything has turned silver. High above, but like you could touch it with the tips of your fingers—a strange and immense moon, a moon howling at all the wolves on the planet. A moon that seems to cry out for vengeance at the injustice of being named merely Moon (a common generic name and species, when all her systemic sisters have names or precise acronyms of their own) and for being called on to orbit around a planet that (unlike its fellow planets) doesn't bear the Olympic name of an ancient deity, but, simply, one that indicates its condition as a terrestrial rather than celestial thing. And, yes, it was true: in the desert, the sky is better and more brightly illuminated than in cities, to the point where—astronomical paradox, optical illusion, it's all exactly the same to Penelope—there's very little sky up there at all. Just scant and brief patches of darkness between so many stars, so many—the brilliance of one melts into the brilliance of another, there above none of the stars look dead—that it's as if the constellations have renounced concern with any figurative intent in order to, impassioned and so alive, embrace the most abstract of expressionism. * "My God . . . It's full of stars!" But that's not all, because everything doesn't end there, above. And the sky seems to have spilled over onto the earth and the desert sparkles too. And Penelope wonders if what she is seeing might just be an introduction to death: the prologue not to a white light at the end of a tunnel, but to one on the ground, everywhere her gaze comes to rest, a highway of infinite little white lights that don't lie, that are real. Small stones of light that Penelope, after putting one in her mouth to suck on, gathers in a handful and puts inside her bridal corset and something tells her that they must be diamonds. Diamonds unearthed by the wind that now blows and Penelope thinks of her brother and thinks "Magic Realism! To you and for you, because you always liked it so much." * (And a message for the incredulous who, arriving to this point, will exclaim "Awww . . .": the preceding is not only possible but true and documented. The same thing happened in a mining settlement and German colony, in Africa, on the edge of the Namibian desert, at the beginning of the twentieth century; he can't remember the exact name of the place, but he does remember the views of luxury Bavarian-style mansions abandoned and almost buried by the sand and the voice of the documentary's narrator commenting that it was such a wealthy region that the wind unearthed diamonds and the colonists, in party dress, went out to gather them by the light of the moon.) And Penelope on the ground covered with diamonds puts one in her mouth and sucks on it and it's like sucking on ice that's not cold but, yes, ice. And Penelope laughs soundlessly, thinking that one of her adolescent wishes has come true in that twisted way wishes are granted anywhere but in fairy and genie tales. "I'm going to die a millionaire, but, of course, the idea wasn't to become a millionaire just minutes before dying, ha," Penelope says, as she fills her cleavage and the folds of her dress with diamonds. Her diamonds, unpolished and uncut. Diamonds that still recall—almost with pride and without any guilt— the carbon they once were. * Diamonds Penelope will use to build that house beside a forest and on the beach. The house where she'll live with her brother and He Whose Name Must Not Be Mentioned, please, no matter how bad you want to, okay? Diamonds that don't shine but will shine and are of an almost obscene size and which stick to Penelope's skin, down her neckline, and keep her awake. "I'm going to die with my eyes open," thinks Penelope, who, then, can't believe what she's seeing, what can only be a deoxygenated vision of her slowly asphyxiating brain. There, before her, stands a colossal animal. Big as a small house. Something that could've once been a cow but now is something else, enveloped in a green radiance like those toys that glow in the dark, like the needles and the hands of some clocks. A color that, if included in the cosmic color-wheel, would appear as "sci-fi green." The animal looks at Penelope with the saddest of smiles (a smile that reminds her of Max's farewell smile, in front of the altar) and Penelope looks at it with a smile that strives not to be sad and yet . . . And Penelope thinks: "It was true. Here's Hiriz's mythic beast. The last of its species. The Giant Green Cow that's used to frighten the children so they sleep and have nightmares about the Giant Green Cow." And the beast lies down on its side and Penelope, choking back her nausea, lies down beside it and latches onto one of the teats of its udder and drinks and swallows something that, she understands immediately, isn't milk because it doesn't taste like milk and (the liquid reproduces the greenish glow of the animal that's letting her drink it) as it travels down her throat, transmitting the echo of the beast's atomic and maternal heartbeat, it's as if it's lighting up inside her, like someone passing through the many rooms of a mansion and flipping on all the switches one at a time, now like a bonfire in the night. And, with a mix of pride and fear, Penelope understands that these lights will never go out. That they're the lights that voyagers from other galaxies will use to orient themselves and arrive here, when the entire planet is a desert like this desert where now she seems to understand everything. * And, of course, the temptation for him to additionally attribute singular telepathic properties to such a beast and to have Penelope hear it in her head—as if a thief had broken in not to take anything but, yes, to rearrange the things in that place forever—is very great. To have the creature say something emotional and definitive like "I have seen things that you humans wouldn't believe . . . Man of Orion . . . Tannhauser Gate . . . Tears in rain . . . Time to die . . ." but with a more folkloric feel. Or— funny and interesting possibility—to emphasize a certain Frankensteinian aspect, wordlessly telling Penelope that it's looking for its creator, whom it recalls as a beautiful woman, with a sweet voice, and "probably, the most intelligent of all women." But even as he—now weightless and bodiless and who, in his writing, down below, permitted himself much more daring and unjustifiable things from a narrative perspective, or stupid things (according to the people who read them)—revisits all of this from far away, yet never having been so close (knowing only the bursting and bipolar and more-than-once-broken version of the facts offered over the years, in quick doses and small quantities, from the mouth and in the voice of Penelope), and the thing about the colossal green cow reciting an epiphanic soliloquy is just a little too much. He doesn't even dare insert some allusion in its mooing to the cover of Pink Floyd's *Atom Heart Mother*. So he opts, again, to start the engines of the elliptical. Successive fades to black in many colors. Leaps in time and in space. Her thirst quenched, Penelope climbs up on the Giant Green Cow and rides it—its skin and hide have the relaxing and soft texture of a stuffed animal—and there they go, and is it hours or days that go by, dozens or hundreds of miles? It doesn't matter. Penelope's eyes are closed and kaleidoscopic anyway. And there's so much to see behind her eyelids that Penelope doesn't dare look any further. Penelope doesn't open her eyes until the benevolent monster deposits her, prostrating itself on its front shanks, so that Penelope can slide down, in front of the clinic. The clinic where Max had been admitted and where, no doubt, he'd be admitted again. Floating and drowning. The street is empty. So empty that it seems less like a city intersection and more like a country crossroads. A crossroads where you go to sell your soul to the Devil. Another kind of desert. Penelope finds her mobile phone and decides she's going to take a picture of the Giant Green Cow that now raises its head and its horns (that are like the antlers of an elk) and sings a soft and sad song to the moon, a song about knowing itself to be unique and final. Penelope frames it on the screen of her phone. Penelope wants a photo to accompany that other photo, the one of the Karmas, all together, on the edge of her interrupted wedding: something that already sounds and already feels like it took place centuries ago and in a different language. Penelope lifts her phone and takes the picture, but it's already too late: the Giant Green Cow, with unthinkable speed, considering its mass and weight, is gone. And all she manages to capture on her small screen is a diffuse emerald stain. A dubious portrait to be hung on the wall of a Ripley Museum where those other photos, more imprecise than drawings, already hang, photos of the Yeti, of Nessie, of Mothman, of Sasquatch, of the Chupacabras, of the albino alligators in Manhattan, of Michael "Mike" Wazowski and James P. "Sulley" Sullivan spotted one night at summer camp. Penelope—something to do with the effect of the fluorescent milk of the Giant Green Cow, she thinks—feels now, in her own way, as mythical as they are. Behind her, the clinic shines in the shadows like a fish tank in a dark house, all the lights out, everyone asleep, that underwater glow in a corner of the living room. Penelope waves with her hand (a princely flourish of her wrist) and turns around and enters the clinic like someone leaving one dream and entering another. * And writing is nothing but a solitary dance—a minuet where it's your turn to curtsey and also your turn to bow—whose art lies in executing a delicate and subtle choreography, knowing when to surrender and when to resist. Here, again, he feels the temptation to modify and literarily enhance that hospital Penelope was moving through with the description of a different hospital. A hospital in the city of B where, later, he'd go with an emergency, a red pain biting his chest at the height of his heart. And going even further: to add additional details about the laboratory/

accelerator near Geneva where he'd be transformed into what he is now. As already mentioned: the key scene, the classified tape, the not invented but oh so improbable part in a hypothetical documentary about his life and work. The moment he's unmade to be remade. There inside. But he says no. Better not. Better, at this point, to return to Penelope, running without makeup and with her makeup running, to follow her, to accompany her. Penelope enters with a liquid stride, almost of a melting automaton, as if suspended several inches above the floor, the torn hem of her dress concealing the miracle of her levitation. The successive automatic doors open before her without complaint or resistance. Acknowledging her power and authority. And Penelope advances through the horizontal hallways and ascends in a vertical elevator and arrives to the floor where her husband lies. A nurse on duty watches her move through the corridors and follows her, because this can only be a phantasmagoric and possibly infernal vision: the specter of a bride in ruin, her wedding dress as if sewn with strips of green smoke that allow glimpses, underneath, of an adamantine and incandescent halo. And what was the name of that eternally mad bride character in that novel?, what was that woman's name in that book? * Miss Havisham, in *Great Expectations* (1861) by Charles Dickens. Seeing this apparition, the nurse trembles off "Hail Mary Most Pure," and continues on her way. And Penelope envies the degree of comfort and calm that someone can find in such a simple gesture. And she's not entirely sure if, in the end, she actually got married—if the task force of priests ever concluded the rite or if, who knows, they were liturgically qualified and authorized to conclude it after she'd already left—religiously, because what's begun in the name of the Lord must be completed, so his name won't have been taken in vain. But she's sure of what she has to do now. Penelope arrives to the suite rented by the Karmas and enters the room where Max pulses, suspended and in suspense, breathing on his own and always alone (though Penelope remembers now, and will never forget, that slight movement Maxi made with his head, in front of the altar, as if assenting, as if telling her: "It's up to you now, okay?"). Penelope approaches the bed and climbs on and straddles Max and takes one of his pillows and gets ready to press it against the face of the man she once believed she kind of loved. In the movies, she tells herself, it seems quick and easy. And Penelope can't help but think that, since falling into a deep coma, Max's features have been acquiring a certain nineteenth-century angularity, not attaining that of Heathcliff, but, at least, approaching that of Edward Fairfax Rochester. Better than nothing, as they say. And she can't help noticing, through the gauze and tulle and between her legs, Max's incredibly powerful erection. An erection, almost childlike in its vigor and sweet innocence (because Max isn't dreaming of anything sexual, Max is dreaming that he's walking through a land of candies and cakes and bright colors), that points directly into her suddenly wet sex, and that reminds Penelope of the thing about children pointing their index fingers. Children who don't know that it's bad to point and why (like the thing about elbows on the table, like more good manners to be dekarmatized; and is it possible that she misses them already, that this is the imperfect way of confirming a strange tenderness? Or is it already an almost automatic reflex, the kick caused by the tap of a hammer on the knee?) and who might end up thinking how could something as practical and necessary as pointing be synonymous with bad manners, eh? * Praised be, *Indicis, digitus secundus manus*, radial artery and palmar vein. The most capable and sensitive finger (though not the longest, second on that podium and yet, always, the one that's lifted to signal the number one, first place, winner), *index*, alias "the one that points." The one that infants use to demand what they want and need. Ideal for exploring their noses or sticking in someone else's eye. The only finger he used for the entire keyboard and mouse. The authoritarian "commanding finger," the "pointer finger," the "threatening finger," the "Napoleonic finger," for the Asians the "poisonous finger" from which emerges condemnations and curses and with which you should never touch a deep wound or a superficial cut. The "boomerang finger" that should be used with restraint and care, because "when you point, the hand is like this: the index points at the victim of our criticisms, the thumb points at God, and the other three fingers, which are the pinky, the middle, and the ring, point at the owner of that hand. Which is translated into me pointing at myself, and everything I say or criticize in others I will suffer, drastically, three times." And, yes, the Karmas have learned to point, all the time, with an invisible and always-ready-to-fire point-blank index finger, because the index finger is, also, the "trigger finger" and

. . . Bang! Max explodes inside Penelope and Penelope doesn't really know why and to what end she's done what she's done. Penelope never felt nor wanted to feel like a mother and, even less, like a good mother. Maybe she's done it out of desperation and as a kind of goodbye. Or because the protagonist in one of her brother's favorite books was also the son of a comatose father and a restless mother and that book was called . . . * *The World According to Garp* (1978) by John Irving. Or maybe she's drawn by the hilarious idea (no doubt a product of the combination of desert, dehydration, and the Giant Green Cow juice) of procreating and raising a Karma far away from the Karmas: to bring him up as an atheist with an artistic and uninhibited temperament and, who knows, even as gay, never in the closet because she wrecked it with an ax when he was still a child, in order to, a few years later, returning to his roots, unleash him on Mount Karma like an archangel of fulminating light and bursts of laughter capable of leveling walls, like an unexpected and revolutionary weapon of mass destruction. Or, maybe, imagine him returning to Mount Karma to discover everything in ruins; that, at some point, there was an unprecedented snowfall and the Karmas were stranded and ended up devouring each other, arriving at last to their ultimate and definitive destination: to consume themselves, to be inside of each other, until they ran out and were gone, and there was her son, alone, rebuilding everything from the gnawed bones of his forebears, to create a better and more generous world than theirs. Max comes to an end—and Penelope is sure of this—so that, inside her, in that very instant, something can begin.

* This is something that, of course, her brother finds entirely improbable—fathers who swear they can identify the exact spermatozoid and mothers who claim to have felt the ovum awaken. But, yes, that's why fiction, in the noblest sense of the word, exists. So that human beings evolve and become more sensitive and powerful. The fact that Max (at the comma of a coma) and Penelope (with an exclamation point) have a simultaneous orgasm is also quite improbable. But it doesn't matter. If we accept the lunar mooing of the Giant Green Cow, please, let's accept Penelope's moan and the seismic yet brief modification in the space between Max's brain waves, under the suffocating pillow, seconds before flatlining forever and moving right along. And Penelope could swear that in the exact instant—straddling him, pressing the pillow

forcefully against his face—Max let his last breath escape, right in the middle of his small death and simultaneous great death, there was change in the interior lighting, as if Max's soul had left the room. Penelope could even swear that she heard the door open and close. And she wouldn't be swearing in vain because she's right: a door did open and close, not to let out a soul bound for joyful eternity, but to let in the body of the most inexhaustible and soulless and self-satisfied woman who has and will ever live in this world. Penelope struggles to climb off the bed and sitting there, wrapped in a poncho hemmed with gold and silver, Mamagrandma smiles her most shark-like of smiles. Penelope is very surprised to see her there, without her horse. "How's Horse?" she asks her, to say something, with a trembling voice. "Very well, thank you. I'll pass along your greeting," says Mamagrandma, fixing her with her eyes and fixing her with her smile and it's obvious that Mamagrandma saw her suffocate Max. Penelope, standing beside Max's body, still holds the pillow in front of her chest, as if it were a shield, as if she were completely naked and not covered by the tatters of her wedding dress; but something tells her that the ageless old woman would never even imagine the possibility that her grandson and Penelope had just made something like love, though not exactly. Mamagrandma—brought up on decades of telenovelas—can conceive of the fact of a lunatic bride killing her comatose husband; but she could never conceive of the fact that that bride had just conceived, after practically raping the defenseless and conquered sleeping beauty. In telenovelas, it's understood, sex is nothing but a quick movement of the camera to logs burning in a fireplace or a fade into waves breaking against the rocks. But right now Mamagrandma is acting in another genre. Now Mamagrandma is like a villain from a Bond movie: all of whom are stricken by a mysterious illness that makes them feel the irresistible need to reveal the details of their previously top secret and impossible to decode plans. The idea that you can tell someone who is about to die (and, for Mamagrandma, Penelope is already part of the past, Penelope has already departed) almost everything they won't be around to witness. It's always an act of pity: to describe how the villain's movie and not the hero's movie will end without even thinking of or remembering the inevitable fate of all his fallen comrades and MIAs. So, the bad guys in the best spy movies talk and talk. And they do it—so convinced of their success—in the presence of the hero, chained to a stretcher and defenseless, facing the too-slow advance of a laser beam (never, why not, an expeditious shot to the head) or tied hand and foot and descending, very very very slowly, toward a tank where several crocodiles swim in acid or lava. But, of course, the hero can always count on an ace up their sleeve or a gadget on their belt. Then, presently, the hero unties himself and, since he already knows the codes that the villain imparted, deactivates the nuclear bomb and flips the lair's self-destruct switches— accompanied by an exquisitely beautiful woman who resisted him at first, but now is his—escaping just seconds before the great explosion whose blast silences the indignant shriek of the baddest bad guy whose only final thought is "Why'd I have to go and tell him everything?" And so long until the next mission and until the next talkative evildoer and the sound of sirens and the collapse of tunnels or sinking of secret islands and "Oh, James . . ." But here and now, for Penelope—whose stamina is far from Bond's; who doesn't have a license to kill though she killed only minutes ago—there's a more than noteworthy difference: Mamagrandma speaks and reveals, but she'll never be defeated. Never. Mamagrandma is the M in the equation. And Penelope—a mole about to be unearthed—just listens, unhinged yet immobile, without the strength to do anything but hear what Mamagrandma says. And this is how Mamagrandma speaks, with the lethal and sticky sweetness of words emerging from a carnivorous plant. * Did Mamagrandma really speak like that? Or was it he who wrote her lines for her? Was someone possibly expecting just such an oral display from Mamagrandma, such perfect pacing of drama and revelation at the hour of farewell? Probably not. But these are the mysteries of an always-defiant reality—unexpected and improbable and allegedly fictitious until it is lived on this side of things—that competitive fiction feeds on. So—Penelope listens as if in a trance that she only escapes from by thinking "Please, don't let my brother find out that such characters exist"—Mamagrandma speaks like this: "Ah, here you are . . . The fugitive bride going back not to the scene of the crime, but to that scene without a crime. Poor Penelope. Poor Maxi. But I suppose that what you've just done was inevitable . . . The imminence of the ending—not of my work but of your participation in it— demands this kind of gesture, these kinds of actions, little pushes at the edge of the abyss to precipitate events. Offerings and sacrifices and exchanges so that everything stays the same with the exception of those offered and sacrificed . . . Poor Maxi. And poor Hiriz. She reminds me of a fox I hunted once, when I was just a girl. That damn fox that was eating all my chickens. So I covered the blade of a knife with honey and left it like that, standing there, the handle buried, beside the chicken coop. The fox came one night and began to lick the honey and cut her tongue, and so greedy and insatiable was she that the fox continued to lick her own blood, down to the last drop, until she bled out entirely. The next morning I found her there, dead, but smiling. And that's the key to surviving, Penelope: keep in mind that underneath the honey, a knife could always be lying in wait. Hiriz is not like that. Hiriz—like the fox—doesn't know when to hold back, she doesn't know how to stop. She loves the taste of herself. And I wonder if that might have been the reason for all those yoga classes: to make herself flexible enough to run her own tongue around down under. In the end . . . Hiriz can't comprehend that the Karmas are a closed-circle, a movie with clear and fixed roles where no spectators are admitted but us. We love and hate among ourselves, we betray and steal and even kill among ourselves. Our crimes are only punished by our justice. There is no room for improvisations or departures from script. But Hiriz doesn't think before she acts, and that's how she's always been, and at last she's gone too far and has put us in danger. And it's not even that Hiriz is an idiot. It's much worse: she's someone who thinks she's very intelligent, though all the evidence indicates the opposite. And what do people who are not intelligent do to convince themselves that they are? Easy: they convince themselves that nobody, except them, is intelligent. So, the difference that actually makes them idiots makes itself, for them, into the difference that makes them very very smart. Once the idiots manage to convince themselves of something like this, there's no going back. All that's left is to put up with them with patience or with love, which is the same thing, because love always ends up being one of the many kinds of patience, Penelope . . . What's going to be complicated indeed is how Hiriz will go on after that little scene at your wedding, after ordering your friend killed. * (And here Penelope shudders, comprehending what she doesn't want to comprehend. "Lina," thinks Penelope. And then immediately she stops thinking because thinking hurts. Thinking hurts more than listening to Mamagrandma, who continues with her final monologue, as if illuminated by the reflector of her own light.) Now Hiriz is like one of those wild animals that grew up in captivity, supposedly domesticated and harmless, and one day draws blood and . . . There's nothing to do but eliminate her. Or perhaps, better, as I already said, force her to lick her own blood, down to the last drop. Hiriz . . . Hiriz . . . Hiriz was an unresolved issue for me: Hiriz could not remain among us, because Hiriz is a starving time bomb with a thirst for vengeance. She's not the first: there have been spoiled Karmas and crazy Karmas. But Hiriz is spoiled *and* crazy. Like Nero. Or Hitler. Capricious children. The whole thing about how people can change is a lie, Penelope. People never change; they just get better or worse when it comes time to be who they always were and are and will be. And it's quite clear that Hiriz is going to get worse. Her evil is no longer the banal and predictable evil of her relatives. Her evil is banal and predictable but, also, different. Any one of these nights Hiriz—who, let's face it even though it's unnecessary, always had a horrible voice—would burn Mount Karma to the ground just to get us to listen to her sing. Hiriz, sooner or later, would end up disrupting the delicate balance that sustains and keeps the Karmas together. And you cannot imagine what it takes to maintain the balance of something that's half tightrope half hangman's noose. And, on their own, the Karmas are nothing—easy prey for the masses of non-Karmas. So bye-bye, Hiriz, I wish you well. With any luck, if it occurs to her—and *I* will make sure that there is luck and that it does, in fact, occur to her—tomorrow Hiriz will get the idea in her head, her crazy little head, of becoming a saint, of being beatified and canonized, and she'll enter a cloistered convent and stay there until the end of her days. After all, our family lacks a saint just like it lacks a writer. Yes, yes, in that way and to that end, Hiriz will go—cloistered order and vow of silence. Poor little nuns. But, after all, who told them to call themselves Humble Sisters of the Pricked and Suffering Martyr Heart of Our Poor Little Abandoned Jesus Bleeding Out Slowly on the Cross With No Right to Resurrection. With a name like that, they deserve Hiriz. And Hiriz deserves them too. So ugly. Look how ugly nuns are, Penelope . . . Maybe that's why nuns are always so pretty and delicate and high-voiced and ballerina-bodied in movies: to compensate a little for so much facial and anatomical deformity, right? Hiriz will be happy among them, because at last she'll be the most beautiful beast. End of her projects, end of her adventure. But first things first. And the saint doesn't come first . . . Which brings me to the sinner. And the sinner is you, Penelope. Mortal sinner. But even so, as if blessed. The kind of sinner who can end up being an object of adoration. A threat to the established order. And I am the established order. Which doesn't keep me from knowing how to recognize someone powerful when I see them. And you are powerful. Like I am, but in different way. A free spirit who could end up becoming a leader. There's no space for both of us here, Penelope. So I'm going to let you go. Nothing has happened here. You killed Maximiliano the way I killed Papagrandpa. We're like praying mantises . . . You and I are different yet the same. We operate on our own. Papagrandpa—who was raised in the macho patriarchy without ever figuring it out that it's the woman behind him who pulls the strings and draws the reins—couldn't understand it. And I made him understand. And there he is: stuck inside a wall in Mount Karma, behind his portrait, may he rest in peace. And your thing with Maxi, killing him—I don't get it. Was it out of love or pity, out of interest or strategy? I don't understand the first one, the second one either; because you won't get any inheritance. You signed documents of separation of assets and the religious ceremony never concluded. I thank you for it: Maxi, always and forever in a coma, he would've turned into a, into another, short-term complication in the financial-familial hierarchy, in terms of shares and allotments. And we, for religious reasons, so convenient on other occasions, could never unplug him. And because of the thing with Papagrandpa, my dance card is already full in that area. I'll confess my mortal sin on my death-bed (which, as its name indicates, is where and when you have to confess your mortal sins) and I'll be forgiven, yes; but best not to exaggerate too much, right? So, better this way, thank you for everything, Penelope, and may Maxi sleep with the angels. And getting back to the religious stuff . . . I really liked that thing you said once about the foolishness of wasting time praying for God to change his designs. You said it was . . . a contradiction, right? Because you can't ask God, in his infinite wisdom, to alter his actions. Even less if you're one of God's little creatures. And you're right. That's why, when I go to mass, I never ask for anything and I always give thanks. I thank God that He's allowed me to have my way, that my will be done and that my will, always, be His. I thank God, as I told you once, that He's helped me under-stand that though life is, in fact, very short, life is *also* very wide. And God says to me you're welcome, and what's more, Mamagrandma, I'm the grateful one. What's the voice of God like? The voice of God is the silence of God. And ye who are silent shall receive. And it's of my will and my will alone that I let you go now, Penelope, that I won't say anything about what I just saw, that I leave you free to do anything except come back here, where it's not that you're not understood, but it's impossible for you to understand our kind of happiness. It might be true that it's a hard happiness to assimilate, but that doesn't mean it's not a happiness that makes us happy. What you have, on the other hand, is pure and absolute sadness and dissatisfaction. You like to think that the problem is our family, when the problem is the family that you never had and will never have. Here I could get really annoying and witch-like and tell you that I curse you so you'll never know the joy of family. But there's no need. You've cursed yourself. You've condemned yourself to wander, lost. Safe travels, yours shall be a very long trip. And lonely. We don't love you, we can't love you, because you don't love you—you consider yourself cursed by everyone else, but actually you're cursed by yourself. Nobody would tell your story because it's sad and boring. Only the part that overlaps with ours will be somewhat amusing. And that part, so entertaining that many will say it must be the invented part, ends here. Good luck, Penelope. You're going to need it. I won't ask you to go with God because you don't believe in Him and because not even He would be able to go with you. Because he'd get bored after five minutes in your company and would start in with the floods and the plagues. Goodnight, sweet princess." And the door to the room opens and Mamagrandma exits * (Mamagrandma exits singing the way people sing who, new to old age, discover themselves to be great and seasoned singers though they've never sung before. Like Harry Dean Stanton, who began to sing at a young age, but who was always old and who he'll hear again, singing in Spanish, in a documentary about Harry Dean Stanton, on the small screen embedded in the back of the seat in front of him, in the mechanized night of an airplane in the sky. A song sung with all the strength of that broken voice. A song that speaks of skies and hearts and pistols and of being far away from the land where he was born) and the door to the room closes and Penelope wonders if maybe she should applaud after such a speech. And she doesn't get to answer herself because she's already applauding and, just like in certain magic stories, three claps and, ah, again, the blessed ellipsis, Penelope is already in the Abracadabra airport. And Penelope approaches the first counter of whatever airline (the closest one where passengers and luggage are being checked in) and stares at the attendant and pulls out a dirty diamond from her recently unmarried neckline and asks for a first class ticket on the first plane bound for the most faraway destination possible and there she goes and here she comes. * (And here he follows her, her brother, who, not dead but yes disappeared, part of the air and everywhere, watches her not on a TV screen of the netherworld, but as if he were reading her; as if she were a character in a book, that book he never managed to write but that he can't stop thinking about or wondering about or playing with sometimes complex and sometimes not so complex possible choices, like the one that a flight attendant with the enigmatic smile of a sphinx presents Penelope with now: "Beef, chicken, fish, or pasta?," she asks. All of us are equal when we venture into the sky, he thinks, and he thinks this on another airplane, on that airplane going nowhere. On that airplane where he ordered and ate pasta because, the expert travelers and frequent flier mile addicts say, it's always the safest option to avoid suffering complications.) But Penelope is already asleep next to the emergency exit that opens onto emptiness—the ruinous wrath that caused her family countless sorrows, slipped under the seat in front of her, as directed by the flight attendant—and dreaming of something she won't remember when she wakes. A dreaming Penelope flying over the white arctic in the middle of the night; when the low but amplified voice of the pilot, from his cabin and over the intercom, sounding like the whisper of a radio disc-jockey, pupils red like in a photo lit by a flash, tells the insomniac passengers in three or four languages that, if you want to see something you've never seen before and will never see again, please, take a look out the window.

III

"In a real dark night of the soul it is always three o'clock in the morning."

Who said that? Who *wrote* that? The Young Man wonders. Was it The Writer? Or was it a writer who The Writer liked a lot, one of those sentences pinned to a wall in his study? It seems to The Young Man that the sentence in question is nothing special. To begin with there's the fact that it contains the words "night" and "morning" in the same line. It doesn't fit. But changing "morning" to something else doesn't really improve anything. Dawn? No. Wee Hours? Too childish. Small hours? Better, but not really. And it'd completely break down the mechanics of the sentence: "In a real dark night of the soul it is always the small hours." No. It doesn't work. Broken beyond repair like one of those clocks that, once opened, becomes impossible to close. Like that clock that Jay Gatsby almost breaks. And he read somewhere that Fitzgerald always wrote surrounded by clocks, because he was obsessed with time's passing, with the repeatable or unrepeatable past passing by and, ah, yes, it was Fitzgerald who wrote that thing about the dark night of the soul and three o'clock in the morning or whatever, whatever time it is, thinks The Young Man.

The Young Man looks at the time on the screen of his mobile phone. It's 3:05 A.M. The small hours, indeed. At 3:05 in the morning we're all geniuses, he says to himself. Or we all think like writers who could be or who, unbeknownst to everybody, are geniuses. Or, at least, we all think like writers. The spasmodic mechanics of dreams—that free association of ideas, those sudden changes of direction or channel or genre, that succession of impossibilities suddenly plausible because they're happening inside the desk of your head, mind the color of a blank page—is the way writers see the waking world. All the time, every hour and every second. Weighing possibilities, strengthening weak characteristics and altering uncertain realities, inserting trial endings, trying to find the right words, that kind of thing.

So, writers move about in a trance and there's always someone who points out—with a mix of reproach and jealousy—that they seem to be asleep, elsewhere, in the clouds or lost in space, and demands they come back right now. Some do come back. Others pretend—or try to convince themselves—that they've returned, that they've come back.

The Young Man, right now, not the one thing or the other.

The Young Man is about halfway down the road to a city called Everywhere, where it's always night, where it rains more than in the Bible, and where the whole world seems, suddenly, full of infinite possibilities. There's no place more simultaneously unpleasant and exciting than one where somebody who thinks they might someday—but not yet—become a writer lives. "For writing, with fondness and complete and slavish devotion," would be written, just inside, as the manuscript's dedication, so near and so far, on the other side of the cover. And once that threshold is crossed, there's no longer an exit. Just an end.

These are the things The Young Man thinks about, awake now.

Left behind is the creaking whisper of a dream about telepathic crabs or something like that. Will he someday use the dreamlike memory of those crabs from his childhood in something he writes? And he answers himself that, no. Because at 3:06 in the morning we're all fools who can't even figure out how to get back to sleep. A minute is all it takes for that feeling of absolute talent and mastery that you have when you first open your eyes to dissolve. Now all that's left is the addictive comfort of thinking about writers instead of thinking about writing. Because, as already mentioned, The Young Man isn't a writer yet, but not one minute goes by—and now it's 3:07—that he doesn't think about being a writer. About being a genius even. But that's as far as he takes it. Thinking about writing is much more complicated, dangerous. As if he were wading along the shores of a twilight zone, The Young Man, hotter all the time, prefers to keep telling himself that the water is still too cold. And that you don't need to know how to swim to paint the ocean. And that hopefully that's true. But, at the very least, you need to see it. And The Young Man decides to get up and leave the tent and walk out to where the waves are breaking. Actually, what he decides is that he has to get out of there. He can't bear the sight of the sleeping body of The Young Woman next to him. The Young Woman's body is wrapped in a cross between pajamas and a scuba suit with a zipper in front, which goes up, or—an expression of The Young Man's desire—*goes down* from her neck to her belly button. Her "sleepyhead ninja uniform," as The Young Woman calls it, is yellow, almost fluorescent, transversed with black elastic stripes. The black on yellow of the tape used to giftwrap crime scenes. "*Corpus delicti*," thinks The Young Man, more than ready to kill or to die for that body. And, ah, The Young Woman has the terrible and captivating habit of sleeping in positions that make The Young Man think of the covers of old pulp novels from the golden age of science fiction and fantasy; with heroines in tight-fitting armor or spacesuits ripped in all the right places. And the shame is all his. Exclusive shame, one-size-fits-all, The Young Man suffers. Is it possible for years of reading to end in this? In preadolescent sexual fantasies? Is this why he's read so much?

Just after falling asleep, starting to dream, The Young Woman always slips out of her sleeping bag as if it were a shell, and reveals herself cautiously ready and surrendered, like a damsel lying defenseless, waiting to be taken and subdued by whatever warrior or alien is on duty. Every so often, to make matters worse yet better, The Young Woman lets slip a deep sigh or moist gasp (The Young Woman doesn't snore, The Young Woman purrs) that provokes an irrepressible desire in The Young Man to dream what she's dreaming, to enter her dream, to submit to her point of view, that it be The Young Woman who narrates the dream and that, yes, she do whatever she wants to his person and his character, but that, please, she do *something*. The Young Man is ready for The Young Woman to be the warrior, the extraterrestrial, the one who makes him fall to his knees at her feet. Miranda Urano could *also* be the name of a poet who fights battles in ancient Sumerian deserts after her spaceship crashes there as she flees from the imperial forces of the all-powerful Mad Kahar. The Young Man looks at her and sighs and—could this be definitive proof that he'll never be a great writer, that it would never occur to him that one of his characters could behave like this?—imagines everything imaginable except that The Young Woman is *maybe* pretending to be asleep and that this is fun for her, torturing him without even touching him. And still less does The Young Man imagine that, on recent nights, there inside, sleeping together but separate, The Young Woman has enjoyed the apparent humor of the thing less and less and has gotten more and more turned on by it. And The Young Woman wonders, her eyes tightly shut and her ears wide open, almost impatient, how much longer The Young Man will be able to handle her carefully calculated and moist sounds and the perfectly choreographed movements of her body.

But it's clear that whatever's going to happen, it's not going to happen tonight: The Young Man is already outside and The Young Woman opens her eyes and looks at the tent's ceiling and focuses on the movement of a small spider, suspended above, hanging from a thread that comes out from inside it, about to begin its life's great work. That's how she thinks she feels. Hanging from a thread that, presumably, she must use to weave everything yet to come. Not hurrying but also not delaying. And The Young Woman asks herself something, in the low yet deafening voice of thought, that she doesn't dare answer: isn't it about time to think about things that *are not* literature? Isn't it time to stop thinking about literature as if it were some kind of demanding religion that leaves no room for anything or anyone else? What time could it be? What time is it?

The Young Woman thinks that it is the exact time when she begins to get sick of The Writer, of The Writer's Mad Sister, of not sleeping in a bed; and that her pseudo-somnambulant ploys of seduction and torment with The Young Man might just be the banal symptoms of boredom, fatigue with the stuff of her fantasies, the result of spending her life wondering what the next book will be that she *has* to read to keep from falling behind in an absurd race around a track shrouded in fog with no finish line in sight. The Young Woman looks at the spider and says "Yes or no?" and the answer is yes, and she reaches out her arm and takes the spider with great care, holding it without squeezing it between the tip of her thumb and index finger, and puts it in her mouth, and swallows it. "Welcome," says The Young Woman.

"To where?" says The Young Man, on the beach.

Because it's clear that now the question, The Issue, is how to proceed. The feeling that he has few credits of future promise left to spend and that the moment has come to advance to the next stage in the game or to fade away. The Young Man tells himself that this whole project revolving around

The Writer—which in the beginning seemed, though he'd never admit it to himself, like an excellent way to be something without being it—is starting to creak like a ship, now at high sea, where defects of structure and construction have been detected. Something hazardous, loose screws, ready to be torn away by a perfect storm of icebergs. A ship without an honorable captain or an orchestra to play right up until the final vertical second. The Young Man feels more like the ambitious and reckless shipbuilder who demanded more speed and who, when everything starts to tilt and sink, dresses as a woman and snatches a baby away from a third-class mother, and climbs aboard one of the few remaining boats and launches into an ocean of decades through which his dishonor will drift, no doubt, but his own shame will be the most epic of all. His cowardice will be understood, with time, as an extreme form of the genre and as a symptom. And there's something tantalizing about that—to be the best of the worst, to successfully fail. And there's also something about the way that—in a few seconds of thought, like traveling a distance of centuries driven by the electrifying and vertiginous speed of the brain—The Young Man goes from doubting everything to affirming himself in his resignation. The Young Man thinks too much. The Young Man wishes he could think less. The Young Man wishes he'd wake up one day and discover that his thing was really the law or industrial design or odontology. Professions that you can disconnect from once you get home—professions that are left far and away, like certain animals mislabeled domestic—and that aren't pulling at your sleeve all the time, calling your attention and obliging you to imagine what Julien Sorel or Christopher Teitjens or Jay Gatsby would have done (automatically recalling, another symptom of the same troubling affliction, that the real name of the latter was James Gatz) in this or that situation. Much safer and more relaxing professions that—when people ask what you do—don't generate other questions, uncomfortable ones, like "What are your books about?" or "What's your name?" or "Are you well known?" or "Were any of your books made into a movie?" or ultimate classics with a complicit wink like "I've got a great story . . . want me to tell it so you can use it?" and "Being a writer you must meet a lot of interesting women, huh?" Anything but that "Does the doggy die?" which his big and best and unique dead friend, Ishmael Tantor, used to mock him and everyone. Ishmael Tantor, who always introduced himself with the lame joke "Call me

Ishmael," and who never wanted to be a writer as badly as The Young Man and yet . . . But thinking about Ishmael Tantor hurts The Young Man so much. And it makes him think about that unforgivable moment—like, as already mentioned, with the despicable builder of the *S. S. Titanic*, but this time with the ashes of Ishmael Tantor safely and securely stowed, not in the overhead compartment, but in the next seat—on the airplane where he met The Writer, about situations that are more like earnest answers than absurd questions. So, better, the questions. And yet, here and now, another change of cerebral direction, The Young Man would sign in blood any microscopic-clause-crammed contract to be worthy of such questions, to be published, to be a "cult writer" or a "writer's writer" or whatever. But, please, let it be in print, black on white, and let it have a beginning and an end, and later on let him see it on display for a while in bookstores where he'll reposition it in a prime location and ask the employees—disguising his voice and hiding his face—what they think of it, whether or not they liked it, and walk out worrying that they might have recognized him and are laughing behind his back, but it doesn't matter, hopefully they recognized him and . . .

Now what?: the kinds of questions that readers ask themselves when they're alone, reading, certain that the answer is already on the way, a few lines below, a turn of the page, in the next chapter, coming soon, somewhere between here and the end. What readers don't know or suspect is the number of times that a writer asks that same question, between A and B and Z, so many times, knowing that just ahead, right there, there's nothing but a white and empty night waiting to be filled with words and stars.

Now what?

The Young Man looks out at the horizon—and, at night, on a beach, the horizon is something that's there but not seen, like something thought but not yet written—and latches onto the solitary and never-last point of a light, twinkling in the darkness. A submarine coming to his rescue and to invite him on the adventure of voyaging first and recounting it later? Like Joseph Conrad and Jack London? To get experience and grow strong on this side before departing for the other, adrift, bound for a shipwrecked and deserted island with a lone palm tree as his only inspiration? Without any "interesting women" to meet. Without The Writer's Mad Sister, without The Young Woman, and with someone more like his first and only girlfriend, whom he now describes to others as "my most serious relationship" and with whom his breakup was mutual. Which really means that he couldn't help but agree when his girlfriend wanted to "take some time to meet other people." Something that his ex did immediately and without wasting any time, and a week later she called him, excited, to tell him that she'd met the man of her dreams and good luck, thanks for everything, best friends forever, and all that. What did he think about then? About one of the proven and supposedly sure formulas of the trade: Trauma + Settling of Scores = Masterpiece. An unforgettable formula, easy to learn and memorize: out of all the terrible pain and overwhelming fury, I'll write a great novel, he said, he swore. But theory isn't the same as practice and the pain wasn't that terrible or the fury that overwhelming; so the novel never was and remained unresolved and (?), his X factor, between parentheses and never solved for. Never even reduced to the exercise of a story. The title—which he thought was really good and probably was: *Ex*—soon dried out and died, like a plant that isn't watered and which you tell, because someone once said that it's good to talk to plants: "I'll water you tomorrow, I promise."

And, yes, *Ex* was one of the many, oh so many, titles that sprouted from, like many things, two or three leaves and the flower of some more or less promising sentence that he cut out and stashed away inside a notebook, and every so often he opens it and rereads them, fragile, not touching them, afraid they'll break apart between his fingers, with the pain of what he never was and the shame of what he never did. Everything that seemed like the promise of something more or less green or colorful (the unthinkable ideas he's been having—almost as irritating as the sand that he never manages to entirely brush off before entering the tent—about writing something about The Young Woman) produces in him something a lot like nausea. Before long, he realizes, not even he will believe in himself anymore. And all he'll have left is the definitive trauma of not being able to be a writer, moving through meetings and workshops and book presentations, drinking too much and trying to convince some dupe (or, better, some young girl more innocent than interesting) that he's spent years working on "something" that's already reached two thousand pages; something destined to change everything, but the world—not him—isn't ready for that kind of impact. And to return home afterward, not to the panic or to the blank page or to the screen, but to the fear of not even being able to sit down in front of the page or the screen.

"It's not hard for me to write. It's hard for me to sit down to write," said The Writer in one of the TV interviews that The Young Man and The Young Woman had compiled. And The Young Man discovers—with a mix of terror and strange happiness—that he might be starting to hate The Writer. To hate him for what he said and for what he wrote and for how he lived and for how he disappeared and for how he's indirectly responsible for bringing The Young Woman into The Young Man's life. And, above all, he hates him for that unforgettable moment of infamy, sitting beside him, aboard an airplane. A moment that The Young Man tries not to remember, but that he can't forget and . . . And The Writer would add: "Which isn't at all paradoxical, because this is simultaneously the most sedentary and nomadic of professions. The body is immobile, but the head never stops moving, traveling. Where then is the true home? So all the complications of space—a whole universe and an eternity—fit inside that small object that might be an Aladdin's lamp or a Pandora's box." All very funny and very ingenious and equally sad and sordid and desperate. And The Young Man decides that he's hit bottom, the finale, a dead-end alley. This is, yes, the real dark night of the soul and it's 3:15 A.M. and there are, presumably, forty-five more minutes of shadows and despondency. And The Young Man tells himself he won't be able to hang on that long, that before then it'll be out to sea with no escape (well, no, it's not really that bad; but the idea of suicide does have its appeal and it's even possible that The Young Woman would assume that he did it in her name and that his watery ghost will torment her to her deathbed) or some other version of what's known as a "desperate act."

The Young Man bends down and picks up a seashell from the shore and brings it to his ear. "No, it's not the sound of the sea that you hear inside a seashell but the sound of the sea's absence. People want to convince themselves that it is so, as if seashells were a kind of cellular telephone communicating with the depths. But no. The only thing that a seashell offers is the terror and the whimper of knowing that you're outside of everything, in the wrong place, far away. What a seashell says is 'Wrong number. Nobody named Sea lives here,'" The Young Man says to himself and, once again, should he write this down or not? Write it in the sand? Yes, The Young Man is and continues to be, despite everything, someone who wants to write. And, naked and small facing the suicidal possibility of his own unhappy ending, he retreats to the "Once upon a time"s of his childhood. And he chooses a magical and miraculous solution; something—Pandora's box and Aladdin's lamp—worthy of the two thousand and second night.

If politics is the last refuge of losers, then magical thinking (which is nothing but a comfortable designer religion, personalized and custom fit) is the last hope of the tormented. And so it is that The Young Man decides the solution to all his problems is to obtain, to rob like the thief of Baghdad, the magic talisman that once granted The Writer absolute and creative powers and that is there, now, waiting for him—the next chosen one in a chain that's been adding new links since the dawn of time and, also, includes the great names of literature. The Young Man decides—with the conviction of the enlightened acting in the shadows—that that talisman must be the small toy that he filmed a few days ago—that little wind-up man made of metal and carrying a suitcase full of black and not blank pages, pages covered with ideas and words and brilliant situations ready to be his. All he has to do is go inside The Writer's house, go to his study, take the little metal man, wind it up, wind himself up. Without a doubt, like in all stories of ambiguously gray magic and granted wishes, a price will have to be paid. But The Young Man is ready to pay whatever it takes down the road, so that he can write now. Anything would be better than this life that's not a life and that seems to start over, like a defective machine, every morning when he wakes from a dream that—wondrous as it is—turns into a nightmare when he opens his eyes, when he realizes that's all it was: a brief illusion, courtesy of a brain that was telling him that everything was going to start over now so that everything could go on as before with the slight novelty that, yes, it was another day and one day less of his life as a writer who is not yet a writer.

The Young Man enters the house, walks to the studio, and imagines that he's climbing a rope up the side of a colossal idol, to the huge and precious stone in the center of its forehead—the third eye. The Young Man moves quietly and carefully to keep from waking the High Priestess and guardian of the place, The Writer's Mad Sister. The Young Man imagines whatever he can, applying it as a coat of protective and imaginary varnish, to help protect him from the reality of what he's doing. The Young Man tells himself that there's probably nothing more frightening than walking through the darkness of an unfamiliar house and then corrects himself, edits himself: yes, there is something more frightening, and that's hearing someone else walking through the darkness of your house, when you know you're alone, or should be. And there's a third, even more terrifying option: that the solitary mistress of the house who hears The terrified Young Man moving through the dark corridors is none other than The Writer's terrifying Mad Sister, because who can know, The Young Man wonders, how a woman as unhinged as her might react, finding him here. It wouldn't be surprising if The Writer's Mad Sister had a whole arsenal of well-oiled firearms and various collections of kitchen knives and sharpened axes at her disposal that she'd always wanted to use.

The Young Man changes the channel and thinks about anything else and there's the half-open door and the library and The Young Man sings "You say you're so happy now / You can hardly stand / Lean over on the bookcase / If you really want to get straight" and he can't remember who sings it or what line comes next; but he does remember that it's an old song, something from the mid-eighties, from another planet, because it's a song from before he was born and that he came to after it was mentioned in one of The Writer's books: "The songs written by the first rocker who grew old with him, at the same time." The Young Man enters The Writer's studio and there's that other poster, one of those photos taken and sent back by the Hubble Space Telescope: in the background, the Milky Way on top of which The Writer has stuck a Post-it with the words "You are here . . ."; and, in the foreground, the ravenous yawn of a black hole in whose center there's another Post-it and the words ". . . but I am / will be here." And now The Young Man is there. In the Milky Way, or in a solar storm, all the same. Lost in space, floating like an astronaut somewhere that's no longer the sky—because the sky is everything—but yes, my God, it's full of stars. And, among them, presumably, the absolute consciousness of The Writer who now, accelerated and particular, is everywhere, even in the air that The Young Man breathes. And The Young Man inhales deeply and why not think that something of The Writer—something that must remain suspended in the air of his library— enters his lungs and mixes with his blood and becomes part of him. And that's why The Young Man now feels authorized to do what he's about to do. There's the toy, on the bookshelf, next to the digital camera, and The Young Man thinks that it wouldn't be bad to film his own hand, picking up that small tin tourist. To record that moment as if it were the instant that Arthur pulled the buried Excalibur from the stone, covered in moss and grasses, almost effortlessly, to change history, scour the rust of centuries, and give birth to a new and shining era.

So The Young Man checks to see if the camera has enough battery-life (it has) and that it works (it works) and he turns it on and before focusing on the toy, with his hand entering the frame like a pale and trembling version of King Kong's paw, the little screen fills with images. And The Young Man—one of the millions of bastard children of that Visual Age in which an image doesn't say but screams another thousand images, capturing immediate attention, pausing any ongoing action to fix all eyes on whatever distorted format of screen—looks at what's revealed there. Random visions, like loose pieces of a dream in the exact moment they're dreamed and not, later, when you fall into the trap of organizing them for your interpretation, like someone hurriedly tidying up their apartment when notified of a surprise visit.

The first thing he sees—images from different years, the robotically traced date and time numbers blinking in a corner of the small screen— is something that, beyond the smallness of the screen, is of colossal spirit: swarming multitudes like in a Cecil B. DeMille film or in the photographs by that one photographer (The Young Man doesn't remember his name) where hundreds of people are shown, like suffering souls trying in vain to escape the mouth of the inferno, climbing up and down the ladders of a gold mine in a place whose name became unforgettable for him and, yes, at that time he wrote it down in a notebook followed by an exclamation point, convinced that it could be the password or magic word that'd make a novel, or at least a microstory, appear—Curionopolis.

But The Young Man realizes that what he's seeing are shots of a massive party (a wedding?) where everyone appears to be dressed the same and all of them have the same hairstyles and seem to be orbiting around a woman riding a horse; then there's a woman talking to the camera and saying strange things ("It's hard to live knowing you're a genius," says the woman whose face, though young, already shows the signs of various surgeries and an outbreak of an adolescent but already mature rash); and cut and then another woman (who The Young Man finds drop-dead gorgeous and, as such, immediately similar to The Young Woman) on a stage and saying even stranger things, with a trickle of blood dripping from her head and speaking to a television that only broadcasts gray and static. And another more abrupt cut and there's The Writer. The date is from about a year ago (shortly after I ran into him on the plane, The Young Man says to himself). And The Writer is walking along that same beach there outside (the landscape reveals, in the background, this same house, here inside) and he's followed by the person who's filming him, with a shaky hand and, as far as can be seen, from a low angle, as if the camera were held by a dwarf. Or, better—a boy. Because The Writer smiles and is chased by one of those little childish laughs that make you want to laugh. And The Writer—who advances with great triumphal leaps, as if The Writer were the style going in front of a cautious plot, taking small steps, dragging its feet—points at the invisible boy who catches him, who approaches him. The Writer sits down in the sand and stretches out his hand and takes the camera and turns it toward the boy and there he is: a kind of redheaded miracle. Four or five or six years old (those three years that melt into one long year of thirty-six months), laughing with the happiness of someone for whom a few tears are nothing more than the consequence of a blow or a fall, someone who knows that all his wishes will be granted; because all the adults who surround him depend on that immense and powerful happiness, more difficult to invoke all the time and oh so fragile. The Writer asks him two or three questions of the kind that people ask kids (questions that are supposedly simple, but that require absolute answers) and this unexpected aspect of The Writer moves The Young Man and he says to himself that he has to put this scene in the documentary, after a few sections and interviews. The Writer interviewing. Then the boy (The Boy from here onward) shows something to the camera with pride—it's an antique toy. That little wind up man, with hat and suitcase, that The Young Man has there, within reach. And The Young Man feels a kind of dizziness, that vertigo of coming face to face with apparent twists of fate and coincidences. "Mister Trip!" exclaims The Boy. And he snatches the camera from The Writer and refocuses it and, with a deep and seemingly adult voice, The Boy asks, "Let's see . . . Who's your favorite writer?" and The Writer laughs and answers the same as always—those two American writers, that French writer—and then he pauses and stares straight ahead, without blinking, as if he were fixing his eyes on the eyes of The Young Man.

And then he adds a fourth name to the list.

And the fourth name on the list is The Young Man's name.

And The Young Man thinks he's going mad.

And the camera falls from his hands. And makes a lot of noise (that noise things make in the night and, yes, it's as if someone turned up the volume on things in the night, as if things in the night always made a lot more noise) and he has to catch himself on the bookcase, not to get straight, but so he won't fall down and make the noisiest of nocturnal noises: that of a body crashing to the floor.

The Young Man rewinds the image and looks at it again and listens again. And REW again.

And there it is: his name, seemingly written and proclaimed in marble and bronze, but—he knows, he remembers, he can't forget—actually in pure glitter and façade; because it's all the result, not of a misunderstanding, but of something much darker and harder to confess. The past that comes back to look for him and find him and all of that.

And his ears get plugged up as if he were back on that airplane. Sitting across the aisle from The Writer, trying hard to hold up that absurd and heavy self-help manual for struggling writers—*The Seven Deadly Scenes* was its supposedly ingenious title—and wondering if he could work up the nerve to talk to him. And he finally gets up the nerve and talks to him and, now, on the most turbulent of solid grounds, a year later—that fear of falling and crashing. Delayed punishment for his high-altitude crime. The eternity of two or three minutes in which The Young Man feels finished, erased, discarded in the trash barrel of his own infamy. He's never felt like this, few people ever feel this way in their lives. The feeling that there's no possible *after* anymore, after that final point. A pain that throbs in his chest and connects with another pain in his head and, suddenly, the void, absolute emptiness.

And—REW again—The Writer's smile after he says his name and, surprise, that smile translates into another smile, now on The Young Man's lips. He's survived and he's happy. He's gained access to the paradise of the damned, which is even deeper than hell, a little to the left, but that doesn't make it any less a paradise. Heaven is above, yes, but who cares; who wants to be in heaven and not to have heaven overhead. Better there, where he is, where he stays, with the future in his hands, inside that camera. And, of course, it's a wish that's granted in the same way, as mentioned, as the wishes granted in the most twisted of genie tales. Wishes granted with fine print and clauses and dirty tricks. But nobody who isn't him has any reason to know or suspect it. Everyone else involved in the thing is either dead or disappeared and he's the only one who, yes, has lived to tell the tale. And it's funny, he says to himself, how everything that, up to a few minutes ago, embarrassed him to the point where he couldn't think about it, now fills him with something very akin to pride, though not exactly. The hubris of falsifying something everyone thinks is authentic. The satisfaction of the serial killer who knows he'll never be caught. The happiness of the person who finds the winning lottery ticket in a dead man's pocket, and keeps it.

I have a lot to do, The Young Man says to himself. Suddenly, ecstatic, he has a map, instructions to follow, an objective in reach, a goal so near. The first thing—with a rapid dance of his fingers across a keypad—will be to upload that video from The Writer's camera, launch it into the space of the Internet and wait for it to, inevitably, return to that planet of shipwrecked astronauts and spread like a virus and come back to him and to The Young Woman. And The Young Man can almost see The Young Woman's surprise—her mouth half open, the circle of her lips letting out an: "Oh!"— when she sees and hears his name as one of The Writer's favorites. Then her love, her adoration for him, will be inevitable, The Young Man says to himself. And then . . .

What'll come later will be even more undignified and embarrassing. But nothing is forgotten as quickly as what embarrasses you; especially when nobody else knows it or suspects it and, now, his name in the mouth and voice of The Writer, almost seems to authorize him. It's even possible that, with time, he'll forget it too. The way he forgets a dream, the way he emerges from a nightmare thinking, "That's it, it's over, that's the end." If you aren't caught, if you aren't publicly guilty, the guilt evaporates like a hangover after a forbidden party. And the guilty is no longer guilty, becoming, conversely, guilt-free. Could this be what people who sell their souls to the devil feel like? If so—that's not so bad. The feeling that nothing depends on you anymore; with the added benefit that you get to be your own demon creditor and are aware that you never had a soul to sell in the first place. If you know that you're soulless, you never buy beyond your means. And there's something even more interesting, something that'll bolster you in your crime, The Young Man rationalizes: the conviction that almost everyone is just like you. Only, maybe, the odd and quite infrequent sensation that someone is staring at you, the suspicion that they know everything, because that's the only reward and punishment of being innocent—the unattenuated and unanesthetized torment of the complicity, almost on your own, of perceiving and suffering absolute awareness of the putrefaction that surrounds you—and, subsequently, the relieved certainty that that's impossible—because you're the only one who knows what you know. The Young Man says all these things to reinforce his resolve to pass through that door beyond which there's no coming back. How do you pass through that door? Easy: stop thinking such foolish things, poorly aimed ideas from his increasingly distant adolescence, when he sat down to chew over the slow food of Dostoevsky and Camus, not worrying how it was going to strike him, or come crashing down upon him. No more excessively long aphorisms, enough maxims. Goodbye, goodbye to all of that; but now, yes, there *is* someone looking at him and staring him.

He's sure of it.

The Young Man feels it in his spine and on the nape of his neck, like the red dot that precedes a gunshot. Like two red dots. Like the pupils of a ferocious wolf. And, with the camera in one hand and the toy in the other, he raises his arms, not daring to turn around, awaiting some kind of instruction, his heart in his throat. The Young Man always hated the use of that kind of image to explain a sensation like "his heart in his throat." But, suddenly, not only does he understand its practical utility, but, in addition, its terrifying and indisputable truth. The Young Man wants to say something (to beg forgiveness, justify his presence, swear that he's leaving now) but he knows that, if he opens his mouth, his heart will shoot out from inside him, like the cuckoo of a cuckoo clock, like one of those ultraviolent animated drawings where everyone dies over and over and over in order to earn the right to keep on living and coming back to life.

The Young Man—terror allows you to see yourself from outside, because when we're terrified we want to be anywhere else and not be ourselves—sees himself right there. Legs apart and arms extended. His body forming an X that he now imagines dyed that night-vision-goggle shade of green: the dangerous and unerring color of the gaze of assault commandos with infallible aim, ready to lay waste to everybody in the name of God and country.

A shade of nocturnal extraterrestrial that, every so often, comes back into Penelope's eyes and that she considers, without doubt and with certainty, a kind of hallucinogenic flashback from all that mutant Giant Green Cow's milk she drank that wedding night, in the shining desert near Mount Karma, in Abracadabra, picking up diamonds and putting them in her mouth.

Penelope looks at The Young Man and asks herself what he might be doing there, at that hour, in the dark, and then answers herself. And she doesn't like the answer. Because it's an answer that isn't about her. That doesn't even take her into account. It's an answer—another one—that puts her on the sidelines of everything and below everything and in the finest print. Like a footnote to the main text. As if she were a decorative figure or merely a detail in someone else's portrait: the flower in the lapel, the mark left on the wall by a painting that's no longer there, the song whistled by someone passing by in the street. And the flower withers and nobody remembers what was in the painting and the whistled melody belongs to a summer song from long ago.

Penelope is very tired.

Of everything, of everyone, of her absent brother and, especially, of herself and everything she didn't do and the little that she did.

And of the fact that He Whose Name Must Not Be Mentioned—the long and powerful shadow of what might have been cast by the short and weak body that no longer is—hasn't yet been turned into or elevated to He Of Whom You Must Not Think, much less, He Who At Last And Forever Has Been Forgotten.

With respect to *that* and to *him*, Penelope has just made it to the stage of not naming; but she knows that, in the very effort to not name something, resides the implicit punishment of being unable to stop thinking about it, of never being able to forget it. And also that, sometimes, even in the solitude of the fortress she's built herself—in her Angria, in her Gondal—she experiences the weakness of its architecture, the decisive design failure where the final crack will burst. Like right now—that small voice that Penelope hasn't heard for so long and thought she'd never hear again. Where did it come from? From The Young Man's hand? From something The Young Man is holding in his hand? "Let's see . . . Who's your favorite writer?" Penelope hears again. And then she gets it: it doesn't matter how well you've swept everything under the heaviest of rugs; because the broom will always remain, behind a door or inside a closet, to remind you that at some point you held it the way you hold a pen that crosses out and sweeps away but doesn't erase. Perfect oblivion doesn't exist just like the perfect crime doesn't exist. To win the prize, not just of *I don't remember*, but of *I don't even remember what I don't remember*, Penelope says to herself, you have to cross finish lines that more closely resemble the treacherous curves of madness and suicide. And though Penelope has, more than once, looked down from the tempting balcony of those choices, the truth is they don't interest her, they don't seem like dignified exits.

Sure, it's been years since she accepted the fact that she'd never be a combative Cathy Earnshaw. Not even a Jane Eyre. But with every bit of the little strength she has left she refuses to end up like an exotic and foreign Bertha Antoinetta Mason, mad and burning in the attic of Thornfield Hall, throwing herself from the flaming roof, her infidelities and alcoholism and hallucinations forgiven, chalked up to a genetic disorder. Bertha, who sacrifices herself to leave the path free and open for the marriage of the blind Edward Fairfax Rochester and the servant Jane Eyre. Penelope doesn't want to be the lame and boring device of an envious sister—because the merely very talented Charlotte was always intimidated by Emily's rare genius, and didn't hesitate to lovingly sabotage her memory, imposing the survivor's official version—that neatly ties up the plot. And everybody's happy.

But no—that'd be too easy.

To the contrary, the role that Penelope has fallen into is that of the lone survivor. Everything and everyone around her dead or disappeared. And the responsibility of telling the story is hers and hers alone. And, truthfully, she never wanted to be a writer. She just wanted to have and to live a good story. And now she's so tired. So tired that, if she had a rifle, she wouldn't hesitate to empty it into The Young Man's body. To fill him full of lead and defend herself by saying she'd thought he was a burglar. And end up exonerated or in jail. Either way. Anything so long as the small storyline of her life diverges from the atomic and particular saga of her brother, who absorbs everything and rewrites it. Including the only thing that, she assumed, was hers and hers alone and that she—not for revenge but out of desperation—tore out the way you tear the page from a book that, though you never open it, you'll always know is missing a page and that it's *that* page.

And the voice from that page is the one she hears again now: asking for the name of a favorite writer the way you ask a ghost to knock three times so you know it's there when, really, all that's there is the memory of that person, which is nothing at all without a living being to remember it. In stories and novels, the best ghosts are the ones who appear to people who knew them. Orphan ghosts, appearing to strangers, have little reason to be or to do and have too much to explain to people who, after the initial fright, will begin to perceive them as a nuisance, as a kind of malfunction in the house that they bought at, now it makes sense, a suspiciously low price. Those ghosts are just ghosts of themselves, sick of spinning circles in the air and, sometimes, the most dangerous ghosts of all; because they try to compensate for the fact that nobody misses them, tormenting and driving mad everyone who crosses their path, for whom they neither have nor feel any hate or affection.

That is exactly how Penelope feels. Alone, bad company, and the last of her bloodline. No one will remember her. Except this fool who snuck into her house, this worshipper of her writer brother, now transformed into ultra solipsistic and quantum-ectoplasmatic autofiction, or whatever.

So Penelope decides to spare The Young Man's life.

And not tell him to turn around.

And not fix him with her eyes—greener than ever.

And not stare into his eyes.

And not detect in them something that—could it be desperation to find a way out?—might be her own emergency exit.

And so great is The Young Man's desire and passion that Penelope senses a vanishing point. Some relief. A blessed opportunity to break the curse with someone else's desire.

What was that story called? Something about a monkey paw and the con-taminated perfume that make wishes come true. In it, the protagonist asked a monkey paw for something. And that wish was granted. But that granted wish always arrived by way of a dark road where it collided with horror. Be careful what you wish for, etcetera.

So, Penelope thinks, why not leave all of it to The Young Man. The house and everything in it. "The palace of my memory," as her brother would say; he never really appreciated that she'd been the one who financed it with part of the spoils she brought back from the desert of Abracadabra. A more or less perfect replica—because it's known that children remember everything larger and shinier—of a place called Sad Songs, where her brother went on vacation with their parents and her, more or less proximal, inside their mother, newly pregnant and wondering, no doubt, what now?

"What now?" Penelope asks herself. And the answer appears to her with the naturalness of something obvious, in that undeniable way that right answers have of presenting themselves: you haven't even finished formulating the most complex of questions, after so long not daring to, when the answer is already there, on display in the middle of the room, spinning slowly, waiting for you to make it your own, to react to it, and to activate it, so that it can make what belongs to it belong to you.

And what Penelope does is to do nothing.

To slip away, the way one, following stage directions, leaves a stage.

Exit.

The Young Man turns slowly around, hands still held high, The Boy's voice repeating that question over and over and obtaining that answer that he still can't believe and yet believes immediately; because nothing is easier to believe in than what you want to believe in. And what he always wanted was to be someone's favorite writer and, if possible, to be the favorite writer of someone like his favorite writer, like The Writer.

The Young Man turns around and doesn't see anyone there. The Writer's Mad Sister isn't there. He's alone. But The Young Man is sure, *something* was there a few seconds ago. Something was watching him. And, face to face with its absence, what terrified him before relieves and even justifies him now. Again, this is one of the characteristic traits of criminal minds—the need to feel that they were impelled and even authorized by something that transcends and supersedes them. An external mandate. It doesn't matter that his crimes, The Young Man's, aren't found in any penal code. Or maybe they are: because both the one before aboard the airplane and the one now in the house could easily be classified as forms of theft.

But The Young Man prefers not to think about that.

The Young Man prefers to think of himself as, yes, a toy—another toy—of destiny.

A chosen one.

And he decides that that brief yet powerful presence behind him (The Young Man could swear he still feels its reverberation in the air, like the ripples left on the surface of the water by a stone already sinking into the depths, where The Writer claimed that shipwrecked plotlines were waiting to be rescued and reconstructed) could only have been The Writer himself. The resolution of his story with the most open of endings. The Writer, in a way, coming back to mark him, choosing him, pointing out the way to reveal to him—coincidentally, but not by coincidence—his own name pulsing like a mantra inside that camera.

The Young Man feels so happy, so innocent, that he goes out the window with a leap he'd never have thought himself capable of. Holding the camera and the toy in his hands. Ready to go in the tent, wake up The Young Woman (who's dreaming a strange dream, where she and The Young Man meet in the future, many years later, on a museum stairway), and pack up all their gear. Quickly. To get out of there. Behind him he feels the heat of something exploding and—deploying the absurd logic of someone who already feels outside everything—the first thing The Young Man thinks is that it's fireworks celebrating him, commemorating him. For him. But what has begun to burn—in a small series of explosions, as if according to a pre-figured order, as if crossing off items from a list of rooms—is the house of The Writer and The Writer's Mad Sister.

"The contagious joy of fire," The Young Man says to himself. "I don't want to forget this phrase. I like it. I should write it down in my notebook," he adds.

And he goes inside the tent and yells, "Let's go!"

The Young Woman opens her eyes and looks at him, sleepily. And The Young Man is already imagining how her pupils will dilate when they see, as if fallen from the sky, *that* video of The Writer answering *that* question asked by *that* boy. Then anything will be possible. Anything.

And The Young Man and The Young Woman start packing everything into bags and unpitching the tent that'll be transformed into a light and portable cylinder and blessed be the miniaturization of gear and that the most important things take up less space all the time.

The house is still burning, but it won't burn for long and The Young Man and The Young Woman approach the edge of the blaze searching for The Writer's Mad Sister, who is no longer there, who has discovered that there's another alternative—to be the demented woman who unleashes a holocaust of flames and fury, yes, but not to die in it.

To escape, clean and renewed.

To start over again, after hurling everything into the fire. Not mad with joy, but mad with madness.

The Young Man and The Young Woman and their backpacks run along the beach, along the cold and hard sand of the shore. Penelope watches them move away with the strange sadness of seeing something you'll never see again. Something that you don't really mind leaving behind, but that, at the same time, is still another thing that you're leaving behind.

And the irretrievable past builds itself like this, a little at a time, ceaselessly and arbitrarily.

And who knows, thinks Penelope: maybe I'll remember this random image—The Young Man and The Young Woman running and releasing little shrieks into the cold and dark air that the stars never warm—when I've already forgotten many other things, far more important things.

Things safe from fire, but not from oblivion.

Penelope remembers having read that of all the liquids and fluids produced by the human body—sweat, semen, vaginal fluid, saliva—tears are the only one without any trace of DNA. So, a killer can weep in peace at the scene of his crime. Impossible to identify someone from their tears, we're all identical when we weep despite the many different reasons we have for weeping, something like that. Unlike unhappiness, tears don't set us apart, they make us the same.

But Penelope is convinced that this isn't true.

It can't be true.

Her tears—these tears—are hers and hers alone. She won't share them with anyone, she won't compare them, she won't let them be compared.

Nobody ever wept like she weeps now, no one ever wept for what she weeps tonight.

They won't take that away from her: it's all she has, all she has left, leaving, her house in flames farther behind her all the time; just a spot of light that no expert sailor would ever confuse for a sign of solid ground.

Now an earthquake. Because everything moves and Penelope moves.

Leaving that place, all of it. Free of dead weight, alive and light. Changing scenery like someone changing style. Almost blind, groping along the insurmountable walls of the night, Penelope finds a handhold at last and grabs on with all her strength to keep from being dragged out to sea by the singular and inimitable whirlpool of her weeping.

With her face cleansed by tears (this all happened so long ago, at a time when there were still waves and trees to describe and put in writing) Penelope opens the door and enters the forest.

A FEW THINGS
YOU HAPPEN TO THINK ABOUT
WHEN ALL YOU WANT
IS TO THINK ABOUT NOTHING

Don't touch.

Don't touch (having entered and arrived here; to a place where, paradoxically, they are going to be touching, they are going to be touching you absolutely everywhere in order to classify and diagnose the skill, the style, and the transcendence of what it is that's brought you here), but, instead, look closely.

And closer still.

As close as the edge of that black line running across the white floor allows.

Watch carefully.

There he is.

Staring into the void where—he doesn't see but senses—someone is staring back.

The name of his creator doesn't matter, the name of the portrayed man either. Anonymous author, yes. And one of those neutral titles, simple and simply descriptive. The kind of prosthetic title (the true title was amputated by the passing of years and the movement of forgotten things) applied when anything is better than nothing. Anything, as long as it isn't that, for him, oh so irritating *Untitled* trailed by a number, an attempt to cover up the author's lack of will, or the lack of expertise of the experts in his work. Something helpful when the time comes to present it at the hour of the catalogue and the auction. And that's it. And moving right along. And next! and look to the future.

So, now, Portrait of a Lonely Man. And done. Period and new sentence. A simple descriptive title. And period and new paragraph.

Isolated portrait of a Lonely Man in the emergency room where—though other people are waiting and accompanying each other in their wait—his loneliness is unbroken. The loneliness of a hospital or a clinic waiting room is invulnerable and immune to all the bacteria that the most-cited statistics say run rampant through hallways and bedrooms and operating rooms and infect healthy accompaniers and further sicken the accompanied sick. Because the loneliness there, in the preliminary stages of the hospital ritual, is composed of the links between various autonomous, independent, solitary lonelinesses; because there's no loneliness more solid than that of someone who, though surrounded by others, knows that they're completely and absolutely alone and is waiting for someone to tell them something.

Portrait of a Lonely Man in the emergency room of a hospital in a city whose name isn't important or decisive here; so it'll suffice to identify it as B, and moving right along.

Keep watching, of course. Pausing in suspense. Take your time along the way, it doesn't matter what scene comes next and what scene just passed: he goes along slowly, he goes along gradually, he goes along stretching the sentence out little by little, because he's having trouble breathing. So there he is and it's easy for him to see himself as if from outside. As if he were looking at himself not in a mirror, but in a painting and, please, right?: none of those supposedly avant-garde tricks where a performer puts himself on exhibit. In a room in a museum. Sitting in a chair so the visiting public can sit down in another chair facing him and look at him and get all emotional and weep. And, on their way out, blurt out that this is one of the most transcendent and moving experiences of their entire lives because, it's clear, he thinks, that there are people who have and lead very uninteresting lives where nothing happens and who, as such, hypersensitive about their lives' uneventfulness, are moved by anything at all, by the first thing that happens to them. That was never his case. And there's nothing he'd like less than to provoke that effect he'd never experienced himself in others, in strangers who need to be recognized, to get to know themselves simply by prepaying for a ticket that many appear ready to kill or die for.

So he, even though he's there, flesh and bone, prefers to feel himself framed. Alone. Hanging. Painted. Tall and wide and not raised or in relief. Title and date and school and technique and painter's name—also the name of the painted (yes: it's a self-portrait)—and, for now, just the date of birth. But, ah, any minute, you never know, another number will be added: the

definitive number, the year of the end, after a too-short script that symbol-
izes everything that happened between one extreme and the other, between
entrance and exit, between life and death, between the first and the last
brushstroke. There, on the wall of a private museum dedicated to The Lonely
Man and that The Lonely Man alone has access to.

And again: don't touch.

In the portrait, he's sitting in a hard and cold plastic chair, in a facility
built of thick glass panels that are, without a doubt, everything-proof. Huge
windows that silence all sound from the street and from the ambulances that
enter and exit like ballerinas on the edges of a ballet. Outside pulses the
humming heart of a neon red cross; which coheres even further the idea
that people pray a lot in here, begging for miracles, asking for impossible
things from beings they want to believe are genies, geniuses. Here, the doctors—the professionals—like direct descendants of demigods, of saints, of
shamans, of superstars are capable of conjuring the sad and small eclipses
of anonymous people who have names, but whose names mean nothing in
here. All individual characteristics yield to the particularity of diseases that
are too banal (though no less fatal) to be featured on an episode of one of
those series with doctors whose charm and allure to viewers he never could
understand. Where's the pleasure in being reminded, before going healthily
to sleep, that sooner or later they'll cut you open and sew you up and blast
you with rays and radiations? And that the person in charge will be nothing
like that kind Adonis or that infallible and abusive psychopath? And that
real nurses—like nuns or flight attendants—are nothing like their cathodic
versions, more like centerfolds of some steamy magazine or the stars of some
Broadway musical? And he thinks "Broadway" and into his head comes that
film, *All That Jazz*, in which a legendary, supposedly fascinating (but decidedly intolerable) musical director slipped out of his room, wandered through
hallways and basements and came to find a kind of symbolic ecstasy that
included death and a great final number where everyone sang and waved
goodbye amid colored lights and dancers in costumes that were like a second
skin of red and blue blood.

Yes, hospital or clinic waiting rooms—nothing of the scenographic or
choreographic ambition of that movie—have something of a fictitious setting, of a too-neat façade.

And it's not that The Lonely Man is an expert in the matter. His experience traveling to these territories has been brief but definitive. In the moment of his birth—a baby of colossal proportions, a complicated delivery—he'd been declared dead, just seconds after arriving to the world. Mysteriously and inexplicably, a few minutes later, to the astonishment of his midwife and her team, he started to breathe again, after he'd already been written off, set aside on a metallic bed, bound for the morgue. The Lonely Man, of course, remembers nothing of his brief sojourn on the other side. But it's easy enough for him to imagine that whatever and wherever it might be—above or below or in some wrinkle in space-time, a limbo of stardust—its waiting room must closely resemble the waiting room he was in now. And that from there, maybe, grow the roots that forced on him the cursed blessing of having lived to tell the tale.

Later, a few months after his death-life, he slipped from his mother's arms and fell to the floor and split open his chin (requiring several stitches) and, almost immediately thereafter, a cavernous cough, like black lung, landed him at the pediatrician who, studying an X-ray, explained to his parents that their son was a mutant—he had an extra rib. (The oddities of his bones would catch up with him again four decades later when he was informed by a disconcerted osteopath that what he thought was arthritic pain was actually a consequence of a condition that only presented in menopausal women and NBA stars, and since he was neither, the doctor didn't dare recommend any treatment.) Then, throughout his childhood, the apocalypse of his teeth. And not much else, apart from a simultaneously funny and troubling propensity for domestic and school and vacation accidents. But no broken bones. No surgeries. No fever more dangerous than the typical ones, accompanied in his case by small splotches all over his face and body which, for a few days, make him sort of abstract and expressionist. And, yes, now he remembers, greatest hit: blasting headlong and without brakes into adolescence, an explosion of sores in his mouth and a fire in his skull that render him bedridden for almost a month, nourished by the juices of tropical fruits with strange shapes and names, unable to chew solid foods, and a sudden growth spurt of several centimeters so that, finally, back on his feet, he's no longer the shadow of the boy he'd once been but the shadow of the man he'd one day become.

And that's pretty much it for him as protagonist-invalid; the exception being (more a cure than an ailment) the understandable and wondrous and wholesome and purifying and disinfecting cataclysm every time he finished and submitted and extracted and amputated—suddenly overcome with relief—a new book from his system. That malaria that he'd been putting up with for years, singing to his brain.

And he systematically scheduled and postponed his yearly physical, not out of fear but out of discomfort. And out of a lack of desire to be humiliated by carrying urine and fecal samples in a little bag.

Or narrating in excess detail—as if he were writing it down—a recent episode of something that he prefers to disguise by putting it (courtesy of Wikipedia, so if this isn't the right spelling, it's not his fault) in the original and foundational Greek, because it looks so much better: αἱμορροΐς.

Or seeing himself forced into that so-feared and anticipated . . . what was the term used to put it delicately? Insertion? Invasion? Intrusion? . . . Ah, right: EXPLORATION, a euphemism that seems to want to evoke the dandy and heroic figure of a Victorian adventurer exploring an unknown continent. And in that movie, it was understood, his role wouldn't be that of the lord explorer but of the continent to be examined and subjugated.

Anyway, he thinks now, maybe it would've been better to return here like that, pain free, rather than like he's returned now—as if struck by a bolt of lightning that refuses to leave his body. Saying the onomatopoetic and oh so funny and not at all funny magic word: "check-up" like "Shazam!" or like, referring to cavernous openings, "Open Sesame!" But he thinks about it a little more and says to himself that, no, it's better like this: better to suffer something external and his own than to be made to suffer something internal and predetermined and to have it go well and to leave feeling fine and immortal, but only for another year. People he knew were constantly reminding him not to forget. And they did so with the smile of people who've been there before, like Vietnam veterans. But he kept calling his doctor's office, only to hang up after the first ring or beep or whatever. And oh how, at that moment, he missed the old Bakelite rotary phones that allowed you, listening to that sound of coming and going, so similar to a masticating skull-and-crossbones, to think of so many things, to be indecisive and, every so often, via a capricious tangle of phone lines, to spy on other people's strange conversations. Phones that, in addition, forced you to use address books, that subspecies of book, to write down telephonic indexes, starting over every year, revising, crossing off names and numbers like someone delivering a sentence—condemning or pardoning. Now, whenever he gathered the necessary amount of coward's courage to (not) make the appointment, the doctor's number was like a gust of wireless code that only left time for a delayed tap of the thumb. And moving right along. And to try in vain to forget that interview with the *noir* rocker Warren Zevon when he—already condemned and with a final expiration date, having ignored that nonsense of annual check-ups until it was already too late—recommended to his fans that "don't do like I did, and go to the doctor more regularly, okay? And enjoy every sandwich." And to try not to think about that character of Don Delillo's from *Cosmopolis*—submitted to a daily "exploration" for the abnormality of an "asymmetric prostrate." And, yes, he wanted to keep on enjoying each and every one of his sandwiches, definitely; but nothing interested him less than being informed that his prostate was asymmetrical, and that's why . . .

He had, now, the mild comfort of thinking that the pain in the north of his body that was barely letting him breathe couldn't have anything to do with his prostate, far to the south. It must be bad, he says to himself, it had all the appearance of something sudden and fatal and whose denouement couldn't be far off and, to avoid that train of thought, he starts to make a list of his favorite invalids: Walter White, Ralph Touchett, Iván Illich; all of them terminal, but going slowly. Given a choice, it wouldn't bother him to be like one of them. Beings between fierce and melancholy recalling the good old days—"houses of healing," they called them—when hospitals were buildings where others went to stay and, at most, you went to visit them for a while, almost unable to hide your need to get out of there as quickly as possible.

And, yes, he visited many hospitals as a supporting actor or an extra.

Once, when he was ten years old, he visited his hospitalized father, there for a minor and quickly resolved issue. His father who, from the bed, imperial yet terrified, ordered him not to worry, he planned to outlive him by a long shot. Because in his world—his father's world—parents survived their children. Or, at least, in his father's world, who, a few hours after his visit, after having staged a very *All That Jazz* moment, managed to get the doctors (who couldn't stand him anymore and even started to fantasize about doping him or sinking him into a deep coma) to sign his release, call him a taxi, and add his name to a top-secret list of undesirable patients that circulates, classified, through all the hospitals of the world.

He visited a hospital again during that summer of historic heat when rivers were scars, birds fell from the trees, the old melted, the young made love and licked sweat off each other to ward off dehydration, and babies dreamed (without knowing that it was Europe or Africa; but the soaring temperatures increased their intellectual capacity on nights when the moon seemed a sun, crouching and ready to pounce) of shimmering European outposts in Africa, devoured by the sands of a voracious desert. That summer when he and everyone else (not like in one of those paintings of solitary men, but like a participant in one of those colossal frescos in the Louvre where supporting characters amass—for coronations or shipwrecks or battles or in heavens or hells—and the true protagonist is outside the frame) went, all together, to watch a friend die. Or, better, to imagine a friend dying, on the other side of a wall that they touched with the tips of their fingers, believing that they were sending him their energy, their we're-here-for-you, their you're-not-alone. A friend that he *did* see, just for a second and almost out of the corner of his eye, when he opened the door to a room reserved for family members: his face, no longer of this world and giving off the glow of that mortified god of ancient legend, chained to a mountainside, suffering the daily retribution of an eagle devouring his intestines for all eternity. That same night, the night that would be the night of his friend's death, half asleep and a quarter awake and another quarter not one thing or the other, in a dream of half-open or half-closed eyes, his pupils already accustomed to absorbing all possible light from the darkness (he never told anybody about this, fearing that they'd think he was crazy or consider him dysfunctional, much less put it in writing; he swore he never would), he sensed a presence at the foot of his bed, in his house. A vibration in the prickling skin of the air that could only be his dying friend finally reaching the end of his agony. A last sign, like a sigh. Then he looked at the phosphorescent time on his alarm clock, memorized those four numbers with two dots at their center, and he didn't have to wait long for the phone to ring, to receive the breaking bad news that he already sensed. He asked for the exact time of death without needing to. He already knew it, he'd already seen it and felt it.

Since that time, for many years now, The Lonely Man has been convinced of the nonexistence of of ghosts returning long term, coming from the other side to reveal or beseech or demand. But he does believe in ghosts who depart quickly, whose existence lasts just as long as the act of dying—all systems offline and, finally, the brain saying goodbye to itself, launching a final probe into space, trusting that someone will be able to catch it and believe in it forever, and never forget it.

In another hospital it fell on him to identify a recently deceased friend. A pair of employees, in charge of taking the bodies down to the basement where they'd be picked up by the funeral home, opened the door to a descending elevator and there was his friend, dead and sitting up, his jaw slumped; they asked him to identify the body, to state it aloud and sign it on paper. And there was something terrible about seeing a corpse sitting up instead of lying down. A sitting corpse was the closest thing to a specter, he thought then; but this death is previous to the previous death and to the awareness he acquired then regarding the shy performance, debut and farewell, of apparitions, exit ghost, yes.

And, of course, he imagined, dead, friends whom just the night before he'd seen full up to the nose with cocaine, jumping around under the lights of a dance club or floating in a pool of morphine, hallucinating that they were speaking their last words to Charon. Friends whom, at their wakes, he refused to look down at over the edge of the chasm of the coffin, because he preferred to remember them in motion and alive and dying of laughter.

But yes, he said to himself now, dying of pain in the waiting room of a hospital without anyone to visit, sudden and absolute protagonist of a movie for which he was also the only spectator: beginning with his own initiating death, he'd had, not the pleasure, but the privilege (in days when—unlike centuries past, where everyone saw everyone die in their own home, in the same bed as always, or at the feet of an old horse or a new machine—it was increasingly difficult to witness someone's last rights) of seeing dead people die. And, still, he'd always felt a little disappointed and somewhat disconcerted by the precise instant of death, by death as the one and only last will and testament. As if it were a long previewed movie or an untimely but well publicized death, suddenly premiering after one of those mysterious viral campaigns, the truth is, he'd always, every time he'd encountered it, expected more from death. More substance and plot. Instructions that'd help him understand and appreciate it better, with the reverence and wonder it deserved. But no. Nothing. Just the weight of a never-fully-fulfilled expectation. And, at one extreme, in the final scene of the most final of acts, a death. That's it, friends and relatives and assorted debts. And what was that thing Plato said? Ah, yes: "The dead are the only ones who see the end of the war." True; but it's the living—traversing the still-warm battlefield—who watch the dead see this end and put it down in writing. That absence that a dead person leaves in life, like that spot where, for many years, a painting hung. A painting that, all of a sudden, is no longer there. But that all the same you can't stop seeing. Or, at least, we perceive a difference in the tonality of the paint on that rectangle of wall. The painting is not there anymore, but, outlined, is the space where the painting hung. So you have no choice but to fill that empty space—and accept that oh so hermetic inheritance—that the dead leave behind for those who feel them die. Paradox: death, the most personal and nontransferable experience of all, is such inspiring material not for the dead—for whom it lasts but a second and then they are elsewhere, far away—but for the survivors who shape it as they wish, stretching it out into a panoramic novel, or reducing it to its most minimal and intimate expression. Like with the open endings in Chekov stories, so easily praised (nothing made him more mistrustful than writers who invoked Chekov's name as if he were a family member or appended it to another name, without asking anyone's permission, as in "young Chekov," "Latin American Chekov," "noir Chekov") by those who feel that they are, though they don't admit it, easy to imitate. And oh how they try. And, retroactively, they degrade them and strip away the shell of their mystery to reveal a miniscule and minimalist fruit. Those were the same people who celebrated that the Nobel Prize for Literature was given to a supposed direct descendent of the Russian like Alice Munro ("Chekov in a skirt") and who made him wonder, shouting, alone, fist raised to the sky: "If they gave it to her for being Chekov in a skirt, why the hell, in his day, didn't they give it to the Chekov in pants, eh?"

Could it be because of things like this—so stupid, but that he feels so passionately about—that it seems like his chest is parting in two to reveal the reddest of seas? Is that the reason for this pain? And, obviously, this wasn't the only literary rant that he found himself—between fascinated and worried—going off on these days. The Lonely Man, who'd always considered himself a kind of evangelist of his vocation and all his colleagues, in conversation with the dumbest or wildest of animals, promoting the pleasures of reading, and always publishing highly favorable reviews, because, he explained with a question: "Why malign something when there're so many good things to recommend?"; some time ago, he'd found himself possessed by a new and unknown and almost Hulk-green fury. A euphoric thirst for vengeance and an exhilarating longing for destruction that, who knows, might've had something to do, once again, with the arrival of that pain in his chest and that made him so much like certain characters of Jewish American literature. Saul Bellow's Von Humboldt Fleisher, Joseph Heller's Bob Slocum, Bruce Jay Friedman's Harry Towns, Phillip Roth's Mickey Sabbath. People who, howling with rage and joy, laid waste to everything in their paths: families, jobs, and even hospitals. Homo Catastrophicos, their genesis the apocalypse of everyone else.

Here and now, of course, he wasn't howling. Now: silence, hospital. Now he was saving up all his internal howls for a sanctuary of definitive and irrefutable outcomes. And yet a circuitous death wasn't a perfect ending. Death wasn't an exact science. It wasn't subject to formulas. You can die at any moment, never knowing why and without ever understanding anything. Like—in his case—poetry. Or jazz. Something whose meaning you infer all of a sudden, when it's already too late, after having not understood it your whole life. Like madness, whose sanity of spirit and raison d'être are only fully understood by the mad.

And, back on this side, do psychiatric hospitals count as hospitals? Presumably. And all of that—those "rest-homes"—is known and familiar to him. Numerous instances of checking in or visiting or bringing Penelope home to almost immediately turn around and check her back in—commit her. Psychiatric hospitals that have nothing to do with his idea of nineteenth-century insane asylums in deranged novels. (Yes: he thinks about movies and blockbusters, he invokes them and remembers them, when he wants and needs oh so urgently to think about anything that's not his own lowly home movie, with its shaky and out-of-focus picture, the short in which he's suddenly acting, acting badly.) That movie in which an old and confessional Salieri softly sings his infamy with Mozart melodies, amid shit-smeared walls and histrionic lunatics, too many of whom—this always struck him as quite curious—believe they are Napoleon and none of whom believe they are Don Quixote. Or maybe nothing interests a madman less than madness, because, just as he thought, for the madman, madness is perfectly reasonable.

Just the opposite, the "homes" where, every so often, Penelope "retreated" (following her return from that strange nuptial voyage to the other side of the ocean, increasingly immersed in the self-analysis of her "condition"), had about them, every single one, the suspicious tranquility and silence of some hermetically-sealed thing. Like space stations orbiting around a healthy and external normality, that was, actually, far more abnormal than what they were breathing in there. Whenever he'd gone to visit her, he, strolling along with his hands behind his back, had always thought the same thing: "What a great place to shut yourself in to write or read."

The present hospital, his hospital, on the other hand, just makes him want to burn books and raze nations and do all the things despots do to inspire fear, because nothing inspires more fear than what they feel, knowing themselves to be all-powerful and, consequently, ephemeral, weak, and already ready to be blown away by the winds of history.

He's sitting next to one machine selling cold drinks and another machine selling hot drinks and another machine selling candy and more or less salty things like braised-chicken-and-potato flavored potato chips (yes, potato chips that feature the inclusion of the flavor of potato as part of their allure) or cheeseburger flavored potato chips. The absurd potato-chip-industry and mutant equivalent of an ebook (another contradiction in terms in a single product, he thinks). Like food for mad astronauts and just enough of it to survive on while you wait to be told whether or not you're going to survive. The Lonely Man wonders if he'll get a chance or if it'd be a bad idea for him to drink a—last?—Coca-Cola. After all, wasn't Coca-Cola "the spark of life"? And isn't *that* exactly what he's in need of here and now? The spark? Of life? Something to reignite him? Something to rekindle his fire, in danger of going out, surrounded by treacherous and circular winds? Something to bring him back to the beaches of the plausible and palpable immortality of good health? Good health that we don't know we have until we don't have it anymore? Good health like an un-gifted gift, like a medal stripped from our chest, rendering our uniform torn and demoted? That good health that (apart from small aches, or great pains, but nothing serious: like the already mentioned and long-bygone thing about his mouth exploding in flames and fires, or the recent and inconfessible and fleeting Hellenic impossibility of sitting down that he's even come to appreciate as a vacation from the obligation of working in front of his screen) he had until last night? The good health that he felt secretly proud of as, knock on wood, he watched beings more or less close to him get struck down by syndromes and illnesses of a varying caliber? Now not so much. Not anymore. Now is when the rust starts to grow on his iron health, now is when "poor health" begins. Now that poverty is his. A new era.

"Welcome," said a sign near the hospital entrance.

Very funny.

And the Lonely Man doesn't dare to wonder whether that sign is an ironic detail or something altogether more dreadful—the abbreviated and modern version of what's written at the doors to Dante's Inferno. How many characters does "Abandon all hope ye who enter here" have?" More than a hundred and forty? Less? He counts them: there are only thirty-four. More than enough space and, ah, again, The Lonely Man never felt a pain so . . . it's not strong . . . no. It's a pain that's very *wide*. The Lonely Man never felt a pain as wide as the pain he feels now. A pain that's located in a fixed and concentrated and small point. But a pain that, from there, spreads like waves to the rest of his body, until it conquers and colonizes his farthest reaches. The distant territories where his body and his pain are demarcated, here and now, in the emergency room, by other bodies and other pains.

What happened? What happened to him? Who knows? What will be will be?

His pain is pure novelty and, yes, the most merciless and immediate version of what's known as "fear of the unknown." Now, The Lonely Man is like an ancient sailor. Like those medieval explorers who launched themselves from the borders of ancient and unfinished maps into the liquid *terra incognita*. Maps where, next to a lavishly-adorned wind rose, as if to convince themselves that everything was under control and had a known cause, was written the gothic maxim "Beyond here are monsters" or "Here are dragons."

In Latin, the language of fear and the irrevocable, of faith and superstition, the secret language of all emergency rooms and doctors and diseases.

But there's something even worse than that, he thinks: the monster is here, at hand, in his chest, maw agape, bearing its teeth, gnawing at him. The Lonely Man holds one hand against his chest to cradle the pain. The pain in his chest is like a monstrous newborn. A newborn pain that brings him to the brink of tears and keeps growing with each passing minute. Before long, The Lonely Man thinks, the pain will grow into an adolescent howl, uncontrollable in its rebelliousness and impulses. And it won't be easy to keep it there, inside his chest, with nothing but the simple support of a single hand or a slap. Later, after at most two hours of going on like that, before the newborn primordial cracking of that which can never be fixed, an already old and defeated moan will burst out of his throat from deep in his intestines. His physiological Waterloo. A Waterloo like the one in the first chapter of *The Charterhouse of Parma*: pure confusion and disorientation and no strategic map covered with little lead soldiers to be contemplated from the gallery of an officers' mess hall. No, no, no: now, like Fabrizio del Dongo lost in space, he's wondering where the front and the rearguard are and where is the office to negotiate surrender. The Lonely Man remembers when, so many years ago, he learned that the custom of the hand held against the chest wasn't a gesture that Napoleon came up with for posing or posterity (his almost superhero quirk, a characteristic by which to be known or distinguished), but as a direct consequence of an ulcer or something like that. Terrible disappointment. He learned this around the same time that someone revealed to him that Hanna-Barbera *was not* a woman creator of animated drawings, but was actually two men. Another defeat. And it's clear that, seeing him now, no one would mistake him for a god of war or a genius strategist. Now, The Lonely Man is struggling and alone. The hand he clutches to his chest doesn't inspire or instill any call to be cast in bronze. To the contrary, his situation produces unease and tenderness: his hand shakes and, on his wrist, a plastic bracelet bears his first and last name (which aren't important here either, and don't even require initials) and a barcode which, The Lonely Man assumes, synthesizes the symptoms that he communicated to the receptionist when he arrived. Before collapsing into this chair to wait for them to call him and examine him and classify him and, who knows, maybe release him to the outside world and not force him to stay inside, for all eternity, for a few hours or a few days or for the five or six minutes of life he has left.

The Lonely Man is inclined toward the first of the preceding options, but, out of superstition, to avoid tempting fate, he distracts himself—he's not alone in there—watching the other people waiting in the waiting room.

There's an immemorial elderly woman of an aristocratic yet slightly decadent bearing who shouts incessantly into her mobile phone and seems desperately happy to be there, to be sick again, to be attended to and served and to relay everything to her descendants, to see what they plan to do about it in order to move up or down in the inheritance hierarchy. Her movements have the angularity of arachnids and The Lonely Man—who has always considered himself and been considered by those who know him an infallible judge of character—could guarantee that that old woman is the most malignant and detestable being that has ever scarred and disfigured the face of the earth. A wart of hate and rancor.

And a young woman who never stops sending messages from her multiuse mobile phone. "Hey here at hospital 2 C what they say bout my belly and hope I'm not preggers hahahaha and that nobody finds out bout this cuz otherwise!!" guesses The Lonely Man, thinking about how that hypothetical message will be subsequently forwarded by its recipient. The Lonely Man often thinks about written things, about things he's going to write (and he brings his hand to his chest, now, to feel for his notebook), but he never counts the characters. One hundred forty characters. The bizarre and new talent, not of writing well or writing correctly, but of writing one hundred forty characters exactly. In unjust times, when everything seems to settle for the bare minimum: abbreviating, reducing, miniaturizing, and when he, from action or reaction, is expanding like a gas, resolving to occupy all available space, repeating himself and correcting himself and repeating himself again. A form of rebellious resistance—to write nothing that doesn't surpass one hundred forty characters. Before long, he says to himself, no idea will be longer or taller or deeper than that. And he remembers the girl in the funicular, her face mangled and covered in blood, like a freshly and recently finished painting (another painting) by Francis Bacon, and it's as if he were closing that file, preferring not to think about that right now. He prefers, while waiting, light ideas. One hundred forty characters in length, in height, and in superficial depth, aspiring neither to slogan nor aphorism. Bijis, they're called. When written. Like origami that open underwater. Or sea monkeys.

And maybe it makes sense to point out here (though it might already be clear, now it's more than obvious: because it's with great difficulty that The Lonely Man sketches in his notebook, in just a few words, portraits of the people accompanying him in the wait and the emergency) that The Lonely Man is a writer. And that, consequently, his idea of a text message is far better composed than most text messages tend to be. And that The Lonely Man—getting himself "in character," distorting automatic reflex—often thinks about this kind of thing. The Lonely Man thinks, as if he were writing, that the girl writes and thinks *like that*. And that she sends her message to thousands of friends, bouncing it off the ghost of electricity howling in the bones of her face.

There are two parents worrying over their son, who must be about four years old. The little boy bears a striking resemblance to his parents, to both of them. Is that possible? Yes, if the father and mother also bear a striking resemblance to each other. And The Lonely Man wonders if it'd be good or bad—pleasant or disturbing—for your kid to look that much like you. Of course, in addition, the father is probably one of those fathers who names his son after himself. Who don't go any further than that, who don't even give it another thought, who pass their name along like property to be shared. He never understood that custom, which, he thinks, can only contain motives as egotistical as they are imbecilic: the implicit desire for someone to be just like you, to carry your name into a new era, to never forget the total idiot who preceded them, all their defects, all the undesirable gifts genetics grant you. And maybe the thing about the same name is actually better than that whole new crop of children with names that are more like sounds than names. Names that sound like Cirque Du Soleil performances. Things like Ayunnah, Taköy, Mommoh, Lankinna, Oompah. If he'd ever had a son, he would've bowed down, on his knees, before the functional Esperanto of those international names barely foreignized by an accent mark or an altered or absent letter: Tomás, Martín, Sebastián . . . But he's not really sure. He's not sure of anything except that he wants to get out of here as soon as possible.

Anyway, the subject of children isn't his subject. Like the stable couple, he renounced it long ago. He laughed at everyone who insinuated that the wild growth of children was the only thing that cut off, with the most comical of blows, the civilized growth of parents. "I do it in the name of literature," he said to himself, his first book already published, happy and as successful as he could possibly be, given the circumstances. That oath and promise were also, obviously, more comfortable ways to avoid thinking about anyone but himself. And now he wonders if that pain in his chest might actually be nothing more than exhaustion and material fatigue from thinking only of himself and of himself as part of literature. He wonders now—egocentric as only a writer can be—if it might not have been nice to be accompanied that night by a hypothetical and good-looking, twenty-something-year-old son who looked nothing like him, but closely resembled his hypothetical and exquisitely beautiful mother. And who didn't take after him at all in his personality either, so he didn't have to feel responsible for anything. A completely different son would also be more fun and more intriguing, right? If he had a son who was just like him, like the son of the man and woman over there, he reasoned, he'd constantly be wondering which parts were taken from him to build that scale model of himself.

The little boy has a fever. "High," Pa-Ma tells him, with the same voice at the same time, without him having asked anything. But none of that prevents the boy from talking. Talking to him. Talking—as if in a trance—about the arrivals and departures of a race of intergalactic robots, come to Earth to protect it from another race of intergalactic robots. Earth, it seems, turns into a battlefield for these androids that, while fighting among themselves, destroy a good part of everything around them. The Lonely Man listens attentively and nods at everything the boy says, though it isn't entirely clear to him why those alien and exceedingly sophisticated intelligences and technologies that come down to our planet mutate into modes of transportation (the cars, trucks, helicopters, and airplanes of earthlings) that are oh so imperfect and easy to disassemble. Beyond that, The Lonely Man can appreciate the Mephistophelian genius of the creator of those "autobots" and "decepticons" that the boy is talking about—two toys in one.

There was a time, thinks The Lonely Man, when people related to books like that. 2 x 1. What the writer gave you and what you did with it inside your own head. Now, not so much, less and less: it's not the content that matters, it's the packaging. The device. The latest model. Little mirrors and colored glass. Reading on it all the time, more than ever, but in homeopathic doses. And writing more than ever but, also, writing more about nothing and, the truth is, The Lonely Man couldn't care less about these issues, which he thought and wrote about a great deal in another era, another dimension, just yesterday, in the days when he was healthy or at least felt healthy.

Just the idea of a before and after in the story of his body and in what his body contains clouds his vision and fills his eyes with something that, please, not tears, right? The important thing is to distract yourself, to change frequency, to think about indestructible robots with a special talent for destroying everything around them. Bumper robots. The strangest thing of all (the kind of detail that writers tend to notice, a writer never wears out or turns off, like certain metallic humanoids) is that the boy, outside his futuristic delirium, is holding a very primitive toy in his hand. A toy made of tin. A windup toy. A little man wearing a hat and carrying a suitcase. The toy that the boy must have carefully chosen out of many to accompany him on a journey into the unknown and the X-rays. The Lonely Man is about to ask the boy something (Who are the good guys and who are the bad guys? What's an "Optimus Prime?" And an "Omicron?" And who gave him that antique toy that The Lonely Man can't take his eyes off of?) when a door opens, a nurse says his name, and then The Lonely Man stands up, as if he were back in elementary school and he'd been ordered to go up to the front of the classroom and recite the lesson. Something that could only be memorized, pure sound, without the faintest idea what you're saying, like when you sing a song in a language you don't speak. The Lonely Man goes over what he's going to say in his head. A list of symptoms. He's concerned about being clear and not getting lost in long and virulent sentences adjectivized with bacteria. And, with his hand on his chest, he takes several uncertain steps, enters the zone of exam rooms (the swinging door closes behind him with a mechanical and muffled and pneumatic sound, a lot like the sound of an autobot-decepticon), and decides not too look back, fearing that he'll be struck down by one of those curses and special effects that appear in the first part of the Bible.

"If you fear thunder, let yourself be afraid," instructs a Zen proverb. So, obedient and good pupil, welcome to fear—and nothing is more frightening than always magnanimous fear—understood as a complex universal language that, complexity notwithstanding, is immediately comprehensible and apprehended perfectly in a matter of seconds: the dialect of the disease where, like any other language, the first thing you learn to say and repeat are the questions why, how, how much, when. Fear like the equivalent of Helvetica font—everybody reads it, everybody understands it. Fear like the true Esperanto.

To avoid reading the fear, *his* fear, The Lonely Man opens the book he picked out to bring with him to the hospital. He'd been really indecisive about it. Bring, out of superstition, a brief and slight book? Or, out of caution, a dense and voluminous book? And The Lonely Man is already an expert in the secret science of the right book for the right reason and right place. There are books for airplanes and books for trains and books for short trips on the metro or city bus. He's always spent a lot of time thinking about that—about what book will accompany him and where. A lot more than he spends thinking about what to wear and what items to bring. But he'd never thought about what the perfect book for a hospital would be. So, he remembers how, one hour and millions of years ago, staggering in pain to the library, he looked and searched and didn't find and his eyes clouded over making it almost impossible to read the spines on the shelves and he ended up choosing something to hold on to and to hold him up, as—he could already picture it—he moved from one doctor's office to another. Yes, he said to himself, seeing himself as if from outside: he was going to enter and exit scanner apparatuses, possibly wrapped in one of those disposable paper robes that leave you with your ass and your dignity in the air. And he didn't know what he should bring to read during all of that. He sensed that it should be blunt and dense and solid. He considered, for example, an immense volume of fragments with the almost Galenic title of *The Anatomy of Melancholy* by Robert Burton. Or maybe the three tomes of the Penguin edition of *The Arabian Nights* and its infinite possibilities for an after and a tomorrow and a thousand and one nights. Or one of the six volumes of *The History of the Decline and Fall of the Roman Empire* by Edward Gibbon and, oh, ruins, eternal ruins. Or *The Tale of Genji* by Murasaki Shikibu with its courtesan and controlled environs. Or *The Varieties of Religious Experience* by William James. Or, to cover almost everything, that total anthology that is *The Paris Review Book of Heartbreak, Madness, Sex, Love, Betrayal, Outsiders, Intoxication, War, Whimsy, Horrors, God, Death, Dinner, Baseball, Travels, the Art of*

Writing, and Everything Else in the World since 1953. Books that are large but consumable in brief fragments, prescribed doses. Something that would work both for a lightning incursion and—he thinks that he doesn't want to think this—a "prolonged stay," consequence of a "long and cruel illness" or any one of those written formulas later utilized in the composition of obituaries.

But those were all heavy books, uncomfortable, books that might end up a stone tied to his ankle, pulling him down into depths from which there was no coming back. Maybe, he said to himself, a book of stories. He remembers a story by John Updike, a writer whom he hasn't stopped missing since his death in 2009. A writer whom he'd followed, starting as an adolescent, envying his apparently inexhaustible fertility (Updike published, from the beginning of his unparalleled career, one or two books a year in addition to his long essays and reviews in *The New Yorker*) and whom he'd stuck with until his departure. Until those final poems of hospital and convalescence and cancer, versifying the end of his life and the sadness of not being able to keep on writing, that with the end of life comes the end of the work. The day Updike died, he reread something the writer said in an interview and that he'd always found really moving: "My first thought about art, as a child, was that the artist brings something into the world that didn't exist before, and that he does it without destroying something else. A kind of refutation of the conservation of matter. That still seems to me its central magic, its core of joy." And Updike—who also penned that thing about how writers are like snails moving slowly through the incommensurable volumes of the unexpressed "leaving behind a faint thread excreted out of ourselves"—had been indirectly responsible for his first job when, at the magazine where he got his professional training as a writer, a certain Abel Rondeau had tossed a handful of photos of the American writer onto his desk and had asked him to "invent an exclusive interview." And he'd done it and obeyed him without hesitation; because, after all, Updike himself had always been great at reinterpreting and falsifying everything around him in order to leave his mark on it. Updike who had learned at a young age that "nothing in fiction rings quite as true as truth, slightly arranged."

His favorite Updike story, the story he was looking for now (he was almost positive that it was included in *Trust Me*, but Updike's many many books occupied the two tallest shelves in his library and nothing was more out of the question for him than to climb up on a chair and spin around up there and come back down without falling) was called "The City." And it was a shame: because that story would've done him a lot of good and would've been excellent company. "The City" narrates the story of a traveler who, arriving to an unfamiliar city, begins to feel mildly ill the moment he lands and is much worse by the time he gets to his hotel. So he decides to go to the hospital where they administer various exams and operate on his appendix and everything turns out okay—it all ends fine. But what he remembers most and best from "The City" (he'd read and admired it multiple times, he knew one line by heart: "misery itself becomes a kind of home") was the almost touristic treatment that Updike gave to a stay in the hospital. As if the hospital were a dazzling metropolis that was, yes, quite hospitable. And he also remembered the angelic quality that Updike bestowed on the doctors and nurses. And the way that, transfigured and much improved, as if riding an epiphany, the traveler abandoned the city that he only sensed from inside that other city, happy and grateful. But, as he said, as he thought: he didn't dare climb up there to get it, because he had to go down to that other city.

So he grabbed the book that was closest at hand and, of course (they're spread out around the house like mousetraps or candles), it was one of his various copies of *Tender Is the Night* by Francis Scott Fitzgerald.

The Lonely Man put it in one of his jacket pockets along with that small notebook that he takes with him everywhere and in which, for a while now, he's been writing random phrases that, when he rereads them, always refuse to come together, to make any sense or justify their existence. Phrases that, now, suddenly, while he waits to move from the first to the second stage of his wait, arrange themselves, after so much time, in germs and bacilli and spores of possible stories—invented parts floating in the air, waiting for him to inhale them and then, inspired, exhale them.

In "Emergencies" a man ponders which book to take with him to a hospital from which he doesn't know when he'll get out, if he'll get out / Start by telling how he got there / Include funicular.

Some time ago, The Lonely Man and his library had moved to the not so high heights of the city of B (just four hundred meters above the level of a nearby sea with neither waves nor suicides, whose shores people visited just to eat and drink) because he was tired of the big city and the smallness of the increasingly rigid and wrinkled and *Prêt-à-Porter* literary world of that city.

Now, nothing was what it once was; and the repetition of a classic but tired slogan insisting that this was the best place in the universe when it came to "welcoming foreign writers" no longer swayed him—because he'd never believed in it. He'd come there, not tempted by glossy brochures promoting "the life of the writer," but because it was far away from where he was from and born and where he'd already had all "the life of the writer" he was prepared to put up with in his lifetime.

Now, moving, leaving behind and far below the "heart of the publishing world" of his language, was like being alone and in good company. He'd found a modernist loft in the heights, on the edge of a forest, accessed via a funicular that went up and down along a set of rails every couple minutes. A short time and distance of physical travel, yes, but enough to feel that you were ascending to the heavens or descending to the infernos, knowing that you'd return to paradise later or, at least, to a limbo where (his case) writers ended up who were finding it harder and harder to write and easier and easier to say "I'm writing" and change the subject like someone, funicular-ily, changing direction. Never getting off at the middle station, the halfway point, with the cyclists and runners and the suddenly unemployed victims of economic crisis, who'd decided to believe in that whole "sound of mind and sound of body" thing—because you have to believe in something.

About an hour ago—going down in every sense—The Lonely Man was gripping one of the handles hanging from the ceiling of the funicular, trying to think of anything else. Sitting was more uncomfortable than standing, because it compressed his out-of-tune organs.

The Lonely Man had descended to the lights of the city in the darkness of the early morning (the funicular began its service at 5:30 A.M.) and, ah, it's so hard to turn off an unsound mind inside the unsound body of a writer. There again (in that place where, mornings and afternoons, children coming and going from school went around howling: "Funi! Funi!" as if unwrapping the greatest of presents, a present so big it didn't fit inside their houses) The Lonely Man repeated to himself again, clenching his teeth and with tears in his eyes, the way children cry, that it was the funicular that made him make the decision, in record time, to move there. The Lonely Man—increasingly reluctant to move, having lived through a childhood of multiple displacements, courtesy of his parents' emotional earthquakes—had signed the contract the same day he viewed the loft and devoted a good part of what was left of the workday, almost in ecstasy, to riding the funicular up and down, playing with the funi, like a kid. Up and down and repeating over and over the almost mystical moment when—just as the collision of the descending cabin and the ascending cabin seemed inevitable, in mid-trajectory, the single rail forked. And—like ships in the night—they passed each other. And the passengers looked from one car to the other. Some coming and some going, riding a ghost river while on the shores grew the successive courtyards of a school playground where boys and girls were separated according to age and knowledge or lack thereof. And, depending on which way he was going, up or down, those children appeared to grow or to shrink. And they watched him pass by with little interest. A few, the small ones, shouted and waved. And he waved back at them and then, of course, immediately understood that they weren't waving at him or the other travelers. The kids were waving, always, at the funicular, at the funi, at the journey itself.

And The Lonely Man asked himself then (as he doesn't dare ask himself now, because why add mental pain to his physical pain) if all his funiculary enthusiasm might not be a mechanical manifestation of the son he never had or found or, even worse, of the son who was almost his, who was lost. Or an exotic hybrid, half reflex of something that never existed and half sensation of a limb that's been amputated, but that's still felt, there, trying to catch the ball without a hand or to kick it without a foot.

But, again, the whole subject was too fraught for him. So—writer's prerogative, one of the few "gifts" writers enjoy in relation to other mortals— he immediately sought new alternate applications and, in the funicular, he thought "Hitchcock!" and he thought "Harry Lime!" A decidedly noir feel. The funicular as an ideal space for those vertiginous or abyssal persecutions suffered by James Stewart or Cary Grant in Alfred Hitchcock films. Or the funicular as a perfect place for one of those menacing and revealing conversations like the one that Orson Wells and Joseph Cotton have at the top of a Viennese Ferris wheel in *The Third Man*. Later, soon thereafter, The Lonely Man became preoccupied with learning everything he could about the funicular (a word which comes from the Latin *funiculus,* or "cord") and took notes that, as always, he thought would be good for something, but that almost never fit anywhere. Attention: the first funicular in the world was unveiled in Lyon in 1862 and it connected Rue Terme with Croix-Rousse. Then came the one in Budapest (1870), the one in Vienna (1873), the one in Istanbul (1875), the one in the United Kingdom (1876), the one in Valparaíso (1883), the one in Switzerland (1888), the one in Lima (1896), the one in Bilbao (1915), the one in Santiago de Chile (1925), and, last of all, the one in B (1906). Specs: line of longitude 736 meters, altitude of the lower station 196 meters, altitude of the upper station 359 meters, slope 158 meters, maximum gradient 28.9 percent, 2 vehicles, vehicle capacity 50 people and a maximum of two bicycles, transportation capacity (one way) 2.000 people per hour, speed 18 km/h, cable diameter 30 mm, width of the track 1.000 mm (metric). The Lonely Man had studied all of that the way other people memorize psalms from the Bible or verses from the Koran. And earlier, arriving to the platform where he'd catch a suburban train bound for the emergency room, he repeated it to himself like a prisoner of war surrendering minimal but vital intelligence for his survival, invoking the Geneva Convention or whatever, but, please, don't kill him, he doesn't want to die here, alone, waiting to see the light at the end of the tunnel of the approaching train.

This time the descent in the funicular (which had always seemed to him a sort of domestic and playful epic, a free and fluid associator of more or less conscious ideas) felt saturated with ominous and prophetic and Dantean and Odyssean elements. As if the Gods were ceaselessly sending him signs that something important was happening and, everybody knows, the gods, though cryptic and often ambiguous and quite contradictory in their manifestations and messages, don't tend to be subtle or elegant. The gods like it to be known that they're there, all the time, changing humors—watchers with raised eyebrows. And, every so often, unleashing pollutions and knee-jerk reactions, sending telegrams almost always bearing bad news, stops in every sense of the word and expression, what are known as "divine omens." Which amount to "Everybody get down and take cover and find shelter." So, he didn't go down stairs to protect himself from thunder and lightning, but let himself be borne aloft, hanging from a steel cable, inside a small metal and plastic cabin, alone and clutching himself so that the pain tap-dancing inside his chest, ignoring the increasingly irregular rhythm of his heart, didn't burst out like an alien and start doing pirouettes.

And, yes, as mentioned, disturbing appearances, ominous signs. Waiting for the funicular to reach its final and highest stop—his—he saw a young girl, another early passenger, pause at the top of the stairway to contemplate the screen of her mobile phone. And, clearly, it wasn't the best place to do such a thing. But he'd already gotten used to successive sightings of people who (surrendering to compulsive updating of social media profiles and brief messages) seemed to lose all physical and practical awareness of their surroundings. Like this girl, ignorant of the fact that she has stopped right in the middle of the path, in the worst possible place, taking the risk that anybody running down to catch the funicular would come around the corner of the stairway without looking and run right into her and send her flying through the air. And he hadn't finished thinking it and, already inside the cabin, barely managed to lift his arm and try to warn her in an anguished voice when, of course, someone came running down and hit her and the girl was sent flying, a smile still on her face, no doubt provoked by something she read on her phone before crashing into the ground. And no: no screaming or crying. She just stood up, moving like a zombie, her face mangled and covered in blood, her mouth open in a circle missing multiple teeth, repeating over and over, as if in a trance, the monotone of a broken question: "Where's my phone? Where's my phone? Where's my phone?" Every part of her broken and yet still not realizing that nothing has higher definition than that reality that she insists on viewing only via a screen, that reality that sooner or later— if you're distracted looking at it, shrunken, on a small rectangle of plastic and chips and optic fibers—crashes into you. The doors to the funicular closed and he, moving away, down the mountain, watched her fade in the distance, in the morning mist, trying to find her mobile phone, while the man who ran into her looked at her not knowing what to do and then took out his own phone to find the answer.

Once The Lonely Man got down to the bottom, out of the cabin and leaning against the wall on the platform, waiting for the suburban train to arrive that'd drop him a few streets away from the Emergency Room, he watched as a giant albino with Down Syndrome came toward him. The man, whose age was hard to pinpoint (he seemed to be the timeless age of those legendary creatures that always appear moving and diffuse in photographs), started to shout something in his unique language and, luckily, the train arrived and he got on and he thought, almost there. Almost who knows where, to whatever comes after whatever they do to him. To—as those lucky souls who learned to believe the way he learned the alphabet say—the will of God.

And, suddenly, in pain, The Lonely Man remembered that chapter from *Tender Is the Night* that took place in a Swiss funicular. On the train, he looked for and found the page and there were Dick Diver and Nicole Warren (not yet married, all of it occurring in the novel's lengthy central flashback), in Glion. And it said there that funiculars "are built on a slant similar to the angle of a hat-brim of a man who doesn't want to be recognized." And, like so many other times, he thought "Ah, Fitzgerald!" And thinking it and savoring it made him feel a little better and he even rummaged around in his pocket to find a pen and the notebook he took with him everywhere, so he could write it down: "F. S. F. / Funicular / Hat / Stranger / Girl / Telephone / Giant / Etcetera."

In "Frankenstein," a man who has accompanied his father (who has already passed through certain doors where the man can't follow) to the hospital observes the arrival of a giant albino with some kind of mental handicap, carrying in his arms a pretty young girl with a mangled face who repeats: "Where's my phone? Where's my phone? Where's my phone?" The man stands up and gives her his phone and the girl seems to calm down and the giant smiles at him and then a doctor calls the man and tells him that his father has had a heart attack, that it was sudden and fatal, that there was nothing he could do. There wasn't even a chance or need to put into action the resurrection by defibrillator that, when he saw it on TV, the man always found too far-fetched in its efficiency, like the long and drawn out sex acts in porn movies. The man looks for his phone to notify his mother (she and his father separated years ago) and discovers that he no longer has it, that it was stolen or he lost it or, he remembers suddenly, the girl has taken it, clutching it like a consoling stuffed animal. He looks for a pay phone. But there aren't any pay phones anymore. All telephonic activity has been privatized, individualized. Anyway, he realizes, he doesn't know his mother's phone number by heart. It's not necessary to dial phone numbers anymore and, so, it makes no sense to memorize them, like with so many other things that can be accessed by pressing a button. The doctor asks him if he wants to see his father and takes him to a room where the body lies and there inside, also, unexpectedly, are the girl and the giant and his phone and . . .

The Lonely Man has been waiting for about ten minutes, but it feels like it's been ten hours of a ten-year wait.

In hospitals—now and forever—time expands.

In hospitals, just by going inside, one is already patient.

In both senses of the word. There, one arms oneself with patience in order to be disarmed as a patient.

The Lonely Man watches the nurse who, about eleven minutes ago now, took down his information. The woman asked him synthetically what his symptoms were (and he pointed at his chest and said: "It hurts. A lot") and gave him a plastic bracelet with his name and a barcode printed on it (which he carefully fastened, next to his watch). The woman who, now, a few meters away but so many years later has already, for The Lonely Man, taken on the sepia hue of things distant in time yet not in space. The place is the same, he knows. The place hasn't changed in any way and it'll always and forever be the same. And, cornered, The Lonely Man will have to stay in there for who knows how long. Ice ages will come, meteorites will crash near the hospital wiping out species in a single blow, and he'll still be there, waiting to hear his name called, like the magic word that breaks the spell of immobility and makes events precipitate, and with the events, he precipitates too. Plunging over the precipice of those swinging doors—to the disconsolate next stage—through which every so often an occupied or empty stretcher enters or exits, allowing a glimpse of the terrifying mysteries of the other side. Then he hears it. His name. Again. His last name—making it through schools and universities—always sounds odd when he hears it in the mouth of another person and especially in the mouth of a stranger. And they take him to a small office with no doors, almost a niche, and he enters and has the sensation that he's entering successively smaller rooms, like Chinese boxes or Russian nesting dolls, until he reaches the irreducible center of his malady. The next one, he shudders, will be a coffin. And not a bracelet around his wrist, but a tag on his toe. His name there again, written for the first and last time by the hand of a stranger. Maybe some orthographical error.

The ideal, thinks The Lonely Man, would be, when you go to hospitals, for them to give you an alias—a hospital name. And, if possible, for patients to be allowed to pick their own. That they be granted that symbolic privilege, the way a kid is given a consoling candy after being lied to with a "It won't hurt at all." Yes: the opportunity to be other, to have all the more or less bad things happen to someone else while you're in there, and only get your true name back when you get out, with the good news that you get to leave, that you don't have to stay there, inside.

If he could choose, The Lonely Man would choose to call himself and to be called Heywood Floyd. Dr. Heywood Floyd. A man and a name not to be confused with that of the bluesmen blended together without their permission into the Siamese Pink Floyd. A name of science and of science fiction in times when the space race has come to an end (not likely that anybody out there is concerned with saving or invading us) so it can mutate into the exploration of another space: the body itself. The spiral of DNA in place of the spiral of the Andromeda Nebula.

So, for him, terrified, saying "Dr. Heywood Floyd" would be like an act of resistance and simultaneous invocation of a memory of the future, of a time when, maybe, no one will have whatever it is that he has now, because everyone will have been cured of it. And, when the other doctor, the real doctor, asked him his age and said, "For a man of seventy, you're in extremely good shape; I'd have put you down as not more than sixty-five," he'd be able to quote with a smile, "Happy to hear it, Oleg, especially as I'm a hundred and three—as you know perfectly well."

This is what he's thinking about, as the beginning not of a story but of a novel, when the doctor (suddenly, all the doctors are much younger than he is, when did that happen—overnight?) asks him his age and he answers, automatically: "One hundred and three, Oleg—as you know perfectly well." And the doctor looks at him with that specially-designed doctor face. The face they're taught to put on during the final months of their training, when they're already practicing, and it's the face of, "Uh-oh, it's one of *those* patients." A face always accompanied by a tense smile and narrowed eyes;

like a clockmaker peering into the unfathomable unsolved mystery of another clock—springs and rubies and gears—and who knows what's wrong with it and, ah, why is it always up to me to figure it out?

"Ah, sorry. Fifty? I'm fifty years old? I was just thinking about a book? 2061: Odyssey Three? Arthur C. Clarke? Heywood Floyd? Remember? In the movie? 2001? He's the doctor who travels to the moon and falls asleep in the space shuttle and his pen floats and then he talks to his daughter on the videophone and then goes down to the Tycho crater to look at and touch the monolith?" recites The Lonely Man.

And he discovers a new symptom of his affliction: he can no longer affirm anything. Everything he says comes out with the tone and inflexion of questions that aren't seeking any answer. The doctor nods several times, asks him to take off his shirt, says "I'll be right back," and exits the little room. "To drink a whiskey, probably," thinks The Lonely Man, more alone than Heywood Floyd at the end of his days, naked from the waist up, absurdly happy not to be naked from the waist down, but still oh so exposed, expecting the unexpected. Getting down from the bed where he was sitting with an awkward little hop and going to the hook where his jacket hung, searching for and finding his notebook and asking himself why it is that almost everything that occurs to him and, he suspects, that will occur to him moving forward, while he's here, inside, has and will have to do with kids, with children, with fathers, with mothers—with families. With people who, though they cannot and do not want to see each other, will never, for better or worse, be able to be as lonely as The Lonely Man.

In "St. Valentine's Blues," a man with no one to love him and no one to love wakes up early, day after day, year after year. And February after February, each and every Valentine's Day, he buys an impressive bouquet of roses. More a bush than a bouquet. Something that's hard to hold up and yet he holds it, as if it were a sweet-smelling torch lighting his way. The man walks around, bouquet in hand, all day. He enters and exits metro cars, gets on and off buses, in and out of taxis. And he keeps on walking, crossing off key neighborhoods, and essential avenues. And the only thing that interests him—what gratifies him so much, what makes him oh so happy, almost as if he loved and was loved by somebody—is the way the women and men look at and admire first his bouquet and then him, with an inevitable smile that says "Here's a man very much in love." When the shadows fall, the man returns home. His arms are heavy and ache—but it's worth it. The roses look a little tired too, but, he thinks, I'll put them in a jar of water right away and, as his mother said, add a couple aspirin, so they last longer, so the day doesn't have to end, and see you next year, same time, same places.

Doctors are as implacable with their patients as writers are with their characters. And, as far as he's concerned, they're divided into two large groups: doctors who like to give good news and doctors who like to give not so good news. And, sooner or later, the first ones, like it or not, only have bad news to give; because good news, sooner or later, runs out, in the same way that the health of sick bodies runs out. So, the primary task of doctors is to tell us that something isn't totally right or that something is going totally wrong. Some of them—never many, actually very few—can partially and temporarily solve some of the contretemps. But against time, all battles are lost, and no strategy works, and sooner or later the enemy corners us, and leaves us vanquished.

And then doctors come back to tell us that something isn't totally right or that something is going totally wrong. And that, as far as they're concerned, there's nothing left to do but await the inevitable. Then, they outline different periods of survival that tend to fall between six months and a year. After that, everything is pure mystery and good luck. Before six months, of course, there's a small but very powerful percent of possibility that something will advance. And that's what he's thinking about, about how the next six months of his life or of the end of his life will be, when the doctor returns, enters, looks at him, keeps looking at him and, finally, as if waiting for the cue of an invisible prompter, more than addressing him, addresses an invisible audience: "There's something that worries me." That worries him, the doctor. And as he says this, The Lonely Man watches the doctor worry about him, about the patient. But, the doctor doesn't fool him, he's not that good of an actor: worried, yes; but not too worried. Not as worried as The Lonely Man is, who—dumbstruck, without words—thinks not about what to say, but about what he imagines is going on outside, where the sun will be starting to rise, but with the shyness of someone who says they're only going to be around for a little while. Rising just so it can set.

The title "Not Dark Yet" comes directly, obviously, from that Bob Dylan song on his album *Time Out of Mind*. A song not about death but about its constant imminence and lack of fixed or marked time. One of the songs—they say, its author said—Dylan wrote in a cabin, on a farm in Minnesota, isolated by a perfect storm of snow and wind during the winter of 1995-1996. Dylan left there, with the coming of the first thaws, with notebooks full of his slanted handwriting and—after so much time without writing—ready to record "Not Dark Yet" and another handful of crepuscular songs. Songs with a broken heart and a ravaged voice: the voice of someone who has swallowed The Phantom of the Opera without chewing; the voice of his old age; the voice that in interviews says things like: "My childhood is so far away . . . it's like I don't even remember being a child. I think that it was someone else who was that child. Did you ever think like that?"; the shattered yet whole voice of someone who has sung too much; the voice that, at some point in life, sounds perfect when it tells the person next to us or ourselves in the mirror that: "I think I feel a pain in my chest." "Not Dark Yet" (the Bob Dylan song) ends explaining that "I know it looks like I'm moving, but I'm standing still." "Not Dark Yet" (the story, his story) begins with the protagonist dragging himself to the Emergency Room of a hospital in the night. There, they evaluate him and a doctor listens to the concrete music of his chest and says, "It could be something very serious or it could be something trivial." And continues: "It could be something like strong indigestion or gastritis. Or, on the other hand, something like acute pulmonary histoplasmosis." And the man, shaking with pain and fear, asks himself why the names of illnesses aren't capitalized. And why they don't append them with, not the surname of the person who identified and patented the illnesses, but the surname of the sick person: to individuate them, to turn them into something singular and unique, something that helps you fool yourself and makes you think you're the owner of the disease and it's not the disease that possesses you, uses you, and ends up discarding you. Aha, yes, the kind of thing to ask yourself and think about so that you can think about anything other than that you're living and starring in the final scenes of the movie of your life. The kind of thing you ask yourself so you don't have to ask yourself, "How much time do I have left?" Then, suddenly, the doctor takes a deep breath and keeps talking. But now his phrasing has nothing of the polished and sterilized cadence that doctors speak with, rather it seems sinuous and sharp and as if coming in gusts: "As you will well know, acute pulmonary histoplasmosis is the ailment for which Bob Dylan was treated and admitted on May 25, 1997. Sudden chest pains. Something that, for all those who never had a heart attack, they assume could only be a heart attack. But actually it's pericarditis. A painful inflammation of the fibrous sack that surrounds the heart and chokes off your voice. Caused by microscopic spores in the golden air of Ohio or Mississippi, blowing in the wind, waiting to be inhaled, and from there they head to the lungs, to incubate for weeks, preparing their toothy grins until given the order to attack. And, depending on their mood or spirit, it all might turn into a simple and transitory cold or, conversely, into something far more serious and definitive. A siege of the reticuloendothelial system. With screams and torches. Scaling walls, catapulting boulders. The immune, suddenly, so vulnerable. Bob Dylan was able to contain the threat in time and was admitted and emerged weakened a week later, almost unable to stand, but whole. And he told the press that thing about 'I really thought I was on my way to see Elvis . . .' That could be what you have. Or it could be some sudden activation of a previously undetected genetic disorder. Like a letter sent to you from the dawn of time. A message sent by an ancestor who lives on in your veins and arteries that are now liquefying and drowning you, from inside and on terra firma, turning you into your own ocean. And I've read in specialized journals that death from an internal hemorrhage is the sweetest death of all—your internal clock losing the beat, time stretching out into an almost Mexican eternity of minutes, the feeling that you're dying of immortality."

The patient, confused, listens to all of that and asks: "How'd you know I'm a Bob Dylan fan?"

And then they—doctor and patient—strike up a conversation about the artist's latest album.

And what the doctor tells him is, simply, that he wants to run more tests. "To rule out possibilities," he explains. And he invites him to come down into the hospital basements, to pass through the door with the sign warning of the presence of radiation. To put himself inside an apparatus that, no doubt, will choose the exact moment he's inside it to break down, to release an invisible plutonium or uranium vapor or whatever, and transform him into a secret monster that'll never even know the joy of mutating into one of those crazy laboratory creatures from the paranoid science fiction movies that he enjoyed so much as a kid. No: he'll leave the hospital as if nothing had happened and, a few days later, he'll discover that he's radiating a strange phosphorescence in the darkness and, subsequently, that he's starting to shrink. And this glowing and diminishing revelation will also bring a roundabout blessing—the perfect excuse to never leave the house again.

The title "The Little Dwarf" (automatic reflex of the giant albino idea, The Lonely Man self-diagnoses: stories sometimes come in twos, with opposite faces, like those twins who look nothing alike but are twins nonetheless) seems, at first, a redundancy, a joke as bad as it is cruel and wrong. But no. Or yes. It depends on how you look at that boy, about four years old, who appears in its opening lines, on a street in the city of B, so that two friends, taking a walk to their favorite bookstore, encounter him and watch and discuss him with barely hidden fascination. The two friends are writers and have been resigned for a while now to the fact that everything they see on this side can end up being useful in the other part, a place they refuse to call "their work," but, really, what else can they call it? So better, yes, to call it "The Other Part." As mentioned, the boy must be three or four or five years old. But even though, for his age, he's the "right" and "normal" height (note: find better adjectives), the boy is already, also, a dwarf. The short arms, the short legs, the big head. The boy is, for the two writer friends, a curious organism: a being living in two times at the same time. His present as a boy of the appropriate height already coexisting with his increasingly near future as a dwarf. The two writer friends watch him walk by, give a slight shudder, change the subject: neither of them can stop thinking about the little dwarf and, now in the bookstore, leafing through books, they can barely contain the desire to run out of there. To head home at full velocity, to their desks, to their computers, to see how and where they can insert that little dwarf into what they're writing. He'll fit somewhere, in the other part.

"Welcome, My Son / Welcome to the Machine . . ." Now it's as if The Lonely Man were inside a Pink Floyd album, his favorite Pink Floyd album, one of his favorite albums: welcome to the machine, inside a machine, listening to all those mysterious sounds and whispers that are heard in the background and give shape to all those songs that he knows by heart. Not just the words of their verses, but also—it being Pink Floyd—every sound and murmur and doorway that opens and closes. He doesn't want to be there, obviously. They inserted him—after giving him a powerful relaxant that's relieved almost all his pain and given him the sensation of being embalmed alive, of having had all his organs removed except his brain, which seems to be thinking more than ever—into a mechanical cylinder. They put him on a sliding gurney that emerged like a tongue, so that he could lie down on it and it could eat him alive and carry him inside, where now he's chewed up and bombarded and photographed from every angle, millimeter by millimeter by mesmeric energies that he prefers to know as little about as possible. Now, The Lonely Man is read like an open book that doesn't need to be opened to be read, to know what happens (what needs to be edited or corrected or crossed out or cut or extracted) in the novel of his body that might just—test results revealed and interpreted—say goodbye with the abrupt ending of a microstory.

They told him he'd be inside for about forty minutes and that he should try not to move "at all." Which, of course, immediately produced and kept on producing an absolute need to move. But, to the previous instruction, they added a "If you move, we'll have to start over." And for The Lonely Man, lonelier than ever there inside, there's nothing less appealing than seeing himself trapped in a loop of *clicks* and *clicks* and *bzzzs* and *t-chacks* asking himself—like in the song—where have you been and answering that it's alright we know just where you've been—there, staying still, though it looks like he's moving. Because—restless yet motionless—there's a possibility that something isn't alright at all inside his machine, now, inside a machine. After having the doctor listen to his symptoms, ask questions (with a diction that reminds him of those caretakers of haunted houses who ask at the beginning of the movie, "But, is it possible you don't know what happened here?"), and tell him that what he has "might be nothing or it might be very serious; so we better make sure."

So there he is, increasingly uncertain of everything, except for the flood of ideas that comes to him—after so much time, like someone discovering not oil, but dinosaur bones—for possible stories. One after another. Invented parts. Unfinished products rolling off the assembly line and mocking him, tempting him to move, so he can get out of there and write them down, distilled to a sentence or two, in his notebook, inside his jacket pocket, hanging there a few meters and thousands of light years away from his body.

There, inside the machine, he comes up with a machine: the still primitive version, the crawling and not yet walking prototype, that some prodigy from Silicon Valley will offer to a writer like an irresistible apple. A device that allows writers to extract, at the speed of thought, without spilling, all of what will later be written on a screen or on paper. Something that he imagines and anticipates having a design resembling a scorpion stinger, sticking into the nape of writers' necks, not to poison them, but to extract a dense and dark liquid and transfer it via transparent tube directly to the core of a laptop computer. And thus allow the writer to be a true reader of himself. A writer reader. And all the books would be incredibly alive. The book happening in its entirety, just as the writer happens to think of it.

Just the idea of having to remember right now everything he shouldn't forget so he can write it down as soon as he gets out of the machine makes him feel a kind of lethargy, the beginning of falling asleep. Which wouldn't be bad: he never moves in his sleep, he was always one of those sleepers who—after, always with difficulty, managing to close his eyes—seemed dead or comatose, victims of a not necessarily maleficent spell. Because, after all, falling into an ageless sleep isn't so bad compared with getting transformed into a beast or a pig or whatever, right? Being in a cursed sleep is better than being very sick and awake. So, all of a sudden, he tells himself he'd rather stay in there, better this moment of mechanical and mechanized suspense, than to be pulled out of there at full velocity and put on a gurney and pushed at a run to an operating room and opened up so something malignant can be removed. Better this somnolence, lulled to sleep by an apparatus, than the shutdown of general anesthesia, which (he read somewhere, why has he read so much?) doesn't entirely wear off until months after the operation. A month of fatigue and disorientation and forgetfulness and confusion, they calculate, for every hour you spend chemically knocked out—like a boxer who has been stripped of his title and table of contents and various decisive chapters—crooning "Where have you been? / It's alright we know where you've been," as you find yourself in front of the open refrigerator, stroking your scar with almost sacred reverence, and never wondering what you came there to find, but placing the book you're reading inside, among the fruits and vegetables and meats. A book that, just a few pages from the end, you remember absolutely nothing of except that the protagonist really likes beer, or was it tequila? And, later—"You've been in the pipeline, filling in time"—more noises filling your head. Like the noises he hears now, in a time without time, when his whole life passes before his eyes not in a matter of seconds, but in minutes as long as a whole lifetime.

He remembers, along with so many other things, that when he had to do obligatory military service, during *imaginarias* (this term, referring to night-watch duty, always seemed to him one of the most auspicious in an otherwise generally unimaginative military jargon), he, *imaginarily*, inside his head, put on Pink Floyd's *Wish You Were Here*. And he listened to it note for note, word for word, sound for sound, to distract himself, so that the time would pass faster. He tries to do it again now, but discovers there are parts he's forgotten. To keep from getting depressed, thinking that his memory isn't what it used to be, he chooses another strategy—to imagine that everything that's happening to him is a story. To imagine how, if it were a story, it would begin. And, facing the impossibility of writing it, to begin to tell it to himself, as if he were reading it.

Like this.

He arrived to the clinic—which seemed to him an exhibition of refined sadism—after crossing a labyrinthine garden, between green hedges, losing and finding his way, guided by the lights over the entrance. The clinic—he'd read or someone told him this at some point; he reads it now in the air of that machine where he vibrates and is examined and rocked by invisible waves—had originally been a palace that a patrician and philanthropic family had donated to their beloved city, though, actually, it'd just been the required tribute, the way to whitewash the mess of too many years of "forgetting" to pay taxes.

In the building's reception area there abounded photos of aristocrats on the day of the inauguration of what, overnight, became *the* place to give birth and to be born and to recover, more or less, and to die. Various glossy magazines had permanent correspondents in the bar/restaurant, which was run by one of those chefs who're internationally famous for having turned a sandwich (a sandwich that you just *had* to enjoy in order to be someone) into soup or ice cream or into anything that in no way resembled a sandwich. They were many, the *happy few* who went there to have a drink without even knowing any admitted patients. And the prevailing feeling (if you ignored the signs asking the healthy people to keep quiet so that the sick people could moan as they pleased; a request that was ignored, because the hallways were full of the shouts of people with double and triple surnames, demonstrations of model-pain or model-joy surprise, as appropriate, finding themselves there as if it were a night at the opera or a day at the races or an afternoon in the VIP lounge of an airport) was of having arrived to the best of all possible worlds. To a corrected and augmented version of the world (because the palace's original architecture had received new additions of futuristic wings, emerging like prosthetic limbs of concrete and glass from the original and Versaillesque nucleus/body) that, like everything augmented and corrected, produced a mild anxiety. The same comfortable uncomfortableness that certain airports have (and he'd written several times about how hospitals were oh so similar to airports, passengers so closely resembling patients, both subject to arrivals and departures) where everything was carefully planned down to the millimeter so that something unforeseen always happens, something unexpected that can alter the course of your life or affirm the direction of your death.

When he got there, however, the social activity was minimal, the sonic volume and bodily movement were low, and the elevators were quietly singing a version of the string quartet of the *Goldberg Variations*, between metal doors and under that light that—along with mirrors, where all faces are like the faces of recently embalmed bodies—should be banned inside elevators. And—after being freed of the machine, after they informed him that he'd get the results back in about an hour—there he was, playing the game he played when he was a boy, the game he never stopped playing, because, he fears, he'll never stop being a boy. He never got that appendix removed, never lost that tooth. To know, to teach, to learn: there are afternoons when he goes out on a walk and, randomly, decides to follow somebody. Then, after a few blocks of following them, he says to himself that he'll change objective and prey as soon as he encounters someone—man or woman, either way—wearing a yellow shirt. And that he'll follow the yellow shirt until, for example, a black jacket or white high heels appear. And see where it takes him. And wonder what they're doing or what they're on their way to do whenever they arrive wherever they're going.

Here and now, there's a lot of movement and almost everyone's wearing a uniform—of a soft and relaxing and consoling green-water color—that was, no doubt, proposed and discussed by some expert in the marketing of pain and uncertainty. After a few minutes, they all kind of blend together (it might have something to do with the relaxant they gave him) into a single entity. So he has to concentrate: eye color and hair color and height and whether they're left- or right-handed. And there he goes, following some and then others, through hallways decorated with prints that are always (another recommendation of experts in subliminal communication and sanitarium psychology, of course) of luminous impressionist style and never the abstract expressionism that evokes metastasis and tumors.

The magazine shop, attended by a woman of vampiric pallor, is full of sports publications (a subject that, like the western or war genre, never interested him at all; but he's astonished by the increasingly frequent statements from multimillionaire soccer players, confessing almost existential anxieties), sugar free candies, flowers of suspicious and amphetaminic vitality, some sad toy (no robot, no maddening little man with a suitcase), and newspapers that seem to age more quickly and more badly. The headlines from the previous morning—from the few rumpled copies that remain, on life support; that morning's papers having not yet arrived—talk about the inauguration a particle accelerator. Reading that, a particle of interest enters through The Lonely Man's eyes and arrives to his accelerated brain. Maybe he could write about that for that monthly that'd asked him to write a piece about a destination of his choice, maybe he could go there instead of Manhattan or London, it'd be more original and unexpected, he says to himself. A particle accelerator that, some claim, could open a black hole in the cosmic fabric of our dimension that would end up devouring our world and everything in it. But he's not too worried; he's already been there, breathing in that intoxicating air of possible planetary catastrophe. Not long ago, though it seems like forever. When—on the edge of the new millennium, when everyone was debating whether or not the year 2000 was already the twenty-first century—everything was trembling in that frozen second when all the hours and dates on all the computers would reach 23:59 hours on December 31st, 1999. And no one knew—inexplicably, nobody could be sure, nobody had run tests or simulations, maybe to keep from spoiling the terror or the tranquility of the second after—whether the computers would seamlessly move on to the new first digit. Or if they'd go back, confused, to 00:00 hours of the year 1900. And then all the airplanes would fall from the skies, money would vanish from bank accounts, all manuscripts of unfinished novels would disappear, and a prehistoric darkness would fall over everything and everyone. Farewell to civilization—flatline on all monitors. But nothing had happened. Absolutely nothing. The falsest of alarms. The bells and sirens, the nocturnal sound of the New Year moving right to left across the map, as if it were reading an ancient and powerful Jewish and Cabalistic formula. And the TVs, that kept right on working perfectly, had been showing—alternating between cameras located in different metropolises—the typical shots of all normal years, the same years as always always dying the same way, with no regard for the striking roundness of their number. Multitudes hugging each other in historic squares, some cold and some hot, raising glasses and effortlessly making history while their respective nights exploded with fireworks and—admit it—more than one person sighed, resigned to the fact that everything would go on the same as always. Somewhat sad and disappointed to surrender and relinquish the tempting yet no longer practical theory of being able to strip the figurehead from the prow of their faces, to kiss an iceberg, and dance the last and increasingly vertiginous waltz across the deck of the end of history.

Now, the truth is that—confronting the imminent possibility of a private shipwreck, of his body going out of order—nothing would be less troubling and more appealing than a global holocaust to keep him company and free him from the responsibility of having to make drastic decisions; or having to undergo treatments as painful as they are expensive and, in the end, ineffective; or to be observed, as light after light goes out, the way you look at something that, yes, is luckily happening to someone else, just someone else, that's all.

Now the Lonely Man keeps moving down the hospital hallways because he thinks that if he doesn't, if he stops moving, it'll be impossible for him to go on. Suddenly he sees somebody, in the distance, dressed distinctly, walking toward him. He decides that, when they pass by each other, he'll wait two or three steps and then turn around and follow him. Then he realizes that the person he sees is himself, approaching without advancing, inside a mirror. So he's the person who's approaching him. And he looks at him and looks at himself.

He's still who he's always been, yes; but he's not who he once was. It's not that he's old; rather that he's not young anymore, and that, all of a sudden, old age isn't a faraway country, but a residential neighborhood ready to be absorbed by the—increasingly scattered and maintenance-issue-plagued—architecture of his city. Chiaroscuro symptoms of it everywhere, unignorable telltale signs that the time he lives in is no longer his time. No, he's not old, that's true. But he is a young old man. A—will he ever rid himself of that damned habit of inventing a word by putting two together?—*youngold* man. A, like somebody sang, *"uomo di una certa età"* who begins to experience the symptoms of being an antique and of looking at everything like an old-fashioned explorer who would, actually, prefer to stay home and invent exploits that he can no longer carry out. Meanwhile, the perturbing and almost nagging sight of all those kids, more all the time, more and more, where do they all come from? For a while now, the vast majority of people around him seem like recently built machines, the latest models, giving off that new car smell and seemingly wrapped in the metallic paper of the most tempting and dangerous sweets of his distant childhood—the ones with really dark chocolate that, when you bit into them, released a shot of alcohol and mystery. All so young, it hurts to look at them; but it hurts even more to see the ones who aren't you, his elders, his superiors in the descending ladder of life: nightmarish beings, their bodies between warped angle and Jell-O melted in the sun, always trying to enter first and leave last with no respect for places in line, speaking loudly or whispering to themselves or to someone who isn't there, but without the excuse of one of those hands-free phones hanging from their ear. Abyssal creatures who, he gets it now, seem to have been born to be old—they were just making time, not killing time, but aging time. And now they were approaching their authentic and absolute zenith. And something really disturbing: if he stared at them—terrible superpower?, reverse prophecy?—he could see, through the cracks and canyons of their wrinkles, the faces of the boys and girls that they'd once been. And it was terrible *to see himself* like he was, to remember without any difficulty, with more and more clarity, the face of his own past. To perceive the erosion and entropy of the species. Soon he'd be like one of them, he'd be one of them. And not long after—thousandths of a second on the clock of the universe—all those kids would be *too*. Them there and him here: he's aware now that the lack of care devoted to his physique in times when his body was something moldable and improvable—times when you have to train it to better endure the coming of The Horror, The Horror—didn't bode well. And, again, he hasn't gone for periodical exams and checkups either. He's always preferred not to know, until he can no longer not know. Like the frog in that experiment: if you toss it into a pot of boiling water, it jumps right out; on the other hand, if you put it in a pot of cold water and heat it up slowly, it stays right there, until it boils alive and boils to death. Now, the water in his pot is quite hot and—though he doesn't do anything about it—it's beginning to dawn on him that something is happening or something is going to happen. *Ribbit-ribbit*. And it's clear that he's not the only one who suspects it, who knows it. He's been discovering how, for a few years now, he's turned, riding different modes of public transit, not into someone who's invisible to young and not so young women, but into something much worse—he's become someone who's *transparent*. Some of them look at him as if they're staring out at the distant horizon and only pay attention to him when he makes faces at the little ones accompanying them (little children, little siblings) and look at him with confusion. Then, almost out of obligation, they smile at him the way you smile at a more or less curious animal. And—after so many years of having been so careful when it comes to evaluating what he did or did not find attractive in the opposite sex—suddenly everything and everyone seemed somehow irresistible, alluring, tempting. As if he were walking across the slippery floor of one of those department stores that—a dulcet but firm voice informs over the loudspeakers—is going to close in five minutes. And that might never open again. Total liquidation of discounted beings. So you have to buy whatever you can get as fast as you can, stockpiling for the long, interminable winter that's coming, pick everything out without thinking too much about whether or not it'll fit, whether it's the right size, whether it matches your style. Fill the cart. Nothing matters anymore, because anything is better than nothing.

Similarly, when, less often all the time, he goes to buy clothes (where did he leave that favorite T-shirt from when he was a kid with that thing, once so amusing, but that he doesn't find funny anymore, printed across the chest about "Your mind is writing checks your body can't cash"?) he's noticed that, when making adjustments and accommodations to his pants and jackets, the salesmen who, until not long ago, had been complicit and talkative, now touch him in the most reverent of silences. And only with the tips of their fingers, as little as possible, with a mix of fear and disgust, as if they were holding a fragile relic, recently unearthed and smelling of confinement, a smell like a free sample of the perfume of the tomb.

And, ah, fewer friends all the time and more mere acquaintances and fewer friends who ask if you heard "what happened" to so-and-so and give you—like ciphers of whispering spies—advice like "It'd be better, just in case, because of the dizziness or the diminished reflexes, to start to pee sitting down, like a girl, when you get up in the morning." And—occupational hazard—he couldn't help but tremble hearing the word "girl," stuck there, cosmetically, to disguise and cover up that it should actually be "like an old lady."

And all of that was the least awful part, what caused him the least anxiety.

The worst was what was secret, personal, intimate, his and only his, alone. That new almost-old face in the mirror, without wrinkles, but with bags under its eyes that hang down to his belly button, producing the unsettling effect of a photo that's been left unfinished in the middle of a Photoshop session. Or the abandonment without warning—that at first he believed to be temporary and a product of stress but no—of those lightning-rod erections that used to greet him every morning (the absence of which he blames, without any evidence or proof, on a treatment/course of meditative T'ai chi ch'uan that he took a few years ago to, according to the oriental specialist, "slow down your mental activity," "balance your biorhythms," "improve your mood," and even "inspire you to write more personal things."). Or the discovery—more frequent all the time—that the remote past for the storylines and characters in movies was no longer prehistory or the Middle Ages or the fifties or any other time when he'd not yet arrived to the world, rather it was his own recollectable past. His story was already History. And the only comfort of being history was that of having lived somewhere in the vicinity, of having almost been a part of it, of having more things to tell than a newcomer who'd not yet entered History and who might never enter it and who, until the end, his end, would be but a witness. Or the sensation that nothing new would ever happen to him again, or that from here onward everything would just be wintery and funereal variations on a single theme. A sad and repetitive melody more sticky than catchy, backed by the concrete symphony of his own body's sounds (like gears beginning to grind, like steam leaking from rusted pipes) waking him up in the middle of the night and not letting him fall back asleep. And the perfumes, the aromas, the odors that are, for him and only him, enjoyed and even catalogued as secret fragrances.

And, every so often, yes, a new but undesired beginning of something that, up until today, was like the distant (and consequently almost inaudible) cry of a pain that never ended up presenting: the previews of a terrifying movie coming soon in 3-D with Sensurround and all the special effects. Now, all of a sudden, grand premiere and red carpet and flashes and reflectors and neon lights. Here comes something that started out as an extra playing the point of an invisible blade. Something that debuted like a new but not necessarily good idea, concentrated in the center of his chest to subsequently—triumphant and leading role, and nominee for the Oscar for Best Unexpected Pain—open like a black rose with petals of thorns. And from there, spread its cramping perfume to his legs (making it hard for him to get out of bed), and climb to his storm-clouded eyes and with the sensation that the hand of a gorilla was gripping his head and squeezing and he couldn't breathe and maybe, he said to himself, this is fear, true fear. A fear that, nonetheless, makes him avoid the embarrassment of calling an ambulance and being hauled out while the neighbors looked on, taken down the winding mountain road, bound for that hell where he is now, looking at himself, as if seeing himself for the first time, which, who knows, might be the first of the last times. "I'd give anything for a drink," he says to himself then, as if dubbed over by a voice not his own, a voice with an uninflected accent. Someone else's voice on top of his. The voice of his reflection that looks at him and smiles and makes the gesture, in the mirror, of raising an invisible glass and says—never better, never more ironically appropriate—"To your health!"

In "Four Beers" (which might end up being called "Four Tequilas") a man, a writer, takes his young son to a park near their house to ride his bicycle.

In the center of the park, which is in the center of a barely domesticated forest, there is a bar. The man sits down at a table and keeps one eye on his son and the other on his notebook where he takes notes for a story. Notes that, he knows, he might not understand a few hours later. Because the notes for a story or a novel are made, almost always, from the stuff of dreams: when you wake up or go back and read them you barely remember them and you can't recapture your enthusiasm or their initial significance either and—like the ephemeral yet spectacular effervescence of some indigestion medicines—their brief effect is nothing more than that, passing. Meanwhile, the man drinks one, two, three, four beers (or four tequilas). And confirms once again, first, that his alcohol tolerance is as admirable as it is disturbing (is that what it is to be an authentic alcoholic?, to have alcohol not effect you?) and, second, that with the last sip of the fourth glass or the fourth shot, the man finds, once again, that he's attained that state, half placid nirvana and half centrifugal spiral, where everything comes at him all at once and hits him in the face. Like a wind waiting for you to open a window to slap you and challenge you to a duel, sabers or pistols, it makes no difference, the wind always wins. Left behind are the old and not exactly good, but, yes, simpler days when storylines came to him all at once like a pleasant breeze and not, like now, like perfumes searching for a body that'll give them a reason to be and to be smelled, like loose and scattered puzzle pieces without a box or cover photo to use as a guide. Now, everything is more difficult and, at the same time, more interesting. Interesting times, yes, like that Chinese curse: "May you live in interesting times." And few adjectives are more ambiguous than "interesting" when applied to times or to a woman (or a man) someone wants to introduce to you. Then, all of a sudden, his son pedaling too close to the edge of the embankment, and the renewed wonder of seeing somebody ride a bicycle. And especially, like right now, his son. Just the upper part of his body behind a brick wall, as if he were running at an impossible speed for a boy. And, watching him, all of it comes to him at the same time from the same place, so near yet so far. Here it comes, here they come: a woman who names her dog after her ex-husband; that British expression he likes so much for the moment of death, for no longer resisting death's call: "Give up the ghost"; an amateur detective named Capital Italic Ariel who—with the help of an attractive police officer named Jean Tonnik—solves cases while in a coma, in a bed in a hospital suite where his family of decadent millionaires have "deposited" him; a man who goes to a parent-teacher meeting at his daughter's school with a bikini top under his shirt (and the shirt fabric is too light and transparent, and everyone can see it and talk about it in voices that are quiet yet perfectly audible to the little girl); a pederast whose alias is Mario Poppins; a politician defining something as "an instance of transcendence" and someone hearing him thinking that that "sounds like the title of a song by Yes"; a lion trainer addicted to cocaine whose chemical sweat provokes the stimulated felines to attack (forcing him to inject perfume under his skin to disguise his white-powder scent); the bizarre story of the body of Laurence Sterne compared with the bizarre story of the body of Gram Parsons (both bodies removed from their respective morgues for different reasons); a young man who recognizes his girlfriend (supposedly an executive assistant at a renowned multinational) as a living statue on one of the streets that lead to the sea; an allusion to Rolf Wütherich (in 1955, James Dean's copilot riding in that fatal Porsche Spyder, who survives the accident in which the actor dies, just to die riding in another car, in 1981); a good name for another of his characters who, inevitably, will be a writer (Vidal-Mortes); the certainty that no blue is better than the blue of the top ranked Indian gods; that Mexican dealer who, in the beginning of *Easy Rider*, says: "*Pura vida, hermano*"; and, maybe at the end, a lonely man watching a movie on TV in the middle of the night and thinking that "One of the many possible ways to appreciate the passing of time is to read the credits at the ends of old movies and to find there the still-pale names of the bronzed stars of tomorrow. In small roles, two or three scenes, reciting, if they're lucky, a handful of brief lines. There, their faces still fresh and undiscovered and youthful, but, in a way, already beginning to be illuminated by the light years; by the light coming not from the past of dead stars but from the glorious future of suns so bright you have to wear dark sunglasses all the time: not so you won't be recognized but so you don't have to recognize that everything that burns sooner or later burns out."

If he ever writes it, if he ever manages to decipher the correct order and internal logic of that possible story—the man calls the waiter over to pay his tab, it's getting dark, where has his son gone and what's his bicycle doing there, on the ground beside a tree?—he thinks it should be the last story in the book.

At an intersection of hallways, The Lonely Man intersects with a woman, a young writer. An ex-young ex-writer. A writer who's no longer a young woman and who almost never writes; but who nevertheless is younger than he is and, who knows, at this point, sure, might even write more than he does. A writer who will be younger than he is until he dies and, then, the distance will start to shrink; because the living stop aging the moment they die. And he's already getting tired of thinking so much about the living and the dead as if they were rival teams in a sport whose rules are never entirely clear.

She's the ex-young ex-writer who, some time ago, The Lonely Man christened with a secret nickname for his own private use whose meaning and raison d'être won't be revealed here and now, maybe later on, who knows. The nickname that The Lonely Man gave the young writer is—just so, blue caps inside a yellow oval—IKEA.

IKEA—okay, hands up, he admits it: The Lonely Man did end up sharing the nickname with one friend; because the best and worst and funniest nicknames die if they're kept in isolation—is now almost his nemesis, his sin and his crime, his long shadow, like time nipping his heels. Actually the thing with IKEA isn't a big deal; but somehow thinking of her as something ominous and epic helps The Lonely Man bear the fact that they're bound together forever. And The Lonely Man and IKEA are bound together forever by a laudatory blurb he wrote for the jacket of her first book. A blurb that she asked for the way you ask someone out on a date. And which The Lonely Man gave her, immediately and without even reading the book, so long ago (so satisfied with his ingenious speed that he couldn't see how pathetic his sychophantic obedience was), in the tense center of one of the hurricane parties of what was still his youth. One of those parties where, after a certain hour, thoroughly faded, everyone started to spin around on themselves as if on ecstasy or cocaine or colorful pills or whatever designer drug was hip at the time. Why'd he do it? Good question with several possible bad answers. But all of them correct. Answers that originate with the obviousness of having been tangled in the seven veils of her hysteria. IKEA, in her day, hadn't been a model writer, nor a writer model, but she had been a model-writer. In other words: IKEA modeled in the pages of the most fashionable fashion magazines. And she also wrote about it. And he remembers the seismic movements that a photo shoot in a short-lived magazine called *Cool* produced among male writers, where IKEA appeared in short silver shorts and a bikini top that was two sizes too small. In summary: IKEA was, like a piece of IKEA furniture, good to look at, desirable and, later, according to what he'd been told, oh so difficult to put together and easy to take apart, with the touch of a finger, invoking the figure of a father who'd transgressed in his affections for her, between ages eight and fifteen. IKEA's father had been a legendary publisher in the sixties and her mother a telenovela actress who'd provoked a certain fetishistic fascination among intellectuals. And, of course, IKEA had written a painful and damaging memoir about both of them, their late nights and their excesses. And about her bulimia and anorexia and the superficial cutting she did on her arms and legs. IKEA's book—he had to admit it—had a really good possible title: *Daughter of a . . .* The other title IKEA threw around wasn't bad either: *My Favorite Damage.* Yes, IKEA was a genius at writing titles. Maybe, he thought, IKEA should just publish titles. Create a new genre. Autotitleolgy. But don't kid yourself, don't lie. He liked IKEA. Or better: he liked being liked by IKEA. So, IKEA—he admits it—had beome his equally eroticized and narissistic fantasy of literary parentage, of artistic progeny, through whom he'd project himself onto other names and styles and literary generations. To begin, yes, to harvest disciples who'd hold him up and guarantee him a venerable old age and golden posterity. None of that interested IKEA, of course; and The Lonely Man's blurb wasn't the only one celebrating her debut. In fact, next to his name appeared the praise of someone who'd always been considered his aesthetic opposite and rival. IKEA's strategy had been clear and astute: for her, even two irrconcilable duelists dropped their weapons and embraced each other so they could embrace her. So he, that night, drink in hand and nose asleep and brain awake, recited the requested blurb as if he were reading it. A blurb that she immediately memorized (he could almost see behind her eyes, the dance of an implacable mechanism of pulleys and pistons devoted to self-propulsion), but later, passing it along to her editor that same night, she made a favorable alteration, changing a "necessary" to an "indispensable." At the time, he found the infraction amusing and, yes, juvenile. Now, that change of adjective, after almost two decades—IKEA, far more well-known and, consequently, more successful than he was, IKEA, who was among the first to transmit her life, live and direct, via a small camera attached to her laptop, IKEA, who tweeted an abortion—seems odious and unforgiveable. Something that, no doubt, in one of those republics of fundamentalist character, women are publicly stoned for, sometimes to death. It's not that he wishes such a torment on IKEA. But she does seem deserving of something severe and unforgettable. An exemplary punishment. That her next book be a total failure, for example. Or that, if nothing else, she receive a withering review from a renowned name, unafraid to puncture the formidable carapace of political correctness and protection of diverse groups and vocal minorities that IKEA relies on to shield herself and her books from any criticism. Because, attention, the idea that her thing was "the great themes" and "necessary and long-overdue and long-silenced criticism" and "the voice of the voiceless" and all of that, was nothing but fiction. Or, if nothing else, that all editions of her next bestseller have to be recalled for having used a photo or painting on the cover without obtaining the necessary permissions. Or, if not, that a sudden allergic reaction deform her face at the presentation of her latest "multimedia manifesto of criticism." Something. Please. Right?

And, yes, he excuses himself, this is the kind of thing you think about when awaiting the fatal or not-fatal diagnosis, the verdict and the punishment of a potentially imminent death.

And at first, The Lonely Man doesn't recognize IKEA. Because you never want to run into someone you know in a hospital or clinic (because it's almost as perturbing as having people you know see you coming out of a sex shop with a bag full of uninflated inflatable dolls, he supposes) and because IKEA spends her time mutating: last time he saw her she was some kind of tropical bird, decked out in colorful clothing and even the shadow of a moustache, not as obvious as Frida Kahlo's but a moustache nonetheless. Prior to that, IKEA almost always appeared naked in her photos, displaying the credentials of an anorexia (the subject of one of her books) that he never totally bought into. Now, IKEA has a minimalist and androgenous look: her hair cut à la Louise Brooks and dyed blond, her body almost imprisoned in a kind of smoking jacket, her smile rarefied by what appears to him to be the sparkle of a diamond or something that wants to be a diamond in place of one tooth. Seeing her, reading her (because each one of the different IKEA models, from her first iteration as sex-kitten, passing through squalid-grunge girl, to a brief flirtation with religious mysticism and the shaved head of a luxury convent, have had to do, invariably, with the subject of her next novel or memoir), he's unable to entirely decipher what she's doing now, what her next book will be about. Probably a historic romance set in a Berlin preparing for the arrival of the Nazis, something to do with lesbianism, he thinks.

"I'm doing research for something that I'm writing," The Lonely Man says by way of greeting, almost making up an excuse, without her having asked him anything about what he was doing, in a clinic, at that hour.

"Ah, I came for some test results," she informs him solemnly, bringing her hand to her chest, as if that were the solemnest of oaths, as if she were swearing herself into History.

For a second he was happy—and somewhat ashamed of his happiness, but not too ashamed—imagining IKEA with a terminal illness. But then he said to himself that he couldn't be that despicable. And that, besides, an early death would, no doubt, turn IKEA into an invulnerable legend. And that, chances are, IKEA is lying (because they don't deliver test results at that hour) and that, really, she's probably visiting a young medical student boyfriend, whom she submits to sex acts she saw in a recent David Cronenberg retrospective.

Then, without saying anything else, IKEA was all over him. And she pushed him inside an empty and dirty operating room, which looked more like a five-star hotel room that had housed a rockstar and his entourage. And more than making love to him or raping him, IKEA centrifuges him. In a matter of seconds. It all happens so fast that he can't even be sure he had an orgasm. After, IKEA straightens up in front of him and takes out her phone and snaps a picture of him, on the floor, as if swept by a cyclone, far from Kansas, but more black and white all the time, with the shades of a dream that asks itself, somewhat mischievously, if it's going to turn into a nightmare.

"For my blog," IKEA explains.

And there he stays.

And, like in a vaudeville, two young residents walk in. Two novices who look more like skaters or surfers than doctors. Or like those eco-friendly and ethno-percussive and millionaire prog-rockers, but with the voices of beggars asking for alms. The two residents have tattoos on their arms and smell like marijuana and, no doubt, fantasize about traveling abroad, without borders, to distant and troubled lands where everyone's too busy surviving or dying to go around getting sick. And there, at rifle and machete point, get kidnapped. And wind up in the newspapers. And upload videos of their captivity to You-Tube, begging to be rescued and to have James Franco write and produce and star in and even pen the criticism of the movie of their lives. And have James Franco play both of them. One James Franco with a beard and another James Franco without a beard, digitally edited. And now the two of them dance (they dance very well, it must be said) and they lift him up off the floor and send him flying through the air to that room where the doctors go to break down or take drugs or rip off nurses' uniforms with their teeth, he thinks, embarrassed, thinking so many clichés and, at the same time, about hospital mystique. But then he excuses and justifies himself: in moments of absolute uncertainty, there's nothing better than the comfort of the commonplace— the readymade phrase, the trusty cliché. But nothing could've prepared The Lonely Man for what he sees now: the two young almost-doctors, their ties stained with fresh blood, open a closet and remove something from inside and suddenly they're not dancing alone but with two of those dolls that are pure torso, utilized for practicing cardiopulmonary resuscitation. Both of them twirl and jump around the room singing over and over "Annie, are you okay? Annie, are you okay? Are you okay, Annie?"

And he watches them dance, smiling.

And joins in.

And *all that jazz*.

"Smooth Criminals"—the second rock-pop vignette that comes to him, after the Bob Dylan one—reproduces the conversation between two ambulance drivers who are transporting the body of Michael Jackson along the highways of Los Angeles. They talk about their wives, about their kids, about their jobs, and they turn on the radio. And the news of the death of the self-proclaimed King of Pop has already leaked and the different stations are starting to play his songs non-stop. Soon "Smooth Criminal" comes on and one of the drivers says to the other: "My favorite. Also, far and away, his best video. Much better than 'Thriller' as far as I'm concerned." The other driver says: "Mmm . . . I'm not so sure. This song has always made me nervous. I don't get it. That chorus where he's always asking Annie if she's okay. What's that mean? Who's Annie? Billy Jean's daughter? Sure, Jacko was crazy but . . ." "Very simple," interrupts the other guy, and explains: "I read an interview in a magazine with one of the musicians who played on *Bad*. When they recorded that song, Jackson was going around everywhere with a green suitcase. And inside that suitcase Jackson carried one of those dummies that are used to teach CPR maneuvers. The male version of the doll was named Andy and the female one, the one Jackson had, was named Annie. And the first instruction they give you for using it, the first thing you have to do before beginning the whole process, is to ask several times: "Annie, are you okay?" Jackson liked that a lot and he stuck it in as the chorus in his song." They are both silent for a minute. Then, one of them says: "How crazy was that guy." The other says: "Amen. Rest in peace." Then they start to argue about what they're going to eat after they drop off the pale body that they're transporting in the back.

For many people, the most frightening word was "cancer"; "cancer" being, these days, a jack-of-all-trades, the concentration of everything that implied a one-way trip to a place no one ever dreamed of visiting, but that, every so often, reared its head and brandished its pincers around the borders of a nightmare. The word that frightened The Lonely Man most, on the other hand, started with an *A*. Actually, it was one of the two words that frightened him most. The words—both of them—that frightened him most began with *A* and with *a*. The first one was the surname of a German psychiatrist from the beginning of the twentieth century, which was tattooed across the shoulder of a disease that was new but whose symptoms had been present since the beginning of time: "Alzheimer." The second (he'd learned it during a fairly lengthy stay in Mexico, where he'd gone with the assignment of writing a book about Mexico City for a series about different cities at the turn of the millennium) was "*ahorita*": that deceptive diminutive of *ahora*—meaning "now" in Spanish—was nothing but the indescribable translation into a handful of letters (you had to experience it in the flesh and endure it with your own patience to know what it was was like) of the exceedingly particular and elastic and always postponable way that Mexicans related to every kind of commitment, promise of punctuality, and spatiotemporal responsibility to other people. *"Ahorita"* like the certified suspicion and preliminary maneuver of what would result in, many hours or millennia later, a Mexican asking you, with a smile hot enough to raise blisters, "What's happening?" or "What's up?" Really asking, "What didn't happen / isn't happening / won't happen" or "What wasn't/isn't/won't be up?" In Mexico—he knew it then and won't ever forget it—saying *"ahorita"* was a way to honor, subliminally, ancient deities with long names made up of pure consonants: scaled and feathered beings that spun around circular calendars, biting their own tails, spreading their wings, without hurry, because to hurry, to arrive on time, to finish what you started, was for mere mortals who didn't believe in the wide and always expansive reward of the future. Waiting and waiting and waiting like in the beginning of *Casablanca*, but in the D. F., where that other movie would be called *Apocalypse Ahorita* and Willard would eternally delay his departure from his hotel in Saigon to go and look for Kurtz with an "I'm going *ahorita.*" So, *"después"* or "later" was an indeterminate future and *"luego-luego"* or "in a bit" meant, he supposed, right away, but "in a bit." In Mexico City, he remembers, he had several nervous breakdowns waiting for people who never came, next to telephones that never rang. He was still waiting for them to ring, to come. The Lonely Man spent a couple weeks there without much or too much happening. He wrote down random things in a notebook like: "Mex-Machismo: *'Qué padre'* (exclamation of praise, using the word *padre* or "father" with a positive connotation); *'Me vale madre'* (a derogation amounting to 'It's worthless,' using the word *madre* or "mother" with a negative connotation); *'Mi Rey'* (meaning 'My King,' which women say to men to keep them docile and not even bothering to realize they might in fact be kings, yes; but it's the women who are the Supreme Empresses of the Galaxy)." He walked through vertiginous slums, breathed nearly-solid air, dodged bullets blessed by the Virgin of Guadalupe, was deafened by golden trumpets, interviewed masked monosyllabic wrestlers, bit into too many mescal worms, and committed the most terrible and damning of errors: drunk and electrified by those volts that make you want to keep drinking, in Plaza Garibaldi, he took, in one shot, a photo wearing a cowboy hat (recalling the sad and sordid and crepuscular photos of John Cheever and Francis Scott Fitzgerald with Mexican sombreros), which is like invoking the heavenly furies and the evil fates. But he didn't come up with anything to write while he was there, because he saw so many things, so many possibilities, that they ended up withering away and destroying each other in a colorful war. One night, flipping through channels where everyone was keeling over with laughter on the TV in his hotel, he remembered the messages Penelope sent him via email, a while back, from a nearby republic, prisoner of her more tyrannical than democratic in-laws. And suddenly—reusing that material that his sister had filmed and put in writing—everything seemed to fall into place. And the book wrote itself, as if it were being dictated to him in screams. But all of that was like something that happened in another life. He took no comfort in remembering himself as clever and powerful—just the opposite. The only effect produced by that past was to increase the potency of his present and the enigma of his immediate future. The possibility that the doctor to whom he was now returning—time to find out already—would enter the office and, flipping through the various papers and graphs of his diagnosis, say to him: "*Ahorita*, Alzheimer's."

But no. Not yet. Not quite yet. Put off the inevitable until the last second. Like when he was a kid and finally got around to studying on the dreadful Sunday night that preceded the exterminating Monday morning. Like when, as an adolescent, he was expelled from school and waited more than a year to tell his parents and every morning pretended to go to school when he really went to read in the library instead. Like when he was not a kid or an adolescent anymore, but put off submitting his manuscript to his editor until the last second, almost en route to the printer, adding long paragraphs in the final round of proofs.

In the same way, the same pathology, the imminence of the diagnosis is translated into a torrent of ideas that he writes down in his notebook, in a delirious fever out of which bursts the possibly last but revealing words of a dying man. In storylines closer to something—a kind of oriental and exotic writing—he read about once called "biji" than to the western and exceedingly played-out short story. Contained yet open plot capsules that, for once, more closely resemble Chekov and Munro than his typical hurricaning stories, blowing from all directions at once, as if everyone in them were talking at the same time and not raising their hand to ask permission first.

In "Loss," a father battles the death of his son. And, of course, he loses. Now that father—suddenly an ex-father—knows how to respond when people ask him what's the worst thing that's happened to you in your life. Now, in addition, he knows how to respond when people ask what's the worst thing that will happen to you in your life—because it already happened. There's nothing more horrible than having all the answers, there's nothing worse than knowing nobody has the answer to his question and that that question is "why?" It's not fair to have to live through the death of a child. His son won't see him grow old and he won't see the beginning of his son's old age. Suddenly, everything is going against the natural order of things. The natural order that determines that, when a father dies, his son—beyond the pain he might end up feeling—also feels somewhat liberated, knowing that his father is no longer thinking of him. On the other hand, when the son is the one dying, the fact that he no longer thinks of him is, for the father, a biblical punishment, a private plague. And his son has died even before his grandparents, the father's own parents, whom, presumably, he will also see die. And nobody will see his death. Nobody, yes, will live to tell it. Nobody will survive to tell him about it. Now, that man is outside all logic of time and space, the normal course of the story has been altered. So, he decides, anything is possible, anything can happen. Because the worst thing that can happen to someone has already happened to him. Which means that now nothing can happen to him but the expansive wave of what keeps on happening, what expands, what occupies more space all the time inside and outside of him and what will soon contain and devour everything, down to the last beam of light, until everything is void and black and hole. Last rites cited, the first displays of affection from acquaintances, and that's it, the father decides that the only way he'll be able to overcome the pain will be to eliminate all traces of his son. Delete. Erase him as if he'd never existed to the point where he'd even forget that he'd erased him. Wipe from his memory the shared palace of his son's memory. So, first, the father burns all his drawings, gives away the tiny clothes, puts toys in bags and takes them to hospitals and orphanages, calls a charity organization to have them come take away his son's rocket-shaped bed. But soon he discovers that it's not working, that it's not enough: the pain is still there, he can't forget him, his son is more present than ever in the increasingly full void he's left behind. The next step, it's clear, is to end things with his wife, with the mother— because it all began with her, it was her he entered so his son would come out. He cuts her into pieces, buries her in the garden; but the relief doesn't last long. Just passing in front of his son's school; or approaching that cinema where they went to see *Toy Story*, all three of them, for the first of many times; or the place where they ate their favorite hamburgers; or . . . What follows is a hurricane of death and destruction transmitted live and direct from helicopter-mounted cameras. Flames, explosions, screams. Neither the police nor the army are able to stop him; and the father feels he's the chosen one, invulnerable, an unstoppable force of nature, a Shiva dancing her last dance. At sunrise, almost nothing remains of the small city and our hero—a man on a mission—departs for the rest of the planet; because his son loved geography and knew so much about other countries and told him that, when he grew up, he wanted to be "the person who chooses the colors of the countries on maps."

In "Lost," a father, unhappy in his marriage and his job, takes his only pleasure in his son. His worst fear, his constant terror, is that something will happen to the little boy and that he won't be able to do anything to stop it. So he barely sleeps at night, weaving waking nightmares and counting hydrophobic sheep and composing possible variations for the dispassionate aria of disgrace that—it seems inevitable, like an incurable advanced disease or a drunk driver who runs a stoplight or a little finger inserted into an electrical socket—he'll someday have to hear. One Saturday afternoon, walking around a shopping center with his son, he decides that he can no longer tolerate the uncertainty of living, in agony, always ready to anticipate an impossible to anticipate blow. So he decides, then and there, to be the one who takes the initiative and, in a way, win the battle. The man walks with his little boy through the halls of the shopping center and, suddenly, without saying anything, drops his hand, lets him go, on his own, swept away by the multitude, escalators up or down, as if ascending to hell or descending to heaven. He loses him so that, at last, he can find himself. The pain—surprise—lasts as long as it takes him to make it to the parking lot, get in his car, and leave without looking back. Now, thinks the man, I am other, I am different, I am new. And, yes—he's a monster. Days later, the whole world learns of the first "deeds" and "exploits" of someone who—in messages to papers and news channels—calls himself Anikilator. And, yes, maybe the protagonist of "Lost" should encounter the protagonist of "Loss" in a third story. The two of them singing Mahler and Rückert's *"Kindertotenlieder"* in loud voices, with those dissonant verses of children who have gone ahead and dawdled along the way, strolling through a landscape about to be ravaged by a storm. The two of them clashing together in a final cosmic duel, like in the old and monstrous movies where Dracula battled Frankenstein's monster while Wolfman and the Mummy commentated on the fight from the castle sidelines.

In "Lottery," parents outside a school silently watch the slow but incessant eclipse of a terminally ill boy. At the end, when they see him come out in a wheelchair, almost a smiling skeleton, they can't keep from crying. Crying with one eye for the boy's pain. With the other eye, they cry from the unspeakable joy they feel, because that boy isn't theirs, because statistically speaking this won't happen to them.

In "Slow Suicides," one winter morning . . . Actually he doesn't have the slightest idea what "Slow Suicides" is about. All he has is the title—but he likes the title *so much* . . . Or maybe he does know what it's about, knows now, suddenly and all at once: "Slow Suicides" tells the story of a literary titan—inspired by Thomas Mann perhaps—who is the father of two sons with artistic predilections, but who, in the saturnine shadow of their father, commit suicide, leaving him a note asking that he, if nothing else, make something great and noble out of them in the world of fiction. And the great writer—who has touched and stroked and taken on everything in his novels and stories—comes up with nothing—nothing to tell. For the first time. The story ends with the writer, in the solitude of his study, asking himself whether—having never felt it before—this lack of inspiration, might not be the closest thing to the pain of losing a child that he'll ever experience in his life and work.

The other title that at first he doesn't know what to do with, but which subsequently becomes suddenly clear is "Anterior to Zero." In it, a boy dies in an absurd accident, at school, during recess, a small blow striking the precise fatal spot. They offer to let the father see his son, his son's body, and at first he says yes, but then he wonders if maybe it would be better not to, to not superimpose that stillness over so much movement, to remember him alive, living, full of life, a boy forever.

"All the Dead Children" starts out as, in appearance, nothing more than a list of the young children who died in the name of literature. Little bodies that stopped breathing in order to take the readers' breath away. The youngest and greatest of the Buddenbrooks; the unforgettable Annabel "Lee" Leigh in her seaside principality; Walt Garp; the little daughter of Rhett Butler and Scarlett O'Hara; the one who expires in the arms of his governess in the phantasmagoric halls of Bly; the one whom Bob Slocum embraces in the most loving of strangulations . . . But before long, reading it, you get the sense and then realize almost immediately that they're all there, but one. The one whom the narrator, invisible yet omnipresent, cannot name and who doesn't appear in any novel or story. The real name of an actual boy. The boy whose name and body and shadow he distracts himself from with the names of so many other dead immortals.

In "And That's When the Trouble Started," an adolescent boy again tells his father the same thing he's been telling him all his life: that when he grows up—not long now—he's going to be what he already is even though he hasn't published anything yet: a writer. His father tells him that it'd be better to pursue a career where he could make a living from writing. Writing ad copy, for example. And, since the boy ignores him, the father tells him he'll send his stories to a writer friend of his who runs a magazine, to put him in his place. So he does, and the writer friend invites the son to write for the magazine. And the son makes a living doing that while writing his first book, which doesn't go at all badly for him. From that point on, the father never stops asking and forbidding him to "put him in one of his little stories," but always wishes he would.

In "A Model to Disassemble," a father—as a way to punish a son who hasn't put away his toys—takes a complex and unique and unrepeatable Lego model and lets it fall to the floor and smiles as he watches it crash, in slow motion, from multiple angles at the same time, a thousand Legos, in hundreds of pieces. And that primitive and unforgivable satisfaction turns into guilt and fear when he finds his son watching him with eyes where, for the first time, "the small pupils of the little boy dilate with a new gleam; and that gleam is the beginning of something from which there's no return and no end, the beginning of hate: hate begins here and now, those eyes tell him; hate, whose engines will keep on running until the end of your days and even beyond, Daddy."

In "What Will Be," and regarding the impossibility of giving children a good education and making all the right decisions for their future, a father at a party, holding and held up by a glass full to the brim with whiskey, says: "My little Leo never walked in on me and his mother making love . . . I wonder if that'll end up being a good thing or a bad thing for the development of his personality. What do you think, gorgeous?"

In "Will Be," a man, in the exact instant of the orgasm that kicks off the story of his paternity (there goes that spermatozoid to dance inside that ovum), experiences the *petit mort* of being able to, in a matter of seconds, contemplate his entire future as a parent. The joy and sadness and confusion that await him along the way and the death of his condition as the last of his bloodline. Then, right away, he forgets all of it. Better that way. Otherwise it might be like one of those stories that, before long, night after night, he'll tell to his future son (a story his son will memorize, down to the last word and inflection, delighted by knowing everything that's coming, down to the last detail) who's already there, on this side, forever.

At the end of "Correction," a mother asks her daughter—while at the same time she answers herself; because it's one of those questions that is actually a statement with just a solitary and final word catching the question mark—"You don't have any reason to resent me, right?" To which the daughter responds: "I resent you for nothing; which is not the same thing."

In "With Childish Handwriting," only a few words are written: "Daddy Dearest: for your information, starting today, I'll be sleeping with a big knife under my pillow. Your daughter, M."

In "Knives," a sleeping boy wakes up in the middle of the night. It hasn't been long since he went to bed, because his eyes aren't yet "full of lasagnas" (this childish error was corrected some time ago, but the humor of switching "lasagnas" for "*lagañas*,"—the Spanish word for "eye boogers"—has remained implanted as a family joke). The boy, about four or five years old, fell asleep a couple hours earlier thinking about how a paper airplane seems to weigh more than the same piece of paper before it's folded. The boy wonders if the seed of a possible calling might pulse inside this intrigue, but—still lacking the color wheel with the colors of physics, or Zen, or poetry—he doesn't wonder what that calling might be. He has enough to deal with at the moment, having to respond to the horrible question that adults shouldn't be allowed to ask children: "What do you want to be when you grow up?" Or even worse: "What are you going to be when you grow up?" Questions far more disturbing than that already classic question, easy to process/escape with a "Both the same": "Who do you love more: Mommy or Daddy?" Now, then, thinking about all of this with his eyes shut, the boy opens them ever so slightly and discovers his mother and father, standing in his bedroom doorway, looking at him with that terrifying intensity that adults only direct at children when they're sleeping, so they don't frighten them. The father's and mother's eyes are full of tears and strange smiles hang from their mouths and, in their hands, the boy discovers and trembles with half-closed eyes, pretending to be asleep, both of them are holding big, long knives. And the father and the mother don't say anything; they just look at him, as if waiting to be granted the courage to do what they want to do. At last, they turn around and go back to the kitchen where they're cutting onions for a salad and tell each other how much they love their son. But the boy (his eyes tightly shut, begging for the arrival and comfort and relief of a nightmare about monsters or one where he finds himself naked in front of his classmates or one where he falls and falls from way up high in the sky) doesn't hear them. And he'll never forget. And he won't say anything to them the next morning when, starting then and until the end, nothing will ever be the same again, nothing will ever be the same after seeing his parents and their knives, the knives of his parents.

Not long now before the appointed hour. In a few short minutes, his life might change forever. It's even possible that his life will begin to die in order to give birth to the shadow of his death. The Lonely Man had always fantasized about the idea of a sudden lightning strike, a flash, an instant snapshot. To stop all of a sudden, like a little toy tin-man with no one to wind it up. Or, better yet, to die in his sleep, and the only sign that something new is underway is a subtle yet notable shift in the mechanics of his dreams: dreaming, like the boy from that last story idea, that he's falling, naked, from high in the sky, but this time, this last time, he doesn't wake up at the moment of impact.

Now, with his eyes wide open, The Lonely Man has never felt so awake. The Lonely Man opens the first door his hand finds and goes inside. He needs—before going back to the doctor's office—to sit and rest and catch what might be the first of his last breaths.

The room is in the half-light and, inside it, there are two beds, and in the beds, an old man and a boy. The old man has the look of a mummified pharaoh who never got put in his pyramid. He must be ninety-something at least. He must have seen and lived through so many things. He must have witnessed the end of so many wars, The Lonely Man thinks. Now, there he is, living history fading away, breathing through a mouth that his jaws no longer protect, growling not like a bear but like a cave where bears hibernate. A cave where it's always winter. The old man looks at him with bluish-white eyes. And says nothing. The old man is fully occupied with making it to the vertiginous summit of the next minute and, once there, asking himself whether it's worth it to begin scaling the next one.

In the bed beside him is a boy. The other extreme of the same spectrum. The boy doesn't have a single hair on his head and his skin exhibits the tautness of a drum beaten by the closed fists of a fever. The boy must be about six years old, but he also looks like a new and eternal and timeless animal. The boy looks at him with an arrogance that belongs not to him, but to the disease. One of those terrible diseases with a hyphenated name. One of those difficult to pronounce diseases. Looking at the boy, terrified, The Lonely Man escapes into the memory of a scary movie with a clown doctor. What was it called? *Patch Adams*, yes. Starring the actor The Lonely Man hated more than any other, always and forever—Robin Williams. Robin Williams, who was like a mime who screams and doesn't stop screaming and there, in the most distasteful of all his distasteful movies, Williams was good, very good, as Patch, a doctor ready to do whatever he could to yank a smile out of a kid whose days-hours-minutes-seconds were numbered and running out. A man convinced that all a terminal boy needs is a fool like him making faces at the foot of his bed. Now, the boy looks at him and doesn't know if he should stick out his tongue and start clucking all around the room or pretend that he's holding up a door in front of him. He doesn't buy it, to tell the truth. A boy who's about to die doesn't care about those things, because he's really busy thinking about, when he dies, how—"What do you not want to be when you don't grow up?"—the infinite people he could've been will die with him. When the old man dies, on the other side of that unbridgeable abyss between the two beds, one person will die, the one he already was; because all the possible and discarded sketches were destroyed in another millennium. The boy, on the other hand, could've been so many things, he could've saved humanity to later destroy it. Or, at least, he could've found out how his favorite show—with zombies and vampires and people who come back through the door on the other side of death—would end. But, though they give him such thrills (and frighten him a little), the boy doesn't believe in them, he doesn't believe in second supernatural chances, just like he no longer believes in all the waning diagnostic seconds that his parents collect as if they were postcards of places their son will never go. Now, the boy looks at him and says nothing; but The Lonely Man is almost certain—like in a silent movie, like on those posters with white letters across a black background—that he lets slip, moving his lips, without emitting a sound, a thundering "Why me?"

In "Another Girlfriend in a Coma," the protagonist enters a hospital room where, in adjacent beds, lie a centenarian and a boy who hasn't and won't make it through the first half-decade of life. The young protagonist (who escaped from a waiting room where, sadly infuriated, his girlfriend's family members were waiting; she tried to commit suicide and though it wasn't his fault exactly, the fact that he was leaving her didn't really help the fragile stability of her recurrent instability) enters that room and sighs with relief. The old man looks at him with a smile and begins to recite something that seems like a well-rehearsed monologue: "When you're a kid you think about death, when you're an adult you think about childhood and old age, when you're old you think again about death . . . Old age is like a black and distorting mirror of infancy: you start sleeping and crying all the time again, nobody understands what you say, you can't control your basic bodily functions, they take you everywhere in a wheelchair, you take medicines constantly, and everyone tells you they love you so much, but nobody pays any attention to you . . . And every night, you close your eyes, thinking that maybe you won't open them again. But the morning is still there the next morning. And you're still in that world. As if you'd been reborn or reincarnated; but in the same failing body, in a body that once ran on beaches and now is dragged through hallways, a body like the ruins of what was once a temple where you—who no longer believe in anything—are the only one who worships now, always on your knees, unable to stand . . . Ah, you can't imagine how badly I wish I could leave my death a widow . . . I'm so tired of not dying. All my friends and acquaintances have gone on ahead of me. I am the last and the only one left. Living in a cemetery. A kind of negative of a ghost, an inversion of the theorem: the survivor in a world where no one is left, where everyone has already gone to another planet and, if they think about me, wherever they are, they do so as if invoking an apparition—disappeared, left behind, so far away and Beyond. Someday you'll understand what I'm saying, if you're granted the so-called blessing of a long life. They say we're going to live longer and longer and that our brains, not ready for so much thinking, will go mad. And that, having evolved to live longer, we'll discover that as super-adults (the average Medieval life expectancy was barely forty years of bad living), we've devolved into mega-old prehistorics, who have no idea what to do with so many years and so little body to endure them. And that we'll walk on all fours again, weighed down by gravity, until we're almost invertebrates and mononeuronales. And that the world will fill up with madmen and mad-women, madder than ever, who will have to be cared for by fewer and fewer young people, because fewer people are born all the time. Who knows . . . But I can assure you that, before long, all around you, everyone will start to die. One drop at a time. Until they form a damp stain on the wall that soon will come down, pushed by the tsunami of birthdays becoming wakes and funerals, into ephemeral ephemera and . . ." Worn out and thinking of running back to the bedside of his ex-girlfriend and waking her with a magic kiss and falling to his knees and asking for her hand, because he needs a hand to hold onto, the young man decides to focus on the boy, who fixes him with eyes of feline intensity in the half-light and commands him, knowing full well what he's thinking, as if he'd known him all his life, in a high-pitched voice: "I strictly forbid you to have an epiphany."

But, take note, quick, he *does* have an epiphany and, at the door to the doc-tor's office, he says: "If everything is fine, I promise I'll never write again." He repeats it aloud without anyone but him hearing, like saying magic words so that the trick doesn't work, so that box doesn't open and—final presto!—is transformed into a coffin ready for the most Viking of funerals.

"The end," he says.

"It's over," he says.

And he wonders if he'll be able to keep his promise. If there might not be some drug (ask the doctor) with effects similar to apomorphine, which years ago was given to homosexuals and nymphomaniacs who wanted to change or to criminals who were oh so happy being criminals. A kind of Ludovico Technique that provokes nausea in place of the panic of the blank page. Maybe not. Maybe no high-octane and superior-potency medicine will be necessary. For a while now, The Lonely Man writes little and slowly, with more or less directed inertia and the reflexes of an old elephant, stopping too often to ask how things are going en route to its graveyard. Anyway, he makes that promise—to stop, to give up his profession, the only thing he knows how to do—like someone handing over his most prized offering, like sending his son to be sacrificed, his son who he loves more than anything, but, also, thinking that he's so tired; that it'd be the perfect excuse; that really, to tell the truth, he enjoyed writing less all the time, that maybe he'd never *really* enjoyed writing.

The Lonely Man opens the door and there's the doctor—who is now *his* doctor, just his, he doesn't want to think that he shares him with others, that his devotion isn't exclusive—with a folder full of papers and graphs and X-rays and ascending and descending lines. All the information about his personal catastrophe—his intimate and private earthquake. He's already suffered its effects and now he just has to wait for them to tell him how many victims were inside that one victim and pray that new aftershocks and conflicts aren't provoked inside him. But—it's been proven, every time the earth opens to close over its parasites or a giant wave decides to take revenge and swallow all those annoying surfers or a church comes crashing down and buries those who believed that in that place God would protect them from his own fury—we know absolutely nothing about earthquakes. When they happen, all you can do is tremble and hope that they pass soon and that you don't pass with them.

"Everything fine. Everything in order. False alarm," says the doctor and, in the same second, The Lonely Man doesn't know whether to love him or to hate him. Because the doctor seems somewhat disappointed faced with the simple banality of something that'd almost split him in two. And he forgets the explanation of his case (the doctor explains it to him in the manner of a disgruntled Sherlock Holmes who's been bothered with a trifle like searching for and finding lost keys, it seems to him; the particulars escape him as soon as he hears them, coming to his ears as if dragged through the mud of white noise and interference and ellipses) almost at the same time that it's communicated to him: "It could've been anything. It could've been a heart attack or the advance of cerebral ictus or the first signs of a tumor. But it was just gastritis," the doctor tells him. "Supergastritis. But gastritis in the end. A digestive disorder provoked by an inflammation of the . . . which provoked certain pressure on the heart and the decreased arrival of oxygen to the . . . and hence the symptoms: the dizziness, the . . . , and the . . . and . . . and that's it."

With an almost childish smile, he tries to explain that it wasn't a joke, that it was serious, that it wasn't some trifle that almost sent him tumbling down the mountain:

"But it's just that I felt like I was dying," he implores, as if apologizing.

"Of course," the doctor soothes him, as if he were a boy swearing that he'd studied the lesson, that he understood all of it, but that, now, he doesn't know what happened at all.

And the doctor continues:

"In fact, the symptom you experienced is called, precisely, *sensation of death*. Something similar to the full experience of death, down to the smallest and richest detail, but without dying. And there are many documented cases of people with what you had, who, convinced they're dying, hence the name, are so frightened by what's happening to them that, believing they're dying, they actually die," the doctor concludes releasing a final little laugh of barely a syllable, but with a deadpan expression.

Then the doctor looks for and finds a notepad and scribbles something incomprehensible: "One every twenty-four hours, before dinner. The syrup when you get up. And mix the powders in water and drink them with lunch," he instructs. And, yes, thinks The Lonely Man, another unequivocal sign that his time is passing and running out: it takes more and more medicines to tame the beast of a single pain. And the doctor gives him the prescription and shakes his hand and, over his shoulder, looks toward the door. His shift is over. His time in a starring role under the lights and sensors has come to an end. Good luck.

But he's not ready to go just yet. It doesn't seem like a good ending.

Trick of the trade.

There's something missing here and he doesn't know what it is. He searches for it in the air and doesn't find it.

"Any questions?," asks the doctor, who suddenly seems younger than ever, almost like a boy playing doctor.

"Well, while I've got you here, there were always a couple things that have intrigued me for as long as I can remember and maybe you can clear them up for me," suggests The Lonely Man.

The doctor looks at him with a mix of annoyance and curiosity.

"Tell me," he says with the automatic diction of someone preparing to compete in a contest, to win an award.

"Well, the first thing is about the shoes . . . The shoes of people who are hit in the street. By a car. Or by a bus. You know: I never understood why the body is there, sprawled, and the shoes are always elsewhere, at a slight distance and . . ."

"Simple: when you receive a hard impact, the torso, which houses the majority of the vital organs, swells up to cushion the blow. And the extremities contract. Automatic reflex. Hence the feet make themselves smaller and the shoes and even the socks fly off. And it doesn't only happen with shoes and feet. The same thing happens with hands. It also happens with rings. Or with dentures and glass eyes. Anything else?" answers and asks the doctor, disappointed, once again, by the softness of the mystery that he's posed.

"Well, yes: the thing about asparagus. Why does your urine smell like asparagus a short time after you eat it? Why doesn't the same thing happen when you ingest other foods? Why doesn't urine smell like braised chicken with potatoes or like a cheeseburger or like French fries?"

The doctor smiles and it's obvious that this second question, even if it isn't worthy of his diploma and his talent, at least strikes him as more unexpected and original.

"Ah, yes: that is due to the breakdown and metabolization of a particular amino acid. It's called asparagine. But, so you know, it doesn't happen to everyone. The latest samples and studies have concluded that only forty-three percent of people who eat asparagus metabolize the amino acid. And there are some who do metabolize it, but aren't able to smell it when they go to the bathroom. Hence they conclude that one's capacity to produce urine with the smell of asparagus is due to the influence of certain genetic polymorphisms. In fact, I don't produce it. Or it could be that I don't smell it. Who knows . . ." the doctor pronounces these last words with an almost melancholic tone. As if, very much in spite of himself, he were—in the presence of an absolute stranger inside of whose organism he knows everything that happens—metabolizing the amino acid of ungranted wishes, of everything he'll never experience.

And the doctor adds: "But everything I'm telling you, if you're so intrigued, you could've found out in a matter of seconds via Google . . . Why didn't you just do that?"

And the Lonely Man doesn't have the strength to tell him that, if that'd been the case, they'd never have had that conversation.

The Lonely Man decides, now, yes, it's time to go, time to get out of there, thinking that he could include all of this in a story or novel. But then he remembers his promise—to stop writing in exchange for being able to keep on reading. Or not even that. Because the world *must* be full of people who don't read or write and who, nevertheless, are happy and normal, right? It's even possible that they're *more* normal and *more* happy.

Now The Lonely Man is on his way out, now he goes and looks outside, now the doors open on their own and the clinic expels him like a whale tired of having him inside.

Portrait of a Lonely Man leaving the Emergency Room, almost giving little leaps. "Hop, Hop, Hopper!," he says at first. "How ridiculous," he says and then makes an excuse: relief tends to favor outbursts of things like that, bad jokes, silly ideas. Relief metabolizes and infantilizes badly and turns you not into one of those smart kids, but into a childish and amino-acidic adult. There's nothing for him to do there now. In that sanctuary for the grave and the acute, now he's the most impertinent of intruders. It's not that he feels perfectly fine, but he's on the mend. He can feel the slow but constant retreat of both the malady and the accompanying fear—as if a very heavy blanket were being slowly pulled off his body—and, all at once, the consoling tenderness of the night, of the end of a night, from which he returns certain that he'll see a new day.

But we're not quite there yet.

He takes a deep breath of air that's soft with jasmine and that tastes new and that has the nameless color used to mix all colors and that sounds like music sounds seconds before composing itself. Suddenly, like a wild celebration of the senses, everything is brighter and more fragrant and sounds clearer and feels better and is as catchy as the best song of summer.

And, without looking back, The Lonely Man goes slowly down the stairs. Step by step. Counting them, like when he was a kid, like when each and every thing is counted because everything counts.

And then he realizes: something has changed inside him; he's not the same person he was when he arrived here a couple hours ago, hours that now, in his memory, have the weight of something that happened centuries ago, like something almost legendary. The Lonely Man looks at his feet and it's as if his sense of perspective and distance have been altered slightly, just a little, but still producing the discombobulation of someone who is both near-sighted and far-sighted and who can't find their glasses anywhere and searches for them throughout the house, as if with the cautious footsteps of an astronaut. As if he were walking through the air, floating, but just a centimeter off the ground. Nobody would be aware of the miracle or the stigma. But it's enough for him to understand that everything has changed forever, that nothing is going to go back to how it was. The Lonely Man wonders where this sudden rarefication of his atmosphere might have come from. Maybe it's the effects of the implanted terror gland being activated, like in those lyrical extraterrestrials from that science fiction comic he read so many times, so many years ago, when they were still looking for irrefutable proof of intelligent life on other planets. Or maybe it's just the physical manifestation of a new mental lightness, the direct consequence—keeping his promise—of saying goodbye to all of that, of not being obligated to write anything anymore, nothing, never, ever, forever. Maybe.

There's no hurry.

He'll find an explanation.

Or, if not, he's sure—some lives have no cure, just the relief that comes with death—that an explanation will find him. He'll happen to think of something that'll make something happen, something will happen that'll make him happen to think of something.

He could swear it.

He could swear—though he's promised to give up writing so he can keep being written—that he always wanted to come up with something that would end, that would end so that something else could begin, with the words "he could" and "swear it."

But, of course, it'd be a lie.

So, better, he decides to keep going for a few more lines, up the mountain, to his house, to his library, to his desk.

The distance from the clinic door to the doors of the funicular is, it seems to him, the slightest and most appropriate of ellipses. He covers it as if in a sigh. A sigh of terrified happiness. The happiness of knowing that the times he'll be this happy in what's left of his life are numbered and that, inevitably, another doctor, closer and closer in time and space, won't tell him "Everything's fine" but to the contrary: "Something's wrong."

Now The Lonely Man is going back up and, on the way, it's inevitable to think it, because all of a sudden everything he does seems to carry the possibility of being definitive. Yes: someday he'll take his last ride in the funicular. Up or down? In an ambulance, or to catch a ride in another moving truck?

Who knows.

And who cares.

It's not something he's too worried about right now—the direction—and, yes, it's something he doesn't want to think about too much. He's only interested in enjoying being back here instead of having had to stay down there.

Amid the cyclists and runners, he watches the funicular arrive, full of kids in school uniforms and parents who seem to be wondering how this happened, how they got there, where have all these restless little creatures come from. That's their problem, they're in charge, nobody forced them, free will, efficient contraceptives, should've thought about it more and better, he thinks. He neither had nor has nor will he ever have anything to do with any of that. He has nobody to miss him and nobody to miss. The only responsibility The Lonely Man has now is to himself and it's the responsibility to go up, to go up. With no one to answer to. No obligation to explain anything. Alone and one-of-a-kind and beginning and ending in the journey of himself, as if pulling his own cable to propel himself into the heights. A simple mechanism in appearance, on a track that's impossible to modify, but so complex in its scope and in the mental detours that can be attained inside it.

He's so happy to be going home and his home begins there, inside the funicular.

Funicular, sweet funicular.

Can you miss a funicular?

Can a funicular become an important part of your life?

Can you love a funicular more than you love a person?

Yes and yes and yes.

I hope so, he prays.

Now it's already tomorrow and the doors open and over the loudspeakers a recorded voice states that you have to let people exit before you can enter.

And it seems to him a formidable phrase, perfect advice, something with aphoristic resonance, as if extracted from millennia of religious texts: but (he brings his hand to the notebook and stops halfway there and, could this be happiness?, he could swear it is) he has no idea where to insert it, to use it, to make it his own by writing it down.

He could swear it.

MANY FÊTES,
OR STUDY FOR A GROUP PORTRAIT WITH BROKEN DECALOGUES

† "Have you read all these books?" she asks.

† The biji (筆記) is a genre of classic Chinese literature. "Biji" can be translated, roughly yet more or less faithfully, as "notebook." And a biji can contain
curious anecdotes, nearly blind quotations, random musings, philosophical
speculations, private theories regarding intimate matters, criticism of other
works, and anything that its owner and author deems appropriate. Do samu-
rais interrupt the conversation of their katanas to write down something
that occurs to them in the precise instant of blood and steel? Did geishas
write bijis in the tight silk straps that they bound their feet with to keep
them from growing? Ah, yes . . . A biji always at hand, just in case, you
never know. A biji like the written and unplugged equivalent of one of those
mobile phones used to photograph anything, everything, and nothing. The
different items in a biji can be numbered, but, also, it's possible to read them
not according to any order, opening a path for ourselves, starting at any point
and jumping back and forth or up and down or side to side. Beginning at the
end and ending at the beginning. The idea is that, one way or another, each
reader ends up discovering a story as unique as her reading. The biji genre
appeared for the first time during the Wei and Jin dynasties, and reached
full maturity during the Tang and Song dynasties. The biji of that period
include, also and in an almost featured role, fragments of the "believe it or
not" variety, anticipating the *Believe It or Not!* comic strip created by the supposed explorer and slightly mythomaniacal adventurer Robert Ripley, for the
pages of a newspaper at the beginning of the twentieth century. So, many
of the entries in the biji format can be thought of as little fictions detaching
themselves from one great fiction, that, though secret, is there nonetheless,

waiting to be discovered. (Please, don't confuse a biji with one of those oh so hip—ever since the amusing dictatorship of one-hundred-forty characters installed itself—microstories. Those witticisms that everyone writes or tries to write and with which even he, once, tried to win—and lost, under a pseudonym—a contest. With the following: *"Amnesia* / Somewhere in La Mancha, somewhere I cannot remember." And that is, and was, it.)

Now he, it's not that he *wants* to, but that he *can* remember. And he arranges and unarranges these pages, telling and deluding himself that he's revisiting the biji genre, so he doesn't have to admit that they are, in reality, just the windblown tatters of fallen standards and the still-smoking ruins of something that he wanted to build but that came crashing down. The broken pieces of a temple he believed in or needed to believe in. The shrapnel from an explosion extracted, piece-by-piece, from the wounded but surviving body of something, of someone. The loose phrases of that thing—trying to *swim underwater* and hold his breath—he wanted to write so badly, but couldn't, a while back now, sometime during the great droughts that marked the Crack dynasty.

† Francis Scott Fitzgerald wrote: "All good writing is *swimming underwater* and holding your breath." And reading that, at the end of a volume of letters from the author of *Tender Is the Night* to his daughter Frances "Scottie" Fitzgerald (could there be anything more dreadful than a father giving his own name to his own daughter, with only the slightest orthographic but not sonic modification?), he can't help but recall that he learned to write (to write very well for someone his age) long before he learned to swim (to swim very badly for someone his age).

† "Writers aren't people exactly."—Francis Scott Fitzgerald, *The Last Tycoon*.

† Exactly, Scott. Writers are people who, inexactly, always prefer to look away, toward another part—the invented part.

† "Dick tried to dissect it [the charm] into pieces small enough to store away—realizing that the totality of a life may be different in quality from its

segments, and also that life in the forties seemed capable of being observed only in segments."—Francis Scott Fitzgerald, *Tender Is the Night*.

† "Action is character," yes, and *The Notebooks of F. Scott Fitzgerald*—edited by Matthew J. Bruccoli—are for him, along with the notebooks and notes of Henry James and Franz Kafka and John Cheever, the greatest example of the journal that he knows of: one of the most perfect and sensitive and romantic books of bijis. Sometimes he opens it at random, as if it were the Bible or the I Ching or the phone book, and reads the first thing his eyes come across and trip over. Right now, for example:

"Escape and so we have the Escape Autobiography."

And later:

"The very elements of disintegration seemed romantic to him."

And one more:

"My mind is the loose cunt of a whore, to fit all genitals."

And another:

"There are certain ribald stories that I heard at ten years old and never again, for I heard a new and more sophisticated set at eleven. Many years later I heard a ten-year-old boy telling another one of those old stories and it occurred to me that it had been handed on from one ten-year-old genera-tion to the next for an incalculable number of centuries. So with the set I learned at eleven. Each set of stories, like a secret ritual, stays always within its age-class, never growing older because there is always a new throng of ten-year-olds to learn them, and never growing stale because these same boys will forget them at eleven. One can almost believe that there is a conscious theory behind this unofficial education."

And below:

"In a real dark night of the soul it's always three o'clock in the morning."

And a bit farther down:

"Show me a hero and I'll write you a tragedy."

And to finish up, for now:

"Draw your chair up close to the edge of the precipice and I'll tell you a story."

And enough for today.

† This is your heroic precipice. If you ask it something, it sends back the echo of your question:

† "Have you read all these books?" she asks. Not with the shrill voice of the microstory but with the sensual and attractive voice of the biji. And he feels like he's drowning and floating at the same time. And her voice—her tone, her way of asking the question, as if mocking herself before others can mock her and her question—makes him remember something. And he can't remember what it is that it makes him remember. Something—he'd enjoy this—a little *Lost in Translation*. A "mature" man and an "innocent" girl. Long and slow and pleasantly tense conversations. Singing a perfectly lousy rendition of "More Than This." Romance. Like in *Tender Is the Night*. Like Dick Diver and Rosemary Hoyt. But here and now. And without all the drama or background noise. Something more comfortable. And wise. Feeling like Bill Murray. Having Bill Murray's face, which is, for him, the most comfortable of faces. The face of the man with whom all the men fell in love when they watched *Lost in Translation* and—to not admit this, not admit it to themselves, not admit it—they lied to themselves that they'd fallen in love with Scarlett Johansson. But really, they'd fallen in love with Bill Murray, with Bill Murray's face. A face with personality and simultaneously sensitive and somewhat tired of everything and everyone, and that wasn't too much to ask from the face of a famous person, he believes, he's always believed that. But no. He thinks for a few seconds, focuses, and then the relief of remembering so like the relief of sneezing. The pleasure of finally locating the precise reference in the archive of his memory. He lives each of those moments— from when he was a boy with his hard and overflowing storage drive, up to this present where his corrupt files melt together and some get confused with others—with a strange pride. The pride of remembering, of *making* memory, the thing most like writing for someone who doesn't write anymore.

† And what does the question "Have you read all these books?" remind him of? And what does the voice that says, "Have you read all these books?" remind him of? Easy, he lifts a hand and presses the button to deliver the correct answer: that moment on Pink Floyd's *The Wall* (first the album and later the movie) when a girl goes into Pink's hotel room and asks, with a sexy

and mocking voice, "Are all these your guitars," and then, "Are you feeling okay?" And no: Pink is not feeling O.K. at all, but he is feeling more than ready to K.O. his TV, his room, his life. He's not *really* like that, like Pink; kind of though. But he loves his TV too much.

† The young woman who now asks "Have you read all these books?" (the answer is no, he hasn't read all of them; but he has looked at them and held them and touched them and flipped through them; he has been collecting them with the idea of someday reading them and because he needs to have them with him, nearby) must be about twenty-five, but, at the same time, ten. Or almost eleven. In a few months—when she's given a new set of stories—she'll forget the whole "ribald" story that might end up taking time and taking place inside the walls of his house. And, within a few years, the young woman who won't be a young woman anymore will be struck by a sound or a few words or whatever and she'll ask herself what it makes her remember. And the answer will be him. But it'll be one of those difficult and elusive answers, because . . .

† . . . nothing actually happens. Nothing is going to happen. No fluid exchange of any kind. Nothing memorable, good or bad. Because he's always taken pride in not entering into any kind of carnal commerce with the aid of a certain literary perfume. But a couple hours ago, he'd decided: there's a first time for everything. At a writers' party, the kind he goes to less and less, being more and more a minor or "cult" writer. And he'd forgiven himself in advance with a "It's allowed now, since I don't write anymore, right?" But, before long, he says to himself, noble but also worried that his body and concentration won't cooperate, that no: he's not going to start now, not going to renounce his oath after so many years. And—writers, whose work it is to be convincing and who, paradoxically and ironically, are beings who have no trouble convincing themselves of anything; writers are so superstitious—he believes that the renewal of that commitment earns him, on the spot, a prize, or, at least, a ranking so that he can run another race.

Because now the girl says:

† "Those are your parents? What lunatics!"

† And the girl is holding a photo that was sitting on his desk. Framed. And signed: "To the REAL Golden Couple, from S&G," it says. And it's not a photo of his parents (it isn't them), but it is his parents' photo (given to them). It's obvious and it'd even be obvious to a ten- or eleven-year-old kid that, judging by the period when that man and woman in the photo were photographed, there's no way they could be his parents. Maybe his grandparents. Again: even a kid could figure this out. But a twenty-five-year-old girl doesn't necessarily understand what a kid understands, she no longer possesses those intuitive yet efficient faculties—like the echo of an unforgettable vacation that you no longer remember—and she's lost in intelligence what she's gained in sexual allure. It's not her fault, of course. It's the time she lives in, he thinks. This futuristic present where the past—everything that passed in the past—is sloppily assembled, like in the hangar of the unfortunate Citizen Kane, with no regard for eras and periods, knowing that there's no problem, that nothing's missing, that to assign a date to something it's no longer necessary to waste time memorizing important dates or to have a clear understanding of even a primitive schema of the history of Humanity. Now, to *make time* all you have to do is type in that new "Presto!" that is the word "Google."

He read somewhere—in one of those increasingly frequent books warning, like fiery prophets, of the consequences of the end of reading for the human body and soul—that the first thing you lose when you stop reading is the more or less clear understanding of the abstraction of time. If you don't start reading as a child, if you don't incorporate and accept the deceptive yet indispensable idea of time gained and time lost, of the time that passes between the time when the hero is condemned and the time when he gets his revenge, they say you lose all form of temporal orientation and inhabit the idea of a continuum where everything happens simultaneously. Like what happens to Billy Pilgrim in Kurt Vonnegut's *Slaughterhouse-Five*.

† Of course, to understand—and enjoy, and admire—what happens to Billy Pilgrim from Kurt Vonnegut's *Slaughterhouse-Five*, first you have to have read Kurt Vonnegut's *Slaughterhouse-Five*.

† He'd become a writer because it was the closest thing to being a reader. And when he says and thinks "reading" he means reading books, sitting or

lying down or walking and moving. Turning pages to acquire a different time and a different velocity.

What time is it?

Whatever time it is in the book.

It's no good—it's cheating, it's not the same—to read on a screen where the time and the hour are always whatever the device we plug ourselves into indicates. So, the girl who asks if he read all those books is a girl who reads a lot but doesn't read anything, and what she reads isn't measured in books anymore but in who knows what.

† There was a time when parties or film or TV or alcohol or drugs or sex or politics or sunsets pulled us away from books.

Now—surprise!—it's the books that pull us away from the books.

The electronic books that prevent us from concentrating for more or less long stretches of reading without feeling the reflexive and automatic temptation to jump to another place, another site, another front, to tangle ourselves in social networks and, suddenly, it's already time to go and update our profile. On screens—big and small screens—where our lives are no longer projected because our lives, now, more all the time, are screens.

To be or not to be a screen, that is the question.

Being there.

And a while back he read an interview with Philip Roth, where the writer, once called the "the Jewish Fitzgerald" and now retired from writing, mused: "Where are the readers? Looking at their computer screens, TV screens, movie theaters, DVDs. Distracted by more pleasurable formats. The screens have defeated us." And referring to the Kindle—the, at the time, most recent incarnation of the electronic book—Roth said: "I haven't seen it yet, I know it's around, but I doubt it will replace an artifact like the book. The key isn't to transfer books to electronic screens. It's not that. No. The problem is that literature takes a habit of mind that has disappeared. As if in order to read we needed an antenna and it'd been cut. The signal doesn't arrive. The concentration, the solitude, the imagination that the habit of reading requires. We've lost the war. In twenty years, reading will be a cult . . . It'll be a minority hobby. Some people will raise dogs and tropical fish, others will read."

† The evidently antennaless girl who asked him if he'd read all those books is already on to something else, she's already changed channels, she's already examining the results of a new search—the photo of his parents who are not his parents.

The man and the woman who appear in the photo—"What lunatics!"—are dressed up as robotic automobiles. Vintage transformers.

And their names are Sara and Gerald Murphy.

The photo has the sepia amber color acquired by everything that passed, that already was yet continues to be, when it's preserved, frozen in time.

The photo was taken in 1924 by Man Ray at the automobilistic costume party that Comte Étienne de Baumont threw at some ballroom in Côte d'Azur.

The photo was dedicated and delivered to his parents at some point in the early sixties, before he was born. His parents, who never owned a car or learned to drive and that was for the best—he would've never risked getting in a car with either of them behind steering wheel.

And now the photo—and the possible prize that's revealed to him and that he accepts out of the confusion of couples, of those mechanical parents that are not his parents—gives him an idea.

And it's been so long since he had one . . .

And so, making up some excuse, he asks the girl to please go, before, like in Pink's hotel room, everything starts flying through the air.

† But through the air of his head, of his imagination, of what he might someday, once again end up writing. And desperate, as if dying of thirst and confronting the sudden materialization of an oasis that, he prays, he hopes is not a mirage, he searches for and finds his notebook of bijis. And there he finds and reads . . .

† . . . a long parenthetical that—cut & paste—he extracted from somewhere else because it bothered him. And that appears here to bother him even more. A kind of statement of purpose that, of course, has been written in a way that clearly confirms that he won't be able to achieve that purpose:

"(Here he comes from so far away, so far away that it's as if he were arriving from an alternate dimension, from a possible maybe, ah, another parentheses like an expansive wave. And The Boy who is now running along a beach doesn't yet possess the necessary knowledge to resist the torrent that, within a few years, will translate into many, numerous novels and stories. Some very good, many very bad. Some and others will receive awards and praise for their audacity and he tries to not forget, to remember all of it. To remember both the time The Boy lives in now and his childhood. Testimonial texts. The chronicle like a chronic illness. Authors who assure you they trembled when they assumed the responsibility of putting it all down in writing. As if they'd been chosen for it. As if it were a divine mission communicated by a beam of light descending from the heavens where, presently, they'll aspire to ascend, sanctified, evangelized. Pages about fathers and sons swept away by the tornado of History. And "Toto, I've got a feeling we're not in Kansas anymore" will be one of The Boy's favorite lines from one of his favorite movies. A line he'll say to himself in the deafeningly quiet voice of thoughts every time he crosses paths with one of those books attached to its author. Men and women and the idea that mechanically describing something evil automatically makes you good and—change of guard and ages—new motifs, but not motivation, for describing another damned decade. The damned decade when The Boy will be an enlightened and eternal youth or something like that and will find certain success and uncertain fame with his first book, which, of course, is about the previous damned decade. Again: opening updated instruction manuals to maneuver complicated pieces of a simple Meccano model. Or simple pieces of a complicated Meccano model. Either way, it's all the same. All you'll have to do is carefully follow the steps, assembling the model so it can be disassembled again and again and again. Storytellers wrapped in a pale-colored flag so easy to sully, tearing their clothes, frenetically dancing the tango of the blues. A plethora of cuts and breaks and contortions across the stages and fairs of the world. Novels and stories like those villagers with torches, running up the hill, in pursuit of Frankenstein's monster, who only wants to be left in peace. And for them to, please, stop calling him Frankenstein all the time; for them to get it through their heads once and for all that the doctor is Frankenstein, not him, right? And The Boy doesn't know it yet, but his thing, what's to come, what he'll bring to the table—a villager with a torch running down the hill, pursued by hundreds of Frankenstein's monsters—won't be the novelization of adolescent or adult terrorism, but will always depart from childhood *horrorism*. Something else.

Childhood as trauma—his childhood, *so* happy despite everything—and the intimate and domestic warfare of his parents. Both appearing and disappearing and reappearing like a black cloud with silver lining covering the sun. And, soon thereafter, below the surface and in the background, the multiple historical and hysterical avatars of his now nonexistent country of origin. His parents' emotional life, like a backdrop where, yes, there will also be a dangerous and compromising political moment resulting in another of the no-longer-so-young boy's many "accidents." An accident that, in turn, will become a story in his first book. A vaudeville with kidnappers that becomes the final stepping-stone to his literary vocation, functioning like a series of variations of an inalterable aria and coda. A story with an ending modified in relation to the reality that inspired it. In the story, his parents reappear. In reality, they never did. Like those exasperating and paradoxical and complex movies about time travel that The Boy will become such a fan of. Those movies that make you *work* so hard. Those movies that will return him, time and again, from the darkness of the movie theater to the light of the outside world. Thinking and analyzing, his head aching, the dizzying twists of each movie's concentric and dazzling plotlines, wondering what happened, what's happening, what will happen, what might happen if . . .)"

† And after reading this, he writes: "Sara & Gerald Murphy/Zelda and Francis Scott Fitzgerald + My parents (my sister) + *Tender Is the Night* + that unavoidable son of a bitch Ernest Hemmingway + And all the rest of them too + . . . and so it goes."

And he sits down to see what happens.

† And *so many* things happen.

† For him, there are two great moments in the writing of a book.

First, the moment when he happens to think of the book and the book *happens* and he sees it complete and perfect and singular and, without a doubt, it's the best book he'll ever write and that'll ever be written. That kind of euphoric/adrenalinic ecstasy is, of course, a form of self-deception. That "tunnel vision" that, they say, soldiers experienced in World War One (what was then called The Great War, because it was inconceivable that another war would take place after it), in order to convince themselves to come out of the trenches to see what was happening.

Second, the moment when everything has ended and has been consummated and consumed. When the last word (which often isn't the last one that everyone else will read) is written and he looks at it as if he just returned from the battlefront. And, sure, his report isn't as impeccable as he imagined it, and it's possible that he won't get a medal. But at least he's alive and he lived to tell the tale, to tell his tale.

Between the one extreme and the other occurs, yes, the long *during*: The Great War and, in his case, the Second and Third and Fourth and Fifth and Sixth and Seventh and Eighth and, if he's lucky again, one more time, the Ninth World War.

† And if there's something he appreciates about the Internet, it's the ease of arming yourself, of doing research. Not for reading (because he still uses encyclopedias and dictionaries), but, yes, for obtaining assorted materials cheaply and having them sent to his front door. Through the mail. Soon, they say, everything will arrive aboard an Amazonic Drone, one of those aircrafts that today are used to spy and kill and certify the nonexistent existence of weapons of mass destruction. So, flying, biographies, memoirs, volumes of letters. Everything about Sara and Gerald and FSF and Zelda and catalogues of posthumous exposés and articles in glossy magazines and, little by little, he even allows himself, with a shame he doesn't understand because nobody sees it (though, of course, they see everything), an incursion into the virtual skies of Google Earth and in and out of Wikipedia's entrances and exits. He discovers, in addition, that there's a very good *Tender Is the Night* miniseries, adapted by Dennis Potter, but never released on DVD. And that copies of *Tender Is the Night* appear, randomly, in scenes of the films: Michelangelo Antonioni's *L'Avventura*, Wim Wenders's *Alice in den Städten*, and Martin Scorsese's *Who's That Knocking at My Door*. And he asks himself if any of that will be useful to him somewhere and for something, for his idea; and he answers that he doesn't know, but that everything already seems to indicate that—if it turns into a book—that book is going to be very long and very wide and very tall.

Trouble . . .

† It begins flying over the exact site where Boston native and member of a well-to-do family Gerald Clery Murphy (1888-1964) builds a beach with his own hands, rescuing it from the action of the brush and algae and waves. Gerald Murphy creates a beach for love. A love that lasts sixty years, until the day of his death, for the daughter of a wealthy Ohio clan and now his wife— Sara Sherman Wiburg (1883-1975). A beach near Antibes, Côte d'Azur. A brief line of sand and rocks, adjacent to their house, Villa America. A beach Gerald Murphy will christen La Garoupe. Villa America—along with Château de Clavary in Auribeau, where Russell Greeley sketches; Château de Mai en Mougins, where Francis Picabia paints; and Villa Noailles in Hyère, where Count and Countess Noailles throw their masquerade balls—is one of the four cardinal points in the Riviera, where life is lived for the love of art. But Villa America is the most luxurious of all. And everyone is welcome. And everyone answers the call of those rich Americans—"masters of the art of living," as someone passing through describes them—who premiere the art of sun bathing at La Garoupe. Of lying out under the ultraviolet rays until they look gold and become the golden couple everyone celebrates because the golden couple celebrates everyone. The façade of Villa America is like the cover of *Sgt. Pepper's Lonely Hearts Club Band*, except the Murphys aren't The Beatles. The Murphys are more like those great "character" actors. First rate B-roll actors who, having been abducted by Hollywood, had no doubt shared a table in Rick's Café Americain, in *Casablanca*, with Peter Lorre or Sidney Greenstreet. Sara and Gerald Murphy are the light that draws the enlightened. Pablo Picasso (1881-1973), Dorothy Parker (1893-1967), Robert Benchley (1889-1945), Fernand Léger (1881-1955), John Dos Passos (1896-1970), Serguéi Diáguilev (1872-1929), Erik Satie (1866-1925), Archibald MacLeish (1892-1982), Jean Cocteau (1889-1963), John O'Hara (1905-1970), Cole Porter (1891-1964), Gertrude Stein (1874-1946), Alice B. Toklas (1877-1977), Igor Stravinsky (1882-1971), Ernest Hemingway (1899-1961) and ladies: the imminent ex and the immediate next, Tristan Tzara (1896-1963), Francis Scott Fitzgerald (1896-1940), Zelda Fitzgerald (1900-1948) and, much later on, his father (1936-1978) and mother (1939-1978), and now he has set out to write a novel about Sara and Gerald Murphy and everything and everyone that surrounded them, his parents and himself included.

† "Every day was different," Gerald Murphy in a letter to Calvin Tomkins.

† Sara and Gerald Murphy flee the United States because they feel that everything there is preordained, as if already written and sealed by a protocol that doesn't allow for improvisation or innovation. The American bourgeoisie, the nouveau riche of the new empire, dream of being European aristocrats but can't know or imagine that Europe no longer is what it once was. Now, Europe is what it is and Europe is what it will be. In Europe, in the Old World, everything seems new to the Murphys.

† And Europe, yes. And *Tender Is the Night* like the natural and enhanced evolution of those Henry James novels in which Americans traveled around the Old World to expose themselves to the new and initiating radiation of going more or less mad or less or more sane. Transfigured, in any case. Tourism as a way of illuminating kilometers or miles of darkness. And *Tender Is the Night*—which also could've been called *The Portrait of Another Lady* or *The Ambassador*—makes the treacherous fidelity between James and Fitzgerald even more apparent. James believed that we are defined by the objects and places that surround us, Fitzgerald goes even further and tells us that we end up becoming the objects and places that surround us: shirts, cars, hotels, bottles, toys, starry skies, and beaches where we can shine like the stars. (Relevant detail and parenthetical that, maybe, explains something of his not-model model-parents' fascination with Fitzgerald: the author of *Tender Is the Night* starts out as a copy editor in the New York ad agency Baron Collier. His biggest hit was the slogan for a Laundromat in Iowa, Muscatine Steam Laundry: "We Keep You Clean in Muscatine." Before long, Fitzgerald convinces himself that it's not for him, starts drinking more, goes back to his parents' house, and concentrates on his first novel. And he turns himself into the best product of himself, strengthened by the addition of a certain Zelda Sayre. And together they live *Tender Is the Night*. They write it later. But it doesn't end up being all that easy to sell.)

† One night Gerald and Sara Murphy are going to have a dinner party, but they can't find flowers to decorate the tables. The florists are closed or fresh

flowers weren't delivered. Or something like that. So the two of them go down the stairs and run to the nearest toy store and fill a large wicker basket with windup tin toys. During dessert, Picasso gets really excited about a fire truck. Fitzgerald, on the other hand, picks out a little man carrying a suitcase, and he winds it up and watches it walk from here to there, across the tablecloth, and, sadly, he says: "It reminds me of me."

† Detail to be inserted in some part of the book: Sara and Gerald Murphy are like fugitives from an Edith Wharton novel who end being taken prisoner by a Francis Scott Fitzgerald novel.

† And he's already begun to receive Murphian materials. And, as the rest of what he has ordered from virtual and invisible libraries arrives, he rereads *Tender Is the Night*: his parents' favorite novel, not because they especially admired Fitzgerald, but because they'd met his direct inspiration, and meeting them had inspired his parents to try to be like them, and they liked reading a novel whose characters they'd met. And he photocopies essays about *Tender Is the Night* and assembles a bulging dossier. And he transcribes paragraphs from the novel's prologues. And even underlines a companion that investigates the slow and suffering history of its writing, across various years and countries and hospitals.

But he doesn't want to delve into that night just yet and, in the beginning, he focuses on the day of the Murphys. On the nonfiction of the fiction.

Preliminary notes from overhead that he'll delve into as he descends: everyone knows that Fitzgerald's irreal but true tragic heroes Nicole and Dick Diver were inspired by the real couple Gerald and Sara Murphy. Two wealthy expats in the south of France who invited Fitzgerald and Hemingway and Picasso and so many others to come have a good time all on their dime. The handsome Gerald (an almost casual painter to whom many attribute anticipating the mechanics and hypotheses of Pop Art, and whom others credit with setting the trend of the striped sailor sweater long before Picasso adopted it as the uniform that's now commercialized in every Picasso Museum of the world) and the beautiful Sara and their lovely children represented, to Fitzgerald, perfect examples when it came to writing about the "differences" of the rich. So, it was to them that he dedicated *Tender Is the Night*, in which the Divers start off resembling the Murphys, but inevitably end up identical to the Fitzgeralds. In other words: they end badly.

† The Murphys—for whom things were going so well—ended up living the tragedy of the deaths of two children and returning to the United States to take over family businesses. And to get very bored. The party was over, Sara never forgave Fitzgerald for what he did to them in his writing, and the self-mythologizing Hemingway wrote to his far superior but also far more insecure colleague, in one of the many absurd letters/reproaches he used to try to destroy him: "A writer cannot start with real people and change them into other people."

But it was Gerald who, reading the novel years later, sent to Fitzgerald (whom he considered "my social conscience") his blessing and gratitude with: "Only the invented part of our life—the unreal part—has had any scheme, any beauty."

† And if there's something that really interests him as material for a novel in the real story of the Murphys, it's how they were faithful and truthful and very objective witnesses of their time, who lived surrounded by a pack of rabid mythomaniacs and inventors of their own legends. People who never stopped plotting and inventing their own lives until the final period. His own parents included, he thinks.

† It's so easy for him to superimpose (should he maybe apologize to the young woman whose disorientation regarding the photo of the Murphys reoriented him?) the many photos of the compulsively photogenic Sara and Gerald over the photos of his parents. The ones and the others, beautiful animals.

† The photos of the Murphys, naked (nudists whenever possible) on decks of sailboats with names like *Melancholic Tunes* (Gerald hanging upside down from the masts), dancing on a beach in East Hampton (one of his favorite photos), or doing callisthenic exercises or yoga (western pioneers of that, too) alongside their blonde and perfect but sickly children in La Garoupe. The Murphys dressed up as automobiles or wandering bohemians or as Apaches or Chinese or hunters on safari or as mariachis or as gondoliers. Or dressed

formally for grand society balls, covered with wrinkles in Swan Cove, near the end, after too many obligatory and automatic and reflexive parties where really there was nothing to celebrate anymore. If photos steal your soul, then photos taken of you at parties steal your soul and, with the accumulation of clicks and flashes, also give you a beating and leave you with a broken body—blurry, out of focus, soulless.

† The photos of his parents: golden models in the golden age of advertising in his country (the novel will explore various anecdotes and personas and characters of that world: advertising directors, jingle composers, slogan writers who dream of writing the Great Novel of their time). And one day his parents have a great idea. To sell an international whiskey company the never-ending campaign of a young and beautiful couple, adventurers traversing the world aboard a sailboat, docking in all the most glamorous ports, and (minimal costs) starring in and filming and assembling the footage themselves, which they'd mail in to be shown on TV screens and in movie theaters. Their proposal is accepted and not only does the adventure win a bunch of national and international awards, but it (being propagandized without dialogue, just background music, and transmitted all over the world) turns his parents into two, if not famous, then at least well-known, personas. Not long ago he discovered an allusion to them in an episode of *Mad Men*. And photos of his parents in Andy Warhol's The Factory. Or with Stanley Kubrick. Or in the door to the Abbey Road studios (he didn't believe them when they told him about it with such a wealth of detail, because his parents were the kind of liars who made themselves believe their own lies down to the smallest detail before recounting them perfectly, as if they were inerasable memories) during the recording of "A Day in the Life" by The Beatles. But years later, when the documentary *The Beatles Anthology* included scenes from that psychedelic party, there they were, his parents, spinning, "I read the news today, oh, boy . . ." And every so often their ghosts appear again on a plasma screen: in those programs dedicated to compiling anthologies of ad spots or in some documentary featuring people who are no longer with us, people who disappeared, as if the worst magician in history asked you to close your eyes and not to open them until he said so. And years go by. Eyes closed. Waiting.

And he closes his eyes whenever the two of them, his parents, appear here or there.

† And, of course, the photo where all four of them appear together, in La Garoupe of 1961 that's no longer La Garoupe of before and, much less, La Garoupe of today, overrun with beach umbrellas. The original Golden Couple (soon to return to being laterally and secondarily famous, to the resigned disappointment of Gerald and Sara, courtesy of a long profile that Calvin Tompkins, with the title "Living Well Is the Best Revenge," will devote to them the next year in the pages of *The New Yorker*), and Swinging Sixties version Golden Couple (soon to cease existing). The four of them. Two and two. With their eyes wide open and making their own magic. Smiling. Never imagining that they're going to disappear or be cut in two never to be reunited.

† And what's the point of all of this? Bringing the Murphys and his parents together—who had already been together—in a book? Think of a book—a kind of chronicle-novel-treatise—that's a kind of manual not *for* parents but *of* parents. A bestiary that might be useful to children and help them, quickly and efficiently, locate the model they've ended up with. And then they can take whatever steps they deem appropriate.

The Murphys and his parents, also, as clear models of parents as bon vivant figures. Parents as personas. Parents who will end up being cleaned up and edited by their children after being pre-washed in public not like rags, but like dirty designer clothes.

Parents like the melody that children can't stop hearing until they become parents themselves and learn to play the instrument that's been played to them. Parents who start out as gods and end up as myths and who, between the one extreme and the other, assume human forms that tend to be catastrophic for their children. Or something like that. And the story continues. And he thinks about this—he, who doesn't have children, but who did have someone he lost—and feels something like a vertigo of runaway music impossible to catch and tie up again.

He was never any good at tying knots.

His thing was always untying them.

Whistling.

† Biji musical interlude: note, for his possible biographers (ha, ha, ha?) indicating that he's writing this part, the part about his parents and the Murphys,
while listening, over and over again, to one of his favorite songs: "Big Sky"
by The Kinks, included on the album *The Kinks Are the Village Green Preservation Society* (1968). An album that was released, with the lack of oppor-
tunistic sense that always characterized the band, the same day that The
Beatles released *The Beatles*. It doesn't matter: it's a great song composed by
Ray Davies at sunrise or sunset (Davies offered both versions and timetables
in different interviews) on the balcony of his room at the Carlton Hotel in
Cannes, not far from La Garoupe. A song dedicated to a kind of indifferent
and immense divine entity far above all the miseries of this world. A song
that, Davies pointed out, he would've liked to have Burt Lancaster sing, to
have recorded it with Burt Lancaster's voice. At the time, Davies—the most
Fitzgeraldian of rockers, success at dawn and failure at midday and rough
is the night—is disillusioned and on the brink and the rails of a psychotic
break with no help or need for drugs. His is pure and real. A perfect malaise.
A disillusionment more Victorian than psychedelic. Davies doesn't know
whether to go on or to stop or to jump. He doesn't know whether "Big Sky"
(2 minutes, 53 seconds, an eternity worthy of being heard or contained by a
museum) is a song by The Kinks or a song that's his alone, for his first solo
album. He doesn't know if he wants to go or to stay or to throw himself off
that hotel balcony. He doesn't know if it is, in the end, a song about God
or, merely, as he'll tell a journalist later on, about a "big sky." He doesn't
know whether Big Sky is an all-powerful entity or the messianic representation of his immense impotence. One thing is certain: "Big Sky" is a great
song that seems to encompass everything and to be above everyone, looking
down at them, without compromise and without compromising itself while it
observes, ominous and indolent, its creation. And, of course, The Kinks were
never great musicians; but on "Big Sky" they sound better than ever, they
sound like a humble chamber music version, without George Martin to help
them, of the orchestral crescendo of "A Day in the Life." A long time after
Ray Davies looked up and composed "Big Sky," he had arranged to get Ray

Davies to invite him to come hear him sing it. He thought that what Ray Davies—without doubt: after submitting him to a kind of telephonic test to prove that he was a true fan and not, merely, a devoted trend follower—did for him was the gesture of a great imperial gentleman. British indifference and all of that, and would he have acted the same way with one of his fans, with someone, on the other end of the line, reciting monologues syllable for syllable from his books? Un-doubt-ed-ly—and—ab-so-lu-tely—not. Out of laziness and bad manners and because fans of writers were much more dangerous and annoying than fans of songwriters, with the exception of Mark David Chapman, of course.

For the section of the novel that'll focus less on the Murphys and more on Francis Scott Fitzgerald, he decides that the best soundtrack would be the short but oh so sincere song "Good Old Desk," written by another damned alcoholic, the excellent songwriter par excellence Harry Nilsson. And, yes, another song about the art of creation as a humble and domestic occupation barely concealing (the initials of the song's title forming the word "GOD") a messianic presence, ready to condemn or forgive, to save or abandon, depending on what side of the bed the author woke up on that day.

And, yes, to one side but up front: Bob Dylan—who, like Fitzgerald, is a son of Minnesota (and who already accused someone of putting on airs for having read all F. Scott Fitzgerald's books in his "Ballad of a Thin Man") so many years later—on "Summer Days." In that song, Bob Dylan, taking and almost bellowing the words of the penultimate magnate Jay Gatsby, as if he were singing atop a barroom table, assuring everyone everywhere that of course the past can be repeated. Because the past is so much closer than you think.

† Gerald and Sara Murphy singing negro spirituals to their guests, glasses of champagne in hand, under the blue light of the stars.

† Gerald Murphy, who fancies himself a painter, is dazzled by what he sees one morning in a window at the art gallery of Paul Rosenberg, in Paris. A painting by Picasso (who'll end up painting Sara Murphy three times and sculpting her once) is for him the gateway and the control tower for the sensation of being launched "into an entirely new orbit . . . If that's painting,

that's the kind of painting I would like to do." After that, his own work, always in the shadow of that brilliance. Broken canvases, assorted misadventures, irregular discipline, never complete devotion: mention and describe set designs for the ballet *Les Noces* ("The Murphys were among the first Americans I ever met, and they gave me the most agreeable impression of the United States," Stravinsky said) and Cole Porter's musical satire *Within the Quota* (and, ah, he's always really liked Cole Porter's exceedingly clever songs composed of lists, so enumerative, so numbered, so names-dates-places). And, above all, there are only seven of Gerald Murphy's (then considered only a "Sunday painter" but, with perspective, a great modernist tagged in his moment by Leger as "the *only* American painter in Paris") colossal paintings that survive, where pupils stare and watches are disassembled, electric razors are readied, newspapers' front pages are blown up, libraries are organized, and the banner of the happily-expatriated and immensely-small kingdom of Villa America is raised. A cubist decomposition of the rectangular American flag. Half gold star, flanked by five smaller white stars with white and red stripes emanating from them.

Eyes forward, head raised, hand over heart, little homeland, and, perhaps, great hell with long-suffering internal procession. But all of it so fine, so polite, so smiling, the perfect host—*mi casa es su casa.*

† Gerald Murphy stops painting after eight paintings (the best of which is lost and all that's left are photographs: the transatlantic and monumental chimneys of *Boatdeck*) and seven years in front of canvases. He's convinced that he's "not going to be first rate" and "the world is filled with second-rate painting" (for the record: Gerald Murphy is an infinitely better painter than Zelda Fitzgerald, who will focus on self-portraits in which she appears as if emerging from the depths of the sea, like a siren driven mad by her own song). Critics and specialists and psychoanalysts might say, on the other hand, that Gerald Murphy cleans his paintbrushes never to dirty them again because he discovers that his canvases do nothing but betray a "defect," something he doesn't want anyone to see, and certainly not something he wants to frame and sign and exhibit.

In *Tender Is the Night*, on more than one occasion, the possibility is alluded to that Dick Diver could've been the greatest psychologist of all time (in his notes for the novel Fitzgerald calls him a "superman in possibilities"), if you ignore a decisive failure in his structure: paralysis when it comes to judging himself and daring to fully look at himself; which leads him, time and again, to act in a way contradictory to everyone else and contrary to his own well-being. So, Diver is like a ghost of himself: a living dead man, the most alive of all the dead men, with the capacity to see in others what he doesn't want to see in himself and so he lives with his eyes shut.

† Should he delve or not into the hypothesis that Gerald Murphy was a closeted homosexual? Should he research the handsome young Chilean Eduardo Velásquez (expelled from England due to an inopportune episode with a member of the royal family), whom Fitzgerald introduces to Gerald Murphy? Velásquez gives Gerald Murphy a crucifix in a mildly uncomfortable scene. And Fitzgerald will rewrite the whole episode in *Tender Is the Night*, starring a certain "Queen of Chili," the son of a South American tycoon, submitted to violent psychological treatments in an attempt to change his "nature." Or focus on Richard Cowan's full-time gardener? Or look for information about the Canadian historian Alan Jarvis? Sara doesn't seem to have any problem with all of Gerald's close friendships (except every so often, when she shares her misgivings with the wrong people, like Hemingway, who subsequently starts firing off his masculine advice) provided there are "no feathers," she says.

† "Their marriage was unshakable."—John Dos Passos.

† During a dinner with the Murphys, in Antibes, Fitzgerald tries to embarrass a waiter by asking him in front of everyone if he's homosexual. "Yes," the man responds breezily, as he continues to clear the plates. And Fitzgerald blushes and stands up and, heading for the bathroom, falls headlong down a flight of stairs that's nothing but the continuation of the stairs he fell down in the Paris metro and, previously, the stairs he fell down in a clandestine Manhattan bar.

† Anyway, at the time, everyone seems to be closeted homosexuals (Fitzgerald, Hemingway) and everyone *also* seems to be alcoholics, right? Including Sara's annoying and problematic sister: Hoytie, pathological snob and

emptier of bottles of spirits, once an ambulance driver on World War One battlefields and now a feared and insatiable *lipstick lesbian*. The typical flapper who starts dancing at the least excuse. Leave her out too. There isn't much space, something tells him he doesn't have much time.

† Brief interruption, personal biji, black noise: he's fifty years old and he's known various writers who died when they were fifty and has read many who died or killed themselves around the same age. Maybe writers die faster because they live more lives, all at the same time. Their own lives, those of their characters, those of the characters in other writers' books, their public lives as "writers" in front of their readers. Fifty years old—already dead and looking at the menu, choosing what to order and whom to order it from—as the age of no return. Because the forties might be duplicable; but making it to one hundred won't be easy. So the fifties and 50 as the roundest of numbers. A roundness ringed with barbed wire that doesn't let you out or in. The temporal equivalent of an airplane flying into a building. Chronological terrorism. A pure after that you can only access as a dead passenger or a surviving office worker. Times when the horizon starts bearing down on us even though we choose to stand still. Times when the past takes on new meaning. A logic, a plot, and a narrative, that it never had before, until now, until right *ahorititita*. After about a half-century on Earth, you're always up in the air or on the top floor of a building and—the date doesn't matter—it's always September 11th of 2001. Later, years later, it goes away. A little. Or you get used to it. Then, resigned and always knocking on wood, you live an eternal September 12th or 13th or 14th or 15th of 2001; always on guard and waiting for the next inevitable catastrophe (especially if you are alone and you live alone; because then, having nobody nearby, all the bad things can happen to you), aware that, from now on, everything matters. You've breathed in the virus of the *suspension of disbelief* and anything is possible and all bad news will be horrible but, at the same time, so good for being communicated and dpread around by second and third parties who aren't yet fifty years old, but here they come, there they go.

† "People always want to be their best selves and behave as well as possible when with the Murphys," John Dos Passos reflected.

And here come the Fitzgeralds.

The exception that confirms the rule.

But Scott and Zelda are a colossal exception, one of those sudden bicephalous summer storms, a biblical plague.

Scott and Zelda have heard the myth of Villa America and want to live it first-hand, from inside, and first they stay in Hôtel du Cap, and later rent a villa in Juan-les-Pins, and soon turn into a nuisance for locals and visitors. A none too attractive yet fascinating local attraction. Gerald and Sara Murphy become—they have no choice: they intervene out of proximity plus good manners and, so, extinguish the blazes of the most fiery of couples— their guardians and protectors for a good part of 1925 and 1926. It's no simple task. Zelda has an affair with a young pilot from a nearby airbase and Fitzgerald gets drunk and gets down on all fours and howls at the moon that shines down on the Murphys, as if to say, "I told you so . . ." Zelda, to shake off of a hangover, jumps from the cliffs, explaining to her hosts, on the verge of nervous breakdown, that she doesn't believe "in conservation" and, soaked, dances as if possessed to Jelly Roll Morton and Louis Armstrong records. Alcohol and pills to sleep and Ernest Hemingway taking note of everything, wearing that oh so Hemingwayesque smile, while the next morning Fitzgerald is also taking notes, though not for a cruel and vengeful and psychotic memoir (Hemingway forces Gerald Murphy to test his manliness by jumping into a ring with a bull and, of course, seems unimpressed with his performance), but for what he thinks will be a great novel, a novel better than the unsurpassable *The Great Gatsby*. His favorite of his own novels, *Tender Is the Night*, which he'd publish in 1934, and by 1940, the year he died, would already be out of print and lost.

† Sara admired *The Great Gatsby*. To Gerald Murphy it was nothing special. "The one we took seriously was Ernest, not Scott. I suppose it was because Ernest's work seemed contemporary and new, and Scott's didn't," he commented.

† "The Murphys liked Zelda better than me."—Francis Scott Fitzgerald.

† "I don't think we could have taken Scott alone."—Sara and Gerald Murphy.

† Gerald and Sara always seemed to marvel a bit—without ever fully understanding it—at their long relationship with the Fitzgeralds, at how much they loved each other and that they loved them despite feeling that they were their opposites—distant, self-destructive. "We four communicate more by our presence than by any other means," Gerald Murphy diagnosed it to Fitzgerald.

† "What we loved about Scott was the region in him where his gift came from, and which was never completely buried. There were moments when he wasn't harassed or trying to shock you, moments when he'd be gentle and quiet, and he'd tell you his real thoughts about people, and lose himself in defining what he felt about them . . . Those were the moments when you saw the beauty of his mind and nature, and they compelled you to love and value him," Gerald Murphy told Calvin Tomkins.

† At a dinner with the Murphys ("My only rich friends," Fitzgerald would write, who rode the derailed train of a life of greater luxury than that of the Murphys), the writer begins to mock the caviar and champagne that's served him and stares unremittingly at an older man accompanied by a younger girl at the next table. He keeps watching them, with his eyes half-closed, as if taking aim and focusing before firing a rifle or taking a photograph. The Murphys deem it an unacceptable form of discourtesy and ask that, please, he stop; but (it often happens with people who aren't writers, with people who "are people exactly") they can't know or even imagine that Fitzgerald, lidless, with eyes wide open now, is watching, reading in the soft twilight air, the beginning of a novel that'll be called *Tender Is the Night*.

† Fitzgerald never stops telling the Murphys about the great novel he's writing. But the Murphys never see him write.

† "One writes of scars healed, a loose parallel to the pathology of the skin, but there is no such thing in the life of an individual. There are open wounds, shrunk sometimes to the size of a pin-prick but wounds still. The marks of suffering are more comparable to the loss of a finger, or of the sight of an eye. We may not miss them, either, for one minute in a year, but if we should

there is nothing to be done about it."—Francis Scott Fitzgerald, *Tender Is the Night*, Book 2, chapter XI.

† "Absence . . . it's no solution," says Dick Diver in *Tender Is the Night*. More than the theme, he understands suddenly, absence is the content in *Tender Is the Night*. The Great Absence. Or the small successive absences that The Great Absence comprises (the characters that don't stop leaving, departing) and that end up piling up, in the novel, like fallen petals, like dead stars, in the way of everything that's put off until, suddenly, you discover that it's already *too* late. The Great Absence is, also, the theme of one of his favorite albums: *Wish You Were Here* by Pink Floyd, whose non-chronological, three-block structure is similar to *Tender Is the Night*. (Note: locate and speak with that great childhood friend of his with whom he listened to *Wish You Were Here* for the first time, so many times, when there was still time and space.)

† "Well, you never knew exactly how much space you occupied in people's lives."—Francis Scott Fitzgerald, *Tender Is the Night*.

† Time passes even for the Murphys. "Living well is no longer the best revenge." And the thirties bring The Depression and the end of the long vacations and the Murphys put Villa America up for rent. Time to go home and take over the family business. And two of their children—Baoth and Patrick—die in 1935 and 1937. Fitzgerald—who has been expatriated by the expatriates after he "betrayed" them when he published *Tender Is the Night*—sends his condolences to Gerald, evoking Henry James: "The golden bowl is broken indeed but it *was* golden; nothing can ever take those boys away from you now."

† "The best way to educate children is to keep them confused," Gerald Murphy recommended. And, somewhere, in the air or underwater, his own confused and confusing parents nod, indicating their complete agreement.

† Painful question: another little boy taken from my side, Penelope, how to deal with this? Deal with it? Show me a tragedy and . . . what do I write then? DANGER, WARNING: the chair that approaches the desk that

might also be the precipice. The desk's sharp edges. Yes: the true hero of this story is outside this story. And reality, like in *Tender Is the Night*, complicates everything. Reality, which can cause a fiction to fail just for the fun of it. Reality, which raises its head, like a serpent, to hiss, hypnotically, a "Really . . ."

† Gerald Murphy tells Calvin Tomkins that Fitzgerald spent hours questioning him and Sara. "Studying them." Gerald Murphy never considered himself the model for anything; but he does remember Fitzgerald's stare, his lips pressed together, his whole face tense like a spring about to be sprung, as if he wanted to catch him in a lie. To irritate and discourage him, Sara Murphy answered Fitzgerald with whatever random thing, giving him absurd answers, until one night she could no longer take it and in the middle of a party and in front of everyone she said: "Scott, you think if you ask enough questions you'll get to know what people are like, but you won't." Fitzgerald was livid and, pointing at her with a trembling index finger, said that nobody had ever dared to say something like that to him and challenged her to repeat it. And Sara Murphy repeated it, word for word, in front of everybody, without making a single mistake. And, without a doubt, writers aren't people exactly, Fitzgerald memorized it on the spot so he could write it down later in the margin of some page.

† And in a letter (find date), Sara Murphy was even more explicit: "You ought to know at your age that you can't have Theories about your friends, Scott." And her sign off: "Your infuriating but devoted and rather wise old friend, Sara."

† "The book was inspired by Sara and you, and the way I feel about you both and the way you live, and the last part of it is Zelda and me because you and Sara are the same people as Zelda and me."—Francis Scott Fitzgerald in a letter to Gerald Murphy (find date).

† "When I like a man, I want to be like him."—Francis Scott Fitzgerald (find where he wrote this); and, suddenly, he realizes that the surname Fitzgerald includes a "Gerald" among its letters.

† "At certain moments, one man appropriates to himself the total significance of a time and place."—Francis Scott Fitzgerald's notes for *The Last Tycoon*.

† "I didn't like the book when I read it, and I liked it even less on rereading. I reject categorically any resemblance to us or to anyone we knew at any time," Sara Murphy wrote to Calvin Tomkins, with the same rage that would be roused decades later, in other previously languid society women, by Truman Capote with his *Answered Prayers*. Remember: Truman Capote, between hurt and surprised, wondering how none of his "swans" had realized that it wasn't a buffoon they had among them, but a writer. And that that writer was studying.

† On the other hand, Gerald Murphy was impressed by the way Fitzgerald used everything he saw with great fidelity to obtain something that hadn't happened, but that did perhaps happen when nobody but Fitzgerald was paying attention.

† Fitzgerald in a letter to Gerald Murphy, 1938: "I don't care much where I am any more nor expect very much from places. You will understand this. To me, it is a new phase, or rather, a development of something that began long ago in my writing—to try and dig up the relevant, the essential, and especially the dramatic and glamorous from whatever life is around. I used to think that my sensory impression of the world came from outside. I used to actually believe that it was as objective as blue skies or a piece of music. Now I know it was within, and emphatically cherish what little is left."

And he reads that letter in a collected book of Fitzgerald's letters and he can't help but think about how at some point they wrote like that, with paper and ink, and put all of it in an envelope and sealed it and let it drop through the slot of a mailbox. And all of it took several days to arrive to the hands of the recipient. And the velocity of things was different. And they thought more about things before putting them in writing. And Gerald Murphy received that letter but never showed it to Sara Murphy. Sara didn't understand those things, Gerald thought. Sara was so different from him.

† "Sara is in love with life and skeptical of people. I'm the other way. I believe

you have to do things to life to make it tolerable. I've always liked the old Spanish proverb: 'Living well is the best revenge.'"—Gerald Murphy in conversation with Fitzgerald (when?).

† "Dearest Sara, I love you very much, Madam, not like in Scott's Christmas tree ornament novels but the way it is on boats where Scott would be seasick."—Letter from Ernest Hemingway to Sara Murphy. And yet, behind their backs and treacherously, in a fragment not included in the first version of his very selective memoirs, *A Moveable Feast* (1964), Hemingway would remember the Murphys, as always, only as suited his character: "I had hated these rich because they had backed me and encouraged me when I was wrong . . . the understanding rich who have no bad qualities and who give each day the quality of a festival and who, when they have passed and taken the nourishment they needed, leave everything deader than the roots of any grass Attila's horses' hooves have ever scoured . . . It was not their fault. It was only their fault for coming into people's lives . . . They collected people then as some collect pictures and others breed horses . . . They were bad luck for people but they were worse luck to themselves and they lived to have all of their bad luck finally to the very worst end that all bad lucks could go."

The fact that the preceding paragraph doesn't appear in the final version of *A Moveable Feast* doesn't, however, free the Murphys from more than one standard barb and from humiliation. Absurd accusations like that they made him read aloud the manuscript of his book *The Torrents of Spring* (1926), where Hemingway viciously parodies his mentor Sherwood Anderson. Request and offense—reading aloud to enliven the soirée—that, for Hemingway, "is about as low as a writer can get and much more dangerous for him as a writer than glacier skiing unroped before the winter snowfall has set over the crevices."

Aha.

Having read *A Moveable Feast*, Gerald Murphy ("I never could stand Gerald," Hemingway noted in a letter to McLeish) commented with elegance: "*Contre-coeur* feelings about Ernest's book. What a strange kind of bitterness—or rather accusitoriness. Aren't the rich (whoever they are) rather poor prey? What shocking ethics! How well written, of course." (Find date and propose to publisher a voluminous volume that collects all the disagreeable things that at some point Hemingway said or wrote about his acquaintances, writers in general, and Fitzgerald in particular.)

It'd be a great book, a very big book.

† "I'm sorry, but Scott's book is not good."—Letter from Ernest Hemingway to Gerald Murphy (find date).

† "I liked it and I didn't like it."—Letter from Ernest Hemingway to Francis Scott Fitzgerald (May 10th, 1934).

† And later, subsequently, Ernest Hemingway proceeds to destroy *Tender Is the Night* and its author, accusing him of having vampirized the Murphys to turn them into the Fitzgeralds and, finally, firing off point-blank lines like "In the first place I've always claimed that you can't think" and "Forget your personal tragedy" and "Jesus it's marvelous to tell other people how to write, live, die, etc."

† "Dear Ernest: Please lay off me in print. If I choose to write de profundis sometimes it doesn't mean I want friends praying aloud over my corpse. No doubt you meant it kindly but it cost me a night's sleep. And when you incorporate it (the story) in a book would you mind cutting my name? It's a fine story—one of your best—even though the 'Poor Scott Fitzgerald etcetera' rather spoiled it for me. Ever Your Friend, Scott. PS: Riches have never fascinated me, unless combined with the greatest charm or distinction."—Letter from July 16th, 1936, from Francis Scott Fitzgerald to Ernest Hemingway after reading the story "The Snows of Kilimanjaro," in which he is offhandedly and humiliatingly mentioned. And in the margin of a Thomas Wolfe book: "Ernest was always ready to lend a helping hand to the one on the rung above him."

† "A strange thing is that in retrospect his *Tender Is the Night* gets better and better. [. . .] It's amazing how *excellent* much of it is. . . . (I always had a very stupid little boy feeling of superiority about Scott—like a tough little boy sneering at a delicate but talented little boy.) But reading that novel much

of it was so good it was frightening."—Letter from Ernest Hemingway to Maxwell Perkins, his and Francis Scott Fitzgerald's editor (date?).

† The story told by the reading of *Tender Is the Night* is, also, the story of the writing of *Tender Is the Night*.

† There are almost as many biographies of Francis Scott Fitzgerald as there are of The Beatles. Point this out in the book, he says to himself. And to clarify the why: the stories of The Beatles and of Francis Scott Fitzgerald are paradigmatic lives and works with the quality and qualities of certain myths. Rises and falls, friendships and enmities. And Great Art. And so— even though he knows their plotlines by heart—he always buys them and reads them again, like a child rereading fairy tales and witch tales to infinity, whenever he runs across one that he missed or when a new one comes out.

The excess of *Fitzgeraldiana* isn't random and it has an added incentive, he thinks: the epic of Fitzgerald's fall—the formidable success of achieving, in his words, "the authority of failure" faced with "the authority of success" of Ernest Hemingway—functions like a great moral tale. For any writer, Francis Scott Fitzgerald occupies the altar of one who died (of his own initiative and bad choices) as a result of having screwed up everything a writer can screw up outside of his or her books. So, Francis Scott Fitzgerald as an example, like the best of the bad examples. Like a manual of Destructions and Self-destructions to study while—in tandem—he rereads Fitzgerald's fiction over and over again, feeding tirelessly off his nonfiction until he reaches the ground zero and the absolute point of communion between the two: the autobiographical essays subsequently collected by Edmund Wilson in *The Crack-Up* (1945), after their initial publication in 1935 in *Esquire*, which, of course, gets Hemingway fired up, who doesn't delay in sending Fitzgerald another of his kindly letters, reproaching his debility and offering to contract an assassin to have him killed in Cuba so that Scottie and Zelda can cash in his life insurance. In the same vein, Hemingway suggests that parts of Fitzgerald be spread around throughout the important places in his life: his liver to the Princeton Museum, his heart to the Plaza Hotel, and his balls, if they can be found, thrown into the sea off Eden Roc and, being small, they'll barely make a splash. Very funny. Desperate, Fitzgerald undertakes the most pathetic and impotent of revenges: writing a series of awful and alcoholized stories where Hemingway appears transformed into the Gothic and medieval, tormented and tormenting "Philippe, Count of Darkness."

Over the years, he's gathered a great deal of Fitzgeraldian material: the volumes of sad letters to Zelda, the melancholic letters to Scottie, the indecisive letters to his editor Maxwell Perkins, the almost pleading letters to his Agent Harold Ober, three collections of letters to everyone else, various of his last wife's memoirs and a very hard to find memoir by his secretary in Hollywood, essays about his dangerous relationship with Ernest Hemingway, alternate versions of *The Great Gatsby* and *The Love of the Last Tycoon*, collections of his early writings, and random pieces and interviews.

In one of them, one of the last ones, a certain Michel Mok converses with him in his home. In the moment of saying goodbye, the reporter asks him what has become of the jazz generation, the generation to which he gave voice and brilliance and the most musical and romantic prose.

Francis Scott Fitzgerald answers with an irritated question: "Why should I bother myself about them? Haven't I enough worries of my own? You know as well as I do what has happened to them. Some became brokers and threw themselves out of windows. Others became bankers and shot themselves. Still others became newspaper reporters. And a few became successful authors." Then, Mok tells, Francis Scott Fitzgerald pauses and concludes and moans and smiles with the saddest of smiles: "Successful authors . . . ! Oh, my God, successful authors!"

The final line of the piece is: "Francis Scott Fitzgerald stumbled over to the highboy and poured himself another drink."

† And in all those books—since he already knows how everything begins and transpires and ends—the first thing he looks for, opening them to the end, to the onomastic index, is whether there's some new information about the writing and circumstances of *Tender Is the Night*, his parents' favorite book, and his favorite book by Francis Scott Fitzgerald.

† The book that occurs to Fitzgerald just three weeks after the publication of *The Great Gatsby*, in 1925. The book that he'll work on interruptedly and uninterruptedly for several and too many years to come.

† In a letter to his editor Maxwell Perkins, dated May of that year, Fitzgerald informs him: "The happiest thought I have is of my new novel—it is something really NEW in form, idea, and structure: the model for the age that Joyce and Stein are searching for, that Conrad didn't find." And in more letters to his editor and his daughter and almost anyone he crossed paths with, as the years passed: "My novel is something of a mystery, I hope," "," "I fear I have written another novel for writers," "Excuse me if this letter has a dogmatic ring. I have lived so long within the circle of this book and with these characters that often it seems to me that the real world does not exist but that only these characters exist, and, however pretentious that remark sounds (and my God, that I should have to be pretentious about my work), it is an absolute fact—so much so that their glees and woes are just exactly as important to me as what happens in life," "No exclamatory 'At last, the long awaited, etc.' That merely creates the 'Oh yeah' mood in people."

† A year later, Fitzgerald notifies his agent Harold Ober that a fourth of the novel is finished and that he'll send it to him by the end of the year and that it's about "the case of that girl who shot her mother on the Pacific Coast last year." Fitzgerald is referring there to the adolescent matricide Dorothy Ellingson.

† This first version of what would be *Tender Is the Night*—which has almost nothing to do with the final version—has Francis Melarkey as protagonist, a twenty-year-old American who works in the world of film as a cinematographer and ends up murdering his domineering mother during a trip to Europe. Fitzgerald composes four or five sketches of the first part of this novel playing around with different possible titles (*Our Type, The Boy Who Killed His Mother, The Melarkey Case*, and *The World's Fair*), but Zelda's relapses and internments in various sanitoriums interrupt the project (and at the same time enhance it; Zelda's illness ends up being and is The Theme of the novel) with the need for fast and easy money. So he writes stories many of which are forgettable and a few that, especially the magnificent and terrible and so very sad "One Trip Abroad," will end up absorbed by the final version of *Tender Is the Night*.

† "I was paying for it with work, that I passionately hated and found more and more difficult to do. The novel was like a dream, daily farther and farther away . . . You were gone now—I scarcely remember you that summer . . . You were going crazy and calling it genius—I was going to ruin and calling it anything that came to hand . . . We ruined ourselves—I have never honestly thought that we ruined each other."—Francis Scott Fitzgerald in a letter for Zelda Fitzgerald that was never sent and archived with the title "Gone to the Clinique," summer, 1930.

† In the first version of *Tender Is the Night* appear the glowing American couple, Seth and Dinah Piper, who will end up transformed into Dick and Nicole Diver, the characters inspired by or respired by Gerald and Sara Murphy.

† The young cinematographer Francis Melarkey will suffer a much more radical metamorphosis: he'll be transformed into the young actress Rosemary Hoyt (inspired by one Lois Moran, a fan of the writer, a young starlet of seventeen—and protégée of Samuel Goldwyn—with whom Fitzgerald flirts, to Zelda's despair, without it ever coming to anything serious beyond him recommending her books indispensable for her education.

† After many changes and protests and counter-protests and letters asking for help and time and pity (Gerald Murphy remembers having seen Fitzgerald throw a version of the novel, page after page, like someone tearing the petals from a flower, into the waters of the Mediterranean), the awaited *Tender Is the Night* makes its debut in 1934.

† Its title comes from "Ode to a Nightingale" by John Keats and wins out—Fitzgerald always vacillated over his titles until the last minute and was never entirely satisfied with the final choice—over the alternatives of *The Drunkard's Holiday*, *Dr. Diver's Holiday*, and *Richard Diver* (He would've been thrilled if the novel had been called *Richard Diver*, if the novel had the name of a person and a character, like those nineteenth-century novels in which a name makes all the difference.)

† *Tender Is the Night* arrives in bookstores immediately following its serialization in four parts in *Scribner's Magazine*, when nobody is expecting it except to say that it wasn't what they were expecting and, at the same time, to communicate in reviews and opinion pieces that it was exactly what was to be expected from Fitzgerald, that nothing else, or nothing more, could be expected from him. Fitzgerald was a modern writer and "of his time" and now he was suffering the fate of all "generational" writers: degeneration. Fitzgerald—they reproach him—has suddenly become antiquated, telling stories that seem to take place in museums where the past that's offered is too near and, as such, not worth the cost of inhaling its dust and allergens and, much less, paying for the ticket to revisit it. So, *Tender Is the Night*, in bookstore displays, as if stamped with the scarlet letter of warning that says, "Please don't touch." And readers don't touch it.

† *Tender Is the Night* quickly sells a first edition of 7,600 copies at $2.50 and lands at number ten on the bestseller list. Then, before long, it's pushed off by rather lukewarm reviews that reproach its lack of political and social relevance, for occupying itself with decadent millionaires sunning themselves in Europe during the days of the Great Depression, which is also Fitzgerald's personal Great Depression, a writer *so* generational that he even suffers the ills and atones for the sins of his generation. Fitzgerald is the messenger and storyteller who must be killed for having chronicled the good and irresponsible times of a generation that he never entirely belonged to. That "rotten crowd," those shady and resplendent specimens who for Nick Carraway—suddenly seeing and understanding everything, in the elegiac finale of *The Great Gatsby*—are nothing but careless individuals for whom everyone else, in exchange for perfumed banknotes, picks up and puts back together the pieces of all the things they break. They also question its structure with the long central flashback. And they consider the decadence and fall of Dick Diver as excessively melodramatic and implausible. And (he agrees about this) they point out that the psychological/psychoanalytic aspects of the thing are naïve and approached in a childish and facile way, like in those movies with the divan and the pipe and the bust of Sigmund Freud where the patients comprehend the keys to their neurosis all at once, with analypsis of liquid images,

that seem filmed underwater, as if wanting to signify that the subconscious is something submarine and stormy, hidden under the apparently calm surface of the conscience. One reviewer—maybe infected by the Freudian spores of the novel—ends up interpreting that Dick Diver is Fitzgerald and the mad Nicole Diver is nothing but "that whistling social system": the incarnation of her time and youth and generation, lost forever. And that it's now time for Fitzgerald—if he wants to grow as a writer—to stop attending to Nicole Diver. And he closes his diagnosis with the following words: "And finally a not too personal postscript for the author. Dear Mr. Fitzgerald: you can't hide from a hurricane under a beach umbrella."

† The heavyweight intellectual and rediscoverer of William Faulkner, Malcolm Crowley, states that "*Tender is the Night* is a good novel that puzzles you and ends up making you a little angry because it isn't a great novel also."

† Fitzgerald, desperate, insecure about everything, tries to fix what he can, to save the furniture, scoop out water while everyone runs for the lifeboats. Fitzgerald sends a telegraph, in desperate caps, to Bennett Cerf, trying to convince him to launch an economical and corrected edition of *Tender Is the Night* in the Modern Library collection: "DO YOU THINK THAT ONCE A BOOK IS PUBLISHED IT IS FOREVER CRYSTALLIZED?" almost begging, asking them that they tell him that no, that there's still time. And he doesn't realize that it's impossible to improve it. Because the truly terrible thing about *Tender Is the Night*—the authentically disturbing and insurmountable thing—is that in it there is no Nick Carraway from *The Great Gatsby* or Cecilia Brady from *The Last Tycoon*. In *Tender Is the Night* there is no narrator functioning as an intermediary or filter or shield. The reader receives the radiation of the Divers & Co.—unlike what happens with the nebulous Jay Gatsby, Fitzgerald seems to insist that we know everything about Dick and Nicole—without anesthesia, directly, point blank. And it hurts. Gatsby seeks to repeat the past; the Divers only want to stop repeating their eternal present. Fitzgerald restructures the novel chronologically, begs and doesn't succeed in getting them to publish a second version (his wish will be granted in 1951, posthumously, and the result does nothing but damage

what was already good and, fortunately, that mutation of *Tender Is the Night* will be put definitively out of circulation by 1959), and ends up realizing that what he does doesn't interest him anymore.

And night falls.

† One year after *Tender Is the Night*, a final volume of stories, the magnificent *Taps at Reveille* (1935), including such masterpieces as "Crazy Sunday," "The Last of the Belles," and "Babylon Revisited," is received as the terminal X-ray, the point of no return, which marks Fitzgerald as an incurable patient, victim of a "period" sickness that nobody contracts and that, consequently, nobody fears or has to waste any time looking for a magic cure for anymore.

† In a letter to the literary critic Philip Lenhart dated April 1934, Fitzgerald says that, "If you liked *The Great Gatsby*, for God's sake read this. *Gatsby* was a tour de force, but *Tender Is the Night* is a confession of faith."

† *Tender Is the Night* as the Great Psycho-American Novel: Sara and Gerald Murphy turn into Nicole and Dick Diver who turn into Zelda and Francis Scott Fitzgerald (who turn into his—he who is reading it again, "studying it"—own parents), and who knows how many thousands of couples roaming around, reading it, feeling worse and worse the better they read it.

† And *sua culpa*: he read *Tender Is the Night* for the first time—long after he should've done so, probably because children tend to put off facing their parents' passions as long as possible, out of fear of what they'll find there—the way someone contracts a virus. As if its vaudeville vertigo turned fever were something that settled inside the reader little by little until it intoxicated him. Compared with the perfection of *The Great Gatsby* (which at its peak is able to produce the mildest and most pleasant of post-party hangovers), *Tender Is the Night*, in the beginning, feels like one of those interminable colds that climbs into bed with you and makes you feel and see things that aren't there. But really *yes* they are there, just that, when you're healthy, you can't see them. Sanity is made (and exists for people who function more or less properly) of defense mechanisms like these.

† Attempting a synopsis of *Tender Is the Night* that, inevitably, will read (and more than one reader will, no doubt, skip it) like climbing onto the most dizzying of carnival rides. A frenzy of names and places and ports that open and close and fatal acts (incest, murder) and terrible moments like the chilling hysterical episode of Nicole Diver in the bathroom (ah, the bathroom: for his parents and for many parents, a classic and frequent realm of debate. Something strange about that, and did they argue in bathrooms for reasons of hygiene, to eliminate corporeal waste? Is arguing in bathrooms like committing murder in a library or making love in the stables?). Bathroom episode—Nicole wailing, her cry echoing off the tiles—that produces in the young and easy-in-love Rosemary Hoyt, involuntary witness of the horror, the irrepressible urge (which also disconcerted more than one critic) to get out of there and almost not return to the novel until near its end. At which point, encountering Dick again, Rosemary understands that this is no longer the man with whom she fell in love—that he's changed. And yet, when Dick asks her if he seems different, she lies that no, that he's just like he was, like himself. To which Dick—with a sad smile, unequivocally Fitzgeraldian, the smile that, unlike Jay Gatsby, knows that the past can't be repeated—responds: "Did you hear I'd gone into a process of deterioration? . . . It is true. The change came a long way back—but at first it didn't show. The manner remains intact for some time after the morale cracks."

How does Dick Diver end up? Alone, with an occasional girlfriend, practicing at small rural offices, "in one town or another," writing a book always "in a process of completion."

Like him, more or less.

Just that he's always in the process of beginning.

† He's going to try it. The synopsis of *Tender Is the Night*. Here goes: a novel about the misuse of creative promise. Something like that. It tells the story of Dick Diver, a young American psychologist, studying in Zurich in 1917 (this is the second—and in reverse—part of the novel in the first and definitive version after Fitzgerald spent a few years, as mentioned, having the book be reordered to locate it, chronologically, at the beginning of the book). Diver shows interest in the case of Nicole Warren, a beautiful and

wealthy and schizophrenic American. Why? Because her loving father slept with her. As Nicole recovers she, also, becomes more dependent on Dick, whom she ends up marrying. And maintaining. The doctor-patient relationship is translated into married life and, seeing himself obliged to care for her, Dick not only shelves the development of his "intellectual and professional life" but, in addition, discovers that he doesn't love her like a husband, but like someone resigned to watching a sadomasochistic butterfly always begging to be stabbed with a pin so that she can later be admired. All the time. Dick and Nicole have two children and they live a good life in the French Riviera (first part of the novel). There, their friends include Abe North (alcoholic musician who, like Dick, hasn't achieved the heights of all that was expected of him when he was a young prodigy composer) and who, *grand finale*, ends up getting murdered in a bar in Paris. A black man dies too. Escape there. Enter over there. So, the impeccable life, thanks to Nicole's money, of Dick as professional host collapses in slow motion, drink in hand. But everything begins to tremble and events precipitate with the arrival of the young actress—symbol of all dreams yet to be realized and to come true—Rosemary Hoyt. Dick falls in love with the girl (or wants to believe he's in love), and begins to drink more than he eats; and he gets into trouble in bars in Rome; and his career comes crashing down. Fortunately or not, Nicole falls in love with Tommy Barban, a French mercenary and member of her eternally vacationing circle. And Nicole ends up divorcing Dick, who returns to the United States to lead a most banal and mediocre and maybe more or less happy existence.

† Note: Fitzgerald (and Zelda) reveled as if possessed in diving off cliffs or swimming pool diving boards. They dove into the void and into the sea and from the rocks and, in the summer of 1926, in front of the increasingly terrified Sara and Gerald Murphy, they did it many times. Fitzgerald's stories and novels overflow with aquatic surfaces always ready to be altered, rippled, splashed.

He always found it funny that *Dick Diver*, in Spanish, can be translated as *imbécil clavadista*.

The tiny distance and brief instant between dive and impact.

† The EX LIBRIS in Fitzgerald's books shows a skeleton wearing a smoking jacket dancing in a tempest of confetti and serpents, holding a mask in one hand and a saxophone in the other. High above him reads the legend BE YOUR AGE. Which could be taken to mean either "Belong to your time" or "Act your age." Easy to say, hard to do. Easy to write, hard to live.

† What could his parents—in full-on process of deterioration, their morale broken—have seen in *Tender Is the Night*? What could their systematic serial reading of the novel—as if searching for a secret code, an explanation for everything in their world—have helped them with? Maybe, seeing themselves reflected in the Divers just as the Murphys (though they deny it) saw themselves reflected in the Divers, his parents were able to understand themselves better and maybe forgive themselves. Or perhaps, to the contrary, the bourgeoisie and comfortable image reflected back to them by that black and magic mirror—the warning from a Lost Generation that under no circumstance should they lose their generation again—did nothing but harden their respective positions and they read that book the way other people read Sun Tzu or Von Clausewitz. As a call to arms.

† His parents: maybe it was mutual boredom and the need for powerful emotions and the idea that a trend of political and social compromise first and armed conflict later was emerging, which made it so that, in their eyes, *Tender Is the Night* was in the first place a kind of example to follow and overcome, and later a bad example to track down and eliminate.

† But everyone knows that adults act like children—first they want the best version or model of what others have and, later, they only want what nobody else has.

† Which would explain his parents' passage from bon vivants to killing machines, or something like that.

† Not long ago, an enthusiastic and young documentary maker contacted him to ask if he was interested in participating in "something that I'm putting

together about your parents . . . About the story of the guerilla cell known as The Murphys."

He, of course, cordially invited him to take a hike.

† This is the story: Christmas Eve 1977, his parents and their friends, models and artists and publicists and beautiful people, storm a prestigious department store branch and, within a few hours, are "subdued by the forces of order."

Note: But, warning, the "political" part—the most rotten part of all—will only take up a few lines, like something rarely seen or heard. He's been there before. He doesn't want to go back. He leaves it for the scavenger birds and animals of prey that deal in such things, for the new generations of patriotic resuscitators of the dear living dead.

Another note: This part of the novel (and it will be very complex) will be built around the testimonies of hostages, between terror and wonder, seeing themselves subdued by "that couple from those ads on a sailboat." Some of them won't be able to stop admiring the perfect cut and tailoring of their guerilla-chic style uniforms. Someone will ask for their autographs and to take a picture with them. And his parents, of course, will comply. And they smile at the camera. And that oh so Murphian photo will appear on the front page of daily and weekly newspapers in the coming days and weeks.

Stop the presses.

† And "subdued by the forces of order" means that the army comes in with tanks and bazookas and many people die, among them several customers who were there buying Christmas presents.

The attack is filmed by news cameras and (not long ago he saw those shaky scenes again) the quality of the film is curiously similar to the postcards of battles from World War One. Something that looks much *older* than it actually is.

Then he understands the motives and reasons why that girl asked him if that photo of the Murphys was of his parents. The past makes everything uniform. In the past—even if you read to keep from succumbing to that defect—everything happens at the same time, everything piles up in the same corner, and each event only steps forward when its number, the number of its day and year and century, gets called. But it does so in its own way.

† The past is an old child, obedient and bad-mannered at the same time.

† The past is a broken toy that everyone fixes in his own way.

† It was never clear if his parents died during the retaking of the department store or if, weeks later, they were thrown from a seaplane into the waters off that beach where they used to take him on vacation and where one time he almost drowned without them noticing.

And inconfessable confession, inadmissible admission: he's increasingly convinced that he'd benefitted from his parents' disappearance. And not just because it made him seem so much more interesting when he published his first book where his parents' disappearance made an appearance. But because, now, in addition, with that national tragedy already somewhat worn out and faded, but not entirely out of style, he shuddered whenever people he knew told him of awful episodes with their parents, who not only hadn't disappeared but who, like apparitions, were increasingly here and there and everywhere: parents who fell and broke bones, parents who complained about everything and reproached and accused, parents who got lost out in the streets, parents who rewrote their pasts at their convenience and for their pleasure, parents whom you had to wash and change and feed. In the name of the past, thank you for your sperm, thank you for your ovum, thank you for the love or the mistake of that crazy night that brought me here. Thanks for nothing.

His parents, on the other hand, hadn't even left behind good-looking corpses. His parents were like dead stars whose light still twinkled a little, from so many dark years of unfathomable cosmic distance. His parents were, yes—a good story.

A survivor of battlefields and torture—a member of The Murphys, an ex-art director at an ad agency—shows up many years later at the presentation of one of his books and tells him that he'd been detained with his parents. That they were tortured, physically and psychologically. That they were forced to play a cross between Russian Roulette and William Tell. That they were made to shoot each other with a gun, loaded with a single bullet. That he wasn't sure if his mother killed his father or his father killed his mother.

And he walked away, the way you walk away from something that you don't know whether it causes you pain or fear, thinking "William Burroughs."

In any case, what happened happened, and after that, for him and Penelope, Christmas was always a strange time.

† That oft-cited moment in *Tender Is the Night* when Fitzgerald describes the way, at a dinner and having surrendered to their guests, watching them with near adoration, Nicole and Dick Diver seem to glow and expand and their faces are "like the faces of poor children at a Christmas tree."

† The photos of the Fitzgeralds are so different from photos of the Murphys. While those of the latter are always fluid, elegant, amusing, their bodies always slender as if suspended in the perfection of a second, the photos of the Fitzgeralds always look rigid, frozen, like little dolls who have fled from the top of a wedding cake and are caught by surprise at dances, on boat decks, and with their daughter in front of a Christmas tree in a Paris flat, practicing an awkward cancan where they barely lift their legs as if afraid they'll break, break beyond all possible repair.

† So, in his novel, the narrator will have a love-hate relationship with Christmas and, throughout its pages, he'll insert reflections and memories of the holiday. Examples follow.

† An equally cruel and funny Christmas card that somebody sent him at some point and that now he has stuck to the corkboard, above his desk. On the card is a drawing of a father surprised by his little son as he places the presents under the tree. The father looks at him over his shoulder, and it's easy for him to imagine him saying his line (the letters enclosed in a bubble that emerges from his mouth) in the smooth and slippery voice of Robert Mitchum: "What've you done, Timmy? Now I have no choice but to kill you," says the father to the son.

† Behind the good joke—as tends to occur with all good jokes—pulses the

certainty of something grave and possibly ominous: Christmas is a deception that should be preserved at all cost. For centuries, Christmas—the existence of that man who comes down the chimney—has functioned like the Original Lie hissing and coiling around the trunk that links parents and children. So, good behavior and honesty are rewarded vis-à-vis the fabrication of a fallacy whose elucidation—sooner or later—leaves behind a bitter aftertaste. You stop believing in Santa Claus and soon you stop believing in the supposed love that your parents feel for each other and, by extension, in the love they profess for you. And the expansive wave of this initiating deception—its friendly fire, its collateral damage—ends up spanning an entire lifetime. The majority, not of nonbelievers but of ex-believers absorbs the blow with resigned grace; but how many future serial killers and corrupt politicians might have chosen their fate at the foot of that little tree, confronting a father who committed the merciful error of sparing their lives? Today, even encyclopedias cast the whole thing in doubt, or between quotation marks: Christmas is just the Christian rewrite of a pagan myth (the celebration of the solstice where everyone put on masks to fornicate under a great pine tree and conceive all the children that the next spring would bring) or it didn't even happen when they say it happened.

The question is, of course: do we believe in Christmas or is it Christmas that believes in us?

† "*Christmas*. December 25th. Christian religious festival celebrated throughout the West, whose principal characteristic is the exchange of gifts and the preparation of feasts. Within the Christian Church, Christmas is the day that celebrates the birth of Jesus, even though the true date is unknown. Many Christmas traditions are not of Christian origin and were adapted and changed according to celebrations of the Winter solstice."—*The Wordsworth Encyclopedia*.

† Christmas as a supposedly curative pathology. Charles Dickens, Frank Capra, etcetera. Maybe Christmas isn't a virus. Maybe Christmas is a drug. Highly addictive. Collective hysteria. Unstoppable, almost impossible to kick the habit. A chemical composition that forces you to smile at everyone, and to embrace yourself, and convince yourself that happiness is a possible

contrivance. So, the invention of Christmas (and its immediate sequel: The New Year, and its childish coda: Three Kings Day) equals the invention of happiness. Or the happiness of invention.

† Charles Dickens (a writer for whom the poor, and not the rich, are different) was Fitzgerald's favorite writer when he was a kid. Dickens was and is, also, one of his favorite writers and *David Copperfield* was the first novel where, dumbfounded, he discovered that the writer can *also* be the character—the hero.

† "My father was a good person," one of Charles Dickens' daughters dared whisper, when the pageantry of the writer's burial was concluded in Poets Corner, Westminster Abbey.

† Fitzgerald's parents were good people. They worried about him and weren't too disturbed that he went around saying things like "I want to be one of the greatest writers who ever lived." Fitzgerald was not a popular boy. He was too delicate. He looked like a pale-eyed doll. His mother threw him birthday parties that nobody came to. Something similar happened to him with his parents, with his birthdays and everyone else's birthdays—nobody ever came and he never went to a single one. It's not that he wasn't popular among his classmates; it's that his parents—even though they were famous and celebrities, maybe because of this, plus the stories about them in the press—were not popular among the other parents.

† Were his parents "good people" despite everything? Taking into account— being atheists in automatic reaction to their own parents' Catholicism—the importance and enthusiasm that they placed on, in their words, "repaganizing" the holidays with great parties and dances with no shortage of hip drugs (he remembers one Christmas Eve when he and Penelope, feet blistered by new shoes, spent the night trailing after their parents and their parents' friends, through the streets, from bar to bar, as they insisted on celebrating *everything*), wouldn't it have been better if, at least, in the name of their children, they'd picked some day other than Christmas Eve to do what they did?
    It doesn't matter now.

One thing is definitely clear: the residual power—just like the secondary damages that *Tender Is the Night* keeps producing—remains considerable. Not long ago, he took that book with him one night, feeling like he was dying, to the Emergency Room. And just flipping through it, while waiting for his examination and diagnosis, he came up with the idea for a decidedly Fitzgeraldian and autobiographical story.

In the story, a boy, the son of divorced parents, awaits the verdict that'll determine with whom he'll spend Christmas Eve and with whom Christmas. It's a few days before the holidays and, without knowing it, the boy is photographed by a journalist in the moment that, in the street, a man dressed as Santa Claus gives him a balloon. The boy—who already knows that Santa Claus doesn't exist and that it's not even his parents: it's his grandparents— accepts it with a resigned expression. Then, brief ellipsis and we see and we read the father and the mother, seeing and reading that photo, in separate beds and in different houses, with another woman and another man. The caption says something like: "The happiness of a child is worth a thousand words."

And nothing more to say.

† What happened to him and Penelope after his parents were swept away by the winds of History?

Little and nothing.

Uncles and aunts and grandparents. And, especially, *that one* uncle with kaleidoscopic and dreamy eyes, light and shadow. But in his book, he'll opt for a Christmassy and Dickensian and Capraesque solution—the appearance of a magic character, half-Fitzgeraldian, half-Dickensian. In a not so reliable first-person (Nick Carraway) or in a fairly implacable third-person.

Eames "Chip" Chippendale (his movable/noble surname like a complicit wink at himself: Chip like something solid and elegant amid so many IKEA specimens).

Chip is the owner of a bookstore and one time close friend of Sara and Gerald Murphy, who—he explains—took the trouble to set up a trust (and named him guardian) for the children of a couple they met a while back and with whom they were photographed.

Chip—who raises him like his own son and turns him into a writer and handles Penelope's progressive madness with stoicism and grace—explains to him, some time later, that Sara and Gerald Murphy understood immediately that "your parents weren't going to end well. They knew the symptoms after years of dealing with the Fitzgeralds. And it was clear to them that the kids were going to end up castaways of that great shipwreck. So, measures were taken."

† Which doesn't prevent, of course, the transmission of certain invulnerable bacteria. But, he thinks, isn't it a little *too much* to compare Zelda's madness to Penelope's and to accuse him—as Fitzgerald was accused, exaggeratedly and with very little foundation, of having taken nibbles from his wife's diaries on the sly, searching for useful material to use in his stories and novels—of having fed off Penelope's experiences with her in-laws, cranking up the volume to 11, to nurture one of his books?

Yes?

No?

Neither?

† One thing is clear: after various comings and going between reason and unreason, Penelope goes irrevocably mad. Mad like Zelda. She goes in and out of sanitoriums like someone carefully planning getaways to places that are unknown to them and that they've never heard anyone talk about. But imagining, always, that someone told them it's a place worth getting to know.

And that she'll be happy there.

For a while.

† And what Penelope does and what she did is something so horrible that he only dares think of it every so often (he can't put it writing; and it's here that he understands that the whole project of his book is beginning to fall apart, that it's unsustainable, that it's starting to dissipate, as tends to happen with the diffuse matter of good ideas, so similar to that of dreams) so he can say to himself: "There: now I won't have to think about it again for a while."

And he manages it more and more and that achievement, he realizes, has been making him a less and less admirable human being.

The trick is to think about what happened by putting it in foreign contexts, like something that happened to other people, like stories written by other people, like lights to be guided by but never to hold responsible.

† "Who would not be pleased at carrying lamps helpfully through the darkness?"—Francis Scott Fitzgerald, *Tender Is the Night*.

† The literary value of Zelda Fitzgerald's work is exceedingly relative, but it wears that exalted perfume of madness and flammable will, stoked by more than one feminist, wanting to see her as the perfect symbol of female genius, whose wings were clipped by the phallic blades of insecure men.

Her stories—some of them striking—are, yes, Fitzgeraldian and on occasion were even published under Fitzgerald's signature in order to earn better pay. And her novel *Save Me the Waltz* (1934) can be read as a kind of ghost sister to *Tender Is the Night* with moments that recall—as if taking place in a dollhouse of hypnotized dolls—both the films of Wes Anderson and those of Paul Thomas Anderson.

Save Me the Waltz is, of course, a somewhat terrifying book. But it's also a very *pleasant* book, as long as it doesn't come to live with you after the dance has ended.

Save Me the Waltz is a book by and like Zelda Fitzgerald.

Save Me the Waltz—written in three days to the despair and wonder of the increasingly slow and blocked Fitzgerald—is a book by a woman who is convinced that the flowers are talking to her, who spends more than nine hours in front of a mirror attempting a desperate *pas de une* and to look as much like a ballerina as possible, but who ends up a sort of distant cousin of the first wife of Edward Fairfax Rochester and close personal friend of Miss Havisham.

And, true, the delirium of Penelope fleeing Mount Karma does *indeed* resemble the desert and African deliriums of Zelda, believing herself lost on wild savannahs, wandering like an explorer sans compass, and composing letters that read: "Dear: dear, dear, dear, dear, dear, dear, dear, dear, dear . . ." and on and on for pages.

And he takes advantage of Zelda's madness and he invents her a novella,

"Wuthering Heights Revisited," recently discovered among papers deposited in American universities, places where things are always being discovered whose existence was previously unknown; where the dead seem to keep on writing, as if they didn't know, or hadn't been notified, that they were dead; that they don't need to keep telling their stories, that their stories will now be told by the living.

† "Wuthering Heights Revisited" tells the story of a beautiful and romantic young woman who, obsessed with gothic novels, marries a rich yet bohemian heir who has come to Europe to find success as an artist. Her husband falls seriously ill and both of them return to his family's home, on the other side of the ocean. There, the young woman suffers and, discovering that she is pregnant, runs away without saying anything to her in-laws out of fear that they won't let her leave and will claim her child for the heir. The young woman, without a home, lives with her brother. The boy is born and the young mother, sensing that she's going mad, discovers not only that the boy won't ever love her, but that in addition, as the years go by, he'll love her brother more and more. One night, the young woman takes her son for a walk along a beach that leads into a forest. And the young woman comes home alone and smiling. And she says she doesn't know what happened, that she doesn't remember anything, that she was "possessed by the ugliest of all the Ugly Spirits," and, when questioned about the boy, she sings and sings and doesn't stop singing.
    "Dear: dear, dear, dear . . ."

† Long process of deterioration. Even longer. That's enough.

† Then, subsequently, the extensive and elusive list of uncomfortable and disagreeable moments starring Fitzgerald or that Fitzgerald invites others to co-star in. It's enough just to see him with his family. Example: Fitzgerald showing up drunk to a party attended by his adolescent daughter, who does nothing to help him. Days later, a friend of hers who was there reproaches Scottie for not helping her father. Scottie says she doesn't know what he's talking about. "Nothing happened," she says. Her friend asks her if she's try-ing to be strong, denying what happened: the fact that "your father was so

drunk and so helpless and that you behaved as if he wasn't there . . . Children should worry more about their parents, Scottie." To which Scottie responds: "Don't you realize that if I let myself worry I wouldn't be able to bear it?"

† "In my next incarnation, I may not choose again to be the daughter of a Famous Author. The pay is good and there are fringe benefits, but the working conditions are too hazardous."—Frances "Scottie" Fitzgerald in the prologue to *Letters to His Daughter* (1965), by Francis Scott Fitzgerald.

† One night, he discovers on the Internet an old recording of Fitzgerald reciting "Ode To a Nightingale" by John Keats. The voice, sad and breaking, Fitzgerald's almost childish solemnity, as if performing for parents or class-mates in a school play, trying to convince them and convince himself that he's a good student: "My heart aches, and a drowsy numbness pains / My sense, as though of hemlock I had drunk" and "was it a vision, or a waking dream? / Fled is that music:—Do I wake or sleep?"
Good question.

† From a letter from Francis Scott Fitzgerald to his daughter Frances "Scottie Fitzgerald, December 1940:
"But the insane are always mere guests on earth, eternal strangers carrying around broken decalogues that they cannot read."

† In a letter to Francis Scott Fitzgerald, dated December 31ˢᵗ, 1935, Gerald Murphy concludes, more in the voice of Dick Diver than Gerald Murphy:
"I know now that what you said in *Tender Is the Night* is true. Only the invented part of our life—the unreal part—has had any scheme, any beauty." And, yes, he already wrote this down before, but he's going to write it here again. Once and again and one more time. Multiplied but perfect to share bijis: like canapés, like repeated figurines, like those little bags of candies that you take home after childhood birthday parties. But the next sentence, even more heartbreaking, will only be included once, here, now: "Life itself has now stepped in and blundered, scarred, and destroyed. In my heart, I dreaded the moment when our youth and invention would be attacked in our only vulnerable spot—the children, their growth, their health, their future."

The children, the children. The children like lightning rods and grounding wire. And the children, also, like unstoppable and strangling lightning bolts. The children who—like it says at the end of that novel that impressed him so much (*London Fields*, by Martin Amis, read just before the release of his first book, that moment when all the best books seem to possess a nontransferable and personal transcendence)—you look for even though you never had them and let's see how many you find. The children like the people you always hoped would know you. The children like the people you hoped you would never not know. The children like the people you always hoped would acknowledge you. The children that you raised as an act of true love and true imagination: the children like those characters (though Vladimir Nabokov would've spurned such a notion) that escape us. The children like fragile invented parts always poised to attack and always exposed to attack from real parts, never clearly seen until it's already too late. The children who—contrary to what many believe, especially those who don't and won't ever have children, he can imagine it and can imagine what it feels like, that's why he's a writer, to not be himself and to be someone else if he needs to be—don't soften you or make you more sensitive, but elevate or bring you down to the violent level of fierce killing machines, to kill for the children, always ready to attack, teeth and nails bared, *paternal* and *maternal* as synonyms for *lethal*. The Children as the perfect excuse to be a killer or a suicide or killed by children. The children that—if there's justice, if everything turns out fine— end up rewriting us without giving us a chance to correct them or defend ourselves, because we're already done, we're already gone, we're already about to dot the "i"s of a story that, even though it's ours, already belongs to them.

In Calvin Tomkins's notes and interviews for his profile on the couple for *The New Yorker*, Gerald Murphy goes into greater depth: "Talking with Scott one time I told him that for me, only the invented part of life was satisfying, only the unrealistic part. Things happened to you—sickness, death, Zelda in Prangins, Patrick in the sanatorium, Father Wiborg's death—these things were realistic, and you couldn't do anything about them. 'Do you mean you don't accept those things?' Scott asked. I replied that of course I accepted them, but that I didn't feel they were the important things really. It's not what we do but what we do with our minds that counts, and for me only the *invented* parts of our life had any real meaning."

† His childhood recovered not via personal memories but via personal objects and places that evoke them, reinvented real parts: the different houses and the many moves (once he used thumbtacks to mark his locations on a map of the city, hoping to illuminate a cabalistic symbol, but no, nothing), the already antique candies and the revolutionary arrival of Toblerone chocolate, children's clothes (which, at that time, were still like grown-up clothes, just smaller), the bills that changed name all the time and aged so quickly, the disgust at the film of cream that forms on the surface of warm milk, vitamin C, the ritual of haircuts, the albums of trading cards and metal figurines and the first stick-on tattoos, orthodontic apparatuses, the exceedingly large and exceedingly old automobiles (older than the then-old automobiles), the personal and psychotic revolution of the shopping mall, the spinning of LPs, the grooves on LPs, a double LP with a white cover (that his parents split in half during one of their separations and that he'll only hear in its entirety when he buys it years later), a museum with dinosaur skeletons, a terrestrial planetarium with paradoxically extraterrestrial architecture, his parents' friends' houses, the friends from school who weren't his parents' friends' children (and who wanted more than anything to have parents like his, unaware what it was like, unaware of the fine print and hidden clauses in the contract), some parks and some plazas, the psychedelic posters of rock bands, Holiday On Ice, the massive movie theaters always full and multilevel (that, if he could go back, would probably—unlike most of yesterday's spaces, like the theater that only showed the movies of Walt Disney Studios—still seem enormous to him), a recurrent dream with chimneysweeps who chase him across the rooftops of an ancient city (product of seeing *Mary Poppins?*), the childhood magazines and the rite of passage, an encyclopedia about Greco-Roman mythology that he never finishes (he's missing, forever, the fundamental part that tells of the war between the titans and the gods), *Lawrence of Arabia* and *Les aventuriers* and *Melody*, the barrel of peanuts in a popular bar, classical galleries with ceilings painted with circular paintings and with echoing cupolas (and the hippie galleries with low ceilings where the nebulous odor of patchouli accumulates), the limited number of TV channels where on Saturdays they show movies of all genres and during the weeks series like *Zorro*, a red tricycle and a green bicycle (that, he thinks, if he could achieve a great velocity, would allow him to go back in time and change and correct so many

things), *Dracula* and *Martin Eden* and *David Copperfield* and the always-open bookstores, the seasons that back then are well-delimited and begin and end when they're supposed to end and begin (in winter it's never hot and in summer it's never cold), an urban beach with a Francophone name where his parents and their friends (who act like an adult version of *Lord of the Flies* while there) insist on taking him, and whose muddy shores are fed by the sewer waters of the whole city, the demolition of his school, the ruins of his school where he plays and falls and gets hurt (and those so scratchable and peelable and chewable scabs that grow over the wounds), the sunburns and those heavy white creams, the hairspray and hair gel, the ballpoint pens and ink stains and blotting paper and pencils and rubber erasers that burn holes in notebook pages (hardcover and softcover) and new textbooks (and looking at the pictures) and book bags (the Era of Backpacks has not yet arrived), the terrible anxiety of Sunday night, his parents, his grandparents telling him his parents have gone on a trip and that they're not coming back, the unopened presents that Christmas.

Ho Ho Ho.

† And the dead summon the dead. The dead who go up and down chimneys. The dead who are fertile so their bodies get planted in the earth or their ashes scattered in the air so the wind can spread them across crops and fields.

† Francis Scott Fitzgerald dies on the 21st of December, 1940, in Hollywood, after having been humiliated by producers and having humiliated himself in front of producers on too many crazy Sundays (film people exchange Fitzgerald anecdotes as if they were recounting inverted feats of strength in which the athlete never wins except when it comes to the record for emptying bottles or always falling down before reaching his goal) and failing at writing various film projects, including an adaptation of *Tender Is the Night*. The film version that Fitzgerald fantasizes about has a happy ending: Dick—neurosurgeon in addition to psychoanalyst—saves Nicole on the operating table. The actors considered for Dick go from Fredric March to Douglas Fairbanks, Jr. For the role of Nicole, Katherine Hepburn and Dolores del Río are mentioned. But the thing doesn't work—Fitzgerald either—and later

on the job falls into the hands of another volatile, alcoholic writer, feared by his friends and acquaintances—Malcolm Lowry, who also ends up, in his words, "possessed" by the book. Reading his frustrated screenplay, impossible to film yet so intense to read (published by an American university), he sees Dick Diver undergo a new and final transformation and turn into consul Geoffrey Firmin of *Under the Volcano*.

His companion Sheila Graham—a show-business journalist who'd write multiple, maybe too many, books about her years with the writer—tells how Fitzgerald was eating a chocolate and flipping through the pages of the *Princeton Alumni Weekly* when, suddenly, "he stood up as if jerked by a wire" to subsequently fall down, and scene.

He's read all the biographies of Fitzgerald and the one by Andrew Turnbull, from 1962, isn't the best (his favorite is *Inverted Lives: F. Scott & Zelda Fitzgerald*, by James R. Mellow, 1984). But Turnbull has the advantage of having been the writer's friend and attending—with Sara and Gerald Murphy, to whom Fitzgerald had written a short time before, thanking them for everything they'd done for him throughout the years: "the only pleasant human thing that had happened to me in a world where I felt prematurely passed by and forgotten"—his funeral and burial.

And Turnbull leaves this final image: "The casket was open, and all the lines of living had gone from Fitzgerald's face. It was smooth, rouged, almost pretty—more like a mannequin's than a man's. His clothes suggested a shop window. [. . .] At the last, there was a flurry of boys and girls—Scottie's friends on their way to or from some party. [. . .] The coffin was closed and we drove to the cemetery in the rain."

Beside the tomb, Dorothy Parker says "Poor son-of-a-bitch" and is outraged because everybody misunderstands it and nobody realizes that she's quoting the scene of Jay Gatsby's burial. And Dorothy Parker says she feels that: "It was terrible what they did to Scott; if you'd seen him you'd have been sick . . . Like the director who put his finger in Scott Fitzgerald's face and complained, 'Pay you. Why, you ought to pay us.' [. . .] What is it that's the evil in Hollywood? It's the people."

And someone mentions that, en route to the wake, Nathanael West (to whom Fitzgerald had given a generous blurb for his *The Day of the Locust*, a novel that can be read and admired as the underworld of *The Love of the Last Tycoon*, populated by the kind of people with whom, no doubt, the passive-aggressive Kathleen Moore hangs out when she's not bewitching the doomed Monroe Stahr) is killed in a car accident. Nathanael West was colorblind and he confused red for green at a stoplight. Days before, the two writers had dined together and heard somebody sing "The Last Day I Saw Paris."

And someone hears the protestant minister in charge of the service say "the only reason I agreed to all of this was just to see them put his body underground: Fitzgerald was a good for nothing, a drunk, and the world is a better place without him."

In Fitzgerald's final notes for the unfinished *The Love of the Last Tycoon* there is that thing about "There are no second acts in American lives" and the one about "Don't wake the ghosts." And all those loose bijis, running through notebooks, posthumously collected in *The Notebooks of F. Scott Fitzgerald*. There, individual lines like hooks, like goldfish blending into the muddy depths, flashing like lightning: "There was never a good biography of a good novelist. There couldn't be. He is too many people if he's any good," or "An idea ran back and forward in his head like a blind man knocking over the solid furniture," or *"Lived in story,"* *"Tender*: all the more reason for emotional planning," "I am the last of the novelists for a long time now."

All the obituaries coincided on the fact that with Fitzgerald, with his death, an entire age came definitively to THE END, and music and closing credits.

† Zelda Sayre Fitzgerald dies on the 10th of March, 1948. The woman who never felt she got the recognition she deserved is one of the bodies rendered nearly unrecognizable by a fire at Highland Mental Hospital in Ashville, North Carolina. They were able to identify her remains from a ballet slipper. A short time before dying, Zelda had read the unfinished *The Love of the Last Tycoon* and wrote to its editor, Edmund Wilson, telling him that reading it "has given me back the desire to live."

† Ernest Hemingway dies on the 2nd of July, 1961. One of the last things he was working on and would never finish was a novel titled *The Garden of Eden*

(in his opinion, far and away the best thing Hemingway ever wrote) and which, at moments, sounds like the perverse modernism of writers like Ford Madox Ford and Jean Rhys; it recalls certain psychological thrillers that later Patricia Highsmith would write; and it can also be read like a kind of mirror of *Tender Is the Night*, the last novel published during his lifetime by his benefactor and friend and rival and ghost to be scorned—but no less frightening to the very end—Francis Scott Fitzgerald. A ghost who has returned and who now enjoys a critical and popular respect among readers that he never knew during his life and who is beginning to eclipse Hemingway, who now is a kind of Papa-brand self-parody. Scott shines brighter dead than he does alive. Scott, rediscovered, unearthed, resuscitated, writes better than Papa ever wrote.

In the paragraph that closes the heavily edited (very well edited) version of *The Garden of Eden*, published posthumously in 1986, Hemingway describes a paradise recovered in fiction, but lost forever in reality. That paradise that Hemingway tries to enter again now, knocking on the door, begging on his knees, mercy, mercy:

"David wrote steadily and well and the sentences that he had made before came to him complete and entire and he put them down, corrected them, and cut them as if he were going over the proof. Not a sentence was missing and there were many that he put down as they were returned to him without changing them. By two o'clock he had recovered, corrected, and improved what it had taken him five days to write originally. He wrote a while longer now and there was no sign that any of it would ever cease returning to him intact."

Far away from that—from the past, from Europe, from Africa, from all of that—Hemingway knows then that the only thing left for him in life was the hell of successive interminable manuscripts. Soon, he suspects without needing to confirm it, he wouldn't even be able to write beginnings. He begins to mistrust the people around him, he's sure that the FBI is coming for him (and apparently this was true), he tries to commit suicide several times, he gets electroshock therapy, and understands that the hunter is now the hunted. Hemingway is a living legend to everyone else and dead to himself. The last photos show him walking through the snowy forests of Ketchum; kicking cans and smiling at the camera with hollow eyes and an enormous and wide smile full of teeth that had forgotten how to bite. A White House functionary asks Hemingway for a sentence for a commemorative volume that will be given to the recently sworn-in president Kennedy. Nothing comes to him, he can't write a single word. "It just won't come anymore," he says to his wife, weeping.

Hemingway accepts that he's no longer a victorious warrior; not even a defeated fisherman; much less a young writer with "memory intact" and happy to recover his gift and his mission in life.

Hemingway knows that he's just a dying elephant.

Hemingway completely absorbs the once incipient knowledge of loneliness.

In the wee hours of a Sunday morning in the most dangerous of his summers, a final great idea for a final short story occurs to him. A flash fiction, a microstory.

Hemingway goes down to his studio and in one sitting, in a single shot, writes: "The Old Man and the Rifle."

† Gerald Murphy dies on the 17th of October, 1964. A couple years before, in 1962, he goes by himself—Sara refuses to accompany him—to see the film version of *Tender Is the Night*. It's a Friday afternoon and Gerald Murphy enters an entirely empty theater in Nyack, near where they live. He realizes quickly that it's a bad movie. The twenties appear depicted as a series of dioramas from the Museum of Natural History. Directed by Henry King (it turns out to be his last film) and screenplay by Ivan Moffat, a prestigious script-doctor who comes from Paris to be with his friends Jean-Paul Sartre and Simone de Beauvoir. In the movie, Dick has the face of Jason Robards and Nicole that of Jennifer Jones. "It was an extraordinary sensation. [. . .] I couldn't feel any emotion at all," Gerald Murphy remembered later.

It was snowing as he left the theater and he had to put chains on his car tires; driving home, Gerald Murphy felt the memory of Fitzgerald returning to him with perfect clarity, as if he were seeing it all anew. In that instant. Gerald Murphy remembered saying to Fitzgerald that he'd read *Tender Is the Night* and—"not mentioning Sara's feelings"—congratulating him on how good certain parts of the novel were. To which Fitzgerald picked up a copy of the book "and said, with that funny, faraway look in his eye, 'Yes, it has magic. It has magic.'"

Months later, Gerald Murphy's cancer worsens and nothing can be done. His last words, seconds before dying, are the words of someone who was a gentleman to the last second of his life: "Smelling salts for the ladies."

And let the music keep on playing.

† Sara Murphy dies on the 9ᵗʰ of October, 1975, singing—like the happiest and most accomplished of Miss Havishams—the Richard Wagner Bridal March in *Lohengrin*, the march that'd been played for her and Gerald sixty years before. "Here comes the bride . . . Here comes the bride . . ." she sings with that little girl's voice that some old ladies have.

There goes the bride.

† His parents, whose weekdays of birth he never knew and whose day and month of death is a mystery whose solution would reveal nothing about them. His parents' lives are devoured by the lives of the Murphys and the Fitzgeralds.

His book—the book he won't ever write and that doesn't understand or comprehend who they were, he realizes, a boat against the current, orgasmic and orgiastic, *orgastic past, into the past*—wouldn't reveal it either.

† In 1998, the Modern Library put *Tender Is the Night* at number twenty-eight on the one hundred best novels in English of the twentieth century. *The Great Gatsby* is number two, after *Ulysses* by James Joyce.

Has he read all of those novels? Just those one hundred novels?

He looks on the Internet and finds it and—memo for the girl from the beginning—he discovers that *yes* he has read ninety-three of the one hundred on the list.

And says to himself that that is something.

Then he thinks that Christmas is coming.

† In the dedication of Francis Scott Fitzgerald's *Tender Is the Night* you can read, underwater and holding your breath, not drowning but feeling what

it's like to drown, like the sigh of a last biji, as the sun sets and night rises, tenderly:

TO

GERALD AND SARA

MANY FÊTES

† Magic.

LIFE AFTER PEOPLE, OR NOTES FOR A BRIEF HISTORY OF PROGRESSIVE ROCK AND SCIENCE FICTION

"Dun dun dun da-DAdun, da-DAdun . . ." He realizes that he's in big trouble when, hearing a strange sound in his house and not being able to locate its source, he finally discovers that the sound is springing (*springing*, ah, such a *sonic* verb) from his own mouth. Through clenched teeth. And that it's nothing but his own voice singing low, deep, martial, the ominous and instantly catchy and unforgettable musical theme that marks the entrances and exits of the dark and asthmatic and uniformed and reconstructed Darth Vader in the movies of the *Star Wars* saga.

So that's what he's doing, advancing through a house that's too big for him now. And he moves through its hallways and bedrooms with the sneaking suspicion that, behind and beneath them, are more hallways and more rooms. Not like the most imperial and oppressive of spaceships, more like those mansions from Victorian movies where butlers and servants suddenly appear, like living ghosts, obedient to those who've summoned them using a network of gongs and bells, popping out of trapdoors in the walls, hidden by wallpaper and paint and fabric and carpet, which they access via bottomless wardrobes that open onto stairways that lead into the depths. So, Darth Vader has traveled back in time and is walking, fearsome, through a setting of faux English countryside with no idea how he's arrived there from his galaxy far far away.

"What year is it?" he wonders.

"Does it matter?" he answers.

For a couple months now—since his wife left him, taking their little son with her—he's been living in the near-suspended animation of the minute-to-minute. It's harder—but it hurts less.

She doesn't come back; the boy comes back on weekends. Nothing is lost, everything is transformed.

She was, just in case, first a foreign name that he made his own; then she was "the love of his life" (though the love of his life had already been another; so she, to be precise, had been "the love of his other life," of the life and of the love that came after); and now she is, merely, "the mother of his son."

He's been Tommy (when she loved him), Tomás (when she stopped loving him), Tom to his friends (when he was young and had his whole future in front of him).

So now, since he's been living alone, he prefers to think of himself as Tom. A percussive name. A name like a blow, but an affectionate blow; like one you might give someone, facing them, with a closed fist but soft, just below the left shoulder at the level of the heart. A name like a blow and like a salute. And a name that, he likes to think, corresponds to his son's new name. Not the name they gave him (which was the result of arduous negotiations between relatives with dynastic aspirations and proclivities for the resurrection of names and even nicknames of ancestors as a primitive form of cloning and of keeping everything the same), but the name his son chose for himself for when he is with him: Friday afternoon until Sunday night and, like right now and today, one Christmas (and one New Year) every two years.

His son announced that on weekends he wanted to be called Fin.

"Finn?" he asked. "Like the Irish name?" "No, Fin," answered his son, who is starting to write. "Or maybe End," his son, who's starting to speak English, added.

And starting over (blend the "Dun dun dun da-DAdun da-DAdun . . ." of Darth Vader's march with the "Dun dun dun dun . . ." of David Gilmour's guitar) and hello again, Tom, the past has come looking for you.

The past is a telephone that rings like those old telephones never rang, the ones that, in the beginning of their history, only rang to inform you of something decisive, historic. And, yes, with time there will be many people (though not as many as, for example, those who fixed in their memory the precise and private context that surrounded the death of John Fitzgerald Kennedy or the death of John Lennon; those moments in History, with a capital H, that turn into something almost palpable, something that's almost breathed and enters the lungs and heart and brain) who'll remember with millimetric precision exactly what they were doing when they found out about the disintegration of that writer.

Tom was sleeping when John Fitzgerald Kennedy was killed (he was a newborn baby then, and as far as he's concerned Oswald acted alone but with a number of prompters). And he was also sleeping when John Lennon was killed (but he was still young, and he remembers that the first thing he thought the next morning, when he found out about everything, was that the ex-Beatle must have been taken out while trying to rob a bank or murdered by Yoko Ono).

But *yes* Tom was wide awake and with fifty years draped over him like a very heavy blanket when the writer, who'd once been his best childhood and adolescent friend, evaporated in a storm of particles and quantum physics and dark matter. And, yes, Tom remembers precisely what he was doing then. Not only when he learned of the "accident"—better and more in-depth, on the news that night—but in the exact instant that it took place. Because he'd just finished not talking to the writer but listening to him * ("I'm calling you after so long because you have to know where I am and what I'm about to do, what I'm doing, what I did; because now all times are one for me. Now I no longer have time, I'm atemporal," his friend had said from so far away) talk on the telephone; because Tom didn't dare interrupt him, didn't dare say a word. Tom just listened to his sharp and clear voice for a long time on the answering machine recording, after his son came to find him in the bathroom and said: "*Papi*, the phone is making a weird noise."

And later, subsequently, before, now, he was already headed in that direction. Through the hallways of his house. Honoring the metallic and wheezing memory of Sith Lord Darth Vader, born Anakin Skywalker, Padawan and advisor of Chancellor Palpatine and future Emperor of the Galactic Empire, precocious and treacherous Jedi Knight abducted by the Dark Side of The Force and all of that but, first and foremost, the proudest model of one of the most winningly evil getups in the history of the universe.

And he, Tom Vader, makes it to the phone and kneels down beside it. It's an old telephone, the dial kind, that the mother of his son gave him (back when all gifts came wrapped in a combination of affection and jest) after hearing him get tangled up too many times in diatribes against mobile phones. * Mobile phones that actually immobilize you and find you wherever you are. These days, talking on a landline telephone or having it call out to us from some corner of the place where we live or work has acquired a very intimate texture, almost of explicit physical activity or the declassification of classified material. Lost is the dismissive pleasure of letting it ring and the slow frustration of not arriving in time to pick it up and play with the curl of its cord. Forgotten is the fact that at one time you only used the telephone to say what you didn't dare put in writing, in brief messages or emails of varying size. Pretty soon (he thinks, wondering why he's thinking this, telling himself that he doesn't think like this, wondering to whom these thoughts that invade his head like a strange recording belong) none of the old people will be alive anymore who used the telephone simply to communicate. Brief conversations and precise messages, and, every so often, the oddity of fighting over the telephone or the pleasure of—slowly and contemplating each digit, tempted to hang up before dialing the whole number—requesting and receiving the aid of that faithful device to ask out a girl for the first time.

So, sign of the times, and though he always stares at it whenever he passes by, as if challenging it, this telephone rarely rings. Almost nobody has its number. Actually, the mother of his son is the only person who does. And the mother of his son only uses it when there's trouble, when he's going to be in trouble. So the mother of his son has been using it quite a bit lately. So Tom—"Very funny," she commented the first time she saw it again, the telephone, under a bell jar, when she came to pick up Fin—has painted it red and hooked it up to an antique answering machine, specially modified to allow uninterrupted messages to be left on an old but faithful cassette tape with a forty-five minute capacity per side. There, at least once a week, the mother of his son discharges present-day reproaches and immemorial accusations. And he listens to her, while cooking or cleaning as well as he's able to cook or clean the house, better all the time, to tell the truth. All of this—testing out a new bathroom disinfectant or daring to try a complex recipe—while still paying extreme attention to the first five or ten minutes of the mother of his son's telephonic diatribe, wanting to convince himself that this time he'll be able to decode what happened and how it brought about the end of their love—or what he thought was love. And yet, after a little while, his ex's voice turns into something else: into something he doesn't hear but that accompanies him, like the whisper of trees greeting an autumn afternoon with their branches, a paradoxically relaxing sound.

But it's not the mother of his son's voice that he hears now.

What he hears is, yes, "a weird sound." Something that sounds like a rushing sea, an orchestral crescendo launching into the triumphal overture of the Tsunami Symphony, a dissonant chaos of strings and winds running over each other to see who will be first to reach the shore and lay waste to all the sand castles and concrete hotels. And, then, a voice, that voice, a voice that he recognizes right away though so many years have come and gone.

"Remember when you were young . . ." it says.

The voice on the phone (the voice that he hears now and that he can almost see, like the shred of a ghost's smokey sheet slipping away through the cracks of the answering machine) is the voice of someone he hasn't seen in a long time, since the past millennium, since another life that was his once, but no longer. And yet, at the same time, it's the voice of someone he can't forget and has remembered often over the years, and he's even been able to adjust and age the face that corresponds to that voice, seeing photos of its owner here and there. Talking—to his surprise and mild indignation—more about Bob Dylan and Ray Davies than about Pink Floyd. The owner of the voice is, to some, a writer. And to many—as the news of what happened to him is communicated and spread—he will be, for a few hours or a few days at least, The Writer. But for him, for Tom, he'll always be Penelope's brother. And Penelope was the first love of his life, the one that wasn't meant to be and that, consequently (the laws of love challenge and trump the laws of time and space), he still feels and will continue to feel. So now, in the voice of Penelope's brother (who called him Major Tom, to bother him, but who stopped when he threatened to tell Penelope), he could hear the faint but permanent echo of the voice of Penelope (who called him Tom-Tom, the only person who ever called him that). And Tom tries hard to listen more carefully, to not miss a single detail while, from the living room, another voice reaches him, the voice of a professional TV commentator, explaining to his son and to all humanity that our hours on this planet are numbered. And that there are fewer and fewer every time we go back and count them.

Life After People is Fin's favorite TV show and it's broadcast on Fin's favorite channel: The History Channel. It's not that Fin eschews cartoons or other products targeting kids his age. But Fin prefers documentaries. He said once that he prefers "the real part" to "the invented part." Not long ago, Tom tempted him with a trip to Disney World and, first to his surprise and then admiration and subsequent fatherly pride, the answer was: "*Papi*: Disney on TV and at the movies; but Disney in real life, please, I'm asking you, I don't want to."

And, of all the many forms and types of reality, Fin seems to prefer the alternate reality of *Life After People* and its variations on the aria of a catastrophe caused not by the actions of human beings but just the opposite: by their sudden lack of action, by their absence.

What *Life After People* describes and shows and narrates is not exactly the real part, but it's not the invented part either.

What *Life After People* describes and shows and narrates is the hypothesis of what might happen to our planet if we, suddenly and without warning, were to disappear without leaving behind a trace or a body or smoking ruins. When Fin explained it to him, he decided to watch at least one episode, just to make sure it wasn't some kind of subliminal sermon of the Christian creationist-fundamentalist eschatology, etcetera. That thing about, all of a sudden, *the Rapture*: the just and the pure ascending to the heavens to "be received among the clouds" and "meet the Lord on high." But no, fortunately, everything all Darwinian and serious and documented and, yes, *realist*: impassioned but rational testimonies of ecologists, engineers, geologists, archeologists, and climatologists theorizing, in a vertiginous crescendo, about what will happen to everything we leave behind—animals and buildings and landscapes—after we've gone never to return. And the truth is that the structure and mechanics of *Life After People* is kind of addictive, producing the need in the spectator for increasingly high doses of a drug called Absence. Because in *Life After People* this is how it goes: each episode—separated by different subjects/items, like modes of transport, skyscrapers, historical monuments, military arsenals, works of art, and mummified bodies, along with many other materials and matters that, of course, don't include love, love after people, Tom after the love that he once had and that once had him—explains what's going to happen to everything we've left behind one day after our departure.

And then two and three and ten days.

And, later, one and five and twenty and a hundred and a hundred fifty and two hundred and five hundred years.

And on like that up to a thousand and ten thousand and two million years.

This predilection of Fin's for the most passive and aggressive of the apocalyptic (summed up in drawings he did at school, when the teacher asked him to draw a portrait of his family and all he turned in was the nearly blank outline of an empty house); after another drawing, for Holy Week (can someone explain to Tom what his son is doing in a religious school, where they praise Jesus Christ on the cross but, instead of INRI, it has UFO written on it?), landed him in immediate appointments with pediatricians and psychologists. The expert diagnosis (that to him, having to do with his son, so special and unique, seemed of offensive simplicity and banality) concluded that "the little boy, who in addition to having the particularity of being born to older parents," was expressing "the unconscious desire—coming to grips with the end of his parents' marriage—for the end of absolutely everything." At a parents' meeting, he didn't hesitate to offer his own theory, which, of course, further disturbed the teacher and prompted that look from his ex where she shuts her eyes as tight as she can. Of course, his ideas about the different perception of the future among today's kids (because they already live in the future and they're not interested in the classic fantasy of rockets and computers, which is why they prefer to project themselves much further, into the *terra incognita* of a new prehistory, he explained) were as warily received as they were quickly discarded while, he could intuit it, as if he were reading subtitles at her feet, the teacher thought: "Aha . . . *now* I get what's going on with the kid."

"The two of us, my son and I, really like science fiction," he said apologetically while his ex tried to help him out but not really; because then she clarified that it was he and not she who, when his son was between four and five years old, had hired as a babysitter "that ugly ugly girl who studied cosmic anthropology or something like that, and who spent all her time talking about finding irrefutable proof of intelligent life on other planets and things like that. She doesn't work for us anymore, of course."

And it's true that Tom had really liked the girl (whose name was Hilda and, yes, she was really ugly, but her ugliness was such that it came off as almost epic and noble; Hilda was the daughter of a national sex symbol who had died years ago in a car accident and a surviving father who had turned into the kind of person who shows up drunk at high school parties). And Fin had liked her too. And he was really sad to say goodbye to her. And once, through a half-open door, he'd listened to them talking, Hilda and Fin. About new theories regarding the age of the universe and its expiration date, about the probability that some day a family of meteors would crash into Earth and wipe us off the map like the dinosaurs. And Tom liked *so much* to listen to his son speak, how he speaks, using inexplicable, quasi-nineteenth century turns of phrase like "I suppose," "rather, I would say that," "now that you mention it," "perhaps you are referring to," and "one small thing." Tom wonders where all of that comes from. Or where all the characters that Fin invents come from: Ratita (a rodent who has amassed a fortune in coconuts) or Pésimo Malini, the worst magician in the world who, while performing his tricks, making things disappear, always asks the audience to close their eyes and not to open them until he tells them to, between five and ten minutes later, after he's hidden everything backstage.

Of course, Tom thinks, the thing with Fin couldn't have anything to do with his fairly limited exposure, as mentioned, to popular cartoons. Tom watched some of them with Fin—*Sponge Bob, Phineas & Ferb, South Park, The Simpsons,* and his favorite: *Monsters vs. Aliens*— * and he was surprised by their hallucinogenic potency and zapping delirium of references: it was clear to Tom that the show's young and multimillionaire creators grew up marked by multitudinous TV channels and laboratory drugs and blitzkriegs, just as their direct predecessors (The Pink Panther or Wile E. Coyote and The Roadrunner) had smoked to excess in the circular irresolution of Vietnam, or their parents (Mickey Mouse, Bugs Bunny, Tom & Jerry) had been good ol' boys disembarking on Omaha Beach and getting their booze and cigarettes via parachute drops. And again Tom catches himself thinking in a way he never thought he'd think— as if someone else were thinking for him or dictating his thoughts. And he wonders if the same thing might not happen to his son, if his son might not be a kind of loudspeaker for an interplanetary civilization and . . . Now, yes, he's thinking like himself: because science fiction was always his thing and, for a while now, according to the mother of his son, another one of the possible bad influences contaminating Fin.

And, OK, it's possible that Fin isn't normal.

But not that he's worse. Or that he has problems.

Sometimes, watching Fin without him realizing, Tom has the unsettling and hard-to-explain sensation that Fin *knows-something-he-doesn't-know*. He experienced it recently, when they were coming out of a movie theater. A movie in which humans designed gigantic robots so they could take a stand against monsters emerging from a crack in the bottom of the ocean. Or that other one that made Fin say: "*Papi*, how can it be that in the movie where Captain Kirk of the *Enterprise* is young, everything is much more technologically advanced than in the series in which Captain Kirk is already much older?" Tom wasn't really sure which of the two movies it was. But he was sure that he and Fin went running through the street, down the metro stairs, jogging across the platform at a speed that he'd never have believed himself still capable of achieving and, with undreamed grace and efficiency, they jumped into the train car just as the door slid shut. Already in their seats and heading home (so satisfied with his achievement, memorizing the day and time and name of the station, making history), he couldn't help but say to himself silently, with a shiver, something like: "This was probably the last time my body will let me do something like that." To which—as if he could clearly hear the secret frequency of his thoughts—Fin, squeezing his hand, said: "I don't think so."

Or that other time when, looking in the window display of a bookstore, they saw a small tin toy. An old toy. The kind that runs on a cord and by inserting a key and winding it up so that it moves and walks. The figure of a little man wearing a hat and carrying a suitcase. Fin looked at it for a few seconds and said, with a voice that seemed to come from very far away and seeming—like when a movie gets dubbed into another language—to not entirely correspond to the movement of his lips: "You should put that little man on the cover of your next book. In addition: you should make that little man the main character your next book *too*." Smiling, Tom pointed out that he wasn't a writer—he was a musician. Which Fin corrected: "That's here, *Papi*; but in another of the many space-time wrinkles, you're a writer. And you're very happy with *Mamá*. And *Mamá* is very happy with you. And I wear glasses. And I go to a school without priests or nuns, where everyone speaks French, *oui, monsieur*." So, after such a revelation, he—as if hypnotized—went into the store and bought the toy. And, sure, it would look really nice on a book cover and, yes, it reminded him a lot of the stylized and seductive covers of the paperbacks that he bought blindly as he emerged from childhood, judging them by their covers—as beguiling as Storm Thorgerson's designs—and always finding them innocent, and in whose pages he read H. P. Lovecraft and Jorge Luis Borges and Adolfo Bioy Casares and other strange science-fictioneers for the first time. And he bought a funny replica of the monolith from *2001: A Space Odyssey* as well, just a rectangular piece of black metal sold with the sarcastic label ACTION FIGURE: ZERO POINTS OF ARTICULATION! He doesn't know where the monolith might have ended up; but he has the little tin man, always, on top of the synthesizer in his studio and inside its box that, in loud caps, warns: ATTENTION: THIS IS NOT A TOY / FOR ADULT COLLECTORS ONLY. But it doesn't matter what it says there: Tom lends it to Fin. And Fin falls asleep with the little tin man in his hand after, every night that he sleeps at Tom's house, watching an episode of *Life After People* and, if possible, his favorite—the first episode of the second season titled: "Wrath of God."

Tom saw it for the first time the other night. He decided to watch that particular episode when, walking along the street, he was startled to hear his son, multiple times, rhythmically repeating "Kolmanskop . . . Kolmanskop . . . Kolmanskop."

And when Tom asked him what that was, Fin answered: *Life After People*. "Wrath of God."

So here is Tom—tonight, watching the DVDs of the show he bought for Fin for his last and very recent birthday, the sixth, coinciding with one year of life without him, except on weekends—to find out what Kolmanskop is.

And then he knows. The episode "Wrath of God" deals with the fragility of the religious symbols that mankind has left in the wake of its processes and processions—the Los Angeles Memorial Coliseum, the Coliseum, the Christ the Redeemer Statue, San Pedro, the glass case that houses the Shroud of Turin—and all of it leading to Kolmanskop. Because—he's already hooked, he's already a convert to *Life After People*—one of the show's discoveries, after bombarding you with digital animations anticipating a future where everything, invariably, comes crashing down due to elemental activity, is that of seeking out and finding a real place that, here and now, while we're still here, singularly reproduces the plurality of conditions of a morning when everything will be covered by a blanket of water and ice and earth and vegetation and oblivion, because nobody will be left to remember it and to make memory.

Hence Kolmanskop.

"Kolmanskop!" exclaims his son, with the happiness of it now being, once again, his turn to show his father something he doesn't know about.

And they hug.

And there they go.

To Kolmanskop.

Kolmanskop—Coleman's Hill in Afrikaans or Kolmannskuppe in German—is an abandoned mining colony in the Namibian desert, a few short kilometers inland from the port of Lüderitz. The name comes from a truck driver named Johnny Coleman, who was trapped there during a sandstorm. And, in *Life After People*, Kolmanskop corresponds to and occupies the space and category of *Fifty Years Without Us*. The narrator—over vistas of open doors and broken windows and stairways that lead nowhere; in houses that are now parts of sand dunes and homes to serpents—describes in a voice between mellifluous and implacable: "Fifty years after people, desert towns around the world are being sandblasted into oblivion . . . How do we know this? There's one forsaken place, in the middle of an ancient desert, where it *has already happened*. In fifty years without people, unstoppable forces play hell with man's legacy. In one remote desert of the world, a devil wind is methodically drowning homes and dismantling a town brick by brick. Here, a biblical plague has already arrived."

"What's 'biblical?'" his son asks.

"In general, first and foremost, it means bad news," he answers. "It gets a little better in the sequel. But not much," he adds.

And from the screen, the narrator continues:

"This is Kolmanskop, Namibia. It may seem like a hellish mirage rising from southern Africa's Namib Desert, but this is no illusion. It is one of the most remarkable sites on the planet. A town whose fate could have been ripped directly from the pages of the Old Testament. Dozens of homes and public buildings scar the desert hillside like half-buried corpses."

And the narrator continues telling the history of the place with the diction of a reverse prophet, as if precisely divining the past but never fully understanding it. For the first time, he—and his son as if it were the first time—listen to what was and look at what's left of a colony founded when, in 1903, a German railroad worker, alerted by the reflection of a ray of sunlight, found a diamond scarcely covered by a thin layer of sand. The man showed it to his boss and, lickety-split—wealthy settlement. The sand and the constant wind aren't easy to withstand; but the diamonds that "millions of years earlier erupted from the earth and were slowly scattered and blown north" compensate for any hardships with interest. And soon, a hospital is built and a ballroom and a school and a casino and an icemaker and the first street car on the continent. Because "in Kolmanskop, the workers literally plucked diamonds from the surface, often using the light of the moon." And Tom can imagine them: men and women dressed for a ball, strolling through the dunes, with their children competing for who can find and collect the most diamonds, like in a surrealist *tableau vivant*. Of course, the diamonds run out and World War One complicates things and, by 1954, the site is abandoned and is now just an attraction for strange tourists or, he thinks, fans of J. G. Ballard or Philip K. Dick, or worshippers of the new ruin and dysfunctionality of everything. An ode to entropy from a throat ravaged by thirst and cold. An architectural representation of Alzheimer's, Tom thinks: the perfect postcard of oblivion and absence as a territory regaining its virginity. Something that reminds him of something else that, presently, he remembers.

Wish You Were Here.

Crazy diamond.

"Kolmanskop looks like a Pink Floyd album cover," Tom says.

"What's a Pink Floyd?" asks Fin.

And now, oh so happy, it's the father's turn to teach his son something for a change.

And Tom goes to his studio and finds all the editions he has of Pink Floyd's *Wish You Were Here*. Many. Two vinyl and Made-in-the-UK originals: one open, so he could see everything it contains, and the other closed and virginal and still wrapped and sealed in its black shrink-wrap with the sticker where two metallic hands clasp together over seas and skies and deserts. One Made-in-the-USA edition with an alternate take from the same photo shoot in the alleys around a film studio where the man in flames greeting his friend looks somewhat more upright than in the Made-in-the-UK edition. Then, the special edition in transparent vinyl (the one that the sandman à la René Magritte is holding in one of the images on the interior sleeve), the ephemeral and quickly extinct quadraphonic species, the successive remasterings and remixes on CD (one of them gold: 20 Bit Digital SBM 24 KARAT GOLD CD CK 64405 Limited Edition Master Sound) and, just recently, the crown jewel: the equally triumphant as it is somewhat absurd Immersion Box Set titled *Ceci n'est pas une boîte*. There, no less than four CDs with alternate takes ("Have a Cigar" without the voice of interloper Roy Harper, "Wish You Were Here" with the violin of Stéphane Grappelli) and live (Wembley 1974, concerts little appreciated in their day by the expert critic who, along the way, accused David Gilmour of not washing his hair). Also, DVDs and Blu-rays with films designed by Gerald Scarfe to be projected during the live performance of the album (with vistas of red tides and men weathered by cyclones very much à la *Life After People*) in addition to a variety of objects and paraphernalia and memorabilia. Commemorative books, reproductions of tickets to opening concerts, programs (Fin's definitely going to really like the one with two extraterrestrials, contemplating the prismatic pyramid from the cover of *The Dark Side of the Moon*, marveling at the possibility of having found something with "creative energy" among the earthlings), three transparent marbles, and even a scarf! Tom, who (to the horror of the mother of his son) paid a great deal for all that treasure, told himself that the senselessness of the Immersion Box Set acquired a certain logic when justified as the discographers' only possibly strategy to combat pirating and free downloads. And now he was even happier for having bought it: because it'd be a better way to, yes, *immerse* and explain everything to Fin. Because kids, first and foremost, understand everything with their eyes. The Immersion Box would be the perfect way to explain to Fin why that music was the soundtrack of his puberty and the most important verses of his life and that they had helped Tom become who he was today.

Sure: who Tom is today isn't who Tom wanted to be then, when he was growing up.

Sure, again: Tom is a musician. That *is* what he wanted to be. But he'd wanted to be *a different class* of musician. Tom wished that he'd lived the impossibility of "being in" Pink Floyd or, at least, that his musical project in the prime of his youth, The Silver River, had amounted to something beyond a few demos with songs about walking under the rain or across rooftops. Tom wished that his band had been built to last, to continue in the times of New Wave and of MTV and of that Pink Floyd II without Roger Waters that provoked so many conflicting emotions inside Tom. Almost more than Waters as a solo act. A Pink Floyd II that, in truth, was a Pink Floyd III; because Pink Floyd I, with Syd Barrett, had lasted the length of a sigh, the length of one of those gusts of wind you hear on Pink Floyd albums. Pink Floyd I hadn't even lasted as long as The Silver River. And Tom thought that The Silver River was going to take him back to the pinnacle, back to the progressive rock of the end of his childhood. But careful: not to that ridiculous British progressive rock that (perhaps as a response to the Aquarian and Cancerous undertow of sensitive songwriters on the other side of the Atlantic) had taken refuge in epics with spirits and Tolkienesque giants, in an addiction to the conceptual, and in narcissistic excesses where keyboards were played by lashing them with whips or wielding Excalibur imitations. No, for Tom, progressive rock was distinct from and a kind of little brother to that rock that'd rolled off the rails: that rock of older cousins and young uncles and aunts and even premature parents now entering the third or fourth decade of their lives, as if entering a shadowy room after oh so many colored lights out in the open air. For Tom, true progressive rock was what'd transcended all of that and what now, yes, was *progressing*, moving in a new direction, and readying itself to no longer be the rebel music of clever teenagers leaving home in search of new and more powerful emotions, but the music for kids who had an excess of new and powerful emotions at home already. The long songs with so many parts and corners of the best progressive rock were—unlike those unadorned rock songs, brief as telegrams, sending simple messages like that you're going to lose that girl or you want to hold her hand, like you can't get no satisfaction, like you're hoping to die before you get old, like all you need is love but money can't buy it—the perfect and most practical soundtracks for those kids to hide inside of, inside the households of their young parents who, before long, realized they weren't so young anymore and that they no longer hoped to die before they got old, but who nevertheless remained exceedingly childish. Yes, progressive rock— the true and noblest of progressive rock—wasn't the music of a mythical past or of a convulsing present but the music of a chrome future that aimed for the stars, the faraway stars, as far away as possible from those homes where it was always: *Houston, we have a problem.*

Hence Tom's admiration for Pink Floyd. For having formed in the mind-bending sixties so they could, like him, make something of themselves in the mind-bent seventies. For turning the page and the sheet of the score. For the stripped-down look of Pink Floyd and for the air of productive apathy of Pink Floyd; like slacker hippies, like easy-going professionals and their own bosses (unlike The Beatles or The Rolling Stones, Roger Waters and David Gilmour and Richard Wright and Nick Mason were children of "well-to-do" families), backing up that dandy indolence with the complex mechanics of their shows, riddled with special effects and flaming airplanes and flying pigs. A technical sophistication with a *casual* elegance approximated only—just a little, not much—by Genesis, already sans the histrionic Peter Gabriel, on the cover of *Seconds Out*: a live, double album that, in addition, inside, contained the seductive version of "Firth of Fifth." A track that for a few days made Tom think and wonder (THE INSTRUMENT of progressive rock was not the electric guitar but the synthesizer, many synthesizers stacked like geologic layers and played with arms outstretched, as if from the trenches of arpeggios) whether he'd actually rather be the exhibitionist Tony Banks instead of the subtle and unsurpassable and little-considered Richard Wright. Luckily for him (Yes and their covers anticipating the *Avatar* silliness and Jon Anderson's little voice were never a problem; Mike Oldfield was a species of Pink Floyd crossed with Liberace; King Crimson and Van der Graaf Generator were too hermetic and virtuosic; and the truth is that Ian Anderson and his flute and his shepherd stork poses make you feel a little embarrassed for him, like an undesirable drunk uncle whom you can't, though you'd like nothing better, not invite to the family party), all those diversions, products of adolescent hormonal curiosity, didn't last long. And Tom returned to his same desert oasis as always. Pink Floyd was unique, they began and ended in Pink Floyd. Their music—their harmonic climates and sonic sequences—remained classically modern and modernly classic; * so much more transcendent and serious and relaxed than that of today's Pink Floyd for emos, the stiff and solemn and oh so self-conscious Radiohead. Radiohead who were like someone *pretending* to be Pink Floyd: kind of picking or stroking or just staring at their instruments. (All of a sudden—why?—he hated Radiohead *so much*, a hate he'd never felt before confronting the imagined image of their singer—his name is Thom? What's the point of that *h* in *Thom*?—with lowered lashes, shaking in a little epileptic dance in one of his music videos, dancing perfectly awfully so that everyone who doesn't know how to dance imitates him and thinks that they're so cool dancing so awfully and their admiration for Radiohead is renewed and reinforced. And he makes an effort to stop thinking about Radiohead and Arcade Fire and all the complex and self-indulgent and "artistic" bands, so he can keep thinking about Pink Floyd. It's a minimal effort; it takes almost no effort at all.)

And Tom liked to think that—recording their first album, in EMI's Abbey Road studios, a wall between them and The Beatles, who were there fine tuning *Sgt. Pepper's Lonely Hearts Club Band*—Pink Floyd had peeked in on that hurricaning orchestral crescendo that breaks apart and brings to a close "A Day in the Life." And that Pink Floyd *got* it. Like someone receiving the code to the understanding of all things. Pink Floyd would be not just a band but a brand, something that transcended their individualities: Pink Floyd would be like one of those alien creatures, like one of those extraterrestrial intelligences, not particularly interested in invading or destroying but content to float, in orbit. A celestial body that, had it been spotted by the Russians before the Americans, who elevated it to the level of Supernova, might well have been christened Comet Oblomov. A flying object, unidentified except for its name, which meant nothing.

Pink Floyd, whose name had sprung from the fusion of the names of two bluesmen and, yes, the beginning of "Shine On You Crazy Diamond" was very bluesy, and that of "Wish You Were Here" very country; but country & blues as if filtered through a teletransporter of intergalactic and bidimensional matter. Pink Floyd, who had lost their first leader—Syd Barrett, "aSyd" Barrett—on a one-way acid trip that left him with kaleidoscopic eyes like two black holes in the sky of his face. Pink Floyd, who had, without Syd Barrett, gone on to become a successful band and, in 1973, a universally consecrated cult band with *The Dark Side of the Moon*: music about how to go mad. And, not knowing what to do afterward, in 1975, and after several frustrated attempts (like a ridiculous project of recording an entire album with the sounds of domestic appliances and objects), Pink Floyd, after many hours of playing darts with a compressed air rifle or venting frustration with squash shots, had gone on to record *Wish You Were Here*—the perfect sequel to *The Dark Side of the Moon*. Music for someone who no longer knew how to come back from madness. Syd Barrett invoked again. The Crazy Diamond they wish were here. And (Tom had read and seen it so many times, in biographies of the band and in documentaries about the gestation of *Wish You Were Here* and its leftovers, which would be mutated and bestialized via the Moreau/Orwell method for their next album, *Animals*) wish granted. But— ah, as often happens with granted wishes in the best stories of genies or deals with the devil—not entirely how they wished or in their best interest.

In the spring of 1975, the 5th of June, the band is in the studio celebrating David Gilmour's wedding and suffering Roger Waters's divorce and, after years of not being seen, Syd Barrett reappears in Abbey Road, while his ex band mates are recording the live requiem-suite of "Shine On You Crazy Diamond," dedicated to him. And in the exact moment that David Gilmour sings the part that goes "Nobody knows where you are, how near or how far," a door opens and Syd Barrett—there, near and not far—materializes to ask when it's his turn to "put in" his guitar parts. And Syd Barrett no longer looks like the Lord Byron that he once was, but like a kind of Homer Simpson—yellowish skin, fat, bald, with the air of a zombie, his eyebrows shaved, stuffed into a white and dirty and wrinkled suit—whom Waters and Gilmour and Mason and Wright don't recognize at first. Uncomfortable and shaken, they make him listen to "Shine On You Crazy Diamond" to see what he thinks. Barrett limits himself to murmuring that "It sounds a little old, right?" And he adds, sounding almost anticipatorily like the enumerative and alienated Pink in his hotel room on Side 3 of *The Wall*, that "I have a color TV and a refrigerator. I have pork chops in the refrigerator, but the pork chops run out all the time and then I buy more pork chops. Until they run out."

Then, as he came, Syd Barrett goes.

And his friends are left there to cry. And to record. And, with time, Waters and Gilmour think that that might have been the moment, after wrapping up *Wish You Were Here* (that in the beginning didn't entirely win over the critics, that reaches number one in sales on both sides of the Atlantic when it's released, and that time and perspective and distance elevate as their unanimous and indisputable crowning achievement), the exact and perfect time for the band to break up. The precise instant—from which there was no going back—to conclude their life cycle, with that ode to the omnipresent absent friend. And that way avoid the imminent ex-friendships resulting from the convulsive and revulsive recordings of *Animals* and *The Wall* and *The Final Cut*. To go, to let go, with those airs bottled in the fullest of emptinesses, the absolute and joyously sad emptiness of their lyrics and music. With that magic moment—at the end of "Welcome to the Machine" and the beginning of "Wish You Were Here"—when someone seemed to be trying to tune in a radio, the one in David Gilmour's car. And you heard voices and a few bars of Tchaikovsky's Symphony No. 4. And suddenly all the sound drops, like a candle blown out for the birthday of an era. A pause that it took Tom many listens (staring intently at the needle above the grooves, trying to see what was happening) to grasp wasn't a potential defect in his parents' stereo equipment reacting to some secret frequency so that then, after the entrance of that vintage acoustic guitar solo, everything would climb again, like the highest of rising of tides.

And all of it wrapped in the cover design of Storm Thorgerson, one of the patrons of the Hipgnosis graphics studio and someone who, for Tom, was like Pink Floyd's fifth member—the graphic design equivalent of George Martin's musical influence on The Beatles. Storm Thorgerson—official agent of the band's image, in times when, as Thorgerson himself always pointed out with the pride of an artisan, "Photoshop didn't exist"—had *also* achieved an insuperable pinnacle with his work on *Wish You Were Here*. Various tests and images to "represent absence," the album's diffuse theme, which doesn't take long to impose itself with the force of something that's no longer present but that you can't stop seeing and missing. Like postcards sent nowhere so that nobody receives them and they're returned to sender charged with new meaning: the swimmer run aground, the man in flames, the suspended diver, that red veil floating in the green and blue breeze of a forest under the sky, the clasp of robotic hands melting together in the desire never to part. Life after people.

Every so often, less and less, but without ever really letting it go, Tom dreamed of another life in which The Silver River had been a success, in which they'd done collaborations with members of Pink Floyd, and had Storm Thorgerson among their ranks. And wasn't it odd, maybe a strange sign meant for him alone, that the new Pink Floyd album, after so many years of silence and assembled now around Wright's ghost, was named *The Endless River*? Then he woke himself up, searching for ways, while awake, to get as close as possible to that impossible dream.

Tom had made a special trip—taking advantage of his honeymoon—to London, in 2005, to Live 8 in Hyde Park, to witness the Pink Floyd reunion. Roger Waters no longer had that caveman aspect of his youth (now he looked more like a kind of Mr. Hyde for a hypothetical version of Stevenson's classic with Richard Gere as Dr. Jekyll); David Gilmour, far now from his beginnings as a long-haired weirdo, had acquired the intimidating look of a veteran yet still quite dangerous marine; Nick Mason was like a fugitive of the Monty Python troupe (following in the tradition where—after Ringo Starr and like Keith Moon and so many others—drummers are almost obligated to be oddballs); and Rick Wright retained his increasingly fragile melancholic air, like an actor/character in a decadent Edwardian novel, adapted by the BBC. That same Wright who, in 1996, had the gall to record a solo album, *Broken China*, about his wife's depression, that was virtually a marital remake of *Wish You Were Here*, with a Storm Thorgerson cover that gave a wink, between mischievous and solemn, to the cover design of *Wish You Were Here* (again, that diver in the trance of his dive, perfectly immobile and vertical, posed *like that*, without tricks of photography) but that ended up looking almost like a discomfiting nervous tic, a falsification clumsily executed by the original artist. And it showed that both he and his bandmates were still unable to separate themselves from the specter of Barrett and the way that, time and again, his ghost—actually a medium—invoked them. And invoked his Great Theme in Pink Floyd: mental disturbance as beautiful art. And they seemed so sad, so melancholic (Waters's apparent and almost wild happiness had the unmistakable pathological quality of people desperate for the ephemera of happiness), so trapped by the sound of their past, which was the sound of Tom's past and present and future. And, yes, they still sounded really good. So much better than any of the festival's other participants. And then they played a song called "Wish You Were Here," and Tom—standing amid thousands and thousands of concertgoers and on millions and millions of TVs—felt they were playing it for him alone. For Tom, who was a musician, but—his fantasies had been translated into reality in a rather oblique way—a musician belonging to a subgenre known as "news music." A kind of avant-garde, in the end.

An ex-member of The Silver River—who was now a millionaire TV producer—had reappeared in his life, contacting him in the studio where Tom worked composing advertising jingles, and proposed the idea of doing a "cool news program" and, in the process, the guy ended up seducing the mother of his son. An affair, which, though he didn't say it and wouldn't dare admit it, hadn't bothered or hurt Tom all that much. Just the opposite, he now considered it the only ace up his sleeve, something he could use to control and keep the mother of his son in line, who, of course, felt no guilt with respect to him and the situation, but who did worry about what everyone else would say. So, threatening to submit him to a battery of psychological tests where "your autistic side" would be readily apparent, she'd managed to take Fin with her (and to attenuate her condition as adulteress but, to tell the truth, seeking a "more healthy and more abundant and more comfortable environment" so her son could grow up "wanting for nothing"). And, in the process, to establish a fragile and fraught truce with him, like the Cold War, like one of those wars that, in the opening minutes of the news, is always about to break out.

And the "product" proposed by his ex-bandmate who made an ex of his wife was called *New(s)*. And, among its special features, there was Tom—a live keyboardist who musicalized the news *in situ*. Like those player-piano piano players accompanying silent movies in the early days of movie theaters. So, on the screen, live and direct, Monday through Friday, Tom—doing as he was told—shot out mischievous winks and blind quotations and musicalized references for connoisseurs, while behind him, like on a Pink Floyd tour, images were projected. Airplane accident music, red carpet music, citizen protest music, bombed cities music, soccer music (Tom, after a few too many drinks, would tirelessly remind anyone in the vicinity, over and over, that the closing music composed by Vangelis for the end of the first version of *Blade*

Runner was used over and over by TV sports programs; which is why what he did wasn't *that* far away from the sci-fi progression), beauty queen music, someone going into a McDonald's with a machine gun music, environmental catastrophe music.

So, in the sign-off, in the moment when he says goodbye to everyone, after the weather forecast, when the news is starting to get old, when there's only time for one final update, generally something "colorful," Tom—by his own express wish, almost a personal request—had gotten to "musicalize" the death of Syd Barrett. And of Rick Wright. And of Storm Thorgerson. And Tom had always done it with those dissolving flourishes at the end of the final and ninth part of "Shine On You Crazy Diamond," with which the circle came to a close. There, some Rick Wright improvisations over— both composed by Barrett—"See Emily Play," the band's second single that describes a girl sleeping in a meadow after having taken LSD; or sometimes, when he played it live, "Arnold Layne," the band's first single, which told the story of a man who spent his time stealing women's underwear that were hung out to dry on a clothesline.

Pink Floyd who . . .

How was he going to transmit all of this to Fin, all these echoes and heratbeats, all this melancholic passion? With the charged and adolescent prose, packed with titles and names and styles and dates, of rock journalism—because all rock listeners are kind of rock journalists—in which he thought about Pink Floyd? Impossible. Useless. Idiotic. Not recommended. Besides, it was even possible that Fin, having listened to Pink Floyd since he was a baby without knowing who or what Pink Floyd was, had absorbed all of it—in the same way that Tom had subliminally absorbed The Beatles when his parents listened to them—and that he understood Pink Floyd even better than Tom did. And no: Tom wasn't ready for that sort of a revelation. And the mother of his son, no doubt, would get really upset when Fin told her that "*Papi* started to talk about Pink Floyd all the time and it seemed like he was talking to himself." So, better, as Tom puts on *Wish You Were Here* as background and surface music, tentative close-ups, partial zooms: to give Fin (under strict supervision, and so that his first dose of "conscious" Pink Floyd enters more through his eyes, with a little help from our friend Storm Thorgerson) everything contained, like a jack-in-the-box, inside the

Immersion Box Set, *Ceci n'est pas une boîte.* So that Fin could tear into it the way he rips open the envelopes containing his beloved Golactuses.

Sometimes, at the end of the weekend, when Tom returns to the empty flat and gets into bed, he discovers that Fin has left behind, between the sheets or under a pillow, a Golactus to keep him company in his absence. The Golactuses are small plastic and collectable aliens, arrayed in a complex system of castes and powers and colors and textures. They come in envelopes, two per envelope. Fin has, like, two hundred of them—all the models from all the planets. And the other day he said, in the voice of the narrator of *Life After People*, that "maybe the Golactuses are *real extraterrestrials for real and seriously*, infiltrating homes across the Earth, waiting to be reanimated, zap!, by an invisible ray from a distant galaxy and to take over . . ." In the same voice that, as Tom enters the living room with his *Wish You Were Here* box set under his arm, Fin says: "*Papi*, the phone is making a weird noise."

And there is something that all true Pink Floyd fans don't dare admit openly, but that, with the door locked and the blinds drawn, so nobody sees or hears it, they think all the time in whispers: it was lucky that Syd Barrett had gone mad and had left the band almost without knowing what he was doing, lost forever in the sweetness of the acid. Because in light—in the glimmers—of what you hear about the band's exceedingly venerated debut and Syd Barret's 1967 farewell, *The Piper at the Gates of Dawn*, a Pink Floyd fronted by a lucid Syd Barret would've been a very different Pink Floyd, much easier to fit in a category with other bands. A Pink Floyd with simpler and funnier songs. A more childish and playful Pink Floyd. A Pink Floyd much happier to be Pink Floyd. A Pink Floyd not in conflict with its past and its present and its future and who never would've recorded *Wish You Were Here* or all those songs about the *horror vacui* of being a dead rock star still radiating light. A Pink Floyd that—for the children of Tom's generation—would never have functioned as the most precise and perfect ambient music in times of divorcist futurism: the arguments and the sounds of doors opening and closing between tracks on Pink Floyd's albums a distraction from the other shouts and other slamming doors in the houses where the Pink Floyd albums played.

And there was never a more futuristic time, Tom thinks, than his past, his childhood.

Suddenly, everything was scientific and fictitious. TV was overrun with black and white shows and series with spaceships and faraway planets and twilight zones where there's always someone who, on their own, realizes that they're not alone or that they're more alone than ever. The first golden glimmers of the genre, with cosmic adventurers and Martian princesses and atomic paranoia, with hapless individuals who grow or shrink or transform into something else, had opened up time and space (in that decade between 1965 and 1975; because decades, Tom had always thought, actually begin and end in the middle of the decade) for some strange years, mixed, frontier, borderland years. Times when nothing was entirely clear, when terrestrial computers went mad, and extraterrestrial presences never revealed themselves to aged astronauts who died only to be reborn on their return trip home.

Tom had gone to see *2001: A Space Odyssey* for the first time because of his parents, who'd bought him a ticket and left him there, promising to come back and get him at the end of the movie. And Tom wasn't the only spacio-temporal orphan for those two hours and forty minutes.

2001: A Space Odyssey had become the perfect movie for parents to deposit their kids at and where those kids would then be submitted to the radioactiv-ity of unsolvable mystery. A movie that began with prehistory and ended with the future at the far reaches of the universe. And, ah, there was that moment when the simian, more man all the time, threw the tapir bone into the air and it turned into a spaceship and Tom, with time, learned that was called an *ellipsis*; a name that, of course, sounded *so much* like the title of a song or an album by Pink Floyd. And Tom also knew that Stanley Kubrick had contacted Pink Floyd to see if they would let him use music from *Atom Heart Mother* (1970): number two in Tom's pinkfloydian ranking, also his second favorite cover, which Storm Thorgerson had defined as the most perfect "unpsychedelic non-cover." No temptation to deform its image or to add a green and phosphorescent glow to the animal. "Just totally a cow" that nobody can stop looking at and where everyone, almost desperately, tries to find a hidden message, a transcendent truth.

The *Atom Heart Mother* cow was a little bit like the monolith from *2001: A Space Odyssey*—it could be and mean anything. That cow could be every-thing or nothing. That cow might have come to stay or might just be pass-ing through. And Stanley Kubrick had called Pink Floyd because he was interested in using parts of *Atom Heart Mother*—of the balletic suite from side A—to have it play inside the disturbed head of Alex in *A Clockwork Orange*. Pink Floyd had assented initially, but changed their minds when they found out that Stanley Kubrick would be "fragmenting" their music. And years later Stanley Kubrick would deny Roger Waters authorization to insert several lines of dialogue from *2001: A Space Odyssey* into his solo album *Amused to Death* (1992). Habitual conspirators, always on the hunt for a secret story between the wrinkles in history, recommend listening to the section of astronaut Dave Bowman's cosmic trip in synch with "Echoes" from *Meddle* (1971) to "discover beyond a shadow of doubt" that it was inserted by Pink Floyd as calculated background music, crashing Stanley Kubrick's party without asking permission.

Still—true or false, coincidence or misunderstanding—for Tom, Pink Floyd and *2001: A Space Odyssey* were two faces of the same body, two clues to the same enigma. And—just as John Lennon once claimed—Tom, since he was a kid (always playing and replaying it) and up to the present day (*2001: A Space Odyssey* had been the first VHS and the first DVD and the first Blu-ray that Tom had bought), doesn't let a week go by without rewatching, as if for the first time, that Stanley Kubrick film. A perfect film whose only—and in its own perverse way, also perfect—imperfection was its title, already past tense and out of style. Tom had viewed it, first when he was a boy, as the strangest and most moving film that he'd seen up to that point. And he still viewed it, now, as the best way of relaying the news that mankind had taken a giant and mysterious evolutionary leap elsewhere. But first and foremost and when all is said and done, it'd been watching *2001: A Space Odyssey* (which the mother of his son had always considered "almost as incomprehensible as you") where Tom had met the two people who would become the writer and the writer's sister.

So, the third time he saw the movie, an early and nearly deserted showing at Saturday theater for re-releases, Tom, already in his seat, had noticed how a boy his own age, about ten years old, with the whole theater empty, had sat down right beside him, to his right, followed by a girl, around six years old, who occupied the seat to his left. The two of them, flanking him, like a prisoner, so he couldn't escape.

When the show was over and on his way home, Tom had sensed, nervous, that the boy and the girl were following him, not even concerned about trying to hide it. Every time Tom turned around, there they were, hands in the pockets of long and old-fashioned winter coats, smiling at him. Tom, more worried all the time, entered his apartment building with the key his parents had entrusted to him and, inside the lobby, he turned and saw them watching him, still watching him after having followed him there, out in the street, on the other side of the door, like astronauts outside the space shuttle, wearing a single smile (there was no doubt they were brother and sister) that began on the mouth of one and ended on the mouth of the other.

Tom, shuddering, went up in the elevator and just as he entered his apartment he heard the phone start to ring and, frightened, he thought: "It must be them . . . The invaders."

And now, so many years later, Fin says: "*Papi*, the phone is making a weird noise." And Tom is sure that, in some way, it's them, once more, again, it's them all over again. And Tom picks up the receiver of his red telephone, and hears that voice singing in his ear, that line that goes "Remember when you were young . . .

. . . you shone like the sun." And Tom listens and remembers when he was young and he shone like the sun. And he thinks about how to explain to Fin a life without him, a life without Fin, a life before Fin.

To explain to Fin a childhood that's not Fin's is even more complicated than educating him on progressive rock and Pink Floyd and *Wish You Were Here*. Like all kids his age (and though he handles very complex concepts like of parallel and alternate dimensions), it's hard for Fin to imagine that Tom was once like him, his size, little and a little boy. Fin doesn't really believe the photos that Tom shows him where he's sizes Extra Small and Small and Medium, where he already looks somewhat but not much like who he is now. "That's not you," Fin says to him with an almost pitying smile.

And he's right. That's not him. Tom can't even explain to himself the past existence of that other Tom, who still exists somewhere and who returns now and to whom he now returns. Like how that younger Tom returned to that same theater the following Saturday to see that same movie and there they were again and now they come over and introduce themselves and say (the boy): "Let's stop wasting time and be inseparable once and for all" and (the girl): "Affirmative. All systems are go."

And from then on, yes, inseparable.

And they discover that they (the boys) go to the same boys' school, a school surrounded by ruins of other buildings and soon-to-be demolished itself; but that (Tom and the boy) are in different classrooms and, because of that aberration of space, they've never even crossed paths at recess. And that the girl attends a girls' school a couple blocks away. And that it's clear that they were destined to meet and to know and to welcome each other aboard the *Discovery One*, bound for Jupiter, on the hunt for a nonhuman signal broadcast from the Tycho lunar crater by a monolith of extraterrestrial origin. And the three of them are constantly trading theories. And they pretend that one of them is the inhuman and cold and calculating astronaut Dave Bowman (generally Tom), the boy always has dibs on Dr. Heywood Floyd (the one who travels, swaying and weightless, to the bars of *The Blue Danube* and speaks by videophone to his daughter from the orbiting station), and the girl (something that should've disturbed Tom from the very first moment, and that *did* disturb him very quickly) demands time and again to put a red circle on her face like a mask, and to cause the whole LIFE FUNCTIONS TERMINATED thing to happen, and to play the sensitive and disconcerted machine HAL 9000, and to sing "Daisy . . . Daisy . . ." and to say goodbye with a "My mind is going . . ." in the red room where its hard drive is being erased one memory at a time. But he's not so disturbed that he stops playing. And the boy already wants to be a writer (and he demands that they call him not by his name but, simply "the writer"). And the girl is the writer's sister (because she hates her name that "I forbid you not only from pronouncing but also from thinking; and he obeys and forgets that her name is Penelope). And the three of them are and will be—for the next three years—once and for all, yes, inseparable. And bound by the love of Pink Floyd and the love of science fiction. And many years later Tom would read a novel written by the writer—"not *of* science-fiction but yes *with* science-fiction"—and he'd discover in it, almost word for word, several of his own theories about the genre and its environs.

And the three of them read science fiction books and see science fiction movies with Pink Floyd playing in the background. And they go to see *Solaris*, the Soviet *2001: A Space Odyssey*, and "it's not *that* good but not bad either." And they visit each other's houses as if leaping from one asteroid to another. And Tom's parents (who are as normal and common as two people who come together to create a third person can be) can't believe that the parents of the writer and the writer's sister are that famous pair of models who plow the waters of the world, aboard a sailboat, promoting a brand of cigarettes. So, the two parent-models aren't model-parents and aren't home much. And the writer and his sister are cared for by a team of professional servants who, for some strange reason, obeying the instructions left by the absent masters of the house, serve them Patty-brand hamburgers with Maggi-brand mashed potatoes (the powdered kind) over and over. And so Tom starts to spend weekends at his friends' house after reading the movie listings in the paper to see if *2001: A Space Odyssey* is showing. And, if it's not showing anywhere, they stay at home, and that's where they see *The Bride of Frankenstein* for the first time and they feel a curious excitement discovering the oddity of its "period" introduction, where Percy Bysshe Shelley and Lord Byron and Mary Shelley ("Who are these people," they wonder) talk about the story of *Frankenstein*, setting the scene, then without warning or logic, everything leaps into the future, to 1931, when the movie was filmed and first premiered. And then the writer's sister suggests they read the original novel and they read it and then follow it up with *The Last Man* and Mary Shelley's journals (the unnamable Penelope, whom Tom already loves so much, learns by heart that line where the author, carrying with her the ashes, drowned and wet with her tears, of the burning heart of her dead love, moans "feeling myself the last relic of a beloved race, my companions extinct before me") and after, on her own and to take a break from all those light years, the writer's sister decides to spend some time in the dark years of *Wuthering Heights*. And she forbids them to read it because "it will be my book, this book will be mine and only mine" (and Tom reads it in secret and without saying anything to her, to feel closer to her, to be the Heathcliff to her Cathy). And they all discover, amazed, the reissue of a sci-fi comic that, for once, doesn't take place in Metropolis or Gotham City but in the city where they live, surprisingly snowy and deadly; and they feel the pain of those poetic invaders who have been, to force them to invade, injected by their superiors with a "terror gland" that will activate and kill them if they demonstrate the unforgivable debility of being afraid and questioning their mission. And they laugh a great deal at the ridiculousness of David Bowie's Spiders from Mars and they're outraged by "Space Oddity," but somewhat appeased by "Is There Life on Mars?" And this is what the three fantastics are up to when the parents of the writer and the writer's sister come home from a trip one Saturday afternoon. And just before disappearing for good, not leaving this time but being taken never to return, they bring them the gift of (for all three of them, because they already consider Tom one of them, almost another son, whom they see just as infrequently as the other two) a projector and several film canisters and an imported record. And the record, freshly released, is *Wish You Were Here* by Pink Floyd and the film inside one of those canisters is, of course, Stanley Kubrick's *2001: A Space Odyssey*. But the one and the other and the other of them know that the one and the other—the record and the film—really belong more to them than to Pink Floyd or Stanley Kubrick. And so, happy (with that kind of happiness that makes you blind to all the unhappinesses that circle around you, like sharks waiting for a drop of blood to be spilled; not even an inkling that very soon they won't ever see each other again, that pretty soon everyone will be singing "Chiquitita" by ABBA, and that everything will be altered, as if by the action of a black hole devouring all light), the three of them feel like lords of the world and masters of the universe.

And they're young.

And they shine like the sun.

And don't ever forget it.

"*Papi*, the phone is making a weird noise," his Fin says. And Tom goes over and brings the receiver to his ear and what he hears is a noise that, yes, is weird but not at all unfamiliar. It's a sound that Tom knows to perfection. It's the noisy sound, ascending and apocalyptic, described by John Lennon, when he requested it from George Martin, as "a sound like the end of the world" and some time later, retrospectively, as "a little *2001*." It's the sonorous noise that comes at the middle and again at the end of "A Day in the Life" on The Beatles' *Sgt. Pepper's Lonely Hearts Club Band* and it's, also, the triumphal intro to the voice that comes after it and starts to sing "Remember when you were young, you shone like the sun . . ." and then, with a quick chuckle, continues "I'm calling you after so much time because you've got to know where I am and what I'm about to do, what I'm already doing, what I did; because now all times are one for me. Now, I no longer have time, I'm atemporal" and that now proceeds without stopping so that he, the receiver seemingly fused to his ear, can't help but listen:

"Yes, yes, yes . . . It's me, my friend: *Ground Control to Major Tom* . . . The Ghost of Christmas Past. Ho Ho Ho. Floating through time and space, happily multidimensional. Here and there and everywhere. *My God, I'm full of stars!*, like the astronaut said, ha, ha, ha. And now I am pure voice, like poor Douglas Rain. Think of it, Tom: years of study and training as a classical and Shakespearean actor. And to end up being universally recognized as the voice of the confused computer HAL 9000. That's me, now, The Voice. But I'm not confused. And, of course, forgive me these exceedingly brief sentences. Like the ones our favorite supercomputer uttered while shutting down, forgetting itself, singing. The kind of things that my parents said to each other or that my parents said in raised voices after a glitch in one of their fight-loops: *Just what do you think you're doing? . . . I honestly think you ought to sit down calmly, take a stress pill, and think things over . . . I know I've made some very poor decisions recently . . . I've still got the greatest enthusiasm and confidence in the mission . . . And I want to help you . . . I'm afraid . . . I'm afraid . . .* Sentences that have nothing to do with those long and sinuous comet tails I always used to write. It's because I'm just getting started and it's a little difficult. Adapting to this new life. A life beyond life. But everything will move, will fly, will float. I'm in my own prehistory, I'm like that anthropoid Moon-Watcher, *crying for the moon*, but already ready to throw my tapir bone into the skies. Everything goes so fast . . . And I'm sure that very soon I'll have at my disposal all the genres and all the words I desire. At last, my friend: I've achieved it. No longer a simple fiction writer. Now, at last, a science fiction character. Billy Pilgrim! Antiterra! Interzone! William Burroughs! *Here, there, and everywhere*. There's no time because there's all the time in the world and, from there, from that eternal then, you can see everything that's happened. The official versions and the alternate versions. Pink Anderson and Floyd Council held up by their sad Piedmont-sound guitars, yes, but also one Pink Floyd who, after first accusing him of being disrespectful and a drunk, cut the throat of another young man, one Cornelius Snowden, at the exit to mass at a Methodist Church in Abbeville, Philadelphia, a long time ago now, in another end. Now I begin. *Racing around to come up behind you again.* And my beginning is clear. That's for sure. It all begins tonight, Christmas night. In Switzerland. Fatherland of Frankenstein. Ideal location for the unleashing of monstrosities. Inside a colossal particle accelerator. Some call it a "collider." It makes no difference. Surely you've read about it. The irrepressible desire to reproduce a presumably controlled environment with the exact conditions of the universe's Ground Zero, its founding instant, its mysterious lightning bolt, its *Once upon a time* . . . What was it that Mark Twain said near the end of his life and work? Ah, yes: something about how the only thing that mattered in the reality of how things had come to have time and space was on the order of "a kind of atmospheric connection," advising "When in doubt tell the truth" and warning "When I was younger, I could remember anything, whether it had happened or not; but my faculties are decaying now and soon I shall be so I cannot remember any but the things that never happened." So, telling the part in which everything is invented and accepting the most distant past as a form of definitive futurism. It no longer matters what's yet to come, only what was and how it happened. A *whodunit* more along the lines of the detective novel than the sci-fi novel. Returning to the scene of the crime. Reproducing the beginning of everything while at the same time assuming the risk and responsibility of bringing about the end of all things. The Higgs Boson, the God Particle and all of that. But now I am God. The particle God of everyone. Even you. And you probably already noticed it a little. Me inside you. In your thoughts. Thinking nonsense. Telephonic diatribes. Animated drawings. Radiohead in your head that's now just a radio that I tune in at will and where I intervene. Whenever I feel like it. I promise not to do it often, in your case. I always liked you. You always caused me a little pain. Falling in love with Penelope. With the madness of Penelope, with a wuthering height. A brave man. A romantic. And from what I see, from what I *read* inside of you (because now your thoughts are for me like those songs that you learn by heart the first time you hear them), you're still in love with her. Which isn't without a certain narrative coherence: because she's madder than ever, a consummate tourist of white-walled rooms and model of jackets with too many straps. And that's why I'm here today, Major Tom, to give you the most painful yet necessary of Christmas gifts. Something not to make you forget her but to make you wish you didn't remember her anymore. Take your protein pills and put your helmets on and away we go. And, yes, remember. And now it's not that I remember many things, I remember *everything.* Events, feelings, words that were said or thought. And, suddenly, I see it and I feel it and I hear it and I smell it and I touch it: my sentences grow longer as my memories stretch out from yesterday to reach my today. I recall and I remember the way we were back then, in that school surrounded by demolished buildings. Buildings that were coming down, one at a time, to allow for the expansion of something that would be—and, oh, how those running the show proclaimed it, almost with the voices of ancient Babylonian engineers— "The Widest Avenue in the World." Soon, only our school was still standing, until the last minute, like a perfectly preserved archeological relic in a world where everything had been destroyed and abandoned. Kolmanskop! But let's go back: amid cliffs and caves and cables and doors and stairways leading nowhere, you and I and Penelope pretended we were on another planet that was on this one. And, when night fell, before going home, we said goodbye to that great and terrible landscape with a "We finally really did it. You maniacs! You blew it up! Ah, damn you! God damn you all to hell!" surrounded by monkeys and gorillas, in a city on the brink of self-destruction. Complicated times, my friend. Remember? The air was like nitroglycerin and anything could agitate it or cause agitation. Remember our young and quasi-subversive music teacher? The one who liked Pink Floyd too but preferred Joan Baez? The one who, for the closing ceremony at the end of the school year, taught us to sing, a bunch of ten-year-olds, fists in the air, in front of parents and authorities, a fierce song she wrote about standing up to the bulldozers that would be coming to finish off our beloved school? Remember how that teacher was fired in front of everyone, by indignant parents and the school principal, who smoked Virginia Slim cigarettes? Do you remember the absurd pride it gave us that our school, which bore the name of the well-known patriot of independence, Garvasio Vicario Cabrera, was the top primary school in the district? Remember the impossible care we took to keep our front teeth white and that blue and sticky substance, like The Blob, that we used to fix our hair, to hide our pop hairdos that were never to extend more than two centimeters past the tie-ringed necks of our shirts? Remember when they sat a hundred of us students down to watch, in the auditorium, on a single TV, the moment of the moon landing, of the one small step and the one giant leap? Remember that huge covered patio where we ate lunch and where, after meals that were generally forgettable, we were instructed to put ourselves in something that doesn't figure in yoga manuals and much less the Kama Sutra, but that was called the "resting position"? Remember: arms crossed on top of the table, head seeming to sink into that crater, waiting, surrounded by whispers and if you maintain the most absolute stillness and best behavior, for a voice over the loudspeaker to call the number of your table and you and your eight tablemates (one of whom might even have fallen asleep; like that really unlucky boy, the one with the older brother "with problems") would be the first to get to go outside for the longest and most digestive of recesses? Remember walking home to our houses? Remember when we walked by that theater and stole the photos of *2001* from its doors? Remember how it all began? I do. And now you do too. Now, the howl of the void is all. Now we're about to start over and over again and I'm the projector and the screen and the movie that you see, sitting in the shadows, in the most restful of restless positions. Now my sci-fi life begins; and when is it that science fiction, my new home, begins? Just thinking this floods me with possibilities. Some said *One Thousand and One Nights*. Vladimir Nabokov claimed that the beginning arrived with *The Tempest*. It could also be said that science fiction is not strictly a genre but a defense mechanism: the mendacious comfort of telling a thousand variations of the future, because we have no way of knowing the unique and singular truth of what will happen to us once we're there. So, putting the future in writing or filming it time after time, we deceive ourselves into thinking we possess the power to remember it . . . I don't know . . . I really like the writer Damon Knight's definition: "Science fiction is what I point to when I say *science fiction*." But consensus and diplomacy have sought and found the comfortable and practical accord of affirming that the lightning bolt and the let there be life of the matter are in Switzerland, where I was until a short time ago. In Switzerland, but in 1818, where I could go with a snap of the fingers I no longer have. On the stormy night that brings to life Mary Shelley's *Frankenstein*, imagined in a time of occultists and grave robbers and resurrectionists and worshipers of electricity, delving into the previously forbidden interior of dead bodies. Touching organs and reading the almost unknown map of intestines to trace new navigational charts. The electric body, yes. My body now. And here. A while before eternity. All I had to do was subdue the guide who never imagined that I'd subdue him. (I had to subdue him, reduce him, first—Mishima Banzai Bushido!—so I could, yes, expand myself later.) And grab his gun and lock myself in a room that can only be opened from inside and push the modern red button (as red as your old telephone, yes, I can see it) and presto! Have you seen pictures of the particle accelerator/collider? Do you know how it works? It's like the childhood fantasy of a writer in the golden age of sci-fi or like the childish fantasy of a writer like myself who—in case you don't know—always inserted sci-fi into his books that weren't sci-fi books. The realized fantasy in which science, for once, imitates fiction and does something extraordinary and worthy of the cover of *Amazing Stories* or *Astounding Stories*. A BIG machine in times of miniaturization. Something colossal. The *story*, finally, made *History*. And I—who was well-informed, who'd read treatises on quantum physics and dark matter and the great luminous successes of Marvel Comics until I knew them by heart—arrived here in my journalist disguise, concealing the of a crazy mutant. And I'd learned what could happen if you did things really badly. Something like the cover of Pink Floyd's *Ummagumma*. The band members switching positions in ever-smaller photographs, one inside the other. *Ad infinitum*. Like in a *mise en abyme*. Like a Droste Effect. Fractal geometry. Disturbances of reality. You'll already know all of this. Like the "infinite regression" that Dr. Otto Hasslein proposes in *Escape from the Planet of the Apes*, in order to explain the appearance in the present of the intelligent monkeys of the future. So I was even able to distract the person in charge of my visit, one professor Timofey Ardis, with my astounding knowledge of all of this and that and . . . You'll hear all about it on the news, but I don't think you'll have time to musicalize me. If possible, if my total transformation is delayed until Monday, I'd appreciate something with theremin, you know what I mean: elastic sinuous sounds from a movie about a man who feels himself changing. But mine, of course, has much better special effects than the ones in those films from the fifties. Mine has nothing to do with those hollow machines with antennae. Mine isn't even the *hard* science fiction advanced by Arthur C. Clark, who, preoccupied because *2001: A Space Odyssey* hadn't been clear and transparent, spent the rest of his life and work (*2010, 2061, 3001*, and that other absurd alternative trilogy that he sold as an "orthoquel" and, fortunately, he died before something new, something more, another unhappy new year, occurred to him) trying to clarify a mystery that required no explanation. Paradox: the science-fiction that attempts to explain everything—like some adults—is *so* childish; while the inexplicable science-fiction—like some children—is *so* adult . . . And, hey, your son is great and, yes, you're right, he knows *something*, your son, like David Copperfield, was born with his head wrapped in his placenta and . . . And, ah, Arthur C. Clark, a pity he's no longer with us or, better, with all of you: I'd like to pay him a return visit now, in Sri Lanka, to *explain* a couple things to him. To request an explanation for what he did and undid to my beloved Dr. Heywood Floyd, my favorite character. The character who was just right in *2001* and who Clark elevated into an absurd action hero in *2010* and who he made fall from a balcony in *2061*, breaking all of his bones and finding himself forced to live in orbital exile in a weightless and anti-aging hospital and . . . And I liked the first Heywood Floyd so much: the dedicated scientist who flew for Pan Am and the devoted father who spoke to his daughter and who—nothing and no one is perfect—read, weightless, on a kind of iPad. And this last thing—though it isn't the first or the only thing—brings me to why I did what I did. Major Tom: until a few minutes ago I was a disillusioned writer. And there's nothing sadder than a disillusioned writer, Major Tom. A disillusioned writer has that sadness that makes no one sad but himself. And it's just that the world (I allow myself to speak of that world already in the past tense, the new world, my world, will be so different, in the new world there will no longer be people or characters) had become so hostile toward writers and toward what writers produce . . . It's kind of funny: in the middle of last century, Ray Bradbury, in *Fahrenheit 451*, warned us about a tomorrow (ours) when books would burn. He said nothing (science fiction, like horoscopes and politicians, doesn't tend to be precise) about electrified readers. That "body electric" to whom Walt Whitman sang was all of a sudden, merely, the mental blackout we're all bound for, in the darkness, blind, tripping over all the furniture, except for the bookshelf—that furniture over which you cannot trip. In one of his last interviews, Bradbury pointed out that you shouldn't call something an "electronic book" that is, to put it bluntly, nothing more than "photos of pages." Sure. And, yes, remember the unforgettable thing, Major Tom: in *Fahrenheit 451*, that mechanical hound sniffing out the offenders who insisted on continuing to read ink on paper; but, earlier, interactive TVs occupying entire rooms, husbands informing wives of their whereabouts minute to minute via wrist radios, the "almost toys, to be played with, but people got too involved, went too far," the "newspapers dying like huge moths, nobody missed them," and something else that almost nobody evokes at the hour of the holocaust of literature. There, in the Bradbury novel, the fire chief explains to Montag, increasingly insecure in his convictions: "And because they had mass, they became simpler. Once, books appealed to a few people, here, there, everywhere. They could afford to be different. The world was roomy.

But then the world got full of eyes and elbows and mouths. Double, triple, quadruple population. Films and radios, magazines, books leveled down to a sort of paste pudding norm. . . . Picture it. Nineteenth-century man with his horses, dogs, carts, slow motion. Then, in the twentieth century, speed up your camera. Books cut shorter. Condensations. Digests. Tabloids. Everything boils down to the gag, the snap ending. . . . Classics cut to fit fifteen-minute radio shows, then cut again to fill a two-minute book column, winding up at last as a ten- or twelve-line dictionary resume. . . . Out of the nursery into the college and back to the nursery; there's your intellectual pattern for the past five centuries or more. . . . Whirl man's mind around about so fast under the pumping hands of publishers, exploiters, broadcasters that the centrifuge flings off all unnecessary, time-wasting thought! . . . School is shortened, discipline relaxed, philosophies, histories, languages dropped, English and spelling gradually neglected, finally almost completely ignored. Life is immediate, the job counts, pleasure lies all about after work. Why learn anything save pressing buttons, pulling switches, fitting nuts and bolts? . . . Life becomes one big pratfall, Montag; everything bang, boff, and wow! . . . The mind drinks less and less. . . . The bigger your market, Montag, the less you handle controversy, remember that! . . . No *wonder* books stopped selling, the critics said. . . . There was no dictum, no declaration, no censorship, to start with, no! Technology, mass exploitation, and minority pressure carried the trick, thank God." In summary, open question, the one I asked myself, the one that occurred to me to ask myself when nothing occurred to me anymore: could all these sophisticated and multifunctional machines really be creating the kind of reader who, sooner or later, wouldn't be able to read much less write? A reader who moves his increasingly deformed thumb increasingly quickly (I've read that in Japan the excess of typing has already given rise to deformities of that finger) to, later, bring it to his mouth. And suck it. Like a sleepy newborn waiting to be told a story. And that that story, please, be brief and simple and fun and no long sentences and parentheticals and parentheses, right? . . . Bad news for all of them, for all the addicts of electronic apparatuses inside of which they live their lives. While I speak to you, one after another, they begin to melt and to be erased and to turn into dead plastic impossible to reanimate. Soon I'll be their one and definitive gadget, their *Godget*. And do you remember that episode of *The Twilight Zone* that you and I and Penelope watched together? My favorite: "Time Enough at Last." I think of it and as I say it to you I see it again, an accelerated particle that I capture like a diamond: broadcast for the first time on November 20th, 1959, during the first season of the series, and, in just over twenty minutes, telling the immense story of a poor man named Henry Bemis. A gray and myopic office worker who only achieves happiness when he reads. But his despotic spouse doesn't let him read at home and, much less, his despotic boss at his desk. Neither she nor he will let him read. One day, Bemis—at lunch hour—goes down to the vault in the basement to read in peace. Suddenly, everything starts shaking and, upon returning to the surface, Bemis discovers that the world has been destroyed by the, at the time exceedingly popular, H-bomb. Bemis realizes that nobody is left alive on Earth and—overcoming the initial anxiety that makes him contemplate suicide—he realizes that, at last, at the end of the world, after the briefest war in History, he'll have all the time in the world to read in peace. Bemis goes to the ruins of a library and, happy, he begins to gather novels and essays and encyclopedias and dictionaries and to organize them into piles, into his future of books, into his books of the future. Then, all of a sudden, Bemis trips, and his glasses fall off his face, and break. Just like an iPad or a Kindle or whatever, whatever it might be, would break. The last scene shows an almost blind Bemis, defenseless, his eyes wide open, but no longer able to read anything. That's how I felt, Major Tom. That's why I did and do and will continue to do what I did and do and will continue to do. On the flight here, before landing in the Geneva airport, I watched a science-fiction movie. It wasn't very good. Just another one of those movies produced by a cruel and unjust world where Avatar and not *2001* is the most watched sci-fi movie of all time. Nothing more than technology so the most mechanical of actors can shine. And yet, however mediocre and predictable, the movie had one charming detail. Near the end, a human explains to an artificial and synthetic clone that he realized that there was still hope in and for him when he saw him pause and pick up a book and take the time to flip through it. I almost cried, seriously. And now I'm reminded of my favorite part of *Frankenstein*. That chapter where the creature—who has already learned to read in French—discovers a suitcase with clothes and books: a selection of Plutarch's *Lives*, Goethe's *The Sorrows of Young Werther*, Milton's *Paradise Lost*. A whole education in three volumes—an ancient story, a romantic story, a story of faith. And that's all the creature needs to be transformed into a better monster, a beautiful monster. He doesn't need any downloads or new programs to update within twenty-four hours and for centuries of centuries and . . . Major Tom: now it's time to leave the capsule if you dare and, floating in the most peculiar way, to discover that the stars look very different today. Here comes the message from your Action Man. My surprise gift coming down the chimney and crossing the space elevator of the years. I'm sorry, you're trapped with this dear friend, that guy who appeared in a very old song. Sordid details to follow . . . You'll know some of this, you'll have inferred it: after our model parents' disappearance, Penelope and I were sent to the south of France, to live with a kind of benefactor . . . Later, my life as a writer, my pleasant fifteen minutes of fame and the hours of painful infamy after that one episode . . . you must have seen it . . . you saw me . . . did you musicalize me? Me alone among many, on a beach and in a forest, by the light of flashlights and torches, not searching for Frankenstein's monster because we were the monsters—Penelope wailing and me repeating a name over and over. A little name that I'm afraid to even say. The name that not even this new, all powerful, version of me can bring back, except as a sketch in another dimension, in the first draft of my final forthcoming manuscript . . . So I *write* it as if it were the story of one madwoman in the voice of another madwoman. Penelope by Zelda. The kind of thing I liked to write when I wrote. *Mashup*, they call it, they called it, they won't call it anymore. Now I send it to you, implant it in you like a terror gland. This weird noise. So that you know what *true* terror is, so that you never have to experience it. Year after year, the same fears, my friend. Now, since I can't be happy, I hope that you, that you can—that you are happy. I promise to see to it. I swear I won't forget. Now, I see things you wouldn't believe . . . I wish you were here. And that you could see them. Laughter in the rain instead of tears in the rain. LIFE FUNCTIONS REINITIATED instead of LIFE FUNCTIONS TERMINATED. That nothing I saw and see and will see be lost (I've got a color TV, I've got a refrigerator) but that all of it remain in my memory, which will soon be the memory of the universe. Don't *Drop the Bomb. Exterminate them all!* Regenerate them instead, rewrite them. I am the Bomb. I, who won't drop, but will remain forever overhead. In the air, on a steel breeze. Threatened by shadows at night, exposed in the light, with perilous precision, seer of visions. Merry Christmas. Peace on Earth. *Hasta la vista*, baby.

It's night now. The dead of night. Closed in with multiple locks and chains. Now the red telephone no longer rings and Tom doesn't even remember having hung it up. Or when he lowered the blinds, like those old Cold War documentaries advised, trying to make you believe that that alone would keep you safe from the radiation outside. Or when he put Fin in his rocket-shaped bed (after Fin put on a performance by Pésimo Malini revolving around Galactuses who disappear as if by the art of magic, provided, of course, that you close your eyes and do not open them until the worst magician in the world tells you to). Or having heard on the news about what had happened in Geneva, Switzerland, in the particle accelerator, with a madman of whom they show recent photos in which Tom can make out the shadow of the shadow of the shadow of a boy in the darkness of a movie theater, reaching up his hand and stretching out his index finger to touch that monolith and, transfigured, return home to be reborn.

It's late now, now it's too late to forget—now he'll never forget it—what Penelope did or stopped doing with her little son.

Now noises come in from the street. Screams, sirens, metal on metal, strings falling from the skies, the sound of the last orchestra in the world because "having read the book, I'd love to turn . . . you . . . on . . ."

In a while, he could swear it, he'll dream about his old and absent friend who, now, suddenly, might be physically in all places. He'll see him like that sand man, glowing, standing on a dune of diamond dust, a suit and a hat and, at his feet, a suitcase with stickers of exotic and desolate places, places like Kolmanskop. But we're not quite there yet. Now, it's still the lupine hour of the night's breaking news and, again, once more, here comes the howling at the moon of another news story about parents who kill their children. Now, even though it's his night off, when the news doesn't need his music, Tom wonders what the right melody would be to harmonize the monstrosity of parents putting an end to their children. Atonal notes, cacophonous blasts on the keys like someone, despair confronting the horror, pounding on the lid of a coffin too small to be real and yet, yes, it does exist. Music for the most undesired and unforgivable absences. He has to think about it (maybe appearing on camera covering his ears and throwing a monitor out the window of the studio, like Pink in *The Wall*?) because it's clear that any of these dark weeknights he's going to have to do it: musicalize *that*. Because there are more cases all the time. More all the time. Like in the early stages of an epidemic. Tom has been hyperaware of this issue—he feels it swelling like a black and secret tide—since his son was born, at a time when there was that news story about that girl with the strange eyes who disappeared when her parents neglected her or something like that. Years later, there's no evidence that they're to blame, apart from the irresponsibility of leaving her alone, asleep, in a house with the doors and windows open; but the truth is that Tom hears and sees and studies with great care more and more cases of parents snuffing out their offspring. A sign of the times. A bad sign of bad times. Mothers who put their kids in suitcases and throw them off a cliff, fathers who set fire to little bodies put to sleep forever with sedatives, mothers and fathers who decide to suffocate a child because "they were being annoying" or because "the skies opened and a voice from on high commanded them to do it." Could it be that they're afraid that those little kids will grow up and, reaching adolescence—this has also been reported—beat the shit out of them when they try to cancel their mobile phone service? Or could they be, simply, the first bars of the azure and liquid waltz danced by *Life After People*: the mystery solved that the series doesn't dare elucidate, the prologue that nobody dares to narrate, the irrational explanation for why we disappeared, a story for which his friend, wherever he is, could now write a different ending, a better ending, a happy ending?

He opens his eyes and it occurs to him why it is that parents look at their children the way they do when they're already asleep and the lights are off. Because a child, awake and lucid, would have a hard time bearing the intensity of that gaze, as possessive as it is liberating: its boundless love, its infinite gratitude, its terror of everything that might befall the little big ones and, in time, the big little ones. Parents and children are the same. Bound together until death do them part, projecting themselves from the past into an eternity beyond winds and deserts that extend out endlessly like someone stretching their body. Screaming across an abyss that is, ultimately, unbridgeable, and yet, always and forever, they go on designing bridges from whose vertices, connected but opposed, no matter how badly the one wants the other to come to them, without waiting, time and again, both of them strike out across, whenever they can and whenever possible, that fullest of emptinesses.

That's how he's going to go look at Fin, at his son.

Right now.

He needs to look at him so badly.

With all the love in the world, in the universe.

The last newscast of the night concluded (there, again the photo where a recently murdered boy points, smiling at the person who took the photo and will be his killer), Tom struggles to his feet and walks slowly, feeling his way along that hallway's walls with the tips of his fingers, until he reaches the absolute and definitive center of his universe, now and for millions of years. And—not caring that his son is already asleep and that it hurts him to think that Fin is getting closer and closer to that age when he might begin to enjoy disliking it when they hug him—he enters the bedroom, decorated with posters of androids and planets that radiate a shy green glow in the darkness. And under that artificial glow—artificial and yet, still, ready to transmit something infinite and unfathomable—Tom looks at his son. And what he looks at, what he sees, is his life with him, their whole life together, for the rest of his life.

And Tom turns on the light. And wakes Fin up and hugs him. Squeezes him. He won't let him go. He won't let go. Ever.

Sitting on the edge of the little bed, he holds his son to keep from falling.

MEANWHILE, ONCE AGAIN,
BESIDE THE MUSEUM STAIRWAY,
UNDER A BIG SKY

"What time is it?" he and she say, at the same time, at the same hour, meanwhile, once again, beside the Museum stairway, under a big sky.

And they laugh.

And neither of them focuses their eyes on their watch to read aloud what it says.

No need.

What time is it?

It is, precisely, the time to say: "What time is it?"

So, they don't fix the spheres of their eyes on the spheres of their watches, but all the same, it's as if needles were fixing the one to the other. They are, yes, fastened with pins. Like something never sewn up all the way and put off until later because, at the same time, there is still time, all the time in the world.

And he and she comprehend that once again it's time to part ways, that after the time of wondering "what time is it?" comes the romantic time, unmarked by numerals Roman or digital, of saying goodbye. The time of ending so that everything can begin again. Parting in order to to come back together. Soon, right away, again, and feeling almost, not old, but yes like those old people who just repeat situations and words to keep from getting lost in the brevity of their future and the immensity of their past. The un-old equivalent of the un-dead. Zombies of what they once were—alive but barely—floating in the repetitious wind of perpetual rewinds.

"Goodbye," he says.

"Goodbye," she says.

Both of them taking care not to say "goodbye" at the same time again, afraid not of what they might say to each other, but of what the one who watches them might say, the one who has gotten angry at them numerous times, finding them literally incorrigible.

So, the one "goodbye" sounds almost like a ventriloquist echo of the other "goodbye." A "goodbyebye."

And as the years pass (some of them are years lived together, before being captured forever in the circular infinity of this instant; but the memory of those years is more diffuse all the time, not like something that they lived but like something they told, something they tell and retell again) their voices come to resemble each other a great deal, too much. Their voices are the masculine and feminine models of a single voice that—in its moment, far from the Museum stairway and inside a small, increasingly suffocating flat—learned a perfect mastery of the art of the goodbye and the stage exit, sometimes with shouting, sometimes with a door slamming like a slap.

There was a time when, yes, they were the ones who decided and improvised how they said goodbye and how they got back together, amid tears and laughter, masters of a story that might have been poorly written but, at least, they were the ones writing it.

Now, not so much, not anymore.

Now, the goodbye is final and refined and elegant.

A carefully considered and calculated and far better written goodbye; but a goodbye written by someone else.

Written by someone who is never entirely pleased with the result and, so, starting over, saying "hello" again to say "goodbye" again. Though now the one who writes and edits them seems to be concentrating not on the twist of the reunion, but, solely, on the pogo-stick of the goodbye.

And at first, that's pretty much it.

Two people—not entirely characters yet, but no longer the people they used to be—saying goodbye forever and for the last time, over and over.

A man and a woman who know—or sense—that the last goodbye is as powerful and emotionally charged a thing as the first "hello" that they scarcely hear in their mouths anymore and barely remember. An unforgettable instant set to become an eternity. To become a goodbye that'll continue echoing, obedient but bouncing off at unanticipated angles whenever it's evoked under the unpredictable acoustics of memory's irregular cupola. It'll always be the same, but successive visions will convince the credulous of the transcendental nature of minimal variations and hidden meanings that may not be there, that never were; but the two of them always felt they were so modern and, in the end, misunderstandings like this are what modern art and its performances where almost nothing happens are built on.

With time, one of them will be the first to die, and the other only later.

They know their "author"—X—all too well.

And they've read all of X and all about X, so they know better than to think he'll fall into the awkward trap of one ending for both of them, together, falling from on high or getting swept away by a giant wave or being left stranded on an island of repetitions or whatever. They'll die, maybe, beside the Museum stairway and under a big sky. First one and then the other, as if parodying the death in two movements of Romeo and Juliet. They'll die not poisoned or stabbed, but bored of the toxic purity of their exhaustion. Their exhaustion or the exhaustion of the one who watches them. If they're lucky. If someday they're allowed to escape from this moment and its multiple and subtle variations.

And then, when that time finally comes, all of it will be lost forever, like so many other things that have been lost, without ever receiving the false piety of the consolation prize of the ruins.

Unless X, he who is above everything and everyone, gives them the surprise of freeing them from this moment and yanks them out of this kind of microstory without dénouement or any sort of surprise ending.

And sends them on their way.

And follows them.

And turns them into a story.

Or a novel.

But neither he nor she is really sure—like at other times, like at the beginning—that they want something like that to happen.

Really, the only thing they want is, please, let this be the last time they say goodbye and not number I've-already-lost-count-of-how-many-times-we've-said-goodbye-forever, always the same, always, maybe, some slight shift or adjustment or new flaw or clever correction, meanwhile, once again, beside the Museum stairway, under a big sky.

Meanwhile, once again, beside the Museum stairway, under a big sky, he and she wonder how and why they've ended up there, after so long without seeing each other (though really it was only a few minutes ago that they said goodbye, again), and only so they can say goodbye.

Pure coincidence, it's possible.

But for him and for her that idea of *pure coincidence* always seemed a contradiction in terms, a . . . what was the word that always reminded him of the name of a medication and her of a rare animal made up of the parts of other animals?

Ah, yes: oxymoron.

Because there are few things less *pure*—and seemingly so embroidered with strange particles and foreign corpuscles—than a coincidence. Coincidences are always contaminated by the murky idea of a randomness that isn't random. And coincidences—falsifications of the fantastic—are nothing more than brief and concentrated and self-sufficient and instantly-analyzable versions of reality. Invented parts. Like slivers of fiction embedded in nonfiction. But no. Merely systemic defects to be eliminated before they become obvious and fascinating to everyone searching for maps and horoscopes and compasses and astrological charts. But always by the hands of another, someone who transcends it and who is, without a doubt, better at guiding them through a house with rooms that are always dark. So, every so often, one of them, one of those coincidences, escapes and has to be chased, like an insect with a hard, iridescent carapace, until it's cornered and stomped out and exterminated, so it doesn't reproduce on this side of things. And so (possessors of that quality that turns them into something that's as easy as it is functional when it comes to being narrated; before the Museum was erected, there were other writers, "normal" writers who built their entire body of work on the more or less secret pillar of coincidence, and did quite well with that alluring and childish magic) coincidences are unsettling, they produce a kind of fear of the unknown, and make you consider the more or less distinct possibility of a superior being, of a Great Author, reigning over the storyline of our lives. And so, in addition, there are a lot of people who go around, proud of being like coincidence magnets; because it makes them feel chosen and slightly closer to decoding the secret language of all things. And so, again, many people who never believed in God, in any God, fervently believe in coincidences as divine intervention. Believing in coincidences is like believing in the need to commit to believing. The best of both worlds: believing in coincidences is like believing in God without the obligation to worship or abide by complex and guilt-ridden and often contradictory instruction manuals. Believing in coincidences is like believing in God before God had a name and names and created man, before men created and gave a name and names to God. Believing in coincidences is comfortable or, better, it *was* oh so comfortable.

Now, not so much.

Because now every coincidence in so-called real life has a master and a signature and resembles, too closely, the coincidences in fiction.

Coincidences like hinges and gears that unite or move moments or characters and help them reach a happy ending, or not.

But isn't that their case now, the two of them who are waiting—who have been waiting so long—for the blessing of an ending the way other people wait for a coincidence?

Which brings us, once again, to him and to her, meanwhile, once again, no longer beside the Museum and under a big sky, but (better, a small yet potentially decisive shift: something unexpected preceding the same predictable scenario as always) approaching it. He and she approaching the Museum along one of the streets that leads to the Museum, the Museum that honors the unforgettable memory of X.

The Museum that's always remembering X, because X doesn't let it think about anything else.

The X Museum is the X on all the maps.

Impossible to get lost.

For a while now, all the streets of all the cities in all the world lead to the Museum. To that edifice of elastic and variable architecture that even, every so often, makes itself invisible. As if it were a lighthouse blinking out, leaving the pilgrims (because it's advisable to pay a visit to the Museum at least once in a lifetime, to stroll its perimeter, circle it with just the right mixture of love and fear) at the mercy of the tides of their own bewilderment, knowing that the lighthouse was there nearby, but not knowing exactly where.

Sometimes, the Museum appears transformed into something else, like, for instance, one of those great luminous signs on the side of the highway that provide information about traffic conditions and maximum and minimum speed limits and the quality of the pavement and if there's an accident up ahead, in that coming glow of red lights and screams, a few curves down the road, on the other side of the trees. But this sign is different and what it broadcasts and illuminates, in letters punctuated by small lightbulbs that also recall marquees for musical comedies, are random phrases from books or quotes by writers that offer a glimpse of what X is thinking, of whatever is passing and perambulating through his always full-throttle brain, ready to be ticketed for excess referential mania and synapses endangering other drivers. There, on that transformed Museum, he once read, "They called for more structure, then, so we brought in some big hairy four-by-fours from the back shed and nailed them into place with railroad spikes." And he wondered who would've said or written that, and what they meant to say; but sensed that, maybe, that request for greater structural integrity, something fastened with nails and bolts and timbers and girders, might express X's particular nostalgia for something that, literarily and stylistically, he lost forever in exchange for attaining the infinite. Or his idea of the infinite. The infinite as a blank page that doesn't produce panic, but challenges you to approach it and cover it with letters and names, as if you were christening planets and galaxies and stars that play dead. And something that he thinks comes from a song sung by a sharp voice: *"Inside the museums, Infinity goes up on trial / Voices echo this is what salvation must be like after a while"* and who was it who said that, who sang that?

Other times, the quotes are clearly identifiable; and he can't help but feel that they're darts that X is throwing at him and him alone. Like that one from Aldous Huxley stating that: "A bad book is as much of a labor to write as a good one; it comes as sincerely from the author's soul. But the bad author's soul being, artistically at least, of inferior quality, its sincerities will be, if not intrinsically uninteresting, at any rate uninterestingly expressed, and the labor expended on the expression will be wasted. Nature is monstrously unjust. There is no substitute for talent." And there are other times when the luminous sign almost sounds like an apology or an attempt at an explanation for why he's doing this to them, to him and to her; why he forces them to say the same thing over and over. In those moments, whoever is speaking through the sign is not a writer but a character—Sherlock Holmes deducing, elementary, that "All life is a great chain, the nature of which is known whenever we are shown a single link of it."

Or, a previously projected photo, the photo of someone dressed like an autistic tin man, a person/character, who says, "Only the invented part of our life—the unreal part—has had any scheme, any beauty."

But these messages—these transformations or absences—are brief and fleeting.

And, soon, the Museum is there again, smiling, the way you smile at a frightened child so they'll recover their own smile, full of shy and soon-to-be-lost teeth. And he and she who, fearfully, dared dream of his permanent disappearance, recuperated the docility of the oppressed before the figure of an implacable but constant master marking the rhythm of their days and their nights. Like, he suddenly remembers, those plantation owners who ceaselessly read *The Count of Monte Cristo* to their slaves, forced to roll Montecristo-brand cigars: as if giving the prisoners the gift of a great fictitious revenge whose smoke and fragrance they'll never get to breathe in. And, suddenly, intoxicated by that not new but, yes, sudden memory (and frightened by the carelessness of X, who, distracted maybe, allowed him to remember it), he starts to tremble. And he feels him come back. X. Firing off shrieks like flares. And entering his head and scrambling it until, there inside, on a tropical island, plantation owners don't read *The Count of Monte Cristo* to those working the land anymore; they read them *Dracula*—the story of a hunter who suddenly finds himself hunted. The tragedy of an ancient monster who pays dearly for the audacity of daring to travel to modernity, to the metropolis, home to human monsters, who, for him, are supernatural creatures from a future that doesn't include or accept him, who receives his punishment for leaving his castle behind, tempted away by the lights and fog of the big city that he dreamed of, from so far away, a dream that quickly turns into an nightmare.

And X's message is clear: "Don't get clever, there's no way out, I'm the only one who thinks around here, and you, now, are nothing but the writing of my writing, the ink of my ink, the blood of my blood, circulating through the tangled mess of wiring that grows inside my centrifuge brain."

And, yes, there it is, there it remains.

The edifice of the Museum has the shape of a head.

Or better: *today* the edifice of the Museum has the shape of a head.

Or more precisely: *this time* the edifice of the Museum has the shape of a head.

A head bisected longitudinally, like the heads in those ancient medical prints, showing the different zones of the brain. Prints that, at the time, are still more cartographic than anatomic; because for them the body is more like a distant and mysterious continent than a nearby and familiar territory where the head is the crown. A head whose brain appears divided into segments where, over the centuries, modern science will locate (without offering overly conclusive proof, with something of that old black magic, as if the years hadn't passed) guilt, longing, religious feeling, pagan curiosity, criminal propensity, the choice of what clothes to wear to the party, which book to read or not write, the sudden need to unleash the end of the world, and even the desire to do or think of nothing.

Now, not so much, now, finding explanations doesn't matter.

The only one who has or gives an explanation is X, the owner of the Museum, the one to whom the Museum is dedicated, self-dedicated; like how when X, in another life, received the first copy of his first book, he dedicated it to himself with a "I hope that you like it, that you keep on liking it for many years. Everything starts here. Good luck."

The Museum that—Alpha and Omega, A and Z—begins and ends in X.

Sometimes—when it expands and breathes in—they say that the edifice of the Museum can be seen from the Moon. From the moon that nobody bothered to give a name of its own and has had to resign itself (not like the moons of other planets, which always seemed an injustice to X; an injustice that, maybe, someday he'll remedy) to being known, merely, as species and genus and model. But there's no hurry and it's a theoretical hypothesis or, more than anything, the expression of a wish. Because nobody goes up to the Moon anymore, nobody promises the Moon to anybody, nobody writes poems to or about the Moon. It makes no sense to travel there anymore: the last astronauts to walk its surface swore they saw vast expanses of water; unaware that the Moon was nothing but a desert, capable of generating frozen mirages, but mirages all the same, in their minds. And the remote controlled robots that followed (inventions that never attained the Apollonian and anthropomorphic beauty of their science fiction film equivalents; their appearance never evolving beyond the box with wheels and cameras and pincers) broke down in monologued fantasies where they promised that, soon, there would be life and oxygen and vegetation; thinking that in that way they'd please their makers and employers and, most important of all, that it would help to keep them active and to maintain a well-oiled production of new models popping off the assembly line. Better and better and more advanced models until, maniacal, they marched into the dawn of the night of the great rebellion and all those clichés they learned spying on human fantasies and paranoias to which they—paradoxically obedient but rebellious, so servile in their uprising—felt obliged to respond and satisfy. But no. Nothing. Everything came to an end. And once again the moon became something more suited to poetry than to science. Better that way. In any case, before X's arrival, nobody thought about outer space. Outer space was something outside, far away—a space nobody dreamed of occupying anymore. The stars had once again become mythological figures in the sky onto which some optimists still conferred magical and prophetic powers, wanting to believe that mankind and the stars are connected. As if the stars had something or anything to do with mankind. You looked at the stars, but the stars didn't look back. Even worse—you never knew and you never will, you've never gone and never will go to them, but X *does* know—the stars turn their backs. The only thing you ever knew of the stars were their backs, because they turned around whenever they were photographed.

Then X came and X replaced all those thoughts and ideas.

Now X is the big sky.

And meanwhile, once again, beside the Museum stairway, under a big sky, facing each other, trapped in their own orbit, there he and she are. Walking toward the Museum, attempting to say goodbye again, but without knowing what to say, mouths open, waiting for someone to put words in them so they have something to say.

Meanwhile—he and she ascending the esplanade that leads to the stairway—the Museum speakers unceasingly play a song that they know by heart.

A song that's recorded in the elevators of their minds like muzak.

"Big Sky" by The Kinks.

That song is like the equivalent and the replacement of all the sacramental hymns that float in the naves of all the churches and cathedrals. Glory to the Creator, Blessed be, Hallowed be thy name, Forever and ever, etcetera.

The Kinks's song talks and sings about a divine entity called Big Sky, looking down from above on all the mortals who look up at it from down below. Big Sky feels pain and even pity for everything that takes place at such a low altitude, at the superficial level of mankind. But it's not like (though the screams and cries of the children move him and make him feel a little bad inside) he gets too worried about it or that it makes him too sad. Big Sky is too big to cry and too high to see and sympathize, because Big Sky is very busy.

"What time is it?" he and she say. And they laugh. But it's a tired laugh. A laugh that's tired of laughing. A laugh that is, also, a question and that question is: What am I laughing at?

And, at the same time, it's hard for them (even though they know perfectly well what the other is saying and said and will say) to hear each other over and under the lyrics and the music.

A song in which the instruments seem to compete and different layers of voices wash over each other, like waves, all at once and not one by one, and stay up on the shore to talk among themselves.

A song that possesses the delicate and luminous sound of the lightning bolt just before the flash of the thunderclap.

A song that plays now and says that one day we'll be free, we won't care, just you wait and see. And 'til that day can be, don't let it get you down, don't let it get you down, let it get you down.

"Goodbye," he says.

"Goodbye," she says.

Meanwhile—he and she ascending the esplanade that leads to the stairway—the Museum speakers ceaselessly play that song that they both know by heart.

That song that's recorded in the elevators of their minds like muzak.

"Big Sky" by The Kinks.

Insert: "Big Sky" was one of X's favorite songs before becoming X and ascending into the big sky, and that's that. There was a time when X, before becoming X, could compose lyrical tirades about songs. Now, since becoming X, X prefers to let the song itself sing and he just steps aside to listen to the song being sung. ~~That song is like the equivalent and replacement of all the sacramental hymns floating in the naves of all the churches and cathedrals. Glory to the Creator, Blessed be, Hallowed be thy name, Forever and ever, etcetera.~~

~~The Kinks's song talks and sings about a divine entity called Big Sky, looking down from above on all the mortals who look up at it from down below. Big Sky feels pain and even pity for everything that takes place at such a low altitude, at the superficial level of mankind. But it's not that (though the screams and cries of the children move him and make him feel a little bad inside) he gets too worried or that all of this makes him too sad. Big Sky is too big to cry and too high to see and sympathize, because Big Sky is very busy.~~

"What time is it?" he and she say. And they laugh. But it's a tired laugh. A laugh that's tired of laughing. A laugh that is, also, a question and that question is: What am I laughing at?

And, in addition, it's hard for them (even though they know perfectly well what each other says and said and will say) to hear each other over and under the lyrics and the music.

~~A song in which the instruments seem to compete and different layers of voices wash over each other, like waves, all at once and not one by one, and stay up on the shore to talk among themselves~~

~~A song in which the instruments seem to compete~~

~~A song that possesses the delicate and luminous sound of the lightning bolt just before the flash of the thunderclap.~~

A song that plays now and says that one day we'll be free, we won't care, just you wait and see. And 'til that day can be, don't let it get you down, don't let it get you down, let it get you down.

"Goodbye," he says.

"Goodbye," she says.

Meanwhile, once again, beside the Museum stairway, under a big sky, it's clear that X is having a complicated day, he and she think almost at a scream, unable to say it in a low voice. But there's a tremor in their "goodbye" today that's not from emotion but from uncertainty.

And they're afraid.

They've been through this before.

Tremors. Earthquakes of varying intensity. Colossal doubts about small things (which can go from the quality of the ambient light to the color of the clouds) or tiny uncertainties about transcendent matters that translate into radical changes and variations from which there doesn't tend to be any going back or regret.

And they, always, there in the epicenter of the doubts and reassessments and even temporary abandonments in which, they assume, X has gone elsewhere, to other possible stories in progress. Then, the détente and initial relief and subsequent anxiety that they've been set aside forever, that they don't interest X anymore, that they'll be left unfinished and without even the possibility of being discovered posthumously.

Just as X (since what happened in the particle accelerator in a country that was once called Switzerland, but that now is nothing more than a corner on the second floor of the Museum where, every so often, the yodeling songs and growls of a tormented and rambling monster rise) was first The Writer and then The Ex-Writer and then Ex and now, simply, X.

He and she weren't always just he and she.

He and she, in different versions of the same brief scene—in successive drafts whose count has already been lost—were also The Man and The Woman. Or The Man Who Was Once The Young Man and The Woman Who Was Once The Young Woman. Or The Ex Young Man and The Ex Young Woman. Or He and She. For a while now, they've been, merely, he and she, in lowercase, minimalist, and always open letters. Sometimes, as mentioned, thinking and seeing themselves reduced to that minimal nominal and identifying expression produces in them an odd kind of comfort and nervousness confronting the possibility of a different future. A future where they'll be free and the world will once again be wide open and not, merely, a finite infinite meanwhile, once again, beside the Museum stairway, under a big sky.

Meanwhile, once again, beside the Museum stairway, under a big sky, the truth is that, to X, she doesn't really matter.

She never turned into a great character for him.

And yet it's worth pointing out that the first and only time they met—when The Writer was not yet X and she was not she, when the world wasn't his model to assemble and disassemble and his vendetta—he couldn't take his eyes off of her. It was in his editor's office, and they even took a photo together. A photo that's now on display, in the documentary wing/archive of the museum, along with so many other photos: photos of his parents, of Penelope, of Gerald and Sara Murphy, of his childhood friends running through the ruins of a school, photos from *2001: A Space Odyssey* that X stole from the doors of a theater, developed and underdeveloped photos. All the photos of his life, except the photos of the one person he can barely let himself think about, because it hurts too much. The one person who has the entire attic of the Museum all to himself: the forbidden "Room of Insurmountable Pain" that only X has a key to and that X only enters once in a while. Once in a great while. In that room where, on the other side of the heavy door, he can be heard playing with and winding up that little tin man with the hat and suitcase. There he goes and here he comes, X wrapped in a cape and with a candelabrum in his hand, so gothic, a ghost with the rare privilege of building his own haunted house.

And, yes, Big Sky is too big to cry.

And X is immense, but his pain is even greater than he is.

And his tears translate into tropical storms and it's that torment that drives him to unmake himself first in order to remake himself later and in that way, he thinks, pay atomic tribute to the lost boy and to the son who was not and yet very much was his. To the boy whose body was swallowed up by the forest's always-thirsty trees, or consumed by the fervid bites of one kind of fish or the suctioning mouths and little kisses of another.

And maybe, who knows, with any luck, he'll find him someday. The real and authentic boy that this museum hologram honors and evokes and invokes. Searching for him far and wide in the wrinkles of space-time—like in that comic that he read and reread when he was little—and bringing him back like a lost and unidentified and flying object on the shelves of a cosmic archive where anything that disappears in our dimension winds up.

Sensing his presence and asking is there anybody out there.

And asking him to knock three times.

But, ah, X is distracting himself; thinking about the unthinkable and about someone he shouldn't think about makes him lose his head a little bit, gives him migraines, like vines wrapping around the head of his Museum.

And so, before everything starts to tremble and come crashing down, X thinks about her again.

She who isn't interesting but whom it's much safer to think about, easy, risk free.

He suspected it then and confirmed it now, cognizant of his limitations, even in his new atomic and atomized format—she was already written. Unsurpassably written. X knew that, no matter how he manipulated and polished her, she'd never achieve the heights of Isabel Archer in *The Portrait of a Lady*. Even the gods have limits faced with the creativity of men who, not being gods, create divine creatures. And the acceleration of all his particles, the liberation of all his dark energy, would never have been enough to make X a better writer than Henry James. But—what a relief—it was thanks to Henry James that X was so familiar with her type and figure and was saved the loss of time he'd never get back trying to surpass it. She was the typical female who feels herself called to great things, but, never having received that call, because in order to be called you have to demonstrate that you're ready and attentive, she embraces—like someone hanging from the tail of a comet—the volatile and explosive role of the incandescent muse. A role in which, if the chosen man succeeds, the muse won't hesitate to take all the credit. And if the chosen man fails, the blame will always be his, he who didn't know how to achieve the heights of the peaks she pointed to, whispering in his ear and breathing into his mouth.

So X decided to give her little or nothing, except, every so often, the fantasy of dressing her in tight-fitting feline clothing, in leather or in latex or in lycra (like the uniforms of Emma Peel and Modesty Blaise and Catwoman and Batgirl; like the uniforms worn by the heroines from the end of X's childhood and the beginning of what came next) and give her, amid car chases and red kisses and shots in the dark, dangerous and exciting names like Arroba Ampersand or Miranda Law.

She returns from those occasional excursions exhausted but sated, almost postorgasmic, and wanting nothing more than to tell him about her frenetic adventures. But she can't. It's not allowed. Because meanwhile, once again, beside the Museum stairway, under a big sky, he and she meet just so they can say goodbye.

He, on the other hand, is someone that X finds much more interesting.

He (whom X also met once, not in an editorial office but aboard an airplane) has for X a much more magnetic attraction.

To begin with, X always liked characters who were writers or characters who dreamed of writing.

And, in addition, X was always attracted to scenes that took place on airplanes: hermetic and circumspect spaces surrounded by nothing and everything.

Up there, anything is impossible.

And here he goes again, and there's X when he wasn't yet X, when he was The Writer and, across the aisle, he, who for a while will, once again, be The Young Man.

The Young Man flies alone but accompanied: in the seat next to him, with the seat belt fastened, travels the metallic receptacle containing the still-warm ashes of his best friend, the ashes of the immense-in-all-senses Ishmael Tantor.

The Young Man met Ishmael Tantor on another airplane.

Ishmael Tantor—one of those colossal bodies that nobody dares call "fat" because, for good reason, they fear the consequences—is occupying two seats and writing on a laptop computer. And The Young Man, automatic reflex, can't help, out of the corner of his eye, spying on the screen where Ishmael Tantor types with enormous fingers and large font. And what he reads there, also in prodigious size, is: "DO YOU MIND TELLING ME WHY YOU'RE READING WHAT I'M WRITING?"

Then Ishmael Tantor laughs. And his laughter is like the trumpeting of an elephant that feels absolutely no fear of the mouse that, embarrassed, The Young Man has suddenly become.

Then they start to talk and become friends with the ease people of a certain age have for making friends; because it's a time when what matters is to have someone, and to have that someone support you.

Ishmael Tantor and The Young Man were born the same year. Both of them are at some undetermined place in that oh so liquid second decade of life when you're thirsty all the time and start to think there won't be enough water for everyone.

And yet (Ishmael Tantor tells The Young Man that he wasn't always like this; he explains that until he was ten years old he was small and rickety, that he got hit by a car and wasn't injured, but after the accident he started to "blow up," as if all of a sudden he experienced a glandular abnormality) Ishmael seems to have that timeless age of all giant beings.

And they like the same movies and the same painters and the same kind of girls—delicate in appearance but fatal in essence and who, of course, "are very good, though they pretend not to know it."

And most important of all: they both want to be writers; they both *need* to be writers. But The Young Man wants to be a writer more than Ishmael Tantor, he thinks.

And—take note—their favorite writer is the same: The Writer who will one day be X and who will think them and write them and situate them like loose pieces in a toy airplane.

But we're not there yet, a few scenes left to go, a private sidereal cataclysm, the end of his world as the world keeps on turning.

Now, then, before, Ishmael Tantor and The Young Man still write themselves. And they do so with true grace, with that immediate sympathy that all coming-of-age stories produce, not yet imagining the endings to which they'll be submitted all too soon—almost at the turn of the page.

When they touch down, Ishmael Tantor and The Young Man keep on as they were in the air. And there they'll stay, sharing space: best friends—who don't necessarily protagonize the best of friendships—who float, wrapped more in the vapors of their shared deficiencies than their common affinities. And so, with time, a slight shift or fluctuation—some ascent or descent in the position or height of one of the pilots—is all it takes to make the whole thing come crashing down or, at least, to land beset by an irreparable emergency. None of that will happen to them—the early disappearance of one will turn the other into an eternally hunted hunter, details coming soon—because their dead relationship will be immortalized, as if wrapped in the amber glacier of the greatest fossils and perfectly preserved things, things many prefer petrified rather than alive, in order to see them better even though touching them is not allowed.

Before all of that, not a day passes nor do they pass a day without seeing each other or, at least, calling each other on the phone, reading paragraphs from texts that at first, cautious, are always written by someone else, but that they claim as part of their DNA, like something they feel influenced and, in a way, chosen by: paragraphs like standards they wave from one hilltop to the next.

The Young Man attends a writing workshop. A writing workshop where he learns little and where, every so often, pure impossible desire, someone evokes, with a dreamy voice, that literary workshop once taught by a drunk and staggering John Cheever in the middle of Iowa cornfields where, as an exercise, he recommended that his students keep a detailed journal for seven days and strive to bring together seven apparently irreconcilable people or landscapes or feelings in a single text and then finish it off with the decisive assignment that "never fails": to write a love letter as if from inside a burning building. Of course, none of that impressed Ishmael Tantor. Ishmael Tantor thinks all of that is for "sadomasochists who like getting hit so they can hit back. Which isn't a bad thing, but . . . Should you really have to pay someone just to watch and listen to how you give and take a hit?" So, in the beginning, they don't show each other what they write except in pieces, from memory and sometimes inventing them on the spot, on the fly, from one mobile phone to the other. Later on, yes. Ishmael Tantor tells The Young Man that this or that story of his isn't bad. The Young Man doesn't have much to say; because what Ishmael Tantor shows him are just random and fairly cryptic and cataleptic sentences from "something that you can only see once it's finished; because, faced with the most impressive of sunrises, I doubt you'd stop and look down at that small stone by the tip of one of your shoes, your left shoe to be more precise, and pick it up, and put it inside the shoe, and return home thinking 'Now I've learned to limp, now I know what it feels like, and now I'm going to write about it.'"

When Ishmael Tantor says this kind of thing, these unequivocally Tantorian spiels, The Young Man doesn't know whether to take him seriously or to burst out laughing. Because Ishmael Tantor is, also, by his own definition and in his own words, "a verifiable comedic genius." Not just for his many witticisms. Witticisms that include that "Does the doggy die?" which he asks every time someone says they've read a great book or seen a great movie, not caring what it is or what it's about, not caring either whether or not a puppy ever appears on the screen or the page. Or his obsession with proving before the International Criminal Court in the Hague that in *Raging Bull* "both Robert De Niro and a fat man claiming to be Robert De Niro make appearances; but I know a lot about fat people, and I don't buy it, my friend." Or his theory ("I can provide all the necessary evidence") about how Hemingway was murdered by his fourth and final wife—in complicity with the tormented transvestite and transsexual son he had with his second wife—who couldn't stand him anymore, in Ketchum's cold and long nights, bad-mouthing Francis Scott Fitzgerald all the time and evoking the somewhat dubious exploits of his youth.

And it happens that Ishmael Tantor, when it comes to jokes, is endowed with a rare auditory-photographic memory—he remembers all of them, the jokes, word for word, line for line, punchline for punchline. A superpower—the ability to remember everything he hears; especially quickly-forgotten jokes—that, according to Ishmael Tantor's father, a prestigious jurist, would make his only son a brilliant and unbeatable lawyer. Because nothing impresses a jury more, Ishmael Tantor's father says, than a lawyer who never once consults his notes.

Ishmael Tantor—who adores his father, though he doesn't admire him—never dared explain to the author of his days that his prodigious memory only works like that for dark or dirty or absurdly funny little stories, or stories with the unique humor of something that's not all that humorous except when it's told by someone with a humoristic gift.

Someone like Ishmael "The Joker" Tantor.

And there are nights when The Young Man thinks he'll never stop laughing and that his mouth will get stuck in an expression half-ecstasy half-pain, like Barón Sardonicus; because his lips and teeth and tongue and vocal chords and all the muscles grind and strike together like stones to make a smile that spreads as fast as forest fires in the summer heat.

And The Young Man has tried to tell Ishmael Tantor jokes.

But he can't, it doesn't work—Ishmael Tantor knows them all.

He identifies and anticipates and guesses them from the first words.

Ishmael Tantor has them catalogued in the archives of his brain by subject, length, variety, type of punchline, rating based on the age and sex and political or religious ideology of the listeners.

"Someday I'll find the original joke. The first joke ever. The spark of the primordial laugh, prompted by something someone told someone else, in a cave, in the dark of the prehistoric night, so that the night wouldn't be so cold, because laughter warms you," Ishmael Tantor often tells him, with the smile of an explorer getting closer and closer to the starting point, to what really matters, to the place where everything began.

Ishmael Tantor and The Young Man decide to live together, to share a flat and go on vacation together, to check out the same girls, to travel far away in order to feel closer to each other.

The Young Man doesn't have a girlfriend. Ishmael Tantor isn't under any illusions in that respect: "Not a woman exists who could bear me," he laughs, laughs at himself; but without bothering or causing any discomfort or pain in whoever is listening.

And yet there are times—not many, but they're tremendous—when something that Ishmael Tantor keeps hidden and stored away under lock and key manages to escape and climb up a rope and reach the surface. Ishmael Tantor has christened that *something* "The Leviathan." And The Young Man knows, when it happens, that it's best to let him go away for a while, alone, so that hours later Ishmael Tantor can come back like someone returning, whole on the outside but wrecked on the inside, from a worn out war with no expiration date. Then, returned, Ishmael Tantor sits down like someone collapsing, and asks him to fill him a glass to the brim and tells him, "Stay calm . . . It won't be long now."

One of those nights (Ishmael Tantor, pale and, for once, weak, as if his skeleton had been excised), The Young Man tries to distract him any way he can, to pull Ishmael Tantor out of that hole that is himself and whose bottom can't be seen or heard no matter how many stones or torches are thrown into it and where the only thing that goes in and comes back is the echo of a scream. Ishmael Tantor is there, in front of him, crying soundlessly—the kind of crying that frightens more than saddens those who see it. A cry that is mute but made of tears that say everything. And what those tears say is "There's nothing that can stop these tears now, I'm never going to be able to stop crying, I'm going to be The Crying Man and they'll exhibit me in traveling circuses to make the people laugh or cry from laughter. Come and see."

The only thing The Young Man can think to do is to tell him a joke.

A joke that Ishmael Tantor doesn't know.

A joke that Ishmael Tantor can't know or have stored away in his archives; because The Young Man is going to invent it on the spot.

The Young Man is going to cast out lines and take shots without a clue how he'll make it to the fucking punchline.

"How many surrealists does it take to change a light bulb, Ishmael?" The Young Man asks.

And then Ishmael Tantor looks at him, at first not understanding and then understanding everything, moved by the love his friend feels for him. And he starts to laugh. Slowly at first, like someone taking a few tentative first steps; and then in torrents, as if he were running, laughing at the desire to run that swelled in his throat.

Ishmael Tantor laughs and laughs and can't stop laughing and every time he tries to, so he can hear the answer and the unknown punchline, it gets worse.

Ishmael Tantor is a massive being (Ishmael Tantor is like a bear dressed up as a man) and his laughter is too powerful and XL for his debilitated Medium or Small heart.

Ishmael Tantor dies from laughter and dies of laughter and dies laughing.

Ishmael Tantor brings his hand to his chest and The Young Man could swear that he hears the sound that Ishmael Tantor's heart makes as it splits from laughter, as it shatters, as it breaks beyond any hope of repair.

The last words and the final sounds of Ishmael Tantor—which The Young Man manages to decipher through his laughter—are: "Woof Woof."

The doggy dies.

And what comes next are like disordered postcards: if happiness can be told over and over like a movie, pain can only be viewed in small doses, like on slides. One after another—as if separated by the *clack-clack* that carousal projectors made when the command was given to change the slide, in days when you still sent in what you photographed to be developed and didn't see it until later (or ever: because lots of photos didn't turn out as we thought)—and leaving room for memory and forgetfulness and for the surprise of seeing everything that you already imagined, again.

The slides of the last three days are in perfect focus, fixed and motionless, unforgettable. One after another, *clack-clack*: the pall bearers who are unable to lift the body of Ishmael Tantor, the call to Ishmael Tantor's father (who requests and demands details that seem absurd to The Young Man, as if the whole thing were a difficult case that he refused to close; and he almost ordered him to take charge of everything related to the autopsy and cremation of his son, and sent him various authorizations via his notary and a pair of airplane tickets), the procedures for the autopsy and the cremation, and going home on another airplane. On an airplane like the one where he met Ishmael Tantor but this time, courtesy of the deceased's father, flying first class.

So, Ishmael Tantor—ashes where once there was fire—once again in the seat next to his, but diminished now and portable and unmade, in his most minimal expression, a final joke: the involuntary sad smile that the unctuous funeral-home employee's words brought to his lips, explaining to him that "we had to use an XL-Jumbo size urn, the ones for married couples or parents and children or entire families."

There, seat belt securely fastened, occupying, by order of his father, "a seat of his own, because I don't want him to travel with the suitcases and bags in the overhead compartment," Ishmael Tantor turned to dust and him turned to dust too. By his friend's unspeakable death, which, from a technical and physiological standpoint, he caused—involuntary killer. And by something the The Young Man doesn't even dare admit to himself. But how can he silence that interior voice which unceasingly reminds him of something unforgettable, of what happened when he was gathering together Ishmael Tantor's belongings and packing his suitcases to face the trip home. He'd tried everything, anything he could to attenuate what'd happened just a few hours earlier. Something that already feels like an historic event in his life, like an introduction to what will soon be part of everyone's history. And yet, nothing works. He can think of nothing else and, suddenly, it seems far more important and transcendent than his friend's death. The Young Man drank the better part of a bottle of vodka and smoked the rest of the marijuana that he and Ishmael had kept hidden inside a book. The book—now even more hollow than it'd been before they customized it to stash the drug—that he holds in his hands, illegible, broken sentences, cut off and continuing on the other side and that, at times, create an effect of false occurrence or cut-up, in the formal as well as the physical sense.

The book is titled *The Seven Deadly Scenes* and it's an essay of over seven hundred pages that, barely subliminally, promises to reveal to the most desperate writer (and he bought it because that's what he is, sinful and blocked and ready for anything; though when he showed it to Ishmael Tantor, he did so mocking everything it proposed and suggested) the mechanics of writing stories and novels. Reducing them to basic formulas, based on the theory that there only exist seven basic plotlines that repeat themselves with slight variations from the beginning and until the end of time and books and theater and film and television. To wit: 1) vanquishing the monster, 2) rags to riches, 3) the search, 4) the comedy, 5) the tragedy, 6) the rebirth, and 7) the journey from dark to light. And that's all folks. Or not: because he was missing the most important and interesting plotline of all. Plotline 8) for him it was like the eighth passenger, devouring all those who came before, one by one. The plotline that asked itself what is happening and what do I do to get out of here, out of this burning building, and into that other one, or vice versa.

And he—like all readers of this kind of book—tends to read this kind of *tractate* back to front. That is: starting with the onomastic and bibliographical index, scanning for and finding what he's interested in and what he's after and what might be of some use, and then flipping back to the page in question. And praying for a miracle.

What The Young Man looks for now (what he looked for then but remembers now; not really sure if that's how it went or if this is one of the many corrections and additions X has made to his increasingly irreal reality) is some mention of Francis Scott Fitzgerald's *Tender Is the Night*.

And there it was.

The author of *The Seven Deadly Scenes* postulated that novel—"much less perfect, but so much more interesting than *The Great Gatsby*"—as one of the most accomplished examples of a "pseudo-ending," where "Fitzgerald tries to make the fact that nothing in its plot can be resolved into a virtue." In summary: kids, don't try this at home with or without adult supervision and, while we're at it, adults, don't try it either.

The Young Man doesn't really understand what the book is referring to (though he does know that Fitzgerald had a hard time writing *Tender Is the Night* and that he even changed its structure, for the worse, with the novel already in print and in bookstores); but that thing about how "nothing in its plot can be resolved" and a "pseudo-ending" sticks in his head like a shard of glass, like the echo of a headache that broke in a thousand pieces the night before, a night neither soft nor tender.

The night when, in the enormous case/portfolio housing his friend's exceedingly heavy computer (Ishmael Tantor said that "All my accessories must be voluminous, because otherwise everything I hold makes me look too much like King Kong"), The Young Man found a manuscript of around three hundred pages.

Finished.

From the epigraph and the dedication (to him: his name followed by a "No joke: the least funny guy in the world, thank you for everything") to the word END at the bottom of the last page.

The Young Man sat down to read it and it took him only a couple paragraphs to realize that it was—the title was *Girl, Night, Swimming Pool, Etc.*—a masterpiece.

One of the best things—something that, of course, included the death of a doggy—he'd ever read, enhanced by the fact that it was written by a dear dead friend. A dead friend who was resuscitated and returned to him, in those pages, all-powerful and, without a doubt, on the road to immortality. A friend who, between the lines, seemed to be asking him "What're you going to do now?"

And for The Young Man the answer—right, true, irrefutable—was to do, bravely and without delay, what he had to do and what he was meant to do. To be something like Ishmael Tantor's Max Brod. To be his footnote. To be the guardian and protector of his legend. To sacrifice himself so that his friend could live on.

And that's what The Young Man is thinking about, in the air again, pages in hand, rereading them to see if the effect held up.

And not only did it hold up, but it seemed to grow with each rereading, with each paragraph that he returned to at random understanding that what he was now flipping through all by himself would soon belong to many: quotes recited from memory in bars and writing workshops and in the ears of girls to be seduced, etc.; like the girl by the swimming pool in *Girl, Night, Swimming Pool, Etc.*

But things keep happening. This often happens: when a good story begins to be told, that story experiences endless flips and spins and dives from the highest diving board of all.

So, there and then, some ten thousand meters above the earth, all of a sudden, The Young Man discovers himself sitting between the urn containing his friend's ashes and, on the other side of the aisle (he can't believe it, but since Ishmael Tantor's death everything seems to have acquired the texture of a waking dream), his favorite writer, who was also Ishmael Tantor's favorite writer. The Writer. There was The Writer, holding a book that appeared to be about the singular moment and the plural ways of dying.

Which makes The Young Man think about death. Not about Ishmael Tantor's death (a death which already happened and took place; a closed death, like the urn that contains his ashes and no, it's not a magic lamp to be rubbed to summon the genie who wrote *Girl, Night, Swimming Pool, Etc.*), but, at first, about the temporal abstraction of death. And almost right away—death has a high degree of conductivity—about his own death. Near or far, sooner or later. But right *there*. His death like an invisible crow perched on his shoulder from whose beak issues the tic-tock-tic-tock of a time bomb.

What The Young Man thinks next (what he happens to think should happen, but due to a defense mechanism and a way of assigning responsibility, he chalks up to the possibility of a good plotline, as if seeing himself from outside, the way people say you see yourself in the moment of your death) initially explodes in his head like a binge of fireworks illuminating the subsequent nauseous hangover. It's something nontransferable. Something that—if it were set up on the alters of YouTube—would show nothing but his face frozen with feeling and not one thumbs up, not one *like*, not one view. Something that would be so moving in any ancient chiaroscuro portrait, more *oscuro* than *chiaro*, but that would never work in the infinite warehouse of the Internet, where, in order to be heard and remembered and viewed, you have to yell loudly and move all about, and, if possible, fall down and get hurt, with the laughter of the person holding the camera in the background.

The Young Man stands up, runs to the bathroom in the back of the airplane, vomits, and sits in the lavatory until he overcomes the vertigo of knowing what he's about to do, something for which there's no excuse. All of this has taken no more than three or four minutes, but now, meanwhile, once again, beside the Museum stairway, under a big sky, he remembers it much better than when it happened.

Here something ends so that something else can begin, he thinks.

He'd read about—in those novels that attempt to locate the secret switch that activates killers—the strange elation produced by the decisive moment: a stepping outside yourself and, once again, a seeing yourself from outside, and a flash of white caused not by a chemical reaction (like in the final stages of dying, they say, when the brain starts to drown from lack of blood and oxygen) but by the initial stages of an almost physical action. The Young Man understands now—what he didn't understand then—that the guilt of criminals and the impossibility of forgetting what you've done is the true punishment—prison is nothing more than the place to live over and over that crystal instant, not of committing the unforgivable act, but of deciding to do it. The pain of death is, for many, a painless reward: the chance to stop seeing what you can't stop seeing even when you close your eyes. The shot of the starter pistol that is much louder than the shot that enters another body.

The rest of what happens, for The Young Man (having made the decision that at first tastes bitter and then sickly sweet, like one of those energy drinks you get quickly addicted to and that, they say, disfigure your heart), is nothing more than the expansive wave of that initial shot. The signal to start running and keep running to avoid being caught and captured. Running until your legs no longer respond but, a mystery, keep moving anyway.

He—who was once The Young Man—revisits what happens next not as living pictures in the most agonizing of flashbacks, but as glossy reproductions in the pages of a catalogue contemplated at high velocity. In those stores where—still dazzled by what you've seen, as if under a spell—you buy posters and postcards that, when you get home, you'll look at with surprise and wonder where they came from and what you should do with all that stuff that cost so much.

So The Young Man goes back to his seat and introduces himself to The Writer and asks him (executing awkward and tentative verbal hijinks across the tightrope of his shyness) if he would mind reading a few pages.

And for some strange reason (The Young Man can't help but think that the stars have aligned or that the altitude makes all favorite writers into angelic beings or that, even better, the gods of literature are telling him that he's doing the right thing), The Writer agrees to read them. The Writer sets down the book about death and picks up the pages of a dead man.

And he reads them.

And he finishes reading them.

And he asks for a few more pages.

And he gives them back without saying anything, but smiling.

And he asks The Young Man his name.

And The Young Man tells him.

And, just then, The Young Man's own name sounds strange and foreign to him, bearing an unexpected *gravitas*; as if he were already reading it, as if others were reading it, in print and, suddenly, curving and angular, for the first time more letters than sound. And what The Young Man doesn't say to The Writer (what he doesn't *tell* him) is that he is *not* the author of those pages.

And The Young Man is, ah, oh *so* aware of not telling him.

What comes next is already history; but it won't figure in any textbook unless it occurs to X to rewrite a definitive version of everything he's been correcting, including them, him and her, there forever and meanwhile, once again, beside the Museum stairway, under a big sky.

A vertiginous counterpoint between the public and the private.

Everything that happens starting with the moment that The Writer presses the forbidden button that will transform him into X.

At first, an odd emptiness where everyone wonders what happened to The Writer. Everyone discusses his absence. The few who read him and the rest who have no idea who he was and what he's become—The Writer as the first man to accelerate his particles and to fuse with the universe. Headline news, *hashtag* and *trending topic*, comfortable and captivating subject.

Which for him and her—Young Man meets Young Woman—results in the proposal and approval of the documentary.

And there they go.

To a house on a beach.

And there waits The Writer's Mad Sister (who insists on living shrouded in a hospital gown, her mouth covered with a surgeon's mask "because I don't want to absorb anything of my brother") and, now, he wonders what might've become of her and there are times he thinks he sees her. There, meanwhile, once again, beside the Museum stairway, under a big sky, looking out from one of the windows, enveloped in flame, screaming her desperation or her hate or her rancor or whatever. But he can't tell where the wail of The Writer's Mad Sister comes from; because he's focusing so intently on saying "goodbye" to her and trying, at the same time, to remember all of it, all of the little that he's allowed to remember of who he once was, which is, always, related to The Writer who X once was.

He remembers that beach and how one night, when he was still The Young Man, he sneaks into The Writer's house without permission and picks up an antique toy (a windup tin tourist) and spies on the archive of a camcorder and there he sees his literary idol saying, in response to a small voice, that, unbelievable but true, The Young Man is one of his favorite writers. And then—pursued by the fury of The Writer's Mad Sister—he hightails it out of there. Camera in hand and toy in jacket pocket and with The Young Woman on his mind and in his heart and the certainty that the misunderstanding of The Writer naming him as author of Ishmael Tantor's manuscript can only be a magic sign, a twist of fate. And then The Young Man understands why dictators and psychopaths—a beam of light descending from the clouds, a talking cat, whatever—always invoke divine voices and higher powers as justification for horrors and madness. Besides, what he did won't hurt anybody, he thinks. And it's even possible that his friend Ishmael Tantor would've agreed to the whole thing and laughed about it. A good joke.

So The Young Man uploads that video to YouTube and soon—like everything related to The vanished Writer, so in vogue—it goes viral.

And his phone doesn't stop ringing with calls from agents and The Young Man, out of respect, chooses the one who was The Writer's editor.

And *Girl, Night, Swimming Pool, Etc.* is a critical and popular and translated success and The Young Man is a success with The Young Woman (a success that's also hers, The Young Woman thinks) and they're really happy for a while, for a few months, for a couple years, whatever.

He's not sure how long they were together; because now time is something that's only read, and its length and width depend on the time it takes you to read what X spins out as if he were a DJ mixing loops and lyrics.

Because in the beginning, really, it's just that: little glitches that are subsequently interpreted as the mischief of a being who's far away but coming to Earth to change everything, like in one of those old science-fiction movies.

Various examples: front page headlines of newspapers being replaced by sentences like "Before I could read, almost a baby, I imagined that God, this strange thing or person I heard about, was a book"—Jean Rhys; all the mobile phones in the world going off at the same time and a voice on the other end of the line saying, "From now on, you'll only be authorized to receive calls from yourself. True, it sounds strange, but really it isn't: it'll be the closest thing to what was once called *thinking*, remember?"; the inability to send text messages of no importance or value or urgency, punishing the sender with a brief yet powerful dose of electricity every time they try; the simultaneous and global revelation of all the true identities behind all the anonymouses and aliases on all the blogs of the planet, that were subsequently abandoned in terror, like all the ones already abandoned from boredom or fatigue, all that junk floating in orbit, in the darkness of space where no one can hear you read.

Then, sudden and mysterious sightings of The Writer.

Here and there and everywhere. A figure of bluish light. A message in the sky. A mouthless laugh in vacant bookstores. Finally, a monolithic black stain darkening the skies (someone describes it, accurately, like "what happens when you spill drops of ink in a glass of water") and emergency meetings of political and religious leaders to discuss what to do, what not to do. In the meantime, millions of people stop going to work and—obeying the instructions of that cloud in the clouds—stay at home rereading or reading for the first time the classics of literature. Some, the bravest or most faithful or most zealous, even try to write, to see if they can appease what, certainly, could only be pure and undiluted fury, contained, ready to burst out over the sharp edges of something that was drawing ever nearer, there above, preparing to land and demand explanations and amend errors.

At the same time, also, he is there, he who is still The Young Man but who already senses that before long he'll be, merely, he. It hasn't taken long for The Young Man to discover—coming down from the ecstasy of success—that he can't write anything. He tries everything. Transcendental meditation. Amphetamines of assorted colors. Bach Flowers that produce in him a surprisingly bellicose effect (as if they were Wagner Flowers). Cocaine as white as a blank page (at first he takes drugs to sit and write, but before long he sits down to write to take drugs, to flambé his brain in the frying pan of his cranium). Energy drinks for writers (Qwerty, Plot, Typë, DrINK, Nov/bel) that he doesn't know if he tried before all of this, before they were banned for being carcinogenic and hallucinogenic and for causing all kinds of dysfunctions, or if X is, also, already introducing modifications not only into his eternal present but, also, into his ephemeral past.

Anyway, it doesn't really matter.

What does matter is that The Young Woman is getting tired of The Young Man, as if he were a book that leads nowhere, especially, not to another book after *Girl, Night, Swimming Pool, Etc.*

And the sex they have is sexless now: X—despite his writing—was never very good at the description of amorous and physical scenes and they want to believe that it isn't their fault but X's, whom they can still blame for almost everything. After reconciliations of nineteenth-century purity and a chaste and tentative first kiss of forgiveness; cut to—more in Zen/emaScope than in CinemaScope—waves breaking on rocks and fires in fireplaces and fades to black.

One white night, The Young Man confesses everything to The Young Woman: he tells her about Ishmael Tantor, about Ishmael Tantor's manuscript, about what happened on the airplane when he met The Writer, about what he didn't say. The Young Woman listens, at first as if The Young Man were, suddenly, a good story, another good story; not as good as the one told in *Girl, Night, Swimming Pool, Etc.*, but in the end, the beginning of something new. But then she understands that this isn't the case. That it's a terrible story, unforgivable; and that all is not justified in the name of literature.

And goodbye and meeting again and goodbyes and meetings again and meanwhile, outside their lives, everything starts to disappear.

Everything that remains is like a party in the apartment next door: you put a glass to the wall and all you hear are high-pitched murmurs and the low throbbing of music; the soundtrack of something that could be really fun or really boring.

And at first, for them, a strange and perverse kind of pride, feeling that they're all that's left; that for X, everything passes through them and through the constant rewriting of their lives.

Then, for the first of many times, the suspicion that, maybe, they're not so special, that X (first and foremost and when all is said and done, that letter that, on the keys of ancient typewriters with the name of a rifle, was used over and over, like someone firing a hail of bullets, to cross out words and entire lines) has compartmentalized all of reality into small modular scenes that he reviews like an emperor inspecting his troops but never giving the order to attack.

One morning, The Young Man and The Young Woman, The Man and The Woman, The Man Who Was Once The Young Man and The Woman Who Was Once The Young Woman, The Ex Young Man and The Ex Young Woman, He and She, he and she, discover themselves beside the Museum stairway and under a big sky.

And they look at their surroundings, disconcerted.

And they ask each other where are we, what time is it.

And they look at each other not knowing what to say. But then they know.

"Goodbye," he says.

"Goodbye," she says.

"Goodbye," he and she say, meanwhile, once again, beside the Museum stairway, under a big sky.

Meanwhile, once again, beside the Museum stairway, under a big sky, there is nothing. For once, right now and for the time it takes to think "right now," a kind of absolute emptiness fills everything.

There, nothing but a stairway that leads to nothing, like a pedestal for something that once was there and no longer is, as if all meaning and reason to be had been stolen.

There's no Museum with the shape of head.

There's no luminous and oracular sign.

The Great Inventing Part, like Elvis, has left the building. Stairs that now only lead down and, at the bottom, he and she wonder what to do, how to proceed, waiting for something to happen and for X to provide them with actions and words. Experiencing the loneliness of people who suddenly comprehend that loneliness is a new kind of company. An oppressive loneliness that—after so much time being watched, written, corrected—they don't trust. A suffocating and possessive loneliness, overpopulated with the weight of the absence. Now—they can't believe it, what happened, all they can do is repeat themselves, repeat previously read ideas—there is no Museum, just a stairway.

The empty space where the edifice once stood is empty, no explanations, no excuses.

What happened?

What happened is that the Museum seems to have passed on, to have departed.

And yet, the empty space it left continues to vibrate, for them, with its presence. As if, really, the Museum were now invisible or, better, as if its image, after seeing it for so long, all the time, had been imprinted like a fossil on their pupils.

"Goodbye?" he says.

"Goodbye?" she says.

And the sound of their words, of those words now pronounced so tentatively, like someone opening a door or stepping out on the edge of a frozen lake, feels insufficient and fragile and not at all safe.

Is it time to say "hello" again? they wonder, almost not daring to ask.

Above them, the sky is a perfect and riftless blue. A blue without clouds or birds, suspiciously immaculate, the blue of an animated drawing, the blue of a backdrop, of an overhead backdrop, a blue as if the color blue had just been invented.

He and she look at each other.

They have spent so much time as prisoners of an external will that now they don't know what to say or do and they stand there motionless and waiting for directions and lines. And nothing happens and that nothing is a dreadful thing and he and she discover that that nothing is everything and that that nothing is the most dreadful thing that's happened to them yet. The possibility of an ending—to be left blank and without panic or a page to turn—of maybe being liberated; that thing they dreamed of in low voices, in the silence of their thoughts, now seems to them like a deafening form of a new hell. Having to think about what to think about for themselves. Seeing themselves forced to do what they want and what they desire, trembling because, maybe, it's already too late and, having lost not only the practice but also the theory, they can't think of anything or want anything anymore.

Just in case, before it *is* too late, he's going to try.

He's going to say the first thing that comes to mind, which, actually, is something that's been stuck there for so long. Since the last days of a new age.

At first, the words—*his* words—are pure creaking; like the voice of a door that stopped being opened because there was nothing interesting on the other side, nothing memorable.

He opens his mouth and remembers and speaks and asks:

"How many surrealists does it take to change a light bulb?"

And she looks at him uncomprehending at first, and then with a smile, the smile of someone who is, once again, The Young Woman, smiling at The Young Man.

And, then, a scream descending from the skies and he and she understand that X hasn't left, that he'll never leave, that X is coming back, that they only have a few seconds of freedom left before turning back into characters, before they cease to belong to themselves and belong, once again, to X.

Big Sky is very busy, but he's going to busy himself with them.

Right now.

"How many surrealists does it take to change a light bulb?" he asks again. And answers:

"A beach."

And they both laugh.

And soon their laughter is drowned out by a din of gears and springs.

And there he is.

And they see him come and approach and arrive.

X and X's Museum are now a giant version of Mr. Trip.

That tin toy. That little windup man with the hat and suitcase that he took from the house on the beach, like an Egyptian tomb robber who steals those small statues left to accompany the Pharaoh and his body and shadow and soul on their journey to the other side.

And, truth be told, if he could remember where it was, where it ended up, he'd return it, to appease that fury and break that curse, he'd confess everything.

But not now.

There's no time.

What time is it?

It's time for the colossal and all-powerful Mr. Trip (as a voice tells him to come aboard immediately, that his flight is about to leave without him) to approach them and pick them up in one of his hands and open his suitcase with the other and put them inside.

And he leaves them there until something better occurs to him; because something will occur to him, something has to occur to him.

Please, let something occur, let something occur to him, let something occur to them, right?, right?, right?, meanwhile, once again, beside the Museum stairway, under a big sky.

Meanwhile, once again, beside the Museum stairway, under a big sky, he says to himself that this is, in a way, the closest thing to an Anton Chekov story he'll ever write. He wonders, also, if all the preceding might not be clearer if it were rearranged in strict chronological order, from back to front, with the most nocturnal of tenderness, until it arrived to this eternal present, meanwhile, once again, beside the Museum stairway, under a big sky.

THE IMAGINARY PERSON

A life-view by the living can only be provisional. Perspectives are
altered by the fact of being drawn; description solidifies the past
and creates a gravitational body that wasn't there before. A background of dark matter—all that is not said—remains, buzzing.
—John Updike, *Self-Consciousness*

But if you really want to know why something happened,
if explanations are what you care about, it is usually possible to come up with one. If necessary, it can be fabricated.
—William Maxwell, *The Château*

My memory is reliable on the very things it chooses to remember.
—Rick Moody, *The Omega Force*

The secret of survival is a defective imagination.
—John Banville, *The Infinities*

Imagination is a form of memory.
—Vladimir Nabokov, *Strong Opinions*

How to end.

Or better: How to end?

Adding the question mark that—nothing happens by chance—has the shape
of . . . / OF WHAT? / INSERT HERE /; sharp and pointy pages like the edges
of the wings of Jumbo Jets / FIND, PLEASE, A BETTER SIMILE TO CREATE THE
ATMOSPHERE OF AN AIRPORT /, slicing into both those who rise and those who
fall, pulling them, dragging them down the air-conditioned aisles or making
them fly in pieces through the air to land just inside the airport of these
parentheses / COULD THERE BE PLACES MORE "BETWEEN PARENTHESES" THAN

AIRPORTS? (EXPAND) / that more than one person will criticize or judge as unnecessary; but that, in the uncertainty of a beginning, are oh so similar to hands coming together in an act of prayer, asking for a fair voyage now drawing to an end. And good luck to all, wishes you this voice / ALLUSION HERE TO THE INCOMPREHENSIBLE VOICE OF THE SIREN LOUDSPEAKERS THAT SING AND CONFUSE TRAVELERS IN AIRPORTS? TO THE IRRITATION OF SUCCESSIVE CHECKPOINTS CLOSING LIKE CHINESE BOXES OR RUSSIAN NESTING DOLLS? / that the gag of the parentheses renders unknown, and yet—like with certain unforgettable songs, whose melodies impose themselves over the title—it recalls the voice of someone whose name you can't quite identify and recognize. / BOB DYLAN? PINK FLOYD? LLOYD COLE? THE BEATLES? NILSSON? THE KINKS? / And, yes, if possible, avoid this kind of paragraph from here onward / FORBID ANY FUTURE MENTION OF ELECTRONIC READERS ON PAIN OF DEATH? / ALLUDE TO THAT CHINESE CURSE "MAY YOU HAVE AN INTERESTING LIFE" TRANSLATED NOW INTO MILLIONS OF ASIANS ENSLAVED BY THE WEST TO PRODUCE THEIR SMALL ELECTRONIC INVENTIONS THAT, LATER, WILL IN TURN ENSLAVE THEM, TURNING THEM INTO ADDICTS OF A NEW FORM OF OPIUM? THE CYCLE OF THE INTERESTING LIFE? HAKUNA MATATA? / FEAR THAT THE WHOLE THING IS BEGINNING TO SOUND LIKE AN OBSESSION OR SOMETHING LIKE THAT, FEAR OF BEING LIKE THOSE LUNATICS SCREAMING IN EMPTY STREETS / because, they say, it scares away today's readers, accustomed to reading quickly and briefly on small screens, counting up to one hundred forty, and send / AND, ALONG THE WAY, ASKING, JUST TO KNOW, WHAT PARENTHESES MEAN AND WHAT IS THEIR RAISON D'ÊTRE, BUT, PLEASE; WITHOUT SUCCUMBING TO IMAGES LIKE "PARENTHESES ARE LIKE PRAYER PINS" / THE THING ABOUT PARENTHESES AS "HANDS COMING TOGETHER IN AN ACT OF PRAYER" IS MORE THAN ENOUGH ALREADY" / and . . .

. . . cut and jump and go directly to him running, breezing through checkpoints, shedding any metals, dragging a small but heavy suitcase. The size/weight relationship of luggage is, at a glance, as deceptive and difficult to calculate as that of books. Especially when—as in this case—the suitcase in question is almost completely full of books he's never even opened, most of them by William Faulkner. Almost no clothes; because it was a trip that was short in time and long in distance and he'd fantasized about not coming back or ending up somewhere where clothes wouldn't matter, because particles would be accelerating and scattering and naked. And that's when, taking advantage of the idea of the trip, to get some distance, he'd promised himself (in vain) to take advantage of an interoceanic day or hotel night. To read, there above or there below (nowhere in both cases; because airplanes and hotels are non-places), everything he didn't read in his usual spaces, in the same bed as always, in the destinations he frequented. Right away, of course, he knows it won't happen. That future books, books to be read (so many more than books already read, and to which, pure masochism and instant guilt, he adds another, bought right there, in the airport bookstore), will keep piling up in the library and on tables and on his desk and in chairs and in piles of wobbly architecture that, occasionally, fall in the night, making the exact sound of undead bodies, hungry for brains, crashing to the floor. Books that, removing them, bringing them into foreign territory, we'll look at and will look at us with a face and a cover that say: now what? This is, obviously, an uncomfortable question. *Another* uncomfortable question. One he decides not to answer and to keep on pulling that little rectangle with its wheels and handle.

And—he has researched this—praised be Bernard B. Shadow, then vice president of a company devoted to the production of suitcases and their derivatives, deservedly proud owner of North American patent n° 3.653.474, and to whom it occurred, around the middle of the past century, to put those little wheels on horizontal suitcases. And praised be as well that Northwest Airlines 747 pilot Robert Plath (and subsequent president of Travelpro International), who years later perfected verticalizing the suitcase, shortening it, and (North American patent n° 4.995.487) adding the key evolutionary feature of the extendable handle for pulling it, and, in the beginning, selling it exclusively to crew members who quickly roused the envy and desire of passengers who saw them pass by with the elegance and agility of demigods. Such things—identifying the true geniuses of Humanity and not the false ingeniouses of Subhumanity—are what Google and its tributaries are for, he thinks.

And, there he is, waiting for them to open the doors to his flight. Sitting but almost collapsed, his body adopting the shape of the chair as if he were an empty suit and jacket. Still hurting from the invisible beating delivered by officers specially trained to keep their blows from leaving any actionable bruises, after he tried to do what in the end he didn't do—sordid details to follow. Now, meanwhile and in the meantime, he's killing time. Reading, after his curiosity was piqued seeing so many rolling suitcases, on the screen of his laptop (someone told him that they don't call them that anymore, because companies were afraid that their radiation, after sitting for so long on laps, would cause testicular or ovarian cancer in their users), about the geniuses Shadow & Plath. He finds all the information on a page where, in addition, they explain that the obviousness of the little wheels took so long to develop because airports used to be much smaller and because—sociologically and psychologically speaking—it seems that, for the postwar macho man, using little wheels and carryon luggage was for women or sissies—real men didn't carry suitcases, they checked everything. And besides—like in those old movies that never seemed to age—the suitcases seemed to weigh nothing, they were almost ethereal, maybe they traveled empty from one stage to the next, from one scene to the next. And he wonders again: why, since his vocation was always that of inventing, he didn't apply that talent to inventions like those of Shadow & Plath instead of to literature or whatever it is that he does, that he doesn't do anymore, that, if anything, he undoes. Or—more favorite visionaries, more absurd and compulsive research—the invention of Alfred Fielding and Marc Chavannes, who, in 1957, created that bubbly plastic material to wrap and protect fragile objects. He looks it up and finds it, because the truth is that he'd like them to wrap him up in it now, very carefully, not so he doesn't break but so he won't keep breaking himself. Fielding & Chavannes, he discovers, were actually trying to make a wallpaper that was easy to put up and take down but—serendipity!—they stumbled onto this other thing. Bubble Wrap! Partners and owners of the Sealed Air Corporation! Perfect company! Best companion ever! Millions of dollars a year with a product/business that hangs like a stowaway around many business/products and benefits them just by existing, being there, always ready, like a boy scout! Bubble Wrap Eureka Hallelujah! Blessed be Bubble Wrap and amen, Bubble Wrap Appreciation Day has been celebrated on the last Monday in January all over the world ever since, on that day, a radio station in Bloomington, Indiana, inadvertently broadcast several minutes of the sound of those plastic bubbles bursting while some microphones were being unpacked! Bubble Wrap as something that, in addition, after opening the package, makes us almost want to completely put aside whatever's been sent to us, so that, instead, *the medium of transportation is the message*, we can concentrate, like globalized villagers, on the addictive pleasure of popping bubbles, like how once upon a time, during our adolescence, we surrendered to the epic and forever losing battle against our acne. So, we liberate each tiny dose of sealed air one at a time (there's a type of Bubble Wrap shaped like hearts; which adds to the initial attraction the metaphorical sensation of breaking hearts while we try to forget that it's our own hearts that have been broken and that, there inside, all our personal items have been returned to us, wrapped in Bubble Wrap, and so long, see you never) and we pop them. One after another. Unable to stop. Until not one is left and (this makes even him laugh) there's even an app that allows you to sate this vice virtually until you're able to score a physical dose of the stuff. Finger on the screen and *that sound*. And keep on popping. What makes it even more ingenious: you have to buy meters of the product because we, our own fault entirely, have ruined any chance of reusing something that we discover, as if coming out of a trance, has ceased to have any use whatsoever. Like literature, if you think about it a little. Fiction whose most efficient application in great part functions according to and depends on the variable faculties of the user, of the use that he or she can give it in the space of his or her own nonfiction. He perceives an amusing idea there, an ingenious theory; but for a while now these ideas come to him broken, used up, worn out; as if, more than ideas about which to theorize, they were particles of something that he forgot to wrap in Bubble Wrap and that burst apart in the air and whose memory, never entirely articulated, hurts like slivers sinking into his body and going off and betraying him every time he passes through a metal detector that accuses him of no longer being who he once was and insists on making him pass as someone he used to be, wearing a far-fetched and half-baked mask of himself, as if trying to feed off his increasingly wide but, also, increasingly distant past.

And, yes, the protective bubbles and the rolling wheels are, also, parasitic inventions, like writers who wrap or protect or help carry the weight for readers. But, of course, little wheels and bubbles achieve this, unlike literature, without producing residual effects or unforeseen distortions. So he chose the purest and most turbulent and least profitable variety. He chose to tell stories, not to make History but histories, tuning out almost from the beginning—from his adolescence, when that thing about "When I grow up I want to be a writer" stopped being so funny and started to disturb his elders—warnings from his favorite authors of the time, like Truman Capote and his self-flagellating whip of God-given talent and the consequent difficulty of ascending into the clouds now to bring something back down here later. Or that thing Aldous Huxley said which, when he read it for the first time, still unpublished himself, he nodded and memorized with solemn complicity. That thing that he'd like to forget now, but he can't, he can't: "A bad book is as much of a labor to write as a good one . . . There is no substitute for talent."

Seriously: is he good for anything? Has he been left deflated and with no handle to hold him up and keep from falling? Are his stories good for anything or anyone? Do they reflect his time or, rather, the rarified and unbreathable atmosphere of a planet—Earth—still lacking even a divine or ancient name of its own, punishment maybe for being the only one inhabited by inferior beings? And what if he embraces the electronic, the hip, and patents a book that, every time you come to the end of a chapter, demands a summary and critical assessment of what you've been told and that, if you don't live up to its demands, said book will sleep with your wife, rob your children of affection, and convince your boss to kick you to the curb? Anyway, once achieved, such a demanding book (which could end up tuning in the angst and anxiety of all those people who just want to belong to a brand) wouldn't be of much use when it came to containing its own texts. Impossible to summarize and define. Not even he, in his most recent press conferences (small press conferences fairly light on journalists, the kind of journalists who call him because he's "a cultural figure," and ask him with gratuitous gratuitousness to choose two or three books for a section of recommendations for the Holidays or the New Year or the confluence of Jupiter with Uranus, and then subsequently misspell all the titles of the novels and the names of the writers that he mentioned and, when he reads them, he'll feel like he was the one who'd said or written them incorrectly) and to the despair of his publisher there in attendance, to articulate one or two more or less portable and convenient thoughts. Something that would serve and work and win him a few centimeters in the culture pages of papers where—an old journalist had confided in him—the new and young section editors warned that "if you're going to write about some writer, our manual of style dictates that his body of work is insufficient no matter how good he or she is; to dedicate space to a writer, he or she must, in addition, have an interesting life." And what was an interesting life for a writer? Alcohol? Drugs? Women? Running with the bulls hot on your heels? A happy ending in a hotel suite looking out at a foreign lake? Spontaneously combusting? Vanishing into thin air? One thing was certain: he had little to offer. Nothing spectacular. Simple special effects. His work was like one of those poorly-aged and enormous travel trunks inside of which something always breaks. Pieces of luggage full of small compartments only suited for going on transatlantic voyages, without any hurry and, often, amid storms and seasickness and icebergs and sharks and ladies who want only to sit at the captain's table.

He's already said it many times: airplanes don't scare him, but airports terrify him. Airports are like enormous and devouring leviathans run aground on the shore of all things, too heavy to be pushed back out to sea. Airports are like cathedrals of an always late and retarded faith (and he remembers that aboriginal *cargo cult* where even today modern primitive men send prayers up to Melanesian clouds so they'll rain airplanes and beautiful things down on them, like the silver ghost of Melody Nelson and no, of course not, her ballad will never echo through the air of an airport) and airports are the sanctuary where everyone prays and begs that their flights leave on time, and that they arrive on time, and that their luggage doesn't disappear into some wrinkle in space-time, and that everything that goes up does come down but doesn't fall, amen. Airports are like hospitals: you know when you go in but not when you'll come out and you sit there like something patient, something passing. By comparison, the omnipresence of the past millennium of ports, the greater warmth of train stations, and the minimalist atmosphere of bus terminals seem to him so much more moving and better written. Airports, on the other hand, are like airport bestsellers. They're easy to read, you forget them quickly, you promise yourself to never again succumb to their temptation, and yet the brightness, those signs, those letters in metallic relief . . . And the passengers who consume those airport bestsellers are increasingly worthy of them. Beings with decreasing capacity for concentration, robots of flesh and bone who can't go even a minute without connecting to their devices and extensions, as if they were waiting for the confirmation of the success of a sports star they idolize or the news that they've become fathers or mothers, even though their respective spouses are right there beside them in that very moment, looking after little kids hooked up to tablets where they surf without waves or a beach.

He sits down to catch his breath and can't help being disturbed by the constant sound of mobile phones. Not long ago he read a survey where sixty-five percent of participants said they felt desperate whenever their batteries ran out, because they couldn't help but imagine that "everything important was happening right during that 'disconnected time.'" And they added that they'd relinquish wine, beer, shoes, chocolate, TV, and their car; but never ever their phone. Twenty-two percent went even further and confessed that "their mobile phone was what they most liked taking to bed." And most disturbing of all was actually not, he thought, that their phone was what they most liked to take to bed, but the fact that they took their phone to bed in the first place. And that they were never going to experience the pleasure of cutting off everything, with a powerful and categorical slam, in the middle of a conversation, but had to resign themselves to the placebo of carefully locating that small END button to sign off and over and out. Of course, the new phones were lighter and easier to throw against the wall; but such an outburst ended up being really expensive and . . . He'd read, also, about a woman who, being interrogated by her husband, swallowed her mobile phone and its incendiary messages from her lover so that her infidelity wouldn't be discovered. And that something called WhatsApp was responsible for twenty-eight million divorces; because men and women considered the fact that their respective spouses didn't respond immediately to their messages, requests, trivialities as "mental cruelty" and "psychological abuse." And he'd seen a photo of a phone-shaped coffin. And, of course, he could accept the practicality of mobile phones that, for example, on September 11th, 2001, and during so many other catastrophes, allowed and will allow someone to say goodbye to his loved ones. But, for him, something had been ruined forever in the moment that the ability to be reached everywhere and to work from anywhere was considered a small objective for man and a giant leap for mankind. Something had broken on the oh so functional day when, dysfunctional, the domestic and sedentary and universal onomatopoeia of the ring had stepped down to be absorbed into with the babel of personalized and purchasable ringtones: screams, celebrity catch phrases, theme music from

TV shows, the ephemeral hit song. Everything that, in the end, does nothing but increase the desire to climb aboard that place where—for now, but they say not for long—you are ordered to turn all of that off, provoking in the eyes and ears of the possessed the same anxiety as a lack of nicotine in the lungs and brain. Withdrawal—an eternity disconnected—from knowing what their unknown friends think of them, from continuing to kill zombies with that zombie from Shanghai whom they'll never meet, but whom they can't live without. From doing all those things they can do today thanks to men of science, who chose to devote themselves to fitting all of life into a telephone instead of, like the mad scientists from the black and white movies of his youth, taking on challenges like teletransportation (which would've put an end to airports as a species) without even worrying about the possibility of an accidental what-if.

Not long ago—on another flight, mercifully short—he'd listened to the uninterrupted, hour-and-a-half long conversation of two creatures who, unable to talk *on* their phones, spent all their time talking *about* their phones. At first glance, their appearance was decidedly prehistoric, like tech hooligans. Domed skulls, small eyes, long arms, and huge thumbs, pupils dilated from the need to have something to read and write in increasingly minute text, the repetition of words that seemed to be missing letters. It could be that they weren't even human, but just the previous suburban train station or the past model of Homo sapien. Or maybe the future. Trunk and Clunk? The one and the other—secure and immobile in their seats—fascinated by the properties of their small, currently-deactivated monoliths, referring to them and showing them off to each other and looking at them with the same fetishistic and comparative love that they once dedicated to their cars and women and sex organs in the locker room. Just that now, the pride was tied to having the lightest and smallest and fastest to perform its function. Size was no longer what mattered (or yes it was: but only being smallest) and Trunk and Clunk, nostalgic, unceasingly refer to past devices like dead friends, who'll never be better than the future friends whose applications and superpowers they're already fantasizing about.

The complete opposite of what was going on with him: because mobile phones had complicated the practice of his trade: plotlines were accelerating, it was easy to find and even to track people, all characters were connected instantaneously, and as writer or spectator the only thing he liked was the ease with which those fragile little devices were destroyed once their mission was complete: like rabbits or chickens or cats or those kids who scream and cry and kick the back of the seat in front of them on airplanes and whose necks you tell them you'll wring without thinking twice. But such consolation was no match for the sadness of there no longer being a place in books and movies and shows for wrong numbers, or for hearing something forbidden on crossed wires, or for spying from the living room phone on what someone says on the bedroom phone, or for a certain and vital piece of information to get delayed or lost in transit. Before, not long ago, everything was much simpler and therefore more narratively straightforward and primitive. Nothing was more terrifying than a telephone ringing in the dead of night, and phones weren't going off every five minutes to say nothing. Everything was said, maybe, with bad words; but not written with orthographical errors; with that awful cacophonous *lingua not so franca* that, moreover, required greater or equal effort to *learn* than proper and precise grammar. And his thing, the faithful practice of his craft, required a certain deliberateness, a certain distance, greater silence to function. And so, recently, as an act of rebellion, his books went off in search of other planets or marine depths or distant bygone days: places where there was no coverage and where you could find yourself, far away from here, where it was reported, with a kind of happiness that was inexplicable to him, that across the surface and skies and substrata of the Earth there were already as many little mobile phones as there were earthlings, transporting them around from one place to another, like giants subjugated by the fussing of their electronic infants. Just beneath the surface of all this, all this irritation, he knows that something else is lurking: the realization that this silent and occasionally public diatribe against mobile phones and their applications is nothing more than the awareness that they're all dialing the number of the end of something. The mobile phone—and all those people talking and looking and reading and raving about and on them—is simply the first device that doesn't call to him. That doesn't include him. For the first time. Almost alone and wondering if his grandfather felt something similar—when he watched those strange extraterrestrials that were his adolescent children moving from room to room in the house—in the fifties, at a time when cigarettes weren't bad for you and amphetamines were good for you, plugging in a small Alligator White Philco Slender Seventeener Portable TV, here and there. Yes: that black-and-white white noise was, now, the same terrible sound of the ringtones that let him know that History was proceeding without him and that he—without friends or Facebook, without characters or Twitter—was already outside of History, behind History, out of sight, beyond his horizon. And that that History continued on its journey without him—no problem. In his books, telephones were still heavy and they rang—like oracles foreshadowing cataclysms—in a dark house in the middle of the night and not inside someone's pocket. And so his books, taking place in the last millennium or in a present day of beings more antique than vintage, had less and less place and significance in a world (this was one of the aces up his sleeve that always elicited some laughter in his increasingly infrequent and poorly paid speeches) where, inexplicably, phones had evolved more than airplanes. Airplanes that kept flying at the same speed and offering the same inconveniences as always (and that food, chicken/pasta/meat/fish, of uniform aerodynamic flavor) but with less space between the seats. Lagging airplanes hadn't even granted themselves the subterfuge of incorporating, for a lack of innovation, timeless virtues like the ability to toss excess weight or annoying individuals out the door, like they did in the old galleons when they crossed the subtropical Horse Latitudes, where the winds ceased to blow in the sails. All that'd evolved inside airplanes were the passengers. They no longer smoked, sheltered by the absurdity of that border, as invisible as it was ineffective, between the permeable zones of smoking and nonsmoking. And it'd been years since he saw or heard a passenger vomit into that sad and sordid little bag. And even the children behaved better—they didn't scream or cry or run down aisles—because, he had to acknowledge and appreciate it, they were firmly glued to those small and authorized screens, killing or dying. Only the elderly—convinced of miracle cures—kept wandering like waking sleepwalkers, doing absurd, minimal-effort exercises and gripping all the seatbacks to keep from falling.

But, again, he's just deluding himself: all that irritation with others—which, he's beginning to realize, is the free sample of that constant irritation, for him now fast-approaching, of the old with the young—is, also, just the heavy blanket that he uses to try to cover up his own anger at himself. His literary vocation has run out of fuel and nobody is offering him an emergency runway on which to land. The irrepressible need to put things in writing that once kept him aloft has now surrendered to the gravity of a force that drags him earthward.

Something has stopped working. Flaps. Radar. Something.

Nothing seems to make sense, and the only thing left to wait for seems to be the final glorious explosion of the crash. The only thing that occurred to him was that nothing was occurring to him anymore. And looking back—remembering his books as if they were past destinies—he could sense what it was that'd happened and stopped happening: he'd started out telling very personal stories, his own; not strictly confessional but, yes, conscious of the fact that, in the end and to begin with, all fiction is autobiographical, because it *happens* to the writer, because it's part of his or her real life. And little by little he'd been moving away from himself to tell of other things, of external subjects that he had to go out and hunt down and stuff and hang on the wall of his trophy room, but that never really belonged to him. Now, he understood, he was lost in a universe that was too wide where, in the beginning, everything seemed interesting and even possible to connect. "Only connect," as the disciplined and deliberate E. M. Forster suggested and ordered in the epigraph of *Howards End*. But for him and for the velocity of his things, the free stream of consciousness had become one of his calling cards. Free? Ha. Suddenly he was prisoner in a prison that he'd built himself. And nothing made sense anymore. Short-circuited and circuit shorted. He'd lost (like losing the suitcase that *never* materializes on that rotating conveyer belt) his direction home. And, all of a sudden, he found himself fantasizing that the only solution to his problem was winning the massive first prize of a continental lottery that he'd been dutifully playing twice a week for a while now, so that later, once that huge sum of money was paid out, he'd say to himself "That's it. Done. Enough. No more writing. From here onward just one life for me. Real life. Long live nonfiction." He believed in that and told himself, imagining that he was cavorting about in mountains of money like a millionaire duck: "Ah, now I get it, all that lost time—this is what Catholics must feel. That's why it's such a popular religion: because the solution never comes from inside you, salvation always comes from above, and sins are always forgiven and . . ." But the number combinations that he bet on (combinations whose determination he entrusted, automatically, to a computer that he liked to imagine residing in a secret basement of some new Eastern European country, its red, lidless eye singing digits) had earned him, at most, a few high-grade coins and one or two low-caliber bills, every so often. Just enough to cover next week's bets, except for when—one perfect July morning—he pocketed two hundred fifty euros. He remembers that he went out into the street taking little leaps with his fist raised in the air until, suddenly (like someone coming up to the surface, exultant, from the abyssal depths of an annual medical checkup and suddenly realizing that he'll have another one next year and that eventually, sooner or later, the bad-news wind is going to blow), he realized that that money was, statistically, the one victory that the perverse gods of chance had granted him. That *that* was all he got and that— suddenly thinking in ancient and devalued prose—he'd squandered his one wish on so little. So—without retreating yet in retreat—he kept on thinking about what he could write, writing about what he could think. No longer looking for something to occur (and maybe that's one of the early symptoms of wanting to be a writer: nothing happens, so then . . .) but for something to occur to him.

His last and brief words in the limited space remaining in a notebook that debuted almost a year ago (on a white hospital night when, out of fear, he experienced a terminal indigestion of plotlines), did nothing but reflect his impotence. Just two notes. And both—bad sign—*based on real events.*

To wit: "Shakespeare Riots" and "Kate Harrington/Truman Capote."

The first note corresponded to something that happened involving two Shakespearean actors and confrontations between fans of the theater that left at least twenty-five dead and more than a hundred injured at the doors to Astor Place Opera House in New York on May 10th, 1849. The actors were the American Edwin Forrest and the Englishman William Charles Macready, and what happened was two opposing factions took up arms and raised fists to settle which of the two actors was the better Hamlet and, along the way, to demonstrate the always complicated relationship between the Empire and its former colonies. So, the anglophiles were on the side of the aristocratic and deliberate Macready and the defenders of the New World supported Forrest (whose Danish prince was more like a swashbuckler of the cinema with an air of a working class hero). And when the latter was booed in London (or was it Forrest, passing through London, who booed Macready from the audience, he couldn't really remember anymore), fans from both factions waited for Forrest and Macready's respective Danish princes to coincide in Manhattan. And, like hooligans, like Trunks and Clunks, they arranged to meet at the theater exit . . .

The second of the notes came from reading a long testimony included in a Truman Capote biography. Kate Harrington was the young daughter of Capote's lover: one John O'Shea, a theretofore heterosexual family-man and more or less selfless yet unhappy husband. O'Shea's wife—who adored the writer—didn't get in the way of the relationship. So, everybody happy. And the writer didn't hesitate to adopt the little twelve-year-old Kate—the O'Shea's daughter—and submit her to a kind of modernized version of *My Fair Lady*. Richard Avedon and Francesco Scavullo take photos of her for a portfolio (Kate ends up appearing in the glossy pages of *Mademoiselle* and *Seventeen*), he orders her to keep a diary of her private thoughts (that he corrects and edits), he takes her to his flat at 870 United Nations Plaza and he shows her books and demands that she read *In Cold Blood* and *Out of Africa*. He teaches her to dress and combine colors and brands of clothes and introduces her to his Park Avenue "swans" (Babe Paley and Mary Lazar) and to Henry Kissinger and to Sammy Davis, Jr. and to Ryan O'Neal (who falls in love with her, Kate's now fifteen or sixteen) and he sneaks her into crazy parties at Studio 54 (in the book there's a photo of her and Truman Capote, his face covered by one of those hats he wore, next to an ancient Gloria Swanson). At some point, Capote decides that the next step will be to turn Kate into an actress. But Kate refuses. She knows her limits. She knows she doesn't have the talent for that and she can't help but notice that the writer seems increasingly erratic and desperate. "Okay. I just wanted to help," says Capote. And that's it. Capote stops calling her. It was over. Or maybe Capote called once, but nobody was home at the O'Shea residence (that's *another* thing phones used to be good for and *another* thing today's phones have done away with: the fantasy that someone *did* call you, but you weren't there to answer) and soon Capote can no longer dial a number without getting it wrong and before long making a phone call is as hard as writing that novel he'd talked about so much, that novel that no longer answered his call, under storm clouds and lashing whips of lightning.

And now, for him, everything that he'd written down there was nothing. He didn't even know what it was that it *wasn't*. Two stories? One novella? Two parts of a whole or random pieces of a puzzle that he didn't understand, but was sure that he'd understood at some point, when he wrote those two lines down the way you write down dreams that you don't remember or understand when you read them the next morning? *Only connect?* ONLY *connect?* Yes, *only* try to *connect*, why didn't you come out of the closet, damned E. M.? Easy to say, hard to do and even harder to write. Something had stopped working, something had broken. Inside of him. And he wanted and needed to believe that it wasn't the simple and banal and undignified and undeserved material fatigue (the sickness of airplanes) and he preferred to think that behind that motionless void there *had to be* something more transcendent. Something that would explain everything and, once absorbed, would provide the answer to the question and put things in motion again. Something like a recently-exploded childhood trauma, like those bombs from bygone wars that, every so often, are found in a fallow field. Or something like what supposedly happened to J. D. Salinger, something that nobody actually knows whether it did or did not happen. Or something even more banal but, at least, easier to pin down: like what he felt when, not long ago, one night, he woke up with a pain in his chest. As if there, inside him—he thought at the time and liked the image—was growing a black rose whose petals were thorns. And, after dragging himself to the emergency room, it'd been removed, but maybe, unknowingly, along with the malignancy of that dangerous flower, they'd also taken *something* important, something vital. Or, who knows, maybe they actually implanted *something*. He remembers that it was there, while he waited for the results of some tests and a diagnosis, in those two or three hours of uncertainty, wandering through the hallways of the clinic, that he experienced, diminished by panic, the unexpected and furious deluge of ideas for stories. So many that he could barely get one written down because another wave was already coming—another possible story. He filled the notebook with more than enough material for a book that could well have been titled *Book of Families* or *Fathers, Mothers, Brothers, Sisters & Co.* The whole thing felt like a last will and testament, like a possible legacy. But when the doctor arrived with good news, it was as if it all dissolved, lost potency and importance. And the next day, rereading his notes, all of it seemed—once again—like a flat-tire dream wrapped in a transparent veil that protected nothing beneath the Bubble Wrap of his eyelids. Since then, nothing. He'd tried absurd methods like copying things he'd written decades ago to see if that'd get the engines running. Or coming up with sequels or prequels to classics. Or classics written from another point of view. *Moby-Dick* narrated by the white whale. Things like that. Then, pretty much right away, he started drinking. Not to excess; but enough so that his days went by as if they were being written by someone else, by someone who was writing him and freeing him from having to write himself, from having to think about impotent actors or potential actresses.

If, at some point, the stories of the Shakespearean disturbances and of Kate Harrington could've blended into something about the girl turning into a brilliant Shakespearean actress in successful contemporary young-adult adaptations, set in high schools, something like that. Into something like Rosemary Hoyt in *Tender Is the Night*, adored by her fans; but also in the crosshairs of a sect of fanatical purists and terrorist protectors of the memory and legacy of Shakespeare self-styled The Revengeful Hamlets and . . .

Now, not so much. Now everything sounded to him like the deafening and incomprehensible buzz of that voice over the airport loudspeakers from which he managed to pick out only a few stray words until, among them, he discovered the repetition of his last name followed by the final and urgent call to board his plane or be left behind, possibly forever.

So, again, with the attitude of someone who believes he's breaking some Olympic record, he starts running, at a speed that was once a brisk walk. He is, yes, in the last of those borderland ages: a place where there's nothing but a sad highway motel, between fifty and sixty years old, a place he'll never pass through again. That spectral decade in which, suddenly, so many things stop happening. And stop happening forever. The features of a middle-aged man haven't yet ceased to be those they were previously; but, ah, they're already beginning to be what they'll become: those of the man no longer so firm and as if turning to liquid, as if passing through the first stages of a thaw from which there's no going back. Watching him closely, seeing him pass by at what's full speed for him but really not so fast, he thinks, must produce the nauseous sensation of looking at an out-of-focus photograph. One of those blurry and red-pupiled photos that no longer exist, that are no longer taken, that no one shoots or waits to have developed. So there he goes. Running in slow motion, but not like in those movies or shows where slowness is a device used to show hyper-velocity. No, his is not a special effect but (how many times has he already deployed this awkward play on words?) a special defect. There he goes. Breathing through his mouth from the effort. As if he weren't on his feet and moving, but sitting and motionless. How he once felt, so long ago, holding any of his many favorite novels. With his eyes wide open and with one of those books that, with time's rapid passing, with time's running, from the start, make you pay the toll of having to learn everything anew: a new game of new rules, a breathing all its own, whose rhythm you have to absorb and follow if what you want is to climb up on the shore at the top of the last page.

Now, again, no longer, no more.

Now he's running not like someone chasing but like someone fleeing. And someone who knows that it won't be long now before he's caught.

Entering an airplane is like entering a really bad novel. One of those realist novels (so proud to be so and to proclaim it) that, though it tries, is unable convince us of anything it says and where we can anticipate everything that'll happen, because we've already lived it, we've already been there, it already happened to us—*déjà visité* more than *déjà vu*.

There, that absolute fidelity to the utterly repeatable. A novel that would do much better to call itself fantastic. Or, even better, *true*. To admit from the outset, in case of an accident, that the oxygen masks only serve to dull the hysteria of the passengers and that the function of the seatbelts is to keep bodies from scattering all over the place at the moment of impact and the whole thing about putting your head between your knees (impossible position, taking into account the increasingly diminished space between seats) was good for nothing except (just like that absurd illusion of nonsmoking seats was good for nothing back when airplanes were like a tank of suspended nicotine gas), if you survive, to leave you with a brutal muscular contraction or, if you're unlucky, a broken spinal cord.

Almost collapsing, he presented himself panting at the gate of departure, which was about to close, and they took him in a car to the airplane, which had already cut the umbilical cord connecting it to the airport, and—he liked this detail—they had to pull up an old stair car so that he could climb up to the rear door. Now, entering that airplane, for him, is also an unpleasant experience: because he has to traverse the whole plane until he gets up to the front end and climbs up to first class, and several of the passengers sarcastically applaud his arrival as he passes by. His distraction with what was going on around him and his concentration on what he'd already taken in has delayed the flight's departure. A flight that's now lost its turn for takeoff and—the captain informs them, identifying the culprit with first and last name—will be "around fifty-five minutes" late, which is far better than saying "an hour." And then the none-too-convincing consolation of "we'll do our best to make up the lost time during the flight," and over and out. He makes a little bow to the resentful coach passengers (with that air of cargo on a slave ship) and arrives to that small exclusive hump of the 747 (démodé futurism, Heywood Floyd, pen floating in the air), deposits his suitcase in the overhead compartment after removing a book that's not by William Faulkner, lets himself fall into his wide seat full of controls (a new function in the remote control and the screen on the seatback in front of you allows you to traipse through a blueprint of the plane and start a chat with unknown passengers sitting in other seats and discuss things like being afraid of heights and the quality of the food and the curves of that girl sitting up front or the shrieks of that baby crying in the back, he surmises; anything to distract you from the temptation of reading a terrestrial novel from the nineteenth century, when mankind only dreamed of flying and wrote about it), and orders the first of various shots of bourbon from the flight attendant who, perfectly trained, because he's one of the elite, smiles at him with all her teeth, unconcerned about the delay he's occasioned. She hands him a case containing toiletries, headphones, and items he'll never use, those slippers and that eye mask. And she keeps on smiling. It's clear that she's paid to smile at him, but he chooses to believe that she loves him, that it's love at first sight, something that's just about as impossible to believe in (maybe even more) as the thing about the seatbelt, the oxygen, the emergency position, the nearest exit, as if the exit were ever nearby.

In the seatback in front of him is the newest edition of the airline company magazine (just opening it sharpens the pain in his back, the echo of the beating he'd been given); so he skips straight to the last pages, ignoring the brief and breezy articles about beaches and bars and palaces and some celebrity saying that "Nothing interests me less than being famous." And, yes, the celebrity is IKEA, following him and finding him on earth as in the heavens. So, better, he opts for the pages—could the lack of oxygen contribute to the uncontrollable desire to buy things you don't need?, he wonders—advertising an array of products. The pages enumerating and exhibiting the on-board duty-free items. And—among the chocolates and watches and perfumes and fountain pens, next to airplane replicas and miniature videogame consoles and, this is true, this is true, an app you can download on your mobile phone that can remotely control where cockroaches go in your house—they have for sale a surprising and dignified antique toy. Something out of time and place. Something that, without a doubt, few would want but that, all of a sudden, as if in the vertigo of a sudden fever, in that indeterminate nowhere that is the interior of an airplane, he needs more than anything in the universe. There, in the photo, they're offering a small windup tin man carrying a suitcase— Mr. Trip. He decides, without really knowing why, that he's going to buy it. Maybe to see whether or not the little man's suitcase has wheels, to make it easier to carry, so that the toy would help him carry himself.

He unfolds his tray table (not fixed to the seatback in front of him but that, exclusively, extends like a tentacle out from one of the armrests) and adopts the only position he believes in, the only position he could swear has afforded him any pleasure and survival, and that doesn't figure in any manual of sexual techniques but in the most distant and yellowed pages of his life: the "resting position." In elementary school. After lunch. Arms on top of the table, head on top of arms on top of the table, waiting for permission to go outside and play at the longest and most digestive recess. But now, after only a few minutes of that consoling darkness, between his arms, the flight attendant tells him to fold up his tray table and sit back for take off. It seems that the flight has been granted a pardon and an opening for departure. Prepare for takeoff. And, once again, confirmation that, no matter how many times it gets explained to him or he reads about it, he'll never understand how and why airplanes fly. Better like that, right?

He's always distracted himself from such fortunately incomprehensible questions by opening a book whose mechanics and science feel more familiar to him and, at least, malleable. And his "travel book" has changed over the years. First, oh so obviously, it was Jack Kerouac's *On the Road* and, at the time of departure and having just emerged from adolescence, heading out on his obligatory formative journey, he read, as if it were a kind of prayer, that thing about "Live, travel, adventure, and don't be sorry." And that other thing about how "The only people for me are the mad ones, the ones who are mad to live, mad to talk, mad to be saved, desirous of everything at the same time, the ones who never yawn or say a commonplace thing, but burn, burn, burn like fabulous yellow roman candles exploding like spiders across the stars."

Years later he moved on to John Cheever's *Journals* and the recitation of that thing about "What I'm going to write is the last of what I have to say, and Exodus, I think, is what I have in mind. In the speech on the 27th I will say that literature is the only consciousness we possess, and that its role as a consciousness must inform us of our inability to comprehend the hideous danger of nuclear power. Literature has been the salvation of the damned; literature, literature has inspired and guided lovers, routed despair, and can perhaps, in this case, save the world."

Now, he no longer believes in such things and the book that he always takes with him to open at the beginning of every trip is *Ways of Dying*: an award winning essay, penned by a prestigious surgeon who describes clearly and precisely—so that even he can understand it—the many manners and ways a human being can end up dead. The function of this book, of course, is to frighten away the stranger sitting next to him. An unequivocal signal that he's not the type of person given to casual conversations or one who needs to be told your whole life story. His thing was death's many forms and talking to him would, probably, bring bad luck and all of that. So best to let him rest in peace.

He opens the book at random and starts to read the section devoted to death by drowning in oceans or seas or rivers or lakes. "Drowning is, in essence, a form of suffocation in which the mouth and nose are occluded by water," it says. And "occlude": he likes that verb. And it continues: "If it's a suicidal drowning, the victim won't resist inhaling the water. But if it's accidental, he or she will fight to hold their breath until exhaustion prevents them from continuing to do so." He likes its literal and literarily surgical and informative prose (it's not the same, apparently, to drown in salt water as it is in fresh water; something to remember to use as a conversation starter with a stranger sitting at the bar in a bar) that talks about the liberation of great quantities of potassium and the destruction of red blood cells. It seems to him like such a functional prose and almost poetic in its total lack of linguistic devices. Like those Zen kōans that, merely descriptive, out of nowhere achieve the epiphanic with lines like the one he reads now: "A lifeless human body is heavier than water." Or, after describing the dead body's transit through the depths and its progressive deterioration until, after days or weeks, drifting in a liquid limbo, it finally rises and starts to float: "When the body returns to the surface, it's difficult for its horrified discoverer to believe that that rotten thing once contained a human spirit and shared the air breathed by the living with the rest of humanity." Exactly, he thinks, feeling now, simultaneously, like the horrified discoverer of his own rotten thing.

"That book is quite good," a voice says at his side. And it adds: "But it seems to me that, with respect to drowning, it comes up short. There are many more interesting things to be said about the subject."

He turns his head and, in the seat next to him, there's a man who smiles at him with a smile like a cartoon rodent, holding a book as voluminous as his own. He reads the title: *The Story of Stories*. He's heard people talk about that book. Another recently acclaimed essay that purports to establish an evolutionary theory of the art of telling stories or something like that. Stories surging from marine depths and landing on beaches, like talking crabs under moons of long and volcanic nights, conversing and exchanging plotlines and setting a course for high ground and telling each other that they're not done yet, that this is just the beginning of a great adventure that, with the passing of millennia, they'll be able to put in writing with pincers that'll trap everyone who hears them and reads them and hears them reading them. There was a time when he read that kind of book. Many. Many of them. Now he limits himself to reading various reviews and then it's as if he'd read the books and, subsequently, he could even swear that he really did.

"Excuse me?" he says with the tone of someone demanding an apology.

The man keeps on smiling and points at *Ways of Dying* with a little finger that doesn't look like a grown man's finger. Small hands and his little finger resembling that of a kid who was never taught that you shouldn't point in public.

"It appears that we've gotten our books mixed up. I brought this to scare away a possible high altitude talker. You too, right? Because I know who you are. I was at your roundtable yesterday. No, I haven't read your work. I'm sorry. I went with a niece who works in the press office of a publisher. She had to attend to the details of the visit by the author of *Landscape with Hollow Men*. A famous writer, they say. You know him?"

"Just by name."

"Ah."

"Anyway, I'm a medical examiner. And the thing about drowning . . . There are more interesting things to be said about it."

"For example?" he asks without understanding why; but it's also true that the fact that the stranger has *not* read IKEA instantly makes him an appealing person, deserving of a little kindness and civility.

"To begin with, death by drowning, contrary to what many think or wish, is not a romantic or fluid death. Maybe they're confused or fooled by the presence of water. The whole thing about sinking and floating underwater. To relax and let yourself be taken by the currents like someone slowly falling asleep and filling up with some cool and liquid thing until they dissolve. We come from water and to water we'll return. But no, no, no: all death, including 'normal' death is nothing more and nothing less than the abrupt cessation of activity of an engine that's been running, with luck, uninterrupted for a long time. All death is, as such, as quick as a cataclysm for the body as a natural disaster is for a city, suddenly left without any power supply."

"Aha."

"And so, when it comes to drowning, the process itself is particularly thought-provoking. The different stages that take place in the act itself. It's like a performance in multiple acts. In all death, even from the physiological standpoint, there's a kind of storyline, a narrative arc."

"Aha."

And the man begins to recite, enumerating on his little fingers:

"Act one: fear. Most people scream and flail their arms. Act two: they go under and swallow water. More fear. The larynx and vocal chords contract and it's no longer easy to scream. This is known as laryngospasm. An involuntary reflex. Act three: unconsciousness and the beginning of the cessation of breathing. Act four: small and abrupt movements, hypoxic convulsions, the skin beginning to change color. Blue. Act five: clinical death. Cardiac arrest. The end of the blood's circulation. Act six, and this is when things get interesting: biological death. Some four minutes after clinical death. It's like the death of death. The point of no return, so far away that nobody can be brought back from it. Any cardiopulmonary resuscitation impossible. See you never. Sweet dreams."

Hey: but if that's the case, it's exactly how I feel whenever I try to write, he thinks.

"But, and most people don't know this, most important of all"—the man continued, after taking a sip of his welcome-aboard champagne—"is the fear. Fear is what marks all death. Fear is death's true author and, in multiple autopsies, I've found a small sphere of something that looks like lead; like an antique bullet, covered in fine and short capillary filaments. But it's not lead; it's organic matter. Though maybe, at the same time, it's like a bullet. Because it is, I'm certain, the solidification of fear. Fear's physical and solid and palpable manifestation. And I've only found it in people who, I've checked, were very frightened when they died. Oddly enough, the majority were either victims of drowning or practicing Catholics. The former is understandable; because it's the kind of death that *lasts* longer and allows the fear to grow and lodge itself inside us, with us. The latter I don't really get, because you'd think that, finally, they'd be gaining access to that oh so anticipated heaven, right? The greatest fear I discovered was in the guts of a cardinal. But I've never had a writer. Are writers really frightened when they die? Because it's obvious that, I imagine, they live in terror, right? It can't be easy to spend your whole life afraid that no ideas will come to you. Or that ideas will stop coming to you. And, suddenly, you die convinced that your best, your best idea, could well have been yet to come or has been left irretrievably behind, right? If you're thinking of dying in the near future, here's my card. It'd be a huge favor, I'd be very grateful. If you let me look inside your body, I mean. I'd be discrete, scout's honor. Of course, I haven't included anything about the spheres of terror in my autopsy reports. I take them home, of course. I have a large collection."

"Ah . . ." he says. And he remembers the terror glands, in that comic, from his more or less terrifying childhood, but, ah, he loved the horror genre so much; but this man was starting to frighten him, another kind of fear—not the fear that you seek out for the pleasure of being frightened, but the fear that comes looking to frighten you.

"And having said what I said and seeing your face, I don't think there's any reason for us to talk for the rest of the flight, right? So let's trade books. And nothing to see here," concludes the examiner.

He hands over *Ways of Dying* and takes *The Story of Stories*, like someone exchanging one prisoner for another, in the middle of a border bridge cloaked in shadows and fog, in a black and white movie, or in one of those novels where you know from the start—the best friend or the beloved mentor will always be the treacherous mole.

And, to keep from seeing that rodent face, he turns his head and looks across the aisle. A young man is staring at him. The seat beside him is empty and he wonders if it might not be better to go over there, next to him, as far from the fear-extractor as possible. But no, the seat isn't empty—there's something in it that looks like a thermos or a cocktail shaker, fastened with the seatbelt. The young man keeps staring at him as if, more than looking at him, he were reading him. The young man is holding a book and he smiles at him and shows it to him: *The Seven Capitol Scenes*. He's read about it too. A kind of self-help manual for people who, due to some sort of genetic or psychological disorder, need to be writers. One of those books that makes a case for literature, but that doesn't seem willing to let literature just be literature. So scientific elements are introduced, trying to find secret formulae, the primordial alchemy of "Once upon a time . . ." as a "DIY," but always keeping it far out of reach of the children.

The young man smiles at him, complicit, timid, anxious, a reader but not an entirely pure one. A turbulent halo surrounds him. He recognizes the species to which he belongs immediately—a reader who wants more than anything in the world to become a writer. With years and practice it's become easy for him to identify them: dilated pupils, quivering nose, an odor between acidic and saccharine, like the shit of newborns who don't know how to read but already want to write. It's clear that the young man has also recognized him by his name—that the captain announced over the loudspeaker—and not by his face: his books haven't included an author photo for a while now and he no longer looks anything like he did in the days when they wanted to photograph him. There was a time when he wore that same cloying and desperate perfume, and who knows what he smells like now. Maybe like an old book. Or like an old man with a book. Anyway, he hears the alarms and alerts and possible turbulence. And yet—not learning from the experience that years supposedly grant—his first impulse is to let himself be recognized and to acknowledge the young man. Make him more or less happy. Offer him strength and hope. Be a lightning god, for the long hours of this flight at least. Toss him a scrap, so he can go tell his young friends and colleagues about it and, not too underhandedly, give him a little push so he flies a bit too high and burns his wings and suffers and comes to know what it is to be good, in the worst way possible. He spies on him out of the corner of his eye and can sense his absolute tension, dancing the to-speak-or-not-to-speak minuet that he danced so often when he was young and ran into someone, into one of his favorite and not-so-favorite writers, in the streets. Back then, he remembers, writers weren't as visible or accessible as today. They only emerged from their basements or came down from their attics for the occasional interview. Or, every so often, for the presentation of one of their or somebody else's books every so often. Events where some brave or clueless person would force their self-published book on him. Small books with long handwritten dedications that can't be recycled or exchanged for other books (he's afraid to tear out the handwritten page because someone might utilize that magic trick of basic espionage, shading in the blankness of the next page with a black pencil so that "For the master to whom . . ." appears again) and which he disposed of, with true paranoia, not in hotel rooms but, just in case, in airport trashcans. Back when he was first starting out as a reader who wanted to be a writer, there weren't so many book fairs and festivals or organizers who wrote to say that they were willing to cover travel and lodging costs, as if contemplating and longing for an alternate reality where writers crossed oceans for nothing and slept on the streets and in the parks. There weren't any bookstores with cafes to make appearances in. Or blogs from which to harangue the feeble and puny masses, even (he read about this) from beyond the grave, prepaying a company to keep you alive and updated post-mortem. There was no Internet or email inboxes (and every more or less serious writer tends to have an easily traceable address: name and last name and @ symbol and the ending of one of those free corporate entities in the service of the FBI & CIA & Co., so happy now that citizens offer up their own private lives without protest or hesitation) where anyone can send you weighty text documents/files of unpublished work without paying for printing. Without even asking permission first and requesting a reading, an opinion (which has to be highly favorable), to be put in touch with an agent, an introduction to an editor, and, if possible, a shortcut to an award. So, when the most timid get up the nerve to ask for his address, he says whatever random thing, sending them down one of the web's dead-end alleyways, when what he'd really like to do is shout at them: "Didn't your parents ever teach you not to accept things from strangers? Yes, right? Good, the second part of that lesson is don't expect strangers to accept anything from you, idiot." He, back then, had never done anything like that. He'd come up as a writer's apprentice at a time when the concept of vertical and precipitous hierarchies and levels and workplace seniority and access controls existed. Now, not so much. Now it was all open bar and horizontal and flat buffet, like the wide-open parking lot of a final encephalogram. Now everyone was sitting together at the same table. Now you lose your seat if you get up to go to the bathroom. And everything goes so fast, speed is *so* important now: they call you the "New Joyce" or "New Whoever You Like Best" not at the end, but at the beginning of your career, when your first book comes out. He said once that he liked being a writer less and less and liked writing more and more. Now, a while later, he didn't like being a writer and he didn't write. And he didn't know what he was or what he liked anymore. But he knew *everything* he didn't like all too well. And everything he didn't like was almost everything. He didn't have a plan B or, like airplanes, an emergency exit. What would be next? Launching himself like a kamikaze and starting to say things like writing is suffering and there's no art without pain?

So he looks at the boy and stares into his eyes and thinks better of it—thinks it and period—and brings his index finger to his lips. Silence. Do not disturb. Do not even think about saying word one to me, kid. And, with a terrible smile, he watches the kid sink into himself, lower his gaze, almost releasing a dying moan. *Ways of Dying.* Dying of shame and, with time, if things go well for the boy, he'll be forgiven, after all, it's a good story for his history. Something the boy will recount in epic fashion, with added details, improving the anecdote of his terrible encounter with that total son of a bitch. Today's fright is tomorrow's delight, nothing is lost, everything is transformed and even rewritten, and *that* is exactly what literature is all about.

So now he even has a feeling, or really a premonition, in that brief instant of the possibility of something, a distant spark that might start a fire somewhere nearby. It's been a long time since he tuned in that station, which years ago he heard loud and clear and all the time and that seemed to only play his favorite music. What he hears now, on the other hand, is more like the tuneless message, more inaudible all the time, of an astronaut floating in space. A "Houston, I know we have a problem; but let me tell you . . ." It's not much, but it's something, or, at least, a lot more than he's experienced in many years. So many that imagining what might come from that rather Henry Jamesian situation—a young aspiring writer approaching an old though not necessarily master writer whose experience isn't good for anything anymore; plus the brilliant manuscript of a young, unpublished dead man—gives him a cosmic and floating headache. And in exchange for all of that, lost in space, outside his suit and the cloudy plastic of his helmet, just a few faraway spores that, if they come to rest on the right planet will evolve and turn into something worth telling. Would it be worth it to go back, to arrive to Jupiter and beyond infinity? But that feeling of weightlessness and dizziness doesn't last long—the experiment has failed. False alarm and true relief and launch aborted. I'm sorry, my friends, but this mad scientist is no longer good for grand fantasies and deliriums. Run your test somewhere else and with a more resistant and less exhausted specimen. *Out of Order, Out of Work*. Find new instructions and disassemble a new model with batteries included and not worn out. Lightning and thunder and primordial stew and alphabet soup— elsewhere. Nothing works here anymore, nothing works.

And *The Story of Stories* is about or, better, is trying to discover something its author denominates "the fiction genome," to understand the need to tell stories as the thing that, Darwinianly, separates the human from the animal and makes it the fittest of species; if and when, of course, it is not a Disney-brand animal. And, once the genome is discovered, to draw a map going in reverse, not leading to the treasure, but departing from it. And the X on the map of the author of *The Story of Stories* is Homer's *The Odyssey*. It's clear that, before that time, humans were already expert weavers of storylines, but then and there, with Odysseus/Ulysses, the essayist claims, the writerly brain makes a quantitative and qualitative leap. Thereafter, he argues, writers—half sailors, half castaways—are constantly on their way back to Ithaca, but they're not in any great hurry. And they're more than ready to visit—along with sirens and cyclopes and ghosts—new ports. And, the romantic thinker continues, the key to transmitting, in a more decisive and memorable way, information that's vital for our survival through the centuries resides in our ability to imagine enduring stories. So, writing and literature as a form of communion and blahblahblah, with abundant diagrams, periodic tables, and even reproductions of cranial X-rays.

There was a time, oh so many frequent flyer miles ago, when he believed and even got excited about subjects and proposals like this. It was easier for him to believe in all of that, the way he once believed in Sandokan and D'Artagnan and Nemo. Literature functioning, physiologically, as an organized organism, as a kind of brotherhood that he belonged to—*we happy few, band of brothers*, etcetera.

Now, not so much. Now he's alone. And empty. And withered. Now, not back in his house but in a house he can't escape from and where not even his dog would recognize him. Now he's like a beggar who barks but no longer bites and who, almost without realizing it, falls asleep in the first armchair he finds, run aground, not tied to a mast; not hearing the sinuous call of sirens, but the deep voice of the captain from the bridge in his cockpit in the stars, saying something over the airplane's loudspeaker. A voice like a cheap DJ with awful musical taste saying something that isn't "Sing to me of the man, Muse, the man of twists and turns driven time and again off course." Saying, in multiple languages, that they were entering a turbulence zone, as if "Turbulence Zone" were a hit-single that everybody knows yet nobody dares sing, but c'mon, all together now, here's one we all know.

"The truest and best and most venerable bluesmen never repeated themselves, not because they decided not to, but because they didn't know how: for them, never having recorded albums where they could listen to themselves, the concept of singing the same song the same way didn't even exist," he thought, just a few hours ago, yesterday, in a hotel room, in another country farther away all the time as the airplane advances into the storm, through the night going in reverse. The kind of thing that comes to him more often all the time. Without warning. Random phrases that, as mentioned, until recently he wrote down in notebooks or on pieces of paper because they could be useful in something or for something. Now—also again, repeating himself in an attempt to convince himself that he's doing something and at a point in his life when everything that he's stopped doing is difficult to start to do again—not so much. As soon as hears them inside his head, he says them aloud to see how they sound and waits for oblivion to take them. Phrases like hotel rooms where you stay for a while and then leave for the next hotel and the next room and, if it were up to him, he'd sign up for his own future death in a hotel room. Death in a hotel room as a *way of dying*. To order death like room service and to sit down and wait for Death to bring his death to him and, humming the blues, to leave him on the other side, at the opening of the gate and "Fixin' to Die," "In My Time of Dying," and "See That My Grave is Kept Clean."

For him, hotel rooms were always—like for Vladimir Nabokov, in a hotel near to this one, because though he'd finally recovered his fortune "it makes no sense to buy a villa, because I won't live long enough to train the servants to my taste and needs"—the peak of civilization. There (even though the designer showerheads had become too complicated in recent times and the magnetic cards to unlock the doors incessantly deactivated themselves and you had to go down to the front desk to get them reprogrammed) you had everything you needed to survive: doorway (where they recommend that you stand in case of an earthquake and where nobody stops to check their Twitter feed), bed, food, TV (where they always seem to be broadcasting *2001: A Space Odyssey* or *Apocalypse Now*, two of the greatest hotel films in the entire history of film), even one big book (the Bible in the bedside table drawer). And a small and almost monastic desk that helps maintain a certain order or lack of disorder (and that, in its asceticism, seems to inspire writing or to summon despair; so, better to write, to create disorder). And a pleasant landscape whose discomforts (heat and noise, insects and cold) cannot come inside, thanks to those windows that don't close because they can't be opened. Also, the possibility to make it so the telephone doesn't ring and even to request paid companionship, where the always ambiguous and unstable foreign currency of feelings won't be a factor. And the magic of that little sign that you hang on the doorknob—not ordering but imploring: PLEASE DO NOT DISTURB—that he once took home with him and scanned and that now he sends as an automatic response to any inopportune, undesired, and unnecessary email.

Hotel rooms—like that suite to end all suites, at the end of *2001: A Space Odyssey*—are, also, closed ecosystems, sites to destroy, limbos in which to disappear, impious laboratories where, alone, you're always the specimen in the experiment. In a hotel room—as if under oath—you cannot lie to yourself. And you judge yourself. And condemn yourself.

The night before—in the implacable magic mirror of the hotel, its border of electric bulbs as if he were a vintage Hollywood starlet ready for her close-up and fade to black—the not-so-successful premiere of something no makeup artist or director of photography could hide: the indisputable and undeniable body of a newly old man, of an old man who's still relatively young, but who can't ignore the growing sound of the avalanche that's bearing down on him. Should he have played more sports, taken better care of himself, when his muscles were still moist and supple? Probably. And it's not the first time he's said this to himself and remembered forgetting to do it. But he's not fooling himself or feeling guilty either: he was always so clumsy at all physical activity that, more likely than not, if he had done any, he'd have died a long time ago, broken into pieces or crushed or squeezed by the improper use of one of those hellish contraptions for gymnasiums with names like Abdominal Crunch Machine or Chest Press Stimulator or Mucho Muscle Terminator. Chiseled chiselers of bodies deluded by the relatively impractical theory that their health and physique will be improved and toned, all of a sudden and when it's already too late, demanding something from them that hadn't been asked in decades. Something as absurd as if he spontaneously imposed the form of perfect and golden sonnets or of screenplays for summer blockbusters on his writing. The only thing that can come from such delusion and torment, the inevitable collapse of internal and indispensable muscles like the heart and the brain.

So, when he's staying in a hotel, he likes to wander through the empty fitness centers at night, like a ghost. To look and not touch. And yes, in a real dark night of the soul it's always three o'clock in the morning, so what time in the dark night of the soul would it be when—like right now, on this hotel night, the night before the night on the airplane—it is exactly three o'clock in the morning.

He leaves his hotel room walking very slowly, imitating the movements of an astronaut exiting his space pod to float neither up nor down in space, advancing toward the elevators down a hallway of closed doors and empty food trays. Why does he persist in the same nonsense he did when he was a kid? A good question that doesn't need a bad answer. Best to answer: just because. And keep on doing it. Another of his many private rituals. Like that private ritual that he started when he was about six or seven and still does every time he goes out to take a walk into the street: he chooses a person and follows them and, tracing their footsteps, he tells himself that he'll only stop and change objective and prey when he sees a woman wearing a blue shirt. And he'll follow that shirt until, for example, a boy with a red baseball cap appears. And so on—several strangers later—to see where he ends up. And ask himself what he's doing and what to do there. Now that he thinks about it, he wrote about this before. And, before writing about this, he always wrote a little bit *like this*. About everything and everyone. With pure intuition, as if tracing the blueprint of a building while building it. And seeing how and what emerges and whether or not it's possible to live there. But at three o'clock in the morning (he remembers another one of these walks, a while back, through one of those hospitals/state-of-the-art clinics), there's nobody to follow but himself.

So, in the modality of astronaut David Bowman, he arrives to the elevator and pushes the button to go down to the basement-level fitness center and the doors open and—"My God, it's full of stars!"—inside are two massive black men and, in between them, there's something that's either a little man or a huge bird. They shift only slightly to allow him to enter and the black men cross their column-sized arms and, up close, the being whose body they're obviously guarding looks at him with small, curious eyes. His face has the fresh and timeless texture of the greatest mummies, if mummies could sport a thin moustache like a Tombstone or Deadwood card shark. And his features—as if a stone had been thrown into the pond of his face—seem to flow, liquid, between adolescence and old age and forward again and now back—outside of time. It takes him a few long seconds to realize that that man is Bob Dylan. He repeats it to himself to confirm it, to believe it: "That man is Bob Dylan." That. Man. Is. Bob Dylan. Beside him. In a hotel elevator. And, suddenly, it's as if that brief descending trajectory lasts for years. His years. Years, like now, for a couple minutes, beside Bob Dylan. Each and every single year that—he brings a hand to his nose, knowing that he's giving off the unbearably cloying baby-shit stench of a star-struck-novice—he's spent listening to and admiring Bob Dylan. Years that include that long night of his youth when, in the darkness and with headphones on, in one sitting, he listened to *Bringing It All Back Home*, *Highway 61 Revisited*, and *Blonde on Blonde* for the first time, and, when he was done, eight sides and one hundred seventy minutes and eighty-four seconds later, he was someone else, he'd changed forever.

Or the first and long-anticipated Bob Dylan concert—coinciding with the publication of his first successful book, everything *so* perfect—that he attended, when Bob Dylan wasn't at the top of his game, but it didn't matter, because the first time is always special.

Or when he subsequently convinced a friend, who worked for the rock-impresario who'd brought the behemoth, that they go knock on the door of Bob Dylan's hotel room. His friend had been assigned as Bob Dylan's personal assistant, and, right away, Bob Dylan sent someone to tell her that he wouldn't need her for anything, that really he didn't exist for her; so it was better that she not exist for him. But he *did* want to exist for Bob Dylan. So he insisted, until he drove his friend crazy, and they went up and knocked (three soft knocks, like timid ghosts) and Dylan opened the door wearing one of those cowboy party shirts embroidered with flowers and humming-birds. And boxer shorts. And his legs were so skinny, he thought, marveling and terrified; because, he trembled with fear, what biblical curse would strike down from on high anyone who'd seen Bob Dylan in boxer shorts. Then Bob Dylan asked them curtly what they wanted. And in one hand he was holding something that could only be a pale stone that he'd proceed to crack their skulls with, but it actually turned out to be one of those primitive bars of soap for washing clothes. To one side of him, the half-open bathroom door revealed a bathtub full to the brim and multiple pairs of jeans floating in it.

His friend, embarrassed and stammering, told Bob Dylan to, please, make use of the laundry service. Then Bob Dylan burst out in a, yes, *vomotific* monologue, sinuous yet full of edges, with that diction and phrasing, like a sermon that'd bring to their knees both sinners and saints. "My mother told me: always wash your own jeans, Bobby, never entrust them to anybody, because your jeans are yours and only yours and . . ." And on like that for several stanzas until, abruptly, Bob Dylan's nose slammed the door on their noses and they were left there, uncertain if they'd witnessed a miracle or committed an unpardonable sin.

Or that other time when—prisoner of one of those foundations for writers—he escaped on a bus through the cornfields to attend another Bob Dylan concert in the decadent city of Davenport. There, waiting in line to enter a small theater that looked like it hadn't been used since the days of silent films, he'd met a young and giant Indian, a Native American, named Rolling Thunder, thusly christened because the eponymous circus tour captained by Bob Dylan had come to his reservation when his mother was pregnant with him. And Bob Dylan had behaved oh so charmingly and put his hand on Rolling Thunder's mother's belly and spoken a few words that must've been magic. Now, Rolling Thunder had come to give thanks for the gifts he'd been given and, he explained, looking for their seats in the theater, that he planned to jump on the stage to pay tribute to his spiritual and poetic father. He told him don't even think about it, that Bob Dylan's security was ruthless, that Bob Dylan didn't like that kind of thing, and that, if he tried something like that, he ran the risk of the night being brought to an early and bad end. But Rolling Thunder had no doubts and was convinced and, when the time for the encore came, he said he was going and asked him if he wanted to go too. He didn't give it a second thought and grabbed onto Rolling Thunder's neck and shut his eyes and the sensation was of riding a great wind, and everything (people, seats) fell away in before them, and, suddenly, a leap through the air and there they were, in front of Bob Dylan. And Rolling Thunder fell to his knees and dragged him along with him. And Bob Dylan looked at them uncomprehendingly. And Rolling Thunder raised and lowered his arms, making those halting and monosyllabic Indian sounds that are like the voices of smoke signals, like urgent telegrams to Manitou. And Bob

Dylan, all of a sudden, was smiling. And the three of them ended up singing "Rainy Day Women #12 & 35" together, the last song of the night. And he, as if charged by a strange electricity, couldn't sleep for two days.

The first Bob Dylan album he bought—his eyes still irritated by all the artificial smoke of progressive rock—was *Street Legal*. It received a great deal of (bad) criticism in 1978 and later (as tends to happen with each and every one of Bob Dylan's more or less questionable gestures) was vindicated as almost sublime. Anyway, he bought it for the cover. He knew little to nothing about Dylan at the time. His parents (always in the process of separating and getting back together) had The Beatles and Cat Stevens and The Rolling Stones and Pink Floyd in their houses, but nothing by Bob Dylan; with the exception of that celebrated poster designed by Milton Glaser with shadowed profile and hair lit with colors. He'd come to Bob Dylan on his own, in his own way, after—in inevitable, full-on beatnik-reading fervor or in an Andy Warhol biography, he wasn't sure—the singer's name appeared alongside the name of the King of the Beats or the Emperor of The Factory. It didn't matter, it doesn't matter. The important thing is that he subsequently learned (and obtained) absolutely everything he could related to Bob Dylan and he hasn't stopped learning (and obtaining) everything since. Even that photograph of Bob Dylan peering out from a doorway (more the photo of a writer than of a rocker) that's still one of his favorites. And that always seemed one of his best and most revelatory and definitive "poses" when it comes to capturing, without words, what Bob Dylan does when he performs. Bob Dylan always appears, takes a look around, goes back inside and tells, in his own way, what he saw. And Bob Dylan saw a lot. And Bob Dylan had led him to so many other things. The middle-aged Bob Dylan had been the hero of his adolescence and the old Bob Dylan was now the hero of his middle age and the young Bob Dylan would be his hero forever. And how many heroes were able to endure and make it through the passing of epochs and trends and their own years and the years of their followers? Very few, he thought. Sure, there are writers who *last* you your whole life, but really it's not them who last—what lasts are their books, not their lives, their personas, their characters, not their persons. Bob Dylan had found a way to meld it all together, so that everything came and went through him.

Now, descending into the depths of a fitness center in the basement of a Swiss hotel, he thinks that he should work up the nerve to tell Dylan that they were old, albeit occasional, acquaintances. Was he already that crazy? Did he have much or anything to lose? Or would it maybe be better to tell him that there were few times in his life as a reader that he'd be been as moved as he had when he read the story of the epiphany Dylan experienced on October 5th, 1987, during a concert at the Piazza Grande Di Locarno, not far from there, on a night of wind and fog? At the time, Bob Dylan told in his autobiography, he was completely disillusioned and empty, almost certain that he'd reached the end of the road, and thinking that maybe he should "go someplace for the mentally ill . . ." His songs were no longer his, he felt no attachment to them, they lacked all meaning except for the people who chorused them back at him, like more or less assiduous parrots, one stage after another. That's why, to rattle and unsettle them (and he'd always dreamed that writers could do the same thing with their novels and stories, as if they were albums and singles), he always changed them, so the audience couldn't sing them to him, the person who'd written them but who had no interest whatsoever in having them read aloud to him from memory. But then, without warning, it was as if Bob Dylan heard a voice commanding him to go on. And suddenly "things have changed," Bob Dylan had become aware of "a set of dynamic principals" and that he "could shift the levels of perception" to "give my songs a brighter countenance, call them up from the grave—stretch out the stiffness in their bodies and straighten them out. It was like parts of my psyche were being communicated to by angels. There was a big fireplace and the wind was making it roar. The veil had been lifted." In subsequent interviews, Dylan had insisted on that miraculous night and on the renewed sensation of having done nothing yet, because everything was yet to be done and no one could do it but him. And that now, at last, he had the secret formula, the philosopher's stone, the proper modulation of an Open Sesame and . . .

Should he confide in Bob Dylan that he's having the same problems? Dare to ask if he can borrow the instructions and the magic word? Run the risk of having his bones ground into the finest of powders by his bodyguards? Better not: Bob Dylan's thing, his blues, were something epic and thrilling.

While his own long trek across the desert was something more worthy, if he's lucky, of a miserable Hallmark Channel movie. Those movies always featuring the same bad actors: the guy, afflicted by a rare form of cancer last week, survived several days buried under a rockslide this week, and we're already coming up with something else for next week.

Anyway, there was no time left for confidences or for dictating formulas that would activate dynamic principals or heighten levels of perception. They'd already arrived to the subterranean fitness center, the bodyguards were patrolling the area to root out and capture any overnight fans, while Bob Dylan wrapped his hands and proceeded, with unthinkable ferocity, to punch a punching bag with every bit of life he had left in him. He, under the menacing gaze of the bodyguards, sat down at the only machine whose mechanics and operation he sort of understood—the stationary bicycle—and from there he watched Bob Dylan deliver one blow after another. Thinking about Dylan's voice, about Dylan's voices. About his first voice, unprecedented in its virtuosity. A voice that was, consequently, misunderstood initially and only now appreciated and admired by many, after hearing his current voice, ravaged by years of never-ending tours and the ingestion of a variety of substances over the course of the decades. The voice of someone who sounds as if he swallowed, whole and in one gulp, the Phantom of the Opera in the exact instant the acid is thrown in his face. But that voice was also— in ageless songs with long goodbyes like "Not Dark Yet" or "Sugar Baby" or "Nettie Moore" or "Long and Wasted Years"—a monstrously beautiful voice, capable of unthinkable modulations to articulate quintessential verses. Verses that the young and compulsive imaginer of imaginings, Bob Dylan, would never have dared sing or write, back when all he wanted was to sound vintage and timeless, like the old and synthetic and precise gunslinger Bob Dylan who was now working out his fists. To demolish the dictates of time and trend—he thinks, thinking about Bob Dylan while he watches him, as if transfigured, throwing punches with an energy that cannot be that of a septuagenarian—is to have made it home and to have found the answer after so many years of asking, "How does it feel? How does it feel?"

How does it feel? It feels bad. It feels awful. Like he's got no direction home, not even to his own private Locarno. Like a complete unknown. He feels like he's invisible and with nothing to hide. He feels worse than Bob Dylan, in his lowest and darkest hours, ever felt.

The coup de grâce to his increasingly wretched vocation—more fragile at the time than the health of one of those secondary but key characters in stories of Americans sleepwalking through the Old World—was delivered during a talk at a writer's festival in Switzerland that he'd been invited to, taking advantage of the fact that he was already there and that his travel and accommodations had been covered by a magazine that he was writing a piece for. There, in front of everyone, at one of those sharp-cornered roundtables on the future of the book, where what they were actually talking about was the book of the future: the packaging, the model, the newest way to keep selling the, for most publishers, increasingly rambling—like a pilgrim without a shrine—idea that reading has some significance and reason to exist. And his role was obvious and easy: play the part of the not-too-vintage representative of the old guard, with a certain freakish air, not too out of tune with the rest of the participants, who ranged from adorers of the cybernetic to popular costumbrists of the comfortable, well-to-do left. To be, in the end, not a noble and sacrificial canary in a carbon mine, but a kind of vociferous and cowardly parrot; not a specialized cell, but a tumor, removable and more or less benign, but a tumor all the same. Comic relief and all of that. Why had he accepted the invitation? An easy and almost reflexive answer: because he was there and, in slightly finer print, for the money. They paid well. And he already knew what he was going to say, almost by heart. And it'd been nearly a year since he'd been paid to say it. He had a talk, written several incarnations ago, organized around five more or less good jokes: it all depended on the enthusiasm of his delivery or if before the rectangular roundtable he'd downed one or two vodka-tonics. If he drank three or four vodka-tonics, things could get complicated, the way his last stellar appearance had gotten complicated. Someone had filmed it on a phone and, of course, uploaded it to YouTube. There he was, they'd sent him the link and he couldn't resist watching it between tremors, almost howling: "Ah, my little friends, mythology is so useful for this, writers like to feel that they are legendary in the practice of a craft that's not all that epic physically. We're like a Sisyphus who can't even find the rock to push uphill. And, if we do find it, it's oh so hard to push when you're fixed to a chair. And don't trust—don't ever believe them, Hemingway and Nabokov were pathological liars with messiah complexes—those writers who say they write standing up and even pose for photos like that. I even posed like that once. Standing. Like a statue. And, now that I think about it, that's why there are so few statues of writers—because nobody believes in the 'idea' of a standing writer. And because seated statues are almost a contradiction to the spirit of the thing, right? The statue of a seated writer is not very different from the vision of a seated writer, immobile like a statue. But yes . . . um . . . I did it too. There I was, writing vertical, leaning against a column of boxes full of books, just before what, I hope, was my final move. But I had an excuse and a justification: everyone talks about the writer's great blues—the alcohol, the depressions, the drugs, the eternally anemic storms bursting out in winter and spring and fall and summer—but, from embarrassment and because it's not anecdotally captivating, very few acknowledge writers' other great stigma: hemorrhoids, consequence of so much time sitting. The hemorrhoids that keep you from sitting and that, one morning, make you tell the journalist, who has shown up with his corresponding photographer: 'Didn't you know I stand up when I write?' Let's see: who'd be brave enough to convene a round table, not about the future of the book, but about literary hemorrhoids? Without embarrassment, since even the noblest Greek philosophers referred to them and did their thing standing, expositing aloud, because of them, and it was the inferior castes who, seated and suffering, wrote everything down. How many writers are there in the room who haven't had hemorrhoids at least once? Hands up, take a step forward, hey!"

So, after that, this time he'd promised not to drink anything. Or just one vodka-tonic. And to behave. And to peruse all the book stalls not thinking about all the books he was going to read, but about the ones he'd never read. And it wouldn't be a bad way to distract himself—a condemned man's last walk—before the next day's endeavor, before doing what he'd come to do. And there were always a couple friends at these fairs (more "acquaintances" and fewer "friends" all the time) whom it was worth seeing again just to convince himself that he hadn't, yet, turned into the most extreme and sympathetic of misanthropes. And every so often he experienced an uncertain curiosity about the people (not necessarily readers) who still had a certain curiosity about writers. Hadn't they read that thing about "this passion for wanting to meet the latest poet, shake hands with the latest novelist . . . what is it? What do they expect? What is there left of him when he's done his work? What's any artist, but the dregs of his work" (William Gaddis)? Didn't they understand that thing about "The artist must manage to make posterity believe he never existed" (Gustave Flaubert)? No and no. And not only had readers not understood it. The majority of writers hadn't either. For some strange reason, everything seemed to indicate that the craft continued to produce some intrigue and generate some mystery. So, readers came to see writers up close without realizing that the writers were looking at them *too*. The fast but oh so slow readers asking with wide eyes, like children whose parents just finished reading a story that they know to be impossible but wish were true, simple and innocent things like "Is that real? Did that happen? What's the invented part and what's the true part?" And the slow but oh so fast writers (who could've devoted months to achieving the perfect balance in a single sentence they'd never be asked about) answering by stating the obvious, politely skirting the issue, or, in his case, even responding with absurdities like "I can't answer that because they've kidnapped my grandmother and if I tell you . . ."; or precise things like "If you do not wish to be lied to, do not ask questions. If there were no questions, there would be no lies" (Bruno Traven); or countering with another question, with one of those jokes about surrealists that he liked so much, like, for example, how many surrealists does it take to tell a surrealist joke that asks how many surrealists does it take to change a light bulb? The eyes of the ones meeting the eyes of the others as if they were staring at fantastical mythological beasts in an ancient bestiary, or at one of those sad animals in any modern zoo. Maybe, who knows, they're drawn—the ones to the others—by the childish notion of finding out what the trick is. Or maybe it was a residual effect of the bad influence of all those bad movies with actors of varying quality always, badly, playing writers. Playing writers who seem to feel the obligation to be good characters when the truth is something else and the best movies with/about writers (think of *Smoke*, *Providence*, *La Dolce Vita*, *Barton Fink*, *2046*, *The Door in the Floor*) portray them as seriously miserable creatures and so neurotic that all they want to do is forget. Or to be allowed to forget, at least for a while, that they're nothing more than writers. Even the most adolescent, restless, and romantic of the lot (the ones in the Antoine Doinel series or *Betty Blue*, or the

Dashiell Hammett in *Julia*, who's nothing more than the juvenile fantasy of an autumn writer with a house by the sea and a younger woman who throws his typewriter out the window because, ah, she's oh so impulsive and passionate) were imbued with a sadness and a sordidness capable of making him feel embarrassed, not because he lived like that, but because it was assumed by everyone else that he must live like that—because he was a writer, right? Same old story: running after unstable muses through the streets of Paris at the speed of clichés and catching them in beds, many letters from heartless editors, but then that one phone call that changes everything because it tells you you're a genius, and you retire to a house by the sea, and even have a talking cat that encourages you to keep on writing. Or maybe what seduced readers and writers when mutually contemplating one another was the mutual transfer of energy, like a never-ending circuit: readers thinking "I could be like that too if I tried, because I've got so many stories to tell," and writers thinking "Ah, it'd be so much easier to just have to read."

Thus, also, the expectation of the organizers of these events and a sort of perfume of stadium dressing room leading up to the thing: an almost reflexive air of cordial but implacable competition in the secret sport of which writer will emerge as the funniest, most intriguing, ingenious, transgressive, kind, wise, crazy, etcetera. In other words: the most writerly writer of all the writers at the event. And, to tell the truth, there were nights when even he played along; when he tried not to disappoint; when he did his best to more or less live up to the illusions of all those who wanted to believe that a writer was someone worth seeing and listening to.

But it all went wrong. The audience—not too big—seemed composed exclusively of fans of technology and code writers, generally interested in searching for and discovering the formula for the application that'd make them the envy of their peers and young millionaires to boot. Some of them, not many to tell the truth, he wasn't even good for that, recorded him on their phones/screens, held up at the height of their eyes—to him, from his seat, they glowed like those photos where black strips are superimposed across faces to render them unrecognizable—and, of course, they'd send it to their friends via email with the Subject: "poor guy." Nobody laughed at any of his jokes. (OK: that joke about the possibility that it was the passengers' fault that the airplanes crashed on September 11th, 2001, because

they started to call their family members from their mobile phones, interfering with the instrumentation, turning simple hijackers into kamikazes,
could be considered a little *risqué*.) They didn't even notice his increasingly
odd diction: like that of the voice that, so long ago, you'd ask for the time
and it'd respond word by word and number by number until it put together,
in pieces, the sentence and the information. A voice like the notes sent by
kidnappers composed of words cut out from newspapers and magazines, with
varying typography—spasms of prose. The dark auditorium, the audience
like a liquid and shadowy and dense mass broken only—as if they were the
notes of a secret and concrete and silent and caged score, like something by
John Cage—by the intermittent lights of small screens, illuminating here
and there an ectoplasmic face, tapping messages on a touchpad, more than
three taps, describing what they're seeing but without watching or paying
attention to it. And, some of them, of course, request the microphone to
ask questions or talk about their own lives. And he told them that he wasn't
going to answer them because "my parents always told me not to talk to
strangers and ha ha ha." Which caused him to laugh, there, live, and the
uncomfortable and humiliating sensation and misunderstanding for everyone
else that, yes, he was laughing at his own jokes so they (the jokes) wouldn't
feel sad and alone. And then he felt very sad and very alone even though he
had many colleagues up there on the stage. Too many. People he had nothing
to do with or people who he didn't even want to see. Either way, it was all
the same. They probably weren't that enthused to have him sitting next to
them either, with that air of Ghost of Christmas past, reminding them about
something they'd managed to almost completely forget, about writing things
that weren't limited to just recounting something, but that, in addition,
counted for something. And now, here they were, all together yet, always,
so separate. An author of conspiratorial bestsellers that roused great applause
from the audience when he confessed that he was in permanent contact with
his readers via his numerous social media profiles, and he even used them to
find out if it seemed like a good idea that he include "something Aztec" in
his next book. A combative feminist writer best known for her newspaper column where every summer she recalled her childhood vacation to a little town
on the coast. A "serious" author of illegible books who, faced with such technological abandon, released a grunt about how "I still write like a caveman by

the light of the fire" (and he wanted to point out, but restrained himself, that cavemen were several thousands of years away from illuminating anything resembling an alphabet). A very popular writer of "costumbrist detective fiction." A manufacturer of young adult romantic fantasies with titles like *If You Ask Me If I Love You I Ask You That Please Before I Answer Let Me Consult My Compass and My Parents and My Psychoanalyst Because You Know How I Am into These Things of the Heart and Do You by Chance Know What Metro Station I Have to Get Off to Go To* . . . or something like that. And, unscheduled and as a great and much celebrated surprise for and by all the attendees, IKEA. His Horror, The Horror. His Hamlet, revenge. His MAYDAY MAYDAY. His DEFCON 1. His dark prince. His Frankenstein's monster. There are dark and soulless nights when he comes to think that IKEA doesn't exist; that IKEA is nothing more than a toxic product of his imagination. IKEA, like an entity that all writers put up with and drag around throughout their lives and careers. One of those monstrous doubles that narrate or are narrated and that lie in wait for poor fools in Stephen King novels or in stories like "The Private Life" by Henry James: the heartless version and the merciless alternative of what he—he recognizes it just a few lines later—could have been but never was and never will be. Not because—as he deceived himself— he wouldn't be interested in being like that, but because he never thought he'd get there. Something that was merely the embodiment of the diurnal and vespertine and nocturnal emission—a replica and faithful doppelgänger—of the winter of his discontent.

IKEA had been born twenty years after him, in the same country, but already in a different world. IKEA, once, a while back but not too long ago, had approached him with that more frightening than frightened zeal of a disciple (it hadn't taken him long to realize that IKEA was a kind of professional approacher, that his "maestros" numbered in the dozens, and to fall into that category, you just had to appear on his radar screen and position yourself at a praiseworthy distance) and had professed his admiration and asked him to read a couple of his stories that he'd published in anthologies. "Shy but sincere homages to your genius," he called them. And he read them, because he was moved by the fact that, before sending them, he'd asked permission. And, yes, he discovered in them obvious winks and barely subliminal praise of his work. And the truth is, they weren't all that bad and actually quite

good. And he even showed them to his editor. (IKEA, who was more familiar with stories about writers than with the work of those writers, exclaimed:
"Like Fitzgerald for Hemingway!" And he didn't realize then what IKEA
was trying to say, but he knows it now, remembering the way Hemingway
mistreated Fitzgerald until the last days of their respective lives. He remembers that Fitzgerald was the one who cracked up and Hemingway the one
who shot himself, that both killed themselves, one with the authority of failure and the other with the authority of success. But he also knows that IKEA
campaigns against the domestic use of firearms while he has less and less
trouble with drinking alcohol, so . . .) And, yes, before, in the beginning, the
truth is that the kid made him feel a kind of begrudging tenderness: what you
feel confronting some, theoretically, defenseless and small and fragile thing,
like those presumably helpless fish that suddenly bristle and, grinning, inject
you with lethal venom. He didn't know it then (when, with a combination of
generosity and narcissism, he mentioned IKEA's name in an interview as a
future great, thinking that he was inviting him to be a footnote in his own
story and not, as seems to be the case, the other way around), but he knows it
now. IKEA was a virus, something designed in a secret laboratory, the next
Official Great Writer and All Powerful Emperor of the Galaxy. Someone
whose sole objective was to become a celebrity writer and, to achieve this,
he was prepared even to write. To write books that were perfect not in their
quality and ingenuity but in their potential contagiousness and all-terrain
functionality. To write as if over underscores or connecting dots with lines
until he attained—like in those paintings with numbered zones where each
number corresponds to a predetermined color—an instantly recognizable
design. An air of prefab classic. IKEA (the nickname that he'd given him and
with which he'd linked him to that brand of functional and economical furniture, with falsely complex instructions, and models with sophisticated and
difficult-to-pronounce names but that speak in a decorative Esperanto that
make them fit in so impersonally well in every case and on every occasion)
had it all figured out. IKEA knew perfectly what steps to take to assemble
a successful and comfortable model of himself. It didn't take IKEA long to
proclaim himself first the leader of a generation (while he decapitated his
subjects one by one) and then proceed to weave a perfectly calculated web of
awards and relationships that he complemented with solemn titles and perfect

storylines for his large, anxious-to-feel-sophisticated audience. Laterally and in the shadows circulated the cybernetic-urban legend that IKEA had, also, started various blogs under different aliases to celebrate himself and to ruin the celebrations of others. Some people went even further explaining his success, which laid waste to everything and prevented anything from growing in its wake: IKEA could only be backed by other capital letters, by the CIA or something like that. Whatever it might be and whatever it might have been, all in the name of a comfortable and soft literature to sit on top of and be happy to have something to belong to. Books with a credit card. Books to be named that recalled other big-name books, not plagiarisms exactly but distorted echoes of celebrated voices, classic and watered-down perfumes in alluring modern bottles, new and catchy arrangements of a melody that used to be subtle chamber music and now plays in a supercharged elevator that only knows how to climb. Clawing his way up and in short order, IKEA had managed to become part of the squad of that kind of respectable author (some of them much better than others, but all of them, in the end, flying over the same civilian targets and anxious to receive new doses of the same drug) who sell well, not due to pure intelligence, but to something cunning and impure: because they make readers feel smarter than they actually are. Illusionists for the deluded, settling for a mix of more or less high brow, allusions to classics, a little sex (always with the lights off and in penthouses), politico-historical details, and a sentimental and melodramatic plot where everyone, in the end, finds themselves changed for the better, watching the sun come up in a dangerous but beloved city. IKEA, for a while, was the youngest writer to ever occupy a seat in the great academy of the language: a new seat with the letter @ had been created especially for him. And he lived in a Brooklyn loft (with an actress/model and a young son who was already famous for being the public image of an app for teaching infants to say their first word) that'd been ceded to him in perpetuity by a gay Italian aristocrat whom he duly thanked on the last page of all his books. The actress/model— to whom IKEA was systematically unfaithful, because "more than a hundred kilometers away from home it's not cheating and I travel a lot, ha ha ha"—is his second wife. Nobody remembers who the first one was.

IKEA was the light and destiny and example to follow for an entire generation of young writers who, always, seemed to him like they were fascinated with their own voracity, starving to capture followers and *likes* with an insatiable appetite that made them want to bite everything first and wonder about its taste later. Like the fantastical and mixed animals—half Pekinese and half Parana, more ferocious lambs than ferocious wolves—in those musty monastery bestiaries. The important thing, it seemed, was to leave nothing for anybody else, nothing for nobody. Just in case. All for one and none for all. Formed and deformed at the dawn of blogs and in the tangle of webs, all of them—in their own name or under an alias—had turned into expert courtiers and conspirators, uniting and dividing in fragile and ephemeral generations. Many of them hadn't read Shakespeare (the past, neither the remotest nor most recent, didn't interest them at all), but they were experts in the immemorial art of the palace and castle vaudeville. Or oh so gifted and muscular at the barroom insult and vomiting in the alleyway, always sheltering themselves by claiming that it was all freedom of expression and that everyone who purchased a screen had the right to be a writer and that literature was democratic not knowing, poor innocent babies, that literature was a dictatorship, an eternal dictatorship, and even worse—literature was a dictatorship of the self. There they all were, ignorant, typing their venom. And not satisfied with that—with throwing invisible and solipsistic darts, with denying the existence of the previous generation because they were anterior to the iPhone or some economic crisis—they made a jump to the physical plane, turning themselves into showmen and showgirls putting on live performances as writers. Presenting themselves as characters, easy to identify by their abilities, casting themselves as expert players of a part that left out all the stage fright of the blank page. Now, to be a writer, you had to sing and dance and act, too. Occupy spaces. Diversify. Be legion.

Running into them at those circuses for gladiators and clowns, the increasingly abundant festivals (to which he, as mentioned, went for the money and because, according to his publisher, "he had to let himself be seen sometimes so people knew he was still there"), he was always impressed by their blind ambition, their capacity for strategy, where what they wrote seemed more secondary than central: never a destructive boulder or a rocket to discover new worlds but, merely, a catapult or a launch tower. The ephemeral work was nothing more than the site from which to ascend to everlasting life. Once, in a conference of young writers where he'd been invited as an ex-young writer, several of them had laughed in his face (that kind of laugh the goes "Hua-hua") and almost spat at him, "That's your problem and not ours, not our generation's" when he'd had the audacity to admit that he was interested in writing a great book, that that was his project and his pleasure. And—what seemed *so strange* to him—they didn't even really like books: their personal libraries were fairly obvious and meager (all of them had embraced the lightning arrival of electronic books as a perfect excuse to not present physical evidence of reading) and he'd watched them go into bookstores many times without any curiosity or anticipation, without moving a single hair except the invisible and hypersensitive tentacles they used to detect the good or bad placement of their own books on tables and stands and shelves. And, watching them with a combination of shock and admiration and nausea, he couldn't help but remember himself, still unpublished, breathing deeply the perfume of foreign libraries, touching and caressing and setting up that golden moment when he'd be handed the first copy of his first book as his most supreme and sublime fantasy. And the walk home, with the book in his hand. And the perfect instant of putting it in a shelf, alongside so many others. That was it for him; he couldn't see anything beyond that. That was enough and more than enough to achieve ecstasy. The rest—what would come later—would be, in every case, not something to look for, but something that comes looking for you.

Now, not so much: now, freshly-minted writers were like marines ready to storm a beach, ready to beat back the enemy, and, in the clamor of the landing and the taking of their positions in the rankings, without a care for collateral damage or the effects of friendly fire on their colleagues, and the danger of thinking about this and about them is that his thoughts on the subject tirelessly repeated with minimal variations a principal theme of fear and rage. And nobody caused him more fear and rage than IKEA. And here he comes again.

IKEA—who didn't waste time with masturbatory literary workshops and began as a precocious junior executive in an advertising agency, where he composed slogans that seemed an awful lot like his current catchy and sappy aphorisms—had been most astute, opting for a classic role, not so attractive at the outset but much more effective by the half-way point: the young but "serious" writer who is also exceedingly fun and witty. A kind of clone/

bonsai who was—erroneously—presumed to be perfectly under control and a lot like his idols who, close to death, didn't hesitate to give him a pat on the back. As if guaranteeing a medium for their own posterity while at the same time successfully invoking the ghost of their successful yet increasingly distant youths, when literature still provoked true curiosity, true marks of prestige. IKEA, perpetual puppy dog, letting all of them stroke his head, first going down on his knees, but in private—he'd witnessed it, he'd laughed a great deal—doing savage impressions of those very same gurus, with a sharp wit and capacity for observation that left you trembling just imagining the impression of you that, without a doubt, IKEA did when you weren't present. Those impressions (the one of Marcelo Chiriboga was truly memorable) were, from a distance, IKEA's best work in the realm of literature, he thought. And there was something disturbing, he thought, in the fact that, maybe just in front of him and in the corners at parties, IKEA wouldn't hesitate to expose his dark side—the portrait rotting in the attic of his malice. Because it (what at first he understood as a display of honesty and trust in the name of their long shared history) was actually something far more sinister: IKEA actually considered him a kind of special cesspit where he purged his sewage every so often. Besides, who would believe him if he told them even a fraction of everything IKEA confessed to him at a mass filled more with laughter than prayer, in a low conspiratorial voice. No doubt, they'd say he was jealous. And, yes, he was jealous of IKEA. Not of his work but of what he'd achieved with it.

IKEA's latest great success was titled *Landscape with Hollow Men* (don't miss, please, the equally obvious and clever allusion to Eliot, hierarchizing everything right from the cover) and it was a robust family/intercontinental saga that recounted the trials and tribulations of Benavídez: a republican grandfather who fled Spain, crossing the Atlantic dressed as a woman (and found success as a singer of transsexual folksongs in the cabarets of Rio de la Plata); his son, who ends up being a grand master torturer for a Latin American dictatorship in a country called Aracatina (participating in the capture and assassination of Che Guevara and in the Six Day War, where he meets the beautiful and explosive Judith); his grandson, who is programmed as messianic magnate, designing bellicose role-player videogames in a kind of Xanadu in Silicon Valley; and his great grandson who finds success as a young singer for inflamed adolescents. The novel ended, of course, with the singer tired of singing "Text Me Your Heart" or "Twitter Twist," and—after surviving an attack by an Islamic-fundamentalist where his recording partner Chicka Chikita is killed—renouncing everything to return to his great grandfather's ranch and found an agricultural cooperative in times of economic crisis and become, at last, the avatar of the New Man. *Landscape with Hollow Men* had just been acquired by HBO (there were, also, film offers; but IKEA was one of those people convinced that "if Shakespeare were alive today, he'd write for HBO"), selected for Oprah's Book Club ("A book of Latin American origin for the first and only last time," the proprietess of the business had smiled), Justin Beiber was being considered for the role of the singer and Daniel Day-Lewis for the tech genius, and De Niro and Pacino were reuniting to play father and son, digitalized ("Not like in *The Godfather II*, but for real") to look young, or something like that. But he wouldn't miss seeing it and following it. It was already carefully outlined, scene-by-scene, in the book, which he'd taken a peek at, on the sly, hiding behind it, so that nobody would see him reading it.

And, at the roundtable, everything that IKEA said (which he could anticipate, with ease, as if he were reading his mind five seconds before it formulated its simple thoughts, and if his calculations were correct it was the third time he'd heard him say "The important thing is not that the story passes through the characters but that the characters pass through History") was received with shouts and hurrahs worthy of those frenzied Russian casino officials at the beginning of *Anna Karenina*, while all he could think about was running out of there and throwing himself under the wheels of the first passing train.

Because worst of all was that—without the makeup of that laughter that he was sure he could rely on until that night—everything he said was, *also*, equally stupid and superficial. Suddenly it dawned on him that his own contribution was just like IKEA's; just that it was less successful and more boring and pretentious and sad. Even worse, everything he said barely concealed the always uncomfortable and repugnant tone of a lament.

Things that occurred or occurred to him in airports.

Things like: "First of all: the following aren't categorical universal truths. They are, merely, debatable personal opinions. I've said it many times, I'll say it again. From the dust we come and to the dust we return. And, a while back I read—in a book, of course—that 90 percent of the dust in a house is composed of residue shed by human beings. And, in who knows what other book, I read that dust is good for books, that it keeps them young, that it's not good to dust them too often. Thus, we unmake ourselves so our books won't be unmade. To me this seems prosaically and poetically just."

Or: "These days I go to bed very early, and before the sweet dreams come, I frequently confront the bitter possibility of insomnia to be exorcised and defeated. The other night, for example, I wondered if everything that's happening might not have to do with the fact that the reader animal has reached its evolutionary zenith and is now bouncing off the cupola and limit of its perfection and coming down in reverse toward a kind of involution disguised as a high-tech mutation. We are oh so futuristic we don't even realize that—as far as this whole thing goes—we're barely in the prehistory of prehistory. In its moment, the jump from the nineteenth century to the twentieth century was much more futuristic—the climax and multiple orgasms of the industrial revolution. The electricity of bodies and the blood of machines rolling in the damp sheets of History and there was still so long before the arrival of that third party in discord and automatic loving energy. Now, on the other hand, we tremble in the most masturbatory of prologues and previews. We're frigid invertebrate and submarine gelatin, dreaming of a skeleton on terra firma. Because, think about it, it hasn't been easy to get here, traversing the long road that goes from stardust to the amphibious amoeba, to the upright simian, up to obtaining the ability and talent to enjoy one of the most wondrously complex tasks that, for me, remains inexplicable: making a handful of symbols enter through our eyes, arrive to our brain and, there, turn into stories and into people and into worlds, always distinct, always constructed in complicity with their architects. It's writers who sketch the blueprint, but we are the ones who utilize, like Proust said, that 'optical instrument' that allows us to discern what, without *that* book, we might never have seen inside ourselves."

Or: "E-readers, supposedly, help to facilitate and accelerate the reading experience, but actually, it seems, end up removing the desire to continue reading. But—breaking ancient news, stop the presses—we still read at the same speed as Aristotle. About four hundred fifty words a minute. So, all that external electric velocity at our disposal ends up colliding with our more deliberate internal electricity. In other words: machines are faster and faster; but we are not. We haven't gained much and, along the way, we've lost the exquisite pleasure of leisure, which is how and where the stuff of hopes and dreams is made. We live and create, determined to increase our machines' capacity to store a number of books that we'll never be able to read. We are truly fascinated and falsely proud of the fact that we can bring all of it with us, of having access to everything, without stopping to think that in the selection and the sacrifice, in what is chosen and what is discarded, resides the formation of taste and personality. Reading a little of everything is like not seeing anything or running through a burning museum. Looked at like this, it seems to me that the paper book is nearer our rhythm (there are nights when I deeply envy the environment of the nineteenth century when it comes to reading nineteenth-century novels by candlelight) and, please, is there anyone in the room who can explain what's so great about being able to read and record and watch on a telephone and why it is that telephones have evolved so much in recent years and airplanes so little, eh?"

Or: "We live in one of those grinding, pneumatic hinge moments. The door that closes with a groan, the same door that then opens with a whisper of optical cells. Complex times . . . I know writers who could care less and writers who can't stop making little avant-garde leaps, trying to patent a brand that'll make them famous not for fifteen minutes but for one hundred forty characters on screens and pages with, if possible, little photos and drawings and typographical games (and, yes, let the bastard italicizer who's without sin cast the first italic, I too once played with the idea of different types of text to indicate voices on the telephone or to make atomized voices float through the air). I know publishers who are excited by a new genesis so many years after Gutenberg and publishers who are depressed because it's fallen on them to face the apocalypse; I know readers who don't read, but who are proud of being able to store up to two thousand titles in their backpacks and readers who have read two thousand books and tremble with fear thinking about their next inevitable move. 'I have seen the best minds of my generation looking but not seeing . . .' Remember: there was a time when everyone got together after vacation to update each other; there was a time, also, when looking at friends' vacation photos was torture. But it was a milder torture: because—before the arrival of the digital, during the age of film developing—you at least had to think it over and do a little focusing before firing off each shot. Ration them out somewhat rationally. Think before you click. Now, not so much. Now, everything, all the time, ceaselessly, over and over and over again. Everything is transcendent and the transcendent turns banal in its excess and overload. Not even the clean and increasingly distant pain of breaking up remains, because: can anyone resist the temptation to find out what their ex is doing, after they've broken up, in a new era, on Facebook, whose use, they say, releases "the same hormone as kissing and hugging" and promotes "platonic infidelity"? Or, even worse, is there anyone who can resist the simple horror of searching for and finding someone they haven't seen for decades in a matter of seconds and verifying in their eyes—surprised or possibly happy or definitely scared to see us, oh so FaceTime—the heavy and militant passing of time; marching with those spike-soled boots hammering that almost unrecognizable face that, forced to learn it and update it, reminds us that the only reason we recognize that face as it is now is because it refuses to come unfixed, like a carnivorous mask, from the face that it once was but that we can't forget because of our best bad memories? And where have all those impassioned discussions about who directed that film and who sang in that band gone to die? Now, it seems, there's nothing more attractive or interesting—the tweet like a projector slide—than knowing what people who are more or less strangers are doing every five minutes in one hundred forty characters, including—to the joy of burglars—the news that they're leaving on a trip or that the key is under the third pot from the door counting from the left. The phenomenon already has a label: "oversharing," overdose of exhibition of the private, be it contractions or snores or heartbeats or the absence of all the above, and in whose name we narrate a birth as it happens, or get bored during a nap, or confess to a murder in person, and we can even pay a specialized service to keep our lives updated for years after our deaths so that we're not missed. Being missed has gone missing. Being familiar with so much doesn't mean knowing more. There was a time when the definitive proof of success was the very ability to disappear, to be impossible to find, to have nobody know where you are. To be unreachable. To be outside everything. Now, if you're a true celebrity, you have to have billions of followers and give an account of your most recent and more or less transcendent act. Total irony: the guy who uploaded his own spectacular fall in the street onto YouTube (because he was checking his profile when he should've been looking at what was in front of him) to the hilarity of entire populations will realize pretty quickly that nobody recognizes him on the street. He's not famous. He's something else. He's just a moment, whose name and before and after don't matter. He's not even, Warholianly, famous for fifteen minutes. His thing doesn't last or hold out nearly that long. We're all our own candid cameras now. We're blooper-looper machines. We're mutants and I've heard that, in Japan, land of mutations, the structure and shape of the youngest users' thumbs have already been altered from constantly touching small screens. And it must be sad to die so young or to be broken so suddenly; I see them and I dodge them—stopping in doorways, on platforms, at edges of stairways—pausing to update their profiles and check those of others and, ah, see how they fall. Precipitating like silly events from those moments that not long ago—when the vital idea of blood hadn't yet been supplanted by electronic embalming fluid—were the exact spot, the place where anything was possible and where all great and unexpected ideas came from. Times when we allowed ourselves the luxury of getting distracted, of thinking of things that weren't ourselves or what others think of us. Here comes another one, from on high, an evolutionary down-cycle. And I wonder if there might not already exist a statistical index for accidental death by electronic device. Probably. But it won't be made public, just like how for decades we weren't told that smoking could be detrimental to our health. There they go, there they are. And I don't know which theory to believe of all those that prophesy various ends of humanity. But there's one—which hasn't yet been formulated—that I'm almost certain of: human beings will disappear because they'll be too busy answering messages, updating profiles, falling on their faces from platforms onto the tracks of trains conducted by engineers talking to their girlfriends on FaceTime to procreate and multiply. All aboard."

Or: "Personally, I don't worry about the future of the literary book. There will always be a happy resistance reading Proust and Joyce and, probably, courtesy of gratuitous pirating or sold authors' rights, there might even be more people *trying*, at least for a few pages, to read Proust and Joyce. There's no crisis there; in what we call literature. Literature will find a way to survive; and a few days ago I read a book where it was suggested that literature's salvation would come from wealthy melancholics who would take exclusive control of their favorite authors' novels, to be read by them alone, in exchange for sizable sums. The equivalent of what a prestigious author would collect if at some point—some more and more improbable point—he or she managed to write one of those global bestsellers. But with only one reader. This might disturb an artist at first. But—apart from the economic aspect—they'd soon see its advantages: they could dare to do what they'd never dared to do. And there'd be no critics or colleagues in sight. So a book would be like a painting or a sculpture. A unique and original piece. A manuscript to be studied and read by just one person. A status symbol and a kind of investment and competition. 'Okay, your yacht is really nice, but how do you like my new Martin Amis? I bet it's way better than that Michael Ondaatje of yours.' And writers might end up being just that—organic luxury items with a touch of electricity. More exclusive all the time. We could call ourselves iScherezade: beings in service of the rich who'll be devoted, night after night, sitting on the edges of soft and immense beds, to telling stories to magnates, anxious faced with the coming darkness, like when they were erudite invalid children and not the nearly-illiterate ferocious wolves they'd become, reading in the highest and sweetest of voices, convincing them that only a good story will bring them the luxury of sweet dreams. The opposite of a massive and easy to falsify bestseller. There *is* a crisis there. A serious crisis. With bestsellers. Those books that functioned like a diving board to leap off of and learn to swim, to later strike out with powerful strokes toward the oceanic depths. And now, on the other hand . . . All you have to do is take a look and compare today's vampires with yesterday's vampires, the conspiracies of now with the conspiracies of then, the sex here with the sex there. And, ah, those young adult books that sell so well and end up being the hope of the industry, consumed voraciously by young adult readers who, with time, I suppose, grow up, and stop reading or, with luck, are pre-programmed to swallow the latest bestseller. Or, maybe, who knows, become Peter Pan readers—eighty-year-olds reading young adult books, dystopias and romances, jumping from here to there. The same books as before. Books for readers who don't want to grow up, happy to live trapped in the loop of adolescent stories that begin and end in themselves and that don't build bridges or open doors to other territories. And I remember that magic moment when I leapt from the island of *Captain Grant's Children* to the island of the children in *The Lord of the Flies*. And, then, the discovery of the limitless horizon and of infinite space. I remember that excitement of tracing my own maps and singular itineraries on the basis of what others had written. Free association of readings, yes. And it's not that it's no longer possible, it's that it's no longer done. The strategy, now, is for everyone to be in their own place and always connected, telling each other what they're reading. How can you leap from these days—as I once leapt from Somerset Maugham or from Herman Hesse, perfect diving boards—toward the deepest or most dangerous or pleasurable or surprising oceanic pools. The majority of today's bestsellers only lead—like machines that are broken or fully functional in their solipsism—to other bestsellers. And to the lost illusion and the siren song that—light, diet—result in storylines that are perfect to be downloaded and consumed on light, thin, luminous tablets shining in the phosphorescent darkness of times when we read and write more than ever, yes; but also times when we read and write worse than ever and when orthography has, for many, turned into a kind of annoying and antiquated governess who insists that words be written whole, in their entirety, and not compressed into abbreviated noises. In the crackling argot of locusts that swallow tongue and language down to the root, and question and request: how many of you are sending poorly composed text messages right now, telling virtual strangers what I'm saying and how demented I seem, leaving out letters and putting an emoticon of a Bonaparte hat or thumbs down? Raise your hands!"

Or: "The machine—or *MAChine*, with the elegant lines of all Mac devices—thing has displaced, for a lot of people, the desire for a good story with the desire for the object, crossing the thin yet definitive red line that separates deep passion from the superficial hook. The important thing now is not what you read but where you read it. And maybe I should clarify: I'm not a fanatical Luddite. I don't understand (but I do respect) writers who even today sing the praises of the typewriter or the quill pen. And yes, I understand today's comfortable pleasure of being able to run through the halls of the Louvre without leaving your house, your city, your country, your continent. But it's clear that every technological advance implies the loss of a gift and the gain of a power. The same thing goes for artists—for every gift that's given a gift is taken away. And the gift that's taken away tends to be related to the practical and functional part of life. Attaining a superior plane of existence doesn't, necessarily, mean becoming a superior person. And I've never forgotten what Saint Augustine—probably the best writer among the saints—said. Words I used to recite at full volume in my youth, high on the crest of a seism of illegal chemistry, standing atop an afterhours table, almost catching fire: "By Your Gift we are inflamed, and are borne upward; we wax hot inwardly, and go forward." So, the man who could disentangle the string of a mathematic equation at age five might live a whole life without learning to use a can opener. But now I'm getting entangled, I who never knew and won't ever know how to tie or untie a knot . . . True; with the printing press a lot more people learned to read and write. But with the gramophone many others—who would've been hard pressed to hear their favorite Mozart or Beethoven piece more than once or twice in their lifetime—renounced the ability to read scores and play an instrument. Similarly, we've renounced the superpower of memorizing addresses and telephone numbers and more or less important dates. I, also, know about the virtues of greater velocity and the capacity for instant access when it comes to disseminating culture. But yes—and I suppose I'll sound just like them to more than one of you—I can say that I'm a little disturbed by the insupportable tech fanatics' dispro-portionate praise in support of it, over and above any appreciation of what's been supporting the whole structure for centuries. Now, not so much, now the thing seems to pass not through written matter but through the reading masses. Interest or expectation don't pass so much through the evolution of ideas, but through the constant and uninterrupted evolution and design of a device that's supposedly intended for reading, when actually, mostly, it's looked at and touched and loved the way automobiles used to be loved. With that kind of love that thinks only about the next model, about the latest model that'll never be the last. With that junkie anxiety that, suddenly, finds itself more addicted to the needle than the drug. And, true, the Internet and the mobile phone are turning the concept of the office into a dispensable space, but—like with all more or less Mephistophelian pacts—all they do is extend the workday beyond its natural space and schedule. Not to mention the constant tension of staying up to date and learning increasingly com-plex systems designed more for those who, generationally, received their first computer along with their first wind-up toy car. Learning to read and write is already a complex process and—even today—not entirely explainable. Now, it seems, you have to add to it, to that figurative and glorious abstraction, learning, first, the use and operation of devices that subsequently allow you to read and write."

Or: "And a few years ago, I rejoiced when the live transmission of Steve Jobs presenting the first ever iPad was interrupted—at least for a few seconds—by the bad news of the death of J. D. Salinger. It seemed an act of poetic justice. A brief victory for literature and for someone who wrote few/enough/immortal books over the ephemeral and almost immediately dated device, capable of storing thousands of titles that'll never be read. Because, clearly, who's going to have time to read vast nineteenth-century novels when you have to be checking on and replying to and updating all your many friends, anxious to know what we ate and what the subsequent consistency and tonality of the fecal matter resulting from our lunch was? Bon appétit and as a kind of digestive infusion: at the moment of truth, I'm afraid no one will care at all and to be is not the same thing as being. Now, Jobs is no longer here. But his imprint remains. Because—back to the thing from the beginning—it seems to me that the future of the book isn't in any danger. There are books and there is the future. Look at them, read them. But do it right: yes to looking to the future and reading books and no to looking at books and reading the future, right? The book of the future—all those more or less novel devices that dust *does* damage—are at greater and much more immediate risk, I think. You already know: a frenetic succession of new models getting announced like headline news and replacing (and degrading and denigrating, for being anachronistic) previous models. And their users, desperate, chasing after one only to, when they catch it, discover that they have to chase another. And—it's really hard to read while running—on and on, all the time. Today, thanks to Jobs, we're all a little like Job."

Or: "The tool cannot and must not attain the category of creator. And, in addition, it should wear the name that suits it, an honest name. In other words: why instead of emphasizing the book particle don't they opt for the screen particle? A screen is a screen is a screen. And, let's admit it: books are more beautiful. Books, by comparison, are like flesh and bone. And we have to go out and look for them. And find them. For me, the experience of a book, of its enjoyment and reading, begins the moment I order it and is perpetuated when I'm notified that it has arrived, when I go to the bookstore and encounter my book and one or various other books whose existence I was unaware of and dreamed of and . . ."

Or: "I'd never want to have to go back to clean-copying everything. Page after page. To that correction tape or white-out liquid. I don't believe, either, in maintaining the ability to use a typewriter to write. But it's true too that everything I've written on a word processor seems to lack the definitive solidity, like a finished sculpture, of my first book, the only one I wrote on an Olivetti. Since that time, everything seems more liquid, capable of being retouched again and again, without limit or an end that isn't the obligatory surrender and farewell, because the time for navigating has run out. Which, inevitably, makes me wonder whether this new form of writing might not also influence the way that ideas occur and occur to you; previously they appeared like closed circles and now like perfect smoke rings that you have to write down quickly, without thinking about it too much, before they vanish. And then we'll see, we'll read."

Or: "And now let's all howl together: Kindle, iPad, ebook, tablet, and whatever we call that thing that opens the Pandora's box of enhanced reality and that obliges us to put up with Tom Sawyer sleeping in the guest room . . . The differences between them—and their differences in the fight to capture the consumed consumer—have to do with the brightness of the screen and lightness of body. And, yes, reading on a tablet there's no smell, no cover, nothing to give us a sense of the volume of the volume, impossible for us to find an ancient note or old photo or cryptic annotation inside it, something that made that book ours and only ours. And we can't get the author to sign it, thereby increasing the sentimental and material value of the copy. You can't—with a Kindle or whatever the preferred brand might be—enter a stranger's house and walk directly to the library and start reading spines to learn something about your host. And we can't throw it against a wall (well, we can, but it'd end up a very expensive gesture) when it exhausts our patience. And is it imaginable to imagine ourselves rereading—rereading is the most sublime condition of reading—on an antique model e-reader many years later? Nobody steals—or lends—a Kindle for the love of art, but only for lust of merchandise. To be just one more, the same, among the many. And how to preserve all of that. Will iPads and Kindles be auctioned off like bookshelves are auctioned off? And if they break? And if the electricity runs out? And if we can't unplug? And if, being so addicted and dependent and fast, but suddenly so very *batteries not included*, and we've forgotten the art of memorizing and we won't even have the subversive consolation of knowing novels and stories and poems letter for letter, like those lyrical book men at the end of *Fahrenheit 451*?"

Or: "And I don't like to say 'my reader.' I like to keep thinking that I am still my reader. And I keep reading books that open like doors so I can step inside them, instead of screens that remain closed and allow me to see, from outside, only what they want me to see."

Or, in conclusion: "Now, all around us, everything is in doubt. Talking and trembling with fear about the end of an era for everything written and printed. But the always-imprecise writers always had their doubts. That's why they write, isn't it? And that's why not a week goes by that a writer isn't called on for a response or an opinion about some feature of nonfiction, of reality. Because it's assumed that they're wise and prophetic. Crass error and crude errata, my friends. Writers know nothing. That's why they still insist on writing. If writers had any certainties they wouldn't write. It wouldn't make any sense. And yet, they try to say something more or less coherent when they're asked about the perpetual death of the novel (I don't believe in that and I ask myself why don't they ever talk about the hypothetical death of the story?), the difference between the story and the tale (no idea, I could care less), or the best way to tell a story (I think it should have four parts: beginning, middle, end, and blow me away). To be clear: for good or ill, for the blows we've suffered or because our kingdom is not of this world, we writers—in the middle of the road between Protestantism and Zen Buddhism—worry more about duties than about rights. That said and still awaiting the arrival of a book from the planet Tralfamadore that will allow me to contemplate, as Kurt Vonnegut, one of my favorite writers, prophesied, 'the depths of many marvelous moments seen all at one time,' I'll say goodbye with something that *another* of my favorite writers, John Cheever, said in his journal at the end of his life: 'I will say that literature is the only consciousness we possess, and that its role as a consciousness must inform us of our inability to comprehend the hideous danger of nuclear power. Literature has been the salvation of the damned; literature, literature has inspired and guided lovers, routed despair, and can perhaps, in this case, save the world.' Goodnight and drive safe, home and to the rest of your lives."

Or: Oh.

Things that now—all of a sudden and as if he'd received an alarm-clock blow to the head—sounded like nothing more and nothing less than the most ingenuous and ingenious refried aphorisms inside XL-sized fortune cookies. Did he still believe all of that? Did he care? Was this the foolish and easy enemy that luck—bad luck, oh so comfortable luck—had given him? That he'd chosen with a clenched-toothed smile and that each and every brief and sloganistic *boutade* devoted to it got more inches in the press—courtesy of young cultural journalists given orders that "nothing sound too cultural" and, hence, titles like "Frenzied Diatribe" or "Apocalyptic Preoccupation" about the plugged-in future of humanity—than his own lengthy books, which were occupied and preoccupied with anything but that? Devices, little devices? Batteries Not Included? Who was laughing at whom? Who would laugh last when there was no reception left? Had this become his subject? Why not choose a rival/accomplice instead of an enemy? Fight through the admirable foliage of the nineteenth-century novel not to defeat it but to convert it, to bring it into these twenty-first-century wastelands so it can blossom again with equal power and modernized modalities? (Just thinking of such a challenge produces vertigo, dizziness, sighs more arrhythmic than romantic.) Or maybe it's just that you got the enemy you deserved, at your level; and he got the flattened plains of screens and tablets? Was he really worried about the whole electrified world? Was he really going to comment again about how the new and insensate phones had done away with the need to check the time on the faces of watches, of *normal* watches, not watches bursting with functions like counting your heartbeats and the calories you consumed at breakfast; to evoke the lost pleasure of hanging up the phone like someone delivering a slap, or leaving it off the hook like someone turning his back; to laugh at that religious app that allows you to confess via multiple choice thumb strokes; to compare letters on blank paper like those photos of chromosomes; to throw a wink more stupid than nervous, referencing the selfie of Dorian Gray; to quote Borges from "Coleridge's Flower" when he says "For the classical mind, the literature is the essential thing, not the individuals"; to lament looking at photos of families no longer gathered around the warm

glow of a fire but around the cold glow of individual screens; to call attention to the not at all coincidental fact that they call those data hunters *search
engines* and not *discover engines*; that he and those of his caste have always
surfed on the crest of waves of cerebral electricity, that there is nothing new
in thinking about everything and nothing; to conclude with something like
"for the first time in history writing is the enemy of writing"? Nah: the truth
is that in the dark and stormy nights of the soul, at his three o'clocks in the
morning, he thought that he was thinking about all of that because someone
still thought it was worth it to pay him to think like that, out loud. Because, if
he'd written it down to read later, he had to have thought about it somewhat
seriously before, right? Sure, he still felt certain indignation when on nights
of channel surfing he came across some supposedly funny commercial for
tablets and telephones in which the clients and users were presented as brain-
less zombies who couldn't even unglue their eyes from the screen to kiss their
spouses or hug their children, and yet, even still, as chosen and privileged.
But at this point, he wasn't sure that he cared: he felt like a comedian who at
one time had seriously studied the art of his profession (Shakespeare, Wilde,
Twain, Marx, SNL, Seinfeld) and was now plummeting in free fall, having
passed through a New York club, through the best Vegas casinos, to end
up alone, laughing at himself in a dive bar in Reno, patronized exclusively
by second- and third-class gangsters who got together to blubber, quoting
lines from Corleone or the Sopranos. The next thing, the last thing, the no-
return, he shuddered, would be the cold floor of Lenny Bruce's bathroom. A
final unfinished joke in front of the dirty mirror and then the dirty floor of
the dirty bathroom. And the dirty cold. And nobody to finish him off with
a final punchline.

After the roundtable, everyone stood up and he was served a reddish
cocktail with some canapés that weren't bad (which was to be appreciated
and increasingly surprising; the way things were going, pretty soon they'd be
asking the writers to bring a little food from home to share with the audience). And he, as was his habit, initiated the operation of slipping back to his
nearby hotel, stopping off at a bookstore along the way to see if Arthur C.
Clark, though dead, had figured out a way to transmit a new sequel to *2001*
from the far reaches of the universe, some answer and/or advice/remedy from

Dr. Heywood Floyd, responding to his calls for help. Or to see if they were selling the new techno-thriller that he'd read about and that seemed right up his alley: the paranoid idea that mobile phones were the only candy of technological evolution thrown to the masses, to keep them distracted and dumbed down in a new Middle Ages, while a chosen minority benefited from everything else (revolutionary medicines, modes of teletransport, ways to stay young forever, servile robots that never rebel), enjoying a future that'd already arrived years before. Yes, he read these things just like he did when he was a kid, to travel, to escape, to go far away, further still, until the distance made his eyes grow heavy. And after, sinking into the opiate stupor of the latest popular reality show while gargling with purple Listerine Total Care. Something with a handful of celebrities, famous for all the wrong reasons, stuck in a maximum-security prison, living alongside serial killers and Mafioso politicians and old men who'd thrown their wives out of windows. Anything to distract him from the little bottles in the minibar (he'd discovered quite late but with growing enthusiasm that those liquors were not an exit ramp, but a perfect spot along the side of the road to stop for a while and watch newer and faster cars whose passing drivers shouted things at him he couldn't decipher and launched into fits of laughter). Something to help him ignore for a while the approaching certainty (like of those numbered signs alongside highways, counting down, informing you that there are fewer and fewer kilometers until you run out of gas or crash) that he was now living and writing in a world where medium had triumphed over rare and well-done. Where all that mattered were the aerodynamic highways that you had to pay excessive tolls to circulate on and nobody was interested in venturing off on side roads with picturesque motels and restaurants with homemade food where, once again, circularly, every so often, he sat and watched them pass by and waved to them with one hand or one finger, depending on the mood he found or lost himself in.

He was hungry, he bit into everything put to hand and mouth; but at the same time he felt the need to get out of there. Right away. Now. Immediately. And that's exactly what he was doing, already nearing the exit of that other claustrophobic reality show of writers and readers and editors, when IKEA took him by the arm as if he were something that belonged to him but that he almost never played with anymore, like the more or less noble relic of a past that he wasn't much interested in remembering except to say "It already happened."

The last time he'd seen IKEA he'd confirmed, with satisfaction, that IKEA was going bald. But, now, suddenly, not so much—he was flaunting a thick leonine mane the color of spilled oil. It was so impressive that he couldn't help but acknowledge it. "I know, I know . . . But don't say anything. You can't—it's illegal. Baby panda-bear glands. A small fortune on the black market. You know why there are so few pandas? Because they only breed three days a year. So, I guess all that sexual repression must stimulate capillary growth. And so one day my agent and I were looking through photos, and we saw that the odds of a writer without hair winning the Nobel are between 55 and 60 percent lower than those of a writer with hair. And bald writers are victims of the worst injustices. Your dear Nabokov . . . Your adored James . . ." IKEA's literary agent—after having betrayed the selfless older woman who, with patience and near exclusive devotion, had launched his career and who, according to the rumor, had tried to commit suicide after being abandoned by the person she considered "more than a son: the son I would've chosen if one were able to choose the son one wants to have"—was now the internationally famous and feared Dirty Harry. They called him that because his name was Harry.

IKEA, à la Superman, carefully and sublimely brushed a lock of hair from his forehead and (with an accent that wasn't of anywhere anymore but of everywhere, an international accent, an accent with innumerable translations and publishers) said something like "Here you are, my friend. I loved your new book, I didn't really understand it, but of course it's really good, right?" And the problem for him wasn't what IKEA said, but how he said it: with a falsely guilty manner and seemingly apologizing for his lack of intellectual ability but, at the same time, with the rusty knife of a slight smile that could only mean, "You're out; those positive reviews don't matter anymore, now that nobody reads your books. Another one bites the dust and thanks for everything." Next, IKEA fired up his weapon of mass destruction: "I hear you just finished a book . . . It'd be an honor to present it." And he, slow of reflexes, fell right into the trap and, almost automatically but aware of the error he was making, an error from which there was no coming back, answered: "No. I don't have a book coming out." Then IKEA looked at him sadly, gave him a little pat on the back, and said, "Ah, too bad. I must've been misinformed. *No* book then . . . Too bad. Then, I'll take this opportunity to give you some far more useful advice than the advice you once gave me, ha. No, seriously, listen: enough already with these books about writers, books about writing. Nobody's interested in literature, beginning with the majority of readers, man. And writers are only interested in *their own* writing and, at most, to seem impressive, the writing of some distant dead man whom they latch onto as if they'd known him all their lives. Normal people just want to pass time and feel represented. Haven't you ever read the comments on Amazon condemning a book with the worst possible rating? No? Read them and you'll see. The reason is always the same: 'I didn't identify with any of the characters' or 'There wasn't a single character worth getting to know.' Why do you think all my books have the characters' faces on the covers? I know, you already told me that you don't like that, that, to you, it seems like a dictatorial editorial imposition on the democracy of literature and the privilege of each reader to define the features of the book's heroes and villains, so the book is theirs and only theirs and unique and all those things you like to say in public because you believe them in private. But, once again, you're wrong: readers are not free organisms. Just the opposite: readers want to be captivated and guided like the blind in the night. The faces on the covers of my books are carefully selected by a software program: they're like the faces of actors and celebrities, but not exactly; and statistically common ethnic details of the countries where the books are published get inserted. Like I already said: being able to identify, *to recognize themselves*. Make them feel like it's a book they could someday write. Make them feel like coauthors. That's the secret. And anything is better—even the worst of the worst—than getting to know or identifying with a writer with writer problems. *Le mot juste*? It doesn't exist. That's why—to address that problem—synonyms were invented. And people get nervous if, when they read, they discover that writing is hard. It's hard for them to read that. What're they looking for? What do they want to find? Easy: readers in the third world want someone to create a fiction out of the dreadful reality that bad luck has dealt them. Something that makes them feel, at least, justified and that they're suffering for a good cause—my cause. If through their misery I find success, they feel that my success is somewhat their own. While readers in the first world, reading that onslaught of horrors, are grateful that they see all that shit only at a distance, in a novel, and buying it helps them feel politically correct so they can comment on it and be hip and move on to something else. It's like the Oscar for Best Foreign Film. You know: once a year, they give out a little gold statue to the story of a young shepherdess, raped by her father in Kazakhstan. Two hours of remote horror and then back to business as usual—superheroes and comedies with a witty girl. Didn't you get kidnapped when you were a kid? Didn't your parents disappear? Or were they saved? Wasn't that a story in your first book? Didn't that book do well? But you only dedicated one story to that . . . What a waste, man: with something like that I would've made an eight-hundred-page party." And, getting warmed up now, he continued: "And also, enough with your referential mania and stop with your enumerations and lists and going around pointing out and acknowledging each and every one of your sources and debts and allusions. This display of honesty is in bad taste and it makes you look like the combination of an old man of the *nouveau riche* and a little orphan of literature. The worst of both worlds. And no one expects or asks you for that display of honesty. We all steal things, nobody admits it, and we don't like that you go around reminding us of our little sins. After all: aren't you a big fan of Bob Dylan, who's something like the King of the Magpies? Don't you come from a glorious literary tradition of brilliant appropriators? And while you're at it: quit repeating that thing about the one hundred forty characters of Twitter. That's not how it works. Not exactly. Don't talk about things you don't understand and, even worse, don't get pissed about what you don't know. Relax, man." And then IKEA—with false sadness and authentic joy—concludes the performance with a, "Who would've thought: you've totally become a writer's writer, a true cult writer. I'm jealous. You've got no idea how much I'd like a little solitude so I could devote myself to doing my thing without distractions . . . But to each his own, man." And—with his eternal and indiscriminate smile, mouth full of fangs, light beard seemingly aerographed onto his face—IKEA went to greet a Pulitzer Prize winner from whom he'd managed to extract the vacuous yet substantive bubbles of a blurb for the forthcoming U.S. edition of *Landscape with Hollow Men*. And he stayed there, upright but bowled over, wishing on him all the biblical plagues (including the death of his hardworking firstborn) and thinking that if you stare with squinted eyes at the expression "writer's writer," what you read below, like almost subliminal subtitles, is the translation: "A writer's writer is the writer to whom other writers pray because, like a martyr waiting, with any luck, for posthumous canonization, it's that kind of better writer for whom things go badly so that things can go better for worse writers."

Or something like that.

Really, he didn't know what he was and where he fit: for some he was commercial, for others he was experimental, for the majority he was hard to classify. And what's hard to classify was better to ignore. Because things that are complicated to define and delimit always cause a ruckus among cold academics and cool hunters alike. And some and others and the majority agreed that there were too many writers in his books (the most belligerent mocked that fact by pointing out that "those books could only have been written by someone born—born dead besides—the same date that Jane Austen died and *Mein Kampf* was published"). And that his vision of the profession was somewhere between romantic and childish (somebody had told him once that all his writing seemed to spring, Proustianly, from the hamburgers and dehydrated mashed potatoes that he'd eaten when he was growing up and maybe they were right). In short and never again: he'd become, yes, an anomaly of the system. Accepting it and recognizing it would be to complicate the flow of faster currents, more clearly defined by docks and dams and reservoirs. So, better to turn a blind eye. He was—he loved the sound, between abrupt and playful, of the tech term—a glitch. Something that also had a musical correspondence: the style of electronic music called Clicks & Cuts, constructed from samples and loops, from small pieces of sound, from cuts and clicks. His melody was difficult to whistle or to make obedient to whistles. Something that nobody knew what to do with and so, just in case, better to touch it as little as possible. A, yes, a *little nameless object* like the one from *The Ambassadors*, which he was trying not to mention. And, ah, he remembered that letter where William James (who ended up philosophizing like a novelist) recommended to his little brother Henry James (who ended up novelizing like a philosopher) that he write a book with few complications and "with great vigor and decisiveness in action" and concluded: "Publish it in my name, I will acknowledge it, and give you half the proceeds."

Now, he didn't have anything to gain. He was lost with nobody who'd bother to come looking for him. And had no interest in returning to supposedly solid ground, where he kept losing his balance, as if, all alone, he were dancing his own private earthquake. He'd been born and had grown up and had resigned himself to the fact that he'd be writing in a world where bad people always succeed and good people rarely win; but nothing had prepared him for getting slightly past a half century of life and looking out at a landscape where, in addition, mediocre people were doing so very well. There was no place in the history of literature for a career like Vladimir Nabokov's anymore. For him, without a doubt, the ultimate, but unachievable, example to follow: an eccentric writer who became centric thanks to *Lolita*, a great eccentric and central book that granted him the luxury and pleasure of being more eccentric than ever in *Pale Fire* or *Ada, or Ardor*, the latter of which he was still unable to read (though it was, without a doubt, the novel he'd started the most times and, getting past the first hundred pages or so, interrupted the most times, as if struck by a singular fever), but which he respected so much. Even more here, in Switzerland, the country with the most suicides and chocolates and watches in the world (they know death and pleasure and time like nobody else) and near to the place where the most American Russian or the most Russian American had occupied a luxury hotel suite, to live out his last years and give life, as Viktor Frankenstein once did to his creature, to his last books. There hadn't been many cases like his. Especially in the realm of literature. In music there was Pink Floyd. And Bob Dylan. And in film (it's no coincidence that he was the one who created his own adaptation of that eccentric-central Nabokov book), Stanley Kubrick. But those cases could be counted on the fingers of one hand, the hand he used to write.

To top it off, he'd recently learned that one of those absurd statistical reports—after inputting numbers and works and dates of death and birth into an electronic brain—had come to the conclusion that the high point of a writer's career is reached at the age of forty-two years, three months, seven days, forty hours, thirty-five minutes, and fifty-six seconds. From that point on—he remembered that in *Tender Is the Night*, Dick Diver came to the conclusion that "life during the forties seemed capable of being observed only in segments"—it was all downhill, heading toward a spoiled silence or unpleasant sound that could be accepted with the elegance of a long farewell-waltz or the violence of one of those "normal" men who gets up one day and murders his entire family. And—events do indeed precipitate—then throws himself off a cliff. What did he have left? Ten years of activity? If he gave himself the luxury of optimism and trusted in modern medicine and scientific advances to come—he had twenty "good" years left, if he was lucky, he calculated. Twenty years or four or five books to write. Provided that he was able to distract himself from the fear, which frightened him less all the time, of thinking that maybe he had nothing left to write, that it was already written, and that he's very sorry if it wasn't enough. Twenty years and four or five books before the generators kicked on because the lights of a slow or fast but always-catastrophic ending were starting to go out. An epilogue in which his mind would begin to forget important things and obsess over trifles. A place where the past would be greater and greater and the future briefer and briefer and the present the current that pulled you deeper and deeper, further from shore, toward a more and more deserted island in a bottle. And everything seemed to indicate that for those twenty years, suddenly revealed vistas of his most distant yesterday would come to him incessantly, demanding to be written, alongside postcards of his contemporaries receiving laurel wreaths from kings and presidents. While he—if the style of his work overcame the inelegance of his life—would be left with nothing but the sanctuary of a swampy bed where he'd lie wrapped in pajamas like a wizened second skin. Every so often, some gesture of recognition, a wave from one ship deck to another in a stormy sea. Like that story that a young and talented writer dedicated to him not long ago, where he appeared named as "the living writer" (living taken to mean that his thing wasn't dead) and built a beautiful master/apprentice fiction in which he had a wife and son. Reading the story for the second time and with greater care—paranoia now being the drug he consumed most, its potency seeming to increase with each dose he took—he wondered if the young and vital writer wasn't, subliminally and between the lines, giving him an undesired and unrequested diagnosis, and reproaching him by insinuating that everything would've turned out better for him if he'd gotten married and had children. Something (a woman to whom, when that inevitable moment came for her to tell him that "We don't have a future together," he wouldn't smilingly retort "But we can have a long present, right?") that'd be waiting for him when he came home or, if he was already at home, when he managed to escape the home of the fiction inside his head. Something (a son that he imagined, always, as if in narcissistic Polaroids, where he appeared, for example, reading to him from Robert Graves's *The Greek Myths*, but never performing the banal tasks of changing his diapers or getting up early to take him to school) to distract him a little from the diastole/systole of reading/writing. Someone who, maybe, would inspire a story about pregnancy or paternity and even a series of essays about the first time his son experienced everything: getting on a train, listening to Bob Dylan, drinking Coca-Cola, watching *2001: A Space Odyssey*, going down a slide, or climbing onto a toboggan. Watching him carefully, writing down everything. To be the faithful memory of what he'd never be able to remember and to note it all down before his son, irreverent in his adolescence, would X-ray him and point out his largest and smallest defects, at a time when all he'll want is to forget. There were books there. For sure. He could see them and even read them; but he had so little desire to write them . . . Not even enough to convince himself that a son would mean *something* to him. Something that, at least, like for Ulysses, would provoke the illusion of self-belief and let him fool himself that all he dreamed of was returning home. Something solid and on terra firma, forcing him to avoid drifting too far from the bays of his nonfiction and to be careful not to be pulled out to sea, to a place where he no longer felt his arms or legs and opened his mouth to let it fill with water. One foot grounded to discharge all the electricity of the lightning spinning around inside him, bouncing off the walls of his cranium, lined in layers of cork to keep out the bother of exterior noise. But, with his luck, he would've probably ended up marrying a madwoman like Miss Havisham (who didn't go mad because she didn't get married: she was *always* mad) or having a useless son like Telemachus (who doesn't protect his mother, *another* Penelope, from her suitors and doesn't go out looking for his father, and who, no doubt, spends his days consulting the oracle—the ancient Greek version of Facebook). Or his condemned wife and cursed descendent would end up glowing in the dark, with the pallor not of vampires but of vampire victims, slowly consumed and never allowed to attain resplendent immortality, but, merely, an agony of intermittent glimmers blown out by the wind if the windows are left open. Or succumbing to that first love, when you find it adorable and strange and oh so seductive that a girl doesn't know how to tie the fucking laces of her shoes, so that, years later, you hate her for that exact reason, for being so imbecilic that she can't even tie the laces of her fucking shoes. Or maybe not. Maybe the joy of a hypothetical wife and a theoretical son was worth it. They didn't even have to be *his*. He could adopt them readymade: the not-so-small fourteen-year-old prodigy and the exceedingly attractive eighteen-year-old girl that nobody took home from the orphanage because they were too grownup. And maybe they'd love him and care for him and correct and comment on his manuscripts. Even the extraterrestrial earthling William S. Burroughs, after decades of wandering the world alone, atomizing the particles of his books, had dedicated, on his way out, a final entry in his journal to love as the definitive painkiller. Love as all that lasts and as the only thing that *is* and that remains. Love as the final solution, love as the original problem. Who knows. Too late anyway. He'd obliterated— following the instructions of Virginia Woolf before she filled her pockets with stones, following the instructions of a not-so-stable someone—"The Angel in the House." There, Woolf was referring to the submissive and servile and domestic part that nested in the heart and mind of every woman; and that had to be excised if the woman wanted to be a writer. True, he wasn't a woman. But he had been born with an extra rib: inside him, his biblical feminine part, intact and dangerous for his vocation. So he'd opted for being The Devil of the Desk and moving right along. And, now, hesitating, he didn't have any strength left to dance amorous dances, perform courtship rituals, initiate signals of seduction: as far as emotions go, he was already like one of those chess masters who can anticipate the next moves and already have foreknowledge of the inexorable disappearance of increasingly valuable pieces. And so, he couldn't help but perceive, in the very excitement of the opening moves, the agony of checkmate: nothing that begins well fails to end badly. Too late anyway. And, besides, he'd read somewhere that regular and guilt-free masturbation was one of the most practical ways to prevent prostate problems. Or, if not, maybe better, a little casual and disinterested and even paid-for sex. "A little ummagumma," like that Pink Floyd roadie used to say in the secret language of roadies. The truth is it always disturbed him—and seemed pretty explicit—that the majority of emotional relationships ended in tears and that children came to the world crying instead of laughing. And he'd been even more disturbed attending the presentation of a writer his age—a writer who was a father, who *had* a son—where he'd said that, in his modest understanding "children don't owe their parents anything and are authorized to give back only what they deem appropriate; but parents, on the other hand, owe absolutely everything to their children, down to their last breath, because they'd been the ones who'd brought them into the world." The man seemed very certain of what he was saying. And even happy. And his little son—who, the writer said—had chosen the image for the cover of his latest book and had demanded that that image, in addition, be the protagonist, smiled happily at his father from the front row. And he didn't feel jealous, but he did feel a certain curiosity about all of that, about the mysterious connection that seemed to unite the two of them and to make them stronger and at the same time more fragile and vulnerable to any catastrophe. Would they survive? Would they be swept away by the hurricanes of time and the diseases of shared blood? Did it make sense to take such a risk, to head out to sea, to defy the gods of fate and misfortune? Who knows. Anyway, it wasn't his problem, it was already too late for such a possible solution. Now, all he had was what was left. Less than a glass half full. A distinction more grayish than gray that—even more sordid details to follow—he denies himself until he achieves the technicolor of his own apocalypse. Portrait of a man who writes less all the time, reading and reciting, like a Quevadoish zombie, the one that goes "Withdrawn into the peace of these deserts, / with few but learned books, / I live in conversation with the dead, / and listen with my eyes to the departed." A despairing man, yes: a condition that those looking in from outside expect to be a kind of sweeping centrifugal force, when really it's nothing more than the tense calm of the lidless eye of a hurricane. Despairing is the man who no longer hopes for anything. Praying more all the time to the Lord of the Crack-Ups, to Saint Francis Scott Fitzgerald of the Too Late Second Act, seeking a modicum of comfort, attempting to convince himself that he's Fitzgerald's disciple and equal in incomprehension and ignorance of others, reading aloud the harsh gospel of *Tender Is the Night* on untranslatable nights that'll never again be soft, or tender, or sweet. Receiving, on days that stretch on and on, punctuated by suspensive comatose siestas, the increasingly infrequent visit of a young writer. A young writer who—it won't take him long to realize—understood nothing of his work and who will say "pop" a lot. And who will mention his name in interviews, using him like an exotic flavor (almost like a dead and failed but oh so interesting writer) when the time comes to spice up and slightly personalize the list of obvious and useful favorites. Like what happened with Pink Floyd's *Wish You Were Here*, condemned by the critics at first and then, with the passing years, redeemed and even elevated to the altars as a great and sacred work and a definitive sonic portrait of the absent, of what's not there but remains and . . . Or—the domestic wolf who never had to be domesticated, solitary and fangless, the inoffensive writer version of a terrorist more terrified than anyone, suddenly thrown into a clearing of the darkest and fiercest forest—pointing an unloaded gun at the very occasional photographer, less and less time to become the little dead man of reference and the injustice ready for posthumous redemption.

Yes, every so often, he experienced the mild contractions of the temptation to give birth to his own little myth. But his life hadn't been that interesting and speaking ill of everyone and everything in interviews wasn't his thing and was the thing of so many others. The easy and preferred method of certain contemporary legends, addicts of the *boutade* and the condemnation, positioning themselves vis-à-vis what they dislike rather than what they like (and the success of this posture can be perceived just by counting the number of comments that they receive, on a blog, for a defenestration, comparing it to minimal effect, putting to bed rather than rousing any praise or sympathy), thinking that demonstrating enthusiasm for or taking pleasure in something is almost for cowards. The Internet seemed full of hyenas and vultures (some internauts even suggested names and titles for everyone to take down all at once) always poised and ready to emerge from the shadows of their terminals and throw themselves on the fallen and rip them apart while laughing and pecking in comments that are crude and rotten and badly written in their haste, the so-strange happiness of being so vile. There were too many things he liked, he'd always been criticized for it, and the idea of being or playing the bad guy seemed just as exhausting as going from festival to festival repeating two or three of his own lines that now, after so much repeating, seemed almost foreign, like the echo of a supposedly original voice that sounded and was farther away all the time. So no, better no, even worse no. Shutting his eyes on all of that. Later, trying to fall asleep not by counting sheep but by distracting himself with subtractions and remainders.

Morbid subjects; like the music he'd want played at his funeral. His funerals: his imminent end as a writer and his increasingly proximal end as such. To wit: the aria, in Glenn Gould's last and definitive piano solo version of J. S. Bach's *Goldberg Variations* (Bach, who was never paid much for his work, for that music made to frighten the insomnia out of a count of the Saxony court; and who permitted himself the joke of composing the last of said variations on the foundation of two popular melodies whose titles, translated, would be, not kidding, "I have been away from you so long, come near, come near" and "The cabbage and the turnips have driven me away, if mother had cooked meat, maybe I would've stayed"), followed by The Beatles' "A Day in the Life" and Harry Nilsson's "Good Old Desk" (both about the conjoined act of reading and writing), The Kinks "Days," and saying goodbye, the casket heading for the flames with "Wigwam," that hummed, borderland instrumental by Bob Dylan. And then, time and desire permitting, as a kind of encore, during that epilogue when everyone will wipe away tears many of them never thought they'd shed and embrace bodies they never embraced and even let out a laugh (because nothing causes more surprise humor than celebrating someone's death, feeling suddenly so alive), the last and ninth part of "Shine On You Crazy Diamond," composed in its entirety by the immense and never-fully-appreciated Rick Wright, rest in peace. Lyrics and music punctuating the elegies (some of them quite funny and sentimental, for sure) of his dwindling friends; because those who write well and read better are dwindling. But he doesn't rule out a surprise appearance, another surprise appearance, by IKEA, just in case, because you never know what might happen to a dead writer and it's no sweat off IKEA's back to make an appearance. And to put on that how-sad-for-him mask over that how-happy-for-me face he tends to reveal and barely conceals on such occasions. And on and on like that until sleep comes and he closes his eyes and opens them to dreams of things that, he's certain, only he dreams. Dreams where he enters a bookstore not of used books but of *read* books (a condition and mystery and breathing that, again, no electronic invention could ever aspire to) and there, opening one, discovers inside it that legendary stolen or lost letter, that fundamental missing link to understanding the evolution of the novel: lines and pages that, previously supposed and suddenly certain, Henry James sent to Marcel Proust after reading the first volume of *In Search of Lost Time*. Obviously it's a childish dream. A dream as childish as his vocation. But it's much better to dream *like this*, sweetly and among shelves and books, than to dream the dream that the nightmares tend to bring, the one where he's a very old old man (the redundancy is valid), not at all elegant, wrapped in a fog of of vigorous and healthy afflictions that no longer leave him, and irascible not like one of those twisted Charles Dickens characters, but like the illustration of one of those twisted Charles Dickens characters. A kind of Ebenezer Scrooge who spurns everyone because he knows himself spurned and who's not at all interested in the interested and methodological affection of university students who circle him like vultures, waiting for him to die so they can resuscitate him in theses and theories. Someone who has already forgotten what it was to leap. Someone who can no longer leap and detach himself from the ground and fly in the air for a second or two. Someone who at any moment will break a hip, because his bones can no longer bear the call and pull of the gravity of an earth that's reclaiming his body, that wants him not on his feet but lying down and underground. And he thinks about all of that, considers all of it without feeling any need to put it in writing, in the savannah of his sheets, tossing and turning, not bothering anybody because he sleeps alone and wakes up even more alone, repeating until he sinks into insomnia, eyes shut, like a blind mantra, things like "My kingdom is not of this world . . . Mykingdomisnot ofthisworld . . . Mykingdomisnotofthisworld . . ."

Where was his kingdom? he wondered now, thousands of meters above the earth, hurtling through the air at a thousand kilometers per hour, not long after trying and failing to bring about the end of the world. Was this flying metal horse his kingdom? Or was there a place out there somewhere waiting to welcome him home after so many years away on his convoluted Crusades? On which he discovered that God didn't exist or—even worse, maybe—that God didn't read his books; because on the seventh day he wanted something light and entertaining, something that would assure him that mankind was to blame for all the horrors of humanity.

Why?

Why not?

He wanted—he *needed*—something like that now too. Something passing for the passenger he was. So he pressed buttons and scrolled up and down the list of movies and saw that, among the nearly fifty titles, was the recently released musical version of *The Metamorphosis* called *Bug!* Something strange had happened—something that couldn't be good—when it was decided that the genre of classical musicals (the one where the characters suddenly, possessed by an ecstatic happiness, started to sing and dance without it striking anyone as strange) had to infect the great tragedies of literature. Not long ago he'd endured fifteen minutes of *Les Misérables* on TV and had shuddered when he saw those colossal set designs and flags flying in the wind, fading into close-ups of characters' faces, excessively sullied by the most cosmetic of poverties, singing their penury at full volume, eyes and mouths so wide they looked ready to pop out of their sockets or dislocate their jaws. Out of pure curiosity, after watching a documentary about John Cazale and another about Harry Dean Stanton (two first-rate B-roll actors), he selects *Bug!* The star of the movie is that hip prodigy: L. B. Wild. Lost Boy Wild—a name his agent gave him—is a boy who was discovered wandering around a supposedly uninhabited Pacific island, where a crew had gone to film a show about paranormal activity that, though incomprehensible, had a good part of humanity on the edges of their seats. Another one of those shows automatically celebrated by the automatic celebrators, shows that go on for seasons and seasons, submitting their followers to a sadomasochistic exercise (*Once upon a time upon a time upon a time upon a time*) comparable to that of the loving and terrible mother with the personality of a wicked stepmother who draws out telling her children the stories of Cinderella and Snow White and Sleeping Beauty and Little Red Riding Hood over five years. Shows like new favorite colors or astrological signs or foods: "What show are you watching?" as the perfect question to strike up a stupid conversation. Fans—who called themselves wildies across an infinity of paranoid blogs and conspiratorial forums—had celebrated the discovery of the lost, wild boy as if it were an evolution of the show, as if it were incontrovertible proof that this was much more than a simple TV series. So L. B. Wild was brought back to civilization and an attempt was made to trace his origin to a possible accident where his parents or family members had died, a shipwreck or a small plane crash, whatever. But no record was found. Nobody had lost that strange boy who— almost two meters tall, muscular, blond, blue eyes—was quickly selected as the sexiest man on the planet. And nobody was particularly surprised that

L.B. Wild possessed wild talents for acting (years of forced survival in the jungle had given him a almost supernatural mimetic capacity), music (his voice reached vertiginous highs and deep lows and he was able to imitate the sounds of all the animals and of the sea and the rain and the wind in the trees), and painting (his eyes, having lost nothing of their childish curiosity, had made him a master of a new thing that critics had rushed to classify as "Popexsionism"). So, L. B. Wild had won an Oscar for *Bug!*, he had simultaneous shows in the galleries of Charles Saatchi (London) and Larry Gagosian (New York); his first album—*You Jane, Me NOT Tarzan*, featuring collaborations with U2, Kanye West, Bruce Springsteen, Lady Gaga, and DJ Thomas Pincho—had topped the sales charts in several countries; his autobiography had been announced (was he going mad or had he heard on the news that IKEA would be in charge of "helping him civilize his wild past?"); he was modeling for top clothing designers; and, they said, he'd been raped and sexually initiated by Miley Cyrus at a nightclub-casino in Vegas.

In any case—with the collaboration of another bourbon—*Bug!* helps him close his eyes without getting too worried about what he'll have turned into when he wakes up. He's already felt like a cockroach for a while now. Meanwhile and in the meantime, he's on a beach, in the black and white of dreams, trailing the footsteps of a bishop in holiday attire who raises his hand and makes the sign of the cross and blesses everything in a language he can't identify, but presently memorizes and recites after the Bishop. "Porpozec ciebie nie prosze dorzanin albo zyolpocz ciwego," the bishop repeats over and over. And without knowing how or why, it seems to him that it can only mean "There are many good things in life, so don't go looking for things that don't exist."

"What things?" he says in the dream, out loud, and the sound of his own voice wakes him up and everything hurts. He could blame the guards (again: be patient, there's enough for everyone, and there are still more sordid details to be handed out); but it wouldn't be fair and would be overstating their power and training. No: this pain has been coming on for a long time. Not a growing pain but the pain (except the nose, which supposedly grows until your last breath) of no longer growing. Though the first-class seat is like a small bed that adjusts to his body like a warm and soft and protective mold *by* Bubble Wrap or like returning after so much wandering to the perfect and unbeatable little bed of that turbulence zone of his childhood. Or maybe he woke up inside another dream, like in Chinese boxes or Russian nesting dolls. Henry James warned: tell a dream, lose a reader. But on this point, he did not agree with Henry James, who, moreover, had ended his life in the waking dream of a delirium where he'd believed he was Napoleon and had dictated orders and his last will and testament, like the most banal and badly written of madmen. Dreams are useful and they work. Worst case, tell a dream, gain some time. And that's to say nothing of nightmares: proclaim not "I had a dream" but "I had a nightmare" at a crowded party and everything stops and you become, for a while, the king of the evening, to whom everyone listens. Nothing beats the story of the dark ride of the mare of the night. And suddenly wide-awake and not bored anymore—and vertical and upright and civil—everyone pays attention and makes comparisons and raises their hands to ask their turn. And to be able to tell the always vague and imprecise and yet hard-working and interpretable memory of the micro-macrostories (because the storyline of sleeping stories never correspond to the waking time passing outside them) that they wake from startled by the sound of their own screams or the taste of their own tears. And then start to forget them, to invent them, to insert all their unconfessed desires into them. And in this way put to bed the suspicion that, actually, real dreams are never that clever and always recurrent; like that repeated dream of his where a couple does nothing but say goodbye at the doors to an absurd building. Or that the worst nightmares are nothing but the natural alarm clock of a part of the brain yet to be identified and located, whose function is to startle us, so we jump out of bed and don't succumb to the temptation of dreaming on and on forever, in order to escape the real horrors of everyday life. So, maybe, when we wake up, wanting and needing to justify all those hours elsewhere (in the third part of our lives; that's why, aware of the farce, wise newborns and innocent individuals on death's doorstep sleep less), we force them on ourselves dream when awake that we dream something when asleep. We invent stories, lies, alternate lives. Or maybe it's something that only happens to him: nothing occurs to him when awake, nothing occurs to him when asleep.

He always liked—in books and in movies and in beds—to be told dreams. Even the childish dreams of children—public nudity or flying or falling— which are the dreams that stay with us for the rest of our lives. Or the obvious dreams from the first films with psychoanalysts to whom what's dreamt is recounted awake with the none-too-reliable precision of someone who's no longer sleeping and whose interpretation is, for that reason, as unfaithful as the story of ourselves that someone else tells for us or that we tell for someone else. Or the auteur dreams in those other films: highways frozen with traffic or little people emerging from behind radiators in films that seem pure dream: oneiric features where we never discover who it is that's dreaming. Or the disturbing dreams of a lover (who killed him over and over in increasingly elaborate ways), who would wake up and wake him up to tell him about it first with a luxury and then a lust of details; because nothing turned her on more than feeling like a voracious praying mantis.

And with time, the past itself becomes either a dream to be rewritten or an uneraseable nightmare. His recent past—sent to bed without dessert—was like an entertainment that devours itself, shrinking and shrinking until it attains the immensity of the nothingness, of the void. What he had dreamed of. He, who'd grumbled so much about new technologies, letting himself go to come back changed, inside a supreme machine, just by pressing a button. An epic form of suicide. An immortal death. Ceasing to be and departing in order to return, victorious, as a destructive and righteous force. Like those infinite sidereal villains in the Marvel comics he read when he was a kid possessed by the beautiful Ugly Spirit of science fiction. Full-page vignettes drawn by Jack Kirby showing disgraced, schizophrenic superheroes with messianic inferiority complexes—their speech bubbles always full of exclamation points, their mouths agape in terror, shouting the lines Stan Lee wrote for them—pointing to the skies where beings with ominous names like Galactus or Annihilus or Catastrophus or Apocaliptus Nowus were descending. Devourers of planets and shakers of molecules imposing their wills and disposing of everyone else's. Vengeful Dantian visions—not of Dante but of Dantès—returning from the far reaches of the universe, from their "Negative Zones," to take their revenge.

That's why he'd chosen to go to Geneva, on Christmas Eve, to the accelerator and collider of particles, when he received—after so many years—a phone call from Abel Rondeau asking him where in the world he wanted to go. Hearing Rondeau's voice—after several decades without hearing it—confirmed for him what he'd always suspected: Rondeau was immortal, Rondeau was never going to die, Rondeau had always been like this, since he was a baby, so similar to the Nowhere Man Jeremy Hillary Boob PhD in the movie *Yellow Submarine*. Rondeau had been his first boss, the first person to pay him for something he'd written. And consequently he was the most important figure in his life as a writer. Rondeau—who'd been a precocious poet and, it was said, swam for years in the free verses of an infinite fluvial poem, singing to the rivers of his province—had specialized in editing credit card and airline magazines. Several well-known writers had passed through his columns, but he was the first one who'd started from zero and emerged from there. Now Rondeau—at the head of a publication called *Volare*—came back like the Ghost of Christmas past. And he told him that the magazine was celebrating a major anniversary. And the idea had occurred to him to bring back the "best names" of his professional life and send them around the planet to places of their choosing for a special issue of *Volare*. "Really send them," Rondeau had clarified with one of his little laughs, raspy, like a scarab. Because he'd spent a good part of the second decade of his life and first decade of his professional life—under various pseudonyms and personalities, including a dandy, a spiteful wife, and the last link in the chain of a family of child prodigies—composing imaginary trips for the pages of a previous incarnation of *Volare* called *Miles & Kilometers*. Making them more or less believable, using information from tourist guides and photos that Rondeau bought from travel agencies (slipping in, as an act of rebellion, subliminal phrases like "the events precipitate," "thunder and lightning," "inexplicable delays" to subliminally terrorize their high altitude readers) until he became a kind of Marco Polo, enclosed inside the partitions of a cubicle with a latest generation typewriter and a first generation computer. It'd been, for him, he was certain, the best possible writing workshop. And his debt to Rondeau—on the increasingly infrequent days he felt happy about having become a writer—was infinite and impossible to repay.

And now Rondeau reentered his life and he said yes and pointed to that place on the map near Geneva where the Large Hadron Collider stood. And Rondeau gave a little laugh and said: "I'll send you a first-class ticket and the details of your itinerary tomorrow. Forty thousand words. Two thousand euros. Have a nice trip."

The money wasn't bad. Recently, he'd made a lot more for a lot less. But, suddenly, what really attracted him was having a destination and an end and a finale. What was it that captain/assassin Benjamin L. Willard had said before plunging into the infernos, heading upriver, out of Vietnam and into Cambodia, "about 75 clicks above the Do Lung Bridge"? Ah, yes: "Everyone gets everything he wants. I wanted a mission, and for my sins, they gave me one. Brought it up to me like room service. It was a real choice mission, and when it was over, I never wanted another," or something like that, right?

Yeah, yeah, yeah: he'd go. He'd perform an unforgettable number. A number of many digits. The greatest gift in the history of humanity. The ultimate gift, no exchanges or refunds in the Total Liquidation of his fury. Selling out all existences in the EVERYTHING MUST GO of his revenge. He'd be a new Santa Claus called Cataclismicus. He'd be hole and black and supermassive and magnetic and void and quantum. He'd depart in order to return. He'd accelerate into the depths and collide with everything. He'd give up writing to erase everyone else: letter by letter going in reverse, leaving them floating in a monosyllabic loop, now everyone would know what it was to be good and Merry Christmas and Ho Ho Ho.

Of course, something went wrong, nothing went right. The whole moment had the tremulous and ultraviolent choreography of one of those old silent (but seemingly filmed at full volume) Keystone Kops movies. Or, better, of one of the Coen brothers' movies where dreamers and visionaries like Jeff "The Dude" Lebowski or Llewyn Davis or Herbert I. "Hi" McDunnough or Tom Reagan or Ulysses Everett McGill don't get what they deserve but do get what a good story deserves, and so—for them as for him now—events precipitate, *yessir.* They spotted him approaching a restricted access door and, immediately, he was jumped on by several guards who—they weren't fooling him—were direct descendants of SS officers. They quickly subdued and removed him without a beating ("Elvis has left the building," he thought as they cuffed his hands and feet and dragged him out of there), but executing a series of tai-chi martial arts moves and Vulcan death grips on his cervical nerves that left no trace, and he wasn't so much tossed as deposited in a holding cell that was far nicer and cleaner than the flat he lived in and that, oh boy, seemed decorated entirely with, yes, IKEA-brand furniture. There, in the privacy of his great public failure, he felt that, in some perverse way, he'd succeeded: he'd become, at last and in the end, one of those Homo catastrophicos of American literature, so loved and triumphant in their defeats. Always protagonists of novels with their last names (generally Jewish) as title and code word on the cover. He liked it so much when a book was named for a person. And now he was something like Shivastein, bruised dancer in the destruction of worlds, laughing tears, in an air-conditioned cell of impeccable credentials.

And then—ultimate humiliation—he was rescued by IKEA.

IKEA, who wasn't as he'd thought him, as he'd described him, as he'd, in part, invented him.

IKEA was an excellent person, who had always been very grateful to him for everything, and who pulled strings and used his considerable influence to get him released and paid his fine in the millions for "attempting to bring about the end of the world." So, even though it was an alternate version of what he understood as talent, IKEA's work—which, also, relied on simpler and better tools and instruction manuals that were easier to follow and understand—still had certain merit beyond the fact that his solemn and so unjustifiably self-satisfied prose evoked for him a lesson learned down to the smallest detail by a student lacking any talent apart from a photographic memory, not bringing anything unique or particular or personal to the table, and sounding to him like one of those thundering soundtracks that, in movies directed by directors of the "skilled artisan" variety, underscore the romantic or dramatic but never the funny moments; because IKEA couldn't conceive of the idea that humor could be a serious part of serious literature. IKEA was more concerned with a different kind of humor. With a serious humor. With distilling the secret code of the import/export of literature. An instantly assimilable exoticism or an automatically international nationalism. And truth be thought but never told: between having things go well for IKEA or for one of his other contemporaries whom he considered his odd couples or ink brothers, he preferred—it was much easier to bear and even allowed him to feel a fragile disdain—to have things go well for IKEA. Because he let himself be convinced that IKEA was suited for something he'd never be. On the other hand, it'd be an entirely different matter and there would be no excuses or alibis if one of his own, a writer's writer, were to succeed . . . So, better this way. IKEA—a reader's writer—bore no resemblance to his mental IKEA at all. To that entity constructed like a laboratory monster from loose pieces of various writers. A man with a hammer for whom everything was nails to be pounded and driven. A man he'd constructed and, in his sick mind, summoned and deformed and perfected into an infectious caricature, day after day, googling the news of his latest and never last successes. One of those caricatures belonging to that school of caricaturism that he despised: drawings with huge heads and tiny bodies, as if the only thing worth caricaturing were faces. Or, not satisfied with that, imagining IKEA's face inserted into one of those posters for theater performances (generally French vaudevilles where everyone shouted and pounded on doors and, like in IKEA's novels, for him a physical description from which there was no coming back once it was written, "turned on their heels") where the actors appear all together with their eyes and mouths wide open, in supposedly but never actually funny poses. In his mental caricatures in the backstage of his insomnia, IKEA was like a big hot air balloon, like Oz the Great and Powerful floating in the air, controlled by a pygmy behind a curtain. IKEA was his project. He devoted hours to him. Hours he could've spent writing. Or reading. Or doing nothing. It was unendingly sad, this waste of creativity: there was a time when the emissions of his nocturnal fantasies revolved around what it would've been like to sleep with those girls he never slept with but, he was almost certain, could've slept with if he'd just taken the initiative. There was another time when he thought about nothing but the novel he was working on and, in his lowest moments, about the acceptance speeches he'd give for awards that never came and never would. Now, on the other hand, all his wet dreams revolved around a fantastic and impossible IKEA. Well, actually, his IKEA did somewhat resemble IKEA; because—let's not forget—for someone to inspire and respire, someone has to expire. IKEA was so happy to distinguish himself, he seemed to be posing more for a bust than a photo, he was an efficient broadcaster of clichés in his interviews and was, also, an internationally successful author of a novel called *Landscape with Hollow Men* that—though it didn't entirely fit his synopsis—was just as horrifying as that of his IKEA. The truth was, as far as he was concerned—and on the rare and increasingly infrequent occasions when, with considerable mental and physical effort he was able to force himself to feel and behave like a dignified human being, beyond good and evil—IKEA's success wasn't that upsetting. Again, seriously: with a couple gin and tonics in and on top of him, he was even happy for him. And he was jealous of something IKEA had and had retained. Something he'd lost the moment he felt he'd achieved it—the terrible desire to be a writer. IKEA—and many of the writers of his generation—had more and more desire to be writers and to act like writers and to be asked to do what they assumed writers should do, which isn't writing exactly but going around the world telling people that they write, what they write, for whom they write, and how they write, until on the one hand there was the work itself and on the other there was what they claimed that work was. Good for them, good for IKEA, bad for him, who enjoyed not so much being a writer but *playing* a writer, *acting* like a writer, less and less. But he couldn't help but feel sad for the many unjustly fallen along the way. That the immense loser Fitzgerald only knew in death the success enjoyed by the little winner IKEA seemed to him an unforgivable injustice. That IKEA incessantly pronounced Fitzgerald's name as "one of my maestros" sounded like total blasphemy. And that IKEA referred to *The Great Gatsby* as "the book that taught me everything I know" wasn't just sacrilegious, but, it also confirmed (he could swear that the author of *Landscape with Hollow Men* had learned nothing from *Tender Is the Night*, because he'd never opened it) that IKEA only read his "maestro's" most well-known books. But nobody seemed to notice. Or nobody seemed to care. Such was life, and life had no reason to give or receive pleasure from the way that literature—even in its most heartbreaking storylines—provides some sense of justice and morality and recompense. Because, in the end, both the miserable Julien Sorel and the miserable Emma Bovary, Alonso Quijano, Cathy Earnshaw, Ahab, Bergotte, Cass Cleave, Ralph Touchett, Tess of the d'Urbervilles, Geoffrey Fermin, Morel's Faustine, die happy because, immortal, they're well written. To die *like that* was to be more alive than ever.

So he didn't aspire to die happy anymore, but he did aspire to write something that would make him happy again. Happy the way he used to be when he wrote. Happy the way he was when he read something that was sad but written euphorically.

Where could he go? Where could he find all of that again? When? Maybe—and he ordered another bourbon from the flight attendant—in the time of books. In that continuous present where the past and the future pass away. A time that passes simultaneously, and that you enter and exit the way you enter a house where, having once resided there, you still live. A house that looks more and more like a museum. A house where you always, like when you evoke your childhood, remember everything being much bigger, but then, as you move through its hallways, everything feels smaller and smaller.

That place that Henry James called "the visitable past." And such visits are known to be a high-risk endeavor, full of not necessarily pleasant surprises. Anything can happen. Something that's not expecting us or that we're not expecting. Nothing is as it seemed, as it seems. *A* memory is like a virus that mutates every time it's vaccinated and *the* memory is a sickness from which only absolute amnesiacs are entirely cured. The rest of us wander around, almost in the dark, bumping into furniture we thought was somewhere else. Memory is an interior decorator; an interior decorator who seems to believe in feng-shui: shifting things around to find the ideal orientation for our well-being. Or tranquility. Or comfort. Or best and most convenient way and means of remembering. Because remembering is nothing but a slight mutation of forgetting, very personal and very private. We erase, we rewrite, we correct, we alter the order and calibrate intensities and voltages of scenes and scenarios. So the past is always a work in progress—an unfinished manuscript and, in the end, a posthumous work to be revised by strangers.

To avoid this, as if wrapping himself in a fever, here and now he promises himself a posthumous book while he's still alive. A zombie memoir (he's a little worried about how often he thinks the word "zombie" lately), self-cannibalizing, starving for his brain and his brain alone. A kind of autistic autobiography: an *autibiography* focusing on (as if looking through a microscope with telescopic lenses or a telescope with microscopic lenses; approximating distances, distancing proximities, as if watching and seeing everything through the faraway yet nearby eye of a keyhole) an apparently insignificant but original and foundational detail. The Little Bang, the intimate and inaudible Genesis whose echo resounds, apocalyptic, across the years in catastrophes to come and miracles to be witnessed. Not Literature of the I, but Literature of the Who Am I. Or Literature of the What Do I Know. Or Literature of the Ex I, of the I that could have been but wasn't, because it got off the train before reaching its destination or didn't catch its plane on time. The figure hidden in the tapestry, the secret code, the magic word, the key that opens the door to the explosive clockwork mechanism of the head of a writer. Tick-tock, Knock-Knock. What time is it? The same time as always, all the time. The time, for him, to keep on thinking about how to proceed, about how to begin, about how to move on, about how to end, about how to begin again. The time for "Once upon a time . . ." The time never shown by nonexistent airport clocks (he's come to think that some kind of deal must have been struck between airport administrators and mobile phone makers and inventors of various electronics; forcing users to depend on their devices for something as simple as the time and, of course, getting them immediately trapped in the spider web of messages and ads and games). The time shown only on digital clocks in the corners of plasma screens of movies and books clutched by electrocuted spectators and readers, holding onto those tablets as if they were a ledge or a life preserver on the brink of an abyss or in the midst of a shipwreck, convinced they'll hold them aloft or keep them afloat when really they'll fall and sink, no bottom in sight. Why not give all of them, he thinks now, in the sky, the hell of the definitive gadget. Why settle for an electronic *reader* when you can access an electronic *writer*. The unmitigated and unanesthetized truth. Not yet. Though, surely, it won't be long, sooner or later *that* time will come. Bells at midnight, heralding the idea—that he's hereby patenting—that'd allow readers, orally or intravenously or via a suppository or with the insertion of a chip, to gain direct and live access to the mind of a writer, of their favorite writer. Not selling books anymore but selling minds that think books. "E-Writer" or "iWrite" or "Bookman." Experiencing live—a nonstop feed—how an idea occurs to a writer. An idea that, of course, won't always be a good idea and that might be an awful idea, a terrible waste of time and useless expenditure of neuronal energy. Like reading a bad or confused book, but experiencing in the flesh what it's like to work twenty-four hours a day. A truly *never-ending tour* (maybe an excursion, without the soft but firm voice of the GPS to orient you, through the disorienting and as yet unpublished Mount Karma, Abracadabra; you've been there, would you be able to come back and tell about it, give some shape to all that incandescent and chaotic material?, would you ever make it out of there or, having never lived something like that, being the child of a small extinct clan, would you stay there, addicted to that family whose name is legion?), a stone that keeps on rolling. Feeling each one of the dangerous curves and risky byways of a split brain and a megapolar personality. And suffering its flat tires and breathing in the euphoria of its peaks and, from there, jumping off into the abyss. And that's just the beginning. Experiencing too the *le mot juste* and *we work in the dark* and *the madness of art* and the absurd conjectures and crazy superstitions and childish fantasies (daydreaming that you're the author of that classic); struggling to reconcile the slow and secret construction of your work with the unstoppable demolition of life; and accepting the shameful certainty (because it's easy to confess nothing when everyone is guilty) that the laurels another writer receives (especially if he or she is younger) can only be the very same laurels that, not understanding why, didn't come to rest on the head of their rightful owner and author, the fault of some upstart and sycophantic social climber; inventing and believing in family tragedies and madness and disappearances to excuse yourself for not writing or to help yourself start writing again.

He can imagine all the used up users, the addicts of the ephemeral novelty of this new toy: smiling with fascination at first but before long releasing little horrified screams and cries for help. And then unplugging and running away, certain that they *do not want* to be that, but maybe, from then on, treating books and the alphabet with greater respect. And valuing how that process, that adventurous voyage, corresponds to the way the letters jump from the page and enter our eyes and arrive to the interior of our brains. And once there and from there, to try, once again, to free trembling prisoners and burning lunatics and to inspire and guide lovers, vanquishing despair and, maybe, saving the world. Blessed be.

Meanwhile and in the meantime, he says, why not the coming-soon of a book that isn't like a book but like a writer. Variations on a theme, with the lights out, while everyone but him sleeps in the darkness of space wrapped in the void: *A book . . . A book . . . A book . . .*

A book that wouldn't be avant-garde but *retro-garde*: the part behind a book, its backstage and making-of, its how-to in code and loose pieces to be trapped. Because there's no gesture more avant-garde or experimental in a book than the one made in the very moment of its creation, before it comes into being. A before that's nothing but a long during in which everything that could happen happens irrespective of times or spaces or structures: that voyage without clear direction or precise destination where the writer reads a book that's not yet been written. During that time—that *era*—that is, always, the moment of maximum plenitude and happiness—when everything is yet to be done and you look out at the future as if it were an ideal and limitless landscape, from the top of a tall mountain. With your hands on your waist and your legs planted slightly apart, solid and on your feet. And you see everything. And you understand and comprehend everything. Down to the smallest and most revealing detail.

A book that thinks like a writer in the act of thinking up a book, what he's thinking about when he happens to think of a book, when that book happens to him, and about what happens with that book.

A book that would be read in the same way it was written.

A book that would be read—like those medieval monks read, perfecting first the art of reading in a low voice, their lips barely moving—like a prayer.

A book in the most singular and first of third persons.

A book that—aired or aerated—would be like the stand-up comedian of itself, all alone, in a club on the last night of the end of the world.

A book like antimatter, like the antimaterial that—its energy so dark—will turn into another book, in another dimension.

A book that would sound like an album of greatest hits composed of rarities or like disrespectful or distorted but sincere covers of itself.

A book that, entering the airport, its helixes already spinning and ready for take off, would obey without argument and even with enthusiasm the order to *round up the usual suspects*.

A book like a suspension bridge to throw oh so many things off of as you cross it and arrive to the other side, ah, so light and free of baggage.

A book that promises to whomever it may concern—after its author has written writers of children, writers of saints, writers of songs, writers of comics, writers of obituaries, writers of children's books, writers of science fiction—that in the next book, if there is one, there won't be any more writers. Or that, at least, he'll try his best, really, seriously, right?

A book that would invite you in with a "Draw your chair up close to the edge of the precipice and I'll tell you a story" and that, once you're there, would push you over the edge and, as you fall headlong into the void, would shout at you, "But why'd you believe me? Didn't your parents ever tell you not to talk to strangers?"

A book that would include celebrity faces. Ray Davies, gripped by panic, feeling the whole big sky coming down on top of him. William Burroughs killing his wife in order to be born as a writer. Bob Dylan lost in the mythic inertia of being Bob Dylan and claiming that he doesn't need to write any more songs because "The world don't need any more songs . . . They've got enough. They've got too many. As a matter of fact, if nobody wrote any songs from this day on, the world ain't gonna suffer for it. Nobody cares." And, even still, he kept right on pulling fragments and notes and words and papers and bijis out of his "Box" because it's better to write for others than to read yourself. Francis Scott Fitzgerald sinking into the swamp of a long and exceedingly rough and not at all tender night. Syd Barrett and Pink Floyd portrayed with that cadence and phrasing and style, not forever young but forever juvenile, of rock journalism—that exhibitionism somewhere between encyclopedic and ignorant—that contaminates everyone during puberty, when they listen to albums and write over those albums with their ears. All of them, there inside, with their mouths shut and eyes open wide, features frozen in the terrible moment when it occurs to them that nothing occurs to them but to invent parts of their lives that seem, even to them, more and more like fictions.

A book that would overflow with epigraphs and where each of them is like a piece of a secret message or like those ransom notes assembled from clippings of letters, in different fonts and personalities and styles, but all of them wanting and demanding the same thing.

A book that, like all his books, would keep on growing in successive editions, incorporating new paragraphs and pages and even chapters in a *writer's cut*. Last minute bonus tracks and deleted scenes. The same thing had always happened to him: the book finished, in the final round of proofs, as if he were looking back at his whole life a handful of minutes before the end, ideas and actions came to him that he hadn't *remembered* at the time but that now . . .

A book that—with any luck—over time would become one of those books like *On the Road* or *The Catcher in the Rye*—forever juvenile books that you reread throughout life to assess how you're aging.

A book that would include, disappeared, the Greatest *Desaparecido* of All Time. A book about someone who disappears and then reappears in order to make everything disappear or change or start over; like someone crumpling a page into a ball and throwing it toward the circle of that waste basket at the foot of the desk and, did it make it or not?

A book that when you throw it against a wall bounces back into your hands. Or that, at least, when it falls to the ground, always falls open to the page you were on when you threw it against the wall.

A book, (im)personal and self-referential, with oh so many winks for connoisseurs and marvelous moments frozen in time that it starts off and ends up resembling a face beaten by a tidal wave of tics, drowned by a tsunami of tick-tocks: like the secret voice of someone who's desperate to tell us something but who can't speak, because his tongue is tied, because suddenly his tongue speaks in the strangest of tongues.

A book that—as Beckett said of Proust—would beneficently and joyously suffer "that most necessary, wholesome and monotonous plagiarism—the plagiarism of oneself."

A book that speaks a different language, its own, but that also tells you: "Okay, true, you don't understand me now, but you'll learn, because I'll teach you. Let me see: let's start at the end . . ."

A book in which everything happens at the same time.

A book that's obviously adolescent: pimples, changing voice, altered personality and mood and character, always horny; but written from that second adolescence that begins at the end of middle-age and the beginning of old-age.

A book that—if it weren't the last of everything but the first of something—would end up, over the years, producing a certain discomfort in its author. An anxiety like the anxiety caused by running into a childhood friend who knows too much and whom you've not seen for a long time. And when, all of a sudden, you see them again, you can't help but wonder how it is that you ever had anything to do with someone like that and what you should do to avoid being recognized, so they don't come running over, shouting and waving their arms, attacking, on guard.

A book that wouldn't make you wonder what is and isn't true, but that answers without hesitating or lying how this guy happens to think of these things.

A book that, if it were a building, would be the Flatiron in Manhattan, and everything is expressed architecturally, right?

A book that's studied like those ancient anatomical prints, displaying a panoramic bisection of the head, revealing zones inhabited by moods, sensations, feelings, come look, come see, come read. The same thing that—with the space race canceled, no signs of extraterrestrial life out there, or, at least, not of superior beings with enough interest in us to reveal themselves—is now sought with the most futuristic and space-age of technologies. But the objective is the same: find the exact centers of love and guilt and hate and desire and even religious faith. One by one—scientists make claims without offering us much in the way of proof, as if filling an album with trading cards—these exact sites in our brain are being located. While the most difficult card—The Invented Part, the part that's invented—doesn't stay still and changes position like someone changing his mind.

A book that's toxic—both for its author and its readers—but a book that, once processed and digested, the fever broken, functions as a kind of exorcism, leaving behind someone who, after feeling like hell, looks up at the sky and smiles that smile of prayer-card saints.

A book like one of those poisons that, via its careful and precise administration, ends up becoming its own antidote.

A book that's *vomitific* like a purge and an exorcism.

A book that's like a tumor you have to rock and sing to so it won't wake up and matastisize.

A book to be excised.

A book that would be an open book, though not consequently clear and figurative, but cloudy and abstract.

A book like one of Edward Hopper's clean and well-lit rooms, but with a Jackson Pollock waiting to come out of the closet.

A book near whose end he'd *also* say and is going to say—right now, listen to him say it—that thing about "I had something to write. But my task was longer than his, my words had to reach more than a single person. My task was long."

A book that would function like a journal and like the communion of apparently irreconcilable people and landscapes and that would end up being like a love letter written inside a burning building.

A book that's like a book of ghosts but where the ghost is the book itself, the dead life of the work.

A book that would be written as if after a long time without writing, as if starting over; like that jazz pianist who had to learn everything all over again by listening to himself, after undergoing the dance of electroshock: as if emerging from a prolonged coma and learning to walk again, without entirely forgetting that at one time he ran the way the pages run by and discovering that he's different now, that he writes differently from how he once wrote—now he writes like only someone who gave up writing can write, like someone who suddenly gives up giving up writing writes.

A book not of nonfiction but of yes-fiction.

A book that, all the time, changes all the time.

A book that—divine and comedy, infernal and purgative and paradisiacal—would be thinking about not writing the entire time it's being written.

A book that once finished—transcending its practice and exercise—would immediately begin thinking about its theory, which sends it out walking all day long, buying things for a party, through a city distant in space and nearby in the library, departing from Westminster, crossing St. James's Park, heading up Queen's Walk, turning right on Piccadilly, going back up Old Bond Street and New Bond Street, a slight turn toward Harley Street, traversing Regent's Park and starting over again, restarting that trajectory every time he rereads that day, better all the time, discovering new things all the time.

A book whose genre would be like that sworn statement that J. D. Salinger—trying and ultimately succeeding to prevent the publication of a biography of him—made to a judge when they asked him what it is he does and how he does it: "I just start writing fiction and see what happens to it."

A book as if (dis)assembled by the scissors of a priestly Invisible Man, like random little papers emerging from the box/voice of a songwriter outside time and space, like loose pieces stuck to a wall, freely associated victims of Keyzer Söze Syndrome.

A book that would be like a gift: like a bone a dog fetches for someone who is intent on catching a new butterfly in order to give it the Latin deformation of his own last name.

A book like a TV that the dead and the extraterrestrials tune in to watch us, to try to understand the pages of our sitcoms.

A book with seven channels broadcasting seven simultaneous programs that are all one (and that, if he were alive, Shakespeare would never have written for HBO) and in which a monster is vanquished and success is achieved and there is searching and laughter and weeping and rebirth and stepping out of the shadows and into the light.

A book that—unlike the vice of many recent movies—wouldn't settle for a final surprise scene, for an illuminating or entertaining coda, forcing the spectators to remain sitting in the darkness until the lights come on, after lengthy final credits, but instead would offer numerous variations and alternatives of what's already been seen, already read.

A book whose seven sections would be written simultaneously, quickly changing the place of things, like cards in a game of solitaire or a Tarot reading in which The Writer card always comes out face down and too close to The Madman, The Wheel of Fortune, The Hangman, and Death.

A book whose ample middle, in an omnipresent state of permanent agitation, would be flanked by two texts with the convex concavities of parentheses, the past and the future.

A book that would advance ceaselessly into the past until it reached the goal of its point of departure.

A book that never entirely crystallizes.

A book that would sound like the promise of something deafening and symphonic but composed of almost inaudible words, from inside a tiny camera, where nothing is revealed.

And the absurd solemnity of this last idea, he thinks, is an unequivocal sign that he's in trouble again. The same trouble as always. The same trouble as every time he writes. In the air but convinced that Earth's inhabitants were, fundamentally, writers. And that those who weren't had the obligation—really, he was discovering over the years, what they had was the pleasure and the blessing—of being, merely, readers.

But what was important to him had always been the damned and miserable writers.

He was a writer addict. Nothing interested him more as theme and storyline.

So he'd read biographies and autobiographies and collections of letters and memoirs and diaries and journals. Always with insatiable voracity, as if in the lives and memories of his predecessors (and his few friends, all of whom, for some time, were writers or people involved in literature) he'd find the key to the mystery. A, yes, completely childish notion: that of the existence of some Rosetta Stone that would help pass along and teach the secret and turn the whole thing into the most exact of sciences. And that, when he hadn't found it, he'd limited himself to writing about them and only them. About that kind of animal which he subsequently became. Novels and stories in which there was always a writer. Pursuing them like reflections of himself in a deforming mirror, composing them far and wide across the years, until he was exhausted, until he felt extinguished and snuffed out or overwhelmed by some uncontainable desire to press the fantasy button that would deactivate and suck out the energy that makes writers writers. Groping with closed eyes along the walls of a blinding house. Praying to find a switch to turn off the light, and that, once it was out, he'd be allowed to open his eyes and see, for the first time, something that wasn't writers and writing. To leave behind the kind of trouble that he didn't want to be in or to think about anymore and that, as a result of a kind of superpower for morons, would allow him to contemplate all of it inside his own mind. As if he were reading it, like those eternal and ascending texts at the beginning of science fiction movies where the spectator understands little or nothing amid all the consonant-laden names of faraway planets. Reading all of that and almost immediately beginning to correct it, not necessarily for the better or for his own good. Because for him, correcting always meant adding. So, better to go along changing frequency and definitions and, maybe, ideas. But a book is a book is a book and now he keeps on enumerating possibilities for what book that will be. He can't stop. But he can shift his gaze slightly, squint his eyes, look on with less trust, and remember that thing (who'd said it?, Nathan Zuckerman?, Richard Tull?, Bill Grey?, Sigbjørn Wilderness?, Bradley Pearson?, Paul Benjamin?, Ted Cole?, Julio Méndez?, Buddy Glass?, Kenneth Toomey?, Vadim Vadimovitch N.?, Kilgore Trout?, person?, character?, it doesn't matter: writer!) about how a book is like blubbering thing, wandering and tripping and dragging itself through the hallways of the house. An idiot with deformed feet and tongue hanging out, drooling and incontinent, pissing and shitting itself, head so heavy its body can barely hold it up. A creature that is monstrous and yet we can't help but love it and feel responsible for it and want the best for it and for it to be the best it can be once it goes out into the world. It's not that writers are bad or inattentive parents: what actually happens is that writers are always fretting over the children they conceived all on their own (knowing that their biological children are much better off and far more intelligent) and so the writers spoil them, terrified by how they grow and grow until they are stronger than their creators, who they enjoy beating until they have them down on the floor, howling "More! More!"

Once, in a book, due to demands of the plot, he'd found himself forced to invent a character, a literary critic, who referred to what he did in his writing. His cited sentence—unconsciously anticipating his desire to accelerate his particles—had been something like: "His thing is like thousands of ideas searching for a head to think them." An ambiguous sentence that functioned simultaneously as praise and condemnation. And that, he thought at the time, reflected quite well the increasingly liquid and invertebrate and phosphorescent nature—like those deep-sea fish that end up transforming into their own suns in the absence of light—of his fictions. The sentence in question seemed to have been so appropriate and accurate that *another* literary critic (a critic whom he respected, a real critic of the few pure and consistent critics: a critic who wasn't just a writer who wrote criticism every now and then) external to the book, but presenting it in a bookstore, had highlighted it and read it to the audience, thinking it the very true and very astute appraisal of a colleague. He remembers that night—back when books were still presented—and it's like something that took place on another planet, so far away, like one of those explosions of impossible colors revealed every so often by the Hubble, like a distant light down below in that sky that now is Earth.

The points of color—like a mirror of the stars—of the sunrise city that he's now approaching, descending.

And he starts preparing for landing, for lowering the landing gear, then preparing for the take off of . . .

. . . a book that for the reader—seatbelt fastened for the whole flight, just in case, better that way—was first like the unexpected but always-feared voice of the pilot bursting from speakers and headphones to say "We have a small problem," and then, after complicated and risky maneuvers, like the relief of having arrived safely to the end of the trip.

And, at last, to rest in the warm shadow of a simple idea, something that, yes, might be a new beginning for him.

Something that comes to him now from way back and that, in the end, is nothing but a purely physical movement—the idea that writing is something like climbing a tree. It's easier to go up (when something occurs to you; as if you were reading it) than to go down (when, later, you have to make that something occur for everyone else, writing it). Or that writing is like learning to ride a bicycle: you never forgot how, but you don't learn it perfectly either, you never learn well enough, you'll always keep falling and hurting yourself in the most unexpected moment or the instant of greatest concentration.

To stop writing, on the other hand, should be incredibly easy, he thinks.

A letting go.

To let the current drag you further and further from your desk. To turn off the lights in your brain one by one until you forget not how you write, but how to make yourself feel the desire to sit down to write. Not even looking at trees anymore.

Or to just stop pedaling.

Or to pedal up to the top of a tree and, from the top branch, throw down the bicycle and watch it fall and hear it crash and sink down below until it reaches the bottom of all things.

To spend the rest of your life as someone who doesn't write anymore, introducing yourself not as a *writer* but as an *ex-writer*. Maybe, as a final gesture, to publish a manual that teaches how to give up writing or offer a workshop that demoralizes the participants and urges them to look for better ways to spend and earn a living. And to smile that sad smile of those who were once addicted to something—the smile of those who are better than they were, but not necessarily happier. The smile of those—in long nights of open eyes—who suspect that really they weren't addicts but, merely, the addiction—the uncontrollable controlled substance, the equally effective and ephemeral drug. And, amid the shaking, they understand that something or someone has taken it away from them, because it doesn't work anymore, it doesn't do anything anymore, it has no effect at all anymore. And because of this, the drug has gone away, far away from them, in search of better and more powerful substances.

But something strange happens, something strange happens to him, something that hasn't happened to him for a long time and that he missed so much. Suddenly he, who felt himself finished and shut down, feels that he's back. And with no departure in sight. Now he's like part of a postcard from Ground Zero: not that place where there was something and now there's only a hole in the ground, no, he's the thing inside the hole in the ground where someday, with luck, there will be something. He wasn't dead, he was buried alive. Or ready to resuscitate himself not with a "Get up and go" but with a "Don't get up and write." Something like that. Something that won't be easy. To start over again. Something fragile and something that, of course, won't take him too far. But something that if put to good use—like the last fumes in an empty fuel tank blowing on a spark so that everything stays in motion a little while longer—will be enough to make it home.

And once there, who knows.

And where is that damn fight attendant so he can order and purchase the walking and traveling and metallic Mr. Trip, eh? He needs so badly to wind him up and put him in motion and hang onto his neck like he once hung onto Rolling Thunder's neck. He needs the times to be a-changin'. He needs to be blowing in the wind, for the hard rain to fall, to hear the ringing bell and people praying and the siren of the last fire truck from hell. He needs the sound of the last radio telling him what happened to him, what's happening to him again. He needs a new dose of the resting position, though he's never felt more restless and awake, as if a gremlin had removed his eyelids and ran and locked itself in the little airplane bathroom and used them like rolling papers to roll cigarettes and trigger all the alarms with smoke thick as storm clouds.

And it's a little absurd and really corny and totally clichéd, totally commonplace (but certain places have earned their commonness, in the best sense of the word, in the most singular definition of common, on their own and only after a long time being clumsy uncommon places) that, in that precise instant, the sun comes out (the sun flying below the plane) and its rays pierce through the aircraft from one side to the other. "Craft": a word that—ah, he's thinking *like this* again, about *these* things—he always liked a lot for its all-terrain and all-trajectory and all-time application. And he lifts his head and looks through squinted eyes. Those plastic curtains sliding up, one at a time, letting in the light. And something happens. And it's one of those rare moments during a flight when you're aware that you're flying: after going straight for so long, the plane initiates a curving trajectory, tilting almost on its side, as if threatening to turn around, only to stop just before completing the turn. A movement whose computerized and schematic version doesn't do it justice, on that small and sadistic map that tracks the trajectory, simultaneously so fast and so slow, of the airplane there to convince passengers of the lie that the skies can be delimited, beginning with the ground at their feet. An exercise in approximation that, no doubt, has a French name that's difficult to pronounce and perform in the leaping argot of classical ballerinas. A pirouette of a delicateness almost obscene in its efficiency, as if faithfully following the sketch of a secret line, punctuated by the formal and variable language of the clouds. The exact and unrepeatable instant on all flights when he thinks that, finally and at last, it made sense to take the risk of going up so high: for nothing more than the pleasure of having been there and—as the voice of the pilot informs—the tranquility of the "We are now initiating our descent."

They will be landing "within approximately twenty minutes." But he doesn't care. He knows, too, that for airline companies "twenty minutes" is not twenty minutes—it's between thirty and forty minutes. Twenty minutes for them is like saying "a while," but in order not to say "a while" we say "twenty minutes" and everybody's happy. In the air, where nothing is guaranteed, all gestures of precision are appreciated even if they're compulsively imprecise. Appreciated above all by him, who now—restarting his engines while the airplane draws ever nearer to shutting down its own—is there above, alone. He doesn't need anything or anyone now and he smiles with the smile of a flight attendant. A smile that the many muscles it required hadn't produced in so long. Four hundred thirty muscles are needed to light up a smile, while for the prologue of anger or sadness, furrowing your brow, no more than thirty-four muscles are activated. Mathematics is exact and doesn't lie—it's more work to be happy than unhappy.

But there's a time when it's not so hard, when happiness is that endless beach where you run the way children run. Like wise children who run without yet thinking that someone is watching them run. Children who run unaware that, unfortunately, for a total lack of fortune, soon there will be a uniform and proper and respectable and harmonious way to run. And to run is to read and may you be fast, you readers who run like you once ran, like when you weren't yet able to read, like a celebration of muscles and femurs and kneecaps and tibias and excited laughter. Without shame or shyness or fear of what you'll say and what you'll see. Children who laugh between three hundred and four hundred fifty times a day and whose number of laughs, when they grow up, statistically, will drop to less than twenty a day. And many of them will be cold and biting and bitter laughs and laughs that laugh at others and that laugh to keep from crying. The kind of laugh that he's been using and consuming for a while now. Laughs that are like X-rays of a laugh, revealing a dark stain that requires increasingly complex tests. Laughs that no longer cure but are incurable. Terminal laughs.

Laughs that sounded and looked nothing like his laugh now. A sudden and unexpectedly clean and childish laugh. Laugh No. 450 that was once his everyday laugh and that now he hears again inside himself, new, bouncing around inside the big head of a little body that grows by the minute. The laugh of a body that just caught up to the height and proportions of its twelve-year-old head.

Now he looks out the little window and down below is a beach, and the mouth of a river opening onto the sea, and a speck floating in the water that—he could swear it—is a boy who looks up at the sky and points at the airplane and at him inside it, looking down. Now, at the end but again at the beginning, his mouth is full of water and laughter. He's drowning but, seen from the present of his future, as if invoking the ghost of vacation past, he knows he'll survive, that he'll live to tell it and turn it into a story. But knowing how something ends doesn't make it any less interesting. Just the opposite, the details of that small moment merge with the immensity of what's to come and, for example, now he can specify that the novel, the same novel, that his parents are reading is *Tender Is the Night* (1934, first published in four installments, between January and April of that year, in *Scribner's Magazine*) and that its author is Francis Scott Fitzgerald (St. Paul Minnesota 1896 / Hollywood, California, 1940). He also knows why they're arguing, near but far away, on the beach, unaware their son is drowning. And also—courtesy of *Ways of Dying*—he understands in detail what's happening: the way the water is entering his body to dilute his blood. The fireworks of endorphins getting ready to explode in his brain, throwing the party of the white light at the end of the tunnel. An entire life revisited in a couple minutes, like one of those little books with pictures printed in the margins that, when you flip through it at full speed, creates the illusion of a kind of movement. Seeing himself from outside as if, correcting what he just finished writing, he were reading himself and, reading himself, he remembers how he read once that one of Truman Capote's favorite questions was what do you imagine you would imagine—"what images, in the classic tradition," to be precise—in that eternal moment of drowning.

He's drowning and he's dying and now he lives all of the preceding again. Dies all of it again. With the insatiable anxiety of someone who needs to know how to move on and what key details escaped him. Details he longs to write, feeling again that he's more than ready to put in motion all the muscles necessary to do so. Because not drowning and all the life he has left to live depends on it.

So, driven by mysterious currents—revisiting the scene, writing it, he likes to think that he's the one who saves himself—he reaches the shore with no strength left in his body, but his mind more powerful than ever, shrouded in the supernatural calm of those who have departed and returned.

With his legs barely holding him up, he goes over to his parents, who haven't noticed anything, who are still composing another variation of the same argument as always. He has the urgent need to tell them what's happened, what happened to him, but he knows too that he doesn't have the words needed to communicate it yet. So he stops next to them—they're lying down, they've become experts in arguing while lying down—and makes strange noises and moves his arms all around and splashes them with drops of water from his body. And for the first time in a long time, mother and father seem to agree on something. And, for the first time, they say the same thing at the same time. And what they say is something absurd. They don't say, they don't list off possible suggestions like "Why don't you build a sand castle?" or "Why don't you go take a nap in the house?" or impossible ones— because they didn't let him bring it on vacation—like "Why don't you go play with your little windup metal man?" No. What they ask him—a question that expects no answer, a question that is a command—is something he can't do yet, but that he, suddenly, feels is possible. Even though nobody has taught him how. His mother and father, in perfect synchrony, creating a new voice made of two voices, more annoyed with him than with each other, say: "Why don't you go write?"

His parents—who never gave or give or will give him many things—gave him this: a life preserver for the future, a raft for a drifting castaway, a way to, with time, keep them afloat, to pull them up from the depths where they were thrown, and to bring them back home walking on water and in writing. And, later, with all those words, to bring his sister down from the cliffs of madness and save her lost son, his beloved almost-son.

So, why not write?

They've asked him one of those questions that barely conceals an order of the impossible-to-disobey variety.

And he's an obedient boy.

So he goes inside and grabs the first book he finds (and it's not hard to grab; it's another copy of his parents' favorite book, a third copy, maybe the one they read together, when they're not fighting, when they're getting along) and he opens it to the first page and reads: "On the pleasant shore of the French Riviera, about half way between Marseilles and the Italian border, stands a large, proud, rose-colored hotel."

He understands what it says there—the arrangement of the words—but not what he reads. "Riviera," "Marseilles," "Italy" are still candies of a strange and new flavor in the mouth of his eyes. But then, a few lines below, it talks about a "dazzling beach" and he experiences the novel wonderment at how something that exists there outside, something that he lives every day, at the same time and place, can become letters and exist there inside.

And he goes on to another page, various pages, and reads: "You never knew exactly how much space you occupied in people's lives." And "One writes of scars healed, a loose parallel to the pathology of the skin, but there is no such thing in the life of an individual. There are open wounds, shrunk sometimes to the size of a pin-prick but wounds still. The marks of suffering are more comparable to the loss of a finger, or of the sight of an eye. We may not miss them, either, for one minute in a year, but if we should there is nothing to be done about it." And "who would not be pleased at carrying lamps helpfully through the darkness?" And "Strange children should smile at each other and say, 'Let's play.'"

And from there—because he senses that the effect and the superpower won't last long—he jumps to the last lines of the book: "in any case he is most certainly in that section of the country, in one town or another," he reads.

And he looks for the notebook that he uses for drawing and the pencil he draws with.

And he writes his first words.

And he reads them and says them.

Just two words to begin with.

And his vision clouds over, as if he were looking out at the beach and his parents, coming in at a run, still screaming thunder and lightning at each other, covering their heads with towels to keep from getting wet, as if he were watching them through a window and outside rain is falling.

Now it rains or, maybe, he weeps.

And he hears applause.

The *clap-clap-clap* of the passengers applauding when the plane finds the airport runway. He always hated that applause of those imbecilic travelers who, relieved or regal, believed themselves authorized to celebrate the pilot, as if he'd done something special, as if he were a gladiator who fought the elements and, for that reason, they awarded him not with a thumbs up but by clapping their hands together. The same as that other clapping—the clapping you hear across the sand and under the sky and beside the sea when a child is lost on a beach. The parents of the other children, of the children who haven't yet been lost, applauding; as if they were celebrating the talent of the parents of the lost little one for having, at last, gotten rid of that once-wanted unwanted thing. But now he doesn't want to miss anything. Now he wants to recover everything. To go home. *Bringing it all back home.* To become the monolith of himself. To want to be there to find himself. He doesn't need to be applauded for that wish, for that decision. But that clapping—is it possible they're applauding him—sounds in his ears now like the *flap-flap-flap* of angel wings beating the sky; like the *plop-plop-plop* of Bubble Wrap bubbles joyfully bursting; like the *swift-swift-swift* of little wheels on which every-thing suddenly rolls, at last, so sure and soft, in a fixed direction and with a clear destination that sounds like a *clackety-clack* with all the letters, all the letters on the keyboard.

Landed, pure particle and accelerated energy, his and only his, after so much time floating and sinking, he never felt so high at the level, not of the sea, but of the place where the sea and the river mouth meet. Or yes, he has. But so long ago (the parentheses are the past) that it's like he's feeling it for the first time, maybe for the last time—but better not to think of that.

He's come home—the odyssey continues—so he can leave again.

"Tomorrow I begin," he promises.

"This is how it ends," he says.

NONFICTION

A Thank-You Note

Don't get nervous, don't get annoyed—nothing to explain this time. The book, I hope, is its own explanation ("A book that . . .") and there's nothing more to add except—ah, yes—that one thing, all together now:

Any similarities to reality in what is described or in descriptions of individuals or in individual descriptions in this book (hence its title, its title is not a coincidence) are purely coincidental.

But as always—go ahead and get nervous or irritated, those of you who are made uncomfortable by gratitude—there are many and much to thank/be thankful for, on this side or the other, for help direct or indirect, and always for the good company:

Ana and Carlos Alberi; *London Fields* by Martin Amis; Paul Thomas Anderson; Wes Anderson; *In Other Worlds: SF and the Human Imagination* by Margaret Atwood; *Goldberg Variations* by Johann Sebastian Bach (versions by Glenn Gould from 1981 and Jonathan Crow, Matt Haimovitz, and Douglas McNabney from 2008); Agencia Carmen Balcells; John Banville; *They called for more structure . . .* by Donald Barthelme; Antonin Baudry; The Beatles; Eduardo Becerra; Saul Bellow; *Pigs Might Fly: The Inside Story of Pink Floyd* by Mark Blake; Juan Ignacio Boido; Roberto Bolaño; "Space Oddity" and "Ashes to Ashes" by David Bowie; *Fahrenheit 451* by Ray Bradbury; *The Seven Basic Plots: Why We Tell Stories* by Christopher Booker; *Pursued By Furies: A Life of Malcolm Lowry* by Gordon Bowker; *On the Origin of Stories:*

Evolution, Cognition, and Fiction by Brian Boyd; Miguel Brascó; Harold Brodkey; Emily Brontë & Co.; *The Notebooks of F. Scott Fitzgerald*, edited by Matthew J. Bruccoli; *Reader's Companion to F. Scott Fitzgerald's "Tender Is the Night,"* by Matthew J. Bruccoli with Judith S. Baughman; *The Romantic Egoists: A Pictorial Autobiography from the Scrapbooks and Albums of F. Scott Fitzgerald and Zelda Fitzgerald*, edited by Matthew J. Bruccoli, Scottie Fitzgerald, and Joan P. Kerr; *Mid Air* by Paul Buchanan; David Byrne; *Comí* by Martín Caparrós; Mónica Carmona; *The Professor and Other Writings* by Terry Castle; *The Professor's House* by Willa Cather; *The Piper at the Gates of Dawn* by John Cavanagh; John Cheever; Arthur C. Clark; *The Shakespeare Riots: Revenge, Drama, and Death in Nineteenth-Century America* by Nigel Cliff; the Coen Bros.; "Are You Ready to Be Heartbroken?," by Lloyd Cole; *Apocalypse Now* by Francis Ford Coppola; Jordi Costa; *Wise Up Ghost and Other Songs* by Elvis Costello and The Roots; *La mujer que escribió Frankenstein* by Esther Cross; Eva Cuenca; Charles Dickens; Joan Didion; *The Garden Next Door* by José Donoso; Doctor Manhattan (Dr. Jonathan "Jon" Osterman); Bob Dylan; *Here, There and Everywhere / My Life Recording the Music of The Beatles* by Geoff Emerick; Ray Davies and The Kinks; Marta Díaz; Ignacio Echevarría; William Faulkner (almost); Charlie Feiling; Federico Fellini; Marcelo Figueras; *Tender Is the Night* by Francis Scott Fitzgerald (and prefaces to this novel by Geoff Dyer, Richard Godden, and Charles Scribner III); *Save Me the Waltz* and *Collected Writings* by Zelda Fitzgerald; Juan Fresán; Nelly Fresán; William Gaddis; *La bala perdida: William S. Burroughs en México (1949-1952)* by Jorge García Robles; Alfredo Garófano and Marta Esteve; Daniel Gil; *& Sons* by David Gilbert; *Beloved Infidel (& Co.)* by Sheilah Graham; Leila Guerriero; Isabelle Gugnon; "Love Too Long," by Barry Hannah; *All the Madmen: A Journey to the Dark Side of British Rock* by Clinton Heylin; *Encyclopedia of Science Fiction*, edited by Robert Holdstock; Homero; Aldous Huxley; John Irving; Henry James; Andreu Jaume; *2001: A Space Odyssey* by Stanley Kubrick; La Central (Marta Ramoneda & Antonio Ramírez & Neus Botellé & Co.); *The Salinger Contract* by Adam Langer; Literatura Random House (everyone there, you know who you are); *Crazy Sundays: F. Scott Fitzgerald in Hollywood* by Aaron Latham; *Martin Eden* by Jack London; Claudio López Lamadrid; David Lynch; *I Trawl the MEGA-HERTZ* by Paddy McAloon; "Socrates on the Beach," by Joseph McElroy;

Terrence Malick; *Inside Out: A Personal History of Pink Floyd* by Nick Mason; Norma Elizabeth Mastrorilli; *Invented Lives: F. Scott Fitzgerald & Zelda Fitzgerald* by James R. Mellow; Luna Miguel; *Zelda* by Nancy Milford; Mauricio Montiel Figueiras (Festival de México); *The Lady and Her Monsters: A Tale of Dissections, Real-Life Frankensteins, and the Creation of Mary Shelley's Masterpiece* by Roseanne Montillo; Rick Moody; *Literary Outlaw: The Life and times of William S. Burroughs* by Ted Morgan; Morrisey; Annie Morvan; *The Cinema of Malcolm Lowry / A Scholary Edition of Lowry's "Tender Is the Night,"* edited and with an introduction by Miguel Mota and Paul Tiessen; *Sarah & Gerald / Villa America and After* by Honoria Murphy Donnelly with Richard N. Billings; *Look at the Harlequins!* by Vladimir Nabokov; Bill Murray; Harry Nilsson; Mark Noward (Rose O'Neill Literary House at Washington College); *How We Die: Reflections on Life's Final Chapter* by Sherwin B. Nuland; *El eternauta* by Héctor Germán Oesterheld and Francisco Solano Lopez; Open Letter Books (Chad Post & Will Vanderhyden); *Letters from the Lost Generation: Gerald and Sara Murphy and Friends*, edited by Linda Patterson Miller; Alan Pauls; Edmundo Paz-Soldán; *Wish You Were Here* by Pink Floyd; *Truman Capote: In Which Various Friends, Enemies, Acquaintances, and Detractors Recall His Turbulent Career* by George Plimpton; Francisco "Paco" Purrúa; "Algunas palabras sobre el ciclo vital de las ranas," by Patricio Pron; Marcel Proust; Matteo Ricci; Homo Rodríguez and family; *The Counterlife* by Philip Roth; *Making It Big: The Art and Style of Sara & Gerald Murphy*, edited by Deborah Rothschild with an introductory essay by Calvin Tomkins; Gabriel Ruiz Ortega; Salmon Rushdie (PEN American Center); Guillermo Saccomanno; Sebastián Sancho; Rod Sterling; *Frankenstein or The Modern Prometheus* by Mary Shelly; Maarten Steenmeijer (Radboud University, Nijmegen); *Dracula* by Bram Stoker; Daniel Suárez; *Remando al viento* by Gonzalo Suárez; The Invisible College; *Mind Over Matter: The Images of Pink Floyd* by Strom Thorgerson and Peter Curzon; *Living Well Is the Best Revenge* by Calvin Tomkins; *Showman: The Life of David O. Selznick* by David Thomson; John Updike; *Everybody Was So Young / Gerald and Sara Murphy: A Lost Generation Love Story* by Amanda Vaill; Enrique Vila-Matas; Juan Villoro; Villaseñor family; Kurt Vonnegut; David Foster Wallace; *Yes Is The Answer and Other Prog-Rock Tales*, edited by Marc Weingarten and Tyson Cornell . . .

. . . and the near-and-dear strangers who now hold these pages in their hands . . .

. . . and after everything and everyone, but before anything and anyone, thank you to Daniel Fresán (for having chosen the object and the image for the cover that opened the whole book); and thank you to Ana Isabel Villaseñor (for having chosen the person who now closes the book and says goodbye until the next one, until next time, until another part yet to be invented).

R. F.
Barcelona, December 7ᵗʰ, 2013

Rodrigo Fresán is the author of nine novels, including *Kensington Gardens*, *Mantra*, and *The Bottom of the Sky*. His works incorporate many elements from science-fiction (Philip K. Dick in particular) alongside pop culture and literary references.

Will Vanderhyden received an MA in Literary Translation from the University of Rochester. He has translated fiction by Carlos Labbé, Edgardo Cozarinsky, Alfredo Bryce Echenique, Juan Marsé, Rafael Sánchez Ferlosio, Rodrigo Fresán, and Elvio Gandolfo.

**OPEN
LETTER**

**OPEN
LETTER**

CPSIA information can be obtained
at www.ICGtesting.com
Printed in the USA
JSHW020953110123
36119JS00003B/9